Jason M

MADE
NOT
BEGOTTEN

(#1 How Women Took Over The World)

First Edition

ISBN

9798345619520

DISCLAIMER

The characters and events portrayed in this book are fictitious or are used fictitiously. Any similarity to real person, living or dead, is purely coincidental and not intended by the author. While some historical figures and events are portrayed, the narrative has been crafted for creative purposes and should not be interpreted as a factual account.

ATTRIBUTES

Unless otherwise indicated, all Scripture quotations are taken from the Holy Bible, *American Standard Version*.

The author generated this text in part with GPT-3, GPT-3.5, and GPT-4.0, versions of OpenAI's large-scale language-generation model. Upon generating draft language, the author reviewed, edited, and revised the language to their own liking and takes ultimate responsibility for the content of this publication.

Special thanks to Grace Whitham, Patricia Yalung, Marina Cintron, Amy Rhodes, Scott Whitham, Corey Barker, Norm Brown, Matt Munse, Tischan and Jedediah Seltzer, and Lori and Guy Kneebone. Your time and effort in reading drafts, providing feedback, editing, and proofreading were instrumental in progressing this work to publication.

Cover picture was licensed from Comaniciu Dan/Shutterstock.com.

DEDICATIONS

This book is dedicated to my greatest motivations in life: Father, Son, and Holy Spirit (My God); Grace (My Wife); Lily (My Daughter); and Elijah (My Son); the Lord's Bride (His Church); and the rest of humanity. I hope and pray that this and the works that follow will, at least in some small way, improve their lives and the world around them.

Chapter 1: Weblog 1 - My Confession

Attention Survivors,

The most challenging thing you do in your life will be to forgive me. I pray you will, for your own sake. *"You will not be forgiven if you do not forgive,"* are the words of Jesus, the one who will judge and decide your eternal fate. Please decide today not to go to Hell because of unforgiveness. The world may feel like Hell now, but I know you will adjust. Forgiveness will only help you with adaptation. It will liberate your mind so you can restore all I have broken.

I do not anticipate, nor request, absolution from justice. It is right and good that I am convicted of damning crimes against humanity. The confession I write in this series of weblogs will seal my fate. If I make it to trial, the law will find me guilty, and I will be executed. I hope that makes it easier for you to forgive me.

I think a trial is unlikely, though. I am afraid that it's more probable I will be killed once I am found. Today, many people are enraged, saddened, and frightened, and some will react and seek vengeance. It's understandable. Nevertheless, after emotions have run their course, those left in the world will still need to fix it.

A critical aim of this confession is that tomorrow's problem solvers know the cause of what is happening now and how it came to be. The information provided is for everyone, even though scientists skilled in the arts of molecular biology and virology may best understand the woes of today with the information I provide. However, the sociologist needs to know too, so that she can heal our society. The lawmaker, so she can protect you from similar misguided endeavors. The governing authority, so she can lead you through these perilous times. The spiritual leader, so she can give you hope. You deserve to know why your world is so different from yesterday's world. How it is you came to this time and place. I don't want you to be fed a lie and base your whole life on it. I hope that having the truth will connect you all because you will *all* need to work together to make it through. Dare I say, you might even come out exquisite, as gold refined in the fire.

The first step to forgiveness and healing begins with confession. So, my first and foremost sin is that I, Virginia Dare Goremen, am the principal engineer of the Sweetvirus, which has caused the death of so many men, and more men to come.

Chapter 2: My Mother

My mother, Milli, had every room in our brownstone professionally cleaned once a month. Our bedrooms, bathrooms, and her study upstairs, and our kitchen, powder, living, and dining rooms on the first floor were thankfully not part of my chores. Milli made it clear that our time was too precious to be wasted on cleaning. I was to make the most of my time learning about the world, how things worked, and where I best fit in.

Milli knew her purpose was in journalism. She worked long hours, many nights, and even traveled on weekends. Almost nothing was off limits in the pursuit of news and her career. She wasn't sure where the quote came from, but would often proclaim, "Journalism can never be silent! It must speak immediately, while the echoes of wonder, the claims of triumph and the signs of horror are still in the air." Her proliferation and the quality of her stories brought her fame. Milli's articles were regularly featured in the Washington Post. She also frequently entertained our Kalorama, D.C. neighbors and dignitary guests with the paragon style of Babe Paley, another reason why she hired professional house cleaners. And while Milli had a very ambitious schedule, prioritizing her profession, she always made sure to carve out an hour between 5pm and 6pm every day to talk with me in our kitchen before the evening news.

One such evening, in the summer of 1974, I watched my mother making dinner from one of our white-backed countertop stools. The kitchen was mostly quiet except for the muted sounds of car engines as neighbors rushed home for dinner, the jingles of cooking, and taps of my foot as my leg bounced in excitement. My t-shirt and jogging shorts and untamed ginger hair, wild as the red light scattered by a dusty sunset, were pretty typical for that time of year. However, I realized that the disheveled appearance was probably too informal for what I intended to share with Milli that night. The 5pm hour had come, so it was too late to change. I eagerly stepped up to the plate waiting for the pitch.

Milli's manicured hands clamped the can opener onto the rim of the salmon tin and cranked with the same dexterity she used to advance the film of her Hasselblad camera. Milli looked so beautiful with her wavy golden blonde hair that fell to her chest and the Valentino skirt suit she wore to work that day. Her sharp features and flawless skin harmonized with our bright white cabinets and stainless steel appliances.

"You know, it's June?" she asked.

"Yes," I answered wryly, knowing where she was going.

Made Not Begotten

She drained the water and dumped the meat into the mixing bowl, waiting for me to answer the implied question. I didn't respond though because in my fantasy *she asked the question.*

My mother shot me a sideways glance but gave in and played my game. A toss right down the middle. "Have you decided on a coll…"

"Nettie Maria Stevens University!" I burst out, walloping her question through the stratosphere, and raising my right fist in excitement like a showman pleasing his audience.

"Hmm," she murmured, which I knew meant she wasn't quite sure how to respond. The expressionless poker face she maintained while crushing crackers into the mixing bowl was a bit irritating.

"I was hoping more for beaming delight."

My mother smirked and turned away. Retrieving the milk, eggs, and butter out of our stainless Viking refrigerator, she started, "It is indeed highly ranked."

I finished her disapproving thought, "…but specifically in science."

"What about Colombia or Harvard?" she asked, pouring the milk.

"So, I could study law?" I answered with a pouty face. It was one of the degree options she mentioned in our last conversation.

"That's not a bad idea," she said, trying to give me credit for her idea. The trite psychology wouldn't work on me again.

My fantasy was killed. "The world was my oyster," was proclaimed in the last three conversations about colleges and majors. She had made some *suggestions* about vocations, or so I thought. Now I'm realizing that they were actually the oyster's pearls and all other options were not as precious or wise in my mother's eyes.

"I already accepted," I said flatly.

My mother winced, crushing an egg in her hand and dropping bits of shell into the mixing bowl. She frowned as she fished the bits out. "We might be enjoying a little extra calcium in our salmon loaf." Then she managed a half smile. "So, does that mean you're official? All of the paperwork is in?"

"People can hear when you're smiling," was one of my mother's proverbs. I could tell from her expression and high-pitched tone that she was insincere and hoping I hadn't officially accepted the offer to attend Stevens University.

3

"What is the problem?" I demanded, not smiling.

She trashed the shell bits and washed the residuals off her hands.

Ignoring my question, she asked, "They have a good law program too, don't they? You really would make a great attorney."

My mother microwaved the butter in a mug. She could have probably melted it on my forehead instead, as hot as I was from my growing anger.

"You're confident, well spoken, and convincing. You would figure out the opposing side's strategy, find the weaknesses, the loop holes, build a great argument, and..." she paused for effect, "...beat the competition. Enough years under your belt, I bet you could become a judge."

"Really?"

"I do."

"No, I mean you don't really intend to support my choice if it's not yours," I frankly stated.

Mother poured in the butter and dashed some salt and pepper into the mixing bowl. Again, sidestepping my sharp challenge to her good intentions, she adjusted her angle of attack, "Do you want to save some time and money?"

"Time more than money."

"You could skip the law degree and still become a judge. There are actually several large states that don't require it before becoming a judge. Montana, Nevada, Arizona, Colorado, Texas, and New York, to name a few."

Curious about this claim, I asked, "How does that work?"

"You just have to be elected by your county."

Milli dug, chopped, and pressed, vigorously homogenizing the ingredients. As she mixed in the opposite direction, she frowned.

"What?" I asked.

She wrinkled her nose, and said, "Well, elections are popularity contests."

I expected her to continue but she just quietly rolled out the mix on the counter top. Now I was playing into her game.

"And?"

"Well, you're not really one for charming the masses."

"Thanks," I replied sarcastically.

She transferred the salmon loaf onto a greased baking sheet and slid it into the oven. Then, she pulled out a box of Misty 120's from her Louis Vuitton bag and lit a cigarette. Milli took a short drag before continuing. Now she could focus on the battle of persuasion.

"Nothing wrong with that. You're just selective with whom you decide to get friendly. Unfortunately for you, being political and charming would be very helpful for winning an election."

"So, you don't think I would be successful?" I asked.

"Well, perhaps you could make enough voting allies and donors to pay for campaigns by winning cases. Having a legal background before being elected a judge is sensible anyway."

"While electing judges without experience is *deplorable* and ousting them is important for the sake of justice, my aim is to become a scientist, not a lawyer or judge."

She raised an eyebrow at me.

"Scientist? You don't even like cooking."

"And?"

"How are you going to endure the tedium of mixing chemicals every day?"

"I would only do that during undergraduate and graduate school. Then, my job would become writing grants, getting funding for my research, and leading my laboratory. My students would do the chemical mixing."

"Ah, so you've thought this through and have an elaborate plan, do you?" she responded sardonically.

"Yes…" I growled, showing my teeth.

Mother knew how to poke the bear in me. She would use my anger to provoke me into arguments. When my cerebral defenses were down, mother would attack with a Trojan horse, something with the appearance of a gift but loaded with argument conquerors.

She flicked ashes from her cigarette and laid it in her ashtray on the counter. Mother turned away from me for a moment and paused. Then, she spun around and clapped her hands. With eyes nearly popping out of her skull, she declared, "I've got it!" (as if she hadn't already considered what she was about to say in advance of the conversation). With an intense stare and toothy smile, she pointed a finger at me, and then both fingers, and pronounced a single word, "Leadership!" The word was delivered like it was a jeweled crown or some talisman of power. I wondered how much time she practiced this in the mirror.

Mother's pointed fingers spread to open hands. Her expression was the same as that of surprise party participants. The recipient of the surprise naturally responds with shock, which decomposes into thankfulness. Not me though. I would play dumb.

"What?"

"What about studying business?" she asked, maintaining the illuminated face.

My simple, bubble-bursting statement was, "Business is not science." As the words came out of my mouth, however, I recognized that it was my intention to run my laboratory like a business. Still, I wasn't going to admit that to my mother.

"No, it's not science." Mother picked the cigarette back up, took a drag, and blew out the smoke. "Be honest though, wouldn't you rather manage an organization, company, or be your own business owner?" Seeming to know my thoughts, she added, "Certainly, you could do better than laboratory-scale leadership."

My irritation was continuing to build. I felt like a human archery target and my mother was trying to fire a perfect robin hood shot to split through the arrow that was already piercing the bullseye of my heart, a shot to rob and replace my passion with the one she deemed best.

"Why business?" I asked with a glare.

"You've always wanted to lead. In elementary school, when bullies started grabbing your hair, you gathered a team of playground bodyguards. You organized the kids on your bus to sing songs for end-of-week ice cream prizes at summer camp. And you were editor for your high school newspaper, which I'm very proud of."

"As you said though… I can lead a laboratory of scientists, and some research groups can be quite large, bigger and more profitable than many small businesses."

"Yes, but there's not enough female-owned businesses out in the world. Several new laws are breaking down barriers for female entry into business ownership here in the U.S. Women are gaining new access to credit and more loans are being approved. Think of the success you could have and how much it could help improve the female condition."

"Leading people is important to me, and I will likely hire more women than men in my laboratory, but I want to be an expert and make significant progress in a specific area of human health."

Mother's poker face was back. Her frustration threshold was much higher than mine but I could tell I was starting to stoke her fire.

Shooting another arrow, she asked, "What about studying medicine? You could make very meaningful progress practicing medicine. There's so few female MDs, and with your tenacity, I bet you could work your way up to a hospital director position and manage all the MDs."

"That's nice of you to say Milli, but I don't *want* to be an MD."

My mother asked me to call her Milli during puberty. She explained that the title mother perpetuated unfair expectations on women and children. "They are titles for hierarchies ruled by men," she said. "The children in families are dependents. The mothers are responsible for the children. The fathers, when they are responsible, are responsible for the bills and family defense. Ours is not the 1950s nuclear family held up high on a pedestal. There is no father here. We run leaner, more efficiently, providing for and defending ourselves. Just two successful women, loving each other and cheering each other on." Milli really was a great encouragement, especially as it related to my education. At the same time, for someone who advocated for egalitarianism, she could be very overbearing.

"No, you're right, Virginia. Bedside manners might be lacking." She said, smirking to dull the sharpness of the barb. "Leverage your strengths, Virginia! With your strategic mind and confidence, you could do a lot better than science. Perhaps in… sales?" Yet another arrow.

I rolled my eyes. "Sales in what?"

"What about medical products? I'm sure there are good commissions."

This was a rather wild shot, and I had enough of being a target. I got off of the stool and balled my fists by my sides. I considered leaving the room, but have never been one to back down in an argument.

"No, Milli. My plan is to study science at Stevens University. You clearly have an issue with it. So, tell me. What in the fiery Hell is your problem with me studying science?!"

"Calm down, Virginia." My mother closed her eyes for a long moment, took another drag, and exhaled some calming smoke.

'Was the truth so much harder to communicate?' I wondered.

A melancholy expression came over her face. "The gender bias is too great in science," she said with a sigh.

I found this very odd coming from a feminist and an overachiever.

She continued, "It doesn't matter what kind of scientist you are, a biologist or a physicist, your achievements will be taken and credited to your male colleagues."

"Why do you say that?"

"Have you read *The Double Helix* by James Watson?" she asked.

"No."

"He used more words to critique Rosalind Franklin's looks and dress than to describe her scientific contributions to understanding the shape of DNA."

She let the point linger for a moment.

"So, what's different about that and other fields?"

"Scientists spend their whole lives researching the same fiery thing and usually become known for just one discovery, if any. It's too much work just to have the credit stolen. A man might take credit for one of my stories, but there's always next week's article. Scientific journal articles take *years* to publish."

"I won't let a man take credit for my work."

"No?" Her face was starting to turn red with frustration.

"No!"

"So, you're better than Franklin? Better than Jocelyn Bell Burnell, who made major contributions to the discovery of pulsars, but only her male colleagues, Antony Hewish and Martin Ryle, were awarded a Nobel Prize for that work. Better than Esther Lederberg, whose husband solely received the Nobel Prize for the first discovery of a bacterial virus, despite her pioneering contributions. Chien-Shiung Wu, whose male colleagues primarily received credit for the theoretical prediction that weak nuclear interactions violated the Law of Conservation of Parity."

"All of these things happened in prior decades," I countered, not really knowing much about her examples. "This is the 70's!"

"Maybe you're right, Virginia, but what if you're wrong? What area of scientific advancement is worth the risk? The opportunity cost of being immensely successful in law, medicine, sales, business management, etc. is too great! You could be massively successful in any of those areas!" she barked.

"I think it's important to understand why some people struggle with having children."

My mother's face went pale as a ghost. She turned away again.

I walked toward her and yelled, "I will be a famous leader in this field of research! I will manage a laboratory of researchers, and expand opportunities for other female researchers!"

Without turning back toward me, she murmured, "Don't be obtuse and waste your life," she warned.

"It's not stupid…"

She turned. With a cold angry look on her face, she cut me off with, "You naive fatuously vacuous girl!" she returned. My mom had never disparaged me so harshly.

I began to cry, and she just let me.

"I thought you would appreciate it… I mean, since you struggled to have me."

"No. It's a bad decision. You will regret it."

My mother walked past me to the hallway and up the stairs. Pausing halfway up, she finished with, "You don't have my support and won't have my help!"

Chapter 3: Weblog 2 - My Good Intentions

Being vulnerable is really hard for me. Please try to find a caterpillar's footprint of common ground, a shared leaf or branch in our stories. I pray it will pupate into understanding and metamorphosize into empathy.

Our current reality is not what I wanted. I didn't want to be a genocidal murderer. No, the desire of my heart was to help people who had challenges with having children; to either run a laboratory or manage a company with scientific teams that characterized the problems and developed therapies for infertility. However, evil men lied to me, manipulated me, and outright forced me to do things that I didn't want to do. I saw red.

Is it not the instinct of a cornered animal to let anger take over? I raged, and it liberated me, again and again. Somehow, my fierce responses never bore serious consequences to my goals, and I believe that this fed my corruption. The pattern developed like the expanding concentric circles of a disturbed puddle. Without resistance, my actions led to the widest ripple, the ripple that has impacted everyone. Men will never have control again, but this is a shallow victory. Nothing compared to the deep pain and loss I see now.

Chapter 4: Grandmother

Grandmother and I were sitting in the drawing room of her mansion. She wanted to talk before I left for college. Her expression was hard to read with the distant look in her eyes; anger perhaps, mixed with longing, sadness, and maybe a touch of regret.

My bags were packed and waiting beside my armchair. An air conditioning blast from a nearby vent in the floor raised goosebumps along my arm. I thought this was going to be a normal send off, something brief and sweet, like, "I'm going to miss you. Try not to party too hard." Instead, she said something odd.

"He'll be dead soon."

"Who?" I inquired.

"Your grandfather," she replied. "I had three other children by that bastard, besides your mother."

'Bastard? Wait…' I thought and then blurted, "I have uncles and aunts?"

"Before giving birth to your mom, I had two boys and a girl. So, yes, you have an Uncle Hubert, an Uncle Xavier, and an Aunt Harriet."

Feeling hurt, I cautiously voiced dissatisfaction, "Why wasn't I ever told?"

This was the first time my grandmother was willing to say anything about her ex-husband, and she had never mentioned having other children with him. My mom told me that it was a very touchy subject. The topic was always quickly changed the few times it came up during my childhood.

"You weren't the only one kept in the dark."

I furrowed my brow waiting for some further explanation, but she just skipped to the resolution.

"When the boys grew up, they remembered me and hired a private investigator to locate me. I met them without their grandfather's knowledge, and still do from time to time. I've had a few opportunities to see my other grandchildren. Besides you, I mean. I intend to see them more once he's gone."

"Anyway, I thought it was important that you know for a few reasons. Someday, hopefully several years from now, you will receive a will from my executor. I didn't want that to be the first time you discovered these other family members."

"Thank you, Grandma."

"You're very welcome. I also understand that you and your mother are not on great terms with each other right now because of a disagreement regarding the educational and vocational path you want to pursue. Don't hear me wrong. I think you should follow your dreams. However, one thing I've learned from this life is that family is the worthiest and rewarding challenge."

I wasn't ready to consider a reunion. My mother had tried contacting me a couple of times that summer, but the continued feeling of betrayal kept me from returning her calls. I thought I might call once classes started, but wasn't sure. I didn't need my mother's support to go after my dream. My grandmother told me long ago that she had a trust set aside for my college education. She showed it to me earlier in the summer, and there was enough for tuition, books, housing, food, etc. with margin for me to attend virtually any University I wanted. Her financial support and encouragement were enough. I also considered waiting to talk to my mother again once I had a semester under my belt and high marks in my classes since my mother cared about success so much.

She continued, "I already alluded to this, but the third reason why I wanted to tell you about your other family members is because I plan to spend more time with them soon. So, if you try to contact me at the house, I may not be there. I didn't want you to worry that something happened to me."

"Do you think it would be good for them to meet me someday?"

"I don't know. I haven't really thought about it. Is that something you would like to do?"

"Yeah, maybe. What are they like?"

"I'm still trying to figure that out myself."

I gathered that going down this line of inquiry wasn't welcome. Even now, the topic was tender.

Chapter 5: Weblog 3 - The Sweetvirus Poison and a Potential Antidote

Viruses in nature have one purpose, to replicate themselves. They are not living things according to our definition because viruses require a host to replicate. Viruses steal resources from their hosts to do that, like blood sucking ticks. While a tick will detach after feeding and molt into an adult, a virus not well-adapted to its host might kill too many cells and kill the host. This is certainly not the goal of viruses because death of the host would prevent further opportunity of replication. Recall how the Coronavirus adapted itself over time, generating a variety of strains that became better at spreading but less lethal to human hosts. Natural viruses adapt to their host environments to improve their chances of replication.

Even though Sweetvirus might seem similar to a respiratory virus, like Coronavirus, it's not. It's so much worse. Yes, you catch it from other people, but you can also just catch it from the air around you, and it will continue to persist in the air. What this means is there are no easy ways to live on the planet and not be exposed to it.

Sweetvirus isn't a natural virus. It's a highly engineered delivery system with a lethal poison inside that is only lethal to men. Currently there is no antidote, so if a man receives the Sweetvirus "package", he will die. No adaptation will take place over time by the Sweetvirus to be less lethal to men because it was engineered not to adapt. The natural adaptation machinery of the viruses was removed and replaced with stabilizing factors.

The incipient Sweetvirus poison came from my work at SMNL back in the 1980s. I was trying to develop a faster method of sequencing the human genome (i.e. find out the series of A's, T's, C's, and G's of all human DNA). What I came up with was REVs (restriction endonuclease type V), which nowadays is better known as CRISPR-Cas. Lay people, please read: *REVs are molecular scissors that cut DNA at targeted locations.*

REVs had an infidelity issue; that is, they were cutting in *the wrong places* too frequently. Later in my career, during my tenure as CEO of Autonoma Inc., I had my R&D team work on improving their fidelity, but they couldn't figure out a solution for the off-target cuts, even after years of research and tens of millions of funding. It turned out that off-target cuts were a symptom of a greater problem. The REVs were degenerate. That is, they cut more places they weren't supposed to as

13

time went on. So, if the REVs were put into a virus and the virus was released, a runaway proliferation of degenerate REVs could theoretically cut the DNA of all humans and kill us all.

Therefore, we developed homing endonucleases as an alternative for REVs and put those into the Sweetvirus. Through a three-month refinement process, the fidelity of homing endonucleases could be made several orders of magnitude higher than the REVs and we found virtually no risk of degeneration.

Why mention REVs then? My imitators and emulators, trying to produce their own Sweetvirus, are more likely to use REVs as the poison in their package than homing endonucleases. A standard molecular biology laboratory at a university could produce a REV in less than a day. I pray they read here that the consequences could be human annihilation and chose not to copy my folly.

[THE FOLLOWING IS FOR SCIENTISTS SEEKING TO FIND A WAY TO STOP THE SWEETVIRUS]

Sweetvirus utilizes the vesicular stomatitis virus glycoproteins to enter a variety of human cell types including retina, respiratory epithelium, muscle, brain, and liver cells.

Sweetvirus is an RNA virus that reverse transcribes itself into DNA once it's inside a cell. Before it can do anything else, it must integrate into the cell's genome in front of a promoter, because it lacks its own. It is designed to integrate in front of a promoter in the Y-chromosome, specifically taxilin gamma pseudogene (TXLNGY) in the male-specific region of the Y-chromosome. The sequence at the integration site is dissimilar enough from all other sequences found in the human genome to prevent integration elsewhere, especially female genomes. Thus, in females it is quickly degraded and cleared by the immune system.

Most genes on the Y-chromosome are only expressed in testes or in very few other cell types. By hijacking the promoter of TXLNGY, the Sweetvirus is able to replicate in a variety of adult male cell types.

The homing endonuclease in Sweetvirus is precisely engineered to cut DYZ1, and only DYZ1, a repetitive sequence only found in the Y-chromosome. The number of copies varies from dozens to hundreds.

Once the Y-chromosome is shredded by the homing endonuclease at the DYZ1 sites, the cell begins apoptosis. In other words, there are too many cuts to repair, so the cell initiates self-destruction.

What we've begun to see on the news are the effects of excessive simultaneous multi-tissue apoptosis. While severe hypoxemia is by far the most common cause of death, there are numerous reports of combinations of psoriasis and dermatitis; Crohn's disease and ulcerative colitis; Alzheimer's, Parkinson's, and Huntington's disease; systemic lupus erythematosus and rheumatoid arthritis; liver fibrosis and cirrhosis; acute kidney injury; heart attack, and heart failure.

You might consider counteracting the Sweetvirus by changing or masking the DYZ1 sequence in the cells of men. Maybe the Sweetvirus could be reprogrammed to replace the DYZ1 sites rather than just cut them. This is just one potential strategy.

Chapter 6: Best Friends

The 1974 Fall Semester Welcome Week at Nettie Maria Stevens University was where I met my best friends. Students helped each other move into dorms. We toured campus and were oriented together. With each event, mixer, social, resource fair, and icebreaker game, our rubber band ball of friends grew. In the weeks, months, and years following, we saw many of these people around campus, in the dining halls, at the arcade, and the disco. It was nice catching up with other students, but I mainly mingled with the ones in my major, developmental biology. Gina, Dan, and Bobby were the other three sides to my social square.

The four of us formally met at the resource fair, but before that, Dan helped move me into my dorm. Dan was tall with wavy dark hair, and was a helpful hard worker as evidenced by the number of boxes he carried. He was also a quiet guy, letting one of the other guys in his parachurch group do the introductions and farewells. They invited me to some event but I didn't bother going. The invitation to "fellowship" just didn't interest me enough. Still, I appreciated their help since my mother was absent.

The Welcome Week Resource Fair was a couple of days after my move in. There were carnival games like wheel of fortune, milk bottle pyramid knockdown, ring toss, balloon pop, and high striker. Everything was set up along Meitner Rd, a straight road in the middle of campus that was surrounded by the Student Health Center, Music and Theater Hall, Student Cinema, Student Center, Gymnasium, the Dining Hall, and some dorms.

A retro-styled leather jacket-wearing slicked-back hair bad boy was hitting on me while I was walking down Meitner Rd toward the games. He looked similar to John Travolta's character in Grease, Danny Zuko.

"Hey, babe. I'm Franky. Who are you with?"

"My name is Virginia. I'm on my way to meet up with my group of friends."

I lied to deter him from continuing his pitch.

"You should ditch them and come with me."

"Why would I do that?"

"Because I'm the fifth member of the Fantastic Four. Stronger than Ben, hotter than Johnny, and longer than Reed. I'm a lady-killer with magic fingers and out-of-this-world moves."

"You sound like the Impossible Man," I said, testing his comic book knowledge of the ironically-named annoying green alien.

"No. Not like him," he laughed.

Then, a handsome, curly blonde-haired fellow with a nice jaw, V-shaped torso, and perky pecs declared, "Wow! They have a high striker!" and challenged everyone within eye shot, "Bet you guys can't beat me!"

The crowds in front of me turned their attention to the grandstanding bragger who was then spitting in his hands and vigorously rubbing them together as he prepared to wield the mallet like the comic book/mythological god, Thor. I saw an opportunity to ditch Danny Zuko's inspiration.

"I bet you could beat him!"

"Think so, red?" he asked, clearly intimidated. His timidness and annoying uncreative pet name referencing my hair color made me even less attracted to him.

Flashing a fake smile, I said, "Definitely."

The lug looked back over toward Thor, now swinging the great hammer over his head. "Yeah, I mean of course I can beat him."

"Go get him, tiger!" I flattered insincerely.

The empty praise gave him enough courage. While he made his way over to challenge Thor, I cut out of the multitude onto the sidewalk and jetted over to the ring toss. The line for this game had dissipated, the crowds drawn away by the high striker's boisterous ringing bell. I could care less about the peacockery. While the muscle men battled, I enjoyed the spoils of not having to wait in line to play ring toss.

"I saw what you did there. Nice move." Gina Bonaccorso whispered.

"Yeah, that guy isn't my type."

She looked around. Whispering again, "I just meant taking advantage of the open ring toss game while everyone was distracted. Quick thinking! What guy are you talking about?"

"One of the guys who is at the high striker. I got rid of him."

"Oh? Why?"

"Outwardly, he presents as a 1950s tough-guy car-racer. Inside, he is just an insecure little boy."

"Franky. Yeah, he tried to charm me too with his shop talk. Plenty of those back in the city."

"He tried some geeky Fantastic Four come on with me. Why were you whispering?" I asked.

"Just didn't want to draw more people over to the ring toss."

"You want to play?"

"No, I just came over to compliment you," Gina said sarcastically. "Pass me over a few rings, chick."

I handed some over and corrected her, "It's Virginia."

She seemed not to mind the correction. "My name's Gina. Where ya from?" she asked with an easy-to-recognize New York accent. Gina had dark hair and the subtle features of Italian ancestry.

"District of Columbia, originally," I answered.

"Ah, you are a cittadina, like me. I'm from New York City, Little Italy."

Gina seemed pleasant, but I didn't think much of her up to that point. What really intrigued me was when she leaned in and whispered, "You know, there aren't a lot of women at this school. We should protect each other, and frustrate all these horny college guys."

I laughed, thinking she might be more serious about her studies than I guessed based on her appearance. Gina didn't wear a bra. Her breasts were perky, well-defined, and much larger than mine. Their prominence on her thin body made them look like cone-shaped air marshal wands directing planes into dock. While one might assume she was luring husbands, bralessness was actually a common practice of the young feminists of my generation.

"What do you study?" I asked.

"Human development."

"Oh really? I…" Before I could finish my sentence, Bobby Steine interrupted me. "Neat! We are HD majors too!"

"Yeah, is that what you were going to say before curls interrupted?" Gina quipped, referring to Bobby's afro.

"Hi, I'm Bobby," he said, continuing to interrupt and force his way into the conversation.

"Gina, and the pleasure is all yours, Bobby." His eyes were sneaking peeks at Gina's landing gear.

"You just interrupted my new friend, Virginia," she hissed.

"Oh, Virginia? I'm sorry," he yielded, turning his attention over to me.

I considered his below average stature, wavy blonde hair, shifty eyes, and slight grin. Bobby reminded me of a shaggy dog waiting for someone to toss him a ball or for a cat to chase. He was no threat. I decided to forgive his rude manner and chuck a ball.

"Is that a Dylan shirt?" I asked.

"It is. You like Dylan?"

"I'm a fan of *Like a Rolling Stone.*"

Bobby smiled a little wider.

"Yeah, it's a good one. What kind of name is Virginia? You from the South?" Bobby jeered.

I couldn't help rile up the pup, "Actually, if you knew basic United States history, you would know that name was given to the first English person born in America. So, it's an English name, and I'm from DC."

"Interesting. I am all the more ready for Trivial Pursuit," Bobby barked.

Dan who stood behind Bobby howled with laughter. I looked up at him and changed the subject.

"I know you. You helped me move."

"They helped you move?" asked Gina.

"No, just the tall one," I mocked, indirectly.

"With so many targets on your face, Virginia, you might want to avoid a firefight," warned Bobby.

Ignoring Bobby, I asked my move-in helper, "What's your name?"

"I'm Dan. Glad I could help."

Dan stuck his hand out and we shook. He was like a gentle giant and I was curious why he put up with Bobby. Considering them together, I thought neither was very handsome, certainly not ugly though. Bobby was like a seven. He had a youthful face but seemed to have received a lower dose of testosterone relative to many of the other muscly males surrounding us on Meitner Rd. That, or he was too lazy to steward it. Dan was lean, tall, and had a strong jawline, but he had a little bit of a Franken-face and walk.

There was a momentary awkwardness because Dan didn't ask any questions, just smiled at me.

Bobby rescued the situation with the question, "Did you girls get the free stuff?"

"*You…* is enough," I insisted.

"What?" Bobby replied, confused by my statement.

"Did *you two* get the free stuff?" I clarified, expressing my dislike of his need to call attention to our sex.

"Not the point, Virgy."

"*Virginia*," I corrected again.

"I've got something to share with you lovely *ladies*."

"Just call us by our names."

"Okay… look over here Gina and *Virginia*," he directed us down the street to a table of free items. "They've got free tie dye shirts, free pennants, coupons for local places… you just have to spin the wheel and you get something. Plus, they have pizza."

We walked over to the table and Gina took a slice of pizza, but didn't finish it.

I gave her an inquisitive look.

She shook her head slightly.

"What's wrong?" Dan asked with a worried face.

"Oh, nothing." Gina looked a little surprised by Dan's genuine concern. Turning away from him, she stopped me from getting a slice and whispered, "That's not pizza."

Gina's kibosh wasn't just because of her refined New York Italian pallet. The pizza from Kung Food Pizza was objectively terrible.

Bobby suggested we get some dessert. "You *two* probably don't like melting in the sun. I heard that there's free ice cream at the library for the next hour, plus they are doing tours. Did you know it's the tallest library in the world by floors?"

"What does that mean– tallest by floors?" Gina asked.

Bobby screwed up his face and responded, "Actually, I'm not sure." Then smiling, he proposed, "Maybe we can find out while we are indulging in free ice cream. Want to go?"

Gina looked at me with some intrigue. I nodded my head.

"Okay, let's go fellas," she confirmed.

"Oh, so *ladies* is not okay, but *fellas* is okay?"

"You have to define your own boundaries, Bobby," I answered with a smirk, and we made our way north to the library.

Outside was a wheelable metal cart, something the University had rented or pulled out of storage for the Welcome Week. It held six tubs in divided sections. An attendant allowed us to have two scoops each, and we enjoyed the ice cream while we waited in line for a tour guide to take us around the library.

I only remember the introduction of the tour; "The Rosalind Elsie Franklin Public Library at twenty-nine floors, including the lobby but not the basement, is the third tallest library in the world. While one in Indonesia and another in China surpass it in terms of height, our library has the most floors. Both of theirs only have twenty-four."

"There you go, mystery solved!" declared Bobby.

Back then, we saw that most floors had curving serpentine bookshelves that extended from floor to ceiling. The shelves formed insulated spaces that kept out noise from other areas. Oversized bean bag chairs littered the floors, which were great for long study sessions and nap breaks. In the pores of the learning sponge, young students also necked and probably even went all the way. The library really hasn't changed much since that tour. The nooks are still so isolated. One could get away with murder if they wanted to.

During the tour, we saw some students writing on glass tables with Sharpie markers. They were racing each other to label the human anatomy, while other students were drawing organic chemical structures. We thought that was really neat. When they were done, the ink was wiped away easily with solvent and a paper towel.

I take it back. Another thing I remember the guide saying at the end of the tour was that, "The library is open twenty-four hours, seven days a week, except for national holidays and during severe weather. The closest shower is over at the Apgar Gymnasium. Otherwise, you can pretty much live here if your dormmates are intolerable, have sex constantly, or tell every Joe Blow it's 420-friendly. Welcome to college."

Walking out into the brickyard, Gina said, "I hope my dormmates aren't like that."

"You ladies smoke pot?" asked Bobby.

"Never tried, I'm a square though," replied Gina.

"Not interested," I answered.

Dan shook his head.

"Yeah, neither have I," conceded Bobby.

"Neat, so, what do you want to do now?" asked Gina.

"Oh, I know what you guys would like."

Guys is an inclusive term in the Northeast, like y'all is in the South. No correction was needed.

"Follow me," Bobby beckoned us toward Hodgkin Street.

Gina looked at me again for approval.

I nodded my head once.

Bobby brought us to the Palatial Pool Hall, aka the Palace. It was a game hall with arcade games, billiards, darts, shuffleboard, and pinball, but it was so much more. Marketing was ramping up in the 1970s with branding, creating characters like Governor Hamburger Head and Alpha-Bitez Warlock. The Palace was Arabian themed with high walls, Middle Eastern carpets, tall curvy pillars, bright colors, and golden domes. Filling the floors below the grandiose architecture were the arcade games, pinball machines, ping pong tables, dart boards, billiard tables, shuffleboards, and food and beverage counters. Popular music played in the background to enhance the ambiance.

"The first several games are on me," offered Bobby, "And by several, I mean three."

"That's okay, I can pay for my own arcade games," I quibbled, knowing where such allowances might lead.

Gina used a different tact, "I'll take your money. Just don't expect anything for it."

"Okay... guys versus girls..." Bobby corrected himself, "I mean you two versus us two, air hockey?"

"What are we playing for?" I asked.

"How about the losers pay for lunch tomorrow?"

"I can get on board with that," I proclaimed with a competitive growl.

Gina added, "Challenge accepted!"

It was a good match up. Bobby and Gina were not above trickery and distraction to secure victory. Bobby mooned us and Gina shook her tits a couple of times. I didn't mind. The antics made the game all the more stimulating. Dan didn't say much but his smirk communicated he was as happy as the rest of us. Gina and I ended up winning three games to Bobby and Dan's two games. I think Bobby threw the last game, letting a few pucks in, to ensure he got more time with Gina the next day. The days turned into weeks of us spending time together. It was easy since we all had the same classes and agreed on a study time.

Our favorite space to study was at the end of the twenty-fourth floor of the library. We quickly discovered that the space was always available and no one ever interrupted while we were studying there. We thought it was because the curvature of the bookshelf made it somewhat hidden. The books in this section were also a little obscure; naval science books in a college without an ROTC program.

We named our study space Ocracoke after the island where it was believed that the pirate Blackbeard stashed his treasure while evading the British navy. Ocracoke was the name I proposed, having lots of familiarity and history with the place because of vacations my mother took me on when I was a kid. The Outerbanks, which included Ocracoke, was the only vacation spot we returned to over the years.

The Lost Colony of Roanoke, geographically close to Ocracoke, was always an included destination in these vacations. It was special to my mother because she and my father went there during their honeymoon. Before I was conceived, they decided to name me Virginia Dare after the first English person born in America.

What I wasn't ready to share with them was that I never knew my father. The story is a bit complicated and trying to describe it makes me feel rather emotional. I worried that if they asked too many questions, I might be overly sensitive and snap at them. The fact is, my father died before I was born. He accidentally electrocuted himself with high amperage while at work. Going through the who, what, where, when, why, and how is just too much for me. That level of vulnerability would require more trust than I've given to anyone before. Either trust, or maybe some drugs. Not that I was interested, but it was the 1970s.

If I did tell them my secret, I think I would probably start with the most objective part, a picture of my father that my mother let me have showing where my Irish red hair and freckles came from, and a beaming sunshine smile that was not inherited.

Chapter 7: N.O.W. 1 - Goreman Claims Responsibility for Sudden Male Deaths

News Of World report Friday, April 21, 2023. Men are dying in the streets. Other men are leaving cities in droves to escape from the invisible sex-specific reaper spreading from highly populated epicenters. Some men are bringing their families. Many men are leaving their loved ones behind. Women left behind are afraid and confused, while others mourn their dead loved ones. SARS-Covid masks are being dug out of junk drawers and grocery stores are being ransacked. While law enforcement is scarce, little vandalism and looting has occurred.

In related news, criminal diagnostics mogul, Dr. Vir Goreman, who went into hiding after warrants were issued for her arrest for alleged human trafficking and identity theft charges, has implicated herself in the sudden throng of male deaths and illnesses around major metropolitan cities around the world. Scientists are working to corroborate her claims that the cause of the deaths is a virus. Authorities are trying to track down Dr. Goreman but have so far been unsuccessful. Her confessions are being written on an encrypted weblog hosted on a virtual private network.

Chapter 8: Bonding

Gina and I paired nicely, a couple of powerful and graceful lionesses with high volume frizzy manes. Gina's brown locks were a bit curlier than mine. Neither of us gave away smiles as we prowled around campus, our faces signaling that we were generally unimpressed. Our hunts were for the ridiculous abstract, geometric, paisley, floral, and other experimental patterns of men's fashion. We also relished gaudy medallions and a hairy chest exposed by unbuttoned wide V-neck collars, roaring at each other's mockery.

Briskly patrolling through our territory from the southern dorms to the northern library, I signaled Gina to look at the flamboyant display ahead of us.

"What's common between this guy and a peacock?" I posed.

"What?"

"Plumage."

"Good one. I thought you were going to say the color contrasts."

The guy apparently saw us looking at him. He pointed at us with twin finger guns and called out, "Hey, foxy ladies!"

"Ha, and look, he's going to display his dramatic courtship dance," Gina said discreetly so only I could hear.

"What are your names?"

With flawless predictability, the peacock with his one-size-too-small outfit, revealed every bulge and curve of his body, bouncing his pectorals, tensing his abdomen, and flexing his arms before us.

We answered in the order he looked at us.

"Gina."

"Virginia."

He paused to let us ask his name. Being aloof though, we didn't. Nevertheless, he continued.

"Where are you two headed?"

"Library," I replied, hoping an apathetic short response missing a definite article would give him a clue.

"Oh, yeah. Whatcha studying today?"

"Chemistry," Gina briefly summarized.

"You like chemistry?" he asked with a mischievous look.

"Sure," she answered.

"Me too!"

"Yeah?"

"Uh-huh! You know if you two were elements, you'd be copper and tellurium, C-u-T-e, cuties."

We stood still, staring at him as if he were a gazelle on the plains of Africa, and we were getting ready to lunge from our hiding spots in the tall grass. His eyes flicked back and forth between the two of us, and his toothy grin started to fade.

"Do you know what happened to the last guy that tried giving us a line?"

I looked in his eyes to make sure he registered my question.

"They, argon," I cautioned.

"Now that's a good one, Virginia," said Gina.

A slight smirk returned to our prey's face.

Reinforcing the point, Gina asked, "Shall we barium, Virginia?"

Then, I could see some realization in his eyes and a little fear creep across his face.

"Yes." I answered. We start with the claws, and finish with the jaws.

"How well do you know your symbols?" I challenged him.

"I know some."

"Do you know the symbols for sodium, bromine, and oxygen?"

"Um. N-a, B-r, and O?" He said, unsure.

"Yes, you're right. Now all together, what's that spell?"

"NaBrO?" he asked, saying the word with a long A (/eɪ/) like "apex" and "nature", and looking as helpless as prey with teeth around his neck.

"Gina, are we interested?" I asked.

"Na BrO," she answered with the correct pronunciation, "gnaw".

You could almost hear his spine being ripped out, and with that, we left his sad speechless carcass behind for the vultures.

Having worked up an appetite from playing with my food, I grabbed some Rich and Fruity's Mediterranean Medley and some HARD Water Berry vitamin water from the vending machines. I inhaled the dried fruit and nuts before heading up to Ocracoke and crashing in my bean bag chair. My friends were lounging in theirs.

Bobby and Dan would never experience Gina's and my brutality, just some playful banter. They were our symbiotic oxpeckers, the birds that eat parasites off of the lions and other large mammals. We could count on them to relieve us of all the little things that sapped our energy, like homework, exams, boredom, etc. They were always there for us and I'm sure the feeling was mutual.

I took a long draw from my drink to moisten my throat and put it down beside me. "Toss me the ball," I urged Dan who looked like he was trying to throw a tennis ball as high as he could without hitting the ceiling tiles.

He threw it over. I caught the ball and spun it confidently, like it was the world in the palm of my hand. This grabbed my friends' attention, and I asked a leading question, "When we complete our degrees in four years, or five in Bobby's case..." I jeered, "...what will we have to show besides our diplomas that will differentiate us from our peers competing for the same jobs?"

Gina joked, "Maybe a husband." We laughed, but I'm sure Gina was only half kidding about wanting to find a husband in college. She was a true lioness, but she also shared with me one night that marriage and kids were definitely interests. Gina knew that she was a stone cold fox, physically in her prime. She liked learning about developmental biology, but wasn't so driven by the subject or her career as to decommission her trappings. Not interested in a horny boy, but a devoted husband with a college degree who would be a fine prize to go with her own college diploma. I, on the other hand, was a starving bear, not to be screwed with, only satiated, and my food was knowledge.

"What about you, Dan?" I asked, tossing the tennis ball back.

"I'm not sure if this is the best plan, but I was thinking of trying to work at one of the labs on campus to gain some research experience."

Dan was a point of stability and a good listener, consistently emotionally tuned into everyone in our group. Doing things the right way, not cutting corners, was important to him. His parents were Methodist, and you could really see his upbringing and faith permeate every aspect of his life. From his diligent study habits to turning down invitations to the disco.

Knowing that he wanted to do a good job, I asked Dan, "How will you know what laboratory to apply to or what research efforts will make the greatest advancements in the field of developmental biology?"

He replied, "I don't know. I figured all labs would be doing something helpful for humanity and that the professor would decide what project to put me on."

Dan tossed the ball back when I held my hands up in a catching position.

"I like your idea of working in a laboratory for some hands-on experience, but just a quick walk down the Ball Hall or the McClintock Hall will show you that some laboratories have more funding and researchers than others."

"Are you saying I should try to get into one of the best funded labs with the most researchers?" clarified Dan.

"I think they have a much better chance of making the greatest advancements."

"Why?" asked Bobby. "Seems like there could be a lot of caveats."

Bobby believed in working smarter, not harder. That's a nice way of saying he was a bit lazy and needed a good reason to do anything. The thing we loved about Bobby was his humor. His light jabbing and jokes brought the release of endorphins, dopamine, oxytocin, and other health-enhancing hormones and cultivated a mirthful mood in and out of Ocracoke.

I tossed him the tennis ball and explained, "Think of it like this. Funding agency grant reviewers give money for good ideas, but they won't keep giving money to laboratories that don't deliver results. If they don't publish impactful papers in respected journals, they won't get more money. More money translates into more researchers in the laboratory."

"Great! Now I know who to steal from," joked Bobby.

"I have an idea," I announced. I held my hands up and Bobby tossed the ball back. I took my biology and chemistry text books out of my backpack and lined them up on edge in front of me.

"What is it?" asked Gina.

"What if we write a literature review? That will help us find the laboratories that are doing the most impactful work. Publishing a literature review will also help us differentiate ourselves from our peers in the job market. We can kill two birds with one stone." Then, I bounced the tennis ball against the first book causing it to domino into the second.

Bobby challenged, "I thought you just said though that the labs with the most researchers were the best funded and the most impactful? Why write a literature review to find out the same information?"

Dan assisted, bolstering my explanation, "I get it. Writing the review helps us know which of the impactful labs are doing research *we want to do*, areas of study *we want to pursue*."

"Right," I confirmed and tossed the ball back to him.

Bobby questioned skeptically, "What makes you such an expert, Virginia?"

Dan held the ball like he was throwing a dart at Bobby. He held his hands up to receive and Dan lobbed it to him.

"I wouldn't say that I'm an expert, but it's very important for me to excel in scientific research."

"Why?" probed Bobby, bobbling the ball in his hands.

"When I'm done with college, I want to manage a laboratory with a research program to find answers to the mysteries of human development. Getting a review published as an undergrad would put me way ahead of my peers. I'd have more time to do research and accumulate more high impact publications than my peers, and be a better candidate for my dream job." What I didn't say to my friends was that I wanted them to help me so I could simultaneously add leadership as a skill on my CV with a practically relevant example. I also didn't want to talk about the deeper why of needing to be successful to prove my mom wrong and shatter the glass ceiling in science for women.

"Wow! That's stellar."

I was surprised by Bobby's quip-free compliment, and further astounded by his vulnerability when he stilled the ball and said, "It's important for me to do well too. Not just because I want to get a decent job, but because my folks aren't thrilled that I pursued science. I'm afraid that if I do poorly, they would stone me to death, at least they would lob remarks of disappointment during family meals, events, and phone calls until I was shamed to death."

"Why didn't they want you to pursue science?" asked Dan.

"They just think I'm missing out on the age of aerospace and computer science. I'm just not interested in those areas though."

Bobby and I shared more in common than I thought. I considered talking about the fight I had with my mother before coming to Steven's University, but decided to keep it to myself. Again, I didn't want to risk my friends' asking questions about such a sensitive topic and me responding emotionally and embarrassing myself. Maybe when they get to know me better and can understand where to tread lightly with certain topics, I thought.

"Way to be brave, Bobby," encouraged Gina.

Bobby blushed and stammered, "Thanks, Gina." Then, he tossed her the ball.

Turning back toward me, Bobby said, "What I mean is that I don't see how I can do well and help write a review article. I mean, I've got classes all day and we're studying in the evenings and on weekends. Are you saying we sacrifice meal times or Palace time? I need that time to keep my sanity."

"I agree with Bobby, time constraints might be an issue. I've got church events and Bible study, besides everything else," said Dan.

"Now hold on!" Gina gripped the ball tight in her fist, and pointed at me with it. "This is Virginia Goreman. Was she not the one who networked her way to the right professors and admins to get involved in planning a guest lecture series? Yes. Did she identify the speakers, coordinate their travel, or set up the venue? No, but she was the lead for promotion of the events and packed the venue, standing room only for five out of six of the speakers. And Virginia Goreman did that while simultaneously doing the same course load we all had. Is she not the queen of time management, the one who introduced us to the Pareto Principle and the Eisenhower Matrix? She is. If she says there's a way, there's a way."

Gina coming to my defense and affirming my efforts warmed my heart, but it was her faith in me that endeared her to me more than ever before.

"Thank you, Gina. The truth is that we will need to make some sacrifices to write a literature review. It takes reading thousands of pages just to write tens of pages. We will have our work ripped apart by reviewers, get rejected by some journals, and even spend hundreds of dollars for processing fees…"

"You're not really selling this," grumbled Bobby. "Why would I sacrifice my grades for this project?"

"Has anyone ever told you that B's and C's get degrees?"

"No, but that's good to hear because I wasn't planning on getting A's anyway."

Gina chuckled at this. Bobby grinned back.

"Why not just have pass or fail then?" asked Dan.

"I agree!" I said, "A caveat to the rule is that grades can be a factor for entrance into graduate or professional school. I'm planning to go to graduate school but I still believe a literature review will be worth more to an admittance committee than a higher decimal place in my GPA."

I could see the wheels turning. So, I turned up the enthusiasm to rally the troops.

"Listen, when it comes time to interview for jobs, our peers will talk about how they worked with restaurant hosts and bartenders to offer exceptional service to their patrons. *We will be able to say that we dove into the mysteries of life!* While others talk about the diligence of coming to work on time and reliably stocking the shelves with groceries after long study sessions the night before, *we will say we overcame the rigorous process of writing, editing, and publishing a scientific literature review!* Hundreds will apply for a position, but *we will get hired because of our impressive intentional college experience!*"

"How can you be so confident though that this is better than just working hard on our studies?" Dan asked, looking a little distressed. I could tell he wanted to be onboard, but was afraid to commit.

"Good question. I met a Ph.D. candidate at a college recruitment fair. She was one of the only women at the fair, so naturally I gravitated towards her. She told me about her career path, what stage she was in, how she got there, where she was going, what her regrets were, and what she would do differently if she could do it all again. Her stories were very transparent and full of sage advice."

"What did she say?" Asked Gina.

"One of the points she made relevant to this conversation was that most people work hard for their education; fewer get educated for their work. We always need to be asking ourselves about the bigger picture and how our short-term goals will actually get us to our long-term objectives."

"Wait. Do you have a topic in mind?" asked Bobby.

"I do! Human prenatal development."

"Babies?" Bobby scoffed.

"Babies!" Gina bubbled, almost simultaneously with Bobby's disdainful response. Gina's face contorted into a glare, hearing Bobby, and Bobby surrendered with a half-smile.

I explained, "It's not just about babies. There is a significant gap in humanity's knowledge of why some pregnancies progress to term while others stop or fail to start. A review of the topic will help me begin a journey toward understanding infertility and perhaps helping people with it."

"That seems like a great idea for your dream job, but what about ours?" asked Dan timidly.

"What do you want to do?"

"I mean I want to help you, but…"

"No, I mean for a career," I clarified.

"I'm not sure, but human prenatal development seems kind of narrow. I'm worried it might pigeonhole me."

"It's more broadly applicable than you might think."

"Really?" he asked with trusting puppy dog eyes.

"Yeah, if you decide to do something in psychology… Well, cognitive abilities and manifestations of disease often begin at the earliest stages of life. Maybe you decide you want to go into technology development. You could help build better tools for *in utero* visualization. Or maybe you want to make the next aspirin. Well, many of the same enzymes involved in human development are altered by pharmaceutical drugs. There are so many houses to build with this strong foundation."

"Fair points," conceded Bobby.

"She's thought of it all, the whole nine yards!" Gina complimented.

"Okay, I'll help," Dan acquiesced.

I turned my focus to Gina. She was normally very positive and encouraging to me. Even now, in the middle of my project proposal, her warm expression felt like some kind of embrace. What I couldn't be sure of and didn't want to assume was that her disposition toward me was confirmation. Any moment the affiliative smile might decay, revealing itself to be a hug conveying spectator support, that she's a real admirer, the most loyal of fans, but not a player on the team.

Searching her body language, I hoped to get a better read, but my chocolate labrador just gazed at me. Needing verbal confirmation, I resigned to straight talk. My lips parted, and I sucked in air, loading the chamber, but before I could fire off the question, Gina answered, "You know I'm with you."

Gina, Dan, and I looked at Bobby in anticipation. He looked at us with his baseline clown mask, lips turned up in a painted smile and teeth peeking out. While his smile was meaningless, a kind of defense mechanism, feelings could be discerned with a number of other clues. His wide and scanning eyes and the tension in his brow revealed some lingering reservations. But he beheld Gina. Participating in the project would mean more time with her. Capitulating to his heart, Bobby surrendered, "I'm in."

"Wonderful! I'm very glad you are all participating," I beamed, the dynamic just wouldn't be the same without Bobby. Plus, managing a three-person team would look better on a CV than managing a two-person team.

With raised eyebrows, Bobby asked, "So, when do we start?"

Chapter 9: Weblog 4 - Attributes of the Sweetvirus

Survival of men is anticipated to be very limited because of the combination of attributes engineered into the Sweetvirus. It's highly productive, has high transmission dynamics, broad tissue tropism, low immunogenicity, and high lethality. This combination of attributes is impossible outside of engineered viruses. Natural viruses are not simultaneously highly successful at spreading and highly lethal. Simply stated, if a virus is quick to kill its host, it generally doesn't spread very far. I will explain how we got around this issue, but I honestly don't know how to stop the virus from spreading.

To deliver poison into humans, I knew I needed a virus that wouldn't activate the immune system, something with low immunogenicity. You see, I can completely gut out a virus that is normally very harmful to humans, which would make it totally benign, at least it could no longer infect and replicate in a human cell. However, if I injected the gutted attenuated virus into a human, their body might over react to the harmless floating bits of virus, "thinking" they were parts of a fully functional attacking virus. Immunoglobulins might bind to block infection. T-cells might search for infected cells to destroy. Sometimes a person's immune system responds too aggressively. In the process of fighting a virus, the body might produce a cytokine storm, overwork its organs, and kill itself.

To get around an overly aggressive immune response, we and other companies have used a modified version of adeno-associated virus, or AAVs, a group of parasitic viruses of adenovirus. Humans have a robust immune response to adenoviruses, but nearly as much of a response to AAVs. Our species probably never developed an immune response to AAVs because the unmodified AAVs couldn't infect and replicate in human cells without the help of the Adenovirus.

While low immunogenicity is a clear advantage for using AAVs in gene therapy applications, they have some key limitations for the application of genocidal agents. The cargo capacity was too small, it was too expensive to scale production, and too challenging to deliver to the masses.

Autonoma Inc. researchers were therefore directed to engineer plant viruses to infect human cells instead of AAV. The differences between plant cells and human cells are substantial. Therefore, plant viruses don't normally infect human cells so there was no reason for humans to evolve immune defenses against plant viruses. So, my team genetically modified Tomato Spotted Wilt virus to have cell receptor binding proteins that enabled infection of a variety of plant and human cells. The team called their great achievement the Sweetvirus because they performed many tests on fruits initially. Subsequent tests showed that the Sweetvirus also infected vegetables, weeds, and insects, but the original name stuck.

A significant benefit of Sweetvirus over the industry standard AAV is that the large capsid more than tripled the packaging capacity. That's what allowed them to fit the genetic elements that were needed for broad infectivity and replication, as well as multiple homing endonucleases.

While it's true that AAV can be produced in large quantities using a combination of insect cells and Baculovirus, this requires special reactors and is much more expensive than our production of Sweetvirus with plants in greenhouses. Furthermore, AAV generally requires time consuming isolation and delivery by injection directly into tissue. Sweetvirus does not. Rather, Sweetvirus collects in pollen, which can act as a vector, carrying the virus right into the lungs of a human host.

Let me be clear. My scientists at Autonoma should not be held accountable in any way for what is happening. They did not know my plans.

Coronaviruses are a much more obvious choice for weaponization. They already infect humans, have many reservoir hosts, spread through the air, have low immunogenicity, and with a genome that's twice the size of Tomato Spotted Wilt virus, there's more space for engineering additional functionality.

If the use of Tomato Spotted Wilt virus didn't prevent my scientists from guessing my intentions to kill people, what should have really thrown them off was the requirement for low immunogenicity. Low immunogenicity is great for gene therapy because you want to cure a disease without creating a potentially harmful immune response. Why would a killer care if their biological weapon caused cytokine storms or other issues before killing their targets? They wouldn't.

What I was trying to achieve with the low immunogenicity was a virus that could infiltrate the human body like a flash mob in a public space. They look like everyone else, so no one suspects. Then suddenly they do this incredible choreographed dance that blows everyone away. In the case of Sweetvirus, the lung tissue is entirely penetrated before the immune system activates, and then it's too late. There's rapid onset of Acute Respiratory Distress Syndrome (ARDS), massive alveoli damage, accumulation of fluid in the lungs, inflammation, culminating in severe hypoxemia (low oxygen levels in the blood), brain damage, other organ dysfunctions, and death.

Here are some more reasons why I chose the Sweetvirus to achieve my misdirected goals.

1) Viral particles can infect a plant and replicate in the cytoplasm of cells throughout the plant. When plants grow, propagate, get eaten, etc., the virus spreads.

2) Pollen can travel hundreds of kilometers/miles from a tree. Imagine how much farther pollen spreads when dispersed from the top of a skyscraper. Autonoma Inc. owns greenhouses in 366 cities, each with over a million inhabitants. The greenhouses are located on top of tall buildings for maximum spreading. Humans are not needed to spread the Sweetvirus, just infected plants and the wind.

3) Pollen exposure diminishes antiviral interferon response, weakening our immunity against respiratory viruses.

4) Thrips and other insects eat pollen, including viral infected pollen. The virus replicates in the midgut epithelial cells and salivary glands of insects. Production of the virus scales up with insects transmitting virus to other plants through feeding activities.

5) Once the virus is released, it would persist, year after year, dormant in roots and seeds in the off seasons, replicating and spreading in open seasons like relentless tidal waves. There would be nowhere for men to hide.

Chapter 10: A crack in the doorway to my soul

Splitting the team up would be more efficient for gathering sources for the literature review. However, I knew that if left to themselves, my team might decide that they didn't really want to do this project. The best balance of efficiency and risk management was making teams of two. I paired smitten Bobby with Gina to scour the bookshelves with the help of the Dewey Decimal Classification while Dan and I searched through the microfiche archives, printing piles of journal magazines that were up to 10-years-old.

Since finding sources and summarizing abstracts and introductions was tedious work, I told my team that I would buy Ninja Stix (cheesy garlic bread) with extra Gore Sauce (marinara) to enjoy while we worked. As we found out from the Welcome Week Fair, Kung Food Pizza's pizza wasn't any good. However, their Ninja Stix were so good that Kung Food Pizza once received a sanitation score of sixty-five (out of one-hundred!), had to shut down for weeks, and when they reopened, people still lined up around the block to get some Ninja Stix.

I spaced out our project time to just two evenings a week to avoid burnout. After a couple of weeks of sorting, we had a few hundred sources. Many journal articles have far fewer references. Having too many sources was a good problem to have for a literature review. It just meant we could cull the best.

The night I thought we had enough, I asked the team, "What themes are emerging?"

"I'm seeing a lot of animals; rabbits, rats, mice and hamsters. Some frogs, toads, other reptiles, sharks, chickens, and pigs," listed Gina.

"That sounds about right. Researchers study many kinds of animals because they can be used to model human features, rather than using humans for studies. I look forward to learning what researchers were doing with sharks as it relates to prenatal development. See anything else Gina?"

"Something about mesoderm and amniotic sacs," Gina replied.

"Okay, sounds good," I encouraged. "How about you, Bobby?"

"Did you guys know that Nettie Maria Stevens, the namesake of our university, discovered sex chromosomes?"

"Yeah, they told us that during orientation. I'm glad you know that now, though," I teased. The others chuckled.

Bobby shrugged off the jest. "Isn't that out of sight though?"

We nodded our heads in affirmation.

"Anyways, I found a lot on the impact of smoking and drinking on development. Also, some articles on routine prenatal care," Bobby responded.

"My articles focus around the mothers' health during pregnancy, and how age, weight, and diseases impact health," Dan answered.

"And mine discuss the roles of fetal genetics in fetal development. Team… you've done a great job!" I said, trying to encourage my team before asking them to do more. "I think we can sort the sources by these themes."

"It's already 5:30pm though," whined Bobby.

"The problem is that our books are due. We just need to write down the names of the works, the page numbers that are relevant to the review, and which group theme they best fit under, and return them to avoid a fine. It shouldn't take more than a couple of hours, especially if we work fast." I wasn't surprised by the unenthusiastic grumblings. "Okay. Let's have a contest. Whoever sorts the most books and journal articles gets two dollars in quarters for the Palace."

Dan, a little confused, asked, "What are you going to do while we sort?"

"Oh, I'm going to help sort too, and if I sort the most then I'm keeping my quarters."

We raced and sorting did take the full two hours. Everyone was pretty competitive, but it was Bobby that devised a quick shorthand and pulled away from the pack to win the quarters.

"Great work! This was a very productive day. Thank you for all your hard work. Now, before we go, I wanted to share something with you."

While looking somewhat apathetic, my friends were still looking at me and listening.

"Don't worry, I won't keep you long. Milli, my mother, taught me this fun way of encouraging teammates when you finish something together. You slap each other's hands in the air."

"Oy vey," Bobby muttered. "You want us to play patty cake?"

"No, not pat-a-cake. Let me show you. Gina, put your hand up."

Gina held a hand up like she was going to push a door open.

"No, higher. Like this."

I showed her what I meant and said, "Leave it up there."

Then, I gave it a light slap.

"Now, instead of just holding it up there. Extend your hand at the same time as I extend mine so that they collide. Ready?"

We missed each other. Smiles started to emerge on the guys' faces as they saw us struggle.

"You guys try," I challenged.

So, they looked at each other and said, "Ready?"

Gina and I missed again but so did the guys.

"Okay, I just remembered a trick." I said, "Look at each other's elbows."

Hands started colliding with that implementation.

"Heyyy!" Bobby exclaimed, getting a real stinger from Gina.

"Wow! That's stellar, Virginia," she cheered.

"It's something that Milli saw the women's volleyball players doing between rallies during the Summer Olympics in Tokyo in 1964."

"Why do you call your mom, Milli?" inquired Gina.

I lied about the time the practice started. Like I had said before, it was during puberty. I also left out a lot of the details about the feminist ideologies that I thought might make Bobby and Dan feel awkward. I said, "When I turned sixteen, my mother wanted me to start calling her Milli because she wanted the relationship to be more adult and egalitarian. Using first names would reduce the perceived hierarchy, she said."

"Mamma would read me the Riot Act if I called her by her first name," said Gina.

"Yeah, my dad would not spare the rod," said Dan.

"I'd be just as red as your hair, Virginia," joked Bobby. "Why did Milli go to the Olympics in Tokyo?"

"She's a journalist and was tasked to cover a variety of stories at the Olympics. Milli was more interested in international politics, especially between the United States and Soviet Union, than the actual games."

"Neat. And what is this thing we are doing called?" asked Gina.

"I'm not sure. Slap hands?"

"That's a terrible name."

"Five plus five?"

"Um, no."

"Fives."

"That's better but…"

Then Dan suggested, "How about high five?"

"Oooo, I like that," said Gina.

"Yeah, good one, Dan!" said Bobby.

"Then, it's agreed. High five!"

"That's super cool that your mom is a journalist. What does your dad do for work?" asked Bobby.

"He died," I said.

"Oh, Virginia. I'm sorry," gasped Dan. His empathetic heart was already driving him to tears.

"It's okay, Dan. I didn't know him. It happened before I was born."

Gina's brow crinkled. With a perplexed look, she asked, "I'm sorry too, Virginia, but how is that possible?"

Chapter 11: N.O.W. 2 - Impersonators Stand in for U.S. President and other Officials During Crisis

News Of World report Saturday, April 22, 2023. N.O.W.'s artificial intelligence facial recognition and communication software detected discrepancies in the face and speech patterns of the U.S. President in his address to the nation this past Thursday. Through further investigations, N.O.W. determined that impersonators were hired to stand in for at least twenty-five Senators and House Representatives. Several other officials have been absent from official proceedings. Impersonators have been identified in fourteen other countries and absentee officials are ubiquitous. Few deaths have been confirmed at this point.

Chapter 12: The Palatial Palace

"My father died while my mother was pregnant with me."

Gina's face relaxed and eyes widened in sympathy. "Oh, sweetheart!"

"That is so sad," agreed Dan with wet eyes and a mournful expression.

"What happened?" Bobby asked in a timid voice. It was starting to become less alarming, but it was still weird hearing such a meek tone from someone so confident.

I briefly considered sharing the story with my friends, but decided that I just wasn't ready to show my deepest, even bloody wound. It wasn't something I wanted to show others because they might want to try to mend it. The problem is that wounds need closure to mend or scar over, and that was impossible for me. The answers and explanations I needed for healing were unavailable, gone with my father's death. I decided it was better to keep my story hidden for the time being.

"Thank you for caring, friends, but I'd rather not talk about it. Can we get back to the project?"

With compassionate frowns they acquiesced.

"So that we don't all have to read every article, we can each take a subtopic and write about it. Each of our writings will be sections of the review. Of the four subtopics we sorted, which do you like the most, Gina?"

"I liked reading about the animal models," answered Gina, wading through the awkwardness to normalcy.

"Any section works for me," offered Bobby.

"I think genetics would be the most interesting for me," said Dan.

I gave him a one-eyed confused squint, thinking he was joking. He picked the one I obviously wanted.

"You didn't like reading about the impact of maternal health on prenatal development?" I asked.

"It was fine, but genetics is the future. Everyone is trying to isolate, sequence, and connect DNA with functions and dysfunctions through the Central Dogma. It's far out," replied Dan with twinkling wide eyes and excited arm motions.

All four of us just learned about the Central Dogma in Dr. Sewer's biochemistry class. This dogma is that DNA is transcribed into RNA and RNA is translated into proteins. The proteins form cells and perform enzymatic functions. Thus, the building blocks of life come from DNA. It really is quite fascinating and *I* wanted to do that section in our review.

"What about toxins? There's plenty of intrigue there with the EPA, NIEHS, and other government organizations getting tons of grant funding to study how humans and consequently U.S. citizens and prenatal citizens are impacted by drugs and chemicals. That's super important," I exclaimed attempting to persuade Dan.

"Do you think so, Virginia?"

"Yeah."

"So, you wouldn't mind me doing the Genetics section?" he said with a toothy smile.

He got me. I blushed a little, not really sure what to say. I couldn't just take the topic from him. He was helping me and I asked which section he wanted to do.

Bobby knew I wanted to do that section as well. He grabbed Dan's arm and pulled him a few feet away and whispered in his ear. After a little back and forth, I saw Dan nod.

Bobby declared, "Only one way to decide who gets Genetics. Pinball at the Palace!"

Gina gave a hardy chortle. "Yeah, let's do it! Great idea, Bobby!"

Gina and Bobby proceeded to start walking through the bookshelves. I looked at Dan searching for some idea of why he was doing this, and feeling ashamed because of my selfishness. His eyes met mine. Dan smiled, nodded, and then turned and followed Gina and Bobby. I tailed them wondering how big of a blunder I had made.

The pinball machines were right by the Palace entrance, where patrons could see us battling. We decided to have our duel by playing the new Queens are Wild machine. The theme of the machine was Poker and was adorned with playing cards that gave the illusion of queens reaching out toward the pinball player. I liked pinball and felt confident in my ability to compete having played it since I was 10-years-old. I looked over at Dan to see if he looked nervous at all. If he was, he was hiding it very well.

Bobby gave a little announcement.

"Today we have a pinball match for the ages. In this corner, we have the Valiant Visionary Virginia, and in this corner, we have the Dedicated Dependable Dan." A couple of patrons stopped to watch. "Now for the coin toss to decide who goes first."

Bobby said more softly, "Virginia? Coin?" Holding his hand out.

I pulled a quarter from my pocket and handed it to him.

"Heads or tails, Virginia?" he said more loudly to attract more onlookers.

"Heads!" I roared, playing along.

Bobby flipped the coin masterly, like a Super Bowl referee. It must have flipped twenty times before he caught it and slapped it on the back side of his hand. For fun, he showed it to Gina. "It's tails, Dan goes first," said Bobby, and he inserted the quarter.

Dan, looking uncomfortable, stood like a statue in front while some patrons crowded on each side of him to watch. He toggled his flippers before pulling the plunger to launch the pinball as if to calibrate himself. The pinball ping ponged at the top a couple of times before dropping into a spinner that redirected his ball toward the bottom right bumper next to his flipper. A good bounce sent it to the left flipper where he barely tapped it, just enough to pass it back to the right, and then he launched it to the top. Bouncing around, it deactivated two out of eight lights. The top bumper hurled the ball back down, and the tip of the left bumper connected with the pinball. Again, this was just enough to pass the pinball to the right flipper, and again it was launched to the top where it bounced around darkening two more lights. His pinch hit-slam combos earned him a couple of replays. As stiff as he was, that pinball wizard had some supple wrists. Each round we switched off. My rounds were a bit more exciting but erratic with buzzers and bells, lights flashing. My uncontrolled full-force slams sent the ball ricocheting all over, and often to the gutters or right through the middle of my flippers. I had no strategy, and quickly lost the match.

"And the winner is Dan. Thank you for watching this program and have a lovely day," Bobby said, waving at the onlookers.

"Congratulations, you've won your choice of which section of our review you'd like to read and write about."

"I think I'll do toxins," Dan said, smiling at me.

I was taken aback.

"If that's fine with you, Bobby," he added, generously offering the option to Bobby before taking it.

"Fine with me, Dan," replied Bobby.

I looked at Dan, admiringly. He won fair and square and handed over his winnings. Why did he do that? What did he want?

"Thank you very much, Dan," I gushed, hoping that's all he was looking for.

"You're very welcome, Virginia," he beamed back. This drooped into a soft melancholic smile, "We just wish that you would open up to us a little."

"We?" I looked around at my friends, realizing that Dan's selection of my genetics section for the review and challenging me to a pinball match for it was a ploy and they were all in on it. "Oh, was that what this was about? I'm not forthright enough? I don't share enough about my past or what I'm thinking and feeling?" I snapped, snarling my teeth and gesticulating with my hands.

Dan and Gina were wide-eyed, surprised at my sharpness. "Relax, Virginia," soothed Bobby holding up his hands, palms out to me in surrender. Some other onlookers exchanged worried glances.

I scanned around, evaluating. This was what I was afraid of; looks of fear on my friends' faces. It wouldn't be long before that would turn into rejection. Part of me wanted to push them away, and end the relationships preemptively to protect myself. I wasn't ready to give up on them yet and start over with others. They had become my pride, a family away from home. Inhaling air and exhaling the tension, my conformist filter returned.

"I'm sorry," I apologized sincerely. "Maybe you're right. You've been vulnerable with me and a shelter in this wilderness. I'm going to try to be less guarded. Please understand that it's hard for me though."

My friends' expressions softened.

Gina broke off, reached out, and embarrassed me. I teared up and was about to sob thinking about how I almost was alone again, when she stroked my back and consoled, "We're here for you, whatever this is." Dan wrapped around the both of us. I caught my breath and calmed down.

"Alright, show's over," Bobby hollered, shewing at a few onlookers.

"You, okay?" Gina asked, stepping back but still holding my shoulders. Dan released.

I managed to let out a, "Yeah," mouth sticky and eyes inflamed. I wiped my tears away to see her warm tentative smile, reflecting genuine concern.

"Yeah," I confirmed a little less raspy and more audibly.

"Good! Then, we need to celebrate our progress!" she declared.

"Four quarters says we beat you, ladies…"

Gina and I looked up at him. "…you two," Bobby corrected, "at air hockey."

"You're on," I accepted, feeling more gratitude than competitive aggression.

"And after that we can play some Terraform Tracey," suggested Gina, knowing that was my favorite game in the Palace.

"That would be great. I want to try and get past level three," I said.

"I'm your copilot, Captain Virginia!"

Gina wrapped her arm around my shoulder and we all started walking toward the air hockey table. Those were the good days. Probably the best.

Chapter 13: Weblog 5 - Save Men and Uninfected Male Biomaterials

If you are a male and somehow you haven't been infected yet, you must find a pollen-free facility. Travel completely covered head to toe, with a gas mask if possible. Seek shelter in places with advanced HVAC systems like clean rooms, medical clinics with HEPA filters, and clean air spas. Go to places where pollen is non-existent, such as Antarctica, the Arctic tundra, high alpine zones, Arctic islands, and polar deserts. You will die if you simply stay in your home. Pollen will get in, you will become infected, and the virus will replicate and spread throughout your body until it can't spread any further.

The Y-chromosome is unrecoverable if we lose its source, the living cells of men. We cannot make Adam from Eve; Adam's cells from Eve's cells. A molecular biologist familiar with the state-of-the-art might know how to insert a whole Y-chromosome into a recipient cell. However, *de novo* synthesis of all sections of the Y-chromosome would be expensive, combining all the pieces together would be challenging, and getting it to fold properly would be impossible. Piecemeal insertion also wouldn't work for many reasons I won't get into.

The good news is that many organizations around the world have cryopreserved cell and tissue samples from all twenty major Y-chromosome haplogroups and all descending groups. The National Institute of Health All of Us Research Program has collected around 1 million samples, and about half are from historically under-represented groups in the United States. The China Kadoorie Biobank and UK Biobank each have about half a million participants. Germany has about two hundred thousand. Several pharmaceutical companies have cell and tissue banks as well. The largest sperm bank in the world has donors from one hundred countries. We can use these cell sources to make men.

However, while these cell banks seem extensive, they only contain about 0.002% of genetic variation (ten million out of five billion genomes). This effectively cuts the genetic variation on the planet in half, since genetic diversity will come almost entirely from females. What this practically means is that there will be many half-brothers; less variety in looks, talents, ability to fight diseases, adapt to environments, etc.

With that, governments and institutions should do their best now to sample as many healthy (virus-free) males as possible, especially in less affluent regions of the World. Save sperm and cell samples first to reestablish the gender balance once the virus has been neutralized. Take samples before transporting men to safety since there is a risk of infection during transport. Better still, airdrop sample kits and instructions for preservation.

I cannot stress enough that Pandora's Jar is open. The spread cannot be controlled. It will forever be in the environment because we cannot kill all of the plant reservoirs. The concentration of pollen and virus in the air will change from season to season, increasing and decreasing, but never ending. You must learn to live with the virus. You must render it ineffective. By no means will this be an easy task, but I have explained how the virus works. So, you have several features of the virus to target.

Chapter 14: Best Friends

First semester exams were wrapping up, and I could taste the bittersweetness of the coming holiday break.

"What's wrong, Virginia? Aren't you excited the semester is almost over?"

I was always impressed by Dan's ability to read our emotions. He could see the most subtle changes in the curvature of a lip or eyebrow, and discern our anxiety or sadness as if it were his own. It was truly a super power, the way he could relax your heart or brighten your day with an empathetic frown, bear hug, or a kind word. Part of the healing experience was derived from Dan's gentle eyes and deep voice. And while generally a quiet person, he would speak up when he thought one of his friends needed support.

"Oh, it's nothing."

While Dan wanted to help, he would stand down if his care was declined. Gina on the other hand…

"You can tell us, Virginia," she pried.

She wasn't one to shy away from reaching into the dark drain and clearing out the nasty debris clanking around down in the disposal.

"I'm just not sure what I'm going to do over the break."

"Aren't you going home?" Bobby asked from his bean bag. The rest of us were sitting at the table. We were in the middle of studying for a final exam.

"Milli and I aren't talking. I don't want to see her… Well, I do, but it's complicated."

"Do you have any other options?" asked Bobby

"Normally, my mom and I would go to my grandma's house. So, my mom will probably be there, and that means I can't go. I'm not in contact with any of my other relatives, and don't really even know where they are."

"I'd invite you to spend the break with me, Virginia, but my situation is complicated too," apologized Gina.

"It's alright, Gina."

"You could come stay at my folk's place," offered Dan, "I'm sure they wouldn't mind."

"Aww. Thanks, Dan. I don't really want to intrude though. I'll just stay in the dorms like the international students. Get a good book to read, maybe three."

While it was kind to offer, I really didn't want to interject myself into someone else's holidays or make them tend to me during their family time. The thing that I wanted was something that no one but my mother could give.

"What are we doing for dinner?" I asked, changing the subject. "What about some Ninja Stix? My treat, in celebration of all the progress we made on our review this semester."

"Sorry we didn't finish a draft like you hoped we would," Gina apologized.

"No, it's okay, Gina. We shot for the sun and hit the moon. Our progress is still impressive."

"Ninja Stix sounds neat to me," sang Bobby.

While on our way to pick up the Ninja Stix, we decided that a sleepover at Ocracoke would be fun and give us the most time to study for finals. We changed clothes at the dorms and came back in pajamas with pillows and blankets in hand. We also commandeered some extra bean bags from other library nooks for makeshift beds.

Gina tapped out about four hours later.

With droopy eyelids, she announced, "Thanks, friends. This was a great study session, but I'm fading. Think I'm going to hit the hay, or bean bags as it were. Can we go over the review questions one more time in the morning?"

"You read my mind. Time to catch some Z's," agreed Bobby.

I thought Dan might want to stay up, as thorough as he was, but he also said, "Yeah, I think I'm also going to call it quits."

"One more run through on the review questions in the morning sounds good to me," I settled.

Gina had started fluffing her bean bag bed.

"Want me to set the alarm for 8:30 am? That way we can get seven hours of solid sleep, and have plenty of time for the questions, showers, and breakfast before our final."

In a very agreeable drowsy state, Gina purred, "Far out."

"Out of sight," Bobby mocked emphatically, diving through the air into his pile of bean bags.

"Stellar," added Dan.

"Awesome," I contributed, completing the colloquial banter.

My sleepy sister lioness could not be roused by yells from us onlooking zoo patrons. Dan and I let Gina be, but Bobby found her rare vulnerability too tempting and decided to see what kind of provocations he could get away with.

Bobby's eyebrow furrowed, "Is that a tooth brush, Gina?"

She was pulling some toiletries out of her backpack and drearily responded, "Yeah. I didn't want everyone smelling my morning breath."

"I wouldn't mind," started Bobby.

Gina smiled; her eyes nearly shut.

"Might make a good alarm."

With no obvious response, Bobby turned up the teasing.

"Gina. Gina."

She looked up and paused. "Yes?"

"Why don't you ever tell a joke with morning breath?"

"I don't know."

"Because the punchline stinks."

The curl of her smile might have grown as much as a stalagmite in a year, almost imperceptibly, but it was something from the stony girl.

"Good thing you're brushing, since morning Ninja Stix breath is probably violent," he bellowed as she zombie walked around the corner toward the bathrooms, ignoring him.

When she returned about ten minutes later still plodding along, we were all laying on our bean bag beds.

"Can you flick off the lights, Gina?" I asked, not sure if the words could be heard or registered by the unvalidated sleepwalker.

Surprisingly, Gina did respond.

"Sure, Virginia. Let me just make sure I have a clear path to my bed so I don't trip…" As Gina approached, she kept her eyelids nearly shut, but her lips widened and parted. With a huge grin, she finished her sentence "…over anything like Bobby's head."

The cat was out of the bag.

Rolling with the ruse, Bobby quipped, "I'm a treacherous obstacle. Beware of the sinkhole in the middle of my mug."

Three out of four of us laughed at this. Gina looked over and saw Dan kneeling over his bean bags, hands clasped, and realized he was silently praying.

"Oo, sorry Dan. Okay if I turn off the light?"

"Yes, copasetic," he replied, still bowing his head.

"Hey, say one for me," joshed the secular Jewish Bobby.

"Praying for all of us, Bobby," Dan earnestly mumbled.

Gina swatted Bobby on her way to the light switch.

"What?" protested Bobby, feigning ignorance.

"Shhh. Stop interrupting him," Gina chided.

While Gina wasn't practicing in college, she still respected Christian prayer because of her Catholic heritage.

When she clicked off the light, Ocracoke was dimly lit by a slight incandescent glow coming from the rooms around the curve of the bookshelf hallway. She made her way around the table and back to her bed, which was next to mine. I heard Dan finish up and get under his blanket.

"Good night!" Gina saluted.

"Sleep tight!" Dan and I echoed.

Our bean bag beds were all pretty close together, close enough to hear Bobby's under-the-cover fart, which got a few chuckles. After a brief moment of silence, Gina started the pillow conversation.

"Can I ask you a personal question, Virginia?"

"Sure."

"Why are you and your mom not talking?"

The stirring around me stopped. I could tell from the quiet that everyone was waiting for my response. I hesitated, having feelings of claustrophobia, but tiredness damped my fight or flight reflex. I remembered that I promised my friends I would try to be more open, and since we weren't preoccupied with anything, there were no good reasons to deny them or delay my response.

"You don't have to say," she reassured me.

"No, I want to tell you guys. I know you all care about me."

"We do," confirmed Dan. His baritone was like a comforting weighted blanket.

"Tell us a bedtime story," solicited Bobby, the tenor buffo.

Their siege with love and humor crumbled the reinforced ramparts of my heart. Going against my fear, I decided they were worth the risk.

"Okay. My mother raised me by herself while simultaneously working as a successful journalist. Her time management skills, fearless adventurous curiosity, and zeal for a news story showed me that anything and everything was attainable."

"Why didn't you follow in her footsteps?" inquired Dan.

Dan had once shared with us that his dad was a missionary before working in his current position in a marketing department at a plumbing supply company. Like me, Dan also wanted to pursue a different vocational path than his parents, focusing more on caring for the physical needs of people rather than their spiritual needs. The book Silent Spring by Rachel Carson was very inspirational. He was struck by the vast ecological impact of pesticides. What made him interested in developmental biology was learning that among other things, pesticides caused egg shells of many bird species to thin, causing reproductive failure, and population decline. He could not see himself evangelizing in third world nations, but he *could* see himself collecting data, analyzing, and writing an altruistic book like Carson's. I think he was curious as to whether we had similar reasoning for not walking in our parent's footsteps.

"It's funny, I think there's a lot of similarities between Milli's goals and my own. For example, we both want to discover and communicate stories. She writes news articles and I want to write journal articles. Milli mainly focused on politics. My interests are in prenatal human development."

"I know you said before you, um, care about infertility and developing cures for miscarriages. Is there a deeper reason, maybe, behind wanting to study prenatal human development?" faltered Bobby. He was able to sense the serious nature of my story, and even had some idea about where it was leading, but apparently found it challenging to discuss the poignant topic he had in his mind.

"Oh, cara mia, did you lose a baby?" cried Gina, groping at me with concerned hands seeking to embosom me.

"No, no I didn't lose a baby. I didn't have a miscarriage," I clarified, slightly annoyed by them derailing the conversation and taking stabs in the dark. I tapped out of her hug like a pinned wrestler.

"Did someone else?" pursued Dan.

"Friends, just give me a couple of minutes to explain," I exclaimed, annoyed.

"Sorry for taking us off track, Virginia," apologized Bobby. I couldn't be too sore with him. His eldest sister had a miscarriage his last year of high school. From that experience, Bobby also learned his mom had one before he was born. So, of course it was on his mind.

I took a deep breath and exhaled, preparing myself to unwind the bandages covering my anguish.

"Milli used to tell me that I was a miracle-child because she and my father had lots of…" I paused, feeling a little awkward. "…well, they tried for years without conceiving. Then, when it seemed like they were never going to have children, my father decided he would find another woman to start a family with. One morning before work, he left divorce papers on the kitchen table for Milli to sign, but then…" I got choked up and couldn't hold back my tears.

"Oh, I'm sorry Virginia," Gina reached over again to embrace me. This time I was glad for it. It was really hard opening up and part of me really wanted to just close off the wound again and hide it from the world, but I decided to be strong.

She was stroking my hair trying to comfort me. "Bella…you don't have to…"

I caught my breath and released more of my pain, "My father was an electrician at a chemical manufacturing facility. The forensics pathologist explained to Milli that he electrocuted himself after failing to verify that the machinery he was fixing was de-energized."

I started balling. Gina hugged tighter. "Shhh shhh. It's okay…"

"Jeez," responded Bobby, probably disturbed from imagining the graphic nature of my father's demise.

When I caught my breath again, I explained, "This was way before the Occupational Safety and Health Act and the Occupational Safety and Health Administration standards were in effect. I considered getting a degree in something where I could make safety rules to prevent the deaths of other peoples' fathers."

My chest tightened and my throat constricted. They waited for me to calm down. I pulled some more air, fighting to lengthen and slow my rapid shallow breaths.

"Milli called my father's death *an irony, a cosmic justice* on more than one occasion. She was pregnant with me when he died. I can't help but think that if we understood infertility better, my parents would have gotten pregnant sooner, my father wouldn't have been so stressed and made the mistake at work, and he would still be alive today."

The tears returned, blurring my vision.

"I'm so sorry," crooned Gina, still holding me.

Dan's voice quavered with sorrow, appreciation, and admiration.

"Wow! Thank you for being brave and sharing that with us, Virginia. I feel like I understand you better now. That is a heavy burden to carry, but your response to the whole ordeal seems very healthy and helpful. Your pursuit is noble. Thanks for letting us be a part of it."

I was greatly relieved. Of all three of my friends, I would have thought that Dan would have been the one to try and heal my emotional gash. Instead, he characterized it correctly as my burden to carry, and committed himself to lightening the load. It was a joyful weightless moment knowing that I had secretless friendships.

"*You're so strong. Thank you,*" Gina agreed emphatically. Still trying to understand, she repeated her earlier question, "Why is your relationship with your mom strained, though? The things she said about your dad were when you were a little bambina, no?"

I wiped my eyes and cheeks with my t-shirt collar.

"Milli taught me to chase hard after what I wanted. When I shared with her that I wanted my education and career to center around researching infertility and miscarriages and developing cures… Well, to put it mildly, Milli changed her tune, arguing that my abilities were a mismatch for science and that chauvinism would prevent me from being successful."

"If she didn't approve, how are you here now?"

Bobby, like most other students, was dependent on his parent's purse to pay for college. He was actually living in his parent's house just off campus, eating their food, and his mother still did his laundry.

"I didn't really need my mom's approval. College expenses were already taken care of by my grandmother who set up a trust for me."

"Wait, the money wasn't even hers, and she still disapproved?"

"Right."

"I can see how that could get awkward during the holidays, but can't you just change the subject and talk about other things when you visit; maybe go to your room if she brings it up?"

"Yeah," Gina agreed, concisely.

Gina tended to clam up when finances were involved, probably hoping to avoid discussing her own. She had shared with us earlier in the semester that her father out of the blue left her mother. When her mother couldn't afford the mortgage, she moved to Arkansas, where she found a better paying job and lower cost of living. Gina was looking forward to seeing her mom's new digs over the winter break. While it was never said, it seemed likely to me that Gina was on some kind of need-based financial aid given the circumstances.

Answering their question, I stressed, "Milli is a fact communicator. Very black and white. In just a couple of sentences she can tell you why something is great or a Dung beetle's dream and support her assertions with statistics, international and demographic comparisons, etc. She's an elite journalist. I'm afraid she's going to tear apart my dreams again and convince me to do something else, and then I won't get a chance to make a difference in something I'm actually passionate about."

There was a pensive silence.

"Well, that makes me want to help you get this review done even more," Dan trilled between sympathy and support.

"Yeah, we're going to help you show your mom that you *can* make a huge impact!" Gina declared, earnestly recommitting herself to my cause and speaking on behalf of the group.

"Excuse me. *We?*" Asked Bobby. "I mean it sounds like Dan's on board, but what am I, chopped liver?"

"Alright, alright. Sorry, I assumed, Bobby. Do you want to help Virginia make a huge impact?"

"We wouldn't be though. Would we? We'd just be helping identify how *someone* can make a huge impact," Bobby corrected facetiously. He was referring to the fact that a scientific review just summarizes the present state of a field of research and what follow-up studies could contribute to its advancement.

Gina got out of bed. I could see her silhouette. She kneeled down and punched Bobby in the shoulder.

"Ow! What was that for?" he complained.

Gina found this amusing so she kittenishly jabbed him a couple more times.

"Ow! Ow!"

"Like Virginia said before, the review is going to show us which laboratories we should work in. The review is just the first step."

Bobby grabbed Gina and started tickling her. She giggled and wriggled away from him, jumping back to her bed. "That's right. Go to bed!" he goaded.

Then Gina pinged to Bobby, pinning him and tickling into uncontrolled laughter. He yelled, "Mercy, mercy," until she relented and ponged again back to her bean bags.

After a moment of peace, Bobby gave an impish threat. "I wouldn't fall asleep if I were you, Gina."

"Try anything Bobby, and I'll tickle you so hard, you'll wet your bean bags."

Bobby started belly laughing which got us all going.

"Good one, Gina."

I felt lighter than air. To be known and still loved is truly a great feeling, maybe the greatest.

"Night, all. Thanks for caring," I concluded.

"Definitely, Virginia. Night, all," saluted Dan.

"Night, all!" Gina and Bobby said in unison and laughed at the timing.

In the morning, we ate some Rich and Fruity's Mediterranean Medley and drank some HARD Water Berry to tide us over while we reviewed the practice questions for the final. We skipped breakfast, but took showers before going to class. When the test was over, we rendezvoused at the Palace. The year wrapped up in fierce competition at the pinball machines and Terraform Tracy. Victory and peace reigned in our lives. It was a beautiful moment for us.

My friends headed out for the holiday break later that day, eager to get off campus. The student exodus left an expansive ghost town. Cold and alone, there was just one thing to do, grab a few science fiction classics from the library and hunker down in my dorm. I decided on checking out Jules Verne's *Twenty Thousand Leagues Under the Sea*, and H. G. Wells' *The Island of Doctor Moreau*, as well as a first edition copy of the book that created the genre, Mary Shelley's *Frankenstein; or, The Modern Prometheus*.

I came out of the dorm for the occasional walk and to sup with the international students at the local eateries that remained open on Hodgkin St. A man trawled around Hodgkin St, hailing the international students, and inviting them to holiday events in his cozy-looking parka. He was a beautiful man in his late twenties or early thirties with a narrow delicate nose, long wavy dirty blonde hair and matching facial hair; Da Vinci's Jesus in the flesh. I might have joined the man if he invited me to an event. A dirty thought crept in my mind that I might have joined him in bed if he asked.

Chapter 15: N.O.W. 3 - Infectious Agent Determined to be Cause of Global Pandemic

News Of World report Sunday, April 23, 2023. The Chinese Center for Disease Control and Prevention, University of Sydney, and Charité – Universitätsmedizin Berlin have published DNA sequences of the infectious agent causing the global pandemic. Preliminary analysis indicates high sequence similarities with Tomato Spotted Wilt virus and xenotropic properties. The qualities of the virus suggest it is able to infect cells of multiple species including humans and plants.

Chapter 16: Reverend Jim

A week and half later, the students came back from holiday break and I saw the golden stranger at the south entrance to the brickyard. One could hear his projected proclamations and queries from far off. While his volume was very inclusive, his words seemed directed exclusively to one young woman that was just a couple of yards away. The frizzy-haired brunette had a smart plaid skirt with a matching green top that looked fantastic on her. The vociferous man's emerald green eyes were fixed on her.

"Do you listen? I mean, do you really try to listen and hear the voice? You know you've heard Him before. He's directed you, warned you, counseled you, and he wants to speak with you again. Will you listen?"

"I would, if it told me where my class was," the approaching young woman trolled. She chuckled mockingly and turned her head to see if her two guy friends liked her joke. They tittered back. The ratio of men to women at Nettie Maria Stevens University was very favorable for even mildly attractive women interested in the opposite sex. So, getting guys to laugh at your jokes didn't necessarily mean you were funny.

The golden stranger returned a generous chortle, which I felt a little envious of. That is until I saw both the young woman and her companions stop and listen to him. He addressed all three now, not just her, and I discerned that his laugh was calculated and an effective lure. Perhaps the young woman would have stopped too if the guys were first snared, but guys are less agreeable. Getting them to stop and talk might have been more challenging. If I was right, the golden stranger was impressively strategic.

"What about you, preacher? Do you know where Livingston Hall is?" asked the young woman.

"Yes, go up these stairs behind me, walk straight until the library is next to you on your right, but don't walk toward it, *walk straight*. Once you can't walk straight any further, Livingston Hall will be the building on your left." Pointing his finger would have sufficed, but it wouldn't have been as engaging or seemingly helpful, which further supported what I surmised to be astuteness.

"And here, take one of these." The preacher handed the young woman a piece of paper.

"Oh, you're hosting a Bible study?"

"Yes, I'm a local reverend and I lead a modern multi-racial interracial church and multiple Bible studies. Come and bring your guy friends."

"Oh, multi-racial, neat! Maybe I will. Thanks for the directions to class, Reverend…?"

"My name is Reverend Jim, and you all are?"

"Nancy."

"I'm Todd."

"And I'm Andy."

I heard them share as I passed by.

"Catch you on the flipside," greeted Reverend Jim as the trio departed at my heels.

Reverend Jim was at the same brickyard entrance the following morning. As I approached, he said to me, "Did you know that your Father in Heaven wants to know you?"

"My father in Heaven?" I questioned, thinking he was talking about my deceased father.

"Yes. Do you know your Heavenly Father?"

"No," I said, still a little confused.

"Do you know Albert Einstein?"

"Of course."

"Harry Truman?"

"Very well."

"Mother Teresa?"

"Somewhat."

"Excellent. Well, the Heavenly Father is smarter than Albert and more powerful than Harry back in 1945 when the U.S. was the only country to have nuclear weapons. Most importantly, He loves you and me *and all of us* more than a thousand Mother Teresas. He's loving us right now by connecting us together. Do you want to know more about Him?" He asked with a captivating green-eyed gaze.

My mother was not interested in *religion*. This word came with a negative connotation in our home. It mainly came up in conversation when she was on assignment and a politician incorporated something religious in a sound bite. She'd say something like, "How disingenuous? Indulging his *religious* constituents for votes in the upcoming election." So, I never had a chance to explore the idea that my father might still be in the ether somewhere, perhaps a destination that I could go to someday. The gorgeousness of the man made his invitation all the more interesting.

"Yes, I would, but I need to get to class now."

"I don't want to hold you up, but what is your name?"

"Virginia."

"Nice to meet you. I'm Reverend Jim."

"Here's a flier for our next Bible study. Hope the time works for your schedule. If it doesn't, my contact info is on the flier. We can always meet at a time that's more convenient for your schedule and talk more about the Heavenly Father."

I looked at the flier and noticed that it said, "Reverend Jim Marshall's GOLDS Church (God's Obedient Latter Day Saints Church)." How perfect of a name I thought for the golden stranger's church.

"Latter Day Saints?" I asked, hoping he would tell me what that was.

"Yeah, we're not affiliated with the LDS Church but some of their beliefs are part of our statement of faith and some of their practices are part of our church covenants. There are many differences though. For example, we are more inclusive. Black people can be priests in GOLDS Church," he advertised.

The jargon like LDS, saints, and covenants was foreign to me. I didn't have time to get clarification so I just said, "Alright, thank you," and continued on to class.

"Thank you, Virginia!"

I was curious about what Reverend Jim had to say and actually planned to try his Bible study. I told myself that 'college is a great time to explore thoughts and beliefs about why things are the way they are.' What I really craved deep down was a little hope that I might meet my father someday. I had a fascinating lecture, an engaging discourse, an interactive class activity, and capped the day off with an Ocracoke group study session. Somewhere along the way, in the busyness, I forgot all about Reverend Jim and the seed he had sown. The birds of the air came and devoured it.

Early in the month of February, Reverend Jim was on campus again giving out flowers and chocolates.

"Here's a flower for you," he said to a young woman who was walking by his spot at the south entrance of the brickyard. "How come this tall handsome stud didn't get you a flower?"

"Yeah, Patrick?" said the pretty young woman.

"Well, it's not Valentine's Day yet," the guy responded defensively.

"Have you heard of the cultural mandate?" Jim asked.

"No, what's that?" asked the young woman.

"It's the command from Jehovah to *be fruitful, and multiply, and replenish the earth, and subdue it; and have dominion over the fish of the sea, and over the birds of the heavens, and over every living thing that moveth upon the earth.* This was the command to Adam and Eve, Noah's family, and everyone in the whole world by extension."

"Interesting. So, your saying Jehovah said to make babies and rule over nature."

"Yeah, basically. Have you been faithful in multiplying or are you at least seeking the right man to lead you and your family?"

"No, just practicing right now, Reverend," the young woman said cheekily, smiling at her friend.

"Hold on one second." He paused the conversation with the young woman, and beckoned to me, "Virginia!" Before I could walk by, he urged me to stay for a moment.

"I've got a flower and a word for you."

I stopped and moved off to the side, out of the flow of students headed to class.

"Just give me one second, Virginia."

I nodded.

He turned his attention back to the couple, "I must warn you that fornication is sinful. However, we have not a high priest that cannot be touched with the feeling of our infirmities; but *one that hath been in all points tempted as we are*; and He shares mercy and grace when we least deserve it."

"Good thing," said the guy.

"Yes. You two should be preparing yourselves for a virtuous life."

"Why?"

"Because the end will come someday, and the righteous and unrighteous will be judged and will either be saved or condemned for the rest of eternity."

"Wow. You really believe that?"

"Yes, you must get ready. Sacrifice and consecrate everything for the Lord."

"What about *now* though?"

"What do you mean?"

"I mean I just want to have fun in college. Let's say you are right. Can't I just sacrifice after college?"

"No, and here's why. Righteousness makes you ready for marriage."

The students looked at each other.

"Trust me, you're not going to want to wait too long after college to get married."

"Why?" said the guy.

"Well, for one, love making is better when you're young. Also, you don't want to be an old dad who can't run around with his boys."

"What does righteousness have to do with getting married?" queried the young woman.

"Think about it. Marriage isn't just supposed to last while you live on this earth. It is meant to be eternal. The unrighteous will be split from the righteous. So, to be together for eternity, you both need to be righteous."

The young woman and guy looked at each other again, the woman with amorous eyes and the guy looking unsure.

"Be righteous, get married, and you will live together forever with your family in the Celestial Kingdom."

"Far out," said the young woman.

"Here's a flier for our next Bible study. Hope to see you two there."

"Thank you, Reverend," said the young woman taking the flier.

Turning his attention back to me, Reverend Jim excitedly proclaimed, "Virginia! It's good to see you! Here's a flower for you."

"Thank you, Reverend Jim!"

"We've missed you at the last four Bible studies."

"Yeah, I've been really busy and just forgot about it."

"I understand. It's easy to forget when you haven't attended," he said and paused.

Right before I was about to say goodbye and continue walking, Jim said, "I'd really like you to come visit. We've had a lot of great things happening at the studies. Students are learning about their Heavenly Father. There's a growing interest in baptism, confirmation, service in mission, and more. Can I give you another flier as a reminder to come?" Again, he pierced my heart firing Cupid's arrows with his mesmerizing eyes.

"Sure."

"Thank you, Virginia! Please come this week if you can make it."

"I'll see if I can. Thank you, Reverend Jim." I was almost certainly going to go. Just wanted to play it cool and not act too eager.

Chapter 17: A New Experience

The Bible study was hosted at Foote, one of the all-female dorms on campus. I was surprised to see two tall muscular black men welcoming me with a hand shake. It wasn't so surprising that they were men. College-aged people in the 1970s, especially the Northeasterners, were sexually liberal, and so finding men in a female dorm was pretty normal. However, races generally remained separated for extracurricular events. This was a sad reality despite the illegality of segregation with the passing of the Civil Rights Act over a decade earlier. Here though, in a multipurpose lounge with three four-seater sofas and lots of extra chairs, a diverse array of men and women, blacks and whites gathered together, and everyone seemed quite relaxed and genuinely comfortable with knee-to-knee, shoulder-to-shoulder proximity.

Reverend Jim's microphone-amplified voice grabbed everyone's attention. "Thank you all for coming! Welcome to our second week of celebrating Black History Month. Just as it sounds, we are celebrating the history of our black brothers and sisters. We do this because, to quote the bold and brilliant Carter G. Woodson, *"If a race has no history, it has no worthwhile tradition, it becomes a negligible factor in the thought of the world, and it stands in danger of being exterminated."* More positively, our black brothers and sisters have an important history and worthy traditions. They must remain a key factor in our minds because they are in the mind of Jehovah. We will *all* stand together worshiping Him in eternity. Warren, hit it!"

Warren, one of the black men that greeted me at the door, pulled out an acoustic guitar from behind him and said, "Sing along if you know the words." He played a few chords and most people in the study cheered, recognizing the song.

"When I die and they lay me to rest,
Gonna go to the place that's the best.
When they lay me down to die,
Goin' up to the spirit in the sky..."

At the end of the song everyone was cheering. "Wasn't that stellar?!" exclaimed Reverend Jim, and more applause followed. "Yes, Warren is very talented. Great to have you all here! Keep packing in. Get comfortable," Reverend Jim said to a few people showing up late. "Thank you for coming. We love Jehovah and we love our neighbors at this Bible study. So, at this time, take a few minutes to greet those beside, behind, and in front of you with the peace of Christ."

A cacophony of noise erupted in the room. People were shaking hands, smiling, and chatting. Jim let that go on for about three minutes.

I met Harris, one of the tall, handsome black men who welcomed me at the entrance of the dorm. I wondered if this was part of Reverend Jim's strategy, to have the welcomers take note of new faces and make sure they were greeted during this interlude. In any case, I was glad Harris came over. He had a great smile with pearly white teeth that were accentuated by his contrasting dark cocoa black skin. Additionally, his rippling muscles and gorgeous center-parted afro made for an attractive package. I found out he was a junior and was studying business management.

"How did you meet Reverend Jim?" I inquired.

"We connected at the disco."

Small talk quickly became interesting.

"Really?"

"Yeah, that funky cat can really boogie."

I chuckled thinking of a man reluctant to give up his youth, and finding some guilty pleasure dirty dancing with college girls. I wondered if the disco was where he compromised his pulpit integrity.

As if reading my thoughts, Harris commended him. "Reverend Jim is the genuine article. He's squeaky clean at the disco. And I really dig him for going. He's a preacher man and more. He's schooling me big time about God, and showing me the ropes on how to run an enterprise."

"How about you? How did you connect?" he questioned back.

"He's talked to me a couple of times at the south entrance of the brickyard."

"There you go. Consistency with outreach." Harris looked around. Probably reminded that he was tasked to mingle with the new attendees. "Glad you came, Virginia. I'll catch you later."

"Thank you."

I wasn't sure if I was coming back. The unfamiliar practices didn't bother me. Rather it was something Harris said. I wondered how Reverend Jim or any reverend who was starting a church could be uncompromisingly virtuous. I mean, everyone needs money to live, and unless he was independently wealthy or had a side job, he needed his congregation to give him money. Even if God was at the forefront of his mind, money had to be in the back.

A straight-haired brunette girl with hot pants who I saw roaring with laughter at Reverend Jim's mildly funny jokes approached me and introduced herself, "Hi, I'm Alice," but before I had a chance to talk with her, Reverend Jim spoke into his microphone.

"Alright. Thank you. Thank you," he addressed the group, and everyone found their way back to their seats and quieted down. "We are going to open up our study in prayer. Please bow your heads in reverence to Jehovah."

Heads bowed and eyes closed. Curious, I peeked a couple of times to see what was going on around the room. Torsos were tilted to varying degrees of reverence, some bouncing their bodies and heads in agreement. Some affirming the prayers with "Yes, thank you, Jehovah." I wondered if anyone in the room was actually interacting with a powerful Being who was capable of answering prayers.

Reverend Jim seemed to think he was, praying, "Thank you, Jehovah, for last week's celebration of the anniversary of the signing of the 15th Amendment in 1870, which guarantees the right for our Black brothers and sisters to vote in U.S. elections. Thank you that this week we get to celebrate the anniversary of the National Association for the Advancement of Colored People that formed in 1909. Black activists and white reformers sought to promote equality of rights and eradicate racial prejudice after a troubling increase in the frequency of lynchings. We are grateful for your Spirit acting upon those people to combat such heinous crimes in the U.S. God's obedient saints said, please bless our nation, Jehovah."

"Please bless our nation, Jehovah," the room responded emphatically.

"We also thank you, Jehovah, for the support of Egypt, Lebanon, Paraguay, Peru, Saudi Arabia, Syria, Turkey, Uruguay, and Venezuela who joined the Allies in the early part of February 1945 to help stop Nazi Germany, Italy, and Japan's pursuit of World domination. We would not enjoy the same freedoms we do today if it were not for our wonderful neighbors. And God's obedient saints said please bless our allies, past and present, Jehovah."

"Please bless our allies, past and present, Jehovah," repeated the crowd.

"Finally, we pray for the South Carolinians whose homes were damaged last year by eight-foot piles of snow collapsing their roofs. We pray for the generosity of Jehovah's people to restore at least some of the thirty million dollars in assets these poor people lost. And God's obedient saints said, please bless us to be generous with what is ultimately yours, Jehovah."

"Please bless us to be generous with what is ultimately yours, Jehovah."

"At this time, we will take up a collection for the South Carolinians whose homes were damaged last year by the largest blizzard in their history."

Warren started playing again. "Lift up your voice to Jehovah if you know this one."

"I can see clearly now, the rain is gone
I can see all obstacles in my way
Gone are the dark clouds that had me blind
It's gonna be a bright (bright), bright (bright)
Sun-shiny day…"

Harris was given one of the collection plates. He walked around the crowd slowly looking into people's eyes with his arm stretched toward them. Most took out their wallets and dropped at least a dollar in the till. I did, feeling obliged because of all of the other participants.

Ken was collecting money on the opposite side of the room. I would have never guessed he would be part of an event celebrating Black History Month. Gina pointed him out a couple of times to me on our hunts. Not really sure how she knew his name, but Ken usually sported a shaggy mullet and his garb consistently included jeans, cowboy boots, and a t-shirt with cut-off sleeves that showed his tattoo montage. He also wore giant tinted sunglasses outdoors and apparently indoors too.

After the benevolence collection, Reverend Jim facilitated a lively and respectful conversation on what the Book of Philemon can teach Christians about reconciliation between black and white communities in modern times. His inclusion of minorities, ability to open interracial dialogue, and his prioritization of prayer and the needs of others kept me coming back week after week to his Bible studies.

Reverend Jim finished with, "Now, I would be remiss in not discussing romance as we approach the amorous holiday of St. Valentine's Day. While it is a minor Church holiday, and highly commercialized, permit me to use it as a tool for edification of the Saints … and all of you."

Chuckles went around the room.

"One of the common yet very important ways that we can bring glory to Jehovah is by filling the Earth with His image-bearers. He wants men and women who are committed to loving and enjoying Him while reflecting His reign and rule over all creation forever. Let me be clear, it is not enough to have offspring. We must raise up children in the ways of Jehovah. Unified, godly, and loving fathers and mothers are prerequisites to GOLDS children. Come back each week and take with you some golden nuggets of wisdom from the Word shared by yours truly, Reverend Jim Marshall. Until next week, stay holy!"

Warren started playing again as another band member, Phoebe, beautifully sang,

"Oh, happy day (Oh, happy day)
Oh, happy day (Oh, happy day)
When Jesus washed (When Jesus washed)
Oh, when He washed (When Jesus washed)…"

Reverend Jim started clapping and everyone else joined in. Warren and Phoebe slowly led the procession of students toward the stairs like a parade. Some students that didn't attend the study came out and joined in the clapping. Reverend Jim cut beyond the front of the line and stopped at the bottom of the stairs while Warren and Phoebe continued playing, singing and guiding the crowd out of the dorm. Jim shook people's hands as they left.

A few days later, I was sprinting to the library through an empty brickyard. I was trying to briskly escape the bone chilling February wind and cold. The buzz of the hive seemed louder than usual. My friends had beat me to Ocracoke, and upon arrival, Dan gave me a Valentine's Day flower. Bobby gave Gina one too. The thoughtfulness of the gift made me feel as warm as the summer. I don't remember if I grabbed Gina or if she grabbed me, but we had a quick huddle and spontaneously decided we would give our kind young men a kiss on the cheek.

We walked over to them with sweet smiles and hands behind our backs and said, "Close your eyes."

Dan was too tall for me to kiss even when I was on my tippy toes. So, I said, "Keep your eyes closed," and I put my hands on his shoulders and pulled him forward. Dan responded, leaning over, and I laid a nice full lipped kiss on his cheek.

He opened his eyes and warmly smiled.

I smiled back briefly and said, "Alright, ready to get back to work, crew?"

No one answered, so I looked over at Gina and Bobby. Gina had her arms wrapped around Bobby's neck and looked like she was Frenching Bobby.

I looked back over at Dan wide eyed. He still had a lingering smile left on his face, savoring our kiss.

Gina and Bobby were really going at it, so I said "Okay, okay. This is Rosalind Elsie Franklin Public Library, not your private dorm room," and pried them apart.

"Whoops," Gina feigned a lapse in judgment, wiping her mouth.

Everyone was grinning except me who just wanted to roll it back to five minutes ago when we were all just friends. What I thought was just an innocent thank you kiss was actually a relationship changer, a boundary mover at minimum. The meaning of the exchange raised a lot of unspoken questions in my friend group.

We worked on the review article, but that evening was full of winks and smirks and other flirtatious nonverbals. I mostly ignored the one's coming from Dan, whereas Gina and Bobby were rather unproductive.

Dan walked me back to my dorm after the study. He seemed to think that he had a chance with me even though I clearly was not reciprocating any nonverbal flirtatious cues. The cheek kiss gave him a burning hope. It was like a surviving ember hours after a campfire. The fire was gone, but it was still red hot and protected from the wind by partially burned logs and ash surrounding it. The only way to put it out was by dousing it with water. I couldn't do that to Dan though. So, I just let it smolder and said, "Good night. Thanks for walking me back to my dorm."

Why couldn't flowers just mean kindness? Dan was smitten, and I'm sure his flowers were part of a plan to ask me out. Did I appreciate flowers? Yes. Was I interested in Dan? No. All the cute guys on campus were, at most, fleeting temptations. Sure, I had fantasies from time to time, frequently actually, but I really didn't want to complicate my life with any kind of romantic relationship. The Bible study was enough of a distraction from what I wanted to accomplish. On the other hand, part of me wished the flowers from Reverend Jim had more meaning, not just a promotional item to lure women to his Bible study.

Jim was really very intentional with his marketing, and more importantly, successful. After Black History Month and Valentine's, word spread of how vocal and inclusive he was, and attendance of black people and women went up significantly; so much so that he had to bud off another study. I stuck with the Wednesday night study. The Thursday night one didn't work well for my schedule because my friends and I often studied for organic chemistry exams that were held on Fridays. "Orgo" was our hardest course that semester.

In March, Reverend Jim was teaching us about Sanctification, the process of becoming holy.

"I'm going to throw out some words you've probably never heard before. I assume that's okay with you since you're in college, and people come to college to learn, right? At least mostly come to college to learn."

A few people chuckled at this.

"The first word is *sin.* Jehovah gave us a little more than six hundred laws to follow which are recorded in the Old Testament; that is all of the books in the Bible before the Gospels. That sounds like a lot of laws to abide by, right?"

Some people nodded their heads in agreement.

"I used to think so too, but those of you studying U.S. Law would probably find this to be comparatively miniscule. I'm looking at you, Nathan."

Nathan smiled and waved. He was studying to become an attorney.

"To put things into perspective, the whole Old Testament, which includes not only the Law, but also the prophets, amounts to about *six hundred thousand words.* Since World War II, the U.S. Congress adds about *six million words* of new law every two years! Can you confirm that I'm telling the truth, Nathan?"

Nathan verified, "Yes, that's about right."

"Wow! *Six million words* every two years. Now the Old Testament seems like light reading, doesn't it?"

There was more laughter in the room.

"The point I'm getting to is that each of you has either *acted against or failed to act on* one or more of Jehovah's laws. Some people forget that He doesn't just have *thou shalt not* commandments. He *also* has *thou shalt* commandments. And doing things he says not to do are just as bad as not doing things He says to do. Some common transgressions include using the Lord's name in vain, being envious of others' fortune, failing to set aside the Sabbath as a day of rest, and failing to honor our parents. Have you good Christians done any of these things?

Reverend Jim searched around the room.

"Be brave," he said, still combing through the crowd.

Nancy raised her hand. The first time I saw her, she was invited to the Bible study by Reverend Jim at the south entrance to the brickyard. He had expertly fished Nancy, and lured two guys accompanying her. The guy friends who laughed at her joke weren't with her now. They must have released Reverend Jim's line, or maybe they left her.

"Yes!" Reverend Jim said excitedly, pointing at Nancy. "That is a confession! Way to be brave! Anyone else?"

Nancy smiled like a child praised by her parents. Everyone needs some validation, but I was irritated by how much she needed.

Then, others started raising their hands.

"Yes! Yes! Yes!" Jim was pointing his fingers at everyone raising their hands.

I thought maybe I was being too judgmental, and considered again what Reverend Jim was saying.

Memories of envious thoughts of my mom's success came to mind. I wasn't exactly sure what honoring fully entailed but thought that if it included obedience, I certainly was guilty of going against her wishes with the pursuit of a degree in Developmental Biology. And I definitely wasn't observing any sort of rest day on a weekly basis. Surprising myself, I raised my hand.

Looking around the room, it looked like everyone raised their hand. One especially guilty-looking guy with a downcast face had two hands up.

Jim said, "So, what you've done is sinned, and having sinned, you are now a sinner. You've gone against Jehovah's rules. When you go against the rules in the United States, you might have to pay a fine, take a class, do community service, or you might have to go to jail, prison, and in the worst circumstances, the electric chair. If you violate the rules of the Supreme Being, the penalty is eternal separation from Him. It's Hell. And who are we to tell the Supreme Being *that's not fair?*"

Reverend Jim dared us, "Anyone want to challenge the all-knowing, all-seeing, all-powerful creator of the Universe?" His normally dreamy beautiful eyes were intensely bugging out of his head.

I wanted to say that it wasn't fair. Why would the penalty be the same for different transgressions? Surely murder must be worse than envy. Silence seemed more prudent since my knowledge on the topic was very limited.

After a few more paces around the room without response, he continued, "God's Obedient Saints, you need your sins paid for to avoid eternal separation. The Israelites used to sacrifice animals to pay for their sins at the Temple in Jerusalem. That stopped because the temple, where they were supposed to do it, was destroyed in 70 A.D. So, you can't do that anymore. *What will you do* to make up for your sins?"

"Truhst in Jee-sus!" said with a long vowel drawl and relaxed pronunciation. It was the indoor-sunglasses-wearing mullet-haired Ken. I was starting to admire his non-conformist true-to-roots style. While we weren't uniting every tribe and tongue in the GOLDS, Ken at least helped improve the motley quality of our crew.

"Yes, that's right, Ken. Let me clarify for those who are unfamiliar with the Gospel and what my brother is referring to. John the Baptist prophesied that Jesus was the

Lamb of God who would take away the sin of the World. Jesus prophesied His own murder and said it had to be so. Since He was without sin, He was like an innocent animal being sacrificed when He was murdered. We won't get into the details of Jesus's murder now, but just know that He was murdered. Since Jesus is God, the sacrifice of His life covers more than just the Nation of Israel for a year. His blood covers the cost of *everyone's* sin throughout the whole World and through the generations. That is, *if you have faith*. Does anyone know what I mean by: *if you have faith*?"

"If we believe," someone piped up.

"Yes! Thank you. Let me provide the actual verse for what we are talking about." Jim opened his Bible to where a bookmark was sticking out and began to read, "Paul tells us in Romans 10 that *if thou shalt confess with thy mouth Jesus as Lord, and shalt believe in thy heart that God raised him from the dead, thou shalt be saved.* Sounds simple right?"

People nodded their heads. "Yeah," someone blurted.

"In a sense it is, but let me ask you this, how do we really know if we're saved? Put another way, what should faith produce?"

"Works!" Alice belted out.

"Excellent, Alice. Yes, Jesus' brother James tells us that *faith, if it have not works, is dead in itself.* Dead!"

He paused for emphasis.

"Yea, a man will say, Thou hast faith, and I have works: show me thy faith apart from thy works, and I by my works will show thee my faith. He says, "Prove it!" Amen?"

"Amen!" some of the attendees agreed.

"Thou believest that God is one; thou doest well: the demons also believe, and shudder. Belief, he's saying, just means awareness. It is not enough to know that the one true God is king of the Universe. Do you just know about God?"

Reverend Jim wheels around asking the question of everyone, *"But wilt thou know, O vain man, that faith apart from works is barren?* Say, "Yes!""

"Yes!" we affirmed.

"For as the body apart from the spirit is dead, even so faith apart from works is dead. So, if you have faith, you are *going* to have works. Do *you*, good Christians, have works that point to your salvation?"

Jim looked around the room for a moment with a giant grin. "Good job. You passed the first test. No gloaters."

A few people chuckled and Alice was doubled up.

"Thank you. In all seriousness though. If you are going to call yourself a follower of Jesus, there are some key ceremonies that you are going to participate in at least once in your life and there are some activities that you're going to do on a regular basis. Again, these are not things that *determine* your salvation, they are merely *evidence of* your salvation.

Chapter 18: Priesthoods

Soon after joining the GOLDS, I learned that they rejected Christian holiday celebrations. Reasons abounded from man-made origins, to pagan traditions, to commercialism. The greatest concern though was that consistent rich, often spontaneous, Christian living would deteriorate into superfluous Christian observances.

"Jesus says *the wind bloweth where it will, and thou hearest the voice thereof, but knowest not whence it cometh, and whither it goeth: so is every one that is born of the Spirit.* Jehovah does not lead you to a life of monotony. We must be agile and listen to the Holy Spirit, go where He wants us to, and do what He wants us to," Reverend Jim sermonized.

It was Spring 1975, and the mainstream rhythms of Christian and Judaic traditions were in bloom. Gina was telling Dan that he shouldn't be eating meat on Fridays and that we should all go out for fish, and Bobby wanted us to do some Spring tidying at Ocracoke. The traditions seemed fun and innocent. Why not join in? I didn't feel like I was diluting the potency of my Christian life, but I also didn't really feel super engaged in church at that point. When James Rupert murdered his brother, sister-in-law, all eight of their children, and his mother on Easter, the deadliest mass shooting to take place at a private home, I took it as a sign that not taking part in the holiday was fine.

It wasn't that I was apathetic about God and faith. Normally, I'd jump right into something like that without looking, hoping there was water down below, but I was already up to my ears with studying, the review, and I was also volunteering on a developmental biology seminar series committee. Guest speakers at other institutions across the United States were invited to give talks for our department. Being involved was great for networking and exposure to the field. With all of these commitments, one night a week for church was enough.

In the absence of standard traditions Reverend Jim pushed forward with the liturgical calendar supplementing with teachings on the sacramental ceremonies of GOLDS Church.

"GOLDS take the following six sacraments very seriously- Baptism by Water, Baptism of the Holy Spirit, the Lord's Supper, Return from the Mission, Sealing, and Holy Orders. Some of the people here today, like Ken, have already started leveling up in the Holy Orders."

The Holy Orders was a sacrament that involved male and female members being called to a Levitical priesthood, promoted through the ranks, and then potentially onto Melchizedek priesthood if members were male. The sex discrimination in the higher order was hard for me to swallow having come from a line of bold feminist women. However, Reverend Jim supported the gender-specific ordinations with a variety of Bible verses so I tolerated the idea, wanting to hear how this compared with my friend's religious traditions. They would be a good soundboard given their heterogeneous backgrounds.

I shared my reservations about the GOLDS practice at Ocracoke the following evening. Bobby poked fun. I gathered that he found it peculiar, and Dan seemed to agree with the exclamation, "Far out!"

"Is it, Dan?" Gina challenged, "Priests are all men in the Catholic Church. Isn't that the case in Protestant churches?" Her words sounded seasoned with bitterness, or perhaps contempt.

"Ah, well," Dan fumbling his words said timidly, "I think women started being ordained about twenty years ago in the Methodist Church. I can't really speak for the rest of the Protestant denominations."

"Not that you asked, but Judaism also has ordained female rabbis," noted Bobby proudly.

"Well, la-di-dah," Gina sneered with hands on her hips.

I sensed that comparison conversations like these might become contentious and decided to discontinue it for the sake of preserving the peace. I didn't see much of a point further discussing other GOLDS teachings with my Ocracoke friends with the apparent variation and dynamic nature of the beliefs and practices in different churches and faith backgrounds. Still wary of the precepts, I decided to ask Reverend Jim some questions directly.

After Bible study one evening, when the only people that were left were Reverend Jim, Ken, and the rest of the cleanup crew, I asked if he had a few minutes to talk.

"Are you good, Ken?"

"Does a redneck raise a flagpole at a mud bog?"

"I'm going to take that as a yes. Thank you, and see you at tomorrow's study."

"Night, Rev."

Ken left us, taking his crew with him.

"How can I help, Virginia?"

"I'm concerned about the practices around priesthood."

"Is it because women can only become Levites?"

"Yes, that is a concern but it's not my main concern."

"What's your main concern?"

"That Melchizedek priests can basically ask anything of Levites. Are male Melchizedek priests asking female Levites for sexual blessings in the GOLDS Church?"

Reverend Jim's eyebrows furrowed and thinned, bouncing up and down, and eyes darted around. His bottom lip curled into his mouth and his teeth chewed the edge of his beard.

"Where is this concern coming from, Virginia? Did you witness something inappropriate among the priests?"

"No, it's just conceivable."

The Levite priests were *at the service of* the Melchizedek priests and responsible for taking care of the church building, its furnishings, and ministering to the GOLDS people. Ministries included, but were not limited to, performing the sacraments, discipling neophytes, being part of the worship band, managing outreach opportunities and missions, and much more. The term ministry was very liberal and could really mean helping with anything the Melchizedek priests considered a blessing to the people and facilities. Besides managing Levites, Melchizedek priests graduated to greater and greater responsibilities from managing parishes to dioceses, a nation or nations, and ultimately global management. They were also primarily responsible for preaching the Word of God, prayer, and presiding over or assisting at official ceremonies.

"Has supervision abuse occurred in this parish before, or other parishes, or dioceses?" I probed.

"Oh, the network is very connected. If those kinds of abuses were happening or had happened anywhere in the GOLDS Church, I would know about it."

He paused and his eyes seemed to search for a remedy from my own.

"I'm glad you came to me about your concern. Supervision abuse is a real and harmful issue in the secular world around us and even in some religious contexts.

These practices we abide by have been handed down through the ages. Levites took care of the tabernacle and temples of Jehovah. Now that Jehovah indwells people, Levites take care of the living temples and their worship environments. Melchizedeks have always benevolently ruled with spiritual crowns and prayed for God's people as priestly kings. These are Jehovah's ways of doing things. GOLDS try to follow them, but are humans imperfect? Yes. Do they sin? Yes. So, yes, the leadership at all levels watches vigilantly for abuse of power. Does that relieve your concerns?"

"No, not entirely. What do you say about the fact that women are not allowed to be Melchizedek priests?"

"Great question." Interrupting himself, "May I walk you back to your dorm?"

"Sure."

We put our jackets on and walked down the stairs and out of the female Foote dorm into the chilly night air. Reverend Jim went into what seemed to be a well-rehearsed answer. He probably heard the question from other braless sexual revolutionaries in the congregation.

He resumed, "The Old Testament details the functions of the Levites, which were only allowed to be men. Then, in the New Testament, we read that women are doing many of the same functions as the Levites. Something changed. What was it? Part of the change seemed to come from Jesus' respect for women. Part seemed to come from the practical needs of the Apostles with dispersing food to widows, etcetera, in the early church after Jesus ascended. While women could now tend to the physical needs of the Church, only men, Jesus and the Apostles, were tending to their spiritual needs. Jesus was part of the Order of Melchizedek and He gave His authority to the Apostles through the Holy Spirit. We do not see this transfer to women and through prayerful deliberations they distinguished their roles. Ever since, we've never had a Melchizedek priest say that the Holy Spirit inspired him to call a woman to the Order of Melchizedek."

"I'm glad you brought that up. It's another thing that bothered me. Are you saying that Jehovah speaks to you and the other priests?"

A member became a priest in the GOLDS Church when an elder was *prompted by the Holy Spirit* to call them to Levitical Priesthood.

"Yes, and many other people."

"How?"

"Different ways. He's given me visions, He's talked to me in a very tiny voice, boomed in a loud audible voice, spoke in dreams, and other ways. One believer in our parish said that Jehovah spoke to him through a flower. You can't limit His creativity."

He grinned and I smirked skeptically.

"The Holy Bible is rich with verses about people hearing from Jehovah, speaking with Jehovah, even seeing Jehovah. The biblical accounts weren't the only times Jehovah spoke to people in ancient times, and he hasn't stopped in modern times. To convince yourself, I would go speak with some of the homeless people downtown. Jehovah tends to be closest to those who need and want Him. I do not wish it on you, but people also tend to experience Him more during tragedy. I know I did."

My cynicism waned as Reverend Jim started tearing up. It was clear to me that at least he believed he had heard from Jehovah. The anecdotal evidence of personal stories was so much less satisfying than the empirical evidence of properly controlled experimentation, but how could one experiment with Jehovah without being irreverent?

"I don't mean to be indifferent to your challenges, but in regards to the practices around calling and promotion of priests, I'm concerned because they seem susceptible to collusions and fraud."

For a moment, it looked like I struck a chord. Jut-jawed, he slowly drug his bottom teeth along his top. Then, illuminating like a bulb, he emitted, "We take the promptings of Jehovah very seriously because direction from God is better than all of man's schemes. Articulating falsehoods in His Name is considerably risky given what happened to Ananias and Sapphira in the Book of Acts."

"I don't know that story."

Reverend Jim intoned, "They were struck dead and drugged out of their home after lying about their charity."

"Well, that is a very serious consequence, but what if the priest is not really a believer. Just an imposter seeking power in the church. Could he not use quid pro quo, exchanging a promotion, position, or planet for some privilege, perk, or pork?"

"Why would a non-believer care to accumulate heavenly treasures? There is much to gain for priests, from better homes and positions in the eternal celestial Kingdom, and Melchizedek priests can even gain planets, *it's true! But!* Why would anyone care to serve diligently for years, their whole lives, if they didn't *believe* they would gain these things? If all they really want is the limited temporal things this world has to offer, they would do much better to pursue them through more direct secular activities. With regards to premarital sex for example, they need only to shake a tail feather at Paradise 54. I appreciate you thinking in the hypothetical, but please think too about the wonderful, inclusive, loving, and edifying experiences you've had with GOLDS."

Reverend Jim was providing wrinkle-free answers, but I remained skeptical that there was lint hiding in the pockets, maybe even a hamper of dirty laundry in the closet. My mood swung with the gentle reminder that the reality of our Bible study wasn't focused on any one sacrament, but on the unification of whites and blacks, women and men, and others in worship of Jehovah, and it made me happy to be a part of something like that. Suddenly, I realized we were almost at my dorm. 'Time flies,' I thought.

When I didn't immediately follow-up with further questions, he jested, "I think with some commitment you could be one of the best Levite priestesses in the diocese."

This light-hearted peace flag was a good way to end the conversation. I had more questions but decided to throw them in the freezer. I could thaw them another time. We exchanged our goodbyes and I entered my dorm.

During Bible study a few weeks later, Reverend Jim announced, "The Holy Spirit has shown me through a vision that Kenneth Boris Musil has earned a level-three job on a level-two planet! That's quite an accomplishment! Give him a hand!" After the clapping slowed, he exhorted us, "Now, go get some gems for your own crowns of glory! I want to come visit your heavenly homes and learn about the rewarding vocations Jehovah has for you!"

Ken led in the rankings of priests at that point in our parish. That was quite an accomplishment for someone who characterizes himself as a "prickly piney-redneck-hybrid, a product of his parents' peoples in New Jersey". Reverend Jim extolled Ken for his gift for service, giving the example of regularly volunteering his time to help move things for church events and Bible study with his truck.

Ken had a handsome "Grabber Blue or Competition Blue" 1970 Ford F150, which the motor vehicle enthusiasts in our congregation gawked over. Once I sat in the back with other GOLDS cruising slowly down Hodgkin St., passing out flags and coke cans wrapped with Bible study invitations. The volunteers had a fun time getting people's attention with the PA system Ken had in his truck. Ken really was very enthusiastic about outreach and serving the body of believers.

In addition to encouraging such enthusiasm for eternal gain, Reverend Jim would also warn against lack of ambition. He quoted an excerpt from the parable of the talents in a recent Hellfire-and-brimstone sermon.

"For unto everyone that hath shall be given, and he shall have abundance: but from him that hath not, even that which he hath shall be taken away. And cast ye out the

unprofitable servant into the outer darkness: there shall be the weeping and the gnashing of teeth."

Both the carrot and stick would have motivated me if I believed. As Reverend Jim said though, "Why would a non-believer care to accumulate heavenly treasures?" Why worry about eternal separation from Jehovah? Why continue participating at all? Upon further reflection, it wasn't because of the GOLDS impact on demographic reconciliation. My role in that was too minor as a mostly quiet attendee. No, I wanted something for myself. I wanted to know if I could really hear from Jehovah. Having direction from Jehovah would be the greatest comfort and security. Hearing from Him now would give me hope that I might hear my father's voice later.

Reverend Jim mentioned tragedy and poverty as more susceptible conditions to hearing God. These sounded frankly undesirable, and the other beatitudes in the Gospel of Matthew sounded similarly dreadful or that I was perhaps too late for the blessings. An audience with Jehovah was probably too much to hope for in my present condition as an entitled American college student. However, I thought maybe by going through the processes of the sacraments, I could be redeemed through the blood of Jesus Christ. Perhaps, by taking on His merit, there might be a conduit to Jehovah. So, I listened intently in the subsequent Bible studies for directions for the narrow way, drinking in the new vocabulary and also getting to know the other members a little better.

I was happy to hear that at least the first sacrament wasn't a flaming coal walk. The sacrament of Baptism by Water actually sounded rather pleasant, and I added it to my calendar for the summer break.

Reverend Jim described it as a, "...joyous celebration where the whole community gets together in the warm month of August at the Ausable Chasm in the majestic Adirondacks. We hike, we camp, we fish, we tell ghost stories, and the most important thing is that a number of new believers get baptized in the river. Before a congregation, the new believer shares their testimony, confesses that they are a sinner in need of a savior, and professes their faith in the saving power of Jesus. After completion of the sacrament, the newly baptized believers are given the title *neophyte...*"

Chapter 19: OBX

Traveling at warp speed, we accelerated without impedance to the Spring semester final exams.

Rosalind Elsie Franklin Public Library inhaled the frosh and exhaled the conscientious and the crammers. The Ocracoke crew was well-prepared. Still, when the last test packet was turned in, we shared in a collective sigh of relief. Many of our weed-out and boring prerequisites were behind us now.

For our first college summer, we decided to take a road trip down to the Outer Banks, also known as OBX, for a couple of weeks. My idea was to pilgrimage to our study group's/nook's namesake. They liked that idea, and really appreciated it when I said I would rent a car and pay for the gas and camp fees. My friends would only have to pay for their food and incidentals. The main reason why I offered to pay was because I didn't think Gina could have afforded to go otherwise. The subtle signs of money issues had appeared enough that there was no longer a question in my mind. I didn't want to embarrass her though by just offering to pay for her expenses. Paying for the whole group wasn't an issue since Grandma's trust fund account was looking very healthy.

I got us a long stately-looking solidly-built 1973 Chevy Caprice station wagon with whitewall tires and prominent chrome grille, trim, and bumpers. There was plenty of room for our luggage and camping gear. The smooth riding, air conditioning, and vinyl upholstery on ample cushioning made for comfortable traveling, like cruising in a speed boat on a placid lake.

As we loaded up the back with our bags, Bobby queried snarkily, "Are you driving?"

"Yeah. Why?" I returned with a glare.

"Have you heard the joke - Why do women drivers get in more accidents than men?"

"Put the kibosh on it, Bobby," Gina barked.

"Unless you would rather enroll in summer sessions," I growled.

Holding up his hands in surrender and smirking, he squeaked, "I just want to be safe. That's all."

"Not to worry. I bet I have more hours on the road than you," I crowed. "Milli taught me how to drive, and I got uber practice taking her pretty much everywhere from the time I got my permit until I left for college. And before you ask, yes, my record is clean."

"Milli really did make you fiercely independent," complimented Gina. I thought of Milli laughing next to me in the passenger seat after we nearly hit a light pole in an empty parking lot. It was when I was first learning how to shift gears and somehow floored it. Thankfully, my quick reaction time helped me veer us away from the pole and cement parking dividers until my mind could reengage and my foot could rediscover the break. Heavy-handed as Milli was, she did prepare me well.

"My mom never taught me how to drive," mumbled Gina, assuming the front passenger seat for the road trip.

We all piled in after her.

"What about your dad?" inquired Dan. "My dad taught *me*."

"No," she muttered, pursing her lips. Hard to tell if she was sad or angry. Maybe something in between.

"Oooo, the power windows are nice!" Gina exclaimed, changing the subject and toggling the switch.

"Was your dad…" Dan reinitiated with concern in his voice.

"Oooo, and air conditioning!" she said excitedly, cutting Dan off.

When Dan tried to speak again, Bobby interrupted with the request, "Virginia, can you crank the radio so we can embody the classic road trip trope?"

"My copilot is in charge of the radio."

"Tuning into the WARP for the top 100, Bobby!"

"Thanks, Gina!"

Dan, who was catty-corner to me in the back, looked uneasy when he realized that the topic was off limits for some unknown reason. I had no clue what Gina's secret was, but realized then that she only ever mentioned her mom, never her dad. A road trip might be just the right care-free environment for her to open up about whatever painful thing she was hesitant to share with us. There was no agenda for this trip though; it was just meant to be a relaxing break with friends.

The first chunk of the drive we made some quick stops for breakfast, lunch, and gas. We relaxed, and mostly just listened to the radio while we cruised down the highway. It was a good opportunity to recharge before the forthcoming fun.

One memorable moment was about six hours into the trip. Gina, who was in charge of the map, commented, "It's weird."

"What's weird?" I asked.

"Did you know that we go just along the edge of Pennsylvania? We never actually go into the state."

"Yeah, Philly is right across the Delaware there," I said, pointing northwest. "There's a highway that takes you through, but Milli found the traffic is better this way."

Bobby antagonized, "Gina! Did you know Pennsylvania just passed a law that lets girls practice and play sports with boys?"

"No, I didn't!" responded Gina.

"Did you *ladies* know they're the first state to do it?" roping me in too.

"Yeah, I saw that in the news," I drawled, anticipating a rude punchline.

"Isn't that great?" Bobby asked us with some excitement.

A little confused and surprised by his enthusiasm, I responded in kind, "Yes, I think that's a great step forward."

"Still not fair though," whined Bobby.

"Why's that?" Gina asked.

"Because girls get two cups, and guys only get one!" He cupped his imaginary breasts.

Gina and I couldn't bite back the laugh. Bobby even got a small smile out of prudish Dan with that one.

When we made it to Washington D.C. a few hours later, we decided to get some portable street vendor food so we could walk around, and see the famous buildings and monuments. Before Milli and I started flying to North Carolina in my early teens, we drove to OBX, and D.C. was a frequent stop. She toured me all throughout the city, hitting every museum and significant historical site over the years. My friends and I didn't have much time for that, but it felt good to be back in the heart of our democracy with them.

Besides the majesty, we got to see democracy in action with protesters rallying, marching, picketing, chanting slogans and advocating their causes at the Capitol Building, National Mall, and White House.

Gina complained, "Ugh! I was hoping for peace to enjoy the giant monuments and broad open landscapes!"

"It's a strategic play by these activists to protest during prime time."

"What do you mean?" inquired Gina.

"People are off work, able to listen, and participate. The evening news will probably show live coverage of the protestors. It's smart thinking on their part," I complimented.

"The Vietnam War is over. The South Vietnamese beat the communists and democracy wins again. Why keep protesting?" she inquired, still annoyed.

"Didn't you see the banners and hear the bellowing? They're protesting the long-term impacts on Vietnamese civilians, the destruction of their homes and the environment.

"Don't forget their lives, the ones lost with the bombing campaigns and chemical warfare," noted Dan.

"Yes, and they're also demanding congressional oversight, more transparency, accountability, and diplomacy for future conflicts," I explained.

"Oh! I thought they were protesting Gerald Ford's insistence on making tripping hazard awareness a key policy initiative," Bobby joked.

I chortled at that. Gina looked confused.

"What's funny about tripping hazards?" she asked.

Bobby and I both erupted in laughter at this. We never bothered explaining that President Ford was clumsy on his feet.

Dan looked like he didn't care for the jokes too much. I thought, "It must be hard to be Republican with all the scandals going on. At least Ford has a chance though at reelection with a successful end to the war.'

There was only one other planned stop on the way down south. We heard from some classmates that there was a grand opening on Friday, May 16th for an amusement park called Busch Gardens: The Old Country. The opening couldn't have been timed better. With our last exam happening the Wednesday prior, we had all of Thursday to get down to Williamsburg, Virginia. When we checked the map, going there only added 70 miles to the drive. The decision was settled with unanimous intrigue for the European theme and youthful ardor for fast new roller coasters.

First impressions of the park weren't stellar. The industrial brewery and warehouses that could be seen on the Monorail disturbed the illusion of the foreign wonderland. We agreed that the immersion wasn't quite as complete as Disney World, at least what we remembered from preteen family vacations.

The rides were thrilling though. Dan, a baritone, cracked us up with his elated soprano screams on the Glissade coaster. We also loved the Sea Dragon boat ride as well as the swing ride with a hard to pronounce German name, and Le Mans Raceway was probably the most enthralling attraction.

At Busch Gardens' Le Mans, loud go-karts gave an illusion of competition. Roads interwoven with natural landscape provided a pleasant fictitious rural circuit. It was far more of a colorful countryside then the sporty grand Le Mans raceway tracks in France that Milli showed me pictures of. The thought was another reminder of my mom. I frowned for a moment, and before I knew it, Dan was giving me a bear hug.

"You, okay?"

"Yeah," I answered. Wanting to be more open with my friends, I told Dan, "I just miss my mom."

Gina was about to get into one of the go carts with me when Bobby protested.

"You were Virginia's copilot all day yesterday! How about you come with me and drive, Gina? I'll give you a crash course!"

She looked at me to check if I was okay with the switch. I nodded. It was a sweet gesture by Bobby given how glum Gina looked after she mentioned that her folks didn't teach her how to drive. Part of me was a little jealous, especially when I saw how much fun she was having with him on the track.

"Everything okay, Virginia?" inquired Dan. "You look a little mad."

"No," I lied. "I was just thinking how funny it would be if I rammed them."

"It's against the rules! You heard the recorded announcement! We'll get kicked off!"

"No, they just say that so unruly hellion kids with spacey parents don't annoy other riders."

I floored the gas and was gaining ground quickly. Dan pleaded with me to slow down and not hit them.

"Who's watching?"

He looked around.

"I don't know, but…"

"Stop worrying. Just relax. Have fun."

Moments later, I was barreling down a shallow hill, picking up a little more speed for the collision. Gina and Bobby were in Lala Land admiring their surroundings when my iron bumper loudly clapped the back of theirs, and jolted them forward.

"Hey! What the Hell?" yelled Bobby.

Two ride referees ran over from some hiding spot with a megaphone.

"Take your foot off the gas! Break and stop the race car!"

My mischievous smile sank into an embarrassed frown as we were rushed off the track.

"Exit the go-cart on the left side," one of the referees sternly demanded. "Frederick will escort you out."

Frederick, who looked more like a Frederico, climbed up on the right side and followed us out the left. Then, getting in front of us he motioned us to follow him.

I looked at Dan and he glared back at me.

"Don't be such a sheep," I mouthed.

Turning my head back toward my target, I saw confusion on Gina's face. Bobby was the only one laughing, which made me feel even more ashamed.

The referee with the megaphone directed Gina to keep driving and followed in the go-cart we were evicted from. Frederick took down our names and birthdays, and said that if we ever disobeyed one of the rules at La Mans or any other ride in the park, we would be denied entry to Busch Gardens.

Gina and Bobby were waiting when we got back to the ride entrance. Seeing them standing side-by-side invoked the jealousy again.

"It's fine. We basically went on all the rides anyway. Let's just go," I ordered with a growl. "We need to hurry. We need to get dinner, go to the campsite, and pop our tents before dark."

My friends followed as I stormed toward the parking lot. I wasn't sure why, but they let me get away with acting badly without explanation. The only person that came close to broaching the subject was Bobby. After I suggested getting Big Chef burgers and French fries at Burger Chef, he quipped, "Those are good substitutes for real European fare."

We arrived at the campground on the north side of OBX above Kitty Hawk a couple of hours later. It was full of campers, and everyone was busy setting up their sites as the sun was setting. A pack of campers just two plots down from ours were playing guitars, bongos, and other instruments. Barking dogs, whining children, the squeaky hinges and slam of metal stall doors against the bathroom wall cinder blocks, chats around cracking fires, and other noises contributed to the lively cacophony around us.

Helpful Dan immediately started pulling out the tents. Our well used rental equipment came from the Stevenson Outdoor Enthusiasts Club.

"Mm, smells a bit musty," commented Bobby. "I'll work on the fire. Looked like they were selling wood at the front of the campground. Want to see what they have in the shop, Gina?"

"Yeah! We should get s'mores stuff if they have it."

After they sauntered off, I slowly walked over to Dan with my arms crossed. Staring, I sought to read his mood but already knew Dan well enough to know he was still upset.

I took up a collapsed pole and started assembling it the way he was.

Hoping to break the ice, I asked, "Did you go camping with your folks when you were younger?"

Dan didn't say anything. I was pretty sure he heard me, but since it was noisy around us, I spoke louder, "You look like you know what you're doing."

Again, no response.

Sure, that he heard me, I advised, "If you don't want to talk, just say so."

"I just wanted you to know what it feels like to be ignored." A retort showing a passive aggressive side I hadn't seen before.

"Oh, revenge! How Christian of you," I drawled.

Ten seconds into the first round, and I connected with a knockout punch. He dropped his scowl; brief introspection terminated into guilt. I wanted to lift my friend back up though and offer peace.

"Look, I'm sorry you felt ignored. You have my attention now if you want it."

He paused, recomposing himself, but then fell apart. His eyes welled up, his face turned red, a vein was pronounced on his forehead, and a thinly but widely parted mouth showed all of his teeth.

Before he started weeping, he got out, "It's just… I want to know what you think of me?"

Unprepared for Dan's crying, pleading red puffy eyes and unassuming posture, I just said what came to me.

"You are a caring guy. You're a great listener. You try to help people the best you can, and give great hugs."

This slowed his labored breathing, but Dan looked like he was waiting for something more, so I continued.

"I feel very lucky to have you as a friend. You're one of my best friends."

Dan walked over the camping equipment with his arms wide. I dropped the pole. He leaned forward, and embraced me. I returned the hug as he continued weeping on my shoulder, and patted his back.

"Are you okay, Dan?"

"Is that all you think of me?" His voice cracked.

"I don't know… Certainly, there's many wonderful things about you."

"I mean, do you think we could be like Bobby and Gina someday?"

"Like Bobby and Gina?"

I pulled back from him. Looking into his focused sincere eyes, I knew I held his heart in my hand.

"Milli told me that it's always best to build strong friendships with years of experiences and challenges to avoid the three-i beast of men."

"Three-eyed beast?"

"No, three-letter-i beast of men."

"What's that?"

"She told me that men tend to become *infatuated* for a couple of years, then decide that there's some *incompatibility*, which leads to them searching for someone else, and the relationship ends with *infidelity*. Infatuation, incompatibility, and infidelity, the three-i beast."

While this sounded like something Milli would tell me, I just made it up. Dan would figure out that I wasn't the woman for him and move on if given enough time. I felt sure of it.

"I get it. You want to make sure love is the real deal. I can appreciate that."

"Yeah, something like that."

"Well, I'm not in a big hurry either."

"That's good, Dan. Taking things slow can really build strong foundations in relationships, romantic and plutonic."

Just then, Gina and Bobby returned with some firewood and s'mores stuff. They were laughing about something.

"Hey Gina, hold my log."

"I thought you liked holding your own log."

"Most of the time."

While their crass flirting continued through the evening, Dan seemed pacified. He was back to his generous servitude.

"Can I help assemble your tent? … I'm headed to the bathrooms. Want me to fill your water? … Can I roast a marshmallow for you? I can brown it perfectly for you… Let me get you a chocolate and graham cracker…"

This kind of attention was normal from Dan. Our task-heavy camping situation just seemed to increase his default helpfulness to an annoying frequency. I was fine with it though. Freed me up to read my Bible. I was trying to get into a routine with a few expert study guides I found at a bookstore. The baptism retreat was happening toward the end of the summer and I was deciding if I wanted to participate or not.

The next morning Dan inquired about me studying the Bible.

"I'm trying to decide if the Bible offers reasonable explanations for who God is, what humans are to Him, and what happens when we die."

This made him very delighted.

"That's great! Would you like me to show you some verses to read that answer those questions?"

"Thank you, but I think I would just prefer working through my Bible study materials."

"Okay, no problem."

I knew that Dan would start sharing verses with me anyway, perhaps study guides, maybe even Christian songs now that he knew what I was interested in understanding. It was something to keep him happily busy.

Besides Bible studies, I brought "The Sheep Look Up" by John Brunner to read on a recommendation from our organic chemistry professor. He marketed it as a timely tragedy to balance our comedic summer breaks. Critics described it as a near-future U.S. dystopia warning of the consequences of unchecked industrial pollution. Parallel interconnected sub-stories describe how different people cope in a catastrophically toxic environment and a hostile desperate society.

I enjoyed reading and relaxing under an umbrella during the day. Plus, it was better for my pale white high-risk-for-skin-cancer skin. My friends weren't as concerned. Dan mostly built sand holes and castles around us. Bobby swam in the waves until he was pruned. Gina oiled her skin and turned on a towel to bronze. Gina and Bobby also took walks down the beach together, not asking if Dan and I wanted to join. They went together like seashells and tidal waves, a couple of sunset sweethearts. Looking at the way they interacted, I didn't really see Dan and I becoming like that.

We had campfires every night and dedicated the first four nights to competitive mini golf tournaments and ice cream. I captured numerous memories with a Polaroid SX-70 that I picked up a few weeks before the trip. I chose this technology because I thought instant prints would be more fun.

Outside the routine, my friends greatly enjoyed touring the Wright Brothers Memorial, where Wilbur and Orville first successfully flew a plane.

We took our time in the museum before walking the vast test track and climbing the sixty-foot-tall granite tower.

"Inspiring!" Dan gawked over the artifacts and captions. "It's incredible what they did!"

"What's boss, Dan?" asked Gina.

"How systematic they were with their experiments; tweak this, fly a few yards, tweak that, fly a few more; so brave; *and so* innovative."

"I'm with you, Dan. We have the benefit of hindsight, but how brilliant were they to be the first to figure out flying without killing themselves?" I agreed.

Dan was daydreaming.

"Dan?"

"Sorry, I just got a little more excited about becoming a scientist." His dreamer contentment brought smiles to me and Gina's faces.

Reaching up and snapping his fingers in Dan's face, Bobby chided, "Stoop a little Dan, your heads in the clouds!"

We took an instant picture on top of the memorial tower capturing the happiness we all shared. Then, we almost lost it in the wind. Realizing the beauty of the continuous panorama background the surrounding flats gave us, we rambled up some sand dunes for another great photo.

As a teen, I didn't realize how easy it was to find great views on OBX for pictures. That's because my mother didn't like bringing her expensive work camera to the beach. She mainly just took pictures in Manteo and at the Lost Colony.

The photogenic aspect of OBX comes from its thin physique. It's like an Atlantic taproot. There is little room for development on either side of the single two-lane Route 12 that runs its hundred-mile length. The surrounding ocean can be seen between clustered houses, businesses, shrubs, and sand dunes. So, we took oodles of pictures as we worked our way down the taproot, spending a day or two at each of the camp nodules, and enjoying the beaches on our journey to Ocracoke.

On the middle Saturday of our two-week trip, we stayed at a very cramped campground, probably because it was the weekend. What made it worse was that the beach was densely packed during the day. Gina complained other people were kicking sand on her when they passed by. Dan didn't have room to make castles so he joined Bobby in the waves, who was actually very happy because almost no one else was in the water. We were all curious about this until he waded through the crowds to report what he heard.

"One of the brave souls that Dan and I body surfed with asked us if we'd seen the movie *Jaws* that just came out? He said everyone and their mother thinks a man-eating great white is going to chew them."

"Wow! It was that frightening?" I thought the director must be cut from the same cloth as Alfred Hitchcock, instilling fear of the benign, like birds and taking showers.

"Apparently so. Care to swim with the sharks as they say? Maybe we can catch the flick tonight if they're not already sold out."

Everybody liked the idea so we went to a nearby shop to use the yellow pages and phone. The closest theater in Manteo had seats available. We reserved them, and immediately headed up for the 8pm showing. Since we were early, I took my friends on a tour of the historic Lost Colony before dinner.

The woods where the first English colony once stood still has ruins of meager earthen barrier defenses and gold prospecting assay wares. The most interesting allure of the site though is the mystery of what happened after John White left in 1587 for England for provisions and when he returned in 1590. At some point the other colonists disappeared. "CRO" was carved into a tree and "CROATOAN" was carved on a colony fence entrance post.

"Doesn't really seem like such a great mystery to me," I started, sharing a simplified analysis Milli once postulated. "Greedy men came looking for gold; brought diseases, death, murdered, burned down a village, stole, and probably raped native women. They didn't get what they came for. So, they left. Then, a second set of poorly-armed non-soldier families came to settle. When John White left with the big scary ship, the natives got their revenge."

I thought I might have sucked the air out of the room, but Bobby replied, "Sad. If only they had the benefit of three hundred years of advancement. Then, they would have known that two wrongs don't make a right but two Wrights make an airplane!"

Dan laughed.

Pointing her finger and smiling, Gina guessed that this was a banked joke. "You've been waiting to say that for almost a whole week, haven't you?"

"Yeah," he admitted.

"The Croatoan helped them though, right?" she verified, changing the subject.

"Yes, it was probably one of the other tribes that took revenge," I clarified.

Dan piped up, "If only someone could find female bones around the colony, details about the bones would help solve this mystery."

"Why women's bones?" asked Gina.

"Because that would differentiate between the first and second set of colonists," I explained.

"Then, if the woman was murdered, there might be marks or holes in the bones from pointy, sharp, or blunt weapons. The site of remains and orientation could indicate a Christian burial, native burial, or haphazard disposal," added Dan.

I think Bobby was trying to be funny, but it just came out spooky when he murmured, "If infant or toddler bones were found, it would be Virginia Dare herself."

While enjoying a nice dinner in Manteo, we allowed ourselves to wax poetic about changing majors, becoming archeologists, getting a grant to search for her remains, writing a bestselling book about it, and retiring together in OBX. Then, watching Jaws made us forget all about it.

While I was glad to have visited the Lost Colony with my friends, Jaws seemed to have made more of an impact, at least on Bobby. He reasoned, "The odds are like three million to one of getting bit, but what if you're the only one in the water." Bobby ended up staying out of the water the next day and thereafter, until the night before we got to Ocracoke.

We were drinking and roasting marshmallows by the fire when a couple came over to our campsite.

"Hey y'all! I'm Rand, the owner of this fine establishment!" He quickly moved around the fire with a vigorous firm handshake. "My lady Flower and I just came by to see how you're doing?"

"And spreading some love and kindness," Flower added.

Rand had a tan at least twice as dark as Gina's, Mohawk hair, surfer build, and the energy of an on-stage rockstar. Flower had a winning combination of a Farrah Fawcett look and apparently Goldie Hawn mannerisms.

Bobby was dumb struck by Flower's charms. Dan sat smiling. Gina eyed Bobby. To avoid them finding us rude or weird, I answered for my crew.

"We are doing well! Thank you for asking!"

"Wonderful!" said Rand. "Glad to hear that!"

"Watcha drinkin'?" Flower nodded toward Bobby's cup.

Bobby was still mesmerized until Gina cleared her throat.

"Screwdrivers," he answered, mindfully renewed.

"Oh, we can do better than that! How about I get you a Tequila sunrise or a Bahama Mama, much more appropriate for the beach?" offered Flower.

"I was going to grab something for myself anyway," extended Rand.

"Any chance you can make a Long Island Iced Tea?" Bobby boldly inquired.

"I certainly can," Rand enthusiastically assured him. "I'll grab you a double?"

"Thank you!" Bobby turned back to Flower. "You always hear about Southern hospitality…!"

"Don't mention it. Every experience is a chance to learn something new!"

"Where are you from, Flower?" inquired Dan.

Mimicking Doug Ingle, she sang, "In a Gadda Da Vida, honey. How about you?"

"The Garden of Eden?"

"You too!" Flower mistakenly took Dan's question as an answer.

Running with it, Bobby joked, "That flaming sword is such a nuisance."

"Yeah!" Flower responded, very earnestly.

Rand returned with Bobby's drink a few minutes later. "Anyone else want anything?"

No thank you responses all around.

"Hey! Do you beautiful people want to feel liberated and more connected with nature?" Flower rhapsodized.

"We don't do drugs," I responded, assuming that's where she was going with the inquiry.

"No, I mean letting it all hang out and taking a delightful moonlight swim."

"Skinny dipping?"

"Yes."

We looked at each other awkwardly, trying to see what everyone thought about this proposal.

While I initially felt a bit squeamish, I seconded the motion, imagining a little harmless fun. "Could be a great memory for us."

"Yeah!" agreed Gina.

"I'm in," tweeted Bobby, cheerful as a morning cardinal. Then, he fluttered over to mine and Gina's tent and dove in with his bag.

"That's our tent," I complained.

"I'll be out in a minute. Just need to change."

"Change clothes? You understand what skinny dipping is, right?" I quipped.

Gina chuckled.

Bobby didn't answer immediately, but when he came out, he chirped, "I grabbed a couple of towels for you ladies. Do you want me to carry yours in my bag too, Dan?"

"Thanks," cheeped Gina.

"Um. I'll just stay here and watch our stuff," responded Dan.

Flower walked around our log circle behind Dan. She softly placed her manicured hands over his shoulders onto his chest, and massaged with her nails.

"Come now. You should feel confident and comfortable in your own body. I'm sure you have nothing to hide, big man," she seduced. "If you did though, the cover of darkness keeps everything private and fun."

She came around to his side, took his hands, and pulled playfully. Dan looked high-school-dance uncomfortable, but stood up knowing she wouldn't be able to pull him to his feet, which would potentially be embarrassing for both of them.

While I was afraid of giving Dan the wrong idea again, I hated how tense he looked.

"You should come, Dan. It will be fun."

That was enough for him.

We took the Chevy and followed them down the road to a secluded section of beach.

Rand and Flower skipped ahead of us on the beach toward the water, peeling and dropping a trail of clothes behind them. Bobby was the first one to follow.

"Race you to the water, Gina!"

They quickly stripped and tore off across the sand into the dark waves. Hoots and hollers were muffled by the crashing waves.

I looked for something to orient to so I could find our garms after we had our fun. While it was a spartan environment, I placed our whereabouts halfway between a gnarly bush and the breach to our parking spot.

Seeing Dan's silhouette motionless, I assumed he was still hesitant.

"Dan, if you really don't want to do it, it's okay."

"I was just waiting for you."

"What? Do you want to race too?"

"Yeah, if you want to."

The desperation was really unattractive, but what could I say?

"Last one in is a landlubber!"

I beat Dan in the denuding but his long gazelle legs outpaced mine. Then, he carved through the waves like the bow of a speed boat. I glimpsed his wide dangle as he leapt over the waves, and wondered if the image in my mind was really accurate. I found myself dwelling on the thought after I dove in the waves and popped up, and was only able to snap out of it when Dan gloated about his victory.

"I hope I didn't make you eat my sand, Virginia. It just wasn't fair, like the fox and the hound."

"How does it feel winning the race, Mary Poppins?" I mocked.

To which he correctly replied, "Supercalifragilisticexpialidocious."

"Very good, Dan," I approved and flashed a satisfied smile, realizing immediately after he probably couldn't see it.

My friends bobbed and splashed for a while. The guys got into a body surfing competition. We watched, floating and bouncing with the waves, occasionally calling out winners and whooping at their muscly silhouettes as they ran back into the waves.

Then, Bobby got into a squabble with Rand. "No, I went farther than you on that one."

"Look up there, buddy. That ain't a blue moon."

"Help me out, Gina. I think this guy has old man vision issues. Who got closer to the shore on that one?"

"Sorry, it was too close!" Gina called back.

"How about we settle this with a chicken fight? Your girl versus mine?" challenged Rand.

"Oo, fun!" hollered Flower.

"A what?" cried Gina, surprisingly not balking at the label "your girl".

Flower poorly explained, "A chicken fight is when two girls get on two guys shoulders and try to knock each other over."

"Like wrestling on piggyback?" Bobby verified.

"Right! Whoever stays up wins! And my Rand always stays up," she bragged suggestively.

"Okay!" agreed Gina.

"Okay!" Bobby excitedly seconded and ran/swam over to Gina in a comical flounder.

"Alright. Turn around. Now stoop down so I can get on your shoulders," she ordered.

"We're too deep. I'm going to drown," Bobby said dramatically, goofing around. "Let's go in a little bit."

After some adjustments and they were up. The veterans were primed and waiting.

"Ready?" they asked.

"We're ready!" Bobby and Gina answered.

"Then, can one of your compadres say three two one go?"

"Three two one go!" I happily complied, excited to watch the match.

I couldn't really see Gina well from the angle, but Flower's blazoned orchestra trumpets waggled and her battle cry was savage. I was surprised Bobby and Gina lasted as long as they did. From the back, it looked like Gina might have had some instinctive Aikido redirects, but Flower's Kung Fu was stronger.

Just before it looked like they were about to go down, Bobby dipped and yelled out, "Something's got me."

Bobby tossed Gina toward the shore. Rand backed up, let Flower down from his shoulders, and they started to swim away as Bobby bellowed, "Help me, Gina!"

Bobby reached out and Gina hesitated for a moment but then jumped toward him to take his hand. Then, Bobby pulled Gina in and gave her a kiss.

Gina pushed him away. I could hear in her voice, she wasn't sincere in her anger, probably altogether enchanted, but she wouldn't just give into his advances. The wisdom she received from her mother was, "Easy come, easy go." She'd make him work for it, and work he was.

"Don't cry wolf you, jerk!" she barked.

Flower and Rand belly laughed, and started wading back toward the group.

We all played for another fifteen minutes or so longer when Flower complained that she was starting to get pruned. Unanimously, we agreed that it was about time to head back to camp.

Bobby rushed out of the water, yelling back to Gina. "Let me go grab your towel from the bag, sweet cheeks."

"You have no idea how sweet they are!" she bragged.

"Just guessing!"

He jogged over to the bag he packed, wrapped himself with a towel. Then, Bobby brought a balled-up towel toward where Gina was coming out of the water, and turned his head.

"Here's one for you! Not looking," he sang.

As Gina approached him, the towel dropped and a sudden flash briefly illuminated her bare body. She shrieked and chased Bobby who had apparently grabbed my Polaroid and a flashbar while he was in our tent.

"You perv!" she screamed.

"Gotta love instant prints, aye Gina!" he bantered, dashing away.

After a short sprint, Gina tackled him from behind.

I could hear grunts and roars and saw Gina crawl up Bobby's back in the moonlight to grab the print from his outstretched arm. After ripping it out of his hand, she stood up and used her hands and the picture to cover herself as best she could. When Bobby flipped over and declared, "Worth it!" She proceeded to aggressively stomp on him and yell, "Yeah, how about now?" While chagrined, she couldn't help but laugh with him between the ows, oofs, and eeks.

When she had enough, she ran back to the bag and covered herself with a towel.

We caravanned back with Flower and Rand, and drank some of their mixed drink offerings to prolong our merriment. Our supercalifragilisticexpialidocious vacation was smoldering though. We fanned the flames as long as we could, but a few drinks doused our embers.

Heading out early the next day, we discovered a hefty balance for the hootch from Rand. Needless to say, we were upset they never mentioned the booze was going on the bill. But they had our information, and we didn't have time to argue. So, I coughed up the cash and we jetted out of there.

The ferry to Ocracoke from the southern tip of Hatteras is free but first come, first serve. So, to secure our spot for the first morning voyage, we arrived a half hour early, and ate our breakfast in line to pass the time. A couple of thick maple bacon donuts and HARD Water Berry made for a great hangover cure.

It's a glorious feeling standing on deck as the ocean wind blows through your hair. The salty spray, the sound of the hungry gulls, a curious whale breaching to take a breath and peak at the ship. The nostalgia was good but doing it with college friends is even better.

Remembering our archeological fantasies, I painted a new picture, "What if in addition to searching for Virginia Dare, we got a grant to find shipwrecks? Did you know there are more than two thousand known shipwrecks in this area alone?"

"Sounds far out, Virginia! Why are there so many wrecks around here though?" queried Dan.

"The shoals. They're underwater sand dunes."

Bobby threw the can at the easel. "Yeah! Let's forget dev bio and become treasure hunters!"

Handing him a second metaphorical can of paint, I provoked, "Could be a load of booty stashed around here somewhere. Blackbeard the infamous pirate was rumored to have hidden his loot around here."

"What are we waiting for then?" demanded Bobby.

"Ah, my friend, I think we would get hung up. To borrow from the famous pirate Mary Read- *As to hanging, it is no great hardship. For were it not for that, every cowardly fellow would turn pirate and so unfit the sea, that men of courage must starve.* I think real life legal complexities would be our noose. If not that, then the fines for not following the regulatory frameworks.

"Well maybe one of us can be a lawyer," suggested Bobby.

"Good idea. What about you?" encouraged Gina.

"I was thinking you. I'll be the boat captain."

The last day in Ocracoke was a bit of a blur. We packed it with tons of site seeing - wild ponies, the lighthouse, the museum, the British Cemetery, Springer's Point Preserve, the burial site of Sam Jones and his favorite horse, and Teach's Hole, where Blackbeard had his last stand before he was slain by the British navy. We spent only an hour at their beautiful beach before catching an evening ferry back to Hatteras. Then, we drove all the way up to Manteo where I reserved a one-night stay at a motel. Just figured that it was important to get a good night's rest in a bed before the eleven-hour drive home.

Gina's mother met us for breakfast the next morning to take her to Arkansas for the rest of the summer. I could see the resemblance, same eyes and hair, but their noses and chins were different.

"Virginia, you are my daughter's madrina," she started.

"Oh, Mamma."

"No, no." Gina's mother drawled, insisting, "Let me say my blessings on your friends."

She took my hands and held them together with her's, pulling me in close. Sincere eyes darted back and forth to each of mine as she prayed, "Che Dio ti protegga."

Gina translated, "That means may God protect you."

I accepted that blessing, hoping that it held real power and not just well wishes.

Gina's mother smiled, released me, and took Dan's hands in the same way.

"Tall with a quiet peace. Let's see if it's true." The short-to-average height woman opened Dan's arms like she was spreading curtains to let in the sun, and embraced him. After a moment of confusion, Dan hugged back the way he does with the perfect strength, tenderness, and optimal wrapping coverage.

"Yes, you must be Dan," she affirmed.

"Yes, ma'am."

"Che tu possa essere sempre felice e prospero."

"That means may you always be happy and prosperous," translated Gina.

Gina's mother patted Dan on the back and released him.

"Thank you," he said earnestly.

"No, thank you, Dan. It's nice to know that my daughter has a caring selfless friend with a comforting hug on hard days."

Dan really beamed at that.

Turning her attention to Bobby, she squinted her eyes and gave him a suspicious look. She folded her arms.

Bobby buried his fingers in his pockets, thumbs sticking out. He was frozen with a nervous grin, eyebrows raised, and was having trouble maintaining eye contact.

"You must be Bobby. I'm sure she's told you that I live in Arkansas, yes?"

"Yes."

"When Gina and I talk on the phone, she tells me that you make her laugh. That's good. Humor is good." She paused. "Just don't make her cry. If you make her cry…," she spoke slowly, quietly, and sternly, "No distance will help you. You'll be sleeping with the fishes." She pointed in the general direction of the Atlantic. "Capeesh?"

"Mamma mia!" Gina looked mortified.

Gina's mother grabbed Bobby's shoulders, startling him, and glared into his eyes. Then, she lost her composure and burst into laughter.

"Oh, my…" he stopped himself. "You had me." He sighed and chuckled.

Gina's mother kept one hand on Bobby's shoulder, and was half smiling when with a stare and pronounced drawl, she made sure that she was only half kidding.

Take good care of my Gina, e possano la tua vita essere piena di benedizioni e gioia."

"That means may your life be filled with blessings and joy," Gina translated, with a look of hope that her mother didn't just scare her new boyfriend off.

Watching Gina and her mother during breakfast, I found their relationship to be very sweet. Countless acts of affection- hugs, kisses, hand holding. They gabbled in Italian, and laughed frequently. Even though their relationship was entirely different from the one I had with Milli, I couldn't help but miss her.

To distract myself, I committed to knocking out another section of the literature review during the summer. Without my friends helping, it wouldn't be as enjoyable, but it would get me closer to seeing my mother again, and I didn't have anything better to do. I already finished my professor-recommended near-future dystopia. It kind of made me want to go into environmental journalism like the character Maxine Lumumba, or an environmental scientist; going beyond just sounding the alarm like Dr. Tucker to inventing actual green technologies to save the planet.

Hormones from Hell I decided were pulling my passion in every direction. Logical analysis of the opportunity cost would tell me that abandoning my current trajectory to pursue treasure hunting or environmental whatever would be foolish. Staying the course is what I would do. The only other pastime this summer not aligned with dreams would be working through more Bible studies.

Chapter 20: Baptism of Water

I was a woman possessed, wholly focused on my plan to become a great scientist when I entered college. The promise, "*I found them that sought me not,*" echoed through time and broadened my horizon from the physical world to the spiritual, the temporal to the eternal.

Reverend Jim was a farm hand, sowing Jehovah's seed in my heart and watering it. I tried learning more on my own about God that summer, but the bookstore studies I found were impersonal and boring.

"These experts use words that mean nothing to me," I complained, showing him my textbooks. He agreed to meet with me first thing in the morning at a local bagel shop. We sat in a corner booth facing the door, a preference of his for some unknown reason.

"I'm glad you came to me. We are in a season of learning about Ecclesiology. There's a fifty-cent word for you. On the surface, it means the study of the Church, including its structure, sacraments, and role in the world."

The Reverend sounded pretentious, like a recording of my cryptic textbooks. Just then, a passionate twinkle appeared in his eye and his lips curled into a knowing grin as he revealed, "The Greek roots tell us a deeper meaning though. The ekklesia are the ones *called out.* Yes, called out from this worldly existence!"

His volume was a bit loud, and I looked around to see if people looked over to us.

"Sorry, I'll try to keep it down."

Lowering his volume, he transferred the fervor to gesticulation and emphasis, "Listen, many of my GOLDS *hunger* for a *deeper, richer, more fulfilling existence.* They want to do Jehovah's *will, every moment of every day.* I'm trying to help them along in their journey *to walk with Him.*"

He paused, searching my face. My heart quickened as I felt palpated by his survey, penetrated by his peer.

"That really doesn't help *you* though because *you're* way at the beginning of your journey. You're not ready to walk with Jehovah yet. You just want to learn *about* God, confirm in your mind of His existence; study His nature and attributes. Right?"

"Yes," I agreed, really appreciating Reverend Jim's empathy and directness.

His intensity softened more to chat. "And that's stellar! It's what we in the biz call theology proper."

"Is there a book you would recommend?"

"Yes, the Holy Bible."

The response felt like a mischievous boy popping an excited little girl's balloon. I was trying to avoid reading thousands of pages of the Bible. That's why I turned to studies in the first place.

Hoping for understanding, I inquired, "What about a study book?"

"As you experienced, the available books in bookstores can be too dense. There are others that you would probably find too shallow."

"Are there no goldilocks studies?"

"I probably could find some digestible books, but you're at a phase right now where it would be best to explore some concepts together. If you would like, I could answer your burning questions and give you a solid foundation of knowledge to build upon, *and* save you a bunch of money on books too."

"Money is not what I'm worried about, it's time."

Shooting me a skeptical look, I goggled back like a hit deer, my sincerity exposed. I saw in the depths of his pupils a hunter who was surprised and intrigued. Coming out from behind the blind, he approached his kill, and discovered that he had bagged a rare animal.

"In that case, answering your questions and pointing you directly to relevant verses would save you time, right?"

"Yes," I admitted reluctantly, lingering on the feeling that for some reason I was being prepped for taxidermy.

"We can start now if you want. What questions do you have?"

As we talked, my concerns evaporated like morning dew with the rising sun. Our first conversation lasted three hours. I proceeded to take full advantage of his offer, meeting him on Mondays and Thursdays, discussing reading assignments he gave from the previous meeting and new questions. I picked his brain before and after many Wednesday night Bible studies, which continued during the summer.

Also, Reverend Jim rented the First Baptist Church building just a half a mile east of campus on Hodgkin Street and one block south on Almeida Ave. He began hosting everything there and initiated Sunday services. Most congregants, including myself, walked or bicycled from the dorms to attend. The location was very convenient and sometimes I would stop by for an impromptu session. I think he might have been a little annoyed by these but nevertheless made himself available.

While we started with theology proper, we quickly graduated to and jumped around topics in Christology (study of Jesus), Pneumatology (study of the Holy Spirit), Anthropology (study of humanity), Soteriology (study of salvation), and Eschatology (the study of Heaven, Hell, end times, and related areas).

By August, Reverend Jim thought I was ready to be baptized. I agreed and joined the group going on the retreat to the Adirondacks.

We rented a mini bus so twenty-five of us could ride together. Since the group included people from Wednesday and Thursday Bible studies, we started the ride playing the name game. "My name is Virginia, and I like vertebrates," was my introduction and it didn't win me any new friends. I tried to think of a Christian "V" word but all that came to mind was the "Virgin Mary." I like her, but it sounded weirder in my head than "vertebrates".

For much of the ride, we listened to tape cassettes. Many of the riders were familiar with Christian music and sang in harmony. I was introduced to Andraé Crouch, The Imperials, and Evie. Reverend Jim said he liked Evie because her songs reminded him of the intro songs in James Bond movies. While aghast by his taste in cinema, I enjoyed the Christian songs.

We fueled up at a burger gas station around noon. Then, we hiked to the Ausable Chasm rafting put-in. Following the yellow blazes took us over the river in multiple places across iron bridges, sometimes wood bridges, that were thirty meters in the air. This afforded several awesome vistas, caverns, rock formations like the "elephant's head", etc. Climbers scaled the rock faces below and others clipped in and shimmied down a long cable in harnesses.

At the put-in, we were split into two groups of ten and one of five. I was part of the latter, and we were paired with another group of four tourists. It seemed like the whole experience flew by. They went through all the safety disclaimers and training, and told us what commands to listen for and how to respond. Forward paddle, back paddle, hold, all stop… we did all the commands keeping the boat on track. We bounced and blasted through the rapids, mist spraying and waves splashing. Cries of jubilation filled the air as we jetted through the chasm. Twenty minutes later we were at the end of the run. While thrilling, I preferred the serenity of the hike better. Overall, it was a nice group-building experience to kick off the retreat.

Our campsite looked like a tent city, probably like a waffle with strawberry topping from above because of the fires in the middle of each quadrant. Rounding out the evening, we gobbled some flame-roasted hot dogs, baked beans, chips, and soda; sang hymns accompanied by acoustic guitar; prayed for the week; and drifted off after Jim's humorous bedtime ghost stories.

Day one successfully broke the ice. Day two was a routine development day. Our first half hour was dedicated time with Jehovah. The instructions were to retreat to seclusion in our tents or the woods and spend time with Him. Practically, that either meant praying or reading the Bible, or some combination.

I went out into the woods and prayed, "Jehovah, speak to me. Pour yourself into my mind. Please." Giving him free reign, I felt an overwhelming peace come over me. Randomly flipping open the Bible, I landed on the beatitudes. It wasn't a section Reverend Jim and I had discussed yet. An initial reading filled me with awe. 'So many blessings,' I thought, 'For so many groups of people!' A closer inspection and it dawned on me that my character wasn't like one of theirs; not mournful, meek, merciful, etc.

Suddenly, I was startled by leaves and sticks crunching loudly near me. Another camper looked like they were heading back to the tents early. The spook only heightened my anxiety.

'Was I blessed?' it asked, and my logic answered, 'Not according to this list.'

Then, concern questioned, 'Is damned the opposite of blessed?'

And dread chimed in with, 'Yes, as different as the clouds of Heaven are from the smoke of Hell.'

Hot and cold fronts crashed together somewhere off the coast of my mind and a swirling hurricane of fear ripped into the peaceful shores of my heart. Acid poured into my gut as the logical argument emerged.

'Many had not and would not be blessed with seeing God. Many will not receive His comfort and Kingdom.' Discouragement gusted in me like a one hundred and sixty mile per hour wind.

'Don't you remember in other places in the Bible, Reverend Jim showed us where Jehovah said many would not inherit the Kingdom?' reminded my insecurity.

The storm turned further inland, stirring my anger and threatening to damage my pride, self-confidence, and self-assurance.

'Wait! These could be fictitious people,' my pride contended.

My confidence supported, 'Yes, it's just impossible, they're idealized characteristics meant to elevate the perfection of Jesus.'

Self-assurance added, "He is the mournful, meek, and merciful One! No one else."

'No!' insisted inadequacy, 'The prophets are specifically noted in the list for being persecuted. They lived and were killed. If we want to be on that list, we too must die for the faith.'

'What does that mean for my dad though?' asked my respect.

To which frustration answered, 'Who knows. You will never find out. There's no point trying to guess.'

When it was time to come back to the tents, anger was incipient but my fear was a category four at least.

Ken intercepted me on my way in. "You see a bear out there, Red? You look pale, even for a ginger."

"I think it's the fear of God."

He smirked and seeing my candor, he inquired, "Yeah? Why?"

"The beatitudes," is all I could force from my lips.

Ken grabbed my shoulders and looked into my eyes. "You're okay."

My security agreed, 'We're okay.'

I breathed deeply and exhaled. "Thanks, Ken."

"Listen, let's talk after whatever the activity is after this meeting."

"Okay."

It was the first time Ken actually said full sentences to me that weren't just greetings. 'Who says a redneck can't be thoughtful and kind?' remarked my appreciation.

Beside our waffle tent city was a pavilion with four picnic tables and two grills.

"Roughly half of the people in this group were baptized the year before. Raise your hand if you are one of those people," Reverend Jim began during breakfast.

The hands went up. I counted eleven, and they started dropping.

"Keep them up, please. All of you who have not yet been baptized, look around at the raised hands. These are the people who are willing to disciple you afterwards. Part of your goal this week is to find a discipleship partner from among these volunteers. Please note that willing does not mean obligated. You've got ample time during meals and in between activities to get to know each other and make your request. I recommend asking someone with whom you have good chemistry. Thank you. You may put your hands down now."

I recognized all of the volunteers from when the Bible study used to meet the same evening, though about half I hadn't talked to before this trip. Considering the benefits of my discipler being in my Bible study (e.g. potentially more common and convenient meeting times), I decided to target those volunteers.

"Now. Get excited because we have a week of great activities for you. Each day after dedication and breakfast," Reverend Jim paused. "Is everyone enjoying their breakfast?"

Wooing and applause erupted.

"Thank Marj and Alice on the grills for the eggs and bacon!"

They smiled and waved in appreciation of the cheering. When that died down, Reverend Jim continued.

"Yes. After breakfast, we will hike for three to four miles. There are different trials for each day. We'll start off easy today with the two-mile Dry Chasm Trail. Halfway on the hike, we will take a snack and reflection break. Then, when we return there will be a break before we eat lunch together at the campgrounds. Any questions about that?"

Someone asked, "Are we going to have different breakfasts besides bacon and eggs?"

"Yes, there will be some variety. Any other questions so far?"

After no one else chimed in, he continued, "The campgrounds have horseshoes and bocce. We will have doubles tournaments with brackets for these and the card game, Euchre, going throughout the week. Doubles means you have a partner."

"Are we assigned partners?" some guy sitting next to me asked.

"You must pick a different partner for each tournament," answered Reverend Jim. "In the afternoon, I will give a sermon as part of a series on baptism. Then, there will be a two-hour period for studying, journaling, reflection, and prayer. We eat a snack and play capture the flag. Sounding good so far?"

"Yes!" several people hollered back.

"Our craft this year will be making flies for fly fishing, and after we eat dinner, we will go fishing. If you don't want to do that there's also swimming. At night, we will take showers, roast marshmallows, play trivia, tell campfire stories, and relax around the fire, or dance, whatever strikes your fancy. I hope you participate in all the activities but don't feel like you have to. Anyone have any questions?"

"When are the baptisms?" someone asked.

"Great question. Saturday morning, in lieu of a hike, and before someone asks, we will be traveling back Saturday afternoon. Anything else?"

People started shifting around in anticipation for the hike.

"Okay then! Let's get ready. We are taking the bus to our hike in fifteen minutes. Please finish your food and help cleanup. We don't want bears or any other animals coming through our campsite, right?"

"Right!" a handful of people responded.

Ken caught up with me after the hike, when I was feeling more like myself.

"Hey Red!"

"Please call me Virginia."

"Got a stick up your britches, Virginia?"

"No, I just think it's demeaning. I'm more than just a red-head, like you are more than just a mustache or a mullet. Aren't you glad I don't call you M&Ms."

"Actually, I'll have to think about that. Them candies are lick-your-digits tasty."

I grunted in irritation.

"You a feminist?"

"I am," I replied proudly.

He smirked, "That reminds me of a yuk-yuk. Wanna hear it?"

"Sure."

His grin widened and he began, "A redneck with seven kids starts calling his wife "mother of seven" instead of by her first name as a joke. This is funny to the wife at first, who laughs when he says it. But a few years later, the redneck is calling her "mother of seven" for everything. "What's for breakfast, mother of seven? My clothes clean, mother of seven?" This becomes very irritating to her. One night, at the end of a contra dance, the redneck yells out, "Mother of seven, time to leave!" The wife finally has enough and shouts back, "After this last dance, father of five!"

"Oh!" I chuckled. "That's a good one."

Taking on a more focused expression, he dove into the deep end, "Anyway, I said I would come talk to ya. Here I am. What was going on this morning?"

While I appreciated his concern when I was in mid-crisis, I wasn't really sure I wanted to open up to this pseudo-stranger. Then, I remembered that we were supposed to be finding a mentor for discipleship. Ken was a redneck to be sure, but Milli always told me not to judge an article by its title. Ken wasn't part of the Wednesday night Bible studies, which was inconvenient, but he was advancing in the ranks of priesthood quickly. Him knowing me, showing me ways I can serve, and being in his prayers could help me in the long run. 'Maybe this conversation was a good test to see if I wanted him to mentor me,' I thought, and taking it a step further, 'Perhaps I could even use the topic as a test for each mentor candidate of interest.'

After a brief deliberation, I answered, "I am concerned that I am not one of the blessed that are described in the beatitudes, and while I might be able to do something about that, my late father cannot."

"You mean you're worried that your pa didn't make it into the Celestial Kingdom?"

"Yes."

"You don't need to worry about that. Becoming a citizen of the Kingdom is easy."

"What do you mean?"

"There's a vast universe out there, full of planets for our heavenly bodies to dwell and explore. Plenty of space for everyone, you know? Your pa just needed to trust in Jesus as his savior."

"What if my father didn't trust in Jesus?"

"Well, did he go to church? Pretty much all pastors in all the churches preach John 3:16 - *For God so loved the world, that he gave his only begotten Son, that whosoever believeth on him should not perish, but have eternal life.*"

"I think he did, at least in his youth."

"Well, there you go. You're smart. Apple doesn't fall far from the tree. I'm sure he got the message."

I considered his logic and felt a little more at ease, but my skepticism presented itself.

"You don't look convinced."

"While I appreciate what you're saying. It sounds..." I hesitated not wanting to offend him.

"What?"

"...too easy," to use his words.

"I can't say everybody, but many people feel that way. The verse that Reverend Jim showed me was Romans 6:23 - *For the wages of sin is death; but the free gift of God is eternal life in Christ Jesus our Lord.*"

Again, I heard Milli's wisdom, 'There's no such thing as a free lunch, certainly not something more precious. There are only loss leaders. The promotion of something must be a fraction of the sale, a tenth or a fifth, more than twenty percent free is rare. You will pay in the end.' I imagined the enormity of what ten times entrance into Heaven might cost given how much retirement in Florida costs.

"I know you need time to think on it. Happy to talk again if you'd like."

"Thank you, Ken."

Later that night, I was surprised when Ken seemed to have volume control issues and he bellowed, "We need to liven things up. Warren, play your guitar!"

Warren started playing something and he yelled to me, "Dance with me by the fire, Virginia."

"No, thank you," I replied, just not really wanting to dance then, but I think he took it personally based on a momentary glare and a frown.

Alice jumped at the chance though, "I'll dance with you, Ken!"

That turned his frown upside down. Warren's playing sped up. We all clapped and bounced our knees with their caper around the fire, smiling and laughing. The guitar picking got to be very fast and so did the rest of the hootenanny.

When the song finished and the applause was over, Ken shouted, "What was that great song? Sounded familiar."

"That was the guitar part of the song Dueling Banjos."

"Who's the band?" sounding a little impatient.

"I don't remember. It's from that creepy movie about the hillbillies raping canoeists."

"Deliverance?"

"Yeah, I thought you might like it," Warren mused.

Few people laughed.

Ken started marching toward Warren. "Boy, you got a smart mouth, don't cha'?"

"That's enough!" barked Reverend Jim.

Ken stopped in his tracks and they both looked over to Reverend Jim. The whole campsite fell silent and those who weren't already watching tuned in.

"We are GOLDS! We run the race with endurance to victory, to Jehovah's Kingdom come! We run against elitism and racism, and beat them. We don't let them put their arms over our shoulders and carry them across the finish line. Do we?"

Ken was flush embarrassed and Warren was avoiding eye contact.

"Do we?" repeated Reverend Jim.

"No," they said in unison.

"No, we leave them in the dust. Now apologize to each other."

They exchanged glances and looked back at Reverend Jim.

"Say I'm sorry for being elitist, and I'm sorry for being racist."

While clearly reluctant, they still apologized in front of everyone. The whole episode of acting badly at a church retreat and responding to parental disciplining caused me to reconsider Ken as a mentor option. Warren told me on the hike that someone had already asked him. So, he was out anyway.

I interviewed Malorie the following day. She was just one of a few women who were offering to help disciple neophytes; eligible because of her Levite priesthood rank. A heartland strawberry blonde beauty, her top priorities were faith, family, freedom, farm, and the fellas.

I first met Malorie last March, after the news aired about victory in Vietnam. The first words I heard her say were, "Soviets are next!" She shared with the Bible study that her father was a Korean War hero and her grandfather was a World War 1 and 2 hero. While I too felt very patriotic after Uncle Sam got another notch in his belt, my prediction was that it would take decades, civil wars, and internal strife to weaken the U.S.S.R. before external forces could break it apart, like Rome and other historical empires of the region.

Malorie and I both weren't busy after lunch because our teams were already knocked out of the horseshoe tournament.

"Would you mind taking a walk with me? I was hoping to get your opinion on something."

Her cheeks dimpled at the request. "Sure, Virginia, let me grab my pop. Would you like one?"

"No, thank you."

"Okey-dokey."

I led her away from the tents to a secluded section of the woods, and settled on some rocks to talk.

"What's the scoop?"

"I'm worried that I'm not one of the blessed that are described in the beatitudes, and that my deceased father isn't either."

"Oh, Virginia!" she said in a mixed tone of pity and relief. "You had me worried you were pregnant out of wedlock or something! You are almost certainly blessed. Purely because you are concerned is a good sign you are blessed."

I considered this, but wasn't sure what she meant, and my puzzling emoted into skeptical pursed lips and a raised eyebrow.

With a military tough composure, she spoke like a drill Sergeant, "Let me spell it out for you, *brainy dummy*."

Lowering her voice and speaking slower for emphasis, she asserted, "You are being humble. God loves and blesses the humble. Argo, you are blessed. Just because it's not in the beatitudes doesn't mean it isn't elsewhere in the Bible."

"I appreciate your generous assumption of my goodness, but I don't think my best friends would characterize me as humble."

She rebuked me, lightly scolding, "How could you let the Evil One disparage you?"

I was taken aback. I didn't expect there to be so much admonishment on a Christian retreat.

"You are His and you are blessed."

"Why do you say that though?" I demanded.

Her eyes flicked to the side, searching for some tangible example.

"Look, I have a feeling about you, Virginia, a discernment."

I rolled my eyes at the unsubstantiated claim approaching vacuity.

"Wait, I know what you're thinking. It's not really fair because we don't hang out. What I've seen though. Listen! What I've seen is that you ferociously consume the Bible. You're like Ezekiel, the scroll eater!"

She wasn't wrong, but unconvinced at this as a virtue, I lightly argued back, "There is no *blessed are the studious...*"

"No, but the first beatitude is *blessed are the poor in spirit.*"

"So, what does that mean?"

"It means you recognize your spiritual poverty, Virginia, and you hunger to know God. Well, He's not only going to just introduce Himself to you, He says He's going to take you into His Kingdom, shug."

Emotions welled up inside me. The sweet sentiment was needed, like warm sun for reptilian blood. Malorie wasn't done blessing me though.

"Virginia, you can't let the Evil One disparage you."

"Why?" I challenged.

"Because, you are meant to be a great leader. The Holy Spirit has shown me this."

The revelation was intriguing with all the shock and mystery of a Tarot card or palm reading. I furrowed my brow, balking at the mysticism. "What do you mean?"

With wide confident eyes, she clarified, "A vision."

"Of what?"

"Honestly, I don't know, I mean I don't understand what I saw, it's weird. What I do know is that you're a leader in the making."

"Stellar!" Sarcastic out of frustration, I decided to walk back toward the camp.

Still sitting on the rock, Malorie hollered, "More important than prophecy is a piece of advice."

I kept walking.

"Stop worrying, Virginia: about your salvation, and about your dad's. Everything will be okay. You just need to trust in our loving God. He won't forsake us."

Malorie was my Euchre partner, and I was glad because her aggressive optimism really paid off in that game. "Skip on a bower, lose for an hour!" she'd chant. That was fun for a one-week tournament but I could tell in a discipleship relationship it would be too much.

I considered a near opposite of her, Felix, the realist. They belonged to the same church, obviously, but beyond that, there were mostly differences. Felix was blonde like Malorie, but a bleached blonde, not strawberry. He was a large not-so merry dutchman from the marshes of coastal Maryland. Instead of farming, he grew up crabbing and deer hunting. Father was a United Son of the Confederacy, anti-patriotic. Mother's nickname was black-eyed Susan, and not because she was a floriculturist. He couldn't wait to leave home and go off to college. Said he'd never look back.

Felix accepted my request to talk, walked back into the woods, and sat on the rocks with me. His response to my question was, "Well, you sure aren't meek."

I assumed the jab was referencing our introduction. On our first meeting, I challenged Felix on his assertion that God was male. "How do you know God is not a woman?" While he did convince me that God presented Himself as male, he didn't have an easy time with it.

I was expecting him to say something more than the insult, but he didn't offer anything else, which annoyed me. Nevertheless, I decided to see if I could draw any other perspectives out of him. Stoking the conversation, I added, "I'm worried about never seeing my father, either because I won't make it to Heaven, or that he didn't."

Stoic as ever, he responded, *"Wide is the gate, and broad is the way, that leadeth to destruction.* Few will find the narrow gate, the narrow way."

"Are you saying he probably didn't? How could you just say that to me?"

"I have no way of knowing. I'm just stating the facts."

Not averse to blunt delivery, I swung back, "Are you so hopeless that you have no hope to give?"

Seemed I struck a chord because he raised his voice. "You want the truth, right?"

"Yes," I said a decibel louder than him.

He took a brief moment to restore composure.

"The truth is that everyone is welcome, but most people reject his invitation. In the Gospel of Luke, chapter fourteen, the Lord tells us a parable about this. A servant is sent out with invitations to a feast but no one comes at first ...*they all with one consent began to make excuse... I bought a field ... five yoke and oxen ... I have married ...* The servant has to go to the *streets and lanes of the city ... gathering the poor, maimed, lame, and blind ... to highways and hedges ... constraining people to come.* There's plenty of space in Heaven, people just decide not to believe, not to

117

trust, and not to accept the invitation for various reasons. My recommendation is to prioritize God in your life and not get too busy with other things."

The comment about plenty of space made me think about its vastness and Ken's logic. I really had no idea whether my father went to church or not, and accepted Jesus as his savior. I never asked and Milli never mentioned it. The only clue she gave me was that my father's folks went to church when they were alive, and were now buried on the church grounds somewhere in Pennsylvania. I reasoned that if they went to church, they took him too. It seemed unlikely to me that he went to church as an adult though since Milli didn't go, nor did she try to take me. I asked Felix, "What if my father went to church as a kid, heard the Gospel, dedicated himself or whatever, but then stopped going to church when he was an adult?"

"I do not know. There are no verses that I am aware of in the Bible about church goers or former church goers feasting with God in Heaven."

"You made it sound so easy though. I mean you basically said God was inviting everyone from everywhere to come to Heaven. Going to churches to find invitees is like going to a grocery store for produce, right?"

"But then your dad left. Sounds like he got busy. Did he ultimately reject the invitation? I don't know."

"Just because he left the church doesn't mean…" I didn't know how to put it into words. My mind just went blank and fear gripped my stomach, lungs, and throat.

Still, Felix responded understanding the essence. "Correct, coming or going to church doesn't guarantee anything."

A stress headache was coming on.

I started, "What if…"

"Virginia," he cut me off, "Do we really need to continue on with the hypotheticals? We could speculate for hours and still not know what happened to your father's soul."

That got me, like a dagger in the stomach. Tears filled my eyes and I started crying like I had received a mortal wound knowing we were too far from the hospital to do anything about it.

"Oh, Virginia. Please don't cry. Look, you want hope. I've got some hope."

"What?" I croaked.

"There will definitely be other people in Heaven."

He said this with an earnest smile, like "other people" was a good consolation. I was completely blinded by my tears, and my headache raged.

Felix continued, "There are some things you can't control. Think about other people you care about, one's that are not dead yet, and what you can do now to ensure you can spend eternity with them. Also, more hope for you - in Heaven, there is no mourning or crying. Somehow even sad things will be well."

I wanted more hope for my father. Felix's solution to forget my father and spend my energy elsewhere was frustrating, even infuriating.

Seeking to assuage the situation for himself, he retreated from my sobbing with a, "I'm going to give you some space and head back to camp."

I watched his blurred figure walking away, and wished he'd come back just so I could push him off of the rocks. 'Maybe it was better this way,' I thought. 'Now I can push him into the chasm during a hike.'

Felix's words haunted me over the next couple of days. My murderous thoughts subsided, and I surprised myself, thinking more and more about the people I still had time to help save from Hell. My father's eternal situation was uncertain and unchangeable. So, any and all efforts including worrying about him were futile. I surrendered my anxiety about my father to God.

Even though Felix was too much of a heartless killjoy for me to ask him to disciple me, I was glad I spoke with him. Contextually his advice was evangelical in nature, redirecting my energy and time away from the dead to the living was sage advice. However, I saw no reason why this couldn't be more broadly applicable. Releasing anxiety about the uncontrollable and the past, and focusing on the controllable and the present for future sake seemed like a prudent philosophy.

On the fourth day of the retreat, a lunchtime announcement was made that all of the disciplers were taken. I thought I made a serious error; that I had been too picky and would now have to wait another year to be discipled. However, Reverend Jim took the leftovers including myself, and I was glad for it. He had already sort of been discipling me with our Q&A sessions and giving me homework anyway. I thought to myself, 'God worked it all out. Maybe I can trust Him with more things and not worry so much about the things I can't control.'

Shortly after the announcement was made, Alice and Nancy came to see me and pulled me away into the woods.

"You lucky goose!" Alice congratulated me. Seemed like she meant lucky duck but maybe was mishmashing silly goose.

"What?"

"Come on!" Nodding her head and gesturing for me to follow them.

After trampling through the underbrush for a little while, I asked, "Where are we going?"

"No where. Nancy and I just wanted to hang out."

Something seemed amiss. Trying to understand the true intent of the conversation, I asked, "What did you mean calling me a *lucky goose?*"

"Just that Reverend Jim took you as a disciple."

"Oh. Yes, that is good news."

"Yes. That is good news." Alice repeated with a little more enthusiasm.

She was mirroring me with her upright posture, the cadence of her walk and swing of her arms, and even my words and tone. She was trying to get me to open up to her. It's a psychological tactic where you make your body language and parts of speech the same as the person you're talking to, putting them at ease and making them feel like you are part of their tribe.

"You don't sound very excited," she probed.

"Well, he was already kind of discipling me."

Nancy, who was also lockstep on my other side, inquired with bewilderment, "What do you mean? Discipling only happens after the baptism sacrament."

"For most of the summer, we've been meeting regularly to discuss spiritual questions I have."

"Ugh," Alice groaned, "You lucky goose!"

A little annoyed and dissatisfied with the previous explanation for the meaning of her odd colloquialism, I snapped, "Why do you keep saying that?"

With that slight departure from pleasantry, Alice could no longer contain her frustration and enthusiasm.

"Are you blind? The man could put angels to shame."

"You think so?" I played dumb, waiting to see where this conversation was going and why we were tramping through the woods.

"Absolutely! I joined the Civil Rights Outreach Committee just to spend more time with him."

"And what do you think, Nancy?" I asked.

"Yeah, he's a hunk. Don't you think so?" she redirected.

I wasn't going to tell them that I participated in some church outreach events to gaze upon his beauty.

"He's not really my type."

That was a bold-faced lie, and my conscience was all over me. Guilt for a white lie was a new sensation, and I wondered if this was a manifestation of God changing me. I knew I had to correct myself.

"I mean, I don't have time for any guys, I'm too busy," I garbled. It was true enough not to offend my conscience.

With what?" challenged Nancy.

"Well, besides discipleship, I'm part of a committee that organizes developmental biology guest lectures and my friends and I are working on a literature review."

They gaped at me with one eyebrow up.

"I'm trying to become a science professor," I simplified.

"Wow. Interesting." Alice replied, unconvincingly. "We should probably head back. Would be a shame if we missed the bus to go hiking."

The sudden plummet in interest from Alice was evidence that she just wanted to know if I was a threat to her pursuit of Reverend Jim. I wasn't sure, in truth. Reverend Jim hadn't come on to me, and I think I annoyed him at times with my questions. Still, Jim and I spent a fair amount of time together and I was objectively better looking than Alice.

Curious about the dynamics and quality of the time she got with Reverend Jim, I feigned interest in her committee. "My guest lecture committee is just five people. How many people are in your Civil Rights Outreach Committee? What's it like?"

"It's just Reverend Jim, me, Warren, and Phoebe. Committee meetings are like double dates."

I didn't really believe her even though Warren and Phoebe were a sweet couple, very affectionate to each other. Some people find pugs endearing, so physical attraction is clearly complex. However, only a deaf man could remain indifferent to Alice's obnoxious guffaw.

"That sounds nice!" I exclaimed, trying to sound more convincing than Alice had before changing the subject. "Are there any guys you're going after these days, Nancy?"

"Not exactly," Nancy hesitated.

I briefly considered how much Nancy had changed since I first met her. Popularity with guys used to be a high priority, then she started going to GOLDS Church, and began spending less time with guys and more time with young women. Now Nancy was helping Alice get information about a potential threat to her love scheme, even though Nancy was apparently attracted to Alice's object of affection. Maybe Nancy was dating someone, so Alice didn't care.

"Are you already dating someone?" I inquired.

"Something amazing happened to her," blurted Alice.

"Alice!"

"Tell her! It's stellar!" Alice urged.

"What?" I asked.

"Earlier in the retreat, during our devotion time, I was praying to God and…"

"And what?"

"He showed me an image of my husband!" she squealed and began jumping up and down with Alice who joined along in the squealing.

"Wow! Really?" The way she said it and her ear-to-ear grin made me believe her.

"Yeah!"

"So, who is it?" I inquired.

"Not sure. All I know is that he's black."

My mind went in a myriad of directions, but my big takeaway was that Nancy was not a contender for Reverend Jim. I made up my delay in response with enthusiasm, "Wow! How exciting!"

"Do you really think so?" she asked.

"Yes! I'm very happy for you."

"Thanks, Virginia."

As we approached our campsite, it looked like everyone was gone.

"Oh, they left us!" declared Alice.

"Reverend Jim did say we weren't obligated to do any of the activities and buses would leave on time with or without us," reminded Nancy.

Recalling a similar situation on the OBX camping trip with the Ocracoke gang, I proposed, "How about we have a little fun while everyone is away?"

They agreed. I explained that Bobby pranked some young women at a couple of the campgrounds we visited by going into the bathrooms when no one was around and drawing large spiders on the toilet paper for them to discover at the apex of relaxation. He successfully induced hysterical Marion Crane shrieks. We decided that it would be more fun to see if we could horrify the guys.

While our campsite was empty, there were still a minority of campers at other sites on the grounds. Alice and Nancy were my lookouts. If anyone was coming, they would warn me with a bird call.

I entered the men's half of the bathrooms undetected. Thankfully, it was empty. Unfortunately, it was fouler than a compost pile. Opening the closest stall, I discovered why; urine was splashed all over the lid and flies played musical chairs on floating turds. They buzzed away after a flush.

Aware of the microscopic bacteria that remained on the seat even after wiping it dry, I decided to put the lid down and sit on it instead. Then, I proceeded to unroll the toilet paper a little, and with my black pen, I drew a large hairy spider. It was actually realistic with the likeness of a wolf spider. I rolled the toilet paper back up so the victim wouldn't see it at first, and moved onto the next stall, having to flush and wipe again to tolerate the space while I worked. Before I could put the lid down though, I heard bird calls.

My fearful soul exited through the stall door and phased through the concrete wall, leaving my body behind to fend for itself. The first instinct of my abandoned flesh was to lock the door, which thankfully wasn't too loud. The second was to rip off my sandals. I thought they would be a dead giveaway that the person in the bathroom was the wrong sex. Nude hairless legs probably just looked like a boy's. Disgusted but desperate, I eased myself onto the bacteria-coated toilet seat, and carefully listened.

The stranger was wearing flip flops. His walk remained at a steady pace from the entrance to the stall door, suggesting he either didn't see my legs or didn't care. The hinges of the stall beside me squeaked as he opened it, came in, and closed the door behind him. A creak and porcelain clap followed as he lifted the lid. I thought he was going to pee because I could see his foot facing the toilet. Mine were shifted to the opposite side of the bowl so he couldn't see them. I heard him mutter, "Hmm" with a slight rising intonation. There was no trickle or splash of urine. I thought he might be onto me somehow and felt my stomach tighten and my heart race. But then his foot moved and the other one was facing in the opposite direction, shorts came down over it, and then the distinct sound of a rear casually settling into a toilet seat.

'One, two, three…' I counted in my mind, trying to calm down and distract myself. On twelve, I was interrupted by more bird calls. Muscles tensed in my neck and shoulders, I felt sweat drip down my back, and anxious thoughts erased the numbers. 'I would be caught, expelled from the campgrounds, and have to go home early and miss the baptism, or maybe even get my whole group expelled. I would be humiliated, the jokes would never end, and I would be forced to find another church.'

Clear pronounced steps of leather sole boots passed the first stall and the bolt of my door rattled in the strike plate as the man hit my door to see if it would open. Scared he would look through the gap between the wall and the door and see me, I covered my hair and face as best I could, sandals still in hand.

I heard a plunk in the toilet to my left, and the second man entered the stall on my right. I was surrounded and instinctually raised my legs up and out.

Peeling my fearful arms from my face, I looked down and saw the second man's boot facing the toilet. There was another plunk in the toilet to my left; then a flush and a couple of rounds of unrolling and tearing of toilet paper on my right. The man with the boots turned around, sat, and settled.

In the moment of silence, I realized the tension in my quadriceps, hip flexors, and lower back muscles that were created from holding my legs up. Laying my shoes in my lap and bracing my legs with my arms relieved the strain momentarily, but I quickly felt my sedentary lifestyle in my aching muscles.

Plunk, the man with the boots broke the silence on the outside.

I knew that dropping my feet back into vision would draw attention. I was also worried that resting my feet against the stall walls would cause them to vibrate and alarm the men. The fatigue became too much though and I slowly relaxed my feet against the sheet metal. There was an audible pop as it compressed. Thankfully, there were no obvious responses from the men around me. My anxiety was relieved, but my physical respite was only momentary. A sharp twinge shot up my hamstring as I strained to maintain my position.

Another plunk came from the stall to my left, some shifting, and then unrolling.

A cacophony erupted to my left: panicked shrieks, creaks and squeaks of the stall door slamming open and banging back into the stop, feet slapping as they sprinted away on a cement floor. Then, giggles from outside.

Looking down, I saw his flip flops and shorts were left behind.

"What was that?" said the man on my right, and it sounded like he was asking me. I didn't answer. Then, he started moving around.

I hurriedly left the stall with sandals in my hand.

Alice and Nancy intercepted me and led me away from the bathroom, along a roundabout way back to camp, back to safety.

"Breathe!" urged Nancy, and I took a few deep breaths.

I could feel the acid in my body alkalizing. The adrenaline from the fear was wearing off. I felt warmth from the vasodilation. Muscles were relaxing, and a smile crept across my face.

"I did it."

"You did it!" congratulated Alice.

My nervous chuckle was followed by a belly laugh from Nancy and Alice went into full guffaw. 'We got away with it,' I congratulated myself.

When the laughter died down, I hugged Alice and Nancy in gratitude and said sincerely, "Thank you for helping me not get caught."

"What are friends for?" offered Alice.

Seeing how cunning Alice could be, I didn't assume a pure intention. Still, the experience together was real and a reason for at least seeing where the relationship might lead.

Light-hearted fun activities made the next two days fly by and I found myself being baptized in the chasm river beside Alice and Nancy.

"Dead in your sin," declared Reverend Jim.

The congregation watched him plunge me cross-armed down into the rushing water. Then, he pulled me up into the cool breeze and exclaimed, "You are raised to new life in Christ Jesus! Go, follow, and obey your Lord who loves you!"

Cheers and applause echoed through the chasm walls, and a powerful warmth came over me.

'Thank you, Lord,' I prayed silently.

I watched the others share their testimonies. Each confessed a summary of their sins and need of a savior, and professed their faith in the saving power of Jesus before they were symbolically buried and resurrected. The sacrament culminated in

Reverend Jim giving a brief benediction and investiture of our new titles, neophytes."

We ate lunch, packed up the bus, and sang together on the way back to campus. The retreat was great, and I knew it because I could feel myself coming down from the high when I was alone in my dorm. In my reflection, I discovered the GOLDS community meant a lot to me, and I was eager to see everyone again the next day at Sunday service. An unexpected takeaway was the influence of Felix; to release my grip on things I couldn't control and redirect my energy to the things and people I could influence.

After the baptism retreat, Reverend Jim began encouraging the congregants to consider engaging in more of the sacraments.

"The second sacrament is Baptism by the Holy Spirit." He explained, "To be baptized in the Spirit, a believer must first learn how to be a follower of Jesus, not just believe. Remember *even the demons believe and shudder*. During the retreat you asked someone to disciple you. Their job is to teach you how to follow the Holy Spirit, and model Jesus. Your job is to learn and emulate. Okay?"

"Yes," some responded.

"Okay?" Reverend Jim said a little louder.

"Yes!" we all exclaimed.

"Excellent. The processes of discipleship in one sense never really ends. I'm still learning even after more than a decade of complete dedication to the pursuit. For equipping you to be used by the Lord, the formal process of discipleship has a normal time range. It can be completed as quickly as one month but should not take more than one year, unless there are extenuating circumstances like unexpected major family obligations or medical challenges. The priesthood prays for you and listens for direction from the spirit when the neophyte is ready. A brief ceremony is held which culminates in the laying on of hands by the elders in the presence of the congregation for the neophyte to receive the Holy Spirit."

I was spiritually hungry and wanted to experience the transformation of the Holy Spirit in my heart and mind. Reverend Jim was very pleased with my ambition and we decided to meet on Monday and Friday nights during the Fall semester. With Wednesday night Bible studies and Sunday services, I realized this would leave less time for studying and working with the Ocracoke crew on our literature review, but it just seemed like the most important thing.

My best friends (Dan, Gina, and Bobby) returned to campus at the beginning of September and I told them about the discipleship schedule. I think Dan probably understood my prioritization because of how important faith was to him, but I think my friends felt betrayed when I stopped working on the review all together for a couple of months. Some days I didn't even show up to our study sessions, and that turned into weeks. I told myself that my absence was just temporary. At my pace, I would be selected quickly by the Holy Spirit for His baptism, and then I could get back to my friends and the review. But suddenly everything, the review, discipleship, and my studies came to a screeching halt when a truck hit me from behind one day while I was walking back to my dorm.

Chapter 21: Tragedy Marketing

I was heading back to my dorm after a Monday discipleship session when I was mowed over. Accounts from witnesses say that they saw a truck drive up on the sidewalk and impact my lower back. I then rolled up on the hood and crossed it sideways before falling face first onto the paved walkway. I have no memory of this, or the time leading up to the hit-and-run.

I woke up in the ambulance on the way to Davis-Emerson Hospital, which is thankfully just a few miles down the road. They explained that I had been in an accident and sustained a concussion, as well as some other injuries. The paramedics gave me medications for the swelling and pain, and immobilized me in a gurney.

Shortly after I arrived at the hospital a doctor gave me a thorough physical exam, took some blood samples, and took intravenous pyelography X-rays.

The testing suggested that I had lacerations on my kidneys. This was confirmed by surgical exploration while I was under general anesthesia. They placed some drains near my kidneys to collect the combined blood, urine, and other fluids emitting from the lacerations. I was given a transfusion for the blood loss.

My pelvis had multiple fractures. These were stabilized with an external metal frame screwed into my bones. The contraption was a shocking site when nurses showed it to me later.

My thoughts were erratic because of the immense pain, but I knew my body was destroyed and that I would be in need of medical care for a long time. After the pain subsided enough to think more continuously, I worried about losing my friends Gina, Dan, and Bobby. I imagined they might come visit me once, twice, maybe three times, but I felt sure they would forget about me. It would be my own fault. I was the one who betrayed them, deprioritizing our study time and literature review project. We were seeing each other just once a week. I wondered how soon visiting me would become too much of a hassle? Without the convenience and habit of meeting in Ocracoke, I knew it was only a matter of time before I was friendless.

When a doctor came to look at me, I saw something in his eyes that I had never seen before. He was a professional and had probably seen his share of gruesome injuries. Even with his ethics and experience, he failed to fully conceal his nonverbal impressions of my condition.

'We're hideous,' declared my discouragement.

'We'll be fine. It's just going to take some time for us to heal," assured my confidence.

'It's just going to take some time…' mocked my sarcasm.

'Are we sure?' questioned my skepticism. 'There is a metal cage sticking out of us.'

'What the Hell?' complained my frustration.

'Remember when we used to get those irritating and nauseating longing looks from testosterone-raging college guys and even professors?' asked my jealousy.

'Yeah,' quickly replied my irritation.

'Yes,' mused my fascination.

'Well, now we will long for their lecherous stares,' cried my insecurity.

'And mourn our youthful beauty,' added my inferiority.

'It's worse than that. I bet some guys will look away for the sake of politeness. It's the less tactful ones I'm worried about who will look at us with pity and even disgust,' furthered my embarrassment.

Then, a wave of despair came over me when I considered my pelvis.

'We'll probably never walk again,' predicted my helplessness.

'We'll be resigned to a wheelchair for the rest of our life!' overwhelmed exclaimed.

'We might have to urinate through a catheter into a bag and empty it multiple times a day,' piled on irritation.

I audibly gasped and started to cry when my line of thinking brought me to the strong possibility that I might not be able to have children.

'Even if our organs and bones healed enough for sex, pregnancy, *and* childbirth, which right now seems inconceivable, no one is going to want to have a child with someone so grotesquely mangled,' lamented isolation.

For hours, the many feelings of fear, sadness, and anger were unrelenting as I lay in the hospital bed immobilized and throbbing in pain.

To my surprise, Reverend Jim came to the hospital with Alice, Nancy, Warren, and Phoebe.

"Hi, Virginia." Reverend Jim waved as he said this, looking unsure if I could hear him in my condition.

I could see the abhorrence and ruth in their expressions, just like the doctors and nurses.

When I didn't respond, Reverend Jim spoke a little louder and slower as if I was at the bottom of a well and he was trying to save me. "Please save your energy. I just wanted to let you know that I saw what happened. I called 911 and reported it to the police."

'What did happen?' I wondered. Trying to speak, I realized I couldn't, and fear and anger continued their onslaught.

"The nurses told me that you are stabilizing well but need time to rest. So, we won't stay long."

'Wait!' I thought, 'You just got here and I feel so lonely.'

"Also, we came by because we wanted to make sure you're being well taken care of and that you know that you're not alone. We are with you in this."

Up to that point, I felt weaker, more vulnerable, more dependent, and yes, lonelier, in that hospital than I'd ever felt in my life. My energy intensive limbic system and cerebral neocortex were surely working overtime with all of the shock, reflection, and adapting I was doing. Plus, I was physically exhausted from the swelling and drugs. Reverend Jim's words and their presence were an emotional solace and a healing salve. Tears clouded my vision and streamed down my face.

"Rest now and we will be back tomorrow," he said with a smile.

Warren started to sing a hymn to me softly like a lullaby and the others joined in.

"Joyful, joyful, we adore You,
God of glory, Lord of love;
Hearts unfold like flowers before You,
Opening to the sun above…"

It didn't take me long to fall asleep.

When I woke up it was somewhat late in the day. Again, Reverend Jim was there. This time he was reading the Bible and writing down notes, probably for a sermon or study.

"Oh, good afternoon, sleepy head."

My lower back and all around my pelvis felt like it was on fire.

"Ohhhhh…" I groaned, and realized my voice had returned. "Please get the nurse for me," I asked Reverend Jim with a very labored and weak vocalization.

He leapt from his chair to chase one down. I really appreciated his hustle, and was thankful that he returned with the nurse who came with water and more pain medications.

"Sorry, Reverend Jim. Can you give me time for the pills to kick in?"

"No problem," he said and went back to reading. I realized my bed was pointed in his direction, and therefore it wouldn't be strange for me to stare in his direction. So, I watched him trying to distract myself while the painkillers kicked in. His face seemed more beautiful than ever with his gorgeous dirty golden mane of hair, perfectly proportioned nose, and youthful blemish-free skin.

"Thank you for coming," I said about fifteen minutes later.

He stood over me and smiled. His teeth were pearls and his eyes were onyx.

"It's my pleasure. The nurse said she's going to bring you a light meal."

"Great. I am hungry," I rasped.

"Me and some of the other congregants are going to bring more in the coming days and whatever else you need once you're back at your dorm."

"Wow, I really appreciate you."

"Happy to help, and we can also take *you* wherever *you* need to go; doctors' appointments, classes, wherever. Is there anything I can get *you* now that would make *you* more comfortable?" He emphasized each of the yous with a toothy grin.

I said, "No," but secretly wished he would reach over and run his fingers through my hair. Then lean in and slowly nibble my neck. I imagined him taking his time, the pressure and kissing building to a passionate hickey. Oh, how that would be a nice distraction. He could spend the whole day covering me with love bruises to match the wounded sections of my body if he wanted to.

While Reverend Jim's presence was much appreciated, I didn't understand why he was being so attentive and thoughtful, making sure to be in the room when I woke up.

"Why are you doing this, Reverend Jim?"

"What?"

"I can understand why you would visit me, but why are you staying by my bedside?"

"I care about you."

His eyes were kind and warm, and I fantasized what it would be like if he actually meant that in an amorous way.

Probably recognizing how his words might be taken, he clarified, "Virginia, I am your brother in Jehovah. And you are also a part of the flock Jehovah has given me to shepherd. I'm here to care for and protect you."

That was a splash of cold water. The sobering truth left me wanting more pain killers.

He continued, his face contorting in grief as he paused between sentences, "Something very sad has happened."

His eyes fell. "I'm very sorry, but I think the person who did the hit-and-run was someone we know."

I furrowed my brow, confused, waiting intently for a clearer explanation.

"I believe Ken hit you."

I stirred. "What do you mean, Ken from church? Priest Ken?"

I sucked in sharply through my teeth and shifted, which brought discomfort in my wounds.

"Please, relax." He looked like he was going to lay his hands on my torso and sooth my pain, but then stopped and retracted them at the last moment, averting his gaze to the ground. Again, self-consciousness afflicted my mind, and I looked down at my swollen mangled body and the stabilizing metal contraption.

"It was too dark to be sure of the color, but I recognized the New Jersey plates," Reverend Jim said, staring at the ground and shaking his head.

"How drunk did that redneck have to be to veer off the road like that, let alone keep going after hitting me?'

Reverend Jim looked up and I saw his droopy sagging eyes. The emotional strain was weighing heavy for him too.

"I'm sorry, Virginia," responding but trying to keep the conversation more constructive. "The police are currently looking for Ken and asked me to let them know if he contacts me. No one has seen him since last night."

An image of the shady redneck with sunglasses came to mind. What I once admired as a true-to-self style, now seemed like the markings of poverty, ignorance, and stubbornness. 'Old high school habits of tailgating, pounding cheap beer, and driving around intoxicated in a giant truck die hard. Instead of hitting a hungry deer crossing a rural road at night and leaving the roadkill for scavengers, he hit me and left. What a low life, trying to hide from this,' I thought.

"Ken hasn't been back to his dorm. His suitemates told me that he attends a class on Tuesday mornings, but he wasn't there. I'm hopeful that he'll be at the Bible study tomorrow night. He's only missed Wednesday Bible study once or twice since he started going."

"He'll miss it if he's hiding from the cops," I hissed.

"If it was Ken, I would venture to guess it was a mistake. He was afraid and bolted, but I believe at this moment he is thinking through the right way to respond."

"Ken needs to turn himself in."

"Yes, it's sad to think about, but temptations come to all of us. Not to excuse his actions. It's terrible what he did to you. I can't help but think that I too would have been tempted to flee the scene if I thought I could somehow escape the consequences of having injured someone badly, or even inadvertently caused their death."

"I wouldn't," I barked.

He pursed his lips, keeping his thoughts to himself.

"What?!"

"Nothing."

After a short pause, I changed the subject.

"What is the penalty for a hit-and-run in the State of New York?"

"Not exactly sure, but I would guess that leaving you there was a criminal offense. So, he will probably receive charges which will go on his permanent record, impacting his future employment, and he'll get jail time and fines. It's possible he could have avoided everything if he stayed with you. Well, except for the fines and an increased cost in car insurance. Still much better than what he's in for now."

"Oh, Hell!" Dread came over me.

"What?"

"There's no insurance to pay for my injuries. Ken's insurance won't pay because there's no proof he did it. I have no car insurance because I don't have a car. So, no uninsured motorist coverage, and my crappy student health insurance almost certainly doesn't cover a hit-and-run."

Reverend Jim's eyes widened with concern, then darted around as if chasing a fly. Then, he closed his eyes and took a deep breath. I wondered if he was okay, never having seen him do that before.

"Everything will be okay." Opening his eyes, he continued, "Don't worry. Once Ken is found, we'll get a confession or other proof, and his vehicle insurance will pay for your medical expenses."

Just then Gina, Dan, and Bobby walked into my hospital room.

"Oh, sweetheart…" Gina said. "We saw the story in The Nettie Plot this morning and got here as soon as there was a break in the class schedule."

The Nettie Plot was the Nettie Maria Stevens University newspaper.

"How are you feeling?" asked Gina.

"Yeah, not great, but the pain medication helps. You're saying that my story is in The Nettie Plot?"

"And the local newspaper! Who knew that all you have to do is get hit by a truck to become famous?" joked Bobby. "You're in it too, aren't you … uh, Reverend?"

"Yes, that's right. Hi, I'm Reverend Jim. What are your names?" He extended his hand.

"Sorry Reverend Jim, these are my friends Bobby, Gina, and Dan," I piped up.

"Nice to meet you all." He finished shaking hands and said, "I'm going to head out so you all can talk. I'll be back later to check on you, Virginia. May Jehovah bless you."

"And you too, Reverend Jim."

"So that's your pastor, reverend, or whatever?" asked Gina, still unclear about the leadership hierarchy of GOLDS.

"Yes. Why?"

"He *is* cute!"

I smiled at this remembering I told her about my attraction several weeks earlier.

Bobby gave Gina a jealous, bothered look.

"But not as cute as you, Bobby," she blurted, rescuing herself.

He grinned and proclaimed, "Yeah, that's right."

Gina rolled her eyes.

Dan looked gloomy and like he was deeply pondering something.

"Everything okay, Dan?" I queried.

In a very serious, heartfelt tone, he implored, "Please don't worry about me. I should be the one asking how you are. I'm very sorry this happened, Virginia. I feel guilty that we weren't there for you."

"Don't say that. I know you all aren't interested in GOLDS. You have your own church and you two don't go to church. There's no reason you would have been walking back from discipleship with me."

The room was silent for a moment. The things that were on the forefront of our minds varied tremendously these days and it felt like a sad reunion where all you have is old memories. Our divergence in thought, the gap of time, and differential experiences were palpable.

Then Bobby said, "What are you going to do, Virginia?"

"I'm not sure."

Dan perked up, "I can bring your homework."

"I can take notes in class for you to read," offered Gina.

"Nobody can read your notes," joked Bobby.

We all laughed. Again, my heart warmed and eyes moistened seeing real intention in theirs, but again wondered how long the care would last before they forgot about me.

"Then, you just need to work out how you're going to take tests until you're better," Dan continued, working out how I could push forward with my classes despite my immobilization.

"What about food?" asked Bobby.

"Jim said he and some other congregants would take care of that."

"You mean Reverend Jim?" Gina smiled and winked at me.

"Stop," I chuckled. "Anyway, Reverend Jim and I are probably going to finish discipleship soon and then I can receive baptism of the Spirit and start taking the Lord's Supper."

"Of course," Bobby commented, sarcastically, "That's what I would do after getting hit by a Ford F150."

"My point is that I will be done with the core sacraments soon! After those are done, I should be able to start working on the literature review with you all again!"

My feigning enthusiasm was met with gentle compassionate smiles. They loved me now, but I still feared that I would be forgotten in my bed.

"Just worry about getting better and keeping up with your course work. We can get back to the review after rehab," Dan spoke softly.

"Rehabilitation is going to take so much time," I complained.

"It will be okay, Virginia. This too shall pass," Dan again responded delicately, his controlled volume and tone helped me dial back my anxiety.

"Thank you all. I really appreciate your help," I said earnestly.

Chapter 22: Accepting Help

One of my fears, being bedridden, was relieved when follow-up X-rays showed very positive early signs of healing. With that, my doctors were ready for me to start rehabilitation. The news brought me to grateful tears, and Reverend Jim and I spent an hour in prayer and worship.

Just when I thought the day couldn't get any better, Reverend Jim told me that with all that we'd been through together, he considered me more than just part of his flock. He actually said, "You're a friend. Call me Jim if you like." My mouth watered as my appetite for Jim grew. Embarrassingly, I actually choked on my saliva and was unsuccessful in stifling my cough. I felt the heat of my face and knew it had turned as red as my hair.

"Are you okay?" He looked genuinely concerned which made the embarrassment fade.

While Jim was helping with spiritual support and my emotional recovery, a team of physical therapists were helping me to regain strength and mobility. My therapy involved improving range of motion, coordination exercises, and strength training for my abdomen, legs, and lower back to support my pelvis. However, I was almost immobile for two months. So, I relied on Dan, Gina, Bobby, Jim, and the other congregants to help me with everything.

Dan, Gina, and Bobby often came to visit me during the day, collecting my homework in the morning to disperse to my professors, and returning with new notes and homework early in the day so I wouldn't be swamped with work in the evenings. Dan also brought me fresh wild flowers each week. I started reconsidering how I felt about him, after seeing his steadfast love for me. He still wasn't much of a conversationalist, but the extroverted part of my personality was satisfied by Gina and Bobby's vibrant and animated exchanges at my bedside.

Alice and Nancy came in the morning and helped me with using the bathroom and washing. I found it difficult to tell them that this was actually the nurses' job. Glad to spend a little time with them, I decided not to risk losing it.

Jim and I ate dinner together most nights. Our routine included watching the news which reminded me of evenings with Milli before I left for college. We'd also talk about what was happening with the GOLDS and on campus.

One night about three weeks after unsuccessful police searches, Jim said, "If Ken's parents are telling the truth, he hasn't come home once. I understand a knee jerk reaction, but my sympathy is running out. He's had enough time now to see the error of his ways. We need to pray that he's not quenching the Spirit."

Quenching the Spirit is a serious accusation with considerable significance. In chapter five of 1 Thessalonians, there's a verse that says *quench not the Spirit*. In essence, this means rebelling against God when He speaks to you through the Bible or through your conscience. It is like pouring water on a fire. Quenching the Holy Spirit is *the* path away from God, toward evil.

I believe that with the help of God, I was feeling less and less angry at Ken. I was even a little concerned because of how long he'd been missing. Part of me wondered if he killed himself, not wanting to face me and what he had done. My imagination also allowed a scenario where someone killed him and stole his truck before it struck me. Furthermore, I thought that if he was drunk when he hit me, he might have swerved off again further down the road. Perhaps he tore through some woods until he finally wrapped his truck around a tree. If that didn't kill him instantly, then maybe his truck went deep enough to be cloaked from passersby until he eventually succumbed to his injuries.

Jim beamed when I offered, "It's still possible that Ken could repent." I learned in discipleship that "repent" is a military term that means to about-face and march in the other direction. If Ken was marching away from God, he *could* turn around and come back.

Jim agreed, "Yes, let's pray for that." We bowed our heads and Jim prayed for Ken to bravely repent, return, and accept the penalty for his actions. Ken didn't return though, even after several more weeks of prayer.

The medical bills started rolling in after a month. I thought about calling my grandma to see if she could help me financially.

Jim warned, "If you want an early inheritance, call your frail old grandmother and tell her that you've been in a serious hit-and-run. Please don't do that. We can take care of this."

"What do you mean? GOLDS Church?"

"Yes, and the greater college community. As Sir Bevis of Hampton said, *many hands make light work*."

"Oh, I couldn't accept charity."

"We wouldn't give you charity. It would be benevolence, which is totally different. Charity supports the church and other organizations that benefit a community. Benevolence is an altruistic act to help an individual who is in trouble. The funds are specifically earmarked for situations just like yours. You would not be taking charity."

Even though he gave clear definitions of these concepts, I couldn't shake a gut feeling that this was wrong, especially since I had resources to help myself.

"Mm. I still don't like it."

"Virginia. Don't be prideful. You will deprive others of the chance to help you out of love and compassion and, in so doing, take away their opportunities to receive eternal blessings from Jehovah."

I felt an acute sense of being cornered. On one side, my conscience was pressuring me not to take the money. On the other side, Jim was pressuring me to take it.

Then, I imagined Jehovah sharing great treasures in the heavens, positions, estates, and even planets; my GOLDS Church congregation waiting in line for their treasures for serving others; and Jehovah passing by on some of them because my pride wouldn't let them serve me.

"I don't want that," I breathed in deeply, exhaling my reservations. "Okay," I agreed.

"Very good. The first thing I'll work on is seeing if the hospital has any debt relief program for situations like this. They actually might."

"Okay, thank you for being such a blessing, Jim."

"It's my pleasure, and listen, I have heard you are ready."

"Ready for what?"

"To be baptized in the Holy Spirit."

"Really?!"

"Yes."

Chapter 23: Weblog 6 - Final Message

My end is near. I can hear them coming. I've been hiding in Ocracoke, in Rosalind Elsie Franklin Public Library at Nettie Maria Stevens University. It's a place where I have some of my fondest memories, where my only real friends, Gina, Dan, and Bobby (God rest their souls), and I used to study together; where we dreamed about making a positive difference in the World.

It's starting to get very loud here. There are sounds of yelling, boot stomps, and automatic gunfire bursts rising through the stacks. I'm fairly certain they are coming for me.

With my limited time, let me finish by again pleading for your forgiveness. Women, I have taken your husbands, fathers, grandfathers, brothers, uncles, friends, and more. Many of you will never have any of these, and I am very sorry for that. I deserve Hitler's eternal destiny, but I hope for grace. Please don't harbor malice for me. It will do you no good.

Redirect your energy toward preserving the men that are still with us. Find a way to undo what I've done and take measures to prevent anything similar from happening. It is up to you to repopulate men on this planet to restart those precious family dynamics we once had.

Life will never be the same for men again knowing what happened. Their esteem will be shattered and they will question their value. It will be up to you, women, to encourage the men, and make them know that their lives really do matter.

Jesus, I recognize that you are both fully God and fully man. Though you are masculine and had all the physical features and urges of a man, you were celibate on Earth, and still wait for the resurrection of all of your Bride, women and men. You are devoted to loving your Church through deeds and prayer. Your love is overwhelming, even to the greatest of sinners.

Though I deserve death for what I have done to your Church, God, you offer me life and a place in your Kingdom. Praise you, Lord, for your mercy and grace! I say these things in faith, trusting the Words of your Holy Bible including those found in my favorite psalm, Psalm 34.

1 I will bless Jehovah at all times:
His praise shall continually be in my mouth.
2 My soul shall make her boast in Jehovah:

The meek shall hear thereof, and be glad.
3 Oh magnify Jehovah with me,
And let us exalt his name together.
4 I sought Jehovah, and he answered me,
And delivered me from all my fears.
5 They looked unto him, and were radiant;
And their faces shall never be confounded.
6 This poor man cried, and Jehovah heard him,
And saved him out of all his troubles.
7 The angel of Jehovah encampeth round about them that fear him,
And delivereth them.
8 Oh taste and see that Jehovah is good:
Blessed is the man that taketh refuge in him.
9 Oh fear Jehovah, ye his saints;
For there is no want to them that fear him.
10 The young lions do lack, and suffer hunger;
But they that seek Jehovah shall not want any good thing.
11 Come, ye children, hearken unto me:
I will teach you the fear of Jehovah.
12 What man is he that desireth life,
And loveth many days, that he may see good?
13 Keep thy tongue from evil,
And thy lips from speaking guile.
14 Depart from evil, and do good;
Seek peace, and pursue it.
15 The eyes of Jehovah are toward the righteous,
And his ears are open unto their cry.
16 The face of Jehovah is against them that do evil,
To cut off the remembrance of them from the earth.
17 The righteous cried, and Jehovah heard,
And delivered them out of all their troubles.
18 Jehovah is nigh unto them that are of a broken heart,
And saveth such as are of a contrite spirit.
19 Many are the afflictions of the righteous;
But Jehovah delivereth him out of them all.
20 He keepeth all his bones:
Not one of them is broken.
21 Evil shall slay the wicked;
And they that hate the righteous shall be condemned.

22 Jehovah redeemeth the soul of his servants;
And none of them that take refuge in him shall be condemned.

Chapter 24: Baptism of the Holy Spirit

In his Sunday sermon, Jim posed the question, "How much better is it to get wisdom than gold?"

Jim forecasted an expansion of age diversity at GOLDS when he started renting a building for church on Sunday.

"Much!" I yelled with some of the other members this Sunday.

"Yes, we know from Job 12 and Proverbs 16 that there is wisdom to be had from the gray-haired among us. Maybe it goes without saying, but the ideal situation is to have representation of people of all ages, to support each other in every season of life. Let's start with wisdom though. Amen?"

"Amen!" agreed the congregation.

In a couple of months, out of the two dozen new members, only two gray heads were added, which was disappointing for us. Thankfully, Jehovah blessed our church with six new men in their forties. I thought these middle-aged men might actually be better for the current phase of our parish. There was a lack of leadership for the increasing number of congregants.

I was exceedingly glad when four of these men, Aliko, Jeff, Elon, and Bernard zealously rose through the ranks and were appointed priests in time for my Spirit Baptism ceremony. There was now a total of seven active Melkizedek priests in the congregation including Warren, who led GOLDS Church worship, and Wolfgang, who helped Jim found this parish. Ken would have made eight. He probably would have been the officiant of my Spirit Baptism ceremony as he was for the other members, but there was still no sign of him. Instead, Wolfgang and Jim would officiate.

On a perfect Fall evening, Jim spoke from the pulpit about our imperfection and the changes we go through.

"While it would be superhuman to follow Jesus exactly, we seek to improve our likeness over the course of Sanctification. When new believers join on this path, Jehovah instructs His followers to share His Holy Spirit to help counsel, convict, and comfort. The Holy Spirit also prays for us, empowers us with gifts and graces, and unites us. Jehovah has told me that Virginia is ready for the Holy Spirit to help her to follow Jesus. Priest Wolfgang, please initiate the sacrament."

Wolfgang walked from a chair on the opposite side of the stage, down three steps, in front of the central altar, and then back up one step. His forehead was notably large, partly because of his receding hairline, and partly because of his smaller facial features. It seemed like his brain was going to burst forth at any moment. He wasn't unattractive. Getting past the fact that he was middle-aged with a lightbulb head, I think some of the other young ladies found interest in his muscular body.

He looked at me sitting in the pew and said, "Virginia, would you please approach the front of the sanctuary?"

I was sitting in a wheelchair because the doctors didn't want me standing, walking, or doing too much of anything while my pelvis was healing. Despite this, it was a joyous occasion, something like a wedding. My long white robe dragged on the floor as I was pushed by handsome Harris from the back to the front through the central aisle. I wasn't the only one wearing white though. The Levite and Melchizedek robes were white too, perfectly matching my escort's ivory teeth.

Wolfgang read from a leather folder he was holding, looking down and smiling at me from time to time. "Virginia Dare Goreman, please respond, '*I do*' or, '*I do not*' to the following statements. Do you confirm that Jesus is the Son of Jehovah, your Savior and Lord?"

"I do."

"And do you commit yourself to following Jesus' example, picking up your cross each day and following Him unto the death of your flesh and your sinful nature?"

"I do," saying it like a marriage vow.

"Do you believe that Jesus purchased the Church with His own blood as we read in Acts 20?"

"I do."

"And do you believe He added you to His Church as we read in Acts 2?"

"I do." I was getting excited anticipating what having the Holy Spirit inside me would be like.

"And do you commit yourself to active membership in this church, using the fruit of the Holy Spirit that comes with His reception, redeeming the times, advancing the Gospel, and seeking to increase those saved and made holy for His eternal celestial Kingdom?"

"I do."

"Then, as a Priest of the Order of Levite, I find that Virginia Dare Goreman is a well-prepared living temple for residence of the Holy Spirit. At this time, I invite the other priests here today to lay your hands on Virginia's head and shoulders in the presence of the congregation."

Wolfgang stepped down from the first step and stood beside me. Two other priests lined up next to him and three other priests stood on the other side of me. Then, three hands, one from each priest, were laid on each of my shoulders.

Jim walked over from the pulpit and down two steps with a jar of oil. "Virginia, please close your eyes." I did. He spoke louder, "Everyone, bow your heads in reverence to God. Jehovah, we thank you for Pentecost and for the outpouring of the Holy Spirit on a large crowd of people like seeds being scattered on the soil. We thank you that your Holy Spirit has since been passed and propagated by the laying on of hands as seen in Acts 8. Virginia has been baptized in the Name of Jesus, she has been discipled, and now we pray that she receives You so that she has the ability to follow Jesus. Holy Spirit, please come."

Jim dripped a little oil onto his thumb and crossed my forehead. "Be sealed with the gift of the Holy Spirit." The oil and light touch on my forehead stimulated my nerve endings, leaving a lingering tingle and warmth.

"You now better resemble our Lord and Savior, Jesus. Born again by the Spirit you are a child of God. Call out to Him."

Grinning from ear to ear, I cried, "Abba, Father!" I was coached to do this, but was nonetheless sincere.

Then, Pastor Jim smacked my face. It wasn't very hard but a little startling. "You too are now a soldier for Jesus, endowed with supernatural strength to bear witness to the Christian faith. I send you out into the World now to fight for the faith. Peace be with you."

"And with you," I replied, again having been coached, and yet still earnest.

A benediction was given at the end of the service and we ate a celebratory meal. Most of the priests were dispersed at different tables. At the central table, I was honored to sit with Jim, Wolfgang, and Cynthia and Roger (the only gray-haired congregants at the time). Mostly we just exchanged pleasantries, but I saw Wolfgang lean over to Jim and ask, "Is everything ready then?"

Jim responded, "Yes. Start the campaign."

Chapter 25: N.O.W 4 - 2023 Pandemic Death Toll Exceeds Spanish Flu Pandemic

News Of World report Monday, April 24, 2023. Body count numbers have started being published online and the death toll at over 100 million people is already higher than the 1918-1919 Spanish Flu pandemic. All computational models indicate fatalities will surpass those from all previous pandemics. The speed at which this occurs depends on what counter measures are taken in the meantime. Disease centers around the world have recommended that men wear distributed gas masks and move to vegetation-free areas until long term strategies can be devised and executed.

Chapter 26: Restored Comradery

The following day, the school and local news reported a missing person, one Kenneth Boris Musil. Now missing for over a month, he is wanted for questioning after the hit-and-run that resulted in multiple serious injuries to Virginia Dare Goreman, another student at Nettie Maria Stevens University.

That week, several GOLDS Church members went around campus with Nettie Plot newspapers in hand. Bobby told me they were saying, "We are part of the local GOLDS Church. We are out supporting our sister, Virginia Dare Goreman, who was a victim of a hit-and-run last month. She was very badly injured, with a shattered pelvis, kidney lacerations, and some brain damage. The person suspected of hitting Virginia has not been located, which means he cannot be made to pay for her medical and physical therapy bills. Living on campus, she doesn't have a car, and so she doesn't have insurance to cover the bills. Our church is looking for fellow students from campus to help advocate for Virginia, and spread this message. For students who don't have time but are still interested in helping Virginia, we are taking donations to lighten the burden of her medical bills."

"Well, I guess a concussion is brain damage, but *shattered* is a little bit of an embellishment. I'll need to talk to Reverend Jim about that. Thank you for letting me know."

I started meeting again with Gina, Dan, and Bobby to work on our literature review now that GOLDS Church discipleship was finished and the sacrament of Baptism by the Holy Spirit was performed. It felt good to reconnect with my friends.

They told me this funny story about some jock gorilla trying to intimidate Dan to kick him off a pinball machine at the Palace. Bobby swooped in and said, "You know I'm sure Dan would be happy to take turns with you. Perhaps you could have a little competition for the cost of games?" The jock said he would destroy Dan in pinball and they should triple the bet. Bobby pulled Dan aside and whispered in his ear. Then Bobby asked, "You're proposing three games worth of quarters for each win?" The jock put his quarters on top of the Terraform Tracy arcade cabinet next to the pinball machine. Bobby signaled to Dan, and Dan put his quarters up next to the jock's quarters. Bobby said, "Why don't you go first?" Every round the jock played, Dan would play until his score was just a little higher than the jocks. The meat head finally figured out what was going on after five rounds of this and stormed off.

That really brightened my mood. Gina smiled at Dan and said, "That was so clever! Brain over brawn."

Then well-meaning Dan killed the mood with the question, "Do you have a lot of medical bills, Virginia?"

"Yeah."

Gina said, "I know what that's like. Sorry, you're dealing with that."

"I think it will be fine. My brothers and sisters at GOLDS are trying to help. Many hands make for light work, right?"

"Yeah, sometimes. No matter what happens. I'm here for you, Virginia. High five?"

I tried to give Gina a high five lying down and missed. We laughed.

"Me, too," agreed Dan, stooping to give me a high five.

Bobby gave me an air five and joked, "Me, too. Just don't ask too much."

"Thanks, guys. So, where are we in the review?" I asked.

"Review. Review. Review," complained Bobby. "You just want me for my smarts."

"Well, you're not exactly a generous lover," I quipped.

My friends laughed.

"Maybe not, but I make up for it in loyalty and entertainment."

"Yes, you do," I agreed, ignoring the slight, knowing that he was alluding to the fact that I prioritized discipleship over the literature review after returning from summer break. "Did you catch up to where I was at the beginning of Fall Semester?"

"Yes, we each finished a subsection," answered Gina, probably also trying to avoid rehashing that situation.

"Nice work. We are getting close. Just two subsections left for each person, right?"

"Well, those plus the future directions, introduction, abstract, and key words," corrected Bobby.

"Right, and we will also need to get some help from professors in the department to get some figures and do preliminary edits for us to revise before submitting to a journal. Do you think we could get it done before the end of the semester?"

"That's very ambitious, Virginia. Even if we could do our parts, you are recovering from serious injuries, you've got physical therapy, and all your daily activities will take longer."

"Yeah, but you guys and GOLDS members are helping me a ton. I don't have to make my own meals. You attend class and take notes. I just need to read them. Jim said he's going to start hosting Bible study at my dorm so I don't have to travel. You're right though, finishing might be a bit too much of a reach. How about we aim to just get the draft done without figures? Then, when we come back from break, we can set up meetings with the professors."

"That seems much more doable," Bobby concurred.

"Let's do it!" exclaimed Gina. My dearest friend was clearly excited to get back in the saddle with me, and I could see in Bobby and Dan's eyes that we had restored our comradery and united purpose. We rain checked the high fives, which would have proved challenging in my condition, for a sunnier day.

Chapter 27: The Campaign

"Hi, sorry to bother you during your dinner. We are part of GOLDS Church, just down the road here."

"Oh, really?"

"Yes, we meet at the First Baptist Church building on Almeida Ave."

"How can I help you?"

"Our sister, Virginia Dare Goreman, was a victim of a hit-and-run last month. She was very badly injured."

"Oh, I'm very sorry to hear that."

"Yes, her pelvis was shattered, kidney lacerated, and she had some brain damage."

"Oh, my."

"The person suspected of hitting Virginia has not been located yet, which means he cannot be made to pay for her medical and physical therapy bills."

"Oh."

"Since she lives on campus, she doesn't have a car. So, she doesn't have insurance with uninsured motorist coverage to pay for her medical bills. Virginia is in major debt now because of this situation."

"Wow."

"Our church and many students in the campus community are standing with Virginia and trying to help get the word out. We are seeking donations from generous Kali neighbors to lighten the burden of her medical bills. Would you be willing to make a donation to help Virginia?" asked the church volunteer.

"Yeah, I can help. Hold on a second."

"My mom gave her a twenty!" Bobby concluded, finishing his account of the solicitation he witnessed.

"Okay," I murmured. "Well, thank Mrs. Steine for me."

"Will do," Bobby consented, aware of my unease about the situation.

"Thank you again for dropping off the class notes for me."

Bobby gave me a thumbs up before leaving my apartment.

I didn't see any money for a few weeks until Jim held an outreach event in the brickyard beside the library. The church members put out several tables. They were arranged purposely into two long lines with a space of about fifty feet between, enough space to fit a semi-truck trailer. Numerous plates of baked goods were displayed on the tables, which drew a large crowd. Signs on the tables recommended donations of $1 for each item (free raffle ticket included).

Jim wheeled me out to make a grand spectacle of my plight. The message was very similar to what the street advocates were saying. Then, he reported success with fundraising so far and pulled another strategic lever I'd seen him use before.

Speaking with a microphone, he broadcasted, "Thanks to the help of the student community here at Nettie Maria Stevens University, we were able to get the word out to the neighborhoods in Kali, other towns surrounding us, and even beyond. GOLDS Church and the supportive community members have been able to raise three thousand dollars to pay off a large portion of Virginia's medical bills!"

The crowds clapped with the cheering church members standing on both sides of Jim and me. The amount raised covered more than half of all the surgical, hospital, and physical therapy expenses.

"Yes, what you've done is incredible. Now, we ask you to help us again! It's November and Fall Break will be here in no time! You will be returning to your homes, in some cases far from here to celebrate Thanksgiving! Thanksgiving is a holiday that emphasizes both gratefulness and giving! Some of you men may be taking part in turkey trots and many of you women will be preparing food for the big feast!"

The church members cheered, "Wahoo!!"

Jim continued, "When you sit down for that feast or at other times during the break, would you please think of and say a prayer for Virginia?"

He paused for effect.

"And if you are so inclined, we could really use your help in closing the gap on the remaining costs of Virginia's medical bills. Please talk to family members and friends and see if they would like to contribute a small donation for Virginia. In this season of gratefulness and generosity, I think you will find that many people will say yes if you ask. Every size donation helps, and it's a blessing to Virginia, you, and the giver. Any donations you receive can be deposited with me whenever you see me on campus. I'm typically here in the brickyard or at the Student Center. You can also come by First Baptist Church on Sunday. It's one block south of Hodgkin Street on Almeida Ave. It doesn't matter if you're a follower, believer, belong to another faith group, or have no faith. The sermons are for everyone."

Jim tapped into a third motivator just in case pulling on heartstrings and making people feel guilty wasn't enough.

"In exchange for your help, we will be doing a raffle. Prizes include multiple chances to win free large Ninja Stix with extra Gore Sauce, a luxury package for The Palatial Palace for you and three friends, and free admittance to Paradise 54 for you and three friends. We have over two hundred dollars in prizes!"

The church cheered again.

"Each five-dollar increment gets you one ticket, and as a thank you for listening, you get a free raffle ticket today plus additional raffle tickets for buying baked goods. Come and get your free ticket from any of the congregants beside us. Please be generous! Jehovah's blessings to you all and your loved ones!"

And with that, the congregants walked out toward the crowd that accumulated between the tables and around the outside of the tables. Some that were manning the baked goods walked from the outside of the tables toward the open side of the square, flanking the students before they could leave. The congregants surrounded the students and talked to everyone they could. They answered questions, gave out free tickets, reminded people about the date and time of the raffle, and made sure the location of the church was clear. They typically ended their conversations asking the students directly, "Can you please ask your friends and family if they can help Virginia?"

These words were hard to hear, but I just reminded myself that it was my prideful sinful nature that had an issue with receiving financial gifts. Instead of my conscience, I was listening to Jim; his logic was stuck in my mind.

I talked to Jim after the event in my apartment.

"I really appreciate what you're doing for me, Jim, but how much more money do we need to raise?"

"The plan is to cancel your debt. The whole thing."

"Couldn't we just call it? I mean everyone's been so generous."

"Certainly not right now. We already paid for the raffle prizes, and invited a ton of students to participate."

"Okay, well after that?"

"I think after that, you will have everything paid for."

"Really? That's great!"

I was more excited about the money raising campaign being over than my medical bills being paid for.

"Speaking of paid for. How would you like your three grand?"

"I can't believe you were able to raise three grand already?"

"It's actually more like four."

"Oh, wow!"

"Yes, but we need the rest as a seed for the fundraisers. We are multiplying donations with Jehovah's help."

This did not sit right with me. I didn't know what to say though.

I think Jim sensed my unease and changed the subject, "Does a check work for you?"

Chapter 28: Return of the Accused

Professors generally accommodated me during my recovery. Public handicap accessibility was mostly nonexistent on campus. Steps and stairs were significant barriers to attending class. This was an issue because quizzes and exams needed to be proctored. My friends talked to the teachers for me, and typically the solution was teaching assistants or the professors themselves would meet me after my physical therapy sessions. I would take my tests with them supervising in Curie Hall, which was next to the Student Health Center.

One professor was unwilling to make any accommodations though. He gave me an ultimatum, "Either you can come to exams, withdraw, or fail. I cannot accommodate individual student's needs. The class is too large." I wanted to argue that helping a disabled person is hardly a slippery slope, but knew it would be futile.

Jim and his strong right- and left-hand men, Wolfgang and Harris, helped me make it to my tests by picking up my wheelchair at the back and sides and walking me up two flights of stairs. They waited for me to finish my test and brought me back to my dorm. The three of them did this for three quizzes, a midterm, and my final exam in mid-December. While I was grateful to all three men, it was Jim who was organizing everything. Through his own effort and the management of others, Jim probably did more caring things for me than anyone else besides my mother when I lived with her.

The Post-Thanksgiving Raffle was a huge hit, at least in my estimation. Students raised another seven hundred dollars. Jim wasn't satisfied though and used a similar strategy and incentives for the Winter Break. Again, he leveraged sacred and national holidays and occasions for family and friend gatherings to raise more money. These manipulations stirred more students to act. When they returned in the Spring semester, they brought back nearly another grand in donations for the New Year Raffle.

Jim didn't give me the raffle donations publicly, the way he had with the first three grand. I didn't want to question Jim about this because he was always with other people and thought it might sound accusatory. Such an awkward conversation would be better in private. Plus, Jim had done so much, and I didn't want to come across as unappreciative. So, I decided to wait, consoling myself that he would come to me in good time.

Then, Ken returned unexpectedly. It had been nearly four months since anyone had seen him. He turned himself into the police and gave the testimony, "I hit the accelerator when I meant to hit the brake. I was afraid I killed someone and of what would happen to me if I did. So, I just ran."

When asked where he had gone, he said, "Canada. I worked at a garage to pay the bills, but my conscience was bothering me. I also wanted to see my folks and didn't want to stay hidden forever."

Ken pleaded guilty. He was charged with a misdemeanor, fined five hundred dollars and had to serve one year in jail.

Jim came alone to my dorm and advised me to sue Ken for medical expenses.

I pushed back on this, "Why? Didn't you raise nearly enough for all of my bills?"

"That's not the point, Virginia. You're not actually suing Ken. You're suing Ken's insurance. He's got motor vehicle insurance, and they should pay for your medical bills as a hit-and-run victim. All of the money that was given for your medical bills can be used for other benevolence and charitable uses."

"I thought you said the money wasn't charity."

"It's not currently, but that doesn't mean it can't be transferred to other areas where there's greater need."

"People gave the money with the understanding that it was for my medical bills."

"Yes, they did, and the money kept you from incurring unnecessary creditor charges. They enabled you to focus on your studies and recover. We had no idea that Ken would ever return, but now that he has, it would be an irresponsible stewardship of the benevolence funds if they weren't reallocated to other needs. In order to do that, you need to take what's rightfully yours from the insurance company."

Again, Jim made a solid argument. He always seemed to know just what to say and the right way to say it. This, coupled with all of the interpersonal care equity, made arguing with Jim impossible. I did what Jim told me to do, and gave him the insurance claim money.

Since that time, Jim's church attendance doubled from about ninety to nearly one hundred eighty congregants. GOLDS Church now had its gray hairs, middle-agers, families, young professionals, and college students. Racial diversity was still evident but less emphasized. Ministries and missions were the big topics now.

Many new members had their first experience with GOLDS Church when students came to their door raising money for my tragedy. It was great advertising for the

Church. It would have been a hard sell to get students to simply advertise GOLDS Church, but my situation gave the perfect excuse for getting in front of locals. Telling them about their affiliation with the new GOLDS Church was passive, and yet the message was potent: This new GOLDS Church was community oriented, cared for its members, and was neat enough for college students to attend. Additionally, many of the students that participated in raising money also joined.

The doctor said I could start moving around campus with crutches in the second week of February. I hobbled and limped my way to church that Sunday and Jim started clapping as soon as I walked through the door. I was just on time so almost all of the congregants had already found their seats. Everyone looked back at me. It was very embarrassing.

Jim said, "Our prayers have been answered. Our sister, Virginia, is on the road to full recovery and is now able to worship with us on the Lord's Day without wheelchair assistance. Praise, Jehovah!"

I walked around to the side aisle instead of going through the middle to my regular seat attempting to hide from all the eyes.

Jim continued with the announcement which caused more to gape. "In case you have not heard yet, Ken Musil has returned to us but is currently serving a one-year sentence. Ken was responsible for severely injuring Virginia. After a hit-and-run, Ken fled to Canada. Though he was gone for several months, he did return, confessed his sins, and is paying for his crimes in jail. Part of Ken's penalty is a five-hundred-dollar fine. While it is my decision alone according to the bylaws of GOLDS Church, I would like your agreement. I want to make a case to you for why I believe we should use benevolence funding to pay for Ken's fine."

The congregation was silent. He had everyone's attention, including mine.

"Ken's actions came from fear. The Devil loves using this tool to drive God's Obedient Saints away from Him. When Ken hit Virginia, the Devil didn't just whisper. He yelled - *Run! Get out of there before anyone sees you! Hide from the consequences! Because they will be severe!* Haven't you heard that voice in your life? Those very words?"

Two or three congregants admitted, though not very loudly, "Amen."

"Oh, okay. Sorry, I didn't realize Jehovah begot more than one Jesus as well as some Jeesicas. Please forgive me," Jim said smiling, "Seriously though. Even if you think you would have made the right decision, stayed, and faced the consequences right then, will you at least admit that there would have been some temptation to leave? Can I get an amen?"

"Amen!" shouted the congregation.

"Okay, thank you. Now, we've established Ken was tempted and he did act on that temptation. He was gone for a long time...like a prodigal son...he worked and lived in Canada, but eventually realized that returning to his family, friends, church, and ultimately Jehovah was better than staying hidden away. Let's not be like the self-righteous older brother, heralding how good we are. No, let us be gracious like his loving father and welcome him back with open arms. Yes?"

"Yes!" bellowed the congregation.

"And you know what the father did. He didn't celebrate with a small young goat. No, he killed the fattened calf for his prodigal son. Let's show our brother Ken the love and grace of our Heavenly Father, and take care of this financial burden for him. Amen?"

"Amen!"

"I am so encouraged by you, GOLDS. Your generosity warms my heart.

Please note that we are not collecting an additional benevolence offering today. Funds are available. So, donations are for the continually important church tithes."

Jim hurriedly communicated that last part like the unintelligible fine print in infomercials.

Chapter 29: N.O.W. 5 - Men Flee to Low Pollen Locations

News Of World report Friday, April 28, 2023. Men are fleeing to low pollen locations in the Arctic and Antarctica. The exodus was initiated after a weblog from Goreman revealed that the Sweetvirus spreads through pollen. Aid workers are ferrying and airdropping cold hardy supplies to rescue new settlements.

Chapter 30: Return of Mobility

Jim and the other congregants stopped coming to my dorm. I agreed with them that I had recovered enough to not need care anymore. Life became very challenging though in my pseudo-mobile state. Getting around campus with my books and crutches was slow and cumbersome. My mind often drifted to brainstorming efficient daily routines. Instead of returning to my dorm two to three times a day, I would leave in the morning and not return until the evening. Lobbies, study halls, food halls, and the library became benches along my daily path.

One huge benefit to being mobile again was that I could pitch the literature review to professors in person. While having the review done by the end of the year was overzealous, my Ocracoke gang and I had a nice draft completed by the end of January.

The four eminent professors we were targeting were Kacy Burch, Jill Burmeister, Albert Corbin, and William Maddox. We hoped they would contribute to our review and hire us or at least allow us to work in their laboratories. Volunteer work was quite common for undergraduate researchers.

Dr. Burch's and Dr. Burmeister's research were both very interesting to me. They were looking for different types of stem cells and trying to discover what they became. The one exception was blood-forming hematopoietic stem cells, which were already being studied by other groups extensively. While their aims were similar, they used different approaches. Dr. Burch used labeling techniques to trace the cell changes in the tissues, while Dr. Burmeister separated cells from embryonic tissue using microsurgical techniques.

Their research interested me because I could imagine using their techniques and the stem cells from a fetus expulsion to potentially identify the cells responsible for the miscarriages. Finding the problematic cells was just the first step. I would need to learn how to genetically analyze them to determine the genetic basis for miscarriages. Early detection would be possible if we knew the genetic basis. The ultimate end goal would be targeted therapeutics to fix the genetic errors before they proliferated and caused a miscarriage.

The fact that these professors doing the research on stem cell development were women also interested me. Perhaps working in their laboratory would help me learn how they made it in a male-dominated profession. I also wondered if they would be willing to help me transition to a professorship after graduate school. Sometimes it's not what you know, but who you know.

Dr. Corbin's laboratory was huge. He was receiving both government and private funding to determine the structures of cell cycle regulatory proteins like cyclins and Cyclin-Dependent Kinases (CDKs). His students primarily used X-ray crystallography and NMR spectroscopy to do this. Computers weren't available. So, physical three-dimensional models were constructed. Knowing the shapes of proteins, the crevices, cavities, the sites of chemical interactions, all would enable the design of other chemicals (drugs) that would interact with proteins. These mathematical models were the beginnings of small molecule pharmaceutical companies.

Researchers in Dr. Maddox's laboratory were developing methods for tissue explant culture. That is, controlled culturing of tissues outside of a human body. Dr. Maddox was primarily interested in understanding the fundamentals of tissues developed, but was also looking to retire with lucrative patents related to tissue culture for transplantation and xenotransplantation (tissue and organs from other species being used for humans).

Both female researchers were willing to contribute figures to our review, help us with editing, and add their names as contributing authors to enhance the reputability of our work. The male researchers praised us for our ambitions, but were unwilling to contribute.

The rest of the semester was like Dante's Inferno, a journey through Hell. Dr. Burch and Dr. Burmeister provided figures and thorough feedback. We made edits and they helped us submit our manuscript to the premier journal, *Journal of Human Developmental Biology*. That journal outright rejected us. So, we resubmitted to *JED Bio*, aka the *Journal of Early Developmental Biology*. No shame in publishing with them. It wasn't the best, but was still a very high-impact journal. This time the editor of the journal sent back reviewers' comments and gave us the opportunity for resubmission after making corrections and expansions in a couple of areas. We did, and after a month of waiting, we received the sweet news that our manuscript was accepted, contingent upon making some minor corrections, and would be published in the following month's edition.

"I know that I said we could celebrate after we published…" I started.

"Virginia!" Bobby yelled, giving me a scowl.

I smiled and continued, "But… but, they have our processing fees, the manuscript has been accepted, the professors say it's as good as published… Let's go to the Palace!"

"Let's go!" yelled Gina.

We ended up going three days in a row. One was just not enough. We were also celebrating the fact that I didn't need to use crutches any more. My recovery was complete. We probably burned through fifty dollars in quarters between the three of us. I felt convicted to ask God to forgive us for the gluttony.

It's funny, when I first talked about how we would celebrate publishing, I told Dan that we could praise Jesus. I said that because it was something that was important to him. Never did I think that it was going to become something that was important to me. In the late nights and the early mornings of those days of celebration, my face was planted to the floor worshiping Him and the steadiness of His hand that guided us to the finish line.

The publication opened doors just like I said it would.

Gina got a position in Dr. Burch's laboratory doing cell lineage tracing experiments. She would use isotopically labeled cells to discover the journeys and fates of cells and how they contribute to the formation of tissues and organs. Bobby also started working in Dr. Burch's laboratory, wanting to work by Gina's side.

I got a position in Dr. Burmeister's laboratory separating cells by microdissection for graduate students. This was a great experience for my scientific goals, but it wasn't enough for me. Dr. Corbin also let me simultaneously work in his laboratory. While he didn't care to put in the effort of helping us with publishing the literature review, he was happy to get additional free labor for his laboratory. My main job was making buffers, mixtures of water, salts, and organic chemicals. Imagine something like an electrolyte drink. The chemicals in them are often used to stabilize or destabilize proteins. Dr. Corbin's students needed the buffers for protein purification. Dan followed me, also working in Dr. Corbin's laboratory making buffers.

Dan and I spent hours and days making buffers together. It was very monotonous work.

"Was this the kind of experience you envisioned would give us a leg up in the job market?" Dan asked sarcastically.

I smiled, "Very funny, Dan. No, but we all have to pay our dues, right? What we need is to ask for experience. *Ask and you shall receive*, right?"

"True."

Dan asked before I had a chance and was allocated time to purify protein with some graduate students. When I asked Dr. Corbin, he said I could pack columns. With that, I realized this work wasn't for me and thanked Dr. Corbin for the opportunity, but said no thank you.

Dan came to my dorm and we talked later that evening.

"Do you like the research in Dr. Corbin's laboratory?" I asked Dan.

"I don't know."

Knowing Dan, I could tell he did have some interest, but wanted to be where I was because he thought there was a chance for more than a friendship.

"You just got the chance to get some purification experience. You should at least give it a try."

"You think so?"

"Yeah. I think having that experience will open doors for you in the near future. The pharmaceutical industry seems very promising."

"I'm just not sure I want to be involved in designing drugs."

"Why? Might be a way to help treat disease, maybe even cure diseases. It's not miraculous, but perhaps this is a way to *do even greater things* than individual healings." I was referring to a promise Jesus made in John 14.

"Wow! I never thought about it that way, Virginia." I saw his face light up and fade back.

"What's wrong?"

"It's just that I was hoping we could work in a laboratory together."

"Dan, I have a very specific question I'm trying to answer and a very specific research goal. You should not follow me. You need to find your own passion."

His eyes told me he had. I couldn't bring myself to crush my friend's hopes. I stood up from my seat and made my excuses, "I feel gross. Need to take a shower. See you at Ocracoke tomorrow?" We were getting ready for exams before summer break.

"Yeah. See you there."

We both half-smiled as he walked out the door.

A few days later, I interviewed with one of Dr. Maddox's postdoctoral students. You didn't talk to Dr. Maddox directly unless you were a postdoc. We learned this when we spoke with him about the literature review. Postdocs received direction from Dr. Maddox and they hired everyone in the laboratory. They managed and trained graduate students, and graduate students managed and trained undergraduate students. As an aspiring leader, I could appreciate the chain of command and delineation of duties. This method of management gave him the quiet and time he needed to write grants, and to help his postdocs become research professors, teaching them how to manage people and write grants.

Dr. Maddox's students were extremely diverse. An Indian postdoc named Onkar interviewed me. He put me under a Chinese graduate student named Jian-Ke.

Jian-Ke was doing xenotransplantation, swapping tissues between mice and pigs. He was trying to see if he could suppress immune response with corticosteroids and other drugs. He was looking at histological markers of rejection, evaluating cellular changes, inflammation, and cytokine analysis by radioimmunoassays.

Jian-Ke had me start with making tissue growth media for him. This was slightly more interesting than buffers, but I wanted more. I talked to different researchers in the laboratory and found out that Diego was developing methods for infecting cells and tissues with viruses for the purpose of introducing DNA. I thought such a tool could help me tremendously with my aspirations. I could use it to determine which DNA sequences were harmful, causing miscarriages, testing the introduction of putatively harmful DNA into healthy control cells. I thought I might even be able to use the tool to add some therapeutic DNA that prevents miscarriages.

"You don't want to talk to Diego though. He's a thorny guy," one researcher told me.

That didn't stop me. A chance to learn skills in virus production, cell and tissue infection, and nucleic acid delivery was too desirable to ignore.

"Hi, I'm Virginia."

"Hello, new girl."

'Girl'. I really wanted to correct him, but didn't because I wanted him to lead and teach me even more. So, I bit my tongue.

"You're Diego, right?"

"Who told you that?"

"Uh, a few people around the laboratory…"

"What do you want? I'm busy."

I was under no delusion that I caught Diego at a bad time. He reminded me of a poison tree frog, dressed in bright aposematic colors warning of the paralyzing, even

163

deadly, venom inside. Typically alone, he deters intruders in his territory with aggressive croaks.

"Well, I was hoping I could help make you less busy."

"Yeah? How's that?"

"I could be your undergraduate student."

"Ha! No, an undergraduate student is the last thing I need. I'm trying to get out of here, not add an extra year of mentoring some boba."

"I'll work very hard for you."

"Um. No."

"What if…"

"La hostia! Didn't you just get hired? You want me to tell your supervisor that you are trying to sell yourself?"

"I would work for them and…"

"Marcharse! Leave!" He exclaimed, stopping what he was doing and shooing me away with his arms.

Diego was making a scene. So, I left.

The thing about poison tree frogs is that other than the venom, they can't really hurt you. Handled properly, indigenous peoples of Central and South America found them very useful. I just needed to learn how to handle Diego properly to use him.

I wanted to transfer over to Diego's project, but it didn't seem likely he would just let me join him. Asking Onkar to assign me to Diego also seemed like a bad idea. It seemed more likely to me that the postdocs asked the graduate students if they wanted undergraduates. I decided to pray for help, and I believe Jehovah answered.

Diego was in the brickyard looking at the flier wall. Events on campus, items for sale, local business promotions and more were posted on the flier wall. This time of year, students posted requests for transportation. Some were selling rides, while others were posting requests. Diego posted a request. I read it after he left. He was looking to get as close to the U.S.-Mexico border as he could. A divine idea came to mind.

Later that evening at Ocracoke, I asked Gina, "Are you going back to Arkansas for break?"

"Yeah. Why?"

"I have a request, but before I ask, how are you planning to get there?"

"Rideshare; paying someone to drive me."

"So, you already have a ride? How many people are in the car?"

"Yeah, it's just me and one other girl."

"Ugh. I almost don't want to ask."

"What?"

"There's this guy who is doing the most fascinating work with viruses in Dr. Maddox laboratory. I really want to work with him, but he won't mentor me."

"I'm not following. What does that have to do with Arkansas and ride share?

"I saw him put a request on the flier wall for a ride as close to the border as he could get."

"Ah, so you are trying to help him find a ride in hopes he will mentor you?"

"Well, yes and pay his way."

"Wow! You really want this."

"Yes, I do."

"Okay. I'll ask the other girl if she's willing to take another passenger for more money."

"Well, wait. There's something you need to know."

"What?"

"Is he a psycho?" asked Bobby.

"No, but he's a jerk. At least he was to me."

"And you want to work with him?" asked Gina.

"More like I want to know what he knows. Extrasensory perception is preferred, but mastery of the technique remains out of reach."

"Haha. Well, I'll still do it for you."

"Wait a minute," demanded Bobby. "Is he dangerous?"

"No. I mean he's a doctoral candidate. He's just not nice."

"Okay," replied Bobby. Gina smiled, "You're worried about me. So cute. Come by my dorm later."

"Yes, ma'am."

"Gag," I joked. I actually thought it was cute the way Bobby wanted Gina so badly. As far as I knew though, they had never gone all the way. I was pretty sure she would have told me.

"Anyway, thank you, Gina. I really appreciate it."

"Anytime, Virginia."

"Please let me know as soon as you can so I can pitch the deal."

"Will do."

Gina's driver said she would do it for the same cost Gina paid. I gave her a big hug and hustled to the Maddox Laboratory.

"New girl again."

"What do you want?"

"It's actually about what you want."

"What I want?"

"Yes, I saw that you were looking for a ride share down to the border."

"Uhh, yeah. Are you spying on me now? Maybe I should call you creepy girl."

"Do you want a ride or not?"

"Where?"

"Central Arkansas."

"How much are you charging?"

"Just the opportunity to be your servant."

"You want to be my chupamedias?"

"I really really want to learn what you know about working with viruses."

"Hm. So, I don't have to pay for the ride?"

"No. I will pay for it."

"Wait, whose driving?"

"It's a rideshare with two girls. One is a friend of mine."

"Hm." Diego thought about this for a moment. "Okay, if you get me a free ride, you can be my chupamedias."

"Thank you!" I jumped at him with the impulse to embrace him.

"Wow! Chupamedias. Relax." He held his hands up rejecting my advance.

"When do we get started?" I asked.

"When I get back. I have to go to the embassy in my country to renew my visa."

"Oh."

"Yeah. Es mierda."

"How long will you be gone?"

"What, you can't wait?"

"No, I just want…"

"Probably a month, give or take a week. Are we done?"

"Yes, thank you again."

"You're welcome, chupamedias. Get me the information about that ride."

"Okay, I will." I said excitedly and left.

I praised Jehovah for helping me get Diego the ride, and shared the amazing story with Jim after our Wednesday night Bible study. Not a lot of people came because they were either studying for finals or had already left for Summer Break. I hadn't told Jim the news about publishing in JED Bio with Dr. Burch and Dr. Burmeister and my friends, so I started with that.

"Virginia. That is outstanding! All this was going on while you were recovering from the hit-and-run?"

"We started the literature review back in the first semester of freshman year."

"And here you are about to transition into Junior year with this notch on your belt," he beamed.

I smiled back appreciating the admiration.

"What are your plans for this summer?"

"Well, I'm hoping to do research with Diego in the second half of the summer when he gets back. I'll probably just be doing microdissections in Dr. Burmeister's laboratory and making tissue culture media for Jian-Ke until then. Other more boring stuff," I simplified.

"It's the summertime. What about for fun?"

"I don't know. I've been starting to do some jogging and aerobics."

"Oh, a regular Kathy Switzer?"

"I wouldn't go that far."

"What about dancing? Do you like disco?"

"I'm not sure. I haven't really tried it."

"Well, I go every Friday night with some of the congregants. You should come sometime."

"Okay, that sounds fun. Thanks for the invite. What time do you all go?"

"We usually go around 10pm and leave by 2am."

"Wow, Reverend! Far out. I think Harris told me you go to Paradise 54?"

"He did, did he? Yes, that's right. What else did he say?"

"Just that you do ministry there and are a good dancer."

"Well, I wouldn't say good."

"I'm sure you're being modest. This Friday after my final exam, I'm going to zonk out, but probably next Friday. Where should I meet you?"

"We meet out in front of the church."

"Sounds neat," I said, trying not to sound too excited.

"Great! I'll see you there." Then, he added, remembering, "And I'll see you this Sunday in church. Right?"

I giggled at his clumsy speech. "Yes, I'll be there."

"Great. Then, until we see each other again, peace be with you."

Again, I giggled at his rare display of dorkiness, "Peace be with you."

I had a giddy feeling walking back to my dorm. 'Was Golden Jim interested in me?'

Chapter 31: Summer Love

Bobby and I bid farewell to Gina and Dan after our last final on Friday. They would be headed back home, Gina ride sharing with Diego. Like me, Bobby would continue working in the laboratory over the summer since he lived nearby. He also got a job working at Kung Food Pizza since he was only working in the one laboratory and not getting paid. Of my friends, I always felt like I was the least close with Bobby, but we definitely warmed up after hanging out and eating Ninja Stix together over the summer. Bobby was a really funny guy.

The person I hung out with the most that summer though was Jim. Jim and I would see each other on Wednesday and Friday nights and Sunday mornings at minimum. Sometimes there were member lunches. The big change though was nights that had all of the features of a date minus the name.

This started with the first disco night. Meeting up with Jim and five other congregants, I realized that I was totally underdressed with my plaid skirt and short-sleeved shirt. It would have been too much to ask them to wait for me, but going alone would have been awkward, and the same was true for leaving the group upon arrival. They welcomed me with hoots, hollers, and hugs. It was time to go to the disco.

We walked a few blocks down Hodgkin Street, sometimes acting cool, sometimes silly. There was a line outside of Paradise 54. Anticipation was high as we waited to get in and the disco did not disappoint. It was dazzling, absolutely mesmerizing.

The first thing that hit me was the lights, the gleam of the disco ball and beams all around ricocheting off of mirrored walls and ceilings. The mirrors also made the interior seem enormous. Then, the pulsating beats rocked me. I could only hear the music while we were waiting in line, but once we were inside the club, I could feel the thumping of the bass in my core. Songs from ABBA, the Bee Gees, Gloria Gaynor, and others would become familiar favorites later in the summer, stirring thrill and excitement when they came on, but this first time was overwhelming and a little intimidating.

Most of the group cut straight for the dance floor when we arrived. Jim somehow knew that I would feel apprehensive. He took me over to the bar and bought me a virgin Daiquiri. I told him that I was only twenty, as I was unaware that it didn't contain any alcohol. It was more of a yell because of how loud it was in the club. That was the only way to talk unless you got close.

Jim leaned in, and showed me that talking in each other's ears could be done at a reduced volume. "Are you asking me to buy you a drink?" The way he said it made me think this was a pass, the first one Jim had ever made at me. It didn't bother me though.

I leaned in and said, "Maybe later," smiling as I leaned back.

"Can you see the dance floor okay?"

"Not really!"

"Let's get a better view from up top!"

"Okay!"

Jim took me up to the interior balcony that wrapped around the dance floor. I realized too late that I was showing the whole club my underwear through the grated mesh-like balcony flooring. It was the last time I would go up there. I only needed a few minutes to study what people were wearing and the way they were dancing, so I would be better prepared for next time.

Women were wearing Halston dresses, wrap dresses, and a lot of form-fitting jumpsuits with sequins and glitter. Accessories like thin necklaces and hoop earrings were common.

Men were wearing pointed V-neck collared shirts, unbuttoned to show their chest hair, and bell-bottom pants. Heavy duty chains and rings were common.

Just about everyone wore bold colorful patterns and platform shoes.

Barry Gibb's "Stayin' Alive" came on and the place erupted. Jim asked me if I wanted to dance.

"No, no…!"

"I don't want to leave you here by yourself! Come on!"

Before I could protest, he took my hand and we started down the stairs to the dance floor. Cutting through the crowd we found our GOLDS brothers and sisters.

They were paired off, spinning and turning together with smooth footwork. Four steps back, four steps forward, a four step turn to the right and one to the left, eight counts of finger and toe pointing, and a culmination in an eight-count arm roll, chest pump, left turn sequence. I was able to pick it up by the end of the song. Later, I'd find out that they were doing the Hustle.

More freestyle dances followed and Jim stayed with me the entire time we were at the club. His external features captivated me as they jumped with the music. My heart leapt when he took my hand and guided me in and around his arms with expert skill. Nothing was uttered while we danced. There was just symbiosis of our bodies, the lights, and the rhythm. At the end of the night, I might have physically left, but I remained cerebrally in that experience for days.

Disco nights soon became precious to me, the favorite part of my week. There were so many aspects of this diamond that I loved - the energy, the fun, the escape, the mystery, the novelty, the art... I couldn't get enough in the club, so I played disco music and practiced my moves in the dorm room. I spent some of my trust to buy new dresses and jumpsuits, and exercised and ate to help me fit into them better.

I'm not sure whose idea it was, but half way through the summer we also started having pancake brunches together on Saturdays. We all knew we would be waking up late, so why not have a nice, recuperating meal together? The house we brunched at was north of campus, so Jim asked if I wanted to walk up together.

One of those Saturdays, I think it was the second or third, Jim said something about the diversity of the soft and hardwood trees in the brickyard. I felt the urge to try and impress him. Maybe it was because of the way he showered me with compliments. I pointed to the tree we were passing by and said, "That one's a walnut tree." This was one of a very short list of trees I actually knew. He said, "Yup, it's a black walnut tree. The wood is great for crafting furniture and the hulls of the nuts can be used for ink or dye. The nuts are not as good as the English Walnut tree nuts, unfortunately." Jim was a fact sponge, and I really liked that about him.

I asked, "How do you know so much about walnut trees?"

"Trees in general. It's part of the curriculum for the two-part summer wood-working course I'm auditing."

"Why are you doing that?"

"I wanted to be more like Jesus. Plus, wooden furniture for churches like communion tables are really expensive. Should have a really nice one finished by the end of the course."

"Really?"

"Yeah. I'm trying to make it very ornate."

"You're so hardworking and meticulous. I'm sure it will be beautiful."

"Well, it will look out of place if I don't emulate some of the loveliest of GOLDS," he said while smiling flirtatiously.

I felt the warmth in my cheeks and didn't really know what to say. We had this history of doing so much together, between him helping me while I was recovering from the hit-and-run, discipling me, and now, with all this attention in and out of the club, I just wanted him to make a move. The brickyard was empty. I wished he'd just kiss me, and then he did.

The shock, the conduction, it was electrifying. Lips like lightning bolts, jolting me to life. The wind howled and the trees clapped for us.

"Wow," I said, smiling and looking into his eyes.

He peered back into mine, also smiling.

Then, he took my hand. Hand-holding turned into arm swinging. Arm swinging turned into skipping. Skipping turned into running and laughing. Then we stopped, and while we were catching our breath, Jim said, "Virginia Dare Goreman, I'm going to marry you."

Chapter 32: Sustaining ####

Jim was probably infatuated. In any case, he was speaking out of turn. Yes, we had history, but I had no idea what his intentions were. I mean, he didn't know what I wanted in life, and I didn't know what he wanted in life. The pleasure and excitement that he brought into mine was intoxicating though. It probably dulled my reasoning to the point of missing some red flags, misclassifying them as just yellow ones. I was enjoying my Jim addiction with my deadened senses, dismissed apprehensions, alkalized gut, and quenched spirit.

Just a couple of weeks later, school was back in session. Bobby must have updated Dan on what was going on with Jim because Dan was waiting for me at my dorm on Wednesday night after my Bible study.

"Hi, Virginia."

"Oh! Dan, you scared me. Welcome back to campus! How was your break?"

"It was okay. I earned some spending cash for Rich and Fruity's Mediterranean Medley and HARD Water Berry for studying and pinball at the Palace."

"Sounds good," I said, but in my mind, these things that I once cherished now sounded immature, unsophisticated, childish even. My pallet had developed and now appreciated bolder and richer flavors of life.

"Are you going to be at Ocracoke this Thursday?"

"I mean probably not this Thursday. It's syllabus week."

"What are you doing then?"

"Um, I don't know." I actually did know. I was planning on seeing Jim. Eating dinner together and making out with him in my dorm room.

"Well, do you want to maybe hang out? Not just us two. I mean, Gina, Bobby, you, and I could get together and catch up. Maybe you could think of another project we could all do together."

"Dan, I'm pretty tired. How about we just regroup next Thursday, okay?"

I started walking toward the dorm before he could answer. Then, the conversation took a left turn.

#1 How Women Took Over The World

"I heard you were dating Reverend Jim."

Feeling a little exposed, I became defensive, and said, "Yeah. So what?"

He replied, "I'm just concerned, Virginia, that he's a wolf in sheep's clothing. I mean, what kind of Reverend goes to a disco with his congregants?"

My face crinkled. The descriptions of pastoral qualities, found in the books of Titus and 1 Timothy, include being above reproach and self-controlled. It was difficult to argue that Jim demonstrated these qualities after experiencing the moves he used on me at the disco and in my dorm room.

Dan continued, "Jim is using God's name for selfish pursuits."

"Why do you say that?"

"Jim is disingenuous. He's a power-hungry con artist running a cult, and he wants to get in your jeans."

I chuckled and responded recklessly, "And you don't?"

The toothpaste was out of the tube and it wasn't going back in. I saw my friend's face shatter and knew what I said was a mistake, but I wasn't brave enough to humble myself and apologize. Exhaustion overpowered my shame and I walked past him into my dorm. Stripping and collapsing into my bed, I looked up at the ceiling and wondered what would be so bad about Jim getting in my jeans? 'This is the 1970s and God is full of grace!'

While I completely ignored the first part of Dan's accusation, there was something to what he was saying. His words lingered in the recesses of my mind and came to the forefront when I witnessed Jim doing or saying something unsavory. Remembering that Jim would call bigots "white-washed tombs," and would quote "Today, this scripture is fulfilled in your hearing" after reading Old Testament passages. It made me wonder if Jim was trying to emulate Jesus or if he was trying to take Jesus' place as head of the Church.

Instead of hanging out with my friends that Thursday, Jim and I ate dinner and had a fencing match in my dorm room until we came dangerously close to regret. I successfully parried Jim's épée, but felt sure that persisting in my *en garde* would not be enough to avoid a touch from his tip and him scoring on me.

Friday afternoon, Priest Wolfgang found me at the Maddox Laboratory and handed me a letter. Diego made a derogatory comment about this interruption. I apologized to Priest Wolfgang, showed him out, thanked him for the delivery, and assured him that I would read it during my break.

The letter read that Jim Marshall was being called to serve in the capacity of a Diocese Bishop and was looking for pledges of sustaining support. Pledging sustaining support to Jim was a no brainer. It felt good to commit my efforts to Jim after everything that he had done for me during my recovery. I thought, 'Whatever he needed…' and told him that night that he could count on me to help sustain him in the challenges that lay ahead with this new position.

The ceremony took place in the afternoon on Sunday.

Priest Adam spoke to Jim and announced to the witnesses, "Reverend James Leonard Marshall, Pastor of the GOLDS in the Perish of Kali, by the authority of the Melchizedek Priesthood, I ordain you as Bishop of the Diocese of the whole of New York State. You are holy, set apart, to preside not only over the current parish, but over all other future parishes formed in New York State during your service. We are confident that many more parishes will form under your leadership and in accordance with Jehovah's will to grow His Eternal Kingdom."

Jim's new duties required him to develop and execute a plan in cooperation with the Holy Spirit for forming new congregations and planting churches in other parts of the state. It didn't bother me at the time that Jim was presenting an ambitious five-step, ten-year plan to the congregation the following Sunday. He said it was provided to him by the Holy Spirit.

The first step was raising money for land and a house in the Adirondacks that would serve as a home for Jim, a place for retreats, baptisms, and possibly other sacraments. He was targeting one year to complete step one. The second step was establishing Bible studies at Parvati and Durga, New York. This would take two years. The third step was developing reverends to preach the Word to new congregations. This would take one year. The fourth was raising funds to rent existing church buildings. Jim calculated that the Church could replicate more quickly by reducing overhead costs with property and building ownership. Step four would take one year. The fifth step was replicating. Instead of Jim going to campuses, he would teach his reverends how to build their congregations. Eventually, when there were enough GOLDS Churches in New York and the Spirit was leading, he would be elevated to archbishop and would train up reverends to go to other states. He anticipated that this would take five years.

I suspected that Jim living away from campus would mean he and I wouldn't be seeing each other as much. This was a very discomforting thought. Part of my mind was trying to guard my heart. It assured me that my studies and research would keep me very busy, and challenged me with the argument that I didn't need to be dancing and eating pancakes every weekend anyway.

Another part of me was lamenting how nice it had been to have a life outside of the classroom and the laboratory. My romance with Jim, Friday night dancing, Bible study, church events and services, all made me feel like a complete person. Jim was connected to everything that made me feel whole. Not having him close by would be hard.

Jim had said that he wanted to marry me. I wondered if he planned to ask me before he moved. If he did, we needed to have more conversations about what we wanted in life. Cerebrally this was my stance, but my body had a mind of its own. After four months of dating, I let Jim dance me into bed one Friday night after the club. I knew what the Bible said about fornication, but we couldn't be called strangers and sojourners to this land. We had crossed many lines, reaching penultimates on multiple occasions. Now, we soaked in each other's bodies.

As the months passed and seasons changed, I spent more and more time at his apartment. We got into a routine that started with eating dinner and ended with breakfast together. Jim would make breakfast, but always ordered food for dinner. I would cook something tasty when it was my turn; a recipe from a friend or just going off of my instinct. He really appreciated this. Between dinner and breakfast, I studied while Jim wrote sermons. Then, we cuddled and watched TV, and I'd sleep over.

One nice memory I have was on an early December evening, the end of the first semester of my junior year. Jim and I were laying on adjacent couches in his apartment. I was studying for a final exam on genetic inheritance. Jim was browsing a travel book about Guyana. He was thinking about organizing international missions.

"Do you know why inbreeding is done?" I asked, wanting to hear his thoughts on what I just read.

"Out of convenience?" he joked.

Chuckling, I replied, "Gross. Was that a joke about incest? You pervert. No, the purpose of inbreeding is to retain and enhance desirable features, like the extra sweetness of an apple variety or the high milk yield of a goat breed."

"I'd like to preserve your sweet cheeks," he said while closing his book, rolling off his couch, and starting to crawl over to mine.

I pretended to ignore him and continued sharing interesting parts of my reading, "Eventually, inbreeding causes harmful genes to accumulate. At that point, thoughtful crosses can be performed to determine if the deleterious genes are dominant, recessive, etc., and avoid them in the future."

"Brilliant!" he said, looking up at me on all fours.

Looking down, I said, "An interesting phenomenon I think you may appreciate is that even better breeds can come from crossing distinct inbred lines. The genes that cause one variety of corn to have higher yields may be different than another variety, and a hybrid might have an additive yield if they inherited both genes. Know what that's called?"

"Nope." Now he was taking my socks off.

"It's called *hybrid vigor* or *heterosis*."

"Interesting." Now he was caressing my feet and slowly working up my legs.

"A variety of commercialized organisms have benefited from this technique. For example, have you heard of Black Baldy cattle?"

"No, I haven't." He pulled his shirt off.

"It's a cross of Black Angus and Hereford cattle. Black Angus calves can often have arthrogryposis multiplex or contractural arachnodactyly (pour joint or hip mobility), neuropathic hydrocephalus (enlarged malformed skulls), and/or dwarfism. Hereford frequently get ocular squamous cell carcinoma, vaginal prolapse, and udder sunburns."

"Yikes, that sounds painful." He unbuttoned my blouse. "I want you."

I continued, "However, the Black Baldy *hybrid* often lacks recessive issues and can be healthier and faster-growing compared to the purebred stock. Generally speaking, the more different the parent breeds, the better the children..."

He leaned in, "That would bode well for our kids, right? One more reason to get married." He kissed my lips. I dropped my book on the floor, missing the table entirely.

Chapter 33: The Engagement Proposal

Jim and I stayed together all winter break, celebrating Christmas and New Years together. We had a lot of time to talk without laboratory work, classes, homework, and studying for exams.

We both shared our reasons for why we did not celebrate holidays with either of our families. I told him about what happened to my dad, and my relationship with Milli. Jim told me that he was an orphan and that he was in and out of the foster care system throughout his childhood. He was never adopted, and didn't really care to keep ties with the different families who fostered him. Jim said that he always felt like he didn't belong, a tag-along or third wheel.

Still, Jim was grateful that people had opened their homes and lives to him, that some people were willing to feed and clothe him. Jim appreciated how each of his foster parents taught him different things about life, and almost all of them taught him about Christianity. Some were Catholic and others were Protestant. The last set of foster parents, before he aged out of the system, were from the LDS Church. Jim told me that there were a lot of doctrines and practices he disagreed with and that the Holy Spirit called him to refine his understanding and start a true, pure, unadulterated Christian faith.

That was the moment I realized Jim's church was solo. I thought the GOLDS Church was part of some larger network because of the way he talked about the hierarchies of priesthood and parishes. I felt anxious with this revelation, but released it to keep my Felix the Realist control and calm. I had a hard time falling asleep though, looping over questions about whether the GOLDS were a cult like Dan had said, what that would mean about my faith, what that would mean about Jim, etc.

In the morning, when Jim brought me breakfast and thanked me for our heart-to-heart, I shelved my concerns. I recognized how happy I was in this relationship, and how much richer my life was since joining the GOLDS. My sentiment became much more positive.

I welcomed Gina and Dan back to campus in January. I asked Dan to forgive me for the harsh rejection, and shared with him that Jim and I were happy, but left out what I learned about the GOLDS being unaffiliated with other churches. He forgave me, accepted that I was in a relationship, and embraced me in one of his life-giving hugs.

My three comrades and I started meeting again in Ocracoke and visiting each other's laboratories. The days of The Palace were over for the Ocracoke crew, at least for me. It just wasn't fun anymore after experiencing disco. Then again, I didn't go to Paradise 54 as much as I had in the summer and last semester either. Jim and I were starting to prefer just staying in and playing husband and wife.

One night, Jim and I were lounging on the couches, talking about this new normal.

"Are you missing going to the disco every Friday night?" I asked.

"No, Thursday nights are enough for me."

"I didn't know you went Thursday nights."

"Yeah, while you're studying in the library, I get plenty of dancing."

"You better not be dancing with other girls."

Jim smiled and said, "I consider it a ministry."

"Whatever."

Studying made me feel horny sometimes. Knowing Jim, I just needed to give him an *in* and he'd be all over me. By *in*, I just mean some little word or phrase that he could run with, some comment he could twist, make a pun out of.

I asked him, "Did you know that Nettie Maria Stevens, the namesake of our university discovered sex chromosomes?"

"I can't say that I did know that. Since you brought it up though, do you think that sex chromosomes were first revealed in the Holy Bible?"

I was a little frustrated that he didn't take the hint. For some reason, Jim was in the mood to pontificate. Out of love, I asked, "No, what do you mean?"

"Jehovah God said, *it is not good that the man should be alone; I will make him a helpmate for him. And out of the ground Jehovah God formed every beast of the field, and every bird of the heavens; and brought them unto the man to see what he would call them: and whatsoever the man called every living creature, that was the name thereof. And the man gave names to all cattle, and to the birds of the heavens, and to every beast of the field; but for man there was not found a helpmate for him. And Jehovah God caused a deep sleep to fall upon the man, and he slept; and he took one of his ribs, and closed up the flesh instead thereof: and the rib, which Jehovah God had taken from the man, made he a woman, and brought her unto the man. And the man said, this is now bone of my bones, and flesh of my flesh: she*

179

shall be called Woman, because she was taken out of Man." Jim spoke slowly to emphasize.

Before I could really think about what he was saying, he rolled off the couch, crawled over, and got down on one knee.

Excited and shocked, I sprung up and stood on the seat of the couch looking down at him.

Jim finished the passage he had memorized, *"Therefore shall a man leave his father and his mother, and shall cleave unto his wife: and they shall be one flesh. And they were both naked, the man and his wife, and were not ashamed."*

He pulled a considerable diamond ring (for a college pastor) out of his pocket and said, "Let's be united, Virginia Dare Goreman. Will you marry me?"

Chapter 34: N.O.W 6 - Diseases from Rotting Corpses Plague Urban Areas

News Of World report Sunday, April 30, 2023. As bodies decompose in buildings and along streets in cities around the world, rodents are consuming the remains and leaving urine and droppings behind. These conditions and biting insects are causing the rapid spread of plague, tularemia, salmonellosis, leptospirosis, Hantavirus pulmonary syndrome, and other diseases. Health agencies are recommending urban cities be abandoned for at least three months until human remains can no longer sustain the life cycles of the disease-causing agents and vectors. Cleanup efforts to reclaim cities are currently being planned by city officials.

Chapter 35: Liberal Arts

After accepting Jim's proposal and a few thousand mental loops around the cerebral hamster wheel that night, I decided to get off and think about what Jim mentioned right before. He asked if I had thought sex chromosomes were first revealed in the Holy Bible?

This was an odd question and maybe he just used it to stumble into the passage he wanted to quote for the marriage proposal. I thought, 'What if he was serious though. What could he possibly mean?'

Jim would have known from high school biology classes that the genetic make-up of women and men are almost entirely the same. The only difference is that women have two X-chromosomes and men have one X and one Y chromosome.

Then, it popped in my head, "*one of his ribs*". Was Jim suggesting that Jehovah had taken genetic materials from the man, represented as "*ribs*" to make the woman? Then, I wondered, had God made Woman by cloning Man and excluding the Y-chromosome?

I never asked Jim if this was his meaning and he never brought it up again either.

I took a couple of really challenging classes the second half of my junior year, and balanced it out with a liberal arts elective. I'm so glad I did because wedding planning took up a lot of my time.

I wanted to take Modern Dance since I had so much fun with disco and it looked really wild and freeing. Unfortunately, it was completely filled up when I tried to enroll. Only a Postmodern Dance class was available that semester, and it just looked strange, not fun at all.

A classmate insisted that I should enroll in a class called, "The Sociology and Psychology of Women." She said it was truly an eye-opening experience. My initial thought was that I was already pretty knowledgeable about feminist issues.

Milli had shared with me some of the issues that she experienced in journalism, either directly or through a colleague. There were numerous laws blocking equality with men. It was illegal for women to be employed in various capacities. We were not provided the same pay or benefits as men, we couldn't work overtime, and we could be fired for getting married or pregnant. It was nearly impossible to own our own business, but if we did, a huge disadvantage was not being allowed to get credit cards. These restraints bothered me, but not as much as they bothered Milli and some of my classmates. I was facing challenges in achieving my goals, but I liked a good challenge, and always found ways through or around them. No legal or societal forces had stopped my progress up to that point.

I wasn't super interested in taking a feminism class, but there weren't many other electives that intrigued me either. I decided that taking this course might help me expand and modernize my understanding and vocabulary in this area.

On the first day of class, Professor de Pizan shocked me with an opening quote I'll never forget. She said, "Women are not born, but rather made." My mind exploded in every direction and the statement made me want to argue. Then she said, "What does this statement mean to you? Take a minute to quietly think about this."

Murmurs rose around the room.

"Quietly!" she repeated and the noise stopped.

I thought, 'I was both created by Jehovah and born from my mother, and maybe someday I too would be a mother.'

Then I realized, '*Women* are not born. Babies are born. Maybe that's what she means. *When I was a child, I spoke as a child, I understood as a child, I thought as a child: but when I became a woman, I put away childish things.*'

Then, I thought of Jim having sex with me, making me a woman. Then, back to my first day of college, back to trying different sizes for my first bra, back to seeing my mom burn hers at a rally.

My mind snapped back when Professor de Pizan started talking again. "Simone de Beauvoir argues gender is a social construct used to oppress women in ours and other patriarchal societies throughout history. Your homework is to read excerpts from her book, The Second Sex," said Professor de Pizan.

'Women are made. Gender is a tool of oppression.' These were new ideas to me. Mother was always talking about ways in which women were oppressed, but we never really talked about why. What did man gain from this oppression? Why would women allow it? Why couldn't we or wouldn't we stop it?

I wondered how the concepts in this course might impact my research, if there were any measurable connections between human development and gender, and how human development might change if there was no gender, many discrete genders, or a continuous gender range.

Why should I assume that Professor de Pizan and her literature was at all authoritative on the subject? An objection came to mind. She was saying something about the syllabus when I raised my hand.

"Yes, please state your name before asking your question." said Professor de Pizan.

"Virginia Goreman. While society might uphold gender as a construct with various institutions and religion, it is nature that created gender. This very university is named after the woman who discovered the chromosomes involved in sex determinism. Animals…"

Professor de Pizan cut me off and said, "Ms. Goreman, while nature might have created sex, it did not create gender. The difference is bits versus roles. The British have a nice word for private parts called bits. I like this word because it contextualizes these organs as small and of limited utility. We have bits and these determine our sex. If you have these bits, you're a female. If you have those bits, you're a male. Our bits do not necessarily determine our gender."

She went on, "While sex and gender are currently synonymous in the majority of cases, it's not always the case. A hermaphrodite may have their sex chosen at an early age by their parents, and their minds may choose differently and be acted upon in adulthood. In ancient cultures, a man with his bits removed was a third gender, a eunuch, who had the role of superintendent of a monarch's harem. Our sex currently limits our roles. This may be important for wild animals who have a survival-oriented moment-to-moment existence. I'll admit that even our primitive ancestors functioned better with sex-based roles. However, modern humans in many contexts are not in survival mode. The eunuch example shows us that we can change our sex, and we will probably be able to do so in more sophisticated ways in the future."

Professor de Pizan turned her gaze from me and looked around the lecture hall.

"In this class, we will spend a good deal of time expanding more on the idea that our roles can be chosen, without altering our bits, and unlike the hermaphrodite, we will someday have more than just two options to choose from. We will discuss how we can liberate ourselves from societal gender role constructs, decouple gender from roles, so you can choose what you want to do with your lives, and your children, if you choose to have them, can choose what they want to do with their lives! Furthermore, we will debate whether this liberation of gender roles improves our society!"

With that, about half the class gave a standing ovation.

Chapter 36: Extreme Feminism

"Shulamith Firestone says we can only achieve gender role liberation if pregnancy and childbirth can be separated from gender."

"I don't think so."

"Why?"

"Physical distinctions. The bits, Professor," one young woman argued.

"Yeah, we will never be on a level ground in terms of strength or speed," said another.

"Never say never," responded Professor de Pizan.

"We can never pop their cherry, grope their cans, bend them over, give it to them family style. I mean like half of the Kama Sutra positions are restricted. I'm NATO, but I couldn't nuke them if I wanted to."

"Thank you, Marcia. You're saying that even if pregnancy and childbirth were gender independent, women will still be dominated in sex."

"Like the Kingdom of Hawaii," Marcia replied.

Some of the class laughed. Professor de Pizan was not amused, but let the noise die down before continuing, "Firestone also says that the goal of feminism should not be just the elimination of male privilege, but of sex distinction itself. One radical solution she offers, that doesn't fix the problem you pose Marcia, but is nevertheless a powerful idea, is that pregnancy and childbirth could be avoided with an artificial womb."

The room seemed to get brighter with so many mental light bulbs turning on. The extroverts could not be contained.

"Is that possible?" one asked, her voice filled with astonishment.

"Not yet, but someday," Professor de Pizan said, her voice filled with hope.

"How would it work? Would the baby need to get moved from the mother's womb to the artificial womb?"

"Actually, egg cells can be obtained by laparoscopy surgery," I explained. "A woman is put under, an incision is made in the abdomen, and mature follicles are taken from the ovaries. Theoretically, eggs can be fertilized with sperm, grow on a plate, then transferred and grown in the artificial womb until ready."

The room went quiet and everyone turned to look at me.

After what felt like a long silence, a classmate commented, "Sounds like sci-fi. You sure Mary Shelly didn't write that with a pseudonym?"

Another chimed in, "Yeah, that's far out."

Professor de Pizan added, "Definitely would make things easier for women. Definitely less painful. No work time off needed or special accommodations. No risk of being fired."

"I think the artificial womb idea would also be good for traditional roles too."

Murmurs went around the room.

"Settle down, class! Please say more, Julia," requested Professor de Pizan.

"Okay, well, I'm the eldest of five siblings. My mom was miserable carrying my youngest brother for nine months while she chased my other siblings around the house. We needed help when she was recovering after his birth."

"Clearly, there are so many benefits, but my mom always makes such a big deal about how she loved feeling me moving and growing inside of her. Wouldn't we miss something special?"

There was a pregnant pause in the room. A classmate, Sharron, started weeping.

"What's wrong?" Many of us were asking.

She was pink around her eyes and heaving a little. "My mom died giving birth…to me."

"Oh, sweetheart." The closest classmates were comforting her while she continued crying.

"I'm very sorry to hear that, Ms. Swift. Class," she called out addressing everyone, "…about three in ten thousand women will die from childbirth in the United States. While this is somewhat rare now, in the 1940s and 1950s when you were born, women died at a rate of six in one thousand, or twenty times more frequently than today."

I chimed in, "More frequently babies die in childbirth, about three in one hundred."

"While we can't know for sure what improvements might be made in the survival rates of babies that are born in an artificial womb…" Professor de Pizan said, looking at me, then turned her attention to the rest of the class and said, "…we can say with certainty that there will be a one hundred percent survival rate for women choosing artificial wombs instead of traditional pregnancy and child birthing methods."

I thought this was a good point. Many women describe pregnancy as beautiful or special. So, maybe feeling the baby moving inside you makes this experience qualitatively superior. However, a no-risk no-pain pregnancy would likely be considered quantitatively better to many women.

Then, I chimed in with a couple of realizations, "Professor de Pizan, no surgery is *complication free*. The laparoscopy surgery to harvest the egg or eggs has some risk. The anesthesia alone has some risk. Also, the artificial womb cannot eliminate sex distinction. Only getting rid of one of the sexes will achieve this end. Here's why. If this technology came out, women would become egg donors. They have to come from somewhere. We women might be compensated in some contexts and countries, but maybe we are made to do it in others. This will never be the man's job and the sexes will remain distinct in this and other ways."

"Right, and we haven't even talked about what happens after the child is born. Women are still more nurturing overall than men and expected to raise the children. Roles are partly connected to emotional dispositions of the genders," another classmate added.

"That reminds me of another quote from Firestone; that *the very institution of motherhood is antithetical to the idea of individuality and autonomy.* Class, what does that mean?"

"If your gender locks you into raising children, how will you be free to pursue your own interests?"

"I can kind of see how artificial wombs might create more freedom. If a man wants to have a baby, he no longer needs a bride. He can just pay for an egg and an artificial womb. I don't think many men would do this though, knowing that they need to raise the child."

"They need the mother to come with the kid."

"Unless…"

"What?"

"The father pays for child raising, too."

"We could operate the same way. Drop our baby or kid off and go to work. Why not?"

"It is only the collapse of this system that holds out any prospect of freedom from the heterosexual nuclear family, which is a factory of women's oppression. That's another Firestone quote. Great discussion, class. That is all for today."

I think that day's class was the second most thought provoking of Professor de Pizan's lectures.

The first was almost certainly her passionate lecture on men, violence, and war. She started with, "It was Fridtjof Nansen who said *war will cease when men refuse to fight,*" Professor de Pizan started. "Fridtjof Nansen was probably referring to humans and not just strictly men when he said that quote. However, at the international level, men make up the vast majority of top leadership. Israel's Golda Meir, India's Indira Gandhi, and Sri Lanka's Sirimavo Bandaranaike are the exceptions. Are men not responsible for the wars that ravish our planet and take away and kill our family members? At the national level, women represent just three percent of congress. Just twelve House seats and four Senate seats. Men were the reason we remained in a failing Vietnam War for so long. Their stubbornness and pride kept them from declaring defeat or suing for peace. Let's skip state and local influences of male power domination for now, and talk about what happens in the home."

"A study by Murray Straus showed that more than half of couples surveyed reported some form of physical aggression in their relationships. Lee Rainwater's *Behind Ghetto Walls: Black Families in a Federal Slum* found that domestic violence was an accepted frequent aspect of life for black families living in a public housing project in Chicago. Two recent studies found physical violence was occurring in 10% of American families."

"It might feel like we are bouncing around a little bit. Stick with me though. We will come back to how male representation and war are related to this topic, but I wanted to lay some foundations close to home to build the argument. How do you think domestic abuse impacts the mental health of women?"

"I think my mom felt afraid of what everyone would think if she said something or left my dad. Her parents, close friends, and church community might judge her."

"Thank you for sharing, Abigail. Would you please talk more about how she might be judged?"

"I don't know. Maybe if she talked about a divorce, they would say it's a sin or something. They might ask questions like - what did you do to make him mad?"

"Very brave of you to talk about this. Did your father abuse you too?"

Abigail immediately started to cry. "Yes."

The classmates around her comforted her.

When she calmed down a little, Professor de Pizan asked, "Did you ask yourself what you did to make him mad?"

"No, I knew. He would tell me. When I was a kid, it was not putting my toys away. When I was a teen, it was leaving the lights on after I left a room. Little stuff like that."

"Thank you, Abigail. Class, acute battering incidence is part of a commonly experienced cycle of violence characterized by Lenore Walker in her 1968 publication "The Battered Woman". She says women experience an accumulation of fear during a tension-building phase with minor verbal and emotional abuse. Then, there is some major physical violence, the acute incident, triggered by something small. And finally, a honeymoon phase, when the abuser expresses great remorse and perhaps promises never to do it again."

"But it never lasts," interjected Stephanie. "It was rare that two months would pass by without my dad exploding. Mom would always forgive him though. She would tell me she didn't have a choice. She was too old to marry again and couldn't support herself."

"Thank you, Stephanie. Class, some might presume that battered women who stay in abusive relationships are masochistic, but you have heard from Stephanie and Abigail, and Walker's study concurs: economic, social, and psychological factors are more prevalent in these situations than fetishes."

"Oh, God!" There was great distress In Stephanie's face and tears welled up and poured down her cheeks. She was fiercely massaging her head. "I need to talk to my mom! God, I am such a bitch!"

"What?" asked the classmate next to her.

"I called her a coward!" Stephanie confessed.

"You may go," Professor de Pizan said. "I'm sure one of your classmates can fill you in on the rest of the conversation."

"Thank you, Professor de Pizan." Stephanie mumbled, as she quickly gathered her things and ran out crying.

"Now. What about the impacts of domestic abuse on children? We heard briefly from Abigail that some experiences are shared whether it's a wife or child. We also saw that children are not always aware of the whole picture as in Stephanie's case. What else?"

"Feelings of fear, sadness, resentment, anger…" someone shouted out.

"Feelings might be directed at dad, mom, themselves, or maybe others not involved. Maybe they plot to run away, take mom away, or seek revenge on dad," added Carly.

"Something I want to bring up briefly before we continue," interrupted Professor de Pizan. "What assumption are we making about the abuser, and is it fair?"

"The abuser is male, and probably," someone said quickly.

"Right, and right. While we don't have much data to calculate the percentage of men who are domestically abused by women with confidence, the data is trending toward less than ten percent of domestic abuse cases. Similarly, FBI data shows that females account for about nine percent of murder arrests. I am currently seeking funding to test my hypothesis that the probability of homicide increases significantly in relationships where there is a history of physical or sexual violence.

Now, Carly, you said that feelings like anger could be directed at someone other than the father, right?"

"I just mean that sometimes when you're angry about something, you might take it out on someone who is not involved. Maybe a friend, coworker, someone who annoys you and you let them have it, even though what they did was minor compared to the person that upset you," Carly elaborated.

"Indeed. There is a certain amount of emotional awareness and control that keeps us from erupting. Recent studies are finding that children who witnessed violence at home don't have this control. They are exhibiting violent or delinquent behavior in higher frequency than other children. Lynn White and Betty Wright's study, 'The Family Context of Delinquency,' found that this effect was especially strong for boys."

The tie back to war was a little frayed in my opinion. Still, it was hard to argue against the fact that men are primarily responsible for more violent activities ranging from domestic abuse to war. I started to add my classmates to my prayer list at night, even praying for their abusers in hopes that there would be peace and redemption. Then, violence happened to me.

Chapter 37: My Baby

On Saturday, May 6th, 1977, I was sure that I had missed my period. I picked up a couple of Crane Home Predictor Tests from the Pharmacy, and saw the red circle. I cried after getting a second positive test. I didn't want to be pregnant in my junior year of college, and I certainly didn't want a baby in the second half of my senior year. However, imagining a little red-haired mini me or curly dirty blonde-haired Jim Jr. made me feel some happiness and excitement.

Jim had given me every indication that he wanted to make me his wife and a mother. So, I made his favorite dinner, eggplant parmesan, lit some candles, put on a sexy dress, and waited for him to get back to his apartment.

"Sorry, I'm late... Oh, what's this? You look dazzling." Jim gave me a nice, full kiss.

"Thank you."

"What's the occasion?"

"I've got some big news to share, but before I do, let me heat up your dinner. I made eggplant parm."

"Slammin'."

When I was done heating up the food, I set it on the table, and sat down beside Jim. "Let's pray so you can go ahead and start eating. I don't want to make you wait."

Jim smiled, "Dear Jehovah...Amen."

I got up and poured a glass of water and sat back down next to Jim. I had planned out what I was going to say, while I waited for him to arrive.

"Aren't you going to get some eggplant parm?"

"I already *ate enough for two*." I just sat there with a dumb wide eyed toothy smile hoping he would get it.

"Okaayyy..." said Jim, looking at me like he was a little concerned. "So, what's the big news you were talking about?"

Since my first hint didn't land, I tried another, "It's actually very *small* news right now. However, it's going to *grow* so big over the next *eight months* that I won't be able to contain it anymore."

"Well, do I get to know in advance?"

I covered my face with my hands and stifled a laugh. Strike two.

Jim put his fork down, leaned over, and put his hand on my shoulder. "Are you okay, Virginia?" He thought I was crying.

"I'm fine right now, but I might start having morning sickness."

"Morning sickness?" He stood up and said, "Holy… Virginia, are you pregnant?"

Score.

"Um. Yes, I am, you thick-skulled neanderthal," I said smiling.

Jim's face looked flat, not sad or happy. His head and eyes were shifting around, and he started massaging his head and pacing the room. Then, I knew something was wrong.

"What is it, Jim? Aren't you happy."

"Yeah…" the way he said it wasn't very convincing.

"You look anxious."

"Um. There's just no way people aren't going to know you're pregnant when we have our wedding ceremony."

I did the math. We sent out invitations for a wedding on Saturday, November 5th. Eight months from now would be January. There would be no way of hiding my pregnancy in the third trimester.

"What if we…" My mind quickly rejected scenario after scenario. We couldn't organize and have a proper wedding before I was showing, and of course people would want to know why we moved the date up. We could lie, but then they would remember after the baby was born, and do the math. "What if we just elope?"

"When the baby came eight months from now, everyone would know that we did it because you were pregnant! Eff!"

I got worried. Standing in front of him and softly gliding my hands up and down his arms seemed like a good idea to calm him down. "It's going to be alright."

"I can't!"

"You can't what?"

"I can't preach purity if I'm not pure! I can't preach holiness if I'm not holy!"

"What about grace though?"

"I'm not worried about Jehovah. He forgives. It's the congregants that won't. They'll leave!"

"Leave?"

"Yeah!"

"Well, so what? I mean, do you really want unforgiving congregants anyway?"

"I need them."

"Need them? For what?"

"To keep the church going. There are some members that give amounts … if they leave, I might have to choose between paying rent for the church or rent for my apartment."

"You can come live in my apartment," I shrugged.

"No… It's too soon. Congregants give the most in December. They want their tithes to count on their tax deductions. We need that money for our house!"

"The one in the Adirondacks?"

"Yes! And if a third, a quarter, even one major donor leaves, then we won't have enough for a mortgage down payment. Worse still, the five-step plan will fail on step one."

"We can just get the house next year."

"No, I said that this plan was inspired by the Holy Spirit. If it fails, many will not have grace. They will say I blasphemed the Spirit, and they will leave!"

I just looked at Jim in his distress.

"It's all going to fall apart!"

He walked over to the back of the long couch and pulled, slamming it to the ground. The side nearly clipped me.

"Jim!"

He was pacing and massaging his head again.

Then, someone knocked on the door. "Jim?! Is everything alright in there?"

"Yes, Stanley! Thank you for your concern!"

Jim went over to his kitchenette. He turned on the sink and began splashing his face.

I wanted to help him, but didn't know how. Sympathy with recognizing and describing his feelings didn't help. Neither did physical touch. Nor did troubleshooting. He wasn't saying anything, so I couldn't just listen. He was having a meltdown.

"Take a deep breath, Jim."

He glared at me. So, I just stopped talking. He turned around and looked at a calendar on the wall with pictures of New York City skyscrapers.

After a minute or two of silence, and without turning back around to face me, he asked, "What do you think about abortion?"

Chapter 38: Virgin Bride

The question confounded me. Just a few months ago, Jim was starkly opposed to abortion.

'He actually gave a sermon responding to the 4th year anniversary of Roe v. Wade!' exclaimed my surprise.

'Yeah, I remember Jim quoting numerous Bible verses including the passage from Luke 1 where Jesus' cousin leapt in his mother's womb and used this to argue that *the unborn child is a life*,' recalled my confidence.

'Yes, and Jim even claimed that pregnancy was designed by God to help us understand the indwelling of the Holy Spirit in the Tabernacle, then the Temple, and finally in us,' recollected my fascination.

Before I could respond to his first question, Jim followed with another still looking at the calendar, "Did you know that in early 1970, when the State of New York removed all abortion restrictions for the first six months of pregnancy, it was the clergy that opened the first abortion clinic?"

I stared at the back of his head.

'What is Jim coming to? Is he really going to suggest that we have an abortion?' asked my bewilderment.

My serenity helped me respond, and not jump to conclusions. "I do. My mother covered the story."

I had shared with Jim that my mom was a feminist.

"What did she think about it?"

"She was a very early advocate for a woman's right to choose. She said *women are not mere vessels. We have lives and responsibilities before, during, and after we give birth. We should be able to decide whether we carry a pregnancy, give birth, and be changed forevermore.*"

"Do you agree with your mom?"

"At the time what she said seemed very reasonable to me, but now I follow Jesus, and I don't believe He would want me to have an abortion, if that's what you are asking."

Then he turned, and I saw a look of desperation.

"What about the clergy who opened the first clinic? Don't you think they follow Jesus?"

"I don't know."

My response seemed to relieve him based on microexpression changes until I finished my thought. "What I remember though from my mom covering the story was that the New York Archdiocese, Cardinal Cooke, spoke out against abortions, and so did the Catholic Right to Life Movement."

Sounding hopeful, he toed for a footing in the dark, "So, you might say that the Church appears to be divided on the matter of abortion?"

"Yes, I suppose," I conceded.

Breathing a sigh of relief, he came close.

"Okay, now listen." He softly placed his hands on my arms, brought his face close to mine, and peered deep into my eyes, to the depths of my heart. "I can tell you are like me. You're a leader." His grip tightened on my arms.

"Ah, Jim. Too tight."

He didn't loosen, but shook me a little, which made me nervous. "You're going to be a great leader," he said sternly.

"Jim!" I altered.

Then he relaxed his grip.

"You just haven't made it to your full potential yet."

He released me, turned around, and walked away from me.

It wasn't clear what he meant, but Jim knew my dream was to manage a laboratory and develop therapies for infertility. So, I assumed that was what he was referring to.

He raised his right hand in the air, pointed as if to Heaven, and declared, "Jehovah has huge plans for you!"

He leaned over and righted the couch. Then, looked back at me and asked quietly, "What is having a baby right now going to do to those plans?"

My discouragement answered, 'No research professor is going to take on a pregnant mother. You'll be rejected by all of them.'

'What about the female professors?' challenged my self-respect. 'They'll give me a shot.'

My inadequacy responded, 'Even if one did, you won't have enough time for your experiments. You'll be too busy taking care of the newborn. You'll have to give up; master out.' That was what happened sometimes to scientists. They'd start a Ph.D. program, but take a master's degree part way through because they couldn't finish their research. There were different reasons for this, but one was because they became overwhelmed with other things in life.

It was almost like Jim could hear my thoughts.

"When you have a baby, there's a lack of sleep, focus, time," he counted, unfurling his fingers.

I looked down, unable to think clearly. His intensity was too distracting.

He pressed me into an embrace, my head tucking neatly into his shoulder, and spoke softly in my ear, "If they even let you into a program, you'll lose your lead, your upper hand, over your peers."

I thought of the literature review and helping organize the seminar series. What good are these advantages if I work slower and take more time off than everyone else in the program? ...If everyone catches up and writes their literature review while I take care of my kid? And when they're done writing their literature review, they'll be more prolific than me in experimenting and publishing. They'll get the rare coveted research professor jobs, not me. All because I'll be too busy with the responsibility of taking care of my toddler.

'Wait a minute. Someone will take care of her, or him, when you need to work,' assured my relaxation.

'Oh, yeah! Who?' questioned my anxiety. 'Not Jim. Not your mom. Not your grandma. Gina might from time to time, but you can't expect her to be available all the time.'

'You and Jim can't afford a nanny like Milli hired when you were a kid,' commented my inadequacy.

'What about day care?' suggested my responsiveness.

'Oh, that's the kind of mother you want to be?' questioned my embarrassment.

'Terrible quality of care at those places. Certainly not the same level of emotional support. Your child will develop slower, and have long term disadvantages from lack of early maternal care,' proclaimed my shame.

'You're not even considering the practical aspects of graduate school,' challenged my frustration. 'Graduate studies is not a normal nine to five job. You work late evenings, nights, sometimes on weekends. What daycare is available for that?'

"Your academic launch is happening now," declared Jim, "But a baby will cause the mission to be aborted. Your professional career, that's meant for space, will plummet back down to earth, smash into pieces in a fiery waste of resources, investment, life…"

'Your dreams and any chance for real impact in this world are doomed if you have this baby,' translated my insignificance.

My heart fell when nothing in me countered this. I lost my stability and put all my weight on Jim, sobbing into his chest.

Jim whimpered, "I'm so sorry, Virginia."

Looking up, I saw tears in his eyes.

"I really thought it would take longer to get pregnant. I should have been more careful. I'm sorry. It's all my fault," he stammered and buried his face, crying into my shoulder.

I was surprised by Jim's apology. He never apologized; was always sure of himself, his actions and convictions were unwavering. What was he sorry for now?

'Getting a congregant pregnant out of wedlock,' proposed my suspicion.

'Putting us in an impossibly difficult situation with an impossibly difficult decision?' suggested my irritation.

'He's genuinely sorry though,' my trust advocated.

'So?' demanded my frustration.

'It means he loves you,' answered my awareness.

'How's that?' replied my loneliness.

'He wouldn't be sad if he didn't care about you, just angry his plans were messed up,' explained my discernment.

Jim, the golden man, pulled back from my shoulder and looked at me with soft, puffy red eyes for a lingering moment. Our pupils were locked with only the microsecond interruption of our moisture sustaining blinks. Deep in his pupil, I saw love. Then, when I refocused, I could see my own love reflecting in his cornea.

"You're going to be my bride."

Dilation, my eyes searching.

He took my hands in his, and affirmed, "I love you, Virginia."

"I love you, too," I uttered sincerely.

"And Virginia, I want to have children with you, lots of them," continued Jim, a look of wholehearted earnestness.

'Yeah,' cried my happiness.

'Wait, settle down. Don't you see what he's coming to,' my awareness pushed back.

"But this just isn't the time for either of us," I said, finishing his sentence.

With a somber look, he pulled me back into his embrace. We wept for what felt like hours, at some point lying down on the rug below us, until we fell asleep.

On the car ride the next day to the clinic, my mind looped. Jim's pastoral reputation and the congregation was at stake, and so was my professional trajectory. So, it had to be done. At least I couldn't see any other options that would allow me to have the life that I wanted.

Part of me was mad at Jim for getting me pregnant, but my logic consoled me, 'We got pregnant once with Jim, so we can again, when we're ready.'

The abortion was fast and singular. Jim waited in the lobby. I had a ten- or fifteen-minute conversation with a doctor, they dilated my cervix and performed the vacuum aspiration in about the same amount of time, and then I lay in bed for about a half hour. We were on the road heading back to campus only a little over an hour later.

The procedure was too easy, like dropping a bomb. Nuclear bombs fall quickly, but fallouts last for a very long time. A slow, painful, crippling sadness, guilt, regret, and anxiety came upon me. I felt isolated, barely able to talk about what had happened or share my feelings with Jim, who was "trying to forget and move on". Also, I wasn't allowed to tell anyone else, again to avoid consequences with the other GOLDS congregants. Not that I wanted the stigma, but I missed being known. My Ocracoke friends had read my whole life book, all the secrets, down to my painful fatherless childhood. Their cognizant love made me feel shameless and powerful. Now, my walls were back up, parts of my life were hidden once again, and again I was redressing my open wounds.

Chapter 39: Perdita

Solitary reflection of the events surrounding the abortion made me realize that my autonomy had been challenged. I wanted to confront Jim for taking my power away, but when thinking about what I planned to say to him, I realized that I had ultimately yielded to his will. I gave him my power, and it was painful to know I had agreed to terminate the life of our unborn child.

I became frustrated at church. Always assuming Jim had imperfections, but now keenly aware that Jim didn't always practice what he preached. My mind scrutinized him more thoroughly, catching each hypocrisy and debating whether or not he should be allowed on the pulpit. Then, when he would ask me for feedback, I'd let him have it. I could see the frustration in his eyes and the wrinkle of his brow, but Jim could somehow flip a switch and with a smile reply, "You're right, I am a sinner in need of a savior."

To channel my stress energy into beneficial areas, I exercised harder, learning new and more strenuous workouts beyond what was instructed during physical therapy. I also worked longer hours in the lab, which pleased Diego. He never asked me what was eating at me. I should have expected him not to care.

I was glad when the Ocracoke crew asked why I was pushing myself harder than ever. I just blamed it on stressful wedding planning. My other friends, Alice and Nancy, were helping me with wedding planning because everything was tied in with GOLDS Church. They noticed that I was making quick decisions rather than enjoying the process. When they asked about my change in demeanor, I said the lab experiments were getting more rigorous and I just didn't have time to perfect everything.

In the evenings, Jim and I would talk openly about the challenges we were having and much of the discussions were around sex.

He'd declare, "I burn for you!"

And, I'd reject him. "I am not in the mood!"

"We can be careful if you are worried about getting pregnant again."

"We certainly would if we did, but we shouldn't be having sex before marriage!"

"Come on. We are committed to each other. We are basically married."

"No. You pushed me to get an abortion because a baby would have ruined your reputation and all the work you've done building your church!"

"Yes, you're right, Virginia, but I still can't change the fact that I burn for you!"

"Take a cold shower!"

When he'd try to kiss me, I'd leave.

During a dream one night, I found Felix the Realist sitting on a rock in the woods of my mind. The only thing I remember is the sensei saying, "Stop exhausting yourself, hammering on basalt. Sculpt with the softer soapstone or alabaster. Give the basalt to the master sculptor."

I wondered if Felix meant that I should call off the engagement, and seriously considered it. During one of my prayers though, I asked God to reveal the meaning to me. It came to me a moment later that Felix was telling me to give my impossible struggles to God and focus on what I could control.

'We must accept the reality that our baby girl or boy is irretrievable, lost,' broached my daring.

'There is nothing we can do about that. It's in the past,' supported my contentment.

'Jim is before us. We can work on our relationship, and prepare for our marriage,' suggested my responsiveness.

'Yes, we can,' agreed my love.

The following day, I found Jim at the end of the walkway leading to the brickyard trying to recruit new Freshman to Bible studies. I pulled him aside and told him I was ready again.

"Really?"

"Yeah."

"How?"

"I can't do anything about Perdita."

"The abandoned princess in that Shakespeare play, umm? What's it called?"

"Yes, *The Winter's Tale*. It's far from a perfect analogy, so don't look into it too deeply, but I want to work things out with you before further tragedy strikes."

"Thank you, Virginia. I'm sorry, I really am, but our child isn't lost and I'm glad you want to recover and redeem what *we* have."

"What do you mean? Of course our child is lost!"

"Shh. Please, calm down, Virginia." Some people moved further away from us as they walked by.

"Listen. Jehovah has our child with Him. He forgives us, and He will reunite us in the Eternal Universe."

"How are you so sure?" I asked, unconvinced.

"You must know by now that if you ask, he will not withhold forgiveness from you. Don't you?"

"No, this is too great of a sin. It's murder."

"Shhh."

"We knew what we were doing! How would it be fair for us to live in the Eternal Universe? How would a God of perfect justice forgive us?" I scream whispered.

"Shhh. It's okay. You're right. Our sin is deserving of death. Remember though, the words of John, that *God so loved the world,* including you Virginia, *that he gave his only begotten Son, that whosoever believeth on him should not perish, but have eternal life. For God sent not the Son into the world to judge the world; but that the world should be saved through him.* Jesus paid for our sin with His life. He suffered our consequences for us."

I sucked in my breath to try and stifle the sudden wave of overwhelming relief, but my eyes blurred with tears. When Jim embraced me, I erupted, my loud cries drawing attention.

"Are you okay?" some Freshman boy asked.

"She'll be okay. Thank you for stopping, kind Samaritan," pacified Jim, in a reverendly way.

Jim whispered to me, "Jesus makes it just and fair for us to spend eternity with our unborn child."

I thought of the baby in the arms of Jesus and this gave me peace.

After I calmed down, Jim asked, "Are you going to be okay?"

"Yes," I said with some sureness.

"Can I make you something tasty for dinner tonight?"

I smirked. "Yeah. Sure."

"Great. See you at my place, 6pm?"

"Okay, I'll be there."

I believed now that our Perdita was with God and that we'd get to see her one day.

Chapter 40: New Home

A couple of months later, Jim and I were doing great, probably the best we had ever been. Jim convinced me to cut out of work early to show me a surprise. I didn't mind surprises but he asked me to close my eyes and not to peek, and then had me keep them closed for more than twenty minutes. That made me a little anxious.

"Where are you taking me? It feels like we've been driving up a peak for ten miles."

"Haha! Maybe so."

"Okay. Will we at least be there soon?"

"As a matter of fact, we are just pulling up to our destination now. Keep your eyes closed."

Jim stopped the car, ran around to my side, and guided me carefully out in front of the car.

"You can open your eyes."

I did and before me was a handsome dark-brown two-story mountain cabin, gables and windows designed for vista and star gazing. It was perched on the left side, and a wraparound stilted porch tapered level to the ground on the right. There, a small alley, divided the cabin and a sizable matching garage, and provided easy access from the driveway to the back. The Fall season further enhanced the introduction with a picturesque backdrop of oranges, reds, yellows, and greens.

"Wow, Jim! What is this?"

"It's our new home, Virginia."

"What? Are you serious!" I was elated, having assumed my first home would be a cookie-cutter starter in a densely-packed low-to-middle economy neighborhood. This vacation getaway was a fantastic surprise.

Jim was grinning from ear to ear as he scooped me up and carried me to the threshold. After a brief struggle for the keys in his pocket, he successfully opened the door and swung me in.

His tour was very rapid. "Here's a little mud room. Kitchen is off to the right. Living room is before us. There's a finished attic bedroom upstairs that I can show you later. And our bedroom and bath are off to the left, in here."

"You're going to show me the finished attic later?"

"Yeah, we need to christen the house," he huffed, turning into the bedroom and dropping me onto the bed. I let out a "wee" and the springs bounced a little. Drawn curtains darkened the room hiding its details and the view ahead. Only his beautiful silhouette could be seen from the residual living room daylight. He pulled his shirt off and reached up my skirt. The ceremony was passionate.

Afterward, while we lay in bed, I asked Jim how we acquired such a neat home.

"A developer was successful in getting approval and permits to create a secluded mountain-side neighborhood, but after the housing market dipped the project no longer made financial sense. About three acres of the total thirty-acre property were cleared but left undeveloped, except for our house. The rest are woods."

"That's amazing. No wonder we were driving for a while."

"Well, the reason you had to keep your eyes closed for so long was because, beyond the property, there are miles of surrounding densely forested State Park."

"State Park?"

"Yeah, we're pretty deep in the Adirondacks."

"So, we're on a mountain."

"Yeah! We are three quarters of the way up Great Dale Mountain."

Jim jumped out of bed. "I want to show you something. Come on," he urged and left the room.

"Where are you going?"

Jim popped back in as I stood up. He took my hand and we jogged down the hall. I couldn't help but giggle. Then, he opened the door and I pulled my hand away to cover myself.

"Jim! We're naked! Close the door!"

"It's okay. No one is around for miles and miles." Jim ran out, buck naked into the cool, fall evening. I just stood in the doorway and watched.

Jim frolicked in the grass, spinning in circles. The sun was setting behind him and the adjacent mountain, darkening his figure. "See. Nothing around us. Just trees and mountain sides."

The view was awesome, a grandness somewhere between looking at the National Mall and looking at the Atlantic from the Wrightsville Memorial. While it won silver for scale, it won gold for vibrancy.

'Well, you haven't really traveled, have you?' mocked my inferiority.

'At least we will have this view for the foreseeable future. More than most can say,' encouraged my pride.

I suppressed my emotions and looked up to the heavens. Wanting to express gratitude to Jehovah for the magnificent front yard view, I whispered, "Thank you, God."

While still safe in the doorway, like a hermit in her shell, I started to feel daring and asked Jim, "Are you sure no one is going to drive up here?"

"No reason to. It's literally just our house at the end of a ten-mile driveway. The mailbox is at the beginning. So, come on! Let your bits waggle!"

"My bits waggle," I repeated laughing.

"I think that's how they say it in Britain. Run free, Virginia, like Eve in the Garden."

"Before the Fall," I specified, smirking.

"Of course."

I wanted to, and I could tell he really wanted me too. I paced a little between the hallway and the porch pretending to debate myself to engorge his anticipation.

"Come on!" Jim urged again.

"Okay!"

With that, I took a couple of steps back in the hallway, then took off running. I spread my wings as I left the threshold, and launched myself off the front porch in his direction clearing the three steps. I landed in the grass, slowed my momentum with a few graceful strides, and transitioned to a playful skip. Wanting to lure Jim, I turned off course and began twirling and whirling in all directions like a bee meandering about the wild flowers. Out of the corner of my eye, I could see my modern dance was exciting him. Jim started moving toward me, and I ran away. The thrilling chase ended with him pouncing on me and a passionate roll in the field. It was our first time outdoors, but I imagined it would not be the last.

"So, why couldn't you have just drawn the curtain and shown me the beautiful view from our bedroom?" I asked, smiling.

"Not as fun."

As the sun set, the radiance of the fall colors on the adjacent mountain sides dimmed.

"What I meant to tell you before was that we got a killer deal on this private peaceful getaway."

"Oh, really?"

"We are deep in the Adirondacks, the sole residence for miles. Homes like these would normally go for like a hundred thousand dollars, but the market conditions, the developer's desperation, and the connection I had through a friend from the club…Well, everything came together."

"Who was that?"

"Who was what?"

"Your connection at the club."

"You haven't met him. Anyway, the stars aligned, Virginia! Speaking of which, wait until you see the stars out here!"

"I bet they're beautiful without the city light pollution!"

"Indeed!"

After the sunset, our body heat could no longer compete with the dropping temperatures. We went in, showered together, brushed our teeth and hair, prayed, and let the crickets sing us to sleep.

The following morning, Jim woke me with a soft shake. He was beside the bed with an index finger against his lips. "Shhh."

"What?" I mouthed.

Jim motioned for me to follow him.

We tiptoed into the kitchen and he pointed, signaling me to look out the window.

I did and glimpsed a stag with a giant rack of antlers and three doe picking around the front yard.

"Wow! So cool!" I exclaimed, forgetting that we were sneaking up on the deer and that they might hear us with their sensitive predator-detecting ears. We looked out the window and giggled, glad to see that they didn't take off because of my mistake. The house apparently had better sound damping than we thought.

Smiling, he handed me a cup of coffee. "Good morning."

"Good morning," I replied, accepting the coffee and returning the smile. "That's really neat to see in the morning. Very different from what I grew up with. We could see a squirrel or cardinal, bunny rabbit at best."

"Mmhmm, and I saw turkeys two weeks ago."

"Turkeys? Two weeks ago? Wait. When did you move in?"

"This past Sunday after church. I came here to do a quick check of the house before signing day. Seven turkeys were in the back. I took it as a *sign* before *signing day*," he emphasized, trying to be funny, and added the caveat, "...even though I wasn't really looking for one."

"Well, if you hadn't gone for it, someone would have gobbled it up." I couldn't help but grin at my witty pun, and neither could Jim.

"Clever."

"Thank you. Yours too."

"Yours was better."

"Well, thank you. You still need to show me the backyard."

"Yes, and the attic bedroom."

"Let's finish our coffee though before we finish the tour to avoid potentially getting it on the carpet."

The green shag carpet was not my favorite, nor was the color theme in general. It was hidden when we arrived by the dim ambient evening light. I think in cooperation with the wood paneling, the carpet and other earthy green, red, brown, and yellow furnishings and decor were meant to give the illusion of continuity between indoors and out. To me, it just looked like a cheap imitation, even dead compared to vibrant life outside.

"Hm. Do you think we can do something about that?"

"About what?"

"The carpet."

"What about the carpet?"

"I mean, can we change it?"

"Why? It's great!"

"What do you mean? It's hideous, like a furry moss."

Jim went quiet, his face scrunched up, and took another sip of coffee.

"We just can't afford any change right now."

'Couldn't be all positive,' stated my disappointment.

'We're used to our mom's bright white, clean, crisp style. That's the city. This is the mountains. Different themes; different feel. Everything's going to be different,' assured my serenity.

"Maybe something we can remodel in the future," I conceded.

This didn't seem palatable to Jim. He looked a little irritated by the comment, and took another sip of coffee.

"Jehovah made this happen, Virginia. The timing of everything was amazing." His volume rose as he said this and continued to. "The congregational contributions needed for the mortgage down payment came in just in time so I could make the offer and the developer went for it…"

I cut him off, "And Praise God, Jim! I didn't mean to criticize the house. You know, most women like decorating. That's all." I didn't love the gender stereotype but knew he would appreciate the simplification.

Jim paused, considering this. The hue of his face was cooling.

Then, he agreed, "Amen," but didn't really reply to the rest of my explanation.

"Speaking of finances, I'm going to need you to contribute to the mortgage. That shouldn't be a problem, right, if you leave the dorm?"

"You want me to live here before we get married? What about the congregants with more traditional values and convictions? Won't they be upset by us shacking up?"

"We can keep it a secret, can't we?"

"I guess."

"So, can you move out of the dorm?"

"Well, I'll have to break the lease, and they'll fine me, but I can do that."

"Great!"

"Well, wait. There is a problem with this plan. How will I get back to campus for classes and work?"

"I'll drive you."

"To Kali, every morning?" I replied skeptically.

"Yes."

"Weren't you planning to start going to Parvati and Durga?" Those cities are way out of the way."

Jim had completed step one of his empire-building five-step plan. He had shared with me and the rest of the congregation that the second step would be setting up Bible studies in other college towns in New York, and he would first target Parvati or Durga.

I added, "You will also need to come pick me up too, and I work late evenings in the lab sometimes. That's a ton of driving and coordination, don't you think?

"It is, but building large organizations is hard work. Same is true for marriage," Jim charmed. "Plus, I won't head to Parvati and Durga every day. I still need to shepherd the flock at Nettie Maria Stevens University."

I agreed, and Jim helped me pack and move the next two days. We talked to the friends that normally visited us (Gina, Bobby, Dan, Alice, Nancy, Warren, Phoebe, and Wolfgang), and asked them to keep our cohabitation a secret.

"As far as you're concerned, I still live on campus," I told my friends.

Dan pursed his lips. I could tell he still had feelings for me but would respect my request.

"You bad girl," teased Gina.

"Certainly, worse than you," barbed Bobby, indicating that they still hadn't been intimate.

Changing the subject, she asked, "Do you need help moving?"

"Yes, please! I still remember how exceptional Dan was when he helped me move into the dorms Freshman year."

Dan smiled at this.

"Will you help me again?"

"Of course," he replied.

"We will too," Bobby conceded. "I mean, you're going to have Ninja Stix, right?"

Chapter 41: Bride

Two months later, it was finally our wedding day. Soon we could entertain whoever we wanted at our lovely home. No more sneaking around. It would feel good to finally make things official too. Love and commitment were enough for us, but marriage *is* important for honoring God.

"We are gathered here today in the sight of God and these witnesses to join together myself and Virginia Dare Goreman in holy matrimony; which is an honorable estate, instituted by God, since the first man and the first woman walked on the earth."

Jim explained to the crowd of witnesses, "Therefore; it is not to be entered into unadvisedly or lightly, but reverently and soberly. Into this holy estate we two people, present before you, come now to be joined. Therefore, if anyone can show just cause for why we may not be lawfully joined together, let them speak now or forever hold their peace."

The idea of Jim officiating our wedding seemed odd to me when he first proposed it. Jim was excited though about the idea. He was convinced it would make the ceremony more romantic with just the two of us on the stage. So, I decided not to argue. I didn't really see a practical issue. That is, until the rehearsal. Normally, the bride and groom gaze into each other's eyes. However, because he was officiating, the groom was busy addressing the congregation, only looking at me from time to time. It was therefore *less* romantic, *less* intimate, like we were having a conversation with a crowd.

After no one objected to our union, Jim continued, "Excellent. Then, Alice is going to read from the Holy Bible."

I was glad Alice was doing the reading; Alice, who had been with Jim since his first Bible study plant and a good friend to me since our baptisms, belted out, "A reading from the Apostle Paul, the first letter to the Corinthians, Chapter 13, verses 4 through 7: Love is patient, love is kind. It does not envy, it does not boast, it is not proud. It is not rude, it is not self-seeking,"

The words sounded preposterous coming from Alice's mouth. She would probably be front and center for the bouquet toss; step on some dresses to ground the competition before leaping for it. She was anything but patient and kind. Even now, she probably envied the fact that I was getting married to Jim and she was not. I wasn't worried about her though. That love scheming lioness would catch a man sooner or later.

She declared, "It is not easily angered, it keeps no record of wrongs. Love does not delight in evil but rejoices with the truth. It always protects, always trusts, always hopes, always perseveres."

I thought, 'These words sound overly ideal. I mean Jim and I got snippy, even bit each other's heads off a few times over stupid little things like closet space, who was making dinner, what we'd watch on TV, etc. Besides the inconsequential, the big thing that Jim failed to do was protect me from the abortion and brave the opinions of his congregants. We persevered though, and now we trusted each other and supported each other's hopes and dreams.'

"Let us pray for this man and woman as they make their marriage vows," finished Alice.

"Thank you, Alice. Let's bow our heads. Father, as Virginia and I pledge ourselves to each other, help us and bless us that our love may be pure, and our vows may be true. Through Jesus Christ our Lord, amen?"

And the congregation emphatically responded, "Amen!"

"Virginia, we have come together this day so that the Lord may seal and strengthen our love in the presence of His word and this community of family and friends and so, in the presence of this gathering, you and I will state our intentions: Have you come here freely and without reservation to give yourself to me in marriage?"

"I have," I answered, not loving the unequivocal statement. Of course, I had my reservations and doubts, who doesn't? Also, "giving myself to Jim" sounds too much like I'm a piece of property.

"I have also come freely and without reservation to give myself in marriage to you," Jim responded. The fair exchange muted my inner feminist alarms.

"Now we will exchange rings that we have selected for each other."

Wolfgang handed Jim my wedding ring. Gina, my esteemed maid of honor, handed me Jim's wedding ring.

"With this ring, I thee wed." Jim placed a golden band on my ring finger, the style nicely complemented the engagement ring.

I repeated, "With this ring, I thee wed," and placed the ring I had chosen on Jim's finger. I was pleased that his expression suggested appreciation for my selection.

"Now let's bow our heads as we pray. May Jesus Christ, Our Lord and Savior, always be at the center of our new lives we are starting to build together, that we may know the ways of true love and kindness. May the Lord bless us both all the days of our lives and fill us with His joy. Amen."

The congregants shouted, "Amen!"

Jim smiled and continued, "Those whom God has joined together, let no man put asunder. In so much as Virginia and I have consented together in holy wedlock, and have witnessed the same before God and this company, having given and pledged our faith, each to the other, and having declared the same by the giving and receiving of rings, I pronounce that we are now husband and wife."

Jim stepped forward, and pulled me in for a passionate kiss.

Hoots, hollers, woots and whistles followed.

Jim and I turned back toward the crowd. Wolfgang said, "Ladies and gentlemen, I present to you Mr. & Mrs. Marshall!"

A cacophony of excitement, clapping, and *September* by Earth, Wind & Fire ushered us from the podium through the crowd into the reception area where everyone gathered around us. That part seemed like it would be more fun during the rehearsal, but the process was too hurried.

We took some pictures together and with the wedding party while the cocktail hour started. Then, Jim and I made our grand entrance. Our first dance was to Debby Boone's, *You Light Up My Life*. Elon gave a welcome speech. We ate a delicious potluck dinner provided by the congregation. It was probably better than anything we could have catered. The admiration and fond memories shared in the toasts were uplifting.

Jim and I skipped the father-daughter and mother-son dances. It was hard, but I decided not to invite Milli since she hadn't tried to contact me since I started college. Jim said he appreciated what his foster parents had provided him but didn't care to keep or reignite those relationships by inviting them to their wedding.

As a proxy, Jim danced with one of his big financial supporters, a wise gray-head named Cynthia. Jim asked me to dance with another deep-pocketed elderly congregant named Pearly. I did, not loving the exploitation of our wedding, but understanding that these relationships were important to the success of the church.

Once that was over, I happily danced with my best friends, Gina, Bobby, and Dan. Their heartfelt congratulations meant so much to me. Bobby couldn't help but rib me.

"You look so *arresting* this evening, Mrs. Marshall. The name is like a badge of honor."

"Haha."

"Don't be a lame-o," chided Gina.

"I'm just saying. Also, Kung Food Pizza, do we still need to order or does Ninja Stix come with the Marshall arts?"

"Come on."

"It's your fault. I didn't think you'd take his name, Mz. Feminist."

"Well, I guess I've softened some of my convictions. I didn't tell you guys last semester because I didn't want to make you feel uncomfortable, but I took a class called *The Sociology and Psychology of Women*. The professor basically wanted us to believe that men were the root of all evil, and that women were systematically oppressed through institutions like marriages, children, families, religion, etc., but that's just not my story."

My friends' bodies continued to sway, bounce, and shimmy to the beat to keep the fun going, but their focus was locked on me, listening intently.

"I'm marrying one of the good guys. He and I are partners, and we're going to take on this world together. We're going to support each other in our dreams until they become realities. We're going to have beautiful children, a red headed girl, and a dirty blonde-haired boy. It's a fairytale in the making. So yes, we are the Marshalls."

"That's wonderful, Virginia, but it doesn't really answer my first question."

"What first question?"

"Do Ninja Stix come with your Marshall arts, or not?"

"You're ridiculous."

I found Jim and we proceeded to make the rounds and thank everyone for coming. It was absolutely exhausting. Much of the wedding after that felt like a blur. I remember cutting the cake and doing the bouquet and garter tosses, which were fun events. It was also sweet to sway with Jim to Frank Sinatra's *All My Tomorrows* for our last dance, and to race under sparklers for the grand exit to Jim's car. I liked the cheering.

From there, we drove about an hour to a hotel near Utica, where we gave each other the best performance we could in spite of our fatigue. It was probably a seven out of ten. Understandable, given the circumstances.

The next day, we proceeded to Niagara Falls for our week-long honeymoon, which thankfully, was very nice, relaxing, and passionate.

It was off season in early November. Fall season temperatures were consistently in the low 50's Fahrenheit during the peak of the day, calling for jackets and warm beverages in hand. We regularly embraced and cuddled, keeping each other warm. We saw all three of the falls, beginning with the elegant Bridal Veil Falls and ending with the grand Horseshoe Falls. I was grateful again to experience another remarkable view.

'Take that, inferiority,' barbed my cheerfulness, recalling the slight a couple months back about not really traveling.

'Oo, Niagara Falls. Aren't we the globe trotter now? Oh, wait, we've never been out of the eastern time zone,' countered my inferiority.

'Just let us enjoy our time,' said my satisfaction, trying to de-escalate the argument.

'Soak it up. We won't be doing much traveling while Jim's growing his diocese or while we're in graduate school.'

That was a bit of a depressing realization.

'What did you expect? We're not a journalist. We're not Milli,' continued my inferiority.

'Yes, but there's scientific conferences. I'll get to present my research,' I remembered.

'Not once we start having kids. We're barely going to have time to do experiments. The good news is that we don't have to worry about getting a passport.'

'We're stuck for a while. Just face it,' my misery chimed in.

'It's all about perspective. We can think of it as just a season. There will be other seasons for travel,' my contentment weighed in.

'As we put it so well at the wedding, let's make this a season of taking on the world together with Jim,' encouraged my optimism.

'We don't want to hear this, but we will be taking on less world in this season and taking off more diapers, many diapers,' complained overwhelmed.

'No, what we need to do is hurry up and get to the next level, become a professor to lead a lab of researchers,' barked my frustration. 'Then, we can use our brains and mouths to manage them and free our hands up to care for our kids.'

'Are we suggesting delaying kids?' asked my inadequacy.

'No, we just need to dig deep, get creative, collaborate to pass off the drudgery, anything to move faster than our contemporaries,' answered my confidence.

Chapter 42: Petty Arguments

"What's going on with the dishes? They're still dirty."

We couldn't afford a washer and dryer which made keeping clothes clean a tedious chore of mine. I washed and rinsed everything in the bathtub because there were usually dirty dishes in the sink. It was too cold outside for a drying line. So, I had to hang them by the fire, and I had to be careful not to block the TV. Jim needed it to relax at the end of the workday. We did have a dishwasher that came with the house though, which seemed to be a huge convenience for the first few months that we lived together. In the dorms, I had to hand wash dishes and dry them in a rack. Now it was leaving some kind of cloudy film on the dishes though.

"I don't know. I've been running the dishwasher like you showed me."

Jim opened the machine door and looked in.

"Well, there's the problem. Hell, Virginia!"

"What!"

"Do you see all that crust!"

"Yeah…"

"That's hard water build up!"

"Okay?"

"So, do you know what to do about that?"

I didn't want to admit it, but I didn't know what he was talking about. HARD Water was a vitamin-enriched beverage in my understanding, not something that caused white crust on the inside of your dishwasher.

"Wipe it down?"

"Yes! With baking soda, or ammonia is better. This isn't the city water you grew up with. It's well water which has extra minerals. Understand?"

I really didn't need one more chore. My plate was already full.

"Can't you do it? I mean, I do the dish washing."

"No, it's all the same thing," he said sternly.

"No, one is an operation. The other is maintenance. Home maintenance is more of a guy thing."

"It's not home maintenance. It's appliance maintenance. Don't be lazy! You're blessed to even have a machine to do most of your work for you!"

"Stop yelling at me! Take a chill pill!"

That was the safe phrase we decided on when one of us was getting out of our heads with anger.

Jim huffed out of the house into the backyard. He had taken to cutting wood to relieve stress when we fought. Good thing too because we needed lots of wood to warm the house and dry the clothes. What helped me sometimes cut through the anger and gain some humility was reading my Bible, but Jim seemed to get annoyed by this based on the looks he'd give me. He even said once, "I wish I had time for pleasure reading."

Later that day he apologized.

"I'm glad you are reading your Bible. It just feels like we're not doing things together."

"What do you mean?"

"I'm over here doing my stuff and you're over there doing yours."

"Well, do you want to do dishes or laundry with me?"

"I just wish we could have our chores done at the same time so we can do things together like we used to do; read our Bibles, books, watch TV, play games."

"I can't. Dishes are dirty after we eat dinner. The clothes need to be soaked in detergent before I rinse and hang them. If you helped me do some of these chores then maybe we could have some time to relax together."

"Why can't you just run the dishes in the morning before we leave?"

"Fine, but I would still need to unload them when we got home. Doesn't save any time."

"The point is that I'm trying to move things around so we have time together."

"It won't work."

"Humor me!" He yelled, frustrated.

"Not if you're going to yell at me!"

Jim threw his head up and clenched his fists. He breathed in deeply and blew out. Looked like he was just about ready to chop some wood. Instead, he stayed.

"Let's talk through this."

"Okay."

"What if you started soaking the clothing first, then prepped dinner and threw whatever into the oven, unloaded the dishes, finished washing the clothes and hanging them, and pulled the food out of the oven, just in time for dinner."

"Food prep takes too long."

"Well, what if you prepped all the food for the meals at the beginning of the week instead of prepping each meal every other day?"

"That doesn't really work. Vegetables would get wilty, soggy, lose their crisp, and brown if cut up ahead of time. Many meats develop odors..."

"Well, you could cook it ahead of time and then just reheat it in the oven."

"Do you really think cooking and reheating would be faster than just cooking once?"

"Yes!"

"No! If you want to save time, buy me a Crock-Pot and a Microwave!"

"I told you already! Those are hundreds of dollars! We can't afford it!"

Instead of walking to the back sliders toward the wood pile, he headed to the front door. I thought he was going to take off in the car. I saw him turn the corner though and walk to the garage through the kitchen window.

I didn't know what he was planning to do there. The only thing in the garage was the Snapper Lawn Mower he insisted on spending our money on, which was a significant portion of my college fund from my grandmother. Over a thousand dollars Jim spent because he had to ride. "There is no way I can push a lawn mower across all these acres," he said. More like, there was no way he could do that and watch TV every night.

When he came back in later, he still sounded frustrated when he promised, "We're going to have money soon and you'll be able to get all the appliances you need. I just need to expand the dioses."

"That would be great."

"How about instead: I believe in you, Jim! I know you can do it!"

"Is it you that's going to do it, Jim, or the Lord?"

Eyes narrowed, jaw and fists clenched, and teeth grinding, Jim walked away. Under his breath, he was muttering something like, "How dare she rebuke me…"

Chapter 43: Turning a Page

"Why do you need to go to campus on a Saturday?"

"Gina needs me."

"You spend enough time with your friends during the week. It's a Sabbath day for us to relax together."

"Don't give me that! We spend time with your friends on Saturdays! Can't you go see Wolfgang or one of your other friends while I talk to Gina?

"I could, but why can't you just talk to her on Monday?"

"It's a crisis! She needs her best friend," I explained sternly.

"What about after church on Sunday?" queried Jim.

"You're not listening to me!"

"Oh, I am! Just not copasetic about our Sabbath getting disrupted."

"Come on Jim! You're supposed to be a reverend! You sometimes need to pastor your flock at inconvenient times, right? Or do you just wait to visit them at a time that works for your schedule?"

"That's enough, Virginia. We're going to go. You don't need to question my pastoral quality."

"Good, can you get dressed and ready to go now?"

"What's wrong with what I'm wearing?"

"You look homeless."

"Excuse me?"

"You need to trim your beard, put on clothes without holes, and maybe take a shower."

"I was just planning on relaxing on a Saturday morning at my home!"

"And now we are going out, so fix yourself up, quickly please!"

"You're a mean little witch!"

"And you're a lazy pecker! I can just go without you! Give me the keys!"

"Fine! Take'em! They're on the dresser, witch."

"Keep calling me a witch and see what kind of rat tails and mouse brains end up in your dinner!"

"How about thanks for letting me use your car?"

I grabbed the keys, slipped on some shoes, and was out the door without reply. It took me a minute to get my bearings and get a feel for the clutch before hitting the gas and flying down our driveway. It had been a while since I'd driven Jim's car. He let me have some fun and open it up on the way to ice cream when we were dating. Nowadays, we got our kicks from increasingly aggressive actions in the bedroom - scratching, biting, smacking, choking, etc. It was an extension of our egotistical struggles for dominance.

Jim's 1971 Viking Blue Oldsmobile Cutlass was a muscle car with Colonnade styling, meaning it had a semi-fastback roofline, a wide C-pillar, and a more squared-off appearance relative to earlier models. Jim explained that the 7.5L Rocket V8 engine made it fast and the FE2 Suspension Package made it smooth. This time of year, we kept the convertible roof down, and the wind felt great through my hair. I blasted the radio as I sped down the back roads and highway.

I didn't really know what to think. Gina was crying when she called me, and she never cries. It had to be something really serious. She was mumbling something about Bobby, but couldn't get it out. The message I understood was, "I need you now."

Gina was half way through a box of cookies by the time I got to her. Her eyes were red and puffy from crying so much.

"He left," she lamented.

"Who left?" I asked.

"Bobby."

"Where?"

"He got a job in California and left without saying goodbye."

"What? Bobby did that?"

I was truly shocked that my goofy friend would do such a thing.

"Yeah."

"What's the story?" I inquired, wanting to better understand why. He had been obsessive about Gina. They seemed so good for each other. It didn't make sense.

Gina admitted, "Things got a bit strained between us."

"What do you mean?"

"You know that I was spending a lot of time at Bobby's apartment last semester."

"Yes."

"We spent many evenings kissing. Our passion increased, and one day he tried to put his hand up my skirt. I smacked him and he got upset. He knew my position and said we were too young to get married."

"Even though he knew I was getting married?" I asked.

"I said that to him, and his reply was that you had become a religious fool, and that even though you grew up in the city, you lacked street smarts."

The words felt like a knife in my gut.

'If Bobby is thinking that way and saying such things, Dan's probably heard it too,' reasoned my anxiety.

'Yeah, they talk all the time, but does Dan also think we are foolish?' asked my hurt.

'Dan wouldn't betray us,' assumed my loyalty.

'Why not? He's already been cynical about Jim and the GOLDS Church,' reminded my insecurity.

Memories of Dan flashed through my mind. Sometimes he looked at me with sad eyes, like when I told him I was dating Jim and when I got engaged. I just thought he was jealous. Maybe the sadness was more than that though.

'Maybe he's worried we are on the wrong spiritual road, the same way we worry for our non-Christian friends and family,' offered my optimism.

'Worry is not the same as judgment though,' noted my irritation. 'His position might have changed when we rejected his interest in more than being friends.'

'Yeah! Maybe after that, Dan lost his concern for our soul! Then, when Bobby spewed his poison, Dan lapped it up like a golden retriever,' barked my hostility.

'It's hard to imagine Dan disparaging us, but we can imagine him listening to Bobby and not rebuking him,' challenged my discerning.

'Silent betrayal is still betrayal,' decided my hate.

'What about Gina?' asked my hurt.

"What did you say when he said that to you?" I asked Gina.

"I said that you were on a journey, actively seeking truth, which is the opposite of foolish. A fool is someone who thinks they've arrived at the truth, is too busy with the lesser things, or unwilling to journey with the rest of us."

"Wow, that's deep Gina, and thank you."

"It's something my mom says sometimes. Don't mention it."

I flashed a smile and continued, "So, then what happened?"

"We kept spending time together in the evening, alone, behind closed doors, and even though I said no to his advances a number of times, he remained persistent."

"But you're a strong person. He didn't wear you down, did he?"

"No, but then he got creative. Bobby took me out to the Empty Orchestra Bar and sang karaoke. He sang Billy Joel's *Only the Good Die Young*, he made a show of singing to me, and a bunch of other people joined in. Do you know the song?"

"Yes."

"I mean the lyrics?"

"Yes."

I knew his songs from the radio.

"He changed *Come out, Virginia* to *Come out, Gina, don't let me wait.* That made me think of you and how much fun you and Jim were having."

'Oh, no! Did our decision to be with Jim influence Gina?' asked my anxiety.

"And with everyone singing, the peer pressure made me feel prudish!"

Gina started losing her composure again and murmuring.

"Then when he and the crowd sang - *You Catholic girls start much too late.* I felt conflicted about where I stood spiritually. I asked myself - I'm not really a Catholic. I don't really know what I am. Why am I trying to keep my virginity?"

Then, Gina started sobbing. I embarrassed her. "I'm so sorry, Gina," I sympathized and comforted her with pats and strokes on her back.

"At the end of the night, he asked me again, and I asked him what would stop him from just leaving me when he got what he wanted?"

"What did he say?"

"I love you. I'm not going anywhere. I made him swear. He did!" She erupted again, and I joined, feeling my best friend's pain and sorrow.

"That was months ago. Why did he leave?"

"I don't know! I mean we started having serious discussions about family. I wanted to have at least a few kids and raise them close to my mom in Arkansas. Bobby wasn't sure how many he wanted or where he wanted to raise them. He was sure he didn't want to settle down yet though. Said he wanted it to just be us for a while. I kept talking about kids knowing they would come sooner or later, and I think he got scared."

"Scared of what?"

"Responsibility."

The gravity of the moment weighed heavy. A page was turning in our lives. We gained independence from our parents entering college, had it for four quick years, and experienced freedom of choice and unhindered expressions of our personal wills. Having grown accustomed to this, losing independence was challenging. To be in a relationship with another meant living within the confines of agreement with someone else, compromising one's ideals, especially when they had drastically different ideas about long term plans.

We didn't hear from Bobby again the rest of the semester, and weren't sure how he finished his finals, if he was able to take them remotely or what. We don't think he even attended graduation. Gina, who had put all her eggs in his basket, couldn't see herself moving out of the college environment now. She reasoned that there was a larger pool of eligible bachelors there compared to smaller professional environments. Gina also didn't want to commit to years of graduate school, going down the same path toward professorship in academia as me and Dan. She would give herself two years to find someone at the University, working as a paid research technician in the laboratory she had been working in, and if it didn't work out, she'd go back to Arkansas to live and work near her mom.

My sweet best friend was wooed, used, and discarded. Bobby had stolen irreplaceable time and a sacred gift Gina had reserved for her husband. I wish I had rejected that selfish opportunist, traitor, manipulator, thief, and coward at Welcome Week.

Chapter 44: Souring Opinions

We had become very busy throughout the week. Saturdays, especially the mornings, were our time for catching up. Our common custom was for Jim to retrieve the newspaper from the box at the end of our driveway, which would take him about thirty-five minutes, and I'd cook breakfast and brew coffee. We would drink our coffee, eat our breakfast, read our newspaper on the front porch, look out at the mountains, and talk.

I had a couple of topics I wanted to discuss that morning. One I thought might be pleasant. The other I thought might start a fight. I decided to lead with the pleasant.

Jim really had impressive leadership skills. He made people want to help in his efforts, and he delegated tasks really well. Jim was very comfortable leading more clever people than himself and enabling them to do significant work on his behalf. I recognized that this was something I needed to work on if I was going to lead a lab someday. So, I asked him about the strategies he was using to grow the church.

"Missions is my key strategy for expanding GOLDS Church."

Missions is the sacrament of carrying out the command of Jesus to *go ye therefore, and make disciples of all the nations, baptizing them into the name of the Father and of the Son and of the Holy Spirit: teaching them to observe all things whatsoever I commanded you.* Melchizedek priests like Jim were in charge of organizing missions, providing the who, what, where, when. Rather than going to Parvati or Durga every day, Jim often sent the Levite priests two-by-two instead to these cities. They found Bible study members independently and followed up on leads that Jim provided. Their activities helped cultivate new grassroots, one thriving Bible study at both college campuses. The Levite priests involved in expanding the Kingdom benefited from raising their eternal status and wealth.

"It would be great if you got involved, since you're a Levite priestess *and my wife*," Jim emphasized.

'We didn't anticipate that argument rabbit hole,' conceded my irritation.

'Just compliment him. That's what you were trying to do anyway,' reminded my thankfulness.

"I appreciate you wanting me to be involved and think it's amazing what you are accomplishing, but I just don't have time."

A full year of graduate school had flown by like it was nothing. I was a machine, making hypotheses, testing from different angles, pursuing lines of inquiry to their termini, replicating findings, reading and writing. I felt as busy as the Arctic tern, those birds that migrate more than twelve thousand miles each year from the Arctic to Antarctic and back.

Jim sighed, disappointed at my answer.

"I'm watching you though, Jim, and I'm impressed by your delegation. My plan is to try to get Dr. Maddox to let me have some undergraduates to train and do the monotonous work for me."

"Virginia, don't just train them to do monotonous work. Do the professors do any lab work?"

"No."

"You want to be a professor, right? Train your students to do all your lab work. Promote yourself by filling up the levels under you until you are effectively a professor. Make it easy for your management to transition you into the role and then make your pitch for professorship."

"Well, it doesn't quite work that way. I have to prove myself scientifically by publishing articles in good journals and defending my Ph.D. thesis before I can be a research professor." Jim was about to cut me off, "…but I hear what you are saying! It's a great point!"

"Yes, leaders lead."

"Speaking of which. Tell me about what's going on in Parvati or Durga."

"The Levites tell me that they anticipate the next Bible study this coming Tuesday and Friday will have fifteen and twenty attendees, respectively. That's up three and four students from last week, or a twenty percent increase."

"And it looks like the students who have been attending are already contributing financially to the church."

"What do you mean?"

"I saw the envelope on the dresser after we got back home last Friday. Looked pretty full. I mean I didn't look inside. Just looked like an envelope full of money."

"Yeah. You're right. The new Bible studies have been generous." Jim agreed with a suspicious look.

"Everything okay?"

"Yeah, why wouldn't it be?"

"No, you just… Never mind. I also meant to say that I am grateful you delegate so well because then I can take your car to work a couple days a week without needing to coordinate with you." I smiled cheekily.

"Why all the compliments, Virginia?"

Somehow, I had made Jim wary.

"Well, you told me the other night that you felt like I used to honor you more before we got married. I prayed about it and realized that I used to praise you more. So, I thought about nice things I could honestly say, and that's what I came up with."

"Well, thank you. I think … Anything else?"

My problem was that I couldn't think of many other things. Since we got married, my opinions of Jim had soured with continual fights. We seemed to argue about everything and neither one of us were the type to back down. Also, without other houses and neighbors nearby to keep us in check, we would raise our volumes, screaming at each other to a degree that would have been impossible for others to ignore. I sometimes imagined that the surrounding wind-blown trees were rooting us on, pumping their woody fists and howling for more.

"I was hoping to serve you a slice here and there darling, not glutton you with a whole pie."

"Fair enough. Thank you again."

He was about to go back to reading the newspaper when I continued.

"Glad we agree on that. Something else I wanted to talk to you about was these recent purchases of carpentry equipment that you are filling our garage with. What is that for?"

"Carpentry."

"Okay, but why?"

"It's a side business to help support the growth of the church."

"Aren't you earning enough with the new Bible studies?"

"Maybe for slow growth, but I want multiplication."

"I thought your key strategy was missions? Seems like this would be a major distraction, no?"

"Jesus and the Apostles had work outside of their spiritual work - fishing, tent making, and carpentry."

"What about the expense? The garage is filled with what looks like several expensive pieces of equipment."

"Yes, there was a sizable upfront investment necessary to make furniture. One needs a table saw, miter saw, band saw, jointer, planer, drill press, router, lathe, belt sander, and other smaller tools. There's something I didn't need to pay for though, which is going to help that venture become profitable quickly!"

"What's that?"

"Look in front of you. What do you see?"

"Mountains."

"And."

"Sky."

"What's on the mountains?"

"Trees. Ah, you mean wood. You're going to use the wood from the trees? Can you do that?"

"Legally, the trees on my acres are my trees. If you're asking about if I can physically do it. Yes, Ken is going…"

My mind erupted.

"Ken, the man who hit me with his truck, is going to come here?!"

"Yeah. The past is the past. Under the bridge. And, as you mentioned, he has a truck. He also has some tree felling experience."

"Of course that redneck does," I responded bitterly.

"Well, it's more his piney side where he acquired that gifting, but it sounds like you still have animosity toward him."

"Jim, I was hospitalized for months, and was in recovery for over a year!"

"Does our Lord not say forgive others as I have forgiven you?"

"Not precisely, but…"

He cut me off. "Okay fine. Our Lord tells us to pray for Jehovah to *forgive us our debts, as we have also forgiven our debtors*."

"I can forgive him and still not want to see his face at my home! It's bad enough that I have to see him at church."

"It's not going to be often, but I need his help."

"Why didn't you talk to me about this?"

"I don't have to tell you about everything I'm doing."

"Is this not our home? Are we not a family making decisions about our present and future together?"

"It is your home, my house. We are a family, but I'm the head of the household. This isn't some two headed beast."

"Excuse me. During our marriage ceremony, right before we were joined, did we not pray that Jesus always be at the center of our new lives *we are starting to build together*, that we may know the ways of *true love and kindness*? How is unilateral decision-making *building together, love, or kindness*?

"What does this have to do with you, Virginia? This is about a side venture to support the church. You won't even participate in missions! No, I'm not going to include you in every decision I make."

"That's a Dung beetle's dream!"

"Is it? Well, are you going to start including me in every decision you make about your future in research and academia? Because honestly, I don't even want you to be doing that."

"Including you in every decision?" I asked, confused about what he meant.

"No, graduate school. It's delaying us having kids and I'm not getting any younger."

"What? I laid out my plan for you while we were dating! There's no surprises in my plan!"

"Except that we talked about trying to have kids once we were married. I mean we hardly have sex anymore!"

"And whose fault is that? I'm too busy being your cook; home, dishes, and clothing cleaner to have any time! Plus, all the fights don't really put me in the mood."

"Most of that work is done by the machines."

"Glad you brought that up. You just bought thousands, probably tens of thousands of dollars, in new carpentry equipment! You couldn't buy a washer and dryer?

Maybe I could find time for your needs if I wasn't hand washing and hanging clothing every evening!"

That was enough for Jim. He threw his newspaper down on the side table and stood up from his rocking chair. He walked away, murmuring as he headed toward the garage, or rather, the new woodworking shop.

Chapter 45: Crumbling Trust

"Why did you leave me here?"

'It was an egotistical power play!' my frustration answered for Jim.

"I thought you were just studying here today," he claimed, walking past me through the bedroom to the bathroom. I followed him.

"It's Thursday. I've always worked at the lab on Thursday since I started graduate school almost two years ago now. I couldn't even call to let them know that I wouldn't be there because you don't have a phone line out here yet!" I barked while he pulled his pants down and sat.

"Can we talk about this in a minute?"

"No! You don't have any problem asking me when dinner is going to be ready from the toilet."

"It's not the same, but I'm sorry, Virginia. It completely slipped my mind. I just wanted to get away after we had our argument earlier."

"About me not wanting to have morning sex?"

"Yeah. I'll try not to let it happen again. Also, I'll make sure we get a phone line in by the end of the month, at least pay for it. I can't control how long it takes for the phone company to hang the line."

'He stranded us! Let him have it! exclaimed my vengeance.

"If you ever desert me here again…"

"Come on, Virginia! It was an honest mistake. Trust me."

Trust was in short supply between us. I asked him one Saturday morning, a couple of months ago, if we could combine our bank accounts. My grandmother's generous college fund had dried up and graduate school pay was pretty meager. Meanwhile, I was still responsible for paying the equivalent of dorm rent, all of the grocery shopping, and filling up Jim's car each week with gas. My balance was declining month over month.

"You need to start couponing. No, we will be keeping our finances separate, and taking care of our divided responsibilities. Be glad you're not paying for the utility bills, taxes, and insurances."

After that, I stopped paying him what I was paying for dorm rent. For some reason he didn't seem to care. It seemed odd to me because he threatened not to let me use the car if I stopped filling up the tank.

To which I responded, "Would you rather take me to work every day?"

And he countered, "Nope, you can just stay home, like a good wife!"

This insult jarred a flashback to when Jim brought me to our new mountain home for the first time. It seemed like a nice getaway from the hustle and bustle of the world, being so far away from it, but I now felt isolated, even held captive.

Less than a month later, it happened again. Jim had left me at the house with no way to get to work. It felt like he was punishing me for not having sex and for arguing with him.

When he returned four hours later, I ran to the hallway by the entrance, got in his face and let the expletives fly.

Jim pushed me hard and I fell backward onto the floor. His eyes were wide. I could tell he was shocked by his actions.

As he reached down, I recoiled, not sure what Jim was doing. He pursued, caught my arms and picked me up, saying, "I'm sorry. I'm so sorry."

I was stunned, not really sure how to respond.

Jim hugged me, and explained, "It was a primal reaction. Please forgive me."

I felt entirely disarmed. I didn't know what to do. What he was saying seemed sincere. It could definitely have been a knee-jerk defensive reaction, nothing intentional.

Jim made sure that I didn't have any injuries and we let the chores go undone that evening. We knew this was a bad place for our marriage, and lamented the death of our youthful love and passion for each other. We prayed that Jehovah would help us better see the problems and change, see our sins and repent, and that our love would be resurrected.

Our marriage had many wounds. We imagined holes in its hands and a piercing in its side as if it were the resurrected Lord. Such markings remained after the resurrection, and helped us remember what happened. More importantly, we believed our resurrected love was now invincible, having been through the worst trials.

The month after that was a sweet time. We were more relaxed about chores, prayed together more, sang worship songs, and took several walks in the brightly-colored woods.

I was free to go to work without hassle, felt very well rested, and productive. One thing bothered me though. I saw Dan holding someone's hands up to his mouth and kissing them.

When the young woman left, I asked, "Who was that?"

"Jacquee. She's my girlfriend."

I had to remind myself that I was married and gave Dan up years ago.

"Congratulations!" I patted him on the shoulder. "What's she like?"

"She's very creative. She's studying figurative painting and her works emphasize the connections between emotions and physiology. I just love how passionate she is. I've never met someone who could be so happy. When Jacquee's sad, I don't like it, but I like that I can help make her happy again."

I wondered if Dan's description of Jacquee was relative to my personality and what other implications there might be. In any case, it sounded like they were good for each other.

"Very glad to hear that, Dan. Happy for you."

The goodness in Dan and Jacquee's relationship made me think of all the good happenings recently between me and Jim.

In fact, later that afternoon, Jim took me on an introductory tour of his woodshop. It was a nice surprise. I had stayed out for a whole year, but had seen wood go in and furniture come out. I was curious what went on inside, but because I knew the site of the expensive machinery would frustrate me, I stayed out. Now Jim was showing me how his lathe worked, putting the finishing touches on the singular leg of our new small circular dining table.

The table belonged in an old farmhouse, but I didn't want to ruin our argument-free streak. I just wished he had consulted me before making the table. Similarly, not having a washer or dryer while seeing the expensive equipment he had purchased without talking to me bothered me. On the other hand, the functioning equipment and the way Jim operated them were impressive. This led me to start looking into his woodshop from time to time to see him working. He never seemed to notice me watching him.

Ken came by about weekly to help Jim chop trees down and move wood into the shop. Jim told me the furniture being taken away in Ken's truck were sold pieces. With the good feelings and grace we had for each other during that time, I found it in myself to seek genuine forgiveness for Ken who I knew was a good, faithful friend to Jim. I also remembered that I had found many admirable things about him before the hit-and-run.

During church on Sunday, I stole a glance at Ken, considering how I might forgive him. He sat with the other Melchizedek priests on the stage behind Jim as he preached. Ken looked the same in many ways. He was still sporting a shaggy mullet, jeans, cowboy boots, and a sleeveless t-shirt that showed off his tattoos. However, he wasn't wearing his signature giant tinted sunglasses indoors. Their absence revealed tired ringed eyes. I could also see from the other side of the church, there were new wrinkles in his face, diminished muscle tone in his arms, and he looked a little heavier in the midsection. Ken had certainly aged faster than his years, maybe because of the jail time or maybe because of the guilt and shame he felt for committing the hit-and-run and fleeing for months. Maybe it was petty, but it felt like cosmic justice that I, the victim, would be in better physical condition after the hit-and-run, save my scars, and that he, the assailant, would look much worse.

To repent of my unforgiveness, I decided to make some lemonade and bring it out to Ken and Jim in the woodshop one evening. As I walked in from the side door announcing, "How would you two like some tasty homemade lemonade?" I glimpsed Ken placing a pile of plastic bags containing round, white disks into the hollow of a wooden leg.

Jim stepped between me and Ken and took the tray I was carrying. "Thank you, Sweetheart! I'll take this. Very nice of you. We are a little busy right now."

"What are those bags?" I tried getting around Jim to point at them, but he moved to continue blocking my vision.

"As I was saying. We are a little busy right now, but how about we all drink a beer together later."

"Jim, what are you trying to hide from me? Or, I should say, what have you been hiding from me?"

"It doesn't concern you, Virginia."

"It certainly does if it's happening here and is illegal!"

"Calm down. It's just a misunderstanding. We will clear everything up later, but right now we are trying to meet a deadline. Please, can we delay this conversation for a couple of hours?"

"Fine, Mr. Marshall, but I had better not find out that you are up to no good!"

"Yes, Mrs. Marshall," he mocked as I left.

Ken left a couple of hours later, not bothering to stay for the beer.

"He wanted to stay but really needed to get the shipments for those orders completed."

"What are you involved in?" I asked Jim.

"I sell pills at Paradise 54. Not me actually, but some of the church congregants."

"Drugs? You're selling drugs?"

"Well, no. Ludes are not illegal. They are just a way for people to have more fun at a disco."

"If they're not illegal, why are you so secretive about them then?"

"Perception, Virginia. Perception is everything. We go to clubs and make great spiritual connections sometimes. The problem is that people believe we are in a place of sin, with fornicators and homosexuals. It's kind of like how some people would get offended if they knew we were living together before marriage. I mean, we used to go together. You know what it's like. What do you think Cynthia or Pearly would think?"

"So, you've got some congregants helping you sell, what did you call them?"

"Ludes."

"And you've got other one's you are hiding the sales from?"

"Yes."

"And why are you selling ludes?"

"I mean, besides helping people at the disco have more fun, lude sales help pay for church and ministry expenses. We can't broadly herald what we are doing at the disco because of associated stigmas, but there's been some good spiritual fruit. We are winning hearts and minds for Jehovah."

Suddenly I remembered Harris commending Jim. Harris had graduated and left to work in hospitality in New York City. We didn't really get to know each other very well, but I remembered him welcoming me to church the first day I came to Bible study. He told me that he really respected Jim, that Jim was "more than a preacher man" and that Jim taught him "a lot about God and how to run an enterprise."

I wanted to believe Jim, but something was off about his story.

Putting on a disarming expression, I complimented Jim, "Wow. Way to get creative, and look at you, boldly going where no reverend has gone before!"

I asked with as much naivete as I could muster, "Where do the ludes come from?"

"They are imported from South Africa."

"Oh! So now you're an international businessman!" I drawled, and then lured with, "Is transport expensive? Why not just get them here in the United States?"

Jim smiled. "Can't, you need a prescription."

Hook line and sinker. "If you get them from South Africa and they are prescription drugs here in the U.S., how are you not running into illegalities with regulations related to trade, patents, and distribution?" Mom taught me some things about drugs when she covered the enactment of the Drug Abuse Control Amendments in 1965.

"Virginia, ..." he looked nervous. "I'm not part of the manufacturing or import side. Neither do I personally distribute. Nothing I do is illegal."

"But you recruit and manage..." I started.

Jim cut me off, "My affiliates would likely be selling these or something else in the disco whether I was involved or not."

"Aren't you curious why these drugs require a prescription?" I asked.

"No," he responded.

"It's probably because they are super addictive, right?" I suggested.

"These were actually created to replace the addictive barbiturates. If they weren't selling the legal ludes, they'd be selling the illegal barbs because that's what everyone in the disco would want," he insisted.

"They might not be illegal to possess, but you know they are illegal to sell," I rallied.

He brushed it off, "It's not a big deal."

I countered, getting to the heart of my concern. "Doesn't the Apostle Paul say in Romans 13 to let every person be subject to the governing authorities, and whoever resists the authorities resists God and will incur judgment?"

He looked me in the eyes and said, "I think you are paraphrasing, but yes, he does, and we obey man's law as long as it doesn't prevent us from obeying God's law. What we are doing is important for advancing the Gospel!" he emphasized, turned away, and started walking toward the back sliders.

I didn't let it go. "You're saying profiting from illegal drug sales advances the Gospel?"

He looked back glaring, "No. Connecting with people at the disco and helping them have more fun helps create relationships, leading to conversations that lead to advancing the Gospel." Jim shut the slider and headed to the wood chopping pile.

Trust was gone between us. Jim was hiding things from me. It made sense now why he didn't want to unite our accounts; being involved in drug sales.

'Is drug money how he was able to afford all of the woodshop equipment?' asked my pensiveness.

'Maybe, but why couldn't he buy the washer and dryer too?' responded my jealousy.

'Because the money is funding the ministry and the church,' scoffed my irritation.

'I don't believe it,' sneered my skepticism. 'He probably has a loan for all the equipment and owes creditors. That, plus paying for the mortgage, renting the church … he's probably underwater.'

'Yup, he's probably working toward profitability on his investment,' confirmed my discernment.

'The problem is more about him keeping us in the dark!' exclaimed my hurt.

'No, the problem is he is involved in drug sales,' challenged my serenity.

'Those are problems but the greatest problem is that we have been and are continuing to be controlled,' claimed my discernment.

'What do we mean?' clamored my surprise, bewilderment, and anger.

'We know what Jim is capable of now. Recall what has happened with his church and our involvement. Have we not been a cash cow for Jim? His attendance on Sundays doubled after people heard he and his congregation were caring for us after the hit-and-run and organizing the medical bills campaigns. Still more joined when they celebrated our literature review publication. Advertising his church to the whole university and beyond in connection with our saga really paid off for Jim. It is unlikely all the money raised was used to pay our medical bills or went into the benevolence funding bucket; most probably went to pay his debts. The insurance money he urged us to claim probably also went to his debts. The money we were paying for rent was helping with his debts. He's been using us.'

'Not to mention manipulating us into getting an abortion so there wouldn't be stigma leading to financial issues with church congregants,' recalled my shame.

'He's a control freak! He officiated his own wedding!' added my anger.

'What are we going to do though?' asked my responsiveness.

'Yes, what will we do?' seconded my vengeance.

'We know just what to do,' answered my power.

Chapter 46: Reclaiming Control

I didn't lose any sleep over the news. In fact, it was one of the best night's sleep I can remember.

It was a Saturday, and Jim was supposed to go get our newspaper, except he was looking at me in bed with an expression of concern, or maybe remorse.

"What is it, Jim?" I queried.

"Are we okay?"

I smirked. 'The dead dog wants a get-out-of-jail-free card,' explained my amusement.

"No, Jim. We are definitely not okay."

He looked at me nervously with furtive glances and then averted his gaze.

"You weren't supposed to find out. I was trying to protect you from it."

"From the drugs? Okay, maybe." I conceded. "Now that I know what you're doing, how much do you owe your lenders?"

Jim looked surprised that I put two and two together. Then, he responded soberly, "eighteen hundred per month."

"Wow!"

"Yeah, but I'll be at twelve hundred per month after just four more payments."

"Make that five, or six, more payments."

"What?" Jim asked, confused.

"Five or six more because you're going to ask for more money to pay for my washer and dryer."

"No. Why should I do that?"

"You should have done it back when you took the big loan for the woodworking equipment. Then, I would have saved oodles of time doing laundry!"

"You've managed."

"I shouldn't have had to!"

"They're your…"

"Silence!"

Jim stopped talking and waited for me, but glared at me with contempt.

"There are going to be some changes around here or I'm going to leave you and report you, Jim."

"Virginia," he pleaded, face contorting to fear and sorrow. "This was all meant to help us. We're going to be rolling in a pile of cash. I just need time to pay off this debt."

"No, you're part of an illegal enterprise, and we will be doing nothing together, certainly not rolling in a pile of cash."

"Virginia!" He bellowed desperately.

"Indeed, we will be doing nothing together unless you meet my demands."

Jim looked at me curiously.

I could have easily used the illegal drug activities as an excuse to get out of this marriage. However, I didn't want to. Part of me still loved my golden man. I still remembered the first time I laid eyes on him and wanted him. I still appreciated him taking the time to answer my questions about spirituality and the Bible. I still remember him tending to me in and out of the hospital after the hit-and-run., and all the fun we had dancing in the discos. We had been through so much and I still imagined a future with him and at least two children. First though, we needed to fix some things.

"I'm going to help you, Jim. You're not going to like it, but I'm going to help you get out of this sinful enterprise you're in."

"I'm listening."

"First thing you are going to do is take on more debt and buy me a washer and dryer."

"I'm not going to…"

"Jim, this is non-negotiable. Either you comply or you're up a gum tree."

"Okay, what else?"

"We are going to fold clothes together while we watch TV."

"How am I supposed to do both at the same time?"

"Trust me, it's not hard. Third, you will never leave me at the house without the car again, unless I have explicitly said that it's okay."

"Fine."

"Fourth, you are going to completely stop being involved and profiting from the drug activities."

He looked at me shocked, mouth open.

"...In six months. I'm giving you ample time to pay off your debt and make arrangements for a clean exit, but you need to get uninvolved, completely break away from it. That includes not doing anything at Paradise or any other discos. The enterprise is unholy and even though people at discos might have a better time when they're high, giving people drugs is supporting their addictions. It's also putting your church and reputation in jeopardy, and my professional future at risk as well. So, you're going to need to stop."

"Is that everything?"

"No. With the extra time that I have from not having to hand wash clothes, we are going to get busy making babies."

"Babies? You want to have children with me?"

"Yes, I do. I still believe in you Jim; your plans to expand the church, your furniture venture, and most importantly, I still believe in us. I don't believe you need a drug enterprise and I also won't be your stay-at-home wife and mother. No, I'm going to help support this family with a second income and we are going to take care of our kids together with the help of daycare and other church friends."

He smiled and said, "Are you saying we are going to have sex every day?"

I chuckled, "Is that all you got out of that?"

"What else was there? No, I'm just kidding. That is a good plan."

"Good! I'm glad you feel that way, and the answer to your question is no, that means sex like every other day. On the off days, you will be updating me on your progress toward exiting the drug business, okay?"

"Yes. Thank you, Virginia."

"You're welcome."

Jim's compliance felt like a real victory for our family. With the changes I had outlined, we were in a much better place in just a couple of months, and we got busy trying to get pregnant. We didn't have to wait long though. We were pleasantly surprised with positive test results just two months after we started trying. In fact, Jim was strutting like a peacock. I had actually been nervous because I thought maybe the abortion might have damaged my reproductive organs, preventing me from having any children or at least reducing the chances of implantation and increasing our wait.

Here I was though, definitely pregnant and very happy. Don't get me wrong, I felt nauseous, tired, and I had to urinate a lot, all of which did not help me advance my research. However, I felt great love for the baby growing inside of me.

Time ticked by and I shared with Jim that the eight-week check-up looked good. The baby's heart rate was normal. With that news, Jim started nesting. He built a crib, rocking chair, changing table, and a high chair in the woodshop. The crib, rocking chair, and high chair went upstairs in the finished attic bedroom to save space since we wouldn't need them for a while. The changing table was a little too big to make it up the stairs. So, we left it in the living room.

Just after the first trimester, Jim started urging me to stay home and rest. He and some of the congregants were under the impression that the baby and I were extremely fragile, and that strain on my pelvis and uterus should be reduced as much as possible. They wanted me resting in bed to help with blood circulation and to avoid complications with high blood pressure and preeclampsia. "Normal physical activity could cause preterm labor!" I was warned by some of the congregants. "Lots of health benefits with bed rest!" I mostly just continued on as normal, remembering the vigorous work schedule Milli told me she had while pregnant with me.

On a couple of occasions, I did give into the urgings of Jim and the concerned congregants. Each time, I invited Gina over to the house to gab, relax, and eat for two. She came in her Dark Jade Pinto sporting an "I heart NY" plate on the front. She said the colors reminded her of the Italian flag and the good parts of the old neighborhood. Learning to drive was something she decided to do with her extra time as a bachelorette.

Even though I took some days off, it wasn't enough for Jim. We had several arguments about my continuing to go in and work long days. I could not stay in bed if I wanted to generate enough data to publish, and my committee wouldn't let me defend my Ph.D. thesis without peer-reviewed published studies. Despite our agreement, Jim left a couple of times early from home so I couldn't get a ride with him to campus. I was shocked at his boldness, that he wasn't afraid I would report him to the police and leave him. He had taken advantage of my love and mercy. Thankfully, the phone line finally was installed. So, the second time he did this, rather than call in my absence, I called a taxi cab to go into work. My tactic achieved the desired outcome. Hating the extra expense for the long taxi ride, Jim stopped leaving me at the house.

The other thing that was building more tension was that I stopped having sex with Jim again. At least we had sex a lot less frequently. I was rarely in the mood, partially because of hormones, I think. However, the bigger issue was feeling stressed about my Ph.D. I was not progressing nearly as fast as I wanted to because of the pregnancy related tiredness, as well as Jim's restrictions and arguments.

Anger percolated until it finally came to a boil. We started fighting just as fiercely as we had been the first year of our marriage, and worse. There was a lot of cussing, screaming, and hitting. No one got badly hurt, but new lines were crossed, seemingly with each subsequent fight. Dishes were thrown, holes were put into walls, and the bedroom door was broken down. We pushed, smacked, and punched each other, never in the face though so bruises were easily hidden. Neither of us wanted to seek help. I didn't have time and Jim was afraid of how it might hurt his image as a pastor. So, we just kept fighting, neither of us giving ground, both arguing passionately for what we thought was best.

I wanted to complete my Ph.D. as proof that I could accomplish something great in science. Stopping my program wasn't an option. Research funding is only awarded for a certain time period and funding agencies require milestone progress reports. Limited or lack of progress is grounds for taking the funding back and giving it to some other worthy pursuit. I told Jim that if I couldn't complete my Ph.D. on time, they would likely confer a Master's degree. It's called Mastering out, and it doesn't require a qualifying exam, to publish anything, make a thesis, or defend that thesis. Basically, it's doing a couple of extra years of classes beyond your undergraduate classes. Mastering out would be a failure to me. Telling Jim about the option was a big mistake because it just made him go on and on about compromising for the sake of the family.

Jim originally claimed that he was concerned about the health of our baby, but revealed in our arguments that what he really wanted was a "pastor's wife".

"You need to submit to my headship and let me lead the family!"

"I'm trying to help you! Your plans are illegal…"

Jim cut me off. "No, I'm stopping…"

"Really?"

"Really."

"Then why is Ken coming so much more frequently and picking up so much more furniture?"

"I'm making the most of my time, but I'm going to stop."

I looked at him skeptically.

"What I want... What I've been saying is that I want your help in growing the church. I need your steady support as my wife."

"I am. I'm working toward creating a second income for our family."

"No, I need you here, at home, now to take care of yourself while you're pregnant, but in the near future, I need you to take care of our child, the house, chores..."

"No!"

"Yes! I need your help in hosting meals for congregants, baking pies for fundraisers and other church events, sending out letters to thank congregants for their donations, scheduling funerals, weddings and other events."

"No! That's nothing remotely close to my life goals, Jim!"

It made no sense to me. I had shared with Jim many times from the beginning what my passions and dreams were.

"Sometimes you have to compromise, even sacrifice your dreams for the good of the family."

My blood was boiling. I stood up from my chair to square up with him and began gesticulating.

"And what are you sacrificing, Jim?"

Jim, remaining seated, rattled off with high volume and some irritation, "Delays in rapid growth! It's going to be a long tedious slog for me to grow the church without my disco ministry. I won't be able to impact nearly as many lives as I wanted to..."

'The diluted nut case is calling his drug distribution a "disco ministry",' my sarcasm noted with hostility.

'Is Jim really so thick though?' asked my bewilderment.

I cut him off, annoyed. "Jim, why don't you understand? I'm going to contribute financially to our expenses with my income! And my salary as a professor will be much higher than what I'm making as a graduate student!"

He immediately responded, "Listen to me, Virginia! It will be peanuts compared to what I have brought in and would continue to bring if I continued doing the disco ministry."

I was taken aback. I actually had no idea how much Jim was making in drug sales. My assumption was that he was maybe doubling his meager pastoral income.

Jim spoke in a calmer tone, "You're worth far more to me keeping our rugrats healthy and happy than forcing me to split my productivity so you can mess around with lab rats and earn a normal wage."

I didn't believe what I was hearing.

My voice modulated with his, and I sat back down. "Are you saying that me making twenty thousand dollars a year wouldn't be helpful for our family's finances? You would rather me stay home?"

"Yes."

Jim blew my mind. His earnest response made me believe that he was indeed making significant money from drug distribution, bringing in five times his income, ten times income, maybe more. That wouldn't be the case though when he stopped. 'Why wouldn't he want our income after he stopped distributing drugs?' asked my confusion.

"When you're not doing the disco ministry, as you put it, you won't be earning nearly as much. Wouldn't a dual income be better in that case?"

"I already said, no." He was stifling irritation, "With your help managing the children and helping me in other ways, I'll be able to build other wealth tributaries."

"That's not what we talked about before we got married."

"Situations change. Better opportunities present themselves. We need to seize the day. Work together for the betterment of our family."

"If I were earning way more than you, would you just give up your dream of building GOLDS Church?"

"That's different."

"How?" I barked.

"It's a calling. It's not just a career!" he justified, "Don't get me wrong, I like what I do and want to do it. The big difference though between our vocations is that God called me to be a reverend. You just *want* to be a scientist."

Jim's simplification made me feel insecure. I wasn't sure if I had a leg to stand on spiritually for my goals. Being a scientist was something I wanted, not a calling. Then, my emotions chimed in.

'It's more than *just want*! There is a passion inside of us,' responded my pride.

'It's a bridge back to our mother!' reminded my hopefulness.

'Yes, and *by succeeding* we will provide a contributing example of success for women who want to be scientists,' affirmed my pride.

'That would also make Milli proud!' added my respect.

'Don't forget the big picture! If we are successful...' began my excitement.

'And we will be successful!' heralded my confidence.

'... we will help numerous families overcome issues with fertility!' reminded my excitement.

'Yes, maybe God didn't *call* us to be a scientist, but that doesn't mean He didn't create us to be one, that He didn't guide us down this path,' rallied my energy.

'Yeah!' agreed my many emotions.

'Maybe God didn't *call* us but He still wants us to use our talents, not bury them!' spurred my energy.

'Yeah!' cheered my emotions.

Jim's work in directing people to God and Heaven is important for many. It was important for me, and I am grateful, but I couldn't help him the way he needed. My dream was important for many people too and it was important for me.

I said to Jim remorsefully, "I'm not who you're looking for."

Chapter 47: Hemmed In

I didn't just leave. Finally seeing, and acknowledging, that we weren't aligned with our dreams and plans was not enough of a justification to do that, not biblically, but I felt like I had been tricked and wanted to go. When Jim didn't stop the drug distribution on the due date I gave him, that still wasn't a reason for divorce.

It had been a month since I had spent time with Gina. She said I could sleep over if I wanted to. I convinced Jim by explaining drive time savings. He wouldn't have to pick me up that evening on campus or drop me back off the next day. I was so excited. We hadn't done this since the Ocracoke days. But it was a bittersweet feeling because what I really wanted to tell her was that I wanted to divorce Jim.

Of course we got Ninja Stix. We couldn't relive the glory days without them. Halfway through the Gore sauce, I told her.

"I've been thinking about divorcing Jim," I blurted and immediately started crying.

"Oh, honey! Come here." Gina hugged me, patting and rubbing my back.

"I... I ..." It was hard getting the words out. I was losing my breath.

"Take your time."

I gave up and just released everything leaving a puddle on her shoulder, and probably made her deaf from my wailing.

When I finally stopped heaving, she asked, "What happened?"

I needed to open up about my struggles. "Jim and I have been fighting since we got married about a lot of stupid little stuff. It's made the day-to-day miserable and sucked the romance out of our relationship."

"Is that why you want to divorce him?"

"That's part of the reason." More tears streamed down my face but I held it together. "He's selling drugs."

"The reverend is selling drugs? What the Hell?"

"Well, technically he's distributing drugs to church congregants, who then sell them."

"Where? How?"

"He gets pills from South America, and uses furniture operations as a front. His dealers sell at the discos and probably other places." In talking to Gina, I actually just realized that the sellers probably do sell at other places besides the discos.

"That's some mafia stuff right there."

"Well, I'm worried that the criminality is going to catch up with us and that there will be major legal consequences for our family to face. Could be when our child is months old, could be when she is two…"

"She? Oh my God! That is so wonderful!" Gina gave me a huge hug.

I didn't mean to let it slip, but was glad Gina was the first to find out.

"Yeah, I finally decided to take the gender test. I just couldn't wait."

"Are you super happy?"

"Yeah! Not that a boy wouldn't have been great, but since it was just me and my mom when I was a kid, it feels like a chance to relive the good and fix the bad parts."

"I totally get it, and you're right, criminality will catch up. So, what's stopping you from divorcing Jim?"

I do not want to just give up. I loved this man, invested a lot in our relationship, and we have a child coming. What God will think about me divorcing Jim is also very important to me.

"Love, all our history, the children, and the Bible."

"What do you mean, the Bible?"

"I couldn't find any verses that would indicate criminal activity as a justification for divorce."

"What if you just separate?" Gina ripped her Ninja Stix in half and dipped one of the pieces in Gore sauce.

"Separate?"

"Yeah, separate. Catholics have been doing it since the Middle Ages."

Gina took a bite.

"What is that?"

"Officially, you're supposed to talk with a priest, but you're not Catholic, and your husband is the reverend. So, I think you can just leave."

The intense reality of being out on my own with a baby was intimidating.

'Your mother did it,' reminded my security.

"You can leave," repeated Gina, "...and your marriage bond stays intact, no sins committed." She continued eating.

"That's not a bad idea."

'No, it's a big relief!' exclaimed my anxiety.

I ripped off a piece and dipped it. The new option made me feel a little lighter. My mind chewed on the idea while my mouth chewed the Ninja Stix. The scenarios running through my brain were anything but optimal, but they were better than staying.

"Not that I'm saying you should do this, but the Catholics also have this thing called annulment," Gina added.

"What's that?" I asked.

"It's invalidating the marriage."

'Invalid was something that happened to a coupon when it expired. How did a marriage become invalid?' asked my curiosity.

"Can you explain more?"

"Um, like the marriage is proven not to be legitimate from the beginning."

"Why?"

"It's a loophole the Catholics came up with because there are so few legitimate reasons for divorce. Plus, it simultaneously takes care of the issue of marriage eligibility. Divorce is one thing, but remarriage, as I'm sure you looked into, also has its own requirements."

That actually wasn't something I had considered. I mean I wasn't really thinking about my romantic future. My mom had shown me that men were unnecessary. I could just push forward without Jim. I had only imagined life *without* him, not life *with* Brad, Ben, Bill, Bob, or Burt.

"I thought if you're divorced then you're automatically eligible."

"I couldn't tell you the Bible verses, Virginia, but my understanding is that the marriage covenant is permanent until either death or in the situation when an *unbelieving* spouse..." she emphasized, "...abandons the believing spouse. Divorce alone is not a justification for remarriage. That's why mama always told me to choose wisely. Maybe I'm too picky though."

Gina looked sad and I knew who she was thinking of.

"Gina, you couldn't have known Bobby was going to abandon you."

"Speaking of unbelievers… It wouldn't have worked anyway. I was a fool to stay with him so long."

"Come on. Don't be so hard on yourself. At least you didn't marry him."

"Mamma Mia!" Gina smirked at my self-deprecation and we ate some more Ninja Stix.

Part of me was curious about what the Catholic church believed were reasons for annulment, but another part of me was hopeful for reconciliation. If Jim and I separated, I imagined that things could get really bad for him. Congregants would stop seeing me coming to church but still see me on campus. Sooner or later, it would come out that we were separated, probably when Jim could no longer claim that I was staying home with the baby. If he kept up with his drug ventures, he'd get caught. Hopefully, in prison, he'd be rehabilitated. I'd visit him with our child and he'd realize God's blessing in us. When Jim got out, hopefully in a couple of years with good behavior, we could rebuild our lives into something beautiful, honest, and strong.

Our conversation lightened into more amusing banter the rest of the evening and I slept so well. Gina had once again proven herself to be my very best friend.

With separation as a new tool, available for protection of my daughter now and a longview for restoration of my family, I began challenging Jim. Initially, I warned him subtly that I couldn't stay associated with him if he continued distributing drugs. Then, I explained that I wasn't going to put myself or our child at risk of law enforcement chaos and consequences as a result of his criminality. His responses became more defensive with each argument.

"If you're just going to focus on graduate school and your career, Virginia, then you don't really care about this family! Why then, should I let you boss me around and tell me what I can and can't do?"

"What you're doing is illegal!"

"Mind your own business and I'll mind mine! You've got plenty to figure out with childcare since you don't plan to watch your own. No need to concern yourself in my affairs," he guilted sternly.

That was enough.

"I want to get separated, Jim."

This took Jim aback. "What do you mean? Like divorce?"

"It's not a legal event. I want to move out, stop living here."

"Until when?"

"Until you stop putting our family at risk for the sake of money."

"Virginia. We just need to calm down."

"No. That's not the only problem. You want a traditional pastor's wife, and I don't want to be that, never wanted to be that, and never will."

"Well, why did you accept my engagement proposal?"

"I didn't. I mean I did, but with the understanding that the support, passion and fun we shared was something that would continue. I had always told you what I wanted to do with my life, the career I wanted to pursue. I imagined that you would be good at being a pastor, I would be good at being a scientist, and both of us would be good together at parenting, sharing the responsibilities together. There was no communicated expectation that I would need to give up my dreams to support yours."

"It's a fact of our society. You can't be a good mom and a good wife and a good professional. Maybe two out of three, but something has to give. Your own mother was an example."

He wasn't wrong about my mother. While strong professionally, even in the absence of being a wife, there were glaring weaknesses in her motherhood.

"...Just like I can't simultaneously be good at being a dad, husband, and pastor. At least not without support. It's impossible to pastor a flock, keep this early momentum going with giving, hire and train staff, and then create sustainability and growth in the organization."

I didn't know what to say. We were going back through the same tired arguments.

He continued, "This needs to take priority, but once the attendance is high and support staff is in place, I don't see why you couldn't go back to doing science, at least part time."

This concession was new but insulting.

"Part-time?"

"Yeah, at least a couple of days a week."

My face must have looked shattered, a myriad of emotions all vying for supremacy. Who would win? Distance, sarcasm, frustration, jealousy, irritation, skepticism, bewilderment, discouragement, insignificance, remorse, stupidity, isolation... who would come out?

Then I had an existential experience of looking at myself, but it wasn't me. It was a different version of me and I was in the post-war Baby-Boomer quintessential 1950s suburbia with my husband Ozzie and our kids David and Rick. I reeled it in and recalibrated. 'That's not what I want. No, I'm a woman, in the prime of my life, a scientist, and it's 1980.'

"Jim, you might need me, but I don't need you," I said and started walking to the kitchen.

"What are you doing?"

I didn't respond; just pulled the phone off of the wall receiver and dialed the same taxi number I used before when he had previously stranded me at the house.

Jim came into the kitchen, ripped the phone out of my hand, and hung it up before anyone answered.

"Are you going to drive me?"

"No. Where would you even go?"

"Anywhere! Wherever I want!"

I walked around Jim, out of the kitchen and into the bedroom. Eventually, I would be able to call a taxi. He couldn't monitor me forever. I wanted to have a bag packed and ready to go. I closed and locked the bedroom door. Then, I locked the adjoining bathroom door which also connects with the living room. I pulled the suitcase out from under the bed and plopped it on top, and started opening drawers and packing clothes.

Jim spoke through the door, "I'm not going to let you do this."

While I was packing, I heard him slide something on the carpet and move it against the bedroom door. A similar sound followed a couple of minutes later. When I was done packing, I opened the door which hinged into the room and saw that Jim had moved the changing table in front of our bedroom door. Similarly, I found the bathroom doorway blocked by the crib.

Normally, I'd have no problem with just climbing over, but at thirty weeks pregnant, it would have been a truly miraculous feat.

"I'm not letting you leave me," he said looking at me from the other side of the changing table.

'He's trying to control us again!' yelled my irritation.

"You have no choice!" I barked.

'Tell him it's just separation,' urged my respectfulness.

'Don't give into our anger,' pleaded my relaxation.

'We need to keep our stress level down. We're pregnant,' reminded my carefulness.

Jim didn't respond.

"Look, Jim. I'm not talking about divorce, just separation."

"Sounds like the first step toward divorce."

"Er!" I gave the changing table a brief frustrated push and it teetered.

'The bastard won't let us out. Threaten him!' demanded my aggression.

"You know, no-fault divorce was just signed into law earlier this year. If you're unwilling to talk about separation with me, then you'd better get ready to argue with the State of New York. I can divorce you without any burden of proof. While we might still be married in the eyes of God, I can be legally divorced, no problem. How's that sound?"

No response.

I started pushing on the changing table which was met with resistance from Jim who was leaning against it on the other side.

"Virginia, this isn't good for you and it's late. Just get some rest and we can talk more in the morning," he urged.

"Do you want any custody rights and visitation? Hm? If you do, you'd better let me the hell out of this room or I will say you are physically abusive and the courts will deny you time with your child!"

Again, no answer.

"Let! Me! Go!" I grunted, continuing to push on the changing table. I felt it move a little bit, which was encouraging, but Jim immediately pushed it back against the doorframe.

"No! You won't get through. Just quit," Jim discouraged.

'We need to move Jim off of the changing table if we hope to push it out of our way,' reasoned my power.

So, I said, "Fine, I'll just go through the bathroom," and swung the door between the bedroom and bathroom. Instead of actually going in though, I pivoted and ran straight at the changing table. My short shorts and loose strapless shirt allowed me full mobility. The whole force of my sprinting rage slammed into the top of the changing table, hands first. The changing table toppled forward and I did too. My feet left the ground following the inertia of my push. My belly landed hard on the top edge of the downed changing table.

"Ohhhh!" Almost immediately I felt a sharp abdominal pain. It was far worse than I would have expected.

Jim rushed toward me. "What?! What?!"

"Ahhhh! Ohhhh! Jim, there's blood." My voice cracked with fear. Bright red gore gushed down my leg from out of my shorts and onto the brownish green shag carpet.

"Jesus!" Jim exclaimed.

"Get me to a hospital, now!" I gasped through the piercing pain.

He had me put my arms around his neck and he carried me out the door and placed me lying down in the back seat. He ran back in to get his keys, wallet, and a towel, and then he sped down the road.

"Where are you going?"

"Grace. It's the closest one."

"They don't have facilities…!"

"They have blood and you're losing too much!"

"I don't care! We have to go to Blackwell!" That was the closest hospital with a full obstetric unit. The baby was who I was concerned about.

"Albany is an hour away."

"Not at night! Speed like your baby's life depends on it!"

"No, Virginia. I can't take the risk."

"Oooooh!"

"What is it?"

"Aghhhh." I breathed in and out.

"Contraction... Jim! We need to go to Blackwell, now!"

"No!"

We bickered angrily until he finally arrived at Grace Hospital. Jim drove up to the entrance and ran out of the car getting the attention of the emergency staff. They ran a gurney to the car, hoisted me on, and quickly rolled me through the halls. The dim regularly-spaced lights above made me feel like I was moving through the Holland Tunnel. The clamor around me was like superstitious tourists and rude locals honking their horns. An announcement alerted everyone that I was in need of blood. The nurse helped me change into a gown and then administered an O-negative blood transfusion within five to ten minutes upon arrival. A doctor examined me, left the room, and came back with a fetoscope.

"The heartbeat of the baby is slower than ideal. We are not equipped here to do anything further for you. We need to get you to Blackwell Hospital because you need emergency surgery."

The doctor waved to the nurses signaling them to take me away. "We will call Blackwell to have a surgical team prepped and ready for C-section."

They put me in the back of an ambulance. Jim followed with his car. Another contraction came. I could tell these weren't rhythmic labor contractions, just random sharp pains.

The ambulance arrived at Blackwell about an hour and twenty minutes post trauma. Jim was left in the waiting room. I was rushed to the OR and a nurse applied some gel and moved a Doppler wand around my abdomen.

She looked at the monitor and wrote something on her chart. I waited for her to say something, but she didn't.

"Do you hear anything?" I asked.

"Ma'am, I'm only a nurse. The doctor will be in shortly to speak with you," she said, wiping the gel off of me and leaving the room.

My anxiety rose like a tidal wave. My heart and hope were like coastal buildings. There was a great anticipation of impending destruction, and yet there was simultaneously courage. An optimism that the enormous swelling doom would crash before impact. The doctor came in and the microexpressions of sadness and dread came through in his eyes and gritted teeth.

"How many weeks along are you, Mrs. Marshall?"

"Thirty weeks," I replied, barely holding it together.

"Mrs. Marshall, you are having a placental abruption and we need to protect you from continued hemorrhaging. We're unable to stabilize your bleeding and at this point unable to detect the baby's heart rate. For you and your child's best interest, we have to go ahead with a stat C-section. Do we have your consent to go ahead?"

Seeing no alternative, I croaked, "Yes."

A nurse quickly came and put a mask over my mouth. "This is 100% oxygen. Breathe deeply. This will give your body oxygen stores for the next step."

I followed her instructions. Minutes later she said, "Okay, count backward from ten."

Chapter 48: Baby Girl

An intense pain attacked me from my abdomen when I came out of general anesthesia. Through gritted teeth, I moaned and huffed.

"Ma'am, are you awake? How are you feeling?" asked a nurse.

My mind was cloudy. Blinking a few times cleared the tears from my vision. Looking around, I realized I wasn't in the same room I had been in when I went under. This room had beige walls instead of white and was mostly empty other than a couple of other beds with instrumentation, a little kitchenette, and chairs for guests.

"Can you hear me, Ma'am?" The nurse opened the curtain behind me, brightening the room more.

"Is my baby okay?" I asked.

"I'm the post anesthesia nurse, Ma'am. I'll let the doctor know you're awake and he'll come in and talk to you soon."

I vomited in my mouth.

"Oh, sweetheart. Here. That's a common side effect of the anesthesia."

The nurse handed me a cup and a washcloth. I spit into the cup and wiped my lip. I disposed of both in the trash can that the nurse held out before me. Then, she handed me another.

"Here's some water. I'll get you some Zofran for the nausea."

Before she left the room, I asked, "Where's my baby?"

"We have your baby in the other room. We can bring her to you soon."

"Please!" I requested, desperately. I imagined my little girl swaddled with a cute pink hat.

The nurse returned with the medication and administered it through my IV. She assured me, "The doctor will be with you in a moment. Here, take this with some water."

I did, and the doctor came in and sat down in the chair beside the bed.

"Hi Mrs. Marshall, I'm Dr. Armstrong. I was the doctor who performed your emergency C-section. You had a case of potentially fatal hemorrhaging caused by a placental abruption. We were successful in stabilizing your bleeding with surgical intervention and Pitocin. Nurse Mary is going to come in and check on you periodically over the next two hours to monitor your bleeding and make sure it's not too heavy."

"And my baby girl?"

The doctor deflated with a sigh, then took a deep breath, and sat down beside me. "I'm very sorry, Mrs. Marshall, but unfortunately your baby did not make it. She had already passed when we got to her."

"Oh! Oh! No…" My eyes instantly flooded. My lungs deflated. My sobs were choked out while my throat tried to pull in air. Reaching lung capacity, the scream cry blasted out. Anger and sadness were everything. I wanted to strangle God. I wanted to throttle Jim.

The doctor reassuringly patted my back, then got up to leave when the comment the nurse made about my baby being in the other room came to mind. "Wait! Doctor, can I see her, my baby?"

"Yes, certainly. Would you like the nurse to put some clothes on her?"

"No, please just let me hold her."

"Mary?" he implicitly made the request.

She left the room.

"We've already taken handprints and footprints for you. We can take some pictures for you as well if you would like."

Red faced and still crying, I murmured, "Later, please."

The nurse came in and handed me my beautiful girl. I wept as I admired her tiny little facial features.

"We'll be transferring you from this room back to labor and delivery in a couple of hours once we're sure your bleeding has stabilized. I'm going to leave now but I'll check in after your transfer. Would you like the chaplain to come and speak with you?"

"Later," I whispered, still looking at my little girl.

"Okay, Mrs. Marshall. We'll talk later."

From time to time, the nurse came in to monitor my vitals, check my bleeding, and ask if I needed anything. The only need I had was for my baby.

Torrential tears came again and again. In between waves of grief, I craved her vitality and prayed that God would miraculously resurrect my baby girl. I imagined her at different ages crawling on a floor, walking in the grass on a summer day, running at the beach in the sun, climbing on rocks and jumping in the Autumn leaves in the woods, alive and laughing. Then, the grief of reality would hit me.

Another nurse came and moved me to a private room in L&D after a couple of hours. The doctor came in.

"Mrs. Marshall, your vitals and bleeding are stable. Are you ready to take some pictures with your baby?"

"Yes," I whispered. My soul had retreated inside the walls of my cerebral castle, busy brewing and stewing. Tossing over short replies to those on the outside was an arduous effort.

"Okay, I'll get the photographer. Did you want your husband to come for that?"

"No." There was no way I could have smiled if he was in the room. He had already ruined everything. I would not allow him to ruin this time too.

"Before I go, do you have any questions for me?"

"No."

The photographer introduced herself, but I forgot her name. She said, "I'll count off three, two, one before each shot so you have time to smile if you wish. Please let me know or raise a hand if you want me to pause or stop for any reason. I will take several shots from different angles and will mail these to your address or P.O. box in a week or two. Do you have any questions?"

"No," I answered.

I wasn't able to smile every time but the photographer was able to capture some.

The destiny I had envisioned was gone. None of these things I wanted for my child would happen now.

The hospital chaplain knocked and cracked the door, "Hi Virginia. I'm the chaplain. May I come in?"

"Yes." I wondered what God had to say to me and thought that the chaplain might be His mouth piece.

"May I sit down?"

"Sure."

He had puffy eyelids and his sclerae were red. His ashen appearance and white collar contrasted his all-black apparel and purple sash. A heavy key chain hung on a belt loop.

"My name is Father Raphael Gonzolas."

Chapter 49: Jubilee

"What is your name?"

"Virginia."

"How are you feeling today? Are your meds making you feel weird? Do you feel okay? I mean, comfortable? Is the lighting okay? Can I get you extra blankets, pillows, and make it a little darker in here, so you're more comfortable?"

"No."

"Is it okay if I say a prayer?"

"Yes."

"Father, Son, and Holy Spirit, Lord…"

The lids of my eyes closed in routine but things felt different than my normal prayer experience. Instead of listening, anticipating, imagining God, I felt injured and distant from Him.

"…thank you for being in the middle of all this with Virginia. We thank you that you ultimately take care of everything including what she's going through. Amen?"

He continued, not waiting for my "amen" agreement. I'm glad, because it just didn't feel that way.

"I'm sorry, Virginia. Please, excuse me. What is your little girl's name?"

This seemed like a strange question to ask someone who just lost a child. Then, I remembered that I planned to name her Jubilee. It was an intentional name meant to celebrate having a girl after having an abortion.

"Her name was Jubilee," I shared.

"Her name *is* Jubilee," he corrected. "Virginia, what is your faith tradition?"

"GOLDS, God's Obedient Latter Day Saints," I said.

"Interesting, I'm not familiar with that one. In your faith tradition, do you believe that God is God of the living or the dead?"

I remembered the verse he was referring to from the Gospel of Mark.

"God of the living," I submitted.

In a quiet slow voice, he encouraged, "So, she *is* Jubilee."

This made me think of Jubilee holding hands with God, which made me feel relieved.

"I know this is a terrible place to be in, and that you must have so many emotions and thoughts about the things you were going to do with Jubilee. How do you feel about these things not working out the way you wanted them to? Are you feeling forsaken, angry, afraid, sad…? What feelings are you having right now?"

With this seemingly thoughtful question, the impenetrable castle gates of my heart were opened.

"Well, it's hard for me to accept. I keep having visions of the two of us enjoying time together in nature, but then reality hits and I see her as she is."

"And you feel sad?"

"Yes, and…"

Raphael cut me off. "Let me read Psalm 23 to you."

He opened his book to a marked page.

"Jehovah is my shepherd; I shall not want.
He maketh me to lie down in green pastures;
He leadeth me beside still waters.
He restoreth my soul:
He guideth me in the paths of righteousness for his name's sake.
Yea, though I walk through the valley of the shadow of death,
I will fear no evil; for thou art with me;
Thy rod and thy staff, they comfort me.
Thou preparest a table before me in the presence of mine enemies:
Thou hast anointed my head with oil;
My cup runneth over.
Surely goodness and loving kindness shall follow me all the days of my life;
And I shall dwell in the house of Jehovah forever."

He repeated the last line slowly and deliberately, "*And I shall dwell in the house of Jehovah forever.* Be comforted by this Psalm, Virginia."

Raphael then switched back to a man that was seeing his mattress and pillow and not me. I realized that he was moving through a checklist robotically and quickly. Again, I closed the castle gates.

"Okay, so I want you to understand that you're by no means obligated to have a funeral or memorial service but we offer these as a means of giving you some closure. We also offer cremation services, if you'd like. Of course, I can also contact anyone you might need or want for practices of your faith tradition. We will send you home with keepsake hand and foot prints. Those come automatically, and you were already asked about pictures with Jubilee."

"Yes."

"So, are any of these services something you would be interested in?"

"Not sure."

"Do you happen to know if your husband needs any spiritual help or support?"

"He's a pastor," I said.

"Oh, good. That's great! Okay, in that case, I'm available and empathetic to what you're going through. Please have the nurses call me to assist you with any of the services Blackwell Hospital offers. Let me pray one more time for you before I leave."

"Okay," I said, knowing it wouldn't take long and zoned out.

When Raphael was done, I said, "Thank you." This visit was clearly an obstruction in this priest's pilgrimage to bed. The way he traversed the impediment with leaps and bounds was impressive though. Raphael honed his craft and found a formula that actually made me feel better, but still got him in and out of the hospital room quickly.

"You're very welcome. God bless you," Raphael said as he left.

Jim was brought to the room about fifteen minutes later. He walked in with a red face, squinted eyes, and a frown. Jim's eyes stayed locked on Jubilee as he came around the bed to get a closer look. "She's beautiful!" He said emphatically but quietly.

I was surprised to hear him say that and my rage was withheld for the moment.

"Can I hold her?" he asked.

"Uh, yes," I said a little reluctantly. Jim picked her up carefully, as if she were alive and slowly sat back into a chair next to the bed. Then, Jim softly outlined Jubilee's lips and other features with his finger. He lightly mashed his nose against hers and kissed her cheeks and lips a couple of times. It was clear that he was trying to control himself. When suddenly the dams broke and raging sobs flowed.

I knew what was going on. Jim and I were the same in that way, at least most of the time. When something sad or painful happened, we'd privately let the tears flow with unrestrained intensity and rage. In this way, the release was brief and complete, and we could focus on regaining our strength and control.

Minutes later, Jim was able to pull himself together. He stoically asked, "Did they take care of you well?"

"Yes, fine," I replied.

"I asked how long they anticipated keeping you. They said patients typically stay for three to four days after a C-section. A couple of days was the minimum. As long as you are deemed medically stable, they can discharge you. That will be better for reducing our out-of-pocket cost if you can manage."

Of course, he was concerned about the money. Neither of us had good medical insurance. I really didn't want to talk with him about this or anything else right now. Expecting that he would want to busy himself to move forward with his life, I asked, "Are you planning to leave?"

"Yeah, I'll come bring you dinner, sleep here, and have breakfast with you, but I'm going to head to work during the day."

I didn't respond, but was glad he would be gone for a while.

"Do you want the baby back?"

"Yes." His question seemed odd to me at first.

Jim handed me Jubilee a little quicker and with less care than he had taken her.

"Now, you're not going to like this, but since you have to be here for at least a couple of days, they are going to need to take her body and keep it cold, *soon*."

He waited for me to say something. I did not. After speaking with Raphael, I was starting to accept the idea of Jubilee as a spirit and associating her less with her fleshly body that now lay on my chest. Her body served as a reminder to me, like a photograph, a footprint, or a grave. The visions of her walking with God in Heaven were the truth.

"A little bit of good news is that we will be able to take our baby home with us. We just need to sign some legal documents. I will get all of that going if that sounds good to you."

"Okay."

"Great! I will do that then. Is there anything else that you need right now?"

"No."

"Okay, then I'll be back later with food." Jim didn't even try to kiss me goodbye before he left the room. He knew better. He knew I was extremely angry at him.

In the walls of my mental castle, there were two things that rankled me about the conversation we just had. First, Jim never used Jubilee's name. He might have forgotten what we planned to call her or thought we would retain the name for a future child, but he could have asked. Second, he never apologized for anything that happened. While an apology wasn't something I typically expected from Jim; he normally had his reasons. However, this event was extraordinarily terrible and clearly his fault, at least mostly. He created strife in our marriage, physically barricaded me, provoked me (a hormonal pregnant woman), and wasted critical time taking me to the wrong hospital. As much as I wanted to react to these things, an argument at this point would be like a toy terrier yipping at a ninety-pound shepherd. Here in my mental castle, I would recover until I was ready.

Chapter 50: Healing

The next couple of days for me were mostly filled with resting in bed with IV fluids. Perhaps I should have taken most of my time in bed reflecting on and emotionally processing the terrible events that led me here. Instead, I spent most of my time fantasizing about playful cherubs and little Jubilee petting and riding tame wolves, leopards, lions and other heavenly animals described in Ezekiel 10 and Isaiah 11. These thoughts were much more comforting than reliving the traumatic night when Jubilee died. I expected to talk to Raphael again, but he never came. I guess he was too busy or thought Jim would minister to me. Jim only talked about the daily happenings. No part of our conversations suggested he cared about my thoughts or feelings.

My physical pain and discomfort were buffered with medications. The nurses continued to monitor my vitals and check my temperature, looking for fever as a sign of infection. They made sure my C-section incision dressing remained clean and dry, drained the urine from my catheter, and recorded everything in their charts.

I only ate ice chips and drank water my first day. The nurses had me graduate slowly to a regular diet; from crackers to Jello, then soup and salad, and finally heartier meals like pizza and rotisserie chicken. They took off my C-section dressing just 24 hours after surgery and told me the incision area looked clean and healthy.

The most important milestone that would signal I was ready to leave the hospital was reestablishing safe mobility. Ambulating around the room with the nurses' assistance was the first step to this end. This was also an important step because they would need to keep a catheter inside me if I couldn't walk to the bathroom. I mastered this ability by the second day and walked around the unit with assistance by the third. My balance was good enough and they deemed me medically stable and fit for discharge.

The doctor prescribed narcotic pain medication for a couple of weeks and stool softeners to counteract the constipation caused by the narcotics. The nurse instructed me not to lift anything weighing over 15 lbs. for the post-surgery healing. Walking was okay, but exercise was not allowed for six weeks. Taking showers was okay, but no baths. One condition that I was sure Jim would have an issue with was no sex for six weeks. He could gouge out his lustful eyes and cut off his hell-bound right hand for all I cared.

The bastard was rushing me out of the hospital. "You're looking much stronger!" "Don't you want to get out of here?" "Don't you want your privacy and independence back?" I did want to leave, and part of me even wanted to go home. I needed time to recover but I didn't like being reliant on these nurses. So, I went along with it, signed the discharge papers, and we left.

A sad moment of reflection came when I was waiting for Jim to bring the car around outside the hospital entrance. The drop-off zone waits for both the mother with her new infant and the woman who lost hers. Both women are rushed from the drop-off zone into the hospital lobby, and both are wheeled out to the drop-off zone hours or days later to go home. Both wait on that curb for the car to be retrieved. They are both helped into the car, but one car has an infant in a secure car seat leaving with them. The other car, our car, does not. Instead, Jubilee would sit in my lap in a small shoebox-sized coffin.

Jim and I drove back to a house that I envisioned would be better characterized as an isolated, ill-gotten, insidious impassive igloo than a home. While we generally were hot headed toward each other, my plan was to recover in my mental castle. Based on previous experience, he would busy himself, making sure my physical needs were taken care of, while ignoring the emotional and spiritual. There would be no fights because there would be little to no communication.

The one thing that I really wanted a say in was where we would bury Jubilee's body. I wanted it to be respectful even though I knew it wasn't her anymore. Jim suggested a spot beside a hickory tree, just a short walk into the woods. He assured me that it had deep roots unlike many of the fir, hemlock, spruce, maples, and birch around, and that it would probably live for a couple hundred years. I knew that Jubilee's impact on me would be deep despite her shallow life, so it seemed fitting.

Neither of us spoke while Jim dug the grave. I thought of new roots making insect highways to her coffin, ants and beetles boring through it, carrying off parts of Jubilee, and returning her molecules to the elemental cycles. Dust to dust. It was fine. Her spirit was safe with God.

Jim broke the silence. "You should be able to distinguish this tree by the leaves and bark compared to the other ones around here, but the easiest way to tell this tree from the others is by the nuts." He picked up a hickory nut, which was very round and about the width of a quarter. "You won't find anything else like this around here, and you see how much the tree litters the ground with these?"

I nodded.

Placing the box beside the hole he started to pray, "Dear Heavenly Father, we have come here this day to commit to your love and care, the spirit of our baby." Then he stopped and said, "I think we should do this with the congregation. I mean we could have a memorial service for her."

'No, funerals are a time for loved ones to mourn. She didn't have time to accumulate loved ones to mourn her," argued my selfishness.

'Maybe Jim wants emotional support,' offered my consideration.

'He sure as hell is not going to get it from us!' spat my hostility.

'It's fine. As long as Jubilee's body is honored, why should we care?' contended my respect.

When I didn't say anything immediately, Jim continued, "It will be good for us to get some support from the congregation, some sympathy."

He waited for me to respond this time, but I just started carefully plodding back to the house.

"Maybe others will have similar experiences," he said to my back. "They can help us put things into perspective."

Visions of *my* experience came to mind. The anger halted me but I didn't turn.

'Fighting in this weakened condition would be foolish,' reminded my power.

'We need to heal before doing anything,' agreed my responsiveness.

'Yes, *and* we shouldn't *just respond* to some provocation.' noted my cunning. 'We need to be strategic about what we do next. It will serve us better.'

"I'll make the arrangements."

Jim rushed to catch up with me and put my arm around his shoulder to help stabilize me. I tolerated this, not revealing my true emotions.

We entered through the back slider door, and immediately saw the changing table, still lying in front of the bedroom doorway and a large blood stain on the carpet, now a dark black color. Jim must have seen my eyes widen. He rushed in ahead of me and muscled the changing table through the front door.

When I entered, a musty, metallic, pungent, even putrid odor assaulted my olfactory receptors. The insult to injury was that the conspicuous glaring blood stain couldn't just be ocularly ignored. Since the crib was still blocking the entrance to the bathroom, I shuffled in through the bedroom, opened the medicine cabinet and applied a generous helping of Mick's MethoBalm under my nose. The menthol was enough to mask the smell and I was able to sleep.

269

For two weeks, I spent most of my time lying in bed. The environment of the quiet house made me severely depressed, and yet I had no ambition to start laboratory work again. I'd previously called in sick when Jim would leave me behind in the morning, but hadn't yet informed my Ph.D. advisor what was happening. I assumed Dr. Maddox gave up trying to reach me after a few days of missing work. This was just a guess though. Without an answering machine, I had no way to know which of the calls were from him, if any. Furthermore, my ambition had temporarily been buried along with my daughter, so I didn't really want to call him.

Jim fed me oatmeal, eggs, spaghetti, soup, and chili. His culinary skills were terrible. I wanted to spit the flavorless microwaved creations in his face, but restrained. Jim checked the boxes, cleaning our clothes and occasionally sweeping. He also replaced the blood-stained carpet with a section that was left over from the installation. He got a small mat to cover the glaringly obvious cut separating the pieces. This also looked out of place, so he got a matching brownish orange patterned mat and area rug.

We had our first fight a week after returning home. Jim was talking about the memorial service and kept calling Jubilee, "the baby," and I just couldn't take it.

"Call her Jubilee!" I demanded.

"Why?"

"Because that was her name!"

"Does this really feel like a joyful celebration to you?"

"It doesn't matter!"

"Maybe we could call her something else, if you really want to name her."

"Her name is Jubilee!"

That was enough for Jim. He yelled back, "She doesn't have a name! She doesn't have a birth certificate!"

"*Jubilee! Should! Have!*" I screamed.

"Well, she didn't. Besides, I already made the brochures and had them printed." Jim said dismissively and walked out of the bedroom.

Before he left out of the back door, I sat up and yelled, "Well, do it again! With her name!"

Jim accommodated my demand later because I said I wouldn't participate in the service if he didn't change the brochures.

Chapter 51: Reopened Scars

The service for Jubilee was on a Sunday after church. More than half of the two hundred plus congregants came. From the window, I could see their cars stretching at least a quarter mile down the road. The sober tone and sea of black-clothed guests were depressing. Forced out of my bed, ripped from my fantasies of being with Jubilee in Heaven, I endured once again the pain of her death.

Jim laid down several white table cloths on the floor from the front door through the living room to the back. He brought guests through to welcome them, thanking them for their financial support that helped us to afford this home, showing them where the bathrooms were in case they needed to relieve themselves or freshen up, and showing them where to drop off their gifts. Gift baskets and envelopes were arrayed throughout our house - stacked in the kitchen, on the couch, and on the floor all the way to the back door.

Seeing the abundance of gifts, I realized Jim's true motivations for inviting the church to the funeral.

'Most of it was coming from the working adults and retirees, not the college students,' explained my greediness.

'Yeah, the college students are like the powerhouses that bring the excitement, energy, and the expansive activity to the church,' answered my excitement.

'The young college students also lure the adults and retirees,' noted seduction.
'...like Aliko, Jeff, Elon, and Bernard. They were probably the biggest financial contributors to GOLDS Church.'

'A lure to the unmarried ones too, like Wolfgang,' agreed my loneliness.

'Well how clever of Jim,' said my sarcasm.

'And it was a handsome college guy who greeted us the first time we went to a Bible study,' recalled my discernment.

'Oh, yes, Harris. Jim basically uses people like assets,' summarized my fascination.

The congregants accumulated in the backyard before the service. Jim put out high-top tables that he built for groups to gather and mingle around while they waited and a couple of long tables for drinks and hors d'oeuvres. He also made some wooden benches for people who preferred or needed to sit. Jim told me he would sell them after the event to make a few extra bucks. Everything seemed to be about money.

At 11:30 am, Jim directed everyone to follow him to the burial site. He escorted me by the arm like an usher at a wedding. We didn't look back but the loud crunching of leaves assured us that many congregants were close behind. A couple of women started to cry, which created a ripple effect, also bringing tears to my eyes.

I really hated that I was starting to cry in front of everyone, them seeing me at my lowest, most vulnerable point. It was humiliating and it was exactly what I was trying to avoid by not inviting Gina or Dan. I knew if Gina looked at me with sorrowful eyes or if Dan hugged me, I wouldn't have been able to hold back my emotions.

Just when I thought I was back in control, I unconsciously touched my stomach. It was soft and squishy in my hands, not firm as it had been just a couple of weeks ago. And with this reminder, many more embarrassing tears came.

When we got to the hickory tree, Jim asked everyone to line up behind each other in a semi-circle in front of its base. I hadn't walked back to the tree since we buried Jubilee's body. My fear of remembering the trauma kept me away.

Jim started, "Dear Heavenly Father, we have come here, this day, to commit to Your love and care, the spirit of Jubilee."

"Our friends have come to surround us with their love, compelled by that which You give all of us. We *feel* their faithful prayers and are *sustained* by their generous gifts. Thank You for blessing us with compassionate brothers and sisters who share in our sense of disappointment and hurt, and walk with us in our healing."

"We thank You also for the comfort of the Holy Spirit, and for Jesus' promise that He is building an eternal place for us in one of Your heavenly mansions. Beyond the pain and sorrows of life, we have peace that we will reunite there in Your presence."

"Jehovah, please help each of us to rise up, wash, change our clothes, and go to church like David did after he lost his child. Let people be bewildered by our worship. Let them ask us why, and let us answer as David did. *While the child was yet alive, I fasted and wept: for I said, Who knoweth whether Jehovah will not be gracious to me, that the child may live? But now he is dead, wherefore should I fast? Can I bring him back again?"*

"We don't know why Jubilee had to die so tragically and early."

'Yes, we know why!' growled my anger.

"But we do know that God will bring her back again. And in the meantime, we are meant to push on. Yes, David lay with Bath-sheba and bore Solomon, the wisest man to ever to live, and after that, the author of Samuel tells us that Jehovah loved him.

So, let us mourn Jubilee today, and do what her name means tomorrow. Help us brothers and sisters," he teared up, "to celebrate God, His eternal promises, and everlasting kingdom."

And the congregation agreed solemnly, "Amen."

Several of the congregants came around Jim and I, and gave us a group hug, which grew and grew until everyone was part of it.

"Thank you everyone," Jim signaled subtly after a couple of moments, and the crowd released.

Jim ushered me through the congregants who parted to the left and right and then followed behind us. Jim stopped beside the alley between the woodshop and house. "Please stick around if you'd like, have some refreshments, and take time to fellowship together. You may exit through the alley to return to your cars when you're ready to go, but please make yourselves at home."

The congregants only stayed for about a half hour. Many of them offered their sympathies on their way out. "Very sorry for your loss," they'd say, shaking our hands. "How are you doing, dear?" they'd ask me. I didn't want to share my grief. I'd just nod my head and half smile. "We are praying for you. If you need anything. Please let us know," they would offer. Other than Alice, Nancy, Warren, and Phoebe, I couldn't tell who really meant it. Then again, it's not like I would have taken them up on it anyway.

That night, Jim watched the salacious comedy, "Three's Company," while he opened packages and envelopes and sorted gifts and money. He maintained control well in emotional situations, but it didn't seem like he was managing grief. It just seemed like he was entirely over the fact that his daughter died just a couple months away from birth, which really bothered me. Nevertheless, I kept my anger to myself.

On the way to my six-week check-up, Jim seemed especially chipper. I came to find out later, it was because he thought we would be having sex that night. He stayed in the waiting room while I met with the doctor.

"How are you feeling emotionally?"

"I'm fine."

He gave me a skeptical look. My feelings weren't something I wanted to talk about, especially not with him.

273

"Fine. Then, I would encourage you to talk with someone."

Gina came to mind. She would feel hurt and disappointed, probably even concerned about why I felt the need to handle it alone. So, I needed to talk to her at some point. Probably Dan too, but I'd let Gina relay it. He might feel jealous about not getting the information first hand, but the problem is that he would feed off of my vulnerability. He would love being able to be there for me, and I just didn't want his kind of over-the-top attention and care.

"Please be honest about this next question," he looked at me with raised eyebrows that were asking, "Okay?"

"Yes, okay," I responded.

"Are you having suicidal thoughts?"

I didn't even have to think about it. "No." Of course I wasn't trying to kill myself. What for? No, there was justice to be done.

After the emotional evaluation, the doctor had me change into a gown. He pushed down near my belly button to see if my uterus had healed well. The nurse checked my vitals and surgical incision. Everything looked good, so the doctor took out my staples.

That night, Jim tried to come on to me. I told him that I wasn't in the mood. He grumbled. This happened about three or four times a week for the next three weeks. I was getting sick of it, so I decided to go over Gina's and finally talk with her about what happened.

"... so I just imagine her with God now."

"Yeah, I believe it too."

"Thanks, Gina."

"What did you mean when you said you felt like you've been on the wrong path lately?"

"Well, I told you about the problems that I've been having with Jim. Besides that, I've had a noble occupational pursuit up to this point, but it's been hard getting back into going to the laboratory. Everything just seems like failure - incomplete experiments, an unfinished degree program, not reconnecting with my mother, a dissatisfied drug dealing husband..."

"Is he still doing that?"

"Yes, and now the loss of our Jubilee! I want something new to pursue. I want to get busy. I want to leave."

I could tell this was disappointing to Gina.

"Where?"

"I don't know."

"Take me with you."

"That would be lovely, Gina. How many suitors am I competing with though?"

Another disappointing look.

"Wait. Are you getting out there, Gina? Are you trying?"

"It's hard for me, Virginia! I'm not brave like you!"

"We went out all the time though."

"As a group!"

My best friend was an introvert, and I'm just now discovering it.

"I always felt comfortable with the Ocracoke crew," she explained. "Now, Dan's always busy with Jacquee, and you live off campus and share a car with Jim. Just me alone feels weird."

"We should go out."

"Really? Like tonight?"

"No, but soon."

Gina smiled. "Are you thinking of going to the disco?"

'If we go to Paradise 54, would we run into Jim?' wondered my concern.

My irritation made the good point, 'What if we do? What can he do to us that he hasn't already done?'

"Yeah, we can do that," I confirmed.

"Okay, but I'm not going to go without you. So, let me know when you're ready. I'm not going to push you. I know you have crazy stuff going on at home, graduate school, and you're still recovering. Just let me know when to put the dress on," she shined like a new hot rod.

I really did plan to spend more time with Gina, but everything changed the next night, and I just couldn't.

I was lying on my stomach on the bed in my silk shirt and shorts reading a week-old Nettie Plot. Jim tossed the sheets to the side, pulled my pants down, and penetrated me. I tried to turn to the side, but he held my sides and just kept thrusting.

"Stop!" I yelled, and tried to twist harder, but he pressed my center down and I couldn't escape.

"What the Hell?! Jim!"

"I am a man and you are my wife," he excused himself and continued humping me harder and harder, faster and faster. "You cannot deny me sex for months."

"No! Stop! STOP!!" I started to scream, but this only seemed to make him thrust harder.

I was crying when he finished. He had taken my power from me.

Jim rolled over to the other side of the bed. "It's not fair, Virginia. You could have taken care of me in other ways when you were healing, and you've been healed for weeks."

Jim reached over my convulsing body and turned off the light. He turned away and put a pillow over his head to muffle the sound of my sobbing. I decided a few minutes later that I wasn't going to wait for him to do this to me again. No, it was time to escape from this ever-darkening hell.

When I was confident that Jim had fallen asleep, I got up and looked for the keys. Normally, he put them on the dresser, but they weren't there. So, I slowly and quietly opened the top dresser drawer, thinking they might have fallen in there and gotten lost in the socks. They weren't there though. I thought it might be in his shorts or pants. Maybe in his hurry to rape me, he had forgotten to take them out of the clothes he was wearing. It wouldn't be the first time that he left them in his work pants. A thorough search in the laundry basket yielded nothing though. Carefully, I exited the bedroom and searched around the living room, feeling in the cracks around the couch cushions and pulling them out for a more thorough check. Nothing. I went into the kitchen next. Nothing on the countertops.

'It's no good. We need to abort," reasoned my success. 'Tomorrow, we'll get the keys and leave.'

The other emotions reluctantly agreed. So, I went back to bed and fell asleep.

I woke up the next morning with Jim on my back again.

"Stop it, Jim!" I yelled. "You can't rape me!"

"No, Virginia. You can't deny me for months and stop me by calling it rape."

"Stop!" I yelled again.

"Just accept it! Stop fighting! Just enjoy it like you used to."

He slammed and pounded on me.

"Enjoy it, Jim. This is the last time. We're getting a divorce!"

Then, he stopped and loosened his grip.

I twisted up and out from under him. Then, I hit him hard in the face.

Jim just looked at me dumbfounded. Then he said, "No you can't. I need you."

"We already talked about this, Jim; the night you killed Jubilee by putting me in a desperate situation and hemming me in with dangerous obstacles. I told you then, and I'll say it again. Yes, I can leave you, and I don't care if you need me to be successful or to live. I hope you fail and die!!"

Jim's face crinkled, his eyes squinted, and he gritted his teeth.

Chapter 52: Addiction and Sobriety

Women statistically become addicted to drugs quicker than men. It was something I remembered Dr. de Pizan talking about in her class. Women don't use as much but nevertheless become addicted faster. I fell for heroin fast.

Mr. Brownstone satisfied me in ways no man ever could. All the pain and disappointment of life fell away – no failed relationships, no failed Ph.D., no failed career, no failed pregnancies, no failed marriage… only blissful relaxation, more relieving than a vacation resort massage, more comforting than laying in warm clean fluffy sheets on a ten-thousand-dollar mattress, more calming than Enya's Watermark, more mindless than watching Saturday morning cartoons, more peaceful than a campfire.

Jim drugged me because I tried running away. It's partly my fault. I was responsive and not cunning. After getting raped, I put on my clothes, went out the front door, and started walking down the eight-mile road toward the highway intersection. Jim pulled up behind me in the car a half hour later.

He yelled out his window, "Please stop. Let's talk."

"Leave me alone!" I yelled behind me.

He pulled up next to me and said, "I can't. You're too important to me."

"For appearances… to make money," I asserted.

"More than that."

"Yes, because you probably will lose money without me."

"Nooo! That's not why," he said in a high tone, trying to assure me that wasn't the case.

"Yes! People don't think well about a pastor whose wife left him, especially one who is supposed to be housebound and in need of his help!"

I was walking in the middle of the road and it was scarcely wider than the car. Jim was partially driving on the road and partially on the dirt and brush of the roadside. The problem was the trees, dips, and large rocks on the sides that forced him to pull back. When another space opened up, Jim returned to my side.

"Virginia, I love you."

"Well, I don't love you anymore."

"Please, we can fix this, work to make a better relationship."

"I don't want a better relationship. I want out."

Then, he drove around me and stopped a few yards up, parked but didn't turn off the ignition, and got out. Walking toward me, he said, "Please, stop. Get in the car and we can talk about this."

"No," I said simply and tried to walk around him, but he sidestepped in my way.

"Get out of my way," I demanded angrily.

"No," he said, smiling with a childish defiance.

I almost smiled back. It was just one of those weird human psychology things where if someone's mad and you smile at them, it's difficult for them not to lose their anger and smirk back. Even harder when you tickle them. It was a hellish annoying trick that Jim would do to me before hugging me and saying he was sorry about some argument we were having. This wasn't about our most recent argument though. Leaving Jim was about leaving ongoing and regular exploitation, oppression, objectification, abuse, and mind games. I didn't smile, and when he reached to tickle me, I smacked him in the face.

Anger flashed across Jim's face. I turned to run, but he quickly caught me by the torso and picked me up off my feet. As he walked backward, I yelled, "Nooo," kicked and flared about.

Jim was trying to hold me with one arm and open the passenger's side door with the other, but lost his grip on me. I wriggled around to face him. I hammered down on his face with my fist and tried to knee him in the groin but didn't connect well.

I don't know exactly what happened after that. I assume that Jim knocked me out with a concussive punch because I woke up with a splitting headache and throbbing pain in the side of my jaw and head. When I woke, we were in the driveway. Jim ripped me out of the car and dragged me to the side door of his woodshop. Jim grabbed a rope and tied my arms and legs. Then, he dragged me into the house, through the back door, and threw me onto the living room floor. He went into the kitchen. I heard some strange noises and a smell like burnt food. Jim came back with a needle. Fearful, and not knowing what it could be, I rolled from my belly to my side, but Jim rolled me back and sat on my rear. He pulled my legs back, ripped off my shoes and socks, and injected me between my middle toes.

Then, nothing mattered. *Nothing mattered.* My life was isolated to two rooms in a small house, I was treated like a caged animal, and it was all good. And after just a few weeks of injections, Jim didn't even have to force it on me anymore. I just let him give it to me.

After five months of injections, I needed it. I craved it and would have withdrawals, chills, hot sweats, and anxiety if Jim didn't give it to me frequently enough. This was just what he wanted, dependence.

Jim was receiving calls from my professor asking for me. He would give excuse after excuse until Dr. Maddox said that I was going to lose my grant funding and Ph.D. candidacy. My professor demanded that he speak with me directly for confirmation that I was aware of this and accepted it. Jim told Dr. Maddox that he would have me call him back.

Jim starved me of heroin for a few extra hours and promised to give me some if I told Dr. Maddox to go ahead and confer a Master's degree to me. "Tell him you are sorry, but recent personal family matters have made it impossible for you to continue."

He also had an idea to make some extra money from his church members. My role was to pretend to have myalgic encephalomyelitis (chronic fatigue syndrome). The congregants would come over. We'd sit together in the living room. I'd act tired and sad. Jim would act supportive. They'd feel sorry for me, and give Jim some money to help pay for my medication, in reality my addiction.

Jim made me say similar things to Gina, Dan, Alice, Nancy, Warren, and Phoebe when each of them called. Nothing else mattered except the bliss that came from heroin and avoiding the pain that came from withdrawal. I did what he said and got my fix.

After a few months of that, things started getting really bad. I couldn't stand not being high and I needed higher doses to achieve the same relaxation. I had terrible mood swings. Blissful when high, but intensely sad and angry when it was wearing off. I'd yell and nag Jim for heroin and he would scream back which would eventually lead to a beating.

Jim was so infuriated with me one day that he let a big secret slip. He had been working on a large furniture piece the last few days, became absorbed, and was late on satiating the monkey on my back that day. I was hitting Jim's arm while he was turning wood on the lathe to make him stop and tend to me.

"Ah Hell! You made me ruin the leg!"

"Give me my brown!"

"Keep it up and I'll have Ken hit you with his truck again."

"Give me my brown!"

It didn't register at first, but the memory came back to me later. Jim didn't just use my drama to grow his church, he probably orchestrated it. At the time, this news simply added to my depression and need for more heroin. My other emotions, like revenge, didn't say anything.

Verbal and physical abuse graduated to neglect. Sometimes he would tie me up with rope and put me outside while he watched TV. The fact that he was capable of such things convinced me that he did indeed have Ken hit me with his truck.

One day while he was working in his woodshop, I was feeling especially ornery, and carved this Jeremiad with a fork into the top of our coffee table. It was one of Jim's earliest and most prized works. I would have used a knife but he got rid of all those from the house by that point.

I am a woman and have become the maid of a man.
I am a woman and have become the prisoner of a man.
I am a woman and have become the punching bag of a man.
I am a woman and have become the scapegoat of a man.
I am a woman and have become the sex toy of a man.
He oppresses me with …
His murderous eyes.
His restricting arms.
His booming voice.
His mocking smile.
His critical gaze.
His pacing feet.
His flying fist.
His penis.

That was the last straw.

"I hope you enjoyed that," Jim started.

I definitely smirked.

"Did you want some heroin?" he asked.

I crinkled my brow, surprised by his offer. "Yes!" I answered emphatically.

"I'm going to need to tie you up again so you don't defame more furniture, or anything else."

"No, Jim. You don't need to do that. I'll just lie down and sleep after you inject me."

"It's just a precaution."

"Please, no."

"Look, do you want the heroin or not?" he said sternly.

"Yes," I responded and submitted to him tying me up. When he was finished, I demanded, "Now, give it to me!"

"No, Virginia. You need a detox."

I frowned, annoyed by the statement. "What the Hell, Jim!"

"The narcotics are just too expensive. Maybe they are helping you get over Jubilee, but you're just getting more and more belligerent."

"Plunge yourself into the eternal Lake of Fire, Jim!"

"See, that's what I mean. We will just need to find another way to get you to start acting like a wife and submitting to my headship."

Jim left me tied up on a mattress for two weeks.

It's very hard to quit heroin. In fact, four out of five people relapse when they try to quit, but Jim gave me no choice. I didn't sleep at all the first night and I had terrible muscle aches. Cold sweats, nausea and abdominal cramps, terrible diarrhea, and vomiting came the second and third day. The severity of these symptoms tapered each day but it was still torture. I'd yell to wake Jim around 2 or 3 am. In retaliation, he tied a sock in my mouth. The second time, I felt something come up and got scared that I'd die choking on my vomit. Jim didn't seem to care. So, I stopped yelling out.

There were waves of darkness and depression, anxiety and fear, anger and hatred. Emotion was everything for that week, like a fever.

Then, one morning the fever broke. I still had some lingering pain and cravings, but I could think again. The thinking was a bit abstract, something like mental jazz, going all over the place.

Jim put his hand to my head. "Yup, your fever broke," he concurred. "How do you feel?"

"My head is a little cloudy," I replied.

"Do you have any cravings?"

"No," I lied. It's true that my body was no longer in withdrawal, but my mind still wanted the pleasure. However, part of me wanted to escape more than get high.

"You need to move around, get your blood circulating."

My muscles ached as I tried to stand up, and I fell over on the first attempt. Jim just watched me, not helping.

Jim opened the slider doors. "Go run around in the backyard, and hose off, you smell terrible."

I was shocked that he was just going to let me out. I just stood there trying to get my bearings.

He didn't bother waiting for me to walk out. Jim headed for the front door, put his shoes on and declared, "I'm going to go get some food from the grocery store."

After he closed the front door, I walked into the kitchen and watched him get into our car and leave.

I looked around for my wallet briefly but couldn't find it. There was no time to waste. I put on my sneakers and headed out the door and down the driveway.

I tried jogging but quickly ran out of steam. Fast walking became tiresome. Still, I pushed forward fueled by anger and fear.

Two miles down the road, Jim popped out from behind a tree. "I suspected as much."

I gasped, shocked to see him there. Hope was chased away and I collapsed to my knees, my head hung as if I was in the gallows.

Jim strolled up to me. "What are we going to do, Virginia? I can't trust you to stay home, can I?"

I had nothing to say.

He picked me up under my shoulders.

"No!" I flailed and struggled trying to free myself, hating even his touch.

"Come on now, Virginia," he said with somewhat of a calm power.

"Get off!" I scratched him fiercely with my overgrown nails.

"Aw, bitch!"

#1 How Women Took Over The World

I woke up head throbbing and tied up some unknown time later.

Jim was sitting on the couch watching TV.

He saw me stir, got up, and put a cup of water to my mouth.

I was very thirsty, having forgotten to bring water when I tried to escape.

As I drank, he proposed an idea.

"Virginia. I can't keep giving you heroin. You've got to learn how to deal with the loss of our child."

I wanted to throttle him for trying to suggest that's all the drugging was about. He held all the cards though, so I just swallowed it down with the water.

"So, here's my idea. Since I can't trust you to stay here in our lovely retreat cabin in the woods, sober up, and renew your mind, we're going to have to do something radical. I still care about you, Virginia, but fixing you is going to take some effort, and not just on my part."

"What?" I snarled.

"I'm going to have to take away all of your clothes, socks, and shoes. I could be wrong, but I think it will be too humiliating for you to venture out down the long driveway and walk the highway naked. If that isn't enough of a discouragement, then it would probably be too painful to walk so many miles barefoot."

With a crinkled brow and enraged face, I was about to tell him to go burn in Hell when he cut me off with a hand.

"Just sleep on it. If you have other ideas, I'm open to them. I just want to repair what's going on in you and in our marriage."

I was stunned.

'How could he think that this was acceptable on any level?' asked my bewilderment.

Jim moved me over so I could watch TV. Later that evening he fed me dinner, tucked a pillow under my head and put a blanket over me.

I remember having an eerie dream of being a bird and playing in the woods.

"Bang!" A shot rang out and I felt a searing pain in my right wing. Then, I was falling down from my branch.

I came to when a cracky prepubescent voice yelled, "Got her Jim!"

I had a splitting headache rivaling the terrible pain in my wing, and no energy to escape.

The youthful Boy Jim came running.

"Oh, no! You're hurt!" he exclaimed, "Let me take you to my home and help you."

Scooping me into a box, I jostled around inside as he trotted home. There, another little boy with gloves held me down while Boy Jim was applying tweezers to my wing. I tried to peck myself free but it only made the boy with the gloves smirk. Boy Jim pulled a slug from my arm. "Look what you did, Ken!"

The same voice from the woods started, "I thought you said…"

"You were just supposed to clip her wing, not break it," interrupted Boy Jim. "I just wanted some of her feathers for my hat."

Boy Ken looked worried. "What can I do?"

"Just go home for a while. Don't tell anyone anything. I'll take care of the bird and let you know when she's healed."

Boy Ken complied.

Boy Jim poured hydrogen peroxide on the wounded wing and wrapped it with a bandage. Not understanding his words or what he was doing, I pecked at him while he did this. Then, he put me into a bigger box and poked holes in it.

In the box, in his shed, I stayed for many sun rises. Boy Jim visited me each day. He fed me and changed my bandages regularly, and talked to me, though I didn't understand his words.

From time to time, he would feed me from his hand. I started to climb onto his hand to more easily reach the food. Sometimes, while I was eating, he would pluck a feather from my tail and put it in his hat. The pain was quick and brief, so I let him do it.

As days turned into weeks, I could see a growing fondness in Boy Jim's eyes. Then one day, he brought a cage and moved me into it, and carefully removed my bandage so I could flutter around. I liked being able to flutter, but wanted to return to the woods where I could fly.

Boy Ken came to visit Boy Jim.

"Check it out! I decided to keep her," Boy Jim said excitedly.

"Why did I have to take the whipping then?" asked Boy Ken

"Because you shot her and our parents found out, but I wanted to thank you because now I can have bright new feathers whenever I want."

Boy Jim took a wad of candy out of his pocket and gave it to Boy Ken. I flew over, and clutched the side of the cage, curious at what I imagined was food being exchanged.

"Oh, you want some?" Boy Jim asked, and pulled another piece from his pocket and fed it to me.

The sweet was the most delicious thing I'd ever tasted. I fluttered around the cage and sang gleefully to make my excitement known.

"Wow! She really likes the candy," Boy Ken commented.

Boy Jim didn't offer more, even with all of my animation.

I thought, 'What could I do to get him to give me more?' Then, I realized, 'My feathers! He loves my feathers. I can just grow more."

I turned around and pushed my tail feathers out through the cage wires.

"Look, she's offering you her feathers for more," observed Boy Ken.

"How about that!" replied Boy Jim. He took a feather and gave me another sweet.

While I enjoyed it, they left.

When Boy Jim returned the next day, I offered my tail feathers again.

"More candy, huh?"

His words were lost on bird-me. I just waited for him to pluck my feather. He did and fed me another sweet.

This happened again the following day, and when he tried to feed me other food afterward, I rejected it. I only wanted the sweets.

My nutrition-poor diet caused me to grow emaciated and my feathers dulled in color after many sunrises.

"You look ugly, bird," Boy Jim complained, with revulsion in his eyes, "Either you eat normal food or you eat nothing," and filled my feeder.

Eventually, I did resume eating and regained my weight after a couple of weeks. My bright colors however were slow to return. Boy Jim started to lose interest in me and forgot to come feed me every day.

Without Boy Jim's sweets or favor, I began to yearn for the woods again. Then, Boy Jim didn't visit me a couple days in a row. I realized I needed to escape or the neglect may be fatal. So, I devised a plan.

When he came, I fluttered around and sang as beautifully as I knew how.

"That's very nice," he complimented, listening and looking at me.

Then, I leapt onto the cage door.

When he opened the cage, I crawled around onto the palm of his hand, and ate some of the food. As he was saying something, I turned to face him and sprang, driving my beak deep into his open eye.

Boy Jim screamed in pain. I flew toward the shed door seeking a gap or hole to squeeze through, but had difficulty finding one.

Holding his eye with one hand, Boy Jim lept after me. Grabbing a broom from a wall, he swung it in the air trying to hit me. Boy Jim's depth perception was off with one eye so I flew from corner to corner evading his swings and trying to find a way out. There was none though.

Eventually, I got tired. My endurance was gone from being in a cage for months. My speed slowed and Boy Jim swatted me out of the air.

My body was hurled a couple of feet. I slammed against the aluminum shed wall with a clang, and plummeted to the cement floor. He lifted his boot and stomped on my head, crushing my skull.

I startled awake, soaked in sweat, heart racing. Looking around and seeing my dresser and the stairwell down to the living room, I realized that I was in bed and had just woken from a nightmare.

I closed my eyes to try and fall back asleep since the loud crickets told me it was still night. Jumping out from behind my eyelids though was the image of bird me's head popping under Boy Jim's boot. The shock acidified my stomach and accelerated my heart again.

Jim had manipulated and used me. I was a broken bird in a cage because of him. There was no way out of this Hell, and I was running out of pleasing feathers. Someday, probably soon, I'd piss Jim off enough and he'd kill me. He wouldn't be punished for killing me though. He would get away with it. Just like he got away with Jubilee's murder, having Ken hit me with a truck, and all the other fiery things he was doing.

A more peaceful image appeared in my mind. Felix the Realist was sitting on a rock in the woods. We were at the baptism retreat years ago. He was giving his sage advice. I didn't get upset at him this time. Instead, I thanked him and released my anxiety about what I couldn't control and the things of the past, and focused on what I could control and the present. There was no point dwelling on regrets, on victimizing myself. For the sake of my future, to save myself, I needed to do something drastic.

Chapter 53: Killing Jim

"What's for dinner?"

"Spaghetti again."

"Why?"

"Jim, I explained to you that I can't devine food. You need to buy me what's on the grocery list since you won't let me leave the house."

"What about your garden? Haven't you been growing veggies? Can't you make something healthy to go with a meal like this?"

"Yes, I can, and we do actually have some greens in the garden. Do you want some steamed greens or raw greens, sweetheart?"

I knew Jim never liked his greens raw.

"Steamed greens," he replied.

"Sure, but I still need you to pick up the food on the list for tomorrow's dinner. You are also running out of crunchy peanut butter and milk."

"Fine, I'll get food tomorrow. When do you need it by?"

"Quarter after five if you want dinner to be ready by six."

Jim grabbed a beer from the refrigerator, turned on the TV, and sat on the couch. I had been building up to this for a whole month. My dutiful routines of cleaning the house, gardening, and preparing meals for him every day earned his trust, at least some.

Jim allowed me to do these things without bondage after my golden globe acting performance. I put on my most sincere face, and assured Jim, "I want to rebuild our relationship, our marriage." Then, I stripped off my clothes, and with a sweet, even seductive smile, I said, "This is my submission to your headship." That was the line I had memorized and was able to regurgitate convincingly without retching.

I went outside and collected some of the pokeweed growing on the edge of the property behind the woodshop. You might have heard of the Elvis song, Polk Salad Annie? It starts…

289

#1 How Women Took Over The World

If some of y'all never been down South too much
I'm gonna tell you a little bit about this
So that you'll understand what I'm talkin' about
Down there we have a plant that grows out in the woods
And in the fields looks somethin' like a turnip green
And everybody calls it polk salad, polk salad

In fact, people boil pokeweed and eat it like cooked spinach or collards. People who eat pokeweed tend to boil it two or even three times to get out all the toxins. I did not. Just added lots of tasty olive oil and salt.

"Time for dinner!"

Jim sat up as I brought his plate to the couch. I sat next to him with my plate.

"Oh, this looks great. I didn't know you were growing greens in the garden. How come you're not eating any?"

"I don't like eating salad or greens with my spaghetti."

"But it's good for you."

"Are you calling me fat?"

"No, I just mean… Never mind."

"I'm just giving you a hard time. Don't worry, I had some veggies for lunch today. Pray?"

"Yeah."

We bowed our heads and closed our eyes.

Jim prayed, "Dear God, thank you for this food you provided. Amen."

"And the hands that prepared it. Amen," I added.

"Yes." Jim shot me a small glare for supplementing his prayer. Jim turned back to the TV and dug into the food.

Looking at the TV, I asked, "How was your day?"

"Fine. I was busy on campus," he said in between bites.

"I thought you were trying to expand out into the county closer to where we live?" I said nervously, trying to distract him.

He paused for a moment, finishing his mouthful, and glared over to me. I looked back at him inquisitively, anxiously waiting for the reply. He looked down at the food briefly, and I thought he was going to say something about it, but then took another sip of beer, and responded to my question.

"I am, but I still need to consistently visit campus to maintain a presence and influence. Like salesmen make sales calls at their accounts, pastors must regularly visit their parish members."

"That makes sense."

We both stopped talking momentarily as the XYZ World News came on and they reviewed the top stories. They were reporting on the heavy security guarding John Hinckley as he was transported to court. He wrote a love letter to Jody Foster about being willing to abandon his assassination plans if he could just win her heart and live the rest of his life with her in obscurity.

"What a nut," said Jim as I sat next to him nude in our secluded cabin.

"Glad to hear President Reagan is recovering well."

"Yeah."

"Is the Fall semester off to a good start?"

"I've been gathering some new congregants. Probably got four more today." He smiled and ate some more pasta and greens.

"How about you? What did you do today?"

"After you left, I cleaned up the dishes, wiped down the kitchen, watered the garden, picked some veggies, swept the floors, washed your clothes, and ate some lunch."

"You should take some time to read your Bible."

"Oh, I did that too."

"What did you read?"

"I read about half of Leviticus."

"Leviticus! I love that book. *And all the tithe of the land, whether of the seed of the land, or of the fruit of the tree, is Jehovah's: it is holy unto Jehovah.* You know that book helped us get this house."

"Yes, I remember," I said, faking a smile.

"Did you learn anything new?"

"Umm. Yeah." 'But what would stroke your ego,' I thought.

"I actually had a question. How was animal sacrifice sustainable with all of the sin going on in Israel?"

"Good question! Actually, it was a pretty good deal for the Levites."

"Oh, really."

"Yeah! One verse says the priest that *offereth any man's burnt-offering shall have to himself the skin of the burnt-offering* and another one says that *the wave-breast and the heave-thigh shall ye eat in a clean place, thou, and thy sons, and thy daughters with thee: for they are given as thy portion, and thy sons' portion, out of the sacrifices of the peace-offerings of the children of Israel*," he rattled off. "Basically, the Levites ate barbecued meat all the time!"

"Ahh, I see. Thanks for clearing that up."

"Yeah, it's too bad that we stopped doing that after Jesus! I would love it if congregants brought me cuts of meat."

"Speaking of barbecued meat. I put chicken on the grocery list."

"Oh, shhh!" Jim shushed me as Dean Pennings started talking. "Listen to this."

"The Soviet Union said that it's no mystery why America shoots its Presidents. The Communist Party blames the violence on ease of availability and cheap weapons…" European news was discussing gun control in the U.S. so XYZ World News decided to report on the same in other countries.

There was a transition to Bruce Lee who started discussing the history of guns in Europe before going into gun control laws in Europe.

"I didn't realize Boy Scouts came from the Swiss. *"Be prepared"* is such a good catchphrase, don't you think?"

Before I had a chance to respond, Jim said, "I bet I could get a home protection training class going over here. Or maybe extreme persecution, family defense, or maybe even apocalyptic training," Jim formulated, talking over the TV.

Dean emphasized the significantly lower homicide rates in other countries compared to the United States.

"Oh wow! I didn't realize everyone received weapons training in Israel," Jim announced.

When the segment was over, I finished what I was going to say before Jim shushed me. "Does barbecued chicken for dinner tomorrow sound good?"

"Yes, it sure does!" he answered enthusiastically.

Jim finished the food on his plate. "Do you happen to have any more of those greens?" he asked.

"Nope. You've eaten everything I collected. I can gather and cook some more if you like."

"When you're done eating, that would be great," he replied.

So, Jim ate a second serving of pokeweed that evening.

As the hours ticked by, I started to worry that I overcooked the pokeweed. I thought maybe I picked them too early and that the plants needed more time to accumulate toxins, or what I thought was pokeweed was actually something else that looked like pokeweed.

Bosom Buddies came on at 9pm and Jim went on a rant about what an abomination it was for Tom Hanks and Peter Scolari to be dressing like women. He was standing up pointing and yelling at the TV looking at me.

"What is the show about, Jim?" I asked.

"They dress and talk like women to live in a women-only hotel!"

"Well let's just see what else is on."

Jim grabbed the remote and found something called Nurse on CBS.

"Oh, this is new," he said.

"Let's give it a try," I suggested.

"Okay. I feel kind of funny," he said.

"Funny?" I inquired, hoping that the pokeweed was finally working.

"Yeah, can you get me some antacids?"

I stood up and headed to the medicine cabinet in the hallway bathroom. "Sure, honey. Did that show make your stomach upset?"

"I don't know. Oooo, excuse me," Jim said, passing some gas. "Feeling some sharp discomfort."

I headed back toward the kitchen to get Jim a glass of water for the antacid. He jumped up from the couch and jetted into the bathroom.

Jim didn't bother shutting the door and a moment later I could hear the rapid hissing gas and plunks of diarrhea.

"Uhhh," he groaned.

I just stood in the kitchen with the glass of water listening.

Then, I heard him vomit, and I rushed over to the bathroom. Jim was hunched over with his arms curled under his knees. I followed a trail of vomit from his feet, across the bathroom mat, up the bathtub/shower curtain in front of him.

"Ohh, Jim."

He looked up at me, eyes tired, a painful worried look on his face, and vomit dripping down his long beard he had been proudly growing for months.

"Do you want the antacid?" I asked, holding out the glass.

Jim waved to indicate he did not, and vomited again onto the curtain.

"What can I do?" I asked.

Jim shook his head and waved me away. I got some towels from the kitchen and cleaned up the vomit on the floor. I took the mat and washed it in the kitchen sink. Then, I did the same thing with the shower curtain. Jim had another smaller evacuation into the tub. I turned on the shower to rinse it away and cleaned up what was on the floor again with a towel. Once the floor was clean, Jim flushed the toilet, kneeled and turned to face the toilet. He started shivering and dry heaving.

"My stomach keeps heaving but nothing is coming up," he said referring to the cramping.

"You should drink something," I said. "How about some water?"

He nodded his head still looking into the bowl.

I went into the kitchen, filled up a glass, and brought it to him.

He drank some of the water and threw it up moments later.

His breathing started getting excited, rapid and labored.

I said, "You need to calm down!"

"Hh-I-hh-can't-hh-calm-hh-down." He put his hand to his heart and said, "My-hh-heart-hh-is-hh-beating-hh-too-hh-fast."

"What can we give you to relax, slow your breathing?"

"Ludes-hh-get-hh-the-hh-ludes."

"Okay, where are they?"

"In-hh-the-hh-bottom-hh-of-hh-the-hh-Cheerios."

I ran back to the kitchen and opened the cabinet where the cereal was. Jim almost always ate the Frosted Flakes and I always ate the Rice Krispies, but the big yellow Cheerios box was always there in the morning. I pulled the box out of the cabinet, opened the top flaps, and looked in. The plastic cereal bag was rolled up neatly to stop it from getting stale too quickly. I pulled the bag out and looked at the bottom. There was just minced cereal dust. I mashed the bag around to see if dispersing the cereal would reveal the ludes. This just revealed more O's. I looked back in the box and then I saw them, little bags of white tablets. I took one and put the Cheerios bag back in the box and the box back in the cabinet.

I brought the small bag to Jim and he took three ludes. He stayed kneeled with labored, rapid breathing. Massaging his shoulders and singing relaxing hymns – Amazing Grace, It is Well with My Soul, How Great Thou Art, Softly and Tenderly, Abide with Me seemed to calm him down. His breathing started to slow. I helped him up, brought him into the bedroom, pulled the comforter off, and turned the sheet out so he could get in.

Jim fell asleep about fifteen minutes later. I turned on the bedroom light and tapped his face to wake him back up as a test.

"Jim, Jim. You can't fall asleep. You might drown in puke."

Jim's eyes blinked and dilated, but he was otherwise unresponsive. Then, his lids fell and he was back to dreamland.

I put the comforter, pillow, some of Jim's clothes, and bathroom towels on the ground beside the bed. I covered this with a cleaned and dried plastic shower curtain. Then, I rolled Jim off of the bed onto the pile. He groaned and shifted a little but otherwise didn't respond.

I left the bedroom turning into the hallway, went out the back door, turned right toward the woodshop. I opened the side door wide so it wouldn't get in my way. Then, I turned on the light. Everything was still and quiet. I could hear the Spring time crickets and Katydids in the woods. Turning on the lathe, the whirring of the rotation drowned out the natural noises.

Going back into the house, I grabbed Jim's boots and cleaned the dirt off of them in the sink and dried them with a paper towel. There was just a little bit of dirt. I left the boots in the living room.

Jim was lying sideways when I came back to him. I turned Jim flat on his back and held his legs up like he was wheelbarrow and pulled toward the hallway door. He slid pretty easily on the curtain, not quite as easy on the carpet. The slightly raised floor threshold strip between the bedroom and hallway didn't seem to bother him. Once I got him out into the living room, I put Jim's boots on his feet. Then, I straddled over him, taking his hands, and pulled to get him to a seated position. Then, I squatted, put his arms over my shoulders, wrapped my arms around his back, pulled back and engaged my glutes to lift Jim. His rear lifted off the ground a little bit, but he proved to be too heavy to get him all the way up. Afraid I might exhaust myself, I lightly slapped Jim's face a couple of times. "Jim. Jim. You fell. I got to get you back up. Come on Jim." Thankfully, his assistance was just enough to pull him up to a standing position. I turned around and draped his arms over my shoulders. I leaned forward so his boots were just off the ground. I jerked Jim up like a backpack to better position him on my back.

Jim's weight was a significant burden. I slowly clomped forward with deliberate steps trying to avoid dropping him. While I didn't think the fall would wake him from his deep hypnosis, I was concerned he might hit his head and get knocked out. Then, I wouldn't be able to get him back up to a standing position again.

To prepare for this physical challenge, I had been doing a lot of squats, lunges, and pushups during the day while Jim was working. We didn't own any weights, and we no longer had luggage or a backpack that could be filled with rocks for use in resistance training. Jim was concerned I might use bags to get away so he sold them. My creative alternative was using our microwave, and putting fruit and vegetables inside to increase the weight as I got stronger. I pushed myself, working up to forty lunges at a time. I reasoned that this would be more than enough estimating the walk from the living room to the woodshop to be around sixteen steps.

The training paid off. Even though his weight was heavier than the loaded microwave, I could bear it; my adrenaline was high and my legs knew what to do. Left. Hold. Right. Hold. Just a small progression forward with each step was important for maintaining balance. I almost lost it when we turned right by the back door to go toward the woodshop. The side planks, calf raises, and single-leg stands I incorporated in my exercises gave me the strength to recover. He gave another groan as we entered the bright and noisy woodshop, but continued to let me walk him forward.

Besides exercise, I practiced my story, what I would tell the police, how I would say it.

Crying, I'd whimper, "I told him to shave it. He didn't listen."

If they asked why he was out so late. I'd say, "He had a habit of working in the woodshop after dinner, late into the evening."

Standing before the lathe, I tried to set his feet down but his knees just buckled. "Hell!" I tilted and heaved him up on my back afraid he was going to slide down onto the floor. I didn't think he would be so limp. I thought I would be able to get behind Jim and drop him neck first onto the spinning table leg. Unconscious, he was just dead weight.

So, now I had a choice to make. I could try to sling him off one side of me toward the lathe and hope he gets wrapped up, or I could try and wake him up enough to stand and guide him. One of the problems with slinging him was that he might just bounce off. Another was that I might miss the lathe entirely. Yet another was that slinging him at the lathe might cause the thin wood chair leg to break or pop out of the chuck. Then, there would be nothing to wrap him up. The problem with trying to wake Jim up again was that he might help me at first and then collapse as soon as I let go of his arms. Jim, in his altered state, helped me get him to a standing position in the living room, but there was no guarantee he'd help me again.

Other solutions eluded me and I thought of more potential issues with slinging Jim. So, I decided to try waking him.

"Jim. Jim. Stand up. Jim. Stand up. I need to brush your teeth."

Jim groaned.

I loosened my grip to test his stability. He started to drop.

"Jim! Jim! Stand up! I need you to stand so I can brush your teeth!"

Another groan. I tried bouncing his feet. Nothing. No resistance.

So, I threw my head back, connecting with his nose.

"Ahhh," he moaned. His legs stiffened up just enough for me to get behind him. He put his hands to face. "Wha?" he started to ask. "So bright."

"Sorry. Sorry. Shhh. Sorry. Jim. We're in the bathroom. Keep your eyes closed. We need to brush your teeth." I guided him a little closer to the lathe, hugging him from behind, holding his shoulders up, and shuffling forward. He took a couple of steps into position.

"Why does it sound like the lathe in the bathroom?"

"Shhh. Shhh. It's just the bathroom fan. Put your arms down so we can brush your teeth."

Jim put his arms down.

"Okay, now open your mouth and lean over the sink slowly so we can rinse your mouth."

Jim opened his mouth and began to hinge toward the high-speed spinning wooden leg. He was actually just a little far out. I pushed him just a little closer as he continued to hinge forward.

Suddenly Jim's beard caught and wrapped around the wood. The rotational force jerked him forward and his neck was pulled down toward the spinning sharply-patterned wood. The edges of Jim's signature "Sharp" Barley Twist turning style that he always bragged about ripped open his throat. Blood splattered everywhere as Jim writhed, unable to escape. While not painless, his death was very fast (just minutes) after his venous and arterial systems were severed.

I went back into the house, and washed up in the bathroom sink with toilet paper. The blood-stained toilet paper and the empty bag previously containing the ludes were flushed down the toilet. Then, I put on a pair of Jim's socks, T-shirts, some draw-string plaid pajama pants, making sure to button the front, and a hooded sweatshirt. I put all of the clothes away that I used to help soften Jim's fall when I rolled him off the bed. I also remade the bed, rehooked the plastic shower curtain, and put the bathroom mat back down, which was now mostly dry.

Now it was time to let out my emotions. I looked at myself in the bathroom mirror and thought about my aborted baby and my miscarried baby, both killed by their own father. I started to yell and cry at the same time. "You killed them! How could you kill your own! They weren't just yours though! They were mine! They were mine…" I sobbed, and then screamed, "Now you paid!" My balling continued for a while. There was a lot to get out, but I was feeling successful in vengeance. I looked in the mirror and saw that my ugly grief-ridden face was perfect. I left the tear streaks for the police.

A month ago, when I submitted to Jim, he took the phone handset and cord off of the receiver and hid them so I couldn't call anyone while he was away from the house. Jim's hiding place was very good but I was able to find it after searching for about a week and a half. Our kitchen cabinets, like many other designs, have empty boxes above them for an aesthetically pleasing smooth transition to the ceiling. It's commonly wasted space in homes. Our empty above-cabinet boxes were covered in a panel decorated with flowery wallpaper. The repetitive units on the wallpaper were three separate sections of flower designs, and it was hard to see the discontinuity crease between each repeating unit. Jim had made it so that the front panels of these boxes could be removed. In the box right above the phone receiver was the hidden handset and cord.

I climbed up onto the countertop, removed the flowery panel, reached up, grabbed the handset and cord, and put the panel back. Then, I dropped down from the countertop, reattached the cord to the receiver, and reset the handset. Finally, I pulled the handset off of the receiver, checked for the ring tone, and dialed 9-1-1.

"9-1-1, please state your emergency."

"There's been a terrible accident! There's blood everywhere!"

"Ma'am, calm down. What has happened? Whose bleeding?"

"My husband cut his neck in the woodshop, and he's not saying anything! Please come quickly with an ambulance!"

"Where are you?"

"I'm at 1 Potters Field Cemetery Road in Hallow Hill Woods State Forest, New York."

"Dispatching emergency units now. Can you get to your husband safely?"

"Yes!"

"Get a clean dry towel and apply pressure on the wound. The responders will be there soon."

"Okay, I'm going! Bye!" I put the phone back on the receiver, strolled into the bathroom, grabbed Jim's shower towel, and went out to the woodshop. His body lay in a pool of blood. I really didn't want to get my clothes bloody but I didn't see much of a choice around it. "No! No! Nooooo!" I screamed pretending to be a hysterical wife. I smirked, dropped to the ground, getting my knees and shins covered in Jim's blood. Then, I realized that if I actually was trying to save him and thought I could, I would elevate his top half. This reasoning and the theatrical spirit taking over my mind moved me to pull and shift Jim so that he was leaning against the adjacent bench. I wrapped the towel around his neck and applied pressure.

A police siren blared down the narrow road leading to our house. I yelled, "We're in here, officer! We're in here!"

The police officer found me and looked around the woodshop, and said, "Ma'am, stay calm. Help is on the way. Keep holding the towel against his neck."

Jim's face was very pale at this point from all the blood loss.

"I need to go secure the area and call in some backup."

I nodded and the officer stepped back out of the woodshop. He didn't return until the EMS came, which was about ten minutes later. One of the paramedics checked

Jim's wrist and indicated there was no heartbeat. The other looked at his watch and said, "Time of death: 10:47pm."

Tears came to my eyes. I wept for the performance, releasing the sadness I had for myself, my failed marriage, my failed motherhood, and my failed career. "Jim, Jim, Jim! Why? Why God? Why?" I moaned.

I heard the officer say to the paramedic, "You don't need to contact the medical examiner, I've already called for the forensics specialist. They should be here in fifteen minutes."

"Ma'am, I'm sorry, but could you please just stay right there and tell me what happened?"

Crying, I'd whimper, "I told him to shave it. He didn't listen."

"You mean his beard?" asked the officer. Most of it had been ripped off by the lathe.

"Yes."

"What was his name?"

"Jim Marshall."

"And you are his wife?"

"Yes!" I pouted and gave him some crocodile tears.

"What was he doing out here so late?"

Pretending to catch my breath and calm down some, I said, "He had a habit of working in the woodshop after dinner, late into the evening."

My other emotions praised my cunning. Being cunning and strategizing was so much better than reacting.

Chapter 54: Get Out!

The forensics team determined that the cause of death was loss of blood from a lathe-induced throat cut. Methaqualone (intoxicant in ludes) was found in subsequent testing. However, phytolaccatoxin and phytolaccigenin, the primary toxins found in pokeweed, were not since they are not part of the typical chemical screen panel. Thus, the forensics report indicated that drowsy symptoms caused by abuse of illegal methaqualone sedatives may have contributed to his accidental death. Officers came back to the house with a search warrant. They found the ludes in the bottom of the Cheerios box and I said that I was unaware of those being in the house. They did not find the drug money or embezzled donations hidden in the decorative boxes above the cabinets.

The officers took me into custody and questioned me about Jim's involvement in the drug dealing on campus, to church congregants, and at disco clubs. I said that I was unaware of these activities. They had to let me go after a few hours because they had no evidence to hold me. The case was closed a few days later.

Since Jim was a pastor of a sizable church, was found to be involved in drug trafficking, and died a gruesome death, the story was broadcast on several news stations. Gina found me at the house the day after the story aired.

"You should just leave," she said, "Start a new life somewhere else. You can never change what happened here. You will never be able to thrive here. Believe me."

I sat on the floor with her, exhausted from reflection, crying, and thinking about next steps. I didn't tell her what actually happened. She believed that my husband's death was an accident.

"I don't have any experience with selling a house, but I know someone whose brother is a real estate agent. I can connect you, and I'll help you clean the house and get it ready to go on the market."

"Gina, I want to finish my Ph.D."

"Didn't you already master out?"

"Yeah, and I don't think Dr. Maddox would take me back, but maybe Dr. Burmeister would."

"Virginia, you know I love you and will support whatever you want to do, but I really think this is a bad idea."

"Why?"

"I'm afraid that everyone is going to make you feel weird. They're going to treat you differently. They will gossip about your situation, they will pry, they will pity... you will be defined by this event."

"Who?"

"GOLDS Church, the college community, your work colleagues, people in the grocery store..."

I thought about my experiences after the hit-and-run. The attention wasn't my favorite. The college community's support was embarrassing. Then, I thought about some of Jim's congregants. The reactions she mentioned actually seemed imminent, and there might also be some misdirected hostility toward me because of the ways he manipulated them. Still, I wasn't prepared to give up my chance to finish my Ph.D. now that Jim was out of the way.

"Finishing my Ph.D. is more important than worrying about how people might treat me."

"Listen. I want to tell you something." Gina paused. Something in her voice suggested that it was a secret.

"Okay."

"Remember when I told you that my papa left my mama, and she had to move because she couldn't afford the mortgage?"

"Yes."

"Well, that wasn't the whole story."

She paused, grimacing anxiously, and nervously grinding her teeth. Her hands were in front of her, clenching and uncurling, her soul wanting to hide but decidedly surrendering.

"What, Gina?"

"I'm sorry I've kept this from you, but it's very hard for me, and I've been labeled and judged too much before. I wanted to leave it behind me."

"Why tell me now?" I asked.

"Because I care about you and I think you might experience the same problems we had."

"What do you mean?"

"Listen. When I was in high school, Mama found out that Papa owed the government over one hundred thousand dollars in taxes from gambling debts. He borrowed money from all of our family friends over the years to feed his addiction. When the collection agencies started getting aggressive, he skipped town, and left Mama to pay off the debt. Our family friends didn't ask Mama to pay them back, but things became really awkward. We regularly saw people talking and staring, clearly having conversations about us. When they actually talked to us, there were often airs of superiority and the conversation almost always turned to the same topic. It felt like we were being interviewed by news reporters, hungry for stories to sell."

I thought of Milli and wondered if she ever made people feel that way.

"I'm sorry that happened to you and your mom, Gina."

"Thanks. There was a silver lining."

"Yeah?"

"Yeah. My grades and test scores were great at the end of high school. With that and the family debt, I became eligible for financial assistance. Nettie Maria Stevens University actually offered me a full ride. It was my ticket out of that nightmare. Mama told me to take it. I was worried that she would get stuck there, but she told me that once I was out of the house, she could work on selling it and getting out of town too. She's still deep in debt but she's got friends and no one treats her weird in Arkansas. That is, besides the usual barbs about Yankees. Mama can handle those though."

"I hear what you're saying but I need to think about it."

"One more thing. Not that it's really relevant to you anymore, but the reason why I knew about separation and annulments was because my mama did them."

Gina started to cry and I hugged her.

"I understand why she did it. I don't blame her. It's just hard to think your parents are never going to get back together. You know?" Then Gina realized, "No, I guess you wouldn't."

"No, I never saw mine together, but I can imagine what it would be like to see them together your whole childhood, and then…" I squeezed tighter.

"Thanks, Virginia. I was supposed to be comforting you." We chuckled.

I didn't want to be comforted for losing Jim. If anything, I wanted to tell Gina about Jim's abuse of me. I knew that I couldn't because it was a motive for murder, and if Gina was ever questioned by the police, the information could be used to convict me.

Gina left a little later. Hours ticked by and I only managed to move from the floor to the couch.

In the late evening around 8pm, I heard a hard knock at the door and lots of yelling.

It was Rick, one of Jim's faithful followers and his dutiful wife, Marge.

As soon as I opened the door, Rick barged in. Marge was pulling on his arm saying, "Stop! Rick, stop!"

I didn't have time to get out of his way. He slammed into me, knocking me over.

Then he turned, and barked, "Where's the money? I know Jim hid it somewhere here, and don't act like you don't know about it."

"Get out of my house," I barked back.

"I'm so sorry, Virginia," cried Marge. "He's not himself."

"Shut up! I asked you a question, First Lady! Where did you all keep the drug and donation money?"

I stood up. "Go to Hell, Rick." I was feeling really defiant and empowered after having just killed another knave.

"Smart mouth for a pastor's wife."

"Pastor's widow," I corrected.

"Fine," he said through gritted teeth. Then, he turned around and headed deeper into the house leaving me and Marge behind.

"Rick, no!" cried Marge.

"Where the Hell do you think you're going?" I challenged.

Rick didn't respond. He went to my couch, ripped out the pillows, and reached in the crevasses.

I pulled on his shoulder and yelled, "Get out!"

Rick twisted his torso, tossing me into my living room wall.

With a war cry, I ran at him, and was met with a gut punch. I heaved on the ground while he moved to the bedroom.

Marge was hysterical. "Rick, stop!"

I heard him pulling out dresser drawers, turning over the mattress, and ripping up something, which I later discovered was the corner of the carpet.

"Rick, you can't do this! If you don't leave, I'm going to leave you."

This didn't provoke any verbal response I could hear from Rick.

I caught my breath and got to a seated position against the wall. I turned my head toward the kitchen, remembering the phone. I stood up and tip-toed so as not to alert them. I softly pulled the phone from its holder. The stupid buttons made a beep each time I pressed them, 9(beep)-1(beep)-1(beep).

Marge yelled, "No, Rick!"

Suddenly he was in front of me. I pressed the speaker button, "9-1-1, what's your emergency?" I yelled, "Rick Tidje!" He ripped the phone out of my hand and slammed it on the holder.

"Now you're in trouble! That was a recorded line. They'll be here in no time."

Rick put his hand up to strike me, but I didn't flinch. "Rick!" yelled Marge. Suddenly, Rick had this look of uncertainty. He looked at the hand he was holding up, and realizing that he was about to incriminate himself, held it out like he was going to shake mine. When I didn't take his hand, Rick grabbed mine with both of his and shook it. "I'm very sorry for my behavior. I don't know what came over me."

"Marge, please tend to any... umm, please tend to Virginia."

Rick rushed into the bedroom, flipped the mattress back on the bed, pushed the carpet flap back into the corner as best he could, and pushed the drawers back in.

"That's not necessary."

"Oh, certainly. It's not a problem. I insist."

He came back out into the living room and shoved the pillows into the couch.

"I insist you leave immediately."

"Certainly. Again, I'm very sorry for my behavior. Come on, Marge. Let's go."

I followed them to the door and locked it behind them. After watching them drive away from the kitchen window, I fell to the floor and sobbed. The police never came. That was enough reason for me to sell the house and move on. I called Gina and asked if I could stay with her for a little while and she welcomed me with open arms. I packed my bags and left for her place that night.

It wasn't hard to sell the house. The interest rates were steep, around seventeen percent, so people were looking for deals. I put an ad in the paper to sell my house for cash, no inspections, and fast closing terms rather than getting a real estate agent. With those conditions, I was out of town two weeks later and headed down South.

I was glad I got to say goodbye to Gina; a little sad that I was in too much of a hurry to say goodbye to Dan. My 1971 Viking Blue Oldsmobile Cutlass had plenty of room for the few possessions I still had left. As I roared down the long driveway for the last time, I took my wedding ring off and chucked it into the woods. The freedom felt so good.

It wasn't clear where I was going to end up down South, or even if I was going to stay there, but it didn't matter at the moment. The freedom felt so good!

Chapter 55: Act 2

Route 81 led me to Harrisburg, PA. I was looking for research-one universities, but found none there. In Roanoke, I found out that Virginia Tech was just a little further down the road. Unfortunately, the University didn't have a Department of Biological Sciences. Finally, I stopped at the University of Appalachia (UApp), which thankfully did have a Department of Biology.

Colleen Blake was a neurobiologist in the department who studied early brain development in mammals. Thankfully, Dr. Blake was looking for graduate students to work in her laboratory. We met with the dean of the college and they were able to transfer all of my graduate school credits from Nettie Maria Stevens University so that I wouldn't have to take any classes during my Ph.D. program. I was grateful for the two-year savings.

Dr. Blake had a joint appointment at Smoky Mountain National Laboratory (SMNL) just thirty minutes down the road in Clingman, TN. She collaborated with the Mouse House at SMNL. We agreed that part of my training would be to learn how to manage and conduct studies with the mice. So, I was given clearance to SMNL and worked both in the Mouse House and in a laboratory space she had in Building 9. I rarely ever went to UApp's campus, except for laboratory meetings, to fill out paperwork, and eventually to defend my thesis.

I started to rebuild my life piece by piece. First by renting a small house in Clingman, then cooking my own food, and then starting to jog up and down the hills of my neighborhood. I considered attending a church to meet people. Every time I did though, I thought about how I would be forced to face *Him*. I could deceive people about the things I had done, but God would always know. I would be reminded of this over and over again with every prominent cross, every artistic representation, Bible reading, sermon, and worship song. My fear of His judgment was too great. So, I stayed away and buried myself in research. There was plenty to do and a lot of Department of Defense funding to do it with because of the ongoing Cold War and now the election of Ronald Reagan.

A critical aspect of SMNL history was its involvement in the Manhattan Project. Briefly, the secret laboratory was created to enrich fissionable uranium and plutonium. These elements would be used in the testing and construction of the nuclear bombs used in WW2. Personnel from SMNL would help set up enrichment operations at the Hanford plant in Washington State. The elements from that plant would also be used to make nuclear bombs.

Nuclear technologies remained a focus of SMNL over the decades. Perhaps not surprisingly, researchers became interested in understanding how biological and environmental systems are impacted by radioactive materials. They created the Health Physics Research Reactor in 1962 to perform radiation exposure experiments. However, the research mainly focused on determining dosage limits and improving radiation shielding. They saw tumorigenesis (formation of tumors), but they didn't have tools to investigate *why* something was a carcinogen, only that *it was* and *in what quantities*.

In the early 1980s, we finally had some tools to understand the molecular mechanisms that caused deformities in people exposed to radiation. We also could discover why the children of those exposed to radiation from the nuclear bombs were deformed. Researchers in my department at SMNL were starting to address these questions by moving portions of DNA from diseased humans into healthy mice, making them "transgenic" mice. Sometimes the transgenic mice grew tumors and we could label the transgenes as "oncogenic".

While we had some tools for these kinds of experiments, it was important to develop more research tools. Without good tools it would be impossible to unravel the mysteries of biology and disease states.

Since Dr. Blake was interested in studying early developmental neurobiology, she wasn't interested in figuring out which transgenes were oncogenic. Dr. Blake was more interested in using transgenic mice to understand which genes were involved in mammalian brain formation. I asked her if my thesis could be on developing a system for transducing (putting transgenes into cells with a virus) and expressing transgenes in specific regions in the murine (mouse) brain and in specific cell-types (neurons, astrocytes, etc.). She agreed, and I set to work.

The key capability of a viral tool is that it can penetrate deep into three-dimensional tissue. This cannot be accomplished with transfection *chemicals* which only allow nucleic acids to enter cells on the surface of tissue. Tissue is a network of connected cells, so penetration into and throughout the network requires cell-to-cell transmission. This is a task well-suited for viruses.

I found that Retroviruses and Adenoviruses were potential candidates for our intended application based on my literature review. Adenoviruses had higher titer, multiplicity of infection, and protein expression. They could also infect dividing and non-dividing cells, whereas Retroviruses could only infect dividing cells. Being able to infect non-dividing cells is an important capability when studying brain cells that don't divide in adult brains like neurons and astrocytes. So, I focused on Adenoviruses but collected some Moloney Murine Leukemia Virus and Friend Murine Leukemia Virus (Retroviruses) for the sake of comparison.

I could have used a shotgun approach, collected all the viruses I could find and see which ones infected different cell types. I didn't want to go on a wild goose hunt for viruses with different serotypes though. So, I came up with a more elegant solution. I found one Adenovirus that infected a wide range of brain cell-types and then altered it to be more selective. Simply said, I created a gene transport system.

Dr. Blake was very pleased with the tools I made, and I successfully defended my Ph.D. thesis just a few years later.

Getting my foot in the door at SMNL was also a key outcome of my Ph.D. Dr. Blake introduced me to Olga Nikolaev and Dr. Louis Thuillier. These two were secretly leading a team to sequence a million Human Genomes to create a Human Genome-Phenome Database.

Olga and Dr. Thuillier knew that if they could correlate mutations with diseases, they could predict what ailments individuals were likely going to have during their lifetimes. They also knew that finding genetic targets was the first step to developing genetic therapies, which could be developed sometime during their lives before a diagnosed disease manifested itself.

Of course, disease is the first target of interest for noble scientists, but other correlations would be of greater interest to the government. Certainly, the scientists were interested in lessening the burden on healthcare, but the government was more interested in making good soldiers and productive tax payers. The prime interest that would drive the development of methods for sequencing the Human Genome and altering the DNA of humans would be the opportunity to make our enemies weaker or altogether eliminate them.

Chapter 56: Frailties

The Genotype-Phenotype Database construction became a concerted effort across the department. Top management told the group leaders that everyone needed to contribute at least a fraction of their time to the project. I got into a habit of working late into the evenings since I didn't really have a life outside of the laboratory. My work ethic and skills were recognized and I made a smooth transition into an Associate Scientist role at SMNL after I defended my thesis.

Reflecting on the new situation that I found myself in, it was like an oasis, resort, borderline Heaven compared to the hell I had escaped. Gina was absolutely right about getting out of town. However, Clingman and the Laboratory weren't perfect. There was a staring problem.

Eyes were on me in the grocery store while I walked through the aisles, waiting in the line at the bank, when I jogged up and down the neighborhood sidewalks, at the bench and in the Mouse House. Perhaps it was the placid inactivity of the valley invoking a worthless boredom and deviseth mischief.

A more generous theory is that the staring came from a mentality passed down by the generations before who were told, "You are now a resident of Clingman, situated within a restricted military area… What you do here, what you see here, what you hear here, let it stay here." Secrecy was a pillar of the community. Many of the residents were recruited to report suspicious activities witnessed at work and around town. So, it might have just been a faithful vigilance.

Amplifying my discomfort of being watched constantly were the sexual innuendos and come-ons of some of my coworkers. Unfortunately, some of the things we were studying *were* stimulating. Let me give you an example.

Gene-phenotype associations are sometimes not as predictive as phenotypeA-phenotypeB. The latter interaction may actually be more strongly correlated. Contributions from multiple genes (gene1, gene2, gene3…) could all impact phenotypeA to some degree, and cumulatively impact phenotypeB too. Besides being easier to interpret an A-B correlation, it's also important for our mathematical models to understand that phenotypeA is a better predictor of phenotypeB than geneA.

All that to say, the personnel often had long complicated discussions about breasts. Multiple genes determine the density of breasts, and the density (phenotypeA) is one of the strongest determinants of breast cancers (phenotypeX) in general, as opposed to a single type of breast cancer.

The density of a breast is not its firmness, as one might presume, but the content of fibroglandular tissue (lobules, ducts, and fibrous tissue) vs fat. The more fibroglandular tissue, the harder it is to see through a breast on a mammogram. The density of breasts has four official categories-A: almost entirely fatty, B: scattered areas of fibroglandular density, C: heterogeneously dense, and D: extremely dense. This qualitative range is much more easily assessed than trying to quantify fibroglandular tissue. It was therefore included in our data collection, and we found it to be a key predictor of breast cancers.

Breast data was the most commonly discussed phenotype among the male researchers at lunch. Coming in close *behind* was butt size, which is associated with genes that determine the origin and insertion points of the gluteus muscles, and the number of fat storage cells.

Talking about breasts and butts in the workplace relaxes sex-related communication, the private becomes public, and people, mostly men, start getting cheeky. "Would you like to volunteer for the study?" wink wink, and "How about a free cancer risk evaluation?" were typical come-ons.

I thought about different strategies to quench their libidos. You had to, because anything other than rejection would give hope, that would quickly transcribe into courage, and translate into come-ons and pressure. It was the central dogma of horny boys. So, I accentuated my teeth while biting into bananas and sausages at lunch. I regularly brought in a small serving of walnuts, shelling them with a nut cracker and smiling as I crushed them. These theatrics ruined aspects of their doctor/patient fantasies, but I needed to poison the other fruits of their minds.

The male mind has an aptitude for delayering women's clothing to bare skin. This is most easily done when clothing is well or tightly fitted. Loose clothing helps, but I went a couple of steps further, creating the appearance of misshapen breasts by ironing creases into my bras, adding dents and lumps, and uneven stuffings. I also stuffed my panties to give the slightest bulge in the back and front.

I also thought of suggesting that I was lesbian, some small comment to deter but nothing too overt in case I needed to deny. Homosexuality was considered a mental disorder by the American Psychiatric Association and one could get fired for "homosexual behaviors" since there were no federal protections against discrimination. So, I decided against using that tactic.

Dr. Thuillier, who was leading the Genotype-Phenotype Database project certainly didn't help the situation. He was an old flirt himself. Sexual harassment going on in the department was no concern to him. Getting a good deal on his retirement home before the economic recovery drove prices up too much was a much higher priority. That, and a nice capstone project at the end of his highly prolific career.

Olga Novikov, who worked in his lab for almost 30 years was the one driving much of the productivity. Her role in the Genotype-Phenotype Database Project was training recruited personnel in standard operating procedures and managing them. I was glad to help Olga with the molecular biology training.

I felt bad for her because she was always overworked and underappreciated. The United States government gave her and her family religious asylum right around the peak of the Cold War after the Soviets were successful in testing nuclear weapons and Communism was spreading through Asia. Dr. Thuillier and SMNL also gave Olga, a woman with Russian heritage, a job in a secure government facility working on secret government projects. Olga would never dream of upward mobility because of the lack of letters after her name. Still, she would work hard in appreciation to her saviors.

When Olga saw that I was serious about helping her, she asked if I could do something more than train personnel, something that would help move the Human Genome sequence along faster. Olga felt a debt to Dr. Thuillier, and wanted to help him finish his capstone project, but after thirty years of the laboratory and him, she was more than ready to retire.

She said to me one day, "The tools ve haff are too slow and dee vorkers are too few. I haff to keep pushing. I haff nyet time to find a vay to meet our deliverable timelines."

"I can work longer hours, Olga, and help more with the training," I offered.

"No, yoo haff dee deep molekyular biolohgy experience. Yoo might be dee most knowledgeable molekyular biolohgist in this place. Can I ask yoo to help me find a faster vay?"

"Yes, I will certainly do my best."

"Moy mily Virginia, yoo are vonderful!"

"Happy to help you, Olga," I smiled.

"I'm counting on yoo, Virginia. These unreliable people are like dee plumber in the drunkard's house."

Little did I know how important this side project would become.

Chapter 57: Tech Dev

Four years after I left, Gina finally made her move. None of the guys she dated panned out; plenty of fools, but no gold. She decided to go live with her mother in Arkansas, and wanted to come visit me on her way. While we had talked on the phone plenty over the years, this was the first time one of us actually came to visit, so it was very exciting.

I took her on a couple of nice vista trails in the Smokey's and to Music City for some live music and dancing. Talking on the phone was fine, but it was a sweet time seeing my friend and talking as we hiked and explored Nashville together. I also really enjoyed introducing her to tasty Southern foods like real BBQ.

She wanted to know how things were getting on at the laboratory. We talked about that from time to time, but I hadn't told her the newest development.

"Olga asked me to help her speed up a project. Don't tell anyone, but they are trying to sequence the entire human genome."

We were alone, sitting on a bald, looking out at the blue and green mountain sides. I didn't care if Gina knew. She was good at keeping secrets and, I thought, why shouldn't a taxpayer know what she's paying for.

"Wow! How big is that?"

"We don't know yet."

"Whose genome is the government sequencing?"

"I don't know. It's got to be a man though."

"Why?"

"It's got a Y-chromosome."

"Then, it's probably Carl Lewis, the fastest man in the world, or Bill Kazmaier, the strongest man. Super soldier stock."

"You're probably right. They're probably interested in making Captain America soldiers or *Sardaukar* soldiers, from the book Dune, to fight our enemies."

"That's cool, Virginia. How do you think you're going to help?"

"Do you remember in the literature review, the section I did on restriction endonucleases?"

"The DNA cutting enzymes?"

"Yes."

"How do those help you?"

"We have hundreds of REs, and each is able to cut some known sequence of four to eight bases. I found that EcoR1, for example, cuts over seven hundred thousand sites. Since we know that EcoR1 cuts the six bases GAATTC, we know where approximately 4.4 million bases appear in the human genome, just with that single RE."

"That's brilliant, Virginia!"

"Well, thank you, but I don't think it's going to be enough. Even with hundreds of REs revealing the sequences of millions of bases each, mathematically, we are probably an order of magnitude away from covering everything. In other words, the REs will only give us about 10%."

"Well, that's not too shabby, but how do you think you can get the rest?"

"I was talking to Olga, and she had a really interesting idea. Something with bacteria."

"What?"

"We know that bacteria can cut the genomes of viruses that attack them, called phage, from work done in the 1960s, but the mechanism was unclear."

"Wow! Microscopic warfare."

"Yes, it's pretty crazy. Well, Olga thinks that whatever mechanism the bacteria are using to cut the phage genomes must be more versatile than the REs."

"Why?"

"Because phage and other viruses are changing their genomes all the time to try to evade the immune systems of their hosts."

"So?"

"So, small bacterial genomes would be unable to encode enough REs to cut all possible invading phage genomes."

"Oh. I get it. Ice cream trucks might carry twelve flavors, but not butter pecan. Can't have something for everyone."

"Right, and whatever mechanism is being used can't cut the bacterial genome, it has to be specific for cutting the phage genomes only."

"Hm. How can it be so precise?"

"We don't know yet, but we think it's going to be the key to enabling us to cut every site in the human genome."

"Wow, genome confetti."

I chuckled. "Yes, I'm going to remember that. Maybe it will help make a good illustration in a presentation to the group. Thank you."

"Happy to do my part for the good old U.S. of A."

Chapter 58: REVs

When I got back after my mini vacation with Gina, I set to work testing Olga's hypothesis that there was a more versatile DNA cutter in bacteria. Over the course of a few weeks, I isolated a few hundred soil bacteria and electrically shocked pieces of phage DNA into them. We discovered that some bacteria incorporated those DNA pieces into their own genome, and that if we subsequently tried injecting the same DNA sequence, it would be cut up rather than incorporated into the genome somewhere else.

Olga thought this was fascinating and urged me to keep going. The months that followed were very exciting.

I tried electrically shocking *different* phage DNA sequences *sequentially* into bacteria. These sections were *incorporated sequentially* in the *same region* of the bacterial genome, almost like a book shelf. Between each "book" was a divider, a repeated DNA pattern.

The clues I uncovered led us to hypothesize that this bookshelf-like organization was a bacterial immune system. It seemed like the bacteria were protecting themselves from becoming phage replication factories by "remembering who invaded". With the records of pieces of invaders on the bookshelf, repeat invaders were identified and cut up before they had a chance to start replicating.

Then, I decided to sequence the regions around the bookshelves to see if there was anything interesting upstream or downstream. I didn't see anything obviously interesting with the first or second bacteria, but when I sequenced the regions in a few dozen, I started to see patterns forming. There was conservation; that is, very similar sequences appearing in many of the bacteria that were likely section encoding enzymes.

There were several more steps, but after months of investigation, I verified that the sequences around the libraries contained enzymes that could cut anywhere in a genome with limited restrictions. We decided to call these type five restriction endonucleases (REVs) because they cut like REs and there were already four other RE types.

I had to tell Gina what I discovered.

"You're not going to believe what I found!"

"What, Virginia?" Gina asked earnestly.

"I found an ice cream truck with every flavor."

"You mean what we were talking about on the trial months ago? The question of how can a bacteria cut up every potential phage that tries to infect it?"

"Yes! I found that some bacteria have enzymes that use a saved piece of an invading phage as a reference to cut up repeat invaders. Better still, I can actually isolate the enzymes that cut the DNA and provide a reference piece, and it will cut a non-phage target DNA; pretty much any piece of DNA I want!"

"How? I'm not following."

"The reference used is a guide ribonucleic acid, or gRNA, to "guide" them to the right target DNA. gRNAs are twenty-or-so base single-stranded pieces of ribonucleic acid that match the target DNA. There is a little more to it, but that's the gist of it."

"That's amazing! But you didn't discover an ice cream truck with every flavor, Virginia. You discovered pizzerias."

"How's that?"

"Well, the pizzeria staff have good memories. They remember their customers' specialty pie orders, and have their delivery men drop the specialty pies off. They don't have to carry every pie. They just need to make the right pie for the specific customer."

I chuckled. "Have you thought about being a teacher, Gina?"

"Might be nice to *guide* students in their academic growth."

"Haha. You would be the teacher that little boys have crushes on."

"Yeah, great. If only some men around here would find me attractive."

"Are you not going on any dates?"

"Couple here, couple there."

"What do you think the problem is?"

I didn't hear anything for a couple of seconds. Then, weeping.

"What's wrong, Gina?"

"I think I'm too old, Virginia."

"Noo. That's not true."

"Yeah, I'm thirty years old this November."

I was also turning thirty in December.

"All the guys that wanted to get married and have kids, already did. All that are left are the ones that don't want to do one or both of those things."

"Have you tried…"

"Yes!" She cut me off. "I've gone to church events, asked coworkers if they know any good guys, gone to dance halls; I'm this close to putting an ad in the classifieds!"

"Jeez, I'm sorry, Gina."

"Not your fault."

Sometimes it felt like it was though. I should have just told that snake, Bobby, to slither off the first time we met back at the Stevens University Welcome Week. I wasn't sure what to say to Gina.

She broke the silence. "I'm sorry, Virginia."

"For what?"

"You were telling me good news, and I brought up my depressing situation."

"It's okay. I'm here for you."

"No, no. This is your big moment. I mean aren't you going to be able to reconnect with your mom now? You did something amazing scientifically! There's no way she can deny it."

She was right. This was a big deal. The problem was that it was a secret, and she was a news reporter.

"I need to publish first. They tell me that some of the things we are working on will get published."

"When will that happen?"

"My management has been pretty vague about that. I mean, you remember the peer review and editing process with our literature review? It can take some time and much is out of our control."

"Ugh. Well, tell me something else that's awesome."

"Okay, Well, I'm pretty sure that with the help of REs and REVs, we're going to sequence the Human Genome much faster than was planned."

"That's amazing!"

"Yeah. Plus, once that's done, we will be able to use the REV technology to quickly identify which other human samples have the same gene sequences and which have genetic variants."

"You mean, did the customer order the same pizza or not?"

"Riiight," I slurred.

"Seriously though. I assume that comparison could be useful for finding disease carriers."

"Yeah, among other things. We know from radiation and transgenic studies some of the gene variants that are responsible for cancer. So, we can find out ahead of time if someone is at risk by taking a sample of their blood and seeing if the REV cuts (present) or doesn't (absent)."

"That's awesome. You said among other things. What else?"

"I don't know. It just seemed like a precision tool like this should have many more uses."

"I'm sure you're right. I gotta go, but thanks so much for telling me the great news. Tela high five, Virginia."

"Tela high five, Gina. Talk to you…"

Before I could finish my sentence, Gina was gone. I think I really struck a chord. Even though my faith was still healing from what happened five years earlier, I said a prayer for Gina, that she would find a great guy soon.

Chapter 59: The Women Behind the Men

The completion of the project was Dr. Thuillier's cue to leave. They gave him a nice retirement party with speeches from various members and a check for his decades of service. It was widely discussed that he and his family would be flying out to their retirement home in the Florida Keys. I didn't necessarily have ill will toward Dr. Thuillier, but it bothered me to see how nice of a package and sendoff he got, and how little Olga received just a short time after he left.

While the economy was bouncing back in most sectors around the country, one sector that wasn't doing well was agriculture. Commodity prices were falling and there was significant overproduction in the U.S. Olga and her husband owned a local farm and were running into debt issues. With the housing market recovering, they decided to sell their land to developers. At the same time, Olga was having to piece together billing hours from different SMNL projects now that Dr. Thuillier was gone. The stress was too much for her and she decided to take her pension and go. My friend, Olga, the elite female scientist, retired with far less compensation and tribute than Dr. Thuillier, whose best accolades were achieved on her shoulders.

When I looked around, I saw that women were generally allocated to more repetitive tasks at SMNL and were either not asked to be part of experimental design meetings or talked over. The leadership was happy to have women perform data analysis and provide reports. There was even some freedom inside experimentation as long as it did not reduce productivity. Gender equality progress was happening in the workplace but the advancements were incremental.

I thought that being part of this Human Genome sequencing project with Dr. Thuillier was going to open doors for me. I was contributing significantly to *the high-profile project* with *the super famous guy*. My assumption was that after doing this, I would be an Assistant Professor at the major research institution of my choice and rivers of funding would flow from the National Institute of Health.

The problem that I discovered was that no paper was written up for publication. Upper management wanted to keep the human genome sequence data a secret, and I was bound to secrecy. This meant that there was no tangible product of my work, and so no potential for recognition and vocational advancement. Worse still, with the project complete, it was unclear what we would be doing next at SMNL. Without work, it was possible that I would be laid off soon.

This fear amplified when a man in full military uniform arrived at the laboratory, and started calling staff into his office, some of them crying or long faced as they were escorted out of the building. This was all very discouraging and I began to doubt my potential for success in science.

When it was my turn, I felt the blood drain from my face.

"Please, come in."

The office I stepped into was very tight with just enough room for the filing cabinets, desk, and the chair on each side. It was borderline claustrophobic with the two military men standing in the corners to my right and left. A quick glance, and I knew they were the ones who were escorting people out of the building.

The man before me looked like a sparkleless diamond. He stood tall with handsome features like a high and tight dirty blonde trim, tan face, a chiseled jaw, bulging chest and limbs, and thin abs that fit trimly in his well-tailored flawlessly pressed long sleeved uniform. He was also simultaneously intimidating with laser-focused probing eyes, droopy brow, crooked polite smile, and continuously stiff posture. The stony demeanor obscured whatever charming aspects might be there.

"I'm Major Lance." He extended his large meaty hand to shake, which swallowed mine. The grip seemed to be carefully controlled to avoid harm but conveyed no hint of warmth or reassurance.

"I'm Virginia Goreman."

He briefly looked down at a file on his desk. "Yes… My superiors have given me command of this facility, and I am conducting interviews for a special project. I think you may be a good fit. Johnson and Davidson, please station yourselves in the corridor until I call you back in."

"Yes sir," the military men harmonized. They saluted and stepped out of the office, closing the door behind them.

The blood returned to my face, and I felt less nervous knowing that this was an interview.

Major Lance continued, "I have some questions for you and I want you to answer as honestly as possible."

"Okay," I answered suspiciously.

"What do you think of the President?"

'Is this a softball?' my anxiety wondered. 'Something to get our lips loose?'

"President Reagan is admirable; strong, assertive, and articulate," I answered honestly.

"What about his policies?"

"I like that he is rebuilding national pride and lowering taxes." I avoided some policies that I felt double minded about.

"What about foreign policy?"

"I like that he's strengthening our military to protect us from the Soviet Union and that he's tough with Mikhail Gorbachev."

"Anything you don't like about his foreign policy?"

"No." I couldn't think of anything.

"Good. Would you do anything to protect your country?"

"Yes. I believe in standing up for what's right and protecting what matters." Remembering that this was an interview, I added, "You can count on me to do my part if you are looking for people to help defend our country."

"I'm glad to hear that. Do you have any prior management experience?"

"Some. I managed a team of four, including myself, to write a scientific literature review during our undergraduate studies."

He looked unimpressed.

I clarified, "I was able to motivate my team to read scientific articles and summarize them while they were doing all their normal studies for four semesters until we completed the project successfully, which included a rigorous peer-review process. Please note that I did that without having managerial authority."

"So, this wasn't like a class project?"

"No, not in the least. I wanted to have an edge over my peers for getting into graduate school. So, I assembled a team to help me complete what is typically one of the first milestones scientists have in graduate school."

"And you did that during your undergraduate studies?"

"Yes."

"Hm." He stuck his lip out, looking more impressed. "How did you motivate your team?"

"I convinced them that it was in their best interest."

"Anything else?"

"I paid for some food and arcade games from time to time for the sake of rest, appreciation, and team building."

"Okay, any other leadership experience?"

"I've trained scientists here in molecular biology techniques."

"Anything else?"

"No, that's it."

"Okay, next question. Do you know if REVs can be used to cut DNA inside of cells?"

I wasn't sure who had told him about REVs or why he was asking about them, but I answered honestly.

"I'm not sure. So far, we've only applied the REVs to naked genomic DNA in test tubes."

"Do you think it's possible?"

"Yes, it would just require some method of introduction of the REVs and gRNAs through cell membranes."

"Great! Then I'm going to give you a trial run. Your job is now to demonstrate that REVs can cut target DNA in cells. That is all. You can leave and ask the soldiers to come back in."

I was surprised by the abrupt ending to our conversation, but wasn't going to complain. I was happy to still have a job.

"Thank you, sir."

Chapter 60: Friendship from Afar

"I'm sorry. Were you really hoping that I was going to come live with you for a while and go on double dates with you?"

"I was," answered Gina, sounding very disappointed. "Mama is trying to do matchmaking with her church friends."

"Oh! Any good ones?"

"Maybe."

"Who?"

"Angelo. He's a transplant too, and Catholic. I'll let you know how it goes."

"You haven't gone on a date?"

"No. We only talked over the phone. It would have been nice if you were here so we could double and ditch."

Double and ditch was a strategy we never got to implement in college because we each only dated one guy. The idea was that we would leave together if one or both of us didn't like our dates. That way we wouldn't have to reject a kiss or whatever the guy had in mind at the end of the night.

"Well, my job isn't exactly secure," I lied. I felt pretty confident Major Lance was going to keep me.

"You're too good at molecular biology, Virginia. They'll definitely keep you if they are trying to do something with the enzymes *you* discovered."

It was nice to hear the praise and that Gina wasn't betting on me coming to Arkansas. Her confidence made me feel less worried that she'd be more disappointed later if I succeeded.

"Thank you, Gina. That's nice of you to say."

"Yeah. Yeah. So, how are you going to demonstrate how awesome you are?"

"They want me to show that REVs work on cells instead of just naked DNA. So, the REVs have to get through the outer membrane and into the nucleus. Those hurdles aren't trivial."

"No, they don't sound like they are."

"There are also other potential issues like the DNA being inaccessible because it's wrapped around a histone or something. I can't worry about that though."

"Are you going to tell me your grand plan or what?"

"What's the urgency?"

"You're keeping me in suspense." She sounded a little ungenuine.

"If you don't want to talk about this, it's fine, we don't have to." I felt a little disrespected.

'Do we bore her?' Asked my pride.

"Sorry, Virginia. It was just hard to hear that you weren't coming to Arkansas. I'm mad with SMNL for not letting you go, not with you." I could tell she was trying to be funny.

"Okay," I forgave, and asked considerately, "Do you want to stop talking about this?"

"No, no. Please tell me about your idea." I was glad because I really did want to share with Gina. I thought it was pretty clever.

"Great! My elegant experimental design will make it easy for me to tell if the DNA in the cell is getting cut."

"How is that?" I could hear the intentional enthusiasm and appreciated it whether it was real or just out of love.

"I'm going to target genes known to be critical for mitosis."

"Ah, I know that word. You're talking about cell duplication genes. If the DNA is cut, the cells won't replicate, but your control cells will. Which also means few cells after a week of incubation, and no DNA cut means many cells. Easy visual test."

"Exactly!"

"That is smart. What are you going to do about getting your REVs into the cells though?"

"I found in the literature that some chemicals can help usher proteins and nucleic acids through membrane barriers. I'll test a bunch to see which one works best."

"I knew you had it figured out! What a science rockstar!" She gushed.

"Stop. Stop." My modesty was obviously disingenuous. My ego loved the compliment.

A month later, I was glad to report to Gina that the experiment was a success, and that Major Lance told me the higher ups were very pleased.

I also wanted to tell her that Major Lance wasn't as polished in his professionalism as I initially perceived.

Chapter 61: D.O.D. Offer

"Major Lance is a chauvinistic pig, far worse than Dr. Thuillier."

"What did he say to you? I'll kill him!"

"You're so sweet. He didn't say or do anything to me."

"Then who? What happened?"

"I came late one night to the laboratory to passage some cells and saw him and Shelly, one of the young Research Associates, in his office. He was…very passionate."

It was shocking and I didn't like that Major Lance was probably abusing his power and maybe the young woman a little based on her gasps, though it was hard to tell. The impropriety was a little exciting; the memory, somewhat amusing now. Looking back, I probably could have walked away sooner but eavesdropped for a few extra minutes more than was necessary to establish the fact. Certainly, peeking wasn't necessary.

Telling Gina about it made her concerned. "Watch out for that guy."

"Thank you. I will."

"Don't keep going late to that lab when there's no one else around."

"Okay, Gina," I said assuredly. There wasn't any point arguing with her, and I would do what I wanted anyway without telling her and getting her more worried.

The following day, Major Lance called me into his office. He dropped a folder on his desk and nodded, signaling me to pick it up, but I didn't. The difficulty came from recalling what I had seen on the top of the desk the night before.

So, he picked it up and held it out. "I'm offering you a senior scientist position. You have the most experience with REVs and viral transduction experience on the team, and some leadership experience. I want you to manage the project and personnel to determine if REVs can work *in vivo*."

The Latin phrase *in vivo* literally means "in the living". Scientists use the term to mean carrying out experiments inside a living organism as opposed to experimenting outside of a living system like with cells on a Petri dish or naked

327

nucleic acids in a test tube. They wanted me to demonstrate that REVs worked *in vivo*, not just on a Petri dish or in a test tube.

I was immediately excited by the offer. Not only was it a promotion, it was a potentially another high-impact project. My initial thought was that cutting DNA inside of cells, tissues, animals, and ultimately humans could lead to cures for various diseases. Cutting DNA in cancer cells for example could kill those cells or whole tumors.

Then, I mentally collected myself and remembered that this was an interview. There were points that needed to be negotiated and I shouldn't appear too eager.

"How much FTE support will I receive for the project? Senior scientists don't manage personnel." I explained in case he wasn't familiar with the SMNL hierarchy system. At the senior scientist level, I had to request full-time employee (FTE) hours from their supervisors.

"Yes, promoting you two levels is not an option. You will need to be creative with motivating your team since they do not report to you. But you shouldn't have trouble with that. You got college students to spend months of time working for little more than pizza or whatever and arcade games," he mocked.

"Yes, sir, but…"

He cut me off. "This is a high priority project, so you will receive the FTE hours you need, and before you ask, if you do well on this project, I will see to your promotion." He shook the folder in his hand, signaling that I better take it.

Staff scientist was the next level up from senior scientist, and all levels above senior scientist would involve giving me direct reports, which is what I really wanted. Beyond staff scientist, there were only two more levels for the scientist track at SMNL, senior staff scientist and principal scientist. If I continued on this track, I wouldn't need to go back to academia and split my time with teaching classes. Yes, I would probably need to transfer to the National Institute of Health (NIH) or National Institute of Environmental Health and Science (NIEHS) because my research in human development would need to better align with the mission of the organization. But this was no big deal. Transfers were common between government institutions. Furthermore, with my experience and the government's resources, I was sure I could have the project done within a couple of years. That kind of rapid rise in the ranks despite my career setbacks was too good to pass up.

Forgetting about the sex scene on his desk, I took Major Lance's folder. He handed me a pen, and I began signing and initialing the forms to accept my new employment. Additionally, a new non-disclosure agreement and non-compete agreement was included. My presumption at the time was that this was to prevent me from taking intellectual property to another organization. I didn't mind since I had already signed papers like these when I first started. Still, I wondered why I would need to sign more now. The legalese was challenging to understand, so I asked what it was about.

"Basically, it says you won't be a traitor and sell information to the Soviets," he said frankly. "I can't tell you more about this project until you sign the documents. What I can tell you is that your funding will be coming from the Department of Defense, and the research will not be published."

Confused, I thought, 'The Department of Defense? Why not the National Institute of Health? Why would the DOD want to fund a technology that cuts DNA?'

"So, the main goal here is not to stop the growth of cancer cells?" I asked.

"You will be stopping a kind of *philosophical* cancer," he replied.

Then, I realized, 'Maybe they don't want to cut the DNA of diseased cancer cells, but the DNA of healthy cells of enemies.'

The idea of creating biological weapons bothered me. However, I didn't really believe that the U.S. would actually release them to kill people unless we were being attacked. A good offense makes the best defense, and defense is important for a country and for an individual. I needed to defend myself against Jim and regain my freedom from him with good offense. Similarly, the U.S. has defended its freedoms with good offense.

With that, I believed that contributing to our nation's offense/defense should come with extra benefits. This interview was an opportunity for negotiation, which I *loved*.

"I am grateful for the opportunity to serve my country and democracy. Thank you. Wars come and go though, so the work may dry up. My employment opportunities outside of government may also dry up since my work will not be published. Can I count on you for a positive recommendation to other institutions like NIH or NIEHS and help with transfer when the time comes?"

"Yes, upon completion of this project, you may request a transfer and I will support it if you like," he replied.

"Can you tell me the salary and benefits for this position?" I asked.

"The annual salary is $30k, we supplement health, dental and vision insurance, and you are eligible to start vesting a pension plan," he said with his small polite smile.

This sounded very good to me, certainly an increase compared to my current salary. However, I knew from my women's studies class in college that we were making something like two thirds of what a man was making.

"$45k," I countered.

"Huh. That's quite a gamble, Ms. Marshall." His polite smile cracking open a little more, "You are a strong candidate. So, I will raise the offer to $35k because of your exceptional skills and experience."

"Perhaps I don't mind some risk. How much would you offer a man for the same job? I think around $43.5k, right?"

"Are *you* sure you're not a man? Ballsy, even antagonistic. What do you think you're going to gain by accusing me of sexism, Ms. Marshall?"

"I saw what you were doing to Shelly last night. The position you were in certainly didn't make me think you are egalitarian."

After a pregnant pause, I countered, "I'm at least worth $42k."

"$42k, and you don't speak of that again."

"Deal."

We shook hands, and I finished signing the paperwork.

Chapter 62: Team Building

'The key to our success will come from personnel management,' started my confidence.

'Yes, because it's a huge project and we can't do all of it ourselves!' Exclaimed my insecurity.

My impatience barked, 'They should have just promoted us so that we can directly manage people.'

'They'll give us the people we need,' replied my optimism.

'But can we get the clever ones?' Asked my skepticism.

'If they're not going to give us carrots or sticks, we need to use psychology again,' petitioned my manipulation.

'Maybe we can motivate some younger team members with free food, but yes, we need to make them want to work on this project to be successful,' agreed my loyalty.

'Agreed,' approved my other emotions.

'Start with the goal!' exclaimed my eagerness. 'Before talking about who we want.'

'Show the REVs can be delivered into humans and cut target DNA,' acquiesced my respect.

'Now the milestones!' Eagerness urged.

'Really?' My irritation asked.

'The milestones! The milestones!' Badgered my eagerness.

'Okay. Okay,' soothed my respect. 'Test viruses and find the ones that spread through tissue well.'

'Lots of virus!' Exclaimed my excitedness.

'We need to show REVs cut many different gene targets in cells because we only know they work consistently on naked DNA,' explained my respect.

'That can be done in parallel,' said my efficiency.

'Yes, then we put REVs that cut DNA targets in cells effectively into virus that spread through tissue effectively, and demonstrate the unified system on mice,' concluded respect.

'Sounds good, but we need to avoid that word *virus*. It makes people think of something contagious, disease, and death. Say *vector* so they think transfer,' suggested my deception.

'Yeah! Yeah! Yeah! Who do we want?' Asked my impatience.

'Definitely Skii,' insisted my power. 'She's the best computer scientist we have in the department.'

Skii was the one who stored the entire human genome into queryable sections for us. After previously working as a human computer for NASA, calculating the trajectories of rockets for accurate splashdown points and other complex problems involving astronomy, navigation, and physics, she became interested in solving data-heavy biology problems. Our department at SMNL had lots of data-heavy biology problems, and with the fastest supercomputers in the world, SMNL was the ideal place for her to make a transition.

'Yeah, yeah, and Ziggy,' recommended my excitement. 'We want him for biochemistry.'

'Yes, and to work with Skii and find us DNA targets,' manipulation agreed.

Ziggy, one of the most senior biochemists in the department, was an expert in enzyme domain structures. He could look at nucleic acid or amino acid sequences and point out sections that encoded enzymes, and in some cases, make predictions of functional categories. I knew that Ziggy liked puzzles and took great pride in solving them. I also knew that he liked praise, especially from Skii. They flirted, even though Ziggy was married and had three kids. While I didn't approve of this behavior, I knew I could use their relationship to recruit and manage both of them.

Ziggy and Skii were working on annotating the mouse and human genomes together and could help me predict which REV targets would be lethal to both. I told them about my work plan.

"Why do you want lethal targets?" Asked Skii.

"To kill mice," I said.

"We have poison and traps for that. Why use REVs?" Asked Ziggy.

"Making cancer models, or mice with tumors, is very time consuming and an unnecessary complexity right now. We'll get there…"

Their faces changed from concern to interest.

"Oh, so you want to use this technology to cut tumor DNA?" Ziggy clarified.

"That's the idea," I answered.

"Oh, cool!" said Skii.

"For now though, whole organism death is similar enough to tumor death. A mouse is similar in size and a mouse dying is easy to visualize and quantify. I just need this nice quick assay to show that REVs work."

"Then what?" Asked Skii.

"Management gives me funding and time to make cancer models."

"Yeah. I guess there needs to be a proof of concept," said Ziggy reluctantly. "It's a shame how many mice we will need to kill."

These mathematicians understood better than most that even the most basic statistical tests demanded dozens of biological replicates per test condition. We would need to do many tests; replicate tests for every vector, every DNA cut site, combinations of vector and cut site, and any other variables we wanted to test like concentration of virus. The numbers multiply quickly.

"Killing mice is a bummer, Virginia," agreed Skii.

'You wouldn't worry so much about the mice if you knew they were a proxy for killing humans,' commented my guilt.

'It's for U.S. defense,' justified my peace.

Ziggy sighed. "If a cure for cancer is possible then I'd like to help," decided Ziggy, looking at Skii fondly.

Skii smiled and agreed, "Me too."

"Thank you. I really appreciate you both," I said sincerely as I left the office.

I was just glad they didn't ask why I wanted to predict which targets were lethal to humans. BS gets smellier as it piles up.

The higher-ups, whoever they were, encouraged me to use curing cancer as a cover story for developing REVs, and I did advocate their propaganda. Certainly some team members might have been able to accept developing weapons for a job; the scientists who worked on the atomic weapons dropped on Hiroshima and Kokura during World War II in these very SMNL facilities decades earlier did. Many today though wouldn't, even if they felt as I did about defense being the best offense. Today's SMNL researchers were passionate about curing diseases and remediating an environment, making up for the harms caused by creation and application of the nuclear weapons. Cree, who was walking down the hall sing-mumbling a lyric from Anarchy in the UK, was that kind of person; a philanthropist and environmentalist.

Cree stopped singing when he saw me. I could see why he didn't want others to know he liked punk rock. Not a good look when you work for the government. However, neither being a philanthropist, environmentalist, nor government worker, necessitates one being establishmentarian.

Cree worked as a histologist, and he was very good at it. Furthermore, he was extremely creative. I really wanted him on my team to compare tissue spread of test viruses.

"Do you mind joining me for lunch?" I asked before he could pass by.

He stopped. "Okay. What time?"

"Noon?"

"Sure."

A couple of hours later, we were deep into a conversation about punk rock artists and their social activism.

"Our government is failing the poor. You need to listen to the Dead Kennedys."

"Okay. I will," I tried to sound earnest to cultivate some favor. "I admire you for wanting to be part of the solution; trying to make what's broken better."

"What do you mean?" he asked.

"Well, you're here, right?"

Cree scoffed. "This is a job. I can do it well with my eyes closed, but I'm not under any delusion that I'm helping anyone. Maybe way down the road, but not now."

"That's true. Our work is mainly about diagnosing disease and better understanding disease mechanisms. We're not developing many cures here at SMNL. Would you want to be a part of one of the only projects at SMNL that is applied if you could?"

"Bloody yeah I would. Are you trying to say that we're doing clinical trials somewhere on campus?"

"Preclinical, but still applied."

"No, I'm sure you're just talking about more mouse killing. Nothing ever comes of it." He started to get up.

I got up and rested a hand on his shoulder. "Wait. Is it going to hurt you to hear me out?"

"Only emotionally with disappointment I suppose." He was very reluctant.

So, I cut right to it. "We are doing a proof-of-concept study to ultimately show we can eliminate malignancies by cutting cancer cell DNA with enzymes."

His mouth still curled in disbelief but his eyes showed more interest. "How's that?"

"You probably know cancer cells are very similar to normal cells so it's difficult for the immune system to detect and fight them."

"Right."

"Just a single base mutation can start the process of immortalization and cause a cell to grow uncontrollably into a tumor."

"Right, and?"

"I've found an enzyme that can cut aberrant DNA, even a single base change."

"You mean an enzyme that cuts the mutated DNA?"

"Yes."

"That sounds incredible." Cree was still sounding skeptical. "Let's say that's true. It somehow cuts the mutated DNA, leaving everything else uncut. Then what?"

"What do you mean, then what?" I asked confused, thinking the consequence was obvious.

"Are you saying the cell just dies?"

I actually hadn't thought much about what happened next. I had only tested cutting naked DNA and genes known to be critical for mitosis. Cutting the latter, specifically in the catalytic domains, stopped growth of cells. I don't know what would have happened if I cut somewhere else.

'We don't actually know!' fretted my anxiety.

'Actually, it's worse. We know the cells weren't dead from live-dead staining. The ones we cut just weren't growing,' clarified my reasoning.

"We're looking into that," I answered.

"Who are *we*?"

"Me, Ziggy, and Skii so far."

Cree's eyebrows rose. He knew their time was in high demand. So, the fact that they were working with me impressed Cree.

"What's your hypothesis?" He asked curiously.

I just guessed. "I think it gets deleted."

"Why?"

"Because we stopped cell growth when we cut the catalytic domains of meiosis genes." In the moment, I just reasoned. "I mean, the site might remain cut, but it definitely can't be repaired correctly because then cell growth would just resume."

"I guess that's reasonable, and as far as cancer goes, you're thinking that deleting a mutated base is going to inactivate whatever is out of control at the genetic level?"

It's funny. Cree was helping me connect the dots that I hadn't yet. My worry transformed to satisfaction.

"Yes."

"Deleting a base wouldn't fix every cancer though, right?"

I thought of a couple of scenarios that it wouldn't.

"Well, no."

Cree paused, squinting and glaring at me.

'He can tell we haven't thought through everything!' exclaimed my anxiety.

'He's going to call BS,' agreed my discouragement.

"So, you have Ziggy and Skii finding the right targets for you and you want me to measure tumor sizes for you and see if treatment groups look different than control groups."

'Oh my God!' my serenity exhaled in relief.

"Eventually."

"What's before that?"

"First, I need you to see if vectors can get through tissue to get to a tumor deep inside."

"Vectors?"

"Yes, I need to see what vectors will actually deliver the REVs."

"REVs are the cutting enzymes?"

"Yes."

While I was explaining that the REV genes would be encoded in the vector genomes for delivery, Cree asked, "Why don't you add the GFP gene to your vector constructs?"

"What's that?"

"Green fluorescent protein, or GFP, is a *Aequorea victoria* jellyfish protein. It was discovered back in the 1960s. If you add the GFP gene and coexpress them with your REVs, you'll know where the vectors spread through the infected tissue because the infected cells will fluoresce."

Not a technique I had heard before, but a super good idea.

"That's a great idea!"

"Don't mention it. As for the project… I'm sure you can tell that I'm intrigued, but let me properly accept. I'll work with you, Virginia. On one condition, you check out the Dead Kennedys."

"Deal," I happily agreed.

'Our team is coming together!' my pride swelled.

'Who's next?' asked my eagerness. 'We need to get recruitment done so we can actually start doing this work!'

'Calm down. It's not like we are going to finish these experiments overnight. Science takes a long time,' countered my peace.

'We need to let the mouse house know the scope of our project so that we can get on schedule,' urged my pensiveness.

'That's nothing to worry about. We used to be one of them!' assured my optimism.

Rex, Earl, Arlo, and Teo were the mouse house team. They were responsible for managing large cohorts of mice for experiments; dozens, even hundreds at a time. They were a cheesy bunch, pun intended. I think finding humor in the day-to-day was a defense mechanism to help with the mass killing and butchering of these defenseless animals. They called it "euthanasia" and "prepping for histology". If you made them laugh, they liked you, and that helped with them prioritizing your mouse service requests, which translated into getting work done faster.

337

"Hola, Vir!" greeted Arlo chuckling.

"Looking extra shiny today!" Arlo had early onset male pattern baldness. So, I usually targeted that when he was joking with me.

"Olá, Vir!" echoed Teo with his Portuguese accent.

"High five, o'clock." I liked to simultaneously poke fun at Teo's persistent five o'clock shadow and give him a high five. I think he kept the rugged stubble because it was the manliest feature of his boyish appearance.

These Mouse House guys both liked joking around with me. When Teo first nicknamed me *Vir* (pronounced Veer), I just assumed he was abbreviating my name and commenting on the fact that I was working with viruses. He and Arlo would chuckle when they'd call me that. That didn't bother me; I actually saw this new name as part of the process of reinventing myself. Vir caught on with many other SMNL coworkers. It seemed odd to me, but months later, Teo and Arlo continued to chuckle when they would call me Vir. So, I finally asked what was so funny, and Teo explained, "Viril means manly in Portuguese and the root vir means man in Latin. We call you Vir because you're like a guy sometimes." My strategies to quench the libidos of my male colleagues apparently backfired, and the nickname was too widely adopted to correct now. My only hope was that the Mouse House guys were the only one's laughing at me.

"Is Earl around?" I queried. Earl was the best person in the Mouse House to work with because had a good work ethic and wanted to be helpful. Even though he liked to laugh with the team, Earl's skin was too thin for jesting. He was especially self-conscious of his slight overbite.

"Yeah, he's in the back cleaning cages," replied Arlo.

Rex, the Mouse House manager, popped out from around the corner. "What can we do for our former colleague?"

I didn't like Rex as much as the other Mouse House guys. There were a number of reasons. He was my former manager for a time, I didn't like certain aspects of his leadership style, and he thought his Castilian Spanish ceceo "s" as a soft "th" pronunciation was more correct or pure compared to Arlo's and Earl's Mexican dialects. I wondered if he was compensating for his wide nose and protruding chin that made him look like a man-witch.

Politely, I said, "Hi, Rex. I'm getting ready to do a big project."

Sounding interested, he asked, "How big?"

"Thousands of mice."

"Thousands? That doesn't sound very precise."

I could tell Rex was already making his normal transition from help to hindrance.

"I don't have an exact number yet. We are still designing the experiments."

"Well, if you think it's going to be thousands, you might be in the queue for a while."

"Rex, come on, you wouldn't leave an old colleague waiting in the queue, would you?"

"We have a limited capacity, and we have to be equitable with all of our researchers, even if they were previously part of the team. I hope you can understand," Rex stonewalled, politely smiling.

'BS!' barked my frustration.

'He's trying to be a good manager,' defended my graciousness.

The mouse house team were salary workers. Most SMNL members that weren't primary investigators, like Skii and Ziggy, were paid off of project hours that charged for their services on a time or deliverable basis. The mouse house team had to be salaried because mouse maintenance was an ongoing thing regardless of project load. Since it didn't matter how many projects they worked on, they tried to do as few as possible, and would put up roadblocks to researchers requesting services whenever they could. Rex didn't want his team working too hard. I thought maybe they would make it easier on one of their own, but nope.

'Ugh! This sucks!' my frustration continued ranting.

'Don't worry. Everything in science takes time,' my peace tried pacifying the other emotions again.

'Not if we have high-throughput robots to do it for us,' proposed my eagerness.

'Touché,' supported my creativity.

'I guess that means we need to recruit some automation experts,' obviated my reasoning.

'We only know two,' furthered my responsiveness.

Ewan was a thick-accented soccer-loving Scotsman. Jolyon was passionate about hiking around and finding waterfalls in the Smokies.

Before working on automation projects for SMNL, these mechanical and electrical engineers coincidentally helped build some of my most cherished college arcade games, including Terraform Tracy. I mean they weren't the game designers or programmers, but they designed the circuit boards, tested the microprocessors, integrated the control panel, monitor, sound system, cooling system, coin mechanism, etc. They made the body for the game soul. I discovered this when they helped us build the custom robotics for the Human Genome sequencing workflow. I had great admiration for these guys and definitely wanted them on my team.

"Hi guys."

"Aye, lass," greeted Ewan.

"Vir!" Jolyon exclaimed, and gave a single wave.

"Ah thocht yer project wis finished?" asked Ewan.

"Yes, the human genome sequencing project is done. I need your exceptional services again."

"Certainly, whit can we help ye wi'?"

"I need an automated feeding, breeding, sanitation, and euthanasia system."

"Are ye talkin' aboot automatin' the moose hoose operations?"

"Yes, they're always backlogged. It's going to significantly slow my project progress. I need a major speed up and scale up of operations."

"Well, that's going to be a *major* capital expense," Joylon emphasized with a little mockery.

'That's what we have *Major* Lance for,' my confidence mocked back.

"I'll need some designs and an estimate to seek approval, but I feel pretty confident that our funding will cover it."

The two of them looked at each other in surprise and then back at me.

"That's pure brilliant!" exclaimed Ewan.

"Yeah, that sounds like a fun automation challenge," agreed Joylon.

"Ye worried at aw aboot puttin' yer auld moose hoose pals oot o' work?" asked Ewan.

"They won't be out of work. There will still be plenty to do with the mice."

Rex's lack of cooperation didn't make me too happy, but I wasn't trying to threaten their jobs. The automation would just make their work different and also easier in some ways. I was sure of it.

Now that I had made lemonade from lemons, I still had a little more recruiting to do. I wouldn't have time to be a virologist, cell biologist, or molecular biologist anymore. My project manager role with progress reports deliverables and personnel management would keep me busy enough.

So, I recruited Shelly and Wren, both young graduate students hungry to learn every technique they could, like me when I was at their stage. Since they were still young and wearing rose-colored glasses, it was easy to sell them the story about developing cancer therapies.

With so much success recruiting, I was already giving my farewell speech to my bedroom ceiling that night.

"Thank you so much for all of your effort. You made tremendous progress toward developing cancer therapies. I'm sorry, but I must say goodbye for now. The government wants me to reallocate and continue the project at…"

'NIH,' advocated my success. 'They're better.'

'Not necessarily,' argued my pensiveness.

"The government needs your expertise now for other urgent projects," I continued.

"No, no, we want to keep working on the REVs with you! Take us with you, Vir! Lead us, Vir!" I answered myself pretending to be my adoring teammates.

"I wish I could. Sorry my wonderful colleagues. All things must come to an end…"

I waved at the ceiling and shut my eyes.

The faster I completed the project, the faster I could start doing public research and earn the recognition I needed to prove to Milli I could be a success in science. She wasn't wrong about how hard it was going to be, but she would be wrong about me being unable to do it.

Chapter 63: *Vivo In* Project

A couple of weeks later, I gave the project kick-off meeting.

"Your managers graciously sponsored this lunch meeting so that I could share with you the objectives of the *Vivo In* Project, or VIP."

Scientists think it's fun to give clever names to their projects, proteins, and pets. For example, the "Ken and Barbie" transcription factor protein was named because genetic mutations caused loss of male and female fly genitalia. Skii named her German Shepherd Kepler after Johannes Kepler, a German mathematician, astrologer, and scientific revolutionary in the 17th century. I wanted a clever name for my project so I went with *Vivo In* Project, VIP. I flipped the words from *in vivo* to *vivo in* to change the meaning to "living in the project", attempting to make light of how all-consuming it would become.

I quickly realized that the suggestive name, and telling potential team members that the project would be "all-consuming", were not good positionings for recruitment. So, I decided to make it an acronym, another favorite thing of scientists. By calling it the "VIP" project I was emphasizing the importance of the project rather than the amount of work it would demand. Psychology. Psychology. *Psychology.*

"Wow, catered! Nice job, Vir!" Arlo, like some of the other poor graduate students, were very happy to get some free food.

Teo added, "And, it's Alfreda's."

"Oh! I love that place!" said Jolyon. Alfreda's really was quite good.

"Please enjoy. Eat as much as you can. I probably won't get any budget approvals for incidentals like this again until the end of the project." This attempt at a joke sounded funnier in my head. Rex, Earl, Arlo, and Teo chuckled a little thankfully and others joined in.

"Please go ahead and eat while I'm talking, and feel free to stop me if you have any questions or comments… You have been chosen to be part of a high-impact project that I've been tasked to lead.

I detected some skeptical murmurs and half smirks. I think the senior members of my team saw me as a naïve upstart with rose-colored glasses. They would later bring me down to Earth with stories of "high-impact projects" ending in nothing, not even a single publication. That was fine with me. Much better than them having suspicions about my deception and the true intent of the VIP Project.

"Since we don't actually know the genetic causes of many kinds of tumors and their prevalence, we are going to tackle something more ubiquitous across cell types as a proof-of-concept, something easy to measure, before we go after specific cancers. Any questions on that?"

No one responded, probably since that was something I talked about with all of the team members prior to this meeting.

"Ziggy and Skii did some analysis and suggested targeting BCL-2, an anti-apoptotic gene. When this gene is overexpressed in B-cells, they don't die, even when their DNA is heavily damaged, resulting in follicular lymphoma. Since upregulation of the gene prevents programmed cell death, also known as apoptosis, we hypothesize that cutting the BCL-2 gene will prevent proper expression and folding of the protein, and induce apoptosis. A secondary hypothesis is that REV cuts alone might not induce apoptosis. Rather, it might only make cells more susceptible to apoptosis with radiation exposure."

Cree queried, "You said we need a gene to target in tissues. How do you know this is not B-cell specific? You know B-cells float in your blood, right? They're not part of tissues. They are part of your immune system and circulate in the lymph nodes, spleen, bone marrow, blood, and a couple of other areas of your body."

At the time, BCL-2 had only been studied in B-cells. "Good question. We don't. We are guessing that different cells also use BCL-2 as an anti-apoptotic factor."

"And that's not a high-risk prediction, given evolutionary conservation," supported Ziggy.

"So, does everyone like BCL-2 as a proof-of-concept target? Please answer honestly. I would really like to hear other ideas if anyone has any," I said, hoping no one actually did.

"Why not just target genes involved in mitosis like you did before?" asked Wren.

"It's not a bad idea. We know which gRNAs will disrupt activity. We've already tested this with cell culture."

Cree explained, "It will be difficult to monitor. Whereas cell death will be easy to see."

"Right, and Cree has devised a clever way of visualizing how our viral vectors move through tissue. They will be tagged with green fluorescent protein. Once we start seeing apoptosis, we can slice the tissue and under a fluorescent microscope with appropriate filters, we should see green spots across the two-dimensional plane of cells."

There was some clammer around the room. I wasn't the only group member that thought the idea was quite clever and powerful.

"These methods sound like they are good time savers, but are we being thorough enough? I mean, how will we know if the cells in tissue are dying because of apoptosis caused by REV cuts and not simply because the virus is killing them, or there is some immune response to the virus or GFP? Or maybe something related to the REVs?" asked Shelly.

"Like what?" I asked curiously. Shelly asked really good questions most of the time.

"You're the expert Vir, so please correct me if I'm wrong, but if the vector we use to infect the tissue integrates into the genome, and we use a constitutive promoter to continuously express the REV, the constant presence of the REV might result in off-target cutting, no?"

It was a valid concern.

She went on, "We don't really know how specific these enzymes are or for that matter if the specificity varies with different gRNAs. Another alternative cause of apoptosis could be the off-target cutting itself. It might cut once, twice, a dozen times, it might cut the genome to pieces."

'The Department of Defense won't care how REVs are killing target humans, just that they were,' argued my efficiency.

'No, but what's the real value of REVs? Not just killing, but selectively killing target populations or even individuals. Otherwise, they might as well release anthrax or drop a bomb,' reasoned my discernment.

'So, it really does need to be precise,' concluded my respect.

"Skii and I have designed the gRNAs to be specific for a single site, querying the entire genome for similar sequences. Also, our *in vitro* results would suggest that the REVs are very specific."

"But how do we know that as the virus replicates and spreads, the gRNAs won't mutate? I think it's likely they will, and when they mutate, they could be targeting something else."

There were pensive looks around the room.

"That's good thinking, Shelly. You've brought us to the precipice of a question we haven't considered. It's a question that could have very important implications in using this technology as a therapy for cancer."

'And assassinations' added my guilt.

"If the virus mutates, could the specificity of the REVs change and cut non-target DNA? That seems plausible. I will add it to the list of possible avenues of investigation."

Before I had a chance to continue, Shelly raised her hand.

"Yes, Shelly?"

"The idea of all tumor cells having the same mutations is idealized. We will likely need to make multiple gRNAs to cut different tumor cells."

"That's another good point, Shelly. Thank you."

"What do you think is more important? The vector or the target?"

"More important for what?"

"For eliminating a tumor?"

"I think both aspects are important. If the REVs make it into the right cell, a tumor cell, then they still need to cut in the right place. If they go into the wrong cell, the REV should have nowhere to cut. If they cut anyway. That's a problem."

Shelly looked like she was thinking.

I concluded, "The combination of requirements should help avoid killing healthy cells and leaving tumor cells behind."

Cells display lots of proteins on their surface, and viruses bind select proteins to phagocytize (enter) the cells. The protein displays on tumor cells are different from healthy cells. Therefore, we hypothesized that we could find or engineer viruses to only enter tumor cells. This would provide a double check. (1) Is it a tumor cell? Yes, then infect. (2) Is the REV target present? Yes, then cut. For the assassination application, there is no check (1). Virus would broadly infect whoever it came in contact with. In that case, if the gRNA mutated, it might potentially cut the DNA of any and all humans. Eventually, I would need a solution for this issue, but for now only check (2) was important to those funding this project. I would therefore give my team the excuse that check (1) is a refinement of the technology. Something for a follow-up study. I would say that demonstrating check (2) needed to be done first in a variety of cells and tissue before graduating to engineering a virus to have cancer-cell infection specificity.

Now was the time for throwing ideas at the wall to see what stuck. It also made people feel heard and respected. It was important for personnel to buy-in.

"Anyone else have anything to add?"

I didn't hear anyone.

"Great! Before we talk about our next meeting, I'd like to get agreement from the team that we use BCL-2 as an *in vivo* REV target for a proof-of-concept."

Shelly thankfully stopped talking after I said that.

Rex piped up though. "One thing we haven't talked about is biosafety. We need protection against these viruses, checks or not."

'Why did he have to say viruses?' grumbled my irritation.

I cleared my throat. "Indeed. In addition to our offices and laboratories in Building 9, we have been resourced biosafety level 4 labs in Building 5. Safety training will begin tomorrow. Renewed training will be available each month. Those working in the building will be required to participate in safety training at least every two months. That's just going to be me, Wren, and Shelly for now." BSL-4 is the highest level of biosafety available encompassing practices, equipment, and facilities. We couldn't be too careful with a technology that spreads through tissue and cuts a gene that everyone has.

"Any other concerns or comments?" I asked.

No one said anything.

"Okay, then please raise your hand if you agree with BCL-2 as a gene target for proof-of-concept that REVs can cut DNA of cells in tissue."

Everyone raised their hands. I got my buy-in.

"Great communication today, everyone. I'm looking forward to working with you on this project. Wren and Shelly, I'll see you tomorrow for training in front of Building 5 at 9 AM."

"Sounds good," replied Shelly.

Wren gave me a head nod.

Most people left together, but Ewan lingered for a moment. It looked like he wanted to say something so I asked, "Something you wanted to talk about?"

"Naw, naw. Just haein' a blether in ma heid. Ah'm no a braw external bletherer. The script seems pure dead brilliant."

I stared at him confused, trying to interpret what he said. Unfortunately, his interpreter Jolyon had already left the room. When I didn't respond, Ewan just said, "Bye!" and left.

"Bye."

Chapter 64: Climbing the Buy-In Ladder

Once you get a little buy-in from your team, it's easy enough to get more. Sales psychologists call this "yes laddering." Get them to say yes to something small and then work your way up to the big sale. I had sold the idea to my team to target the BCL-2 gene but had no intention of stopping at a single proof-of-concept for REVs. There were three main reasons to test as many REV targets as I could. (1) Science often fails. (2) I might never have as much funding at my disposal as what was currently available at SMNL, hundreds of millions of taxpayer dollars. (3) The more data I could generate now, the more preliminary work I could use to request grant funding later.

I went to Ziggy's office after the meeting with the whole team. His was just down the hall from mine on level two of Building 9. I knocked on the door and he welcomed me in.

"Hi, Vir. What can I help you with?"

"Hi, Ziggy. Thank you for helping me identify the BCL-2 gene as a good target for testing the effectiveness of REVs."

"You're welcome. My manager told me that I would be billing more time to the REV project. What else can I help you with?"

"I like the target you and Skii found, but don't you think that basing our results on a single assay is a little dissatisfying?"

"I thought this was just supposed to be a proof-of-concept?"

"Yes, but what if it doesn't work? What if the cells don't die with or without radiation exposure?"

"You're right. It probably would be good to make some backup targets. I'll work on that."

That was yes number two on the ladder. Time to go higher.

"Thank you. Another scenario that I think we need to consider is if the cells die."

"Isn't that what you want with this assay?" queried Ziggy.

"Yes, but how can we be sure the REV didn't cut off-target, causing the cell death?"

"I'm not sure. It would be challenging to prove. You don't know the location of the off-target cut. Also, to check for cuts, you need to sequence, and to sequence, you need to shear the DNA first into small pieces. So, it becomes challenging to know if an end of DNA was produced by a cut or a shearing artifact. There's also the third option that it's neither, perhaps something biological we weren't aware of. Yes, that's a very tricky problem."

"I have a solution though," I proclaimed, perking up.

"What?"

"My solution is to simply accumulate consistent results. I want to see cell death when we cut a critical gene, and growth when the target is non-essential for life. We repeat it enough times until we convince ourselves that the phenomenon is real."

"So, you want twenty or so different targets?" inquired Ziggy.

Psychologically, I knew it would be difficult for Ziggy to say no after saying "yes" to my prior requests. I asked, "That would be great; thank you, but how hard would it be to predict all cuts in the human genome that would be lethal?"

"Hm. I would think it would be very hard. I mean the human genotype-phenotype database helps us predict which genetic variants are likely responsible for everything from brown eyes to webbed toes. Obviously, it tells us a lot about disease, but not death. It's made of data from living humans, not dead cells."

"I see what you mean," I said, a little concerned that the ask might have been too big. After a quick deliberation in my mind, I decided to reframe the request. "I was thinking you and Skii might be able to set up some kind of query to predict all of the important regions based on conservation across the genome. I would think that more conserved, less variable, regions would suggest they were more important."

"That's a pretty great idea, Vir. Let me think about that." Ziggy looked around the roof of his skull and then snapped back, "You may need to do a screening experiment."

"What do you mean?" I asked, excited that he was troubleshooting with me rather than making excuses to not work on the project.

"I mean an experiment that targets every important region of the genome simultaneously rather than individually. Cut every site once in a population of the same cell type. Wait a few days or whatever to let the cells grow out, double five times, so the final population is 32X the original number of cells. Then, sequence to see which mutations are only present once or not at all. Those are the ones that failed to replicate. While death is not the same thing as not growing, it will narrow our candidates down."

"That sounds good, but how would I cut every site and only cut once in each cell?"

"You're the virologist, Vir. Is there a way to infect all the cells, one virus per cell?"

"Yes, if I know the multiplicity of infection, I can combine the right ratio of cells and virus so that each cell gets infected once on average."

"Okay, and can you make a library of about one hundred thousand gRNAs?"

"Yes, but why one hundred thousand?

"I'm guessing you'll want to cut a few sites in the protein-coding region of each putative gene? You might find that a partially truncated protein still works well enough."

"Yes, that sounds good! How will you decide what sites to target for REV cuts though?"

Ziggy said, "I'll have Skii look for domains that look like catalytic domains, cofactor-binding sites, coenzyme-binding sites, and membrane-binding domains. How about we say minimum of two cut sites, maximum of six, and an average of four cut sites? That should cover the majority of scenarios. I'll let you know if we run into a situation where we need more cut sites."

"Perfect! When you say "we", are you referring to you and Skii?"

"Yes, you really need me and Skii to figure out your targets together. Alone, I can only examine sequences with my eyes. With Skii, I can explain what I'd be looking for and she can write a program to search for all of the sequences that match my criteria in the entire database."

"I can do that. How much time do you need with Skii's help?"

"Probably a month to start?"

"A month?" I asked in a challenging tone.

"Yes, do you think that's long? It's actually a conservative estimate. I suggest requesting six months if you would prefer to make a safe request to my manager."

"I'll see what I can do."

"Vir, the other thing that Skii can incorporate is your idea about evolutionary conservation. Before I pick sites in the protein-coding regions that look important to me, I'll have her compare all of the available genomes to find the most conserved regions first."

"That's good justification."

"Yes, and let me also say that I can't solve these problems in a reasonable amount of time without Skii's computational skills."

"Thank you for helping me with the justification. Hopefully, that will be enough to get the time." I needed to balance sounding positive with making sure he didn't abuse the system just so he could spend more time with Skii and not get the work done.

"It's going to be great for you though, Vir. After you do the screen, the follow-up experiment is easy. Let's say we find nine hundred and sixty cuts that are low in abundance in the sequencing reads. You just need to see which of those cuts kill the cells. So, in your subsequent experiment, you can grow ten 96-well plates, the same clonal population in each well. Apply a homogenous population of virus containing just one of the candidate gRNAs to each well. If the REV cuts are lethal, you'll see it with a live/dead stain."

"That does sound great!"

"I'm curious, Vir. How do you package a REV gene and one gRNA into each vector particle?"

"It's going to depend on the chosen vector, and the vector is going to depend on the chosen cell type or types."

"Why is that?"

"Some vectors use common DNA replication, but others use rolling circle replication, reverse transcription, RNA-dependent RNA replication, and other replication mechanisms. Vectors that replicate differently will require different genes for packaging. Vectors also have different envelope proteins they use to enter different types of cells. The cells they can enter define their tropisms. So, I need to decide what cell type or types we are going to experiment with. Then, I need to find a good vector to work with, make the REVs, and package them up in the vector. It's going to be a while before I can run the screen. I actually need to decide on a cell type, make a clonal population of tons of it, freeze it down, and sequence it before you and Skii find the targets for gRNA design."

"How long do you think that will take?"

"A week to decide on the cell type, two weeks to grow fifty liters of it and freeze aliquots, and a week to sequence. So, let's say a month to two months."

"That works for me," said Ziggy. "One more question that just came to mind."

"Yes?"

"What if we targeted key functions of cells that would result in the fatality of an animal, like the rhythmic contraction of cardiomyocytes?"

"Not a terrible idea, Vir, but I like the high-throughput screening idea a lot better and here's why. If you mutate the important parts of the gene responsible for the rhythmic contracting, you'll need to prove the effectiveness of the mutation not only at the cell-level, but also at the organ-level or whole-animal level. Working just with cells is much faster."

"I do want to get things done faster."

"Plus, you'll get less information for the time and resource investment. We're going to get a lot more data from the screen experiment."

"Good points. Thank you for your ideas and help."

"You're welcome, Vir. Let me know what cell type you decide on."

I left Ziggy's office already knowing that I wanted to use A549, alveolar basal epithelial cells that became carcinomic tumor cells and were isolated from a 58-year-old Caucasian male back in 1972. Other immortalized model cell lines like HEK293, HeLa, SH-SY5Y, Jurkat, U937, HepG2, HCT116, and MCF-7 cells had their own advantages and team members might ask why we weren't using one of these. I would tell my teammates that I chose it as a model for lung cancer, great for drug metabolism studies and other trendy study designs of the period. In actuality I was interested in this cell line because it would allow me to study viruses with the highest potential for transmissibility; respiratory viruses.

Later that evening, I called Gina to update her.

"I got Ziggy. Skii was next. I needed her help bypassing the change control procedures with the human genotype-phenotype database."

"What do you mean?"

"The human genotype-phenotype database came out of the Human Genome Sequencing Project…"

"I remember that. You said it had like a million human genomes with paired clinician-validated phenotypes like green eyes, cystic fibrosis, and webbed toes. You knew what genotype caused people to have web toes because you had about 350 web-toed people's genomes in your database. True positives, true negatives, blah, blah… my question was: what did you mean by change control bypassing?"

"Ah. Well. You understand that we can't mutate people's genomes to see if a genotype causes a phenotype. In other words, we can't try to give someone webbed toes."

"Yeah."

"We certainly can't give them cancer or other diseases."

"Right."

"And we can't give unproven cures to diseased humans."

"Right."

"So, how can we be sure that a specific cancer is caused by a specific genotype?"

"The human genotype-phenotype database?"

"Not quite. Correlation isn't causation. The database is where we start and where we end. Skii can help me make a hypothesis and find genotype-phenotype associations worth testing, but we can't go further than a prediction with the database. Then, after my team tests a hypothesis, Skii can help me put the test results into the database as metadata. She can do this in half the time of any other computer scientist because she has final approval for what goes in. All the others need to submit a request for her to review, approve or reject, and finalize. Does that answer your question?"

"Yes, but can't you just not add the metadata?"

"No, we are legally bound whenever we use the database to generate hypotheses, to include those as well as the experimental designs, and the results. And I'm going to need to add metadata to multiple spots on every gene. It will be the largest metadata entry to date."

"Why? I'm going to make a population of cells, each with a single genome cut, and see which cuts stop growth and even kill the cells."

"I think I've got it. You're looking for more gene targets that can be easily assayed for your proof of concept of REVs. You'll cut all genes to find which cut sites are lethal, and then you'll have Skii put benign, stasis, or fatal in the metadata for each cut site."

"Yes, something like that. I imagine that there could be a number of other phenotypes, even just with cells."

"And how do you prove that a specific cancer is caused by a specific genotype?"

"You should know the answer to this." My tone was playful. I would have been wagging a finger if she was standing in front of me. "It's the same way we would prove a genotype causes webbed toes. With mouse models. Change their genomes and then look at the toes. Change their genomes and look for the cancer. That's the only way to prove a genotype causes a phenotype."

"Right! Yikes, I'm already slipping! The mind is making room for new work-related information and challenges."

"It's okay, Gina. You were right about the lethal cut sites in cells! I'll see if they are also lethal in tissue and then mice. Death will be an easy to visualize phenotype."

"Thanks."

"Speaking of work, how is your new job going?"

"Retail management at Wal-Market is not as different from lab management as you'd think."

"No?"

"I mean the tools are different and there's things I need to do now that I didn't before; like work with cash registers, the inventory control system, payroll systems, security systems, etc. There are more tasks but they're simpler. I think I like it better."

"That's great to hear!"

"And how are things going with Angelo?"

"I mean he's not smart, but so far he's alright."

"Yes?"

"He brought me flowers the other day?"

"Oh, that's right, he works at your store!"

"Sometimes. He normally works at the other store, but he picks up occasional shifts when people call out."

"What does he do again?"

"Warehouse associate. Drives the fork lifts, stores and moves goods, stocks shelves, and helps with inventory. It's blue collar but there's more to life than intellectual stimulation and money…" I heard a reluctance in my best friend's voice as it trailed off.

My tone got more serious. "Are you worried that you'll be settling if you pursue a relationship with Angelo?"

"No, I'm more so afraid that you won't like him."

That felt like an arrow to my gut.

'Why is she worried that we won't approve?' asked my surprise.

'Why does she feel like we have to approve?' added my serenity.

'Well, we are her best friend. Our opinion means a great deal to her,' answered my respect.

'We need to be careful here. We helped her choose badly last time," warned my inadequacy.

"I just care about you."

"I know you do."

"Okay, I'm glad you know that. Now, you say Angelo's not smart, he's not intellectually stimulating, and he doesn't earn much money."

"Yes, but he's also a former New Yorker from the old neighborhood, a Catholic, he brought me flowers, we have nice times together, and…" I heard Gina choke up. "He knows how old I am and was still asking me questions about how big of a family I wanted…" I could hear her weeping over the line.

"Oh, love. Shh. It's okay. It's okay. I'm not trying to get in the way of your happiness. When I meet him, I'll be nice to him even if he thinks a mitochondrion is someone with anxiety problems. We can talk about non-science stuff."

"Really?"

"And you're not going to get jealous and smash into our go-cart when you see us laughing?"

I had forgotten I did that.

"Yes, that was immature of me."

She sniffled and deeply exhaled. Then, her tone completely changed. "Great! So, when are you coming to meet him?"

Chapter 65: Falling Down the Buy-In Ladder

All SMNL members in the biological sciences division were eager to use the genotype-phenotype database. They wanted to know which ion channels, membrane transporters, signal transduction proteins, regulators, etc. were predicted to be associated with a particular disease condition or even just an undesirable feeling, like pain. So, then they could work on finding a drug to alter its function. They all had dreams of finding the next Aspirin, Clopidogrel, Metformin, Omeprazole, Statins, or Warfarin, and SMNL licensing their intellectual property to big pharma and retiring with a huge bank account.

Since the database was so valuable for finding targets, a committee decided that we needed safeguards to prevent users from incorporating erroneous information in the metadata or accidently altering the foundational data. So, only a few computer scientists in the department were given read, write, and execute privileges on the database. Researchers couldn't make direct changes. Access for researchers required billing a computer scientist's time to work on the database. While Skii wasn't the only computer scientist who had -rwx access, she controlled all change approvals. In other words, Skii was responsible for finalizing every change that was made to the database.

Reviewing the changes involved meetings and discussions that often took about the same amount of time as working with the first computer scientist to submit the change request. So, Members quickly realized they could cut the process time and cost in half if they just billed Skii's time to submit the change request and approve. That would remove the review process. That's why everyone wanted Skii, including me.

Even though Major Lance promised I would get the resources I needed, I was still a Senior Scientist, not a Member. Skii had no reason to prioritize working on my project. Rather, it might hurt her in the long term. It was important that she stay in the good graces of the Members who would support her with their grant funding for decades to come rather than me who had funding now but no track record of success or guarantee of funding beyond the next two years. And yes, Major Lance had the authority of brass, but brass could go just as fast as it came. Skii would need more reasons to work with me. So, I appealed to her data hungry nature.

Skii was very interested in my idea to compare all of the human genomes we had in the database to measure genetic conservation of regions in the Human Genome. She gave me the compliment, "Finally, a researcher who knows how to leverage big data!"

As sympathetic as I could sound, I said, "I understand how taking too much of your time can cause problems for you. I need to work on some other parts of the VIP project that will take me a month or two. Will that give you enough time to work through your current requests?"

"That should be enough time."

"Great! Can I ask your management for just a month or two of your time, at say the beginning of March?"

"That's a hefty amount of time, but I think we can swing that, especially if I layer in other projects."

"Great, thank you, and then we can reevaluate to see if you can find any additional time among your other commitments."

"Right on, Vir. Thanks for understanding."

Two months flew by as I trained Shelly to work with the A549 and other cell lines, use the sequencing instrumentation, and prepare plasmids for Cas9 and gRNA expression. These techniques would become Shelly's main responsibilities. Wren was trained on these methods at the same time as Shelly so he was familiar with these technologies. However, he would be responsible for other parts of workflows. The division of labor was meant to improve productivity. For example, Shelly's plasmids would be transfected by Wren into cells for viral packaging. Wren would passage viruses he isolated from patient samples with cells Shelly grew for him.

Then, Skii and Ziggy worked on the project for a couple of months. Things were going pretty smoothly until the mouse house team found out what the automation team was working on for me. I asked them to join us in a meeting with the other members of the project so we could resolve any issues. I really needed the teams to work together to automate mouse house processes.

I called a team meeting to discuss progress, challenges, and concerns. Skii and Ziggy started by reviewing the work they did to predict which genome cut sites were lethal for human cells, the lethal cut sites Shelly confirmed with human cells, and the predicted corresponding sites in the mouse genome.

"You are planning to kill mice?" questioned Rex.

"Yes," I answered.

"Why are you wanting to kill mice?" asked Rex.

"Yeh, wit they dae tae ye?" joked Ewan.

357

"No seriously," said Rex, "I mean, usually for cancer therapy projects the research teams make cancer mouse models and then track things like tumor size. If you're trying to cure cancer, why are you killing healthy mice? That's going to be a lot of annoying paperwork."

Everyone turned their heads toward me waiting for a response. A pregnant pause and I thought I was going to let Schrodinger's cat out of the box.

My whole project team (Skii, Ziggy, Shelly, Wren, Ewan, Jolyon, Cree, Rex, Earl, Arlo, and Teo) were all looking at me waiting for an explanation on how using REVs to kill mice would help us develop a therapy for lung carcinoma.

I said, "Making cancer mouse models with tumors is an unnecessary complexity, initially. However, we will get there eventually. For now, whole organism death is similar enough to tumor death and easier to visualize and quantify. We needed a quick assay to show us that REVs are working *in vivo* first before spending the time to make cancer models."

Rex would not drop it, "Just because killing mice is easier than making mouse cancer models and trying to cure them is not a valid reason for killing mice."

"No, but the efficiency of exchanging a healthy mouse gene with a mutated human gene is a rare event. We would need to euthanize more mice to make the model than what I'm proposing."

"You're saying that your proof-of-concept experiment will require killing fewer mice than how many we euthanize to make a mouse model?"

"Yes," I said.

"I am not convinced that our Animal Care and Use Committee will approve your research protocols. If you haven't submitted your proposal yet, please indicate that you will make animal models, and the animals lacking the intended mutations will be eliminated with your ulterior method rather than humane euthanization."

"Thank you for the recommendation, Rex." I did everything I could not to sound sarcastic.

I honestly didn't know what proposal Rex was talking about. No one ever talked about the requirement when I worked in the mouse house.

"Also, do you have any anticipation of what death by your method will be like for the animal?"

"Sorry?" I was dumbfounded by the question.

"Will it be fast or slow? Will the animal suffocate from lung damage?"

"If the REV cuts cause apoptosis of the lung cells, the rate of transmission of the REVs will be what determines how fast the lungs lose their functionality. I'm going to work with Wren to find a vector that rapidly spreads the REVs through the lungs, as fast as possible."

Rex reworded his question, "And will the animals die of asphyxiation?"

"Yes."

Another pregnant pause. I suppose he was allowing me time to explain why I thought that was okay.

"Vir, I really don't think you are going to get approval for these research protocols. It's one thing to kill cells, it's another thing to cause distress, pain, and suffering in animals. I would highly recommend you rethink your experimental design."

I was thoroughly embarrassed. I could feel the heat of my cheeks and forehead. I didn't have a good answer for Rex. So, I just said, "Yes, let me work on that."

"Sounds good, Vir. Let's meet again when you've worked those issues out."

Then, everyone got up and left the conference room.

Chapter 66: Accelerating Mouse Model Creation

I left the building to vent my rage.

SMNL is a fairly long campus. Aven Valley Rd is the 6-mile main drag that connects the two main guarded campus entries. There are also side streets, gravel roads, and dirt trails. It's a great campus for badged employees to go on contemplative walks and runs for exercise or to work out some stress. It's also a great campus to get pissed and scream at the heavens when myopic bridge trolls who don't like doing paperwork put roadblocks in the way of your research progress. After exercising your legs and/or lungs, you could take a shower on the first floor of Building 9; a warm shower for cleaning up or a cold shower for chilling a blood boil.

Right outside of Building 9 was a beautiful trail that went deep into the woods to an area called the burial site. When I first started at SMNL, I thought this was a human burial site because the historic Aven Baptist Church on campus had a cemetery and at one point it was Native American land. One day while eating lunch in the commons, I asked what the large cement cylinders sticking out of the ground were. My colleagues told me that radioactive waste from the development of atomic weapons during WW2 was buried in them. This made me wonder what else was buried beneath the surface of this secret facility.

Despite the suitability of our roads and trails, I rarely saw others on campus partaking. One exception was Shelly. She was a very fast runner, much faster than I was. Shelly told me that she could knock out a few miles, take a shower, and be ready for work before most personnel were on campus. Her intensity was inspiring. Shelly was also typically one of the last teammates to leave in the evening. I didn't discourage it. Lots of students work late hours in laboratories and she was very good at her work. While I liked her zeal, my competitive nature sometimes didn't appreciate how good she was at seemingly everything.

"Hi, are you okay?" Shelly asked me after I got done screaming at the sky.

"Oh!" I turned around, startled to find her just a couple of yards behind me.

"That meeting was rough," she sympathized.

"Yes," I said, not really sure what else to say.

"Sounds like you're going to need to make the mouse models. Is that right?"

"Yes, probably."

"I'm sorry about that."

"Mm. Thank you, Shelly. It's ultimately just a delay."

"I'm not sure if you'll think it's worth it, but I had an idea that might help you speed things up."

"Oh yeah, what's that?" I asked.

"I read your work on early developmental research a few months back. It's incredible. I can see why the mouse house hired you."

"Thank you, but what's your idea?"

"After I read your work, I talked to Arlo to learn more about the methods used to make mouse models, and discovered that the normal pronuclear injection procedure has a low efficiency of generating transgenic mice, between 1 – 5%."

"Yeah, and you probably also know that it's a very laborious process."

"Because of the low efficiency, they have to collect hundreds of embryos, perform as many injections, and screen as many pups by Southern blot."

"Right."

"So, since the low efficiency of the pronuclear injection procedure increases the time so much by increasing the work at each step, I tried to think of an alternative procedure that could result in a much higher efficiency of generating transgenic mice."

"Okay, what's the procedure?"

"I'll tell you, but before I do, do you remember the surprise observation we had when we did the REV screening experiment?" Shelly asked.

I did remember. We discovered from the sequencing data that in many cases a few bases were being removed around the sites we targeted REVs to cut and then the DNA was rejoined. This didn't happen with our *in vitro* studies when we were just cutting naked nucleic acids with purified REV enzymes. We hypothesized that it must have been something in the cells. While the observation was interesting, I didn't want to deviate from our goals to investigate. While I moved on with the project, Shelly had apparently considered the observation more thoroughly.

"Yes, we saw that some bases were removed around the cut sites and the ends rejoined."

"Right. After thinking about this, I realized that since the cut site was deleted, the site couldn't be recut."

"Yes, what's your point?" I queried.

"Well, doesn't that sound like DNA repair, something similar to what Evelyn Witkins observed in bacteria, right?"

It did sound like DNA repair, but I wasn't sure what Shelly was getting at.

"And?"

"Well, what if instead of killing mice, we make a mutant p53 mouse model and try to cure it?"

The p53 protein, also known as the "guardian of the genome" is a tumor suppressor protein, able to arrest growth in the G1/S phases when DNA damage is sensed, activate enzymes to repair the damage, and initiate apoptosis in cells with irreparable DNA damage. These mechanisms thus protect the errors in the genome from being replicated in daughter cells. We knew some gene mutations that would deactivate this protein and result in a variety of cancers in different tissues.

While I thought about this idea, Shelly added, "I'm guessing the number of p53 mutant mice with tumors would be super high, like more than 90%."

I was sure that there would be a learning curve and some method development troubleshooting, but I liked the idea.

"That's a very interesting idea, Shelly, but how would you then cure the tumors with REVs? I mean, removing bases around the mutation probably wouldn't restore activity."

I was already impressed by Shelly's idea. Little did I know that the next thing she was going to say would be absolute brilliance.

"What if we force the cell to do homologous recombination?"

Homologous recombination means swapping out one gene sequence for another.

"We can give the cell a DNA template. When the REV cuts, don't you think homologous recombination will be preferential over deleting bases and reconnecting ends?"

A cell would almost certainly prefer to repair its DNA by replacement with correct DNA; the fact that we have two sets of chromosomes is evidence enough. Shelly's solution was brilliant and elegant. It would allow REVs to be used as a tool for insertion and not just deletion mutations, for repairing genes and not just making disease models! Then, I realized that I needed to be careful in my response. I didn't want Shelly to outshine me.

"Correct! My thoughts exactly." I just reiterated what Shelly was saying in my own words and expanded to the terminal logical conclusion.

"Oh, you were already thinking about this too?" she queried.

"Yes, I was just upset because... well, can I be honest?"

"Of course!"

"I was upset because making mouse models and curing the mice with REVs is going to take so much extra time compared to just killing the dumb mice."

I could see she was believing me.

I continued. "We kill them all the time. We make them for a purpose and extinguish their lives when we're done. If we were so focused on their wellbeing, we would create some kind of mouse resort for them to retire to after their service. Rex and team could take care of them until they die of old age. Sure, euthanasia is going to be less stressful and painful than asphyxiation. I see Rex's point, but the speed of this project is so much more important than considering the feelings of the damned doomed mice."

"Right, we need to save people's lives," Shelly encouraged.

"Exactly. That's why I was thinking of getting some of their mice with cancer from another group, pretending like we were trying to cure them with the REVs, kill the mice as intended with the REVs as a proof-of-concept, and then pretend like the experiment failed."

"Oh, that would be faster. You should just do that," Shelly nodded her head up and down in agreement.

"One of the major issues with my idea is that Rex will almost certainly realize what happened, and he will make my life even harder than he already has. Please don't tell anyone I told you that," I urged.

"No, no. Of course not."

"We'll, I'm glad we had this talk, Shelly. I think it's pushed me more toward making the mouse model, and the p53 gene is a great target. There are a few others I'm considering. I'll let you know what targets you need to design gRNAs for the experiment later this week. Come on, let's head back.

Shelly's ideas were problematic. If I allowed her credit for those ideas, she could have carved out a career from my project and eclipsed me. Ask the Chinese. It's one thing to make black powder that treats skin diseases and acts as an insecticide. It's quite another thing to repurpose it into gunpowder.

Before I could act on this new plan though, I needed to convince Major Lance to give me the extra resources and time to get it done.

Chapter 67: Conditional Funding

Major Lance agreed that there wasn't a good way to get around the issue of convincing the mouse house and other group members that asphyxiating mice was ethical. He approved extra funding and time for me and Shelly to make a p53 mouse model and cure it.

Wren was right around Shelly's age but he never really stood a chance with her because of his short pointy nose, freckled face, eyebrow scar, and long slender limbs. She still spoke to him. "Yo! What's up?" she'd say because Shelly knew he was into rap music. Wren would slow down, freeze, and become distracted whenever she was around. It was cute at first, but became troublesome because of the mistakes.

Mistakes when working with human pathogens were not only bad for productivity, mistakes were dangerous. While far from the worst thing that could have happened, we irretrievably lost a number of isolates because they were passaged to the wrong cells and another time because the CO_2 incubator concentration was too high. When Shelly wasn't around, Wren hummed, clicked his lips, beatboxed when he got really into the music coming from his headphones, and moved along swiftly completing all his workflow tasks.

Thankfully, Wren spent almost all of his time in Building 5 working with virus and infected tissue. Whereas Shelly spent almost all of her time in Building 9 working with REVs. REVs outside of a viral vector are basically harmless because they are unable to penetrate into human cells. BSL-4 safety precautions are just not necessary with naked REVs. However, BSL-4 safety was needed for working with the human pathogens, and the viruses were needed for delivering the REVs to cells throughout a human's body, their organs and tissue, and to other humans.

I observed that the separation of Wren and Shelly was helpful for productivity, and decided to further reduce their interactions by eliminating every reason for Shelly to be in Building 5. She wasn't happy about this because she wanted the viral packaging experience, at least that's what she told me. I didn't acquiesce to Shelly's preferences because her complaints didn't impact her productivity.

In Building 5, Wren processed samples of blood, a variety of tissues, nasal swabs, buccal swabs, urine, and feces collected from patients at local hospitals and clinics presumed to be infected with viruses. Wren became an expert hand processing hundreds of samples per week, isolating the viruses, figuring out how to culture and preserve them.

The variety of viruses collected from the local hospitals and clinics in eastern Tennessee proved to be limited. We acquired a virus that worked well enough for infecting A549 cells for the screening experiment that I previously talked about. However, the variety he collected up to that point was far from my vision of a vector bank that I could use for optimizing REV transmission.

I asked Wren if he would be up for some traveling to collect viruses elsewhere if I could get funding allocated for it. At first, he didn't like the idea since he would have to miss college classes. I explained that this was important for project progress and that the option to work locally might not be available in the coming months. Wren was disappointed but was ultimately okay with just finishing up his course work at the University of Tennessee. He felt like the experience he already received would enable him to find a well-paying job. Since the stick didn't work, I tried the carrot. I told him that I was talking about going to California.

"You mean where the movie stars are?" he asked.

Smiling, I said, "Yes, where the movie stars are."

Wren agreed to go as long as he could add an extra week to his travel time for vacation. I found it amusing that keeping this job was not enough of a reason to travel and miss school but that a Hollywood vacation took precedence over attendance in class. Wren's request was approved. Major Lance got me the funding. Like every good Terminator fan, Wren didn't miss the opportunity to assure us of his return.

"I'll be back."

We knew from the news that Los Angeles was experiencing an HIV/AIDS epidemic primarily among gay males and drug users. I was able to get funding and approvals to send Wren to the institutions involved in care and research. He isolated HIV from a little over a hundred individuals in just two weeks. Titers from plasma were very high before the patients went on antiretroviral treatments.

During his extended stay, Wren enjoyed the Hollywood Walk of Fame along Hollywood Boulevard and Vine Street, held his hands against the prints of his favorite stars at Grauman's Chinese Theatre, got a photo of the Hollywood Sign, and went on multiple studio tours for the behind-the-scenes movie production experience. One trip made him a hodophile. When he returned, he suggested that I send him to New York City. "Lots of diseases there, right?" His interest was really in going to the hotspots of rap innovation in New York City and Long Island. I told him we had some other priorities, but that New York City was a definite possibility for future travel.

To determine which viruses we should save for our vector bank, we used a modified version of our sequencing pipeline to find the unique ones. We got some assistance from Ewan and Jolyon who added some additional capillaries and incubators to our sequencing instrumentation. Since HIV is an RNA virus, we had to reverse transcribe the viral genome into DNA and amplify before sequencing.

While we saw some matching HIV genomes, there were very few. The variation was high. In fact, almost all of the HIV viruses contained at least a couple of mutations and several had large rearrangements. Wren noted that the genome was so volatile, it would even change with cell culture passages.

Virologists had a general appreciation that viruses could change with serial passages in cells and animals. Pasteur back in the 1800s passaged rabies between rabbits, dogs, and monkeys noting changes in virulence (ability to cause damage to a host). Since then, researchers have developed serial passaging strategies to lower virulence while retaining comparable immunogenicity (stimulation of an immune response) for live attenuated vaccines. Similar strategies are used to increase virulence or transmissibility (ability to pass from organism-to-organism or cell-to-cell easier). With empirical testing and our sequencing pipeline, we were able to begin to see which genetic changes brought about these altered fitness levels and functions.

While some cell types are easy to transduce (infect with a virus) for passaging purposes, others are recalcitrant. Keep in mind that I'm talking about individual cells. Transducing human tissue and organs would have far more challenges to solve. The challenges would amplify when we tried infecting whole organisms, defended from viruses by physical barriers like their skin and mucosa and their immune systems; even harder with humans who could wash their hands, take antiviral medication, quarantine and isolate, and potentially get vaccinated. The viruses Wren was filling our bank with would give us more troubleshooting options.

I started sending Wren on field sampling expeditions, and had him travel to Mexico and Guatemala. Then, to Côte d'Ivoire, Ghana, Togo, Benin, and Nigeria. Then, to China, to Indonesia, and finally to India. These were known global hotspots of emerging zoonotic diseases, where viruses that previously infected animals were evolving to infect humans.

Wren was very successful in isolating numerous viruses from the herpesviruses, papillomaviruses, polyomaviruses, adenoviruses, anelloviruses, parvoviruses, circoviruses, and other viral families. We discovered that very few viruses could be used as vectors because they either did not transfer efficiently between cells, they caused cancer, and/or they killed cells. We didn't investigate the mechanisms of these failures, just kept testing until we could find useful viral vectors.

As planned, Cree added the GFP gene to the viruses Wren collected using state-of-the-art molecular cloning techniques. This made them fluoresce so that we could easily track their spread through tissue under a microscope. We could semi-quantitatively measure the efficiency of the spread by the intensity of the fluorescence. The higher the green fluorescent intensity, the more cells were infected. Speed of spread was less important than the ubiquity of cellular dissemination. REVs in more cells should translate into more apoptosis, a stronger likelihood of organ failure, and ultimately human death. We still measured the fluorescence at several time points post viral inoculation to characterize these rates for comparing viruses.

While Wren was busy collecting viruses from around the world and Cree was preparing strains for organ dissemination assays, I thought of another way to fill our vector bank. I asked Major Lance to request strains from an organization that had been collecting viruses since its inception back in 1946, the United States Centers for Disease Control and Prevention, also known as the CDC.

With all of the recent requests: the p53 mouse model, Wren's travel, and now this CDC viral transfer request, I wasn't surprised when Major Lance called a meeting to talk about expenses.

"Please close the door," he said as I stepped into his office.

"You wanted me, Major?"

"Vir, I know you want to amass a wealth of data, materials, tools, experience, and accolades for your future positions and career. I can appreciate that, and I think it's great."

"Thank you, Sir."

"However. Having your project members traveling and involving other agencies in this project exposes the project. I'm going to say *excessively and unnecessarily*," he emphasized.

"But sir, the team including Wren assures me that they are keeping the project a secret. There are no leaks as far as I can tell."

"It's one thing to tell family members. Indeed, it's often unavoidable but thankfully a historically benign source of leaks with secret projects. It's another thing to be seen outside of the United States collecting viruses. And yes, the Soviets are watching. It's yet another thing for me to make requests to the higher up decision makers at the CDC who approve transfer of infectious agents."

"Are the interactions between agencies documented?" I asked.

"No, they are not, because I won't allow that. However, I have to work twice as hard to protect us and hide what's going on here. The normal processes for approvals are not trivial, but having to cover our tracks is extremely complex."

"Are you saying that you're not going to make the request to the CDC?"

"Yes, I might not, and I also might stop seeking approvals for Wren's travels. Besides the excessive exposure, it's not cheap."

I could tell something was off. Something in his eyes.

"But Major, I thought there was plenty of funding available. Didn't Ronald Reagan double the defense funding budget?" I knew he did and he tripled the national debt to $2.9 trillion during his presidency.

"Yes, well, the money isn't really the issue here. It's more the exposure. We're getting on people's radar, and the extra work I need to do to protect us… I mean how important are these virus collections to you?"

"Very important. The risk is that our pool would be too limited for the vector screen and we would end up having to select a vector that's suboptimal for delivery of the REVs, or we have no vector that was suitable at all. The effectiveness of the technology is strongly dependent on the viral vector."

"You've already collected thousands though. Is there really that big of a risk?" he asked.

"There's a lot of redundancy though in our bank. The same kinds of viruses with mutations and shuffled around genomes. Not having the right kinds of viruses in our bank is a *big risk*," I emphasized.

"How big of a risk are you willing to take?"

His question was kind of confusing.

"Um. I don't know," I said.

"Well, I'm taking a big risk, right?" Major Lance said, getting up out of his chair.

I just stared. Still confused.

"Right?" He asked again.

"Right," I said, even though I didn't understand.

"Well, if I'm taking a big risk, shouldn't you have to take a big risk?"

"I guess," I said. "What did you have in mind?"

Major Lance walked around his desk with his hands in his pockets, he stopped about a foot and a half in front of me. Looking down at me in the chair, he said, "I've got a *big* risk."

In my peripheral vision, I saw his pants twitch. I looked straight ahead and saw his erection forming.

I stood up and tried to move around him in the space between him and his desk to exit the office. He grabbed me, swung me around, and bent me over his desk. I felt him push up against my glutes. It was summer and hot, even in the laboratories and offices, so I was wearing a dress. He kept me bent over with one hand on my back and pulled up my dress with the other hand.

Major Lance pressed himself against my exposed glutes, and my anger took over.

"No!"

I did a backward mule kick connecting with his nerve cluster. He yelped like a dog and staggered back, enough for me to get away and open his office door. I took a few steps down the hall before turning back and returning.

I peeked into his office and he was sitting on the ground, eyes shut, leaning against the chair that I had been sitting on holding his crotch with both hands. I looked around the hallway and then stepped in.

Quietly and sternly, I said pointing my finger at him, "If you ever try anything like that on me again, I will make *you* into a bank of the worst human pathogens in the world." Then, I left, shutting his door on the way out.

The first CDC request I submitted to Major Lance before this incident was for influenzae viruses. In 1986, two years prior, the U.S. experienced the largest influenza B epidemic in twenty years. Institutions all over the United States collected a couple thousand isolates and sent them to the CDC for further analysis and storage. With Major Lances help, we were able to get these strains as well as many influenza A (H1N1) "Swine Flu" strains. Wren propagated these for sequencing. We also collected some Respiratory Syncytial Virus (RSV) from the hospitals in Philadelphia that isolated them from the 1981 outbreak in the neonatal intensive care unit, Measles from northeast hospitals isolated during outbreaks in the 1980s prior to elimination of the virus from circulation.

Major Lance approved my requests from that point forward and his eyes never so much as lingered on me again. I'll never know the whole truth, but it seems like the big risks he was alluding to weren't lies.

Chapter 68: Automation

The new REV-based DNA insert/replacement method was saving the mouse house team a significant amount of time on making mouse models. The researchers were thankful for the faster turnaround times for mouse house services. This innovation put me in a very favorable light across the department, even though Shelly was actually the one who came up with it. The favor didn't do me much good though. I wasn't given any preferred access to the mouse house services. I was still in the same queue as everyone else.

So, I used the favor to get Rex and team to start working with Ewan and Jolyon on the automation of the mouse feeding, breeding, sanitation, euthanasia operations.

Ewan assured me that it "Cannae bae harrder than puttin ae pinba macheen togither."

It was.

Nine months later they were finished with construction, beta testing, polishing, launch, and were now receiving feedback from members. They came up with a matrix of boxes and tubes that reminded me of a series of high-density circuit boards. Sensors monitored where mice were at all times within the matrix. This was especially important for cleaning, sanitation, lactation, weaning, and mating procedures.

For cleaning and sanitation, the tubes and locking release hatches allowed for cleaning liquids, sterilization liquids, and dry air to flow through and around the mouse containments. The sensors and camera were waterproofed to avoid the need for any disassembly, dusting, or other manual procedures. Liquids were recycled a few times to reduce waste.

A mouse mother and her pups cohabitated a single box during lactation. The mouse mother would decrease the amount of milk she would feed to the pups and increase the amount of solid food she would give over the course of about three weeks. Pup stirring would reach a critical point around the three-week mark of this weaning period, and when the mouse mother ventured out to get a pellet from an adjacent apartment, a release hatch would close separating the mouse mother from the pups. Other release hatches would open and close to further separate the mother from the pups and make room for the pups to venture out into their own isolated apartments.

Each isolated mouse had regular access to a "duplex apartment". These were the size of two shoeboxes and opaque. One side of each single apartment had a transparent tube that the mouse would enter into to receive a treat. A sensor would cause a feeder to release a single pellet of food. While in the tube, the weight and temperature of the mouse would be measured and recorded in real time. The mice would have to leave long enough for the scale to zero out, and they would receive an additional pellet upon return to the tube. This trigger would stimulate regular visits for weight data collection. In addition to weight monitoring, a single picture of two sides of the mouse would be taken when it entered the tube. Each connecting tube within the matrix including the one between apartments in their duplex was opaque allowing privacy to the mice. While the release hatch was locked and sanitation operations were underway on one side of the duplex, the tenant could enjoy a pellet in the transparent tube in the other apartment.

During mating, the connection tube and release hatches enabled controlled commingling.

When it was time for euthanasia, the feeding tube doubled as an opening for gas. Mouse carcasses were incinerated to limit biological waste.

Additional sections of tubes were designed for exercise and behavioral/memory testing.

I don't remember all the questions Ewan and Jolyon received about their automated mouse system, but one of mine was, "Why did you design it this way with no way to see into the apartments?"

Ewan responded, "Jolyon ower haur can dee-stress bae findin watterfawhs oan tae weekends in tae Smokies. Theese littul creeturs cannae esc-ape onywhaur, evvur, iff thur expozed const-antly wit transp-arent con-nektion tyoobs and apairtments. Meec are verr-eh feerful privaht creechurs. They nid to be hiddun er at leest feel hiddun."

Ewan's intuition about the mice was right on. The stress of being watched and interacted with by humans was killing many of the mice. The team saw a substantial drop in "spontaneous mortality with unknown cause" just a few weeks after starting to consistently use the automated operations.

A couple of months later, Teo noticed that under these automated conditions, weight loss was an early sign of imminent death. He proposed performing a powered study to look at this and other potential markers like elevated temperature, hypothermia, labored breathing, etc. to determine if a composite scoring system could be used to make decisions about increased monitoring or euthanasia. Teo got approval, completed the study, helped initiate new standard operating procedures, and published a paper in the Laboratory Animal Care Journal. These were some of the measurable beneficial outcomes of the mouse house automation initiative.

The automation initiative more than quadrupled the number of mice that could be managed simultaneously. In consideration of the movement toward 96-unit conventions in high-throughput molecular biology operations, the automation team made the matrix 96 shelves by 96 rows (9216 duplex apartments). The total square footage of the facilities housing these mouse apartments was approximately 10k sq ft. The expansion broadened the experiment possibilities for researchers both in terms of throughput and scale. This would be the most significant outcome of the automation initiative.

Rex and team's responsibilities shifted from mouse management to data collection and analysis, and automated operations management. Rex commented early on in the transition that his wife liked that his clothes didn't smell as bad when she was doing the laundry. Earl was happy because Rex had more time to teach him about mouse house and personnel management. Earl had aspirations to start his own mouse house at a research-one university. Arlo was happy that the mating procedures he took lead on were easier. Teo liked learning new graphing skills and found his aptitude in data management.

Processes that remained manual for various reasons included embryo harvesting, vector application, *in vitro* culturing and fertilization, genetic engineering, and treatment applications.

My team had everything ready to go once the operations at the SMNL mouse house were humming and it was our turn.

"Alright stud! Have fun!" said Arlo as he opened the release hatch to introduce the sire into the apartment of the dam which had recently superovulated.

Arlo was actually just talking to a computer monitor with squares and pipes that kind of looked like a Pac-Man map. The tubes were colored green when the release hatches were opened, red when they were closed, and yellow when they were opening or closing.

A mate pair of mice would normally produce between twenty to forty embryos with sibling genetics. We were generating all of our test subjects from just a single pair because we wanted to attribute the tumorigenesis and cure to our REVs rather than differing genetic backgrounds of our mice. One challenge with this was a mouse mother couldn't carry dozens of mice to term. Six to twelve is the normal range of pups. After the embryos were collected from the dam, they would be implanted into surrogate mouse mothers.

Arlo explained, "I'll collect the embryos tomorrow morning, and you want me to culture for two days before IVF, right?"

"Yes," I answered.

"Okay, your mice will be born in about three weeks. I'll keep you updated, or rather an *automated email* will be sent to your computer informing you that the mice were born." He emphasized and smiled, clearly pleased by the new technology.

"What else will the system send me?"

"Daily movements, weight and temperature data, and pictures. This will just be the mouse mother during the lactation period. You'll get data on the pups after weaning."

"Is there an email message that indicates the mother has been separated from the pups?"

"Not currently. However, I don't see why that couldn't be included in the programming."

"Let's go talk to Jolyon together."

"It's fine. I don't need to go. Just let me know if he can do that for you. I'm sure he'll say yes."

"That's true. Okay. Well, before I let you go..." I could tell he was in a hurry. "My plan is to inject the first vector solution directly into the lungs of twenty of the mice. The remaining eight will be injected with saline solution. I'm anticipating tumors within one to two months after the first vector injection. So, I'm just going to split the difference and inject the second vector six weeks after the first vector injection. Half of the group that got the first vector injection and half of the group that got the saline will be injected with the second vector. The other halves will be injected with saline to control for stress to the mice caused by injections in general. Can you anesthetize as soon as the mother is separated from the pups and six weeks after the first vector injection?" Introducing gasses for anesthesia through the feeding tube was another capability of the system.

"So, basically you want anesthesia at three weeks and nine weeks?" He asked me.

"Well, that sounds good, but the three-week mark is a little variable, right? I mean it depends on when the weaning happens."

"Rather than allowing the automated protocol to tell us when the mother is separated from the pups, let's set a date for exactly three weeks. That way the separation doesn't accidently occur in the middle of the night and some of the pups wander into other apartments."

"Sounds good. Is that something I have to talk to Jolyon about too?"

"Yes, ask him to program a separate protocol that locks the mother out exactly after three weeks and keeps the pups together. We'll resume normal automated operations with your cohort once you've applied the first vector."

"Perfect."

"Great, let's plan for that."

We couldn't apply the first vector that caused a loss-of-function in p53 to the embryos before IVF. The function of p53 is too important for development. Even if it were possible, we wouldn't want tumorigenesis in all the cells, tissues, and organs throughout the mouse. We just wanted tumorigenesis in the lungs.

The surrogate mouse mothers carried twenty-six of the twenty-eight fetuses to term. Only two were reabsorbed. This was very normal since miscarriage and reabsorption rates are between 5% and 15% for laboratory mice. All mice were injected as intended by the experimental design subtracting one mouse from the group of four that were to receive two saline injections and one from the group of four that were to receive just the second injection.

The ten mice that were injected with both the first and second vectors had very small tumors as determined post mortem in the histology report from Cree. The ten mice that only received the first vector had more and larger tumors. The groups that received saline or just the second vector were tumor free.

The fact that the REV treatment kept the tumor size down was a tremendous preliminary result for us, and after two more successful experimental replicates, we were celebrating with champagne at a resort. Everyone on the team was invited, even Major Lance, who paid for the celebration.

We didn't go too far, just to the Smokies. Major Lance rented a large fourteen-bedroom cabin with an incredible view for the week. It was just a few miles outside of Pigeon Forge, where there was some fun touristy stuff to do. We also ate dinner together there at a different restaurant each evening. Jolyon led a few hikes during the week. Almost all of the team members went on at least one hike with him. The team members also played cards and boardgames, chatted out on the cliffside deck, read books, and enjoyed the jacuzzi at night.

Major Lance tried to just take the men golfing. I protested, and Skii, Shelly, and I joined. Skii and I both played terribly. Skii actually gave up about halfway through and just hung on Ziggy's arm while he drove the cart; they both had too much Pigeon Forge moonshine that day. Shelly on the other hand had the third lowest score in the group. I asked her how much she had played before on the sixteenth hole after slicing my ball into the woods and seeing her execute a perfect fade on a dogleg right. She said it was her first time, which made me so angry and jealous. I had to remind myself that we were celebrating a significant milestone in the REV project to keep my external calm.

I gave a short speech the final night to prepare my team for the final push.

"Ladies and gentlemen." I paused to wait for the side conversations to stop. "*Ladies and gentlemen*, you have accomplished something enormous. We've shown that REVs can be used as a therapy for cancer remission!"

Everyone clapped.

"And let's not minimize the other accomplishments, showing that REVs could cut naked DNA, predicting and confirming hundreds of fatal cut sites, showing that REVs cuts could be repaired by cells when they weren't fatal cuts, demonstrating that REVs could induce insertion events, and that REVs could be used to make disease models. You all…"

Everyone clapped again.

"Yes, yes." I paused and clapped too. "You all are doing premier level research that will one day be declassified and help save numerous lives, perhaps even your own family member, friend, coworker… maybe it will help you. You should be proud of that."

More claps and lots of smiles could be seen around the room.

"And we cannot forget our enabling technology contributions. Automating so many of our mouse house processes has accelerated the timelines of other important projects going on in our department."

"Vir, we appreciate you proposing the automation initiative, and thank you for the fat check, Major Lance," said Rex.

Major Lance smiled.

"Your high-efficiency alternative to microinjections was also super, Vir!" declared Arlo and clapped. Everyone else followed.

"Thank you."

"Yae dae an amazin job leeding this praject, Vir!" said Ewan, and everyone clapped again.

"Thank you. I couldn't have done any of this without everyone's help. Please, let's have another round of applause for you and your other team members." Everyone clapped again.

"While I would love to continue celebrating in the beautiful Smoky Mountains of Tennessee, we still have some work to do. The goal of this project was to demonstrate *in vivo* REV cuts in humans, that is human tissue."

A pregnant pause.

"We are so close, but so far from this end. Wren has collected a bank of vectors. Our first task is to find out which vectors will disseminate best through tissue. Continuing with our previous experiments, we will work specifically with lung tissue. Our second task will be to modify the vector's genomes to transduce (transfer) the REVs and gRNA. The goal will be to induce apoptosis in tissue. Again, this is just a proof-of-concept. Once we can show that REVs cause apoptosis throughout a section of tissue, future studies will aim to modify gRNAs and vectors to target specific cancers."

I waited to see if there were any objections. The energy of the room suggested strong buy-in.

"We know several REV targets that kill cells because of our screening experiments, so we no longer need to aim for BCL-2 and rely on radiation to induce apoptosis. We are just going to pick a couple dozen of the REV targets that killed the cells the fastest and see which ones induce apoptosis in tissue."

Another moment to allow objections. Everyone was still good.

"Now, let's raise our glasses. I know we are going to finish this project well. I also know that you are all going to continue to be superstars wherever you go next and whatever you do next. I know this because you are all incredibly talented researchers, technicians, and scientists, and it has truly been my honor to have worked with you on this project.

After we knock out these last experiments, after I submit the final report, I'll be moving onto the next phase in my career. I've always wanted to lead a laboratory as a primary investigator. Leading you in this endeavor has set me up for my dream job. So, from the bottom of my heart, thank you! Thank you so much! Cheers to our bright futures!"

One of the issues with being a leader of personnel is that you can never tell them that leadership will be changing. People get scared. The anxiety of not knowing if your new leadership is going to be better or worse than the leadership you've grown accustomed to causes all kinds of problems. People transition to a new project or department, they find a new job at another company, they retire, etc. The sad truth is the news of changing leadership never helps complete a project; it only makes things unstable.

Chapter 69: RENDS

Upon returning to Clingman, Tennessee and SMNL, Shelly and I went on a walk down the burial ground trail. She said she was eager to share something with me.

I asked, "What did you want to talk to me about?"

"I was thinking about the original proof-of-concept target," she began.

"BCL-2?" I asked.

"Yes. We showed that deleting regions of the BCL-2 gene caused cells to be more susceptible to apoptosis when you applied radiation."

"Right. We saw with gel electrophoresis that the genome was shredded by the radiation and unrepaired."

"Exactly. I'm glad you said that."

"Why?"

"Because it's what I thought before I came up with the idea."

"Okay," I said.

"I think there may be a way we can induce apoptosis without radiation."

"Yes, we already know several cut sites that will cause apoptosis." I was feeling a little impatient.

"Technically, we just know several sites that will kill cells. We don't know if those cuts induced apoptosis or some other type of death like necrosis."

"Why does it matter?"

"Well apoptosis is non-inflammatory, whereas other types of cell death like necrosis can be inflammatory. It would increase danger to a patient if a therapy caused such a response."

Preliminary work by researchers in cell biology suggested there might be a variety of ways cells could die. The scientific community didn't know much about their mechanisms, what caused them, etc. While the way a cell died probably wouldn't matter if REVs were used as a weapon, it would matter if they were used as a cancer therapy, and I needed to maintain the illusion to keep my project team happy and working hard for me.

"That's actually a good point, but surely out of the twenty-four cut targets, one or more of the mutations will induce apoptosis and not necrosis or other unknown inflammatory cell death pathways."

"Right, but I think there's another way we could induce apoptosis that would utilize a mechanism that we have some knowledge and understanding about. Wouldn't it be better not to have to try and explain why some fraction of these two dozen mutations cause apoptosis?"

"Well, I see your point. It's definitely not ideal to just say these cut targets induce apoptosis. It's not really science if you don't explain why. So, what's your idea?"

"What if we targeted sites that were highly repetitive in the human genome to make lots of cuts?"

"You mean one REV that targets a sequence that repeats several times?"

"Yes, and the REV will cut each instance of the target sequence."

"Hmm. So, you think that multiple cuts will induce apoptosis?"

"Yes. We know that given enough damage to the genome, a functioning p53 protein will induce apoptosis. While we traditionally think about the damage being caused by radiation, why would that have to be the case? Why couldn't it just be a ton of REV cuts?"

Again, a simple and elegant solution. This woman was so infuriatingly brilliant. We had been making gRNAs to cut single sites with REVs up to that point. Cutting multiple sites was a clever novel idea. Thankfully, it wasn't as extraordinary as her last idea, using REVs for rapid genetic insertions. So, I didn't mind letting her have the credit.

"That makes a lot of sense. Did you have a target sequence in mind that appears a lot in the genome?"

"Well, I've been talking to Skii a little bit about this. I hope you don't mind."

Actually, I didn't really like that. So, I said, "I'd prefer for you to talk to me first about REV project related matters before talking with the other team members."

Researchers are busy. I didn't want Skii or anyone else getting annoyed and complaining to management that Vir's project team members are taking too much of their time. Plus, it would be significantly harder to take credit for Shelly's ideas if she already told everyone.

"Understood. Sorry," Shelly replied.

"That's okay. Just don't let it happen again, please. So, what did Skii say?"

"She told me that there are several good candidates. Skii said that about two thirds of the human genome consisted of repetitive sequences. She also said that some sequences are only found to be highly repetitive in people with certain diseases like Friedreich's ataxia. So, those are obvious therapy targets."

"Indeed. Did you get some sequence targets from her?"

"I did."

"Any idea which one you want to target to test this hypothesis?"

"So, you like the idea?"

"Yes, why wouldn't I?"

"I just know that you want to get this project done and move onto your dream job."

"Well yeah, but this should be quick right? I mean, you just need to design the gRNA, package the virus, transduce the cells, see if they die, isolate the DNA and run it on a gel to see if the REVs shredded the DNA, right?"

"Yeah."

"And what does that take you, maybe eight hours across a single week, practically no extra time if you do it side-by-side with the other twenty-four queued up targets, right?"

"Yeah, I can just add it in with the other targets."

"Sure. I'm good with that then. I think it's a very clever idea. In fact, go ahead and do half a dozen of those. They might turn out to be better proofs like you said because we have an understanding of the mechanism involved. Just don't tell anyone else about it for now."

Shelly gave a "whoopsie" grimace and said, "I already did though."

I gave an exacerbated glare back and said, "Who else did you tell?"

Her eyes dramatically shifted up and to the right indicating that she was a little anxious and searching her memory.

Shelly responded, "Umm, I was talking about the idea at the lunch table. So, Cree, Wren, and Arlo."

Sighing, I said, "That's okay. Just don't do it again."

Shelly proposed six targets based on Skii's recommendations. With her experiment, we discovered that cutting repetitive sites across the genome was effective in initiating apoptosis without the use of radiation. We also found that REVs cutting multiple different sites using a cocktail of gRNAs also worked; yet another good Shelly idea.

When we showed the results in a laboratory meeting, Cree suggested we call these restriction endonuclease nuclei death shredders (RENDS). The team loved the name and quickly adopted it. Thankfully, my team still seemed clueless with regards to the true purpose of this project even with this evocative name.

Chapter 70: Spy

I turned a new page when I left for Tennessee, trying to leave the bad parts of my past behind. Never did I think that I could recover my life so quickly. Here I was though just eight years later with my Ph.D., creating revolutionary breakthroughs in viral and molecular biology, and leading a world class team of scientists.

One thing that hadn't changed was my desire to reconnect with my mother. If anything, it was more pronounced than ever. I felt alone in my post college high security world. Unfortunately, the secret nature of the VIP project prevented it from being something I could tell Milli about. The one hope that kept me going was the assurance that its success was going to be a bridge to a new position and project that I could share with Milli.

Then, I could reconnect with my mother, and tell her that she had been wrong. That *I am* a highly successful scientist. In the same conversation, I wanted to forgive her for discouraging me right before college as well as thank her for encouraging me throughout my entire childhood. Most importantly, I wanted to tell her that I loved her for the woman she made me. This fantasy looped in my mind. These things I would say. How she would respond. The smiles. The hugs. The crying. The mental image was so beautiful.

My hope of a successful future in science and reconnection with my mother was resurrected in me when I started at SMNL. This hope was so precious to me to the point where it became an idol in my life. If I'm honest, it was more important to me than anything and I would not allow anyone to take that hope away. Someone tried to, though.

I entered Building 9 late one evening to finish designing some viral screening experiments. Major Lance was doing something in his office. Perhaps fooling around with Shelly again. They had continued even after I called him out, but my kick wasn't strong enough to stop him entirely from taking "big risks" with female coworkers. It seemed safe enough to enter after I heard sounds of typing and mouse clicking. I wanted to avoid scaring him by letting him know that I was working in the building, but I startled him with my knock anyway.

"Sorry to scare you, Major. Working late?"

"Whew, no problem. Yes, and you?

"Trying to finish up some experimental design so my team will have everything they need to hit the ground running tomorrow."

"Keep up the good work. What can I help you with?"

"Nothing right now. I was just trying to make you aware of my presence so that I wouldn't startle you."

"Something to work on then, I suppose. Shelly is also here somewhere."

"Thanks for letting me know. I'll go say hello to her too."

Then I remembered that Wren was looking for a promotion and raise. He had made himself very important to the success of the project by becoming exceedingly proficient at traveling to various locations around the world, safely transferring human samples back to SMNL, isolating, passaging, and banking them. We now had over ten thousand viruses in our bank and were ready to start comparing their abilities to spread through tissue.

Wren was a viral virtuoso but didn't like experimenting in the laboratory nearly as much as traveling the world for collection. Travel seemed like it would diminish or possibly stop though since we had a nice collection now for our experiments. So, he demanded a better title and more money. I had experienced Wren's entitlement attitude before but the brazen ultimatum that he would leave if I didn't meet his demands demonstrated how unappreciative he was. Wren would not have been so skilled if I hadn't trained him, and he would have never been able to travel as much if I hadn't successfully advocated for it and procured the funding. Unfortunately for me, getting another person humming on the bench like Wren would cost a lot more than a raise. It would certainly slow progress down. I was too close to finishing the final project milestones. So, I decided to bear with his cockiness, get him the raise, and push toward completion.

"Major Lance, there is one thing you could help me with. Wren has proven himself to be a valuable asset to our group, and I think it's time to promote him. Could you please change his title to Associate Scientist II and increase his annual salary by $10k?"

"How about $5k?"

"$7k"

"Fine, Vir. Is there anyone else on your team in need of a promotion at this time?" He asked sardonically.

"No, just Wren."

"Fine. I'll submit that request first thing tomorrow."

"Thank you. Hope you have a good night, Sir." I was able to bravely face this man who had assaulted me because I had fought back and was victorious. When I said "Sir", it was for the sake of maintaining professionalism, not out of respect for him. Still, cordiality was important for the day-to-day fluidity of our activities.

"Have a good night, Vir."

I went to Shelly's desk. Her bag was there and some other items, so I knew she was still around. I looked in the breakroom, in the BSL-2 labs, in the -80C freezer room, in the media prep room, the women's bathroom on the second floor, and the showers on the first floor, but couldn't find her.

After giving up my search, on the way back to my office, I heard a noise in Skii's office. Opening the door, I saw Shelly with a flashlight. Flicking on the room light, I inquired, "What are you doing in the dark?"

Then, I saw a SCSI drive with a parallel port sticking out of Skii's computer. Shelly saw my wide eyes, my expression of unmistakable surprise and awareness. She leaped out of her seat toward me. I screamed and ran down the hall. "Help!" I shrieked. Right after my third holler, Shelly's shoe pounded into my back, sending my torso flying forward. Thankfully, my forearms protected my face from smacking the floor, but I hit it hard and slid several feet.

Shelly said "I'm sorry" and was about to punch me in the face, when Major Lance yelled down the hall, "Stop!" Shelly took off in the other direction. Major Lance had his walkie-talkie and was describing Shelly's appearance as he ran past me. Just before Shelly was going to turn the corner, Ewan jolted a metal cart in her path from a side door. She flipped over it and clattered into the wall head first. She was down moaning when Ewan stood over her. "Donnae muv!" He was holding a 1L glass graduated cylinder like a baseball bat. Shelly, head down, pushed up to her knees. She swung her leg, catching Ewan's ankle, dropping him to the ground, the cylinder exploding as it landed beside him.

Major Lance leapt over Ewan and connected with Shelly's face with a right hook and a left jab to her gut. Shelly, who was almost a foot shorter than these men, looked like she was fighting trees. Yet with the power of a raging hurricane, she uprooted Major Lance, and cut him down like a master logger with a karate chop. She then collided with Ewan, and felled him onto the turned-over cart with a jump-kick to his chest. Shelly ran to the stairs and presumably out the front door of Building 9. It was the quickest way to the surrounding woods, which extended for miles. Security apprehended her about twenty minutes later. The dogs found her hiding in some leaves.

Security drove us to the gate where an ambulance took us to the hospital. I was mostly fine, but wanted to make sure Major Lance and Ewan were okay. She could've killed me if they hadn't showed up. After they were admitted into the ER, I went home to sleep.

When I woke up, I remembered that Shelly was a spy and that she had attacked me. I gazed at the ceiling as I reconciled this fact in my mind. I was working at a secure national laboratory. A spy working among us was not out of the realm of possibilities. No, it made a lot of sense actually that a spy would be assigned to steal information about the REV technology.

Shelly had let us stereotype her as a clever pupil to be taught in the ways of scientific research and a horny college girl to be screwed. But she was a secret agent, sent to infiltrate our facilities and extract classified information from us. My reaction to the deception was split. I was impressed by Shelly's skills and cunning, and simultaneously resolved more than ever that the U.S. needed to stay technologically ahead of our enemies.

Why the apology though before she almost punched me? I was her enemy, leading the development of the REV technology for my government's military, which might be used against her people. Perhaps she bought into my speeches about the technology being used for cancer therapy, or at least that I believed this story. Or perhaps Shelly appreciated my leadership, tutelage, kindness to her, and felt bad that she was going to need to hurt me? Maybe she didn't like hitting civilians or women. Maybe she liked that I was a woman, leading men, on a top-secret science project. I doubted that I'd ever have a chance to find out.

Ewan would likely be on his back for a week and then crutches for five more, according to the doctor. Major Lance's recovery from a herniated disk injury was also estimated to take about six weeks.

I didn't need to replace Ewan because he could do most of his automation work sitting down. I did have to replace Shelly, and because training was going to set us back, I was allowed to resource two FTEs instead of just one. Her replacements did just fine and we were able to catch up on our deliverables by the following quarter.

The U.S. government was aware that the Soviets were stealing our technologies. The Defense Intelligence Agency, or DIA, was supposed to be protecting the U.S. and our allies from their spies. I never saw DIA agents though. The lack of security was surprising to me given what we were developing.

Thankfully, Major Lance was able to convince upper management to take better precautions with our enormously expensive secret data after Shelly almost stole it. Candidates interviewing for the research positions were more rigorously screened before coming to campus. A card access reader was installed on the door of the data storage room that housed our computers with the Human Genome and Phenotype databases as well as all of our experimental REV data. We also hired 24/7 security guards for Building 9. They mostly stayed in an office by the front entrance and walked the halls every couple of hours.

Building 9 had a corridor style layout with a central rectangular hallway on each floor that allowed access to mostly offices lining the perimeter and mostly laboratories in the middle. On Wednesday, March 8, 1989, Ewan and I were walking toward each other on the second-floor corridor of the back side of the building. He was briskly rolling a metal cart.

At first, this gave me a sense of relief, that things were returning to normal. The ghostly images of Ewan splayed across a turned over metal cart with glass everywhere was being overwritten, or at least shuffled to the back of my mind.

As Ewan and I came closer and closer to each other in the hallway, I noticed that the cart had a sterilization bin on top with books inside. It is very unusual to cart around books in a sterilization bin. Usually, sterilization bins contain autoclavable glassware, metalware, and plasticware.

"Awrite, Vir?" asked Ewan.

My walking slowed as my mind tried to make sense of what was in Ewan's sterilization bin. Ewan, on the other hand, did not slow down.

"Awrite, Vir?" he asked again a little louder.

Realizing I hadn't answered his first greeting, I looked up for a moment and said, "Hi, Ewan. Yeah, I'm good," and then went right back to staring at the bin. I even stopped and turned to look a little longer as he passed me. I saw a monolayer of books on automation, some biology texts, and even a couple of Sci-Fi novels. Something wasn't right. It looked as if there was something hidden under the books; metal, flat, and shiny things.

Before he was too far away, I asked, "What's with the books?"

With his back to me now, not stopping or turning around, he replied, "Just giein' the place a wee Spring tidy up."

I thought this was very odd. Most people just collect more books, cluttering their offices to show how educated and knowledgeable they are. Cleaning out books almost only occurred when staff were moving offices or retiring. Ewan was not an exceptionally tidy person. If anything, he was probably on the messier side of the spectrum.

I looked in the direction he had come from and started walking fast, then faster, and soon was jogging to the end of the hall to the data storage room. I held my card up against the card reader, and when the door opened, my fears were confirmed. All I needed was a glance to see that the hard drives had been removed from the stacks.

The data storage room was on the opposite side of the building from the elevator. Ewan would need to use the elevator to get down to the first floor before leaving the building because he had the cart. I didn't need it though. I jetted over to the stairwell, sprinted down to the first floor and hurried to cut Ewan off before he left the building.

'What was he going to do with the drives?' I wondered. Maybe the Soviets paid him to steal the drives. He was clearly desperate. No telling what he would do if I confronted him. Of course, the 24/7 guard was nowhere to be found. I doubted that I could physically stop Ewan. He wasn't in his prime, but he was still stronger than me.

Ewan turned the corner into the front hallway where he would try to exit to the parking lot. I was already between him and the door thanks to the glacier-slow hydraulic elevator.

"Oh, hi. Long time, no see," I joked insincerely.

Ewan stopped. I noticed the sheen above his brow now.

"I was trying to catch you because I need your help moving Rad2," I said.

Chapter 71: Rad Threat

Before Jim killed our babies and threatened my life, I didn't believe there was a violent bone in my body. My intellect, my ability to maneuver, or juke my opponents that wanted to trap me, was how I effectively progressed throughout life. Violence was just unnecessary. Jim dulled my will though. He chained my heart. Then, he actively oppressed me with manipulations of Holy Scripture, guilt, shame, sex, and with bondage and isolation. Jim made a significant error though. He failed to preoccupy me, which gave me space to think.

The first and hardest step to killing Jim was convincing myself that I had to. The desire for revenge for the murder of my unborn children boiled inside me, but my conscience reminded me of Paul's words in Romans 12, *"Avenge not yourselves, beloved, but give place unto the wrath of God."* My sinful flesh, or perhaps the Devil himself presented a loophole, though. I allowed myself to be convinced that I might be killed if I didn't kill him first. Again, my conscience or maybe the Lord reminded me that Jesus was oppressed and afflicted, yet did not open his mouth as he was led to the slaughter as a sacrificial lamb. The footing I found to stand on was defense of others. Jim had shown himself to be a wolf in sheep's clothing, not only manipulating me but all of his congregants. He killed our unborn children and had me hit with a truck. Jim was dangerous and needed to be stopped.

I had my reasons and you know the rest of the story. The first time is hard, but after killing once, the mental/emotional brick wall is smashed through and the wreckage is relatively easy to step over a second time. It's not like you want to kill. I'm not a psycho, hungry for blood. I doubt that many people who have murdered are seeking new opportunities to step over the mental wall again. It's just that the path stays open as an option for resolving future challenges. Why? I think the experience is not something that one wants to process. It's not like you can get help without incriminating yourself. One tries to think about something else when it comes to mind, but it never gets resolved or repaired. Furthermore, you never know what conditions might bring the evil back out until the decision is right in front of you again and you're flooded with emotion.

"Can it no wait?" asked Ewan, reluctant to help me with my request.

"It won't take long. Just need it shifted and it's too heavy for me," I urged.

Saying no to the boss is not advisable for job security and advancement under normal circumstances. This was not normal circumstances though. Ewan might have been very well paid by the Soviets and was not worried about job security. He might have just knocked me out to expedite his escape. However, that might have made it harder for him to leave the campus if someone saw him do that. So, helping me quickly with my request would allow him to leave without suspicion and be well down the road before we realized the hard drives were missing. When the alarms were finally raised, no one would guess he had the hard drives. The spy could leave the country in a matter of hours.

Ewan rolled the cart to the side of the hallway so it would be out of the way, and we walked a couple of doors down to the irradiation room.

The irradiation room was next to the stairwell I had just come from. The floor dimensions were probably about 18' by 24'. Safety gear like lead jackets and face shields hung from the walls. Heavy 6'x 6' square metal tables, separated by about four feet, were in the center of the room. Each table had a single Rad unit on top, each were fairly heavy and a couple of cubic feet in size. A large drum for collection and disposal of radiated materials was against the wall next to the door. Shielded glass allowed observers in the hallway to watch radiation procedures from a safe vantage.

Rad2 was one of two units we had in the irradiation room. It was generally used for single or multi-beam irradiation of subcutaneous tumors in mouse models.

"Whaur dae ye want tae shift it?" he asked.

"Over to the edge of the table, please," I replied. "Oh, and can you please hold it here, and here?" I pointed to some indentations on the sides. "Please move it slowly. It's heavy, but it's also a fragile instrument and jostling it could misalign the inner components. If that happened, we would need to recalibrate it."

"Weel, mebbe ah shouldnae be daein' this? Whit aboot giein' the maker a bell an' haein' them dae it? Doesnae the department fork oot for a service contract?" Ewan asked.

"No, it's okay, we've done it before. While we do have a service contract, getting the technicians to come on campus requires lots of paperwork. Please, just be slow and steady," I said. Ewan's automation work never required him to get trained on or use these irradiation machines.

As soon as he was in position, I said, "Let me turn on the light so you can better see what you are doing and the alignment." I turned on the machine and dialed it up to the highest setting. I stepped back, slowly walked around the table, and squatted down, pretending to evaluate the orientation, height, and levelness of the machine.

Ewan shifted the machine near to the edge of the table. Crouched down under the machine with the light directly over his head beaming him. He looked over in my direction and asked, "Is that awricht? This licht is pure roasting. Ah feel like ah'm in a sauna or somethin'."

I said, "Please align the edge of the base with the edge of the table."

He did and asked again.

"Thank you, Ewan," I said, going back around and turning the machine off. It was hard to see in the low light but his multitone skin suggested erythema. "Before you go, could we do the same thing with Rad1?"

"Aye," he said reluctantly.

Rad1 had a different head and was generally used for open field irradiation of cells or tissue in a Petri dish, 96-well plate, or on a glass slide. We used it for testing whether cutting the BCL-2 gene with REVs significantly increased apoptosis with radiation, a potential cancer co-therapy.

Again, he got in position, I turned on the machine, fully dialed it up, and stepped backward to distance myself.

"Dae we really need the licht oan? It's pure baltic."

"It's for your safety."

The light shone on his head as he slowly and carefully shifted the machine to the edge. Then, I turned it off, and thanked him again.

"Did you talk to Jolyon about the new automation project?" I asked, trying to stall.

"Project?" he asked, confused by the question since I had just made it up.

"Did he not talk to you about that yet? I need you two to make a tool that transfers nanoliter liquid volumes."

"Wit fir?"

"For…for cells, individual cell sorting."

"Wye?"

"All sorts of things. We can identify the cells that are in a tissue. We can evaluate how each tissue cell type responds to REVs. We can better understand which cells are resistant to viral infection and then further process those cells to determine why.

Then, we can take that information and change our infection strategy and retest using the same sorting technology."

"Customized precision sup handling. Git some speccies fae fabrication or computer engineering fae that drudgery."

"How would you do it?" I asked.

"Dinnae teach yer Granny tae suck eggs! Buy a fluorescence activated cell sorter. That's wit it's fae!" he said and started walking toward the laboratory door.

I couldn't think of what else to say. "Where do you get one?" I blurted.

"Dunno," Ewan replied and was just reaching for the door when I said, "Wait!"

He turned around, "Ye winnae haud me, Vir. Yer bum's oot the windae."

I took a deep breath. "I know." I continued, "But yours is too, Ewan. Why are you taking the drives?"

"Ye know wye," he replied.

"Maybe, but I'd still like to hear how much they're giving you before I call security."

"Givin' me?" he asked.

"Yeah, how much are the Soviets giving you for the drives?"

"No a bawbee. Yeez got me wrong. Ye're playin' wi' a wasps' nest. Urp. Sorry." Ewan dry heaved. The ARDs symptoms were already showing.

"What did you say?"

"Ye claim," Ewan paused hinging at the mid-section. He came back up and continued, "Sorry, but ah'm feelin' awfy mingin' aw a sudden. Got a stoatin' sore heid and a bit daft."

"Please, I want to hear what you have to say" I urged, trying to look as attentive as possible and thinking what I'd do next.

"Awright, Vir. Ye're sayin' it's gonnae be a pure magic fix for cancer and aw sorts o' wonky genetic bother, but wha' if the U.S. goverment is chuckin' cash at yer scheme 'cause they're plannin' a pure jobby of a mass Soviet cull? Gie that a wee think?"

"That would be terrible, but why would you think that?"

"The U.S. goverment cannae nuke 'em cause if the Soviets spot 'em, it's game oan—they'll gie it laldy back."

"Yes, mutual assured destruction."

"Even if the U.S. goverment could, they're no wantin' mair nae-go areas like the yin in Ukraine."

"That's a good point, Ewan," I placated, sure there were many factors in deciding whether to drop a nuclear bomb besides whether or not the area could be inhabited afterward. Long-lasting radioactive isotope contamination certainly did not stop the U.S. from continuing to develop these weapons. In fact, they performed a nuclear test at the Nevada site the next day on November 9th.

"…But are we not in an arms race? What's wrong with being more strategic and powerful than our enemy? Avoiding death by his hand? The Soviets are bent on World domination, and they would not hesitate to kill us if they thought they had an upper hand. Are we not lucky to be alive?" I asked.

"Him that's born tae be hung will nivver be drowned."

Ewan's head, face, and even neck were looking very red. I could see him better now from the light of the windows.

"So what, you're just going to give them the hard drives to even things out?" This was not something I considered before. The nuclear stalemate had kept the people of each side relatively safe during the Cold War. It's likely that both sides having REVs would work effectively the same way.

What was the purpose of Ewan's altruism though? Why not take some money from the Soviets to start over somewhere else? This perplexed me until he said, "Naw, ah'm plannin' tae pure wreck the drives."

Acid welled up in me. "Why would you do that?"

"I dinnae want tae be held accountable fae fowk's deiths," he answered.

This was more serious than I thought. Ewan didn't need to get out of the country. All he needed to do was get outside, find a fist-sized or larger rock, and smash the hard drive shell with enough force to scratch the platters. That would make the data irretrievable. The radiation poisoning would take too long to stop him from doing that. I needed to act fast.

"But, Ewan. You are accountable. You've been an asset to our team and helped us speed up the innovation process tremendously by automating many of our tasks."

"The script wis keepit fae us. Ah'd nivver hae got involved if ah'd kent the moonstrosity."

"We have pioneered what will become major historical innovations. Association with the project will accelerate my career and the careers of your colleagues. You are brilliant Ewan and I really appreciate what you've done for us." My words were genuine and he deserved gratitude.

"Ah definitely didnae dae it for a leg up or onybody else's in the U.S. goverment."

"Nevertheless. And, why do you keep saying, U.S. government like it's a separate entity? You are a U.S. government employee. Right? You might not have contributed your skills to REVs project to help advance your career, but you did work for pay."

"Ma heid's mince. Wit we gabbin' aboot?" Ewan was starting to look disoriented.

"We are talking about why you helped with the REVs project."

Ewan took a step toward me. I stepped back, more worried about being exposed to radiation. He was certainly emitting radiation after those high dose X-ray applications.

"Noo jist haud on! Ye're speirin' at me why ah did this. Wit aboot yersel?"

"If we didn't develop this then the Soviets would have," I answered.

"Ye knew the script for yonks, in didnae let on tae us?"

"Yes, and after the incident with Shelly, it's all the clearer to me that we urgently needed this technology in hand."

"Ah'm pure done in. Wha' have ye…?" Ewan started to ask, stumbling now. It was easy enough to evade him by circling around the tables.

"I had to stop you, Ewan. Destroying the hard drives would have set us back by years and cost U.S. taxpayers billions of dollars. It would not have stopped REV development, by us or the Soviets. You nearly cost us the edge in the arms race. I saved you from being a traitor, Ewan."

He was showing signs of disorientation. Ewan hobbled toward me like a resurrected Egyptian mummy, unable to see his pursuant well through the facial wrappings. I evaded him by running around the heavy metal tables where Rad1 and Rad2 sat. His eyes were locked on me with some animosity but his face also looked troubled. He was probably concerned about the variety of sensations he was feeling as his organs malfunctioned.

Ewan suddenly stopped, turned, and headed toward the door. I grabbed a radiation face shield from the wall, leaped forward, and threw it at his head. The face shield slapped the back of his head before clattering to the ground. It wasn't heavy enough to even cause him to falter.

'What are we going to do? Stop him!' Cried my desperation.

Then, Ewan stopped and brought his hand to the top of his head. "Ow," he said in surprise, turning toward me. A look of shock came over his face. "Owww! It's roasting. It's pure roasting!"

Ewan's eyes were alert. He slowly dragged his fingers against his skin toward his back. Some of Ewan's hair sloughed off. Then, he started patting and scratching his skin. The face shield impact seemed to have activated a sensation like Hell's itch. "Owww, stoap, stoap, stoap!" He buckled, dropped to his hands and knees, and evacuated the contents of his stomach. He then dry-heaved a few times while simultaneously trying to scratch with one hand.

Ewan looked up at me and began speaking nonsense, "Searen searn searn sykeee agnella whishummmm ye see 'em drummmm rummmm mummmm." He tried to get up, but slipped in his vomit and slammed his head against the edge of the heavy metal table, which knocked him out. A pool of blood ran from his head and mixed with the vomit.

'Oh, God!' screamed my shock.

'Put back the face shield. He didn't use proper protective equipment and killed himself.' It was the first story my responsiveness could think of.

I picked up the face shield that I had thrown and placed it back on the wall.

'We need to make it look like an accident,' added my responsiveness.

I walked round Ewan and shifted Rad1 slightly from the side of the table being careful not to step in the fluids. I turned on the machine, which was still dialed all the way up. The light shown on Ewan's face and shoulder.

'We need to distance ourselves from this,' fretted my anxiety.

'We need to cover our tracks,' warned my responsiveness. 'Get out of here and put the drives back.'

I took a deep breath.

'Stop looking guilty,' strongly advised my confidence.

I left the room with my shoulders back, and walked down the hall to collect the cart with the hard drives.

Chapter 72: Clean Up

Before getting to the cart, I saw Ziggy walking down the hall. He greeted me and I returned the sentiment. As I was approaching the cart, Armand turned the corner. He was just another employee who worked in the building. I greeted him as well and walked past the cart until he turned to walk out the building entrance. Seeing me pushing the cart might draw suspicions since I hadn't done wet lab work in years, and carting around books supplemented the oddity.

After retrieving the cart, I hurried to the elevator and got in before anyone saw me. The glacier-slow elevator speed gave me time to think.

When the elevator opened, I peeked out to see if anyone was there. No one was, so I pulled the cart out and pushed it into Shelly's old office. Again, pulling my shoulders back, I confidently turned the corner and walked into the main corridor. Teo, one of the mouse house guys, was walking away from me and exited via the stairway a moment later. I hurried over to Rm 215 and entered. Thankfully, no one was in that laboratory room. I cut a four-foot section of off-white surface liner, which is normally put on the carts as a stable cushioned moisture-absorbing material for drying cleaned glassware. I quickly folded it and put this in one of two Styrofoam coolers that were stacked beside the refrigerators.

I slowly cracked the door to listen for anyone in the hallway. Not hearing anyone, I quickly wheeled the two Styrofoam coolers from the laboratory to Shelly's old office. I pulled the surface liner out and dropped it on the floor.

Suddenly I heard a commotion. Carlos was yelling in the hallway, "Something terrible has happened to Ewan! Please help!" He continued to cry out until people started coming out of their offices and laboratories. Most people were at lunch around this time but a few came out and asked him what was going on.

"I don't know! Please come quickly," he said and the others followed.

I gently closed the door and hurriedly stacked the books into the Styrofoam coolers. I put these on the lower-level cart rack. I then shook open the surface liner and draped it on top of the hard drives.

Suddenly, an ear-piercing alarm went off and an emergency message started looping. "There is an emergency. Stop what you are doing and exit the building. Emergency responders are on their way." I cracked the office door and heard more doors open, slam, and shoes shuffling. After a few seconds, I pushed the cart into the hallway and sprinted with it to the computer room. I quickly slotted the hard drives into the housings. I then flew back down the hallway. I left the cart off to the side and took the two coolers into Ewan's office. I hurriedly arranged the books on the shelf, carefully left the office, and returned the coolers and cart to our laboratory.

As I was leaving the laboratory, I saw men in hazmat suits coming down the hallway. "Ma'am, you have to leave now. Brody, please escort this woman out of the building." I followed the one called Brody while the others went door to door checking to see if anyone else was still on the floor. He asked me what my name was and I answered, "Virginia Marshall."

People were assembling in the front of the building as if it were a fire drill. Jolyon was crying on Carlos' shoulder. I walked over pretending not to know what was going on and preparing myself to conjure crocodile tears, knowing this was particularly important for acceptance of my alibi. I held my eyes wide like I was in a staring contest. Then, I covered my mouth with my hand, took a few big yawns to lift my soft palate and several shallow breaths in my upper chest to activate my stress hormones. Finally, I thought of my unborn children, how I never got to hold them, smell their heads, and kiss their cheeks. I allowed myself to recall my pain of never becoming a mother, not because of genetics but because of Jim's will and because I didn't stop him. I almost cried too early thinking about these things, and just managed to release the tears while Jolyon was beginning to tell me about Ewan's charred and bloodied body being taken away in an ambulance.

After a short hug and cry with Jolyon, a police officer came over and said, "You won't be permitted into the building for at least 72 hours, possibly longer. However, you can't go home until we've collected statements from everyone here."

My heart quickened.

"Who is the division leader?" The police officer asked.

"Major Lance, but he's not here," said Jolyon.

"Who is next in charge?"

"I guess that would be you, right, Vir?" asked Jolyon.

"Well, I'm a project lead. It would probably be one of the members. Not sure, but how can I help?" I replied.

"Please come with me. You'll be the first to make a statement."

The officer walked me over to a police car that was about fifty yards away from the crowd. The engine was running, the radiator was kicking on, and the lights were flashing. I was taken around to the side of the car opposite the crowd where there was an officer with stunning long red hair. He was in a non-committal posture with the door open and tactical footwear planted on the ground. I imagined him either pounce out after someone or swing back in to take off with siren blaring. His head was down and he was writing something in his notebook.

Without looking up, he requested with a slight Irish accent, "Please state your name for the recording," and pointed to the recorder that was on the roof of the car above his head.

"Virginia Marshall."

The officer raised his bright green eyes to meet mine. I imagined that his richly colored features might be distracting and throw liars off their game while he interviewed them.

"I'm Officer McElrath. Please give your account from the beginning of the day in as much detail as you can remember."

"Okay. I came into the office around 9 am. I pretty much wrote like mad, working on my grant proposal all day long."

"Did anyone come to talk to you?"

"Yes, Rex and Earl asked me how many mice I would need for our experiments in two months."

"And what time was that?"

"Around 10am."

"Anyone else talk to you or see you?"

"Ummm, ah yes, Pascal saw me in the parking lot this morning and we walked in the building at the same time. The security guard saw both of us enter. Also, Ziggy and Armand saw me in the hallway a little before the alarm went off."

He took a note.

"The hallway that Ziggy and Armand saw you in, was that on the first floor or second floor?"

"The first floor."

He took a note.

"And is that the floor your office is on?"

"No."

He took a note.

"So, what were you doing in the hallway on the first floor?"

Ewan splayed out on the ground of the irradiation room in a pool of blood and vomit came to mind.

"Lunch. I was getting my lunch from the refrigerator in the kitchen downstairs."

"Did you eat downstairs?"

"No, I took my food back up to my office."

Another note.

"Did you do anything else while you were downstairs?"

"I took a quick bio-break and washed my hands."

"Was that before or after retrieving your lunch?"

"Before."

Another note.

"And what were you still doing in the building after the alarm went off? The hazardous materials team said you were the only person they had to escort out."

"I took a minute to quickly finish my lunch and then I went to the data storage room to make sure our data was secure for whatever emergency was going on. Then, I was checking the laboratories to make sure no one was left behind and no Bunsen burners were left on. I was coming out of one of the laboratories when they found me."

"Let me get this straight. You finished your lunch, walked to the data storage room, checked to see if your data was secured, walked to your laboratories and checked for personnel and if anyone left Bunsen burners on, all while the alarms were blazing?"

"Correct."

"And was the data secure?"

"Yes."

"And did anyone leave any Bunsen burners on?"

"I didn't find any left on."

"Okay. Thank you for your testimony. You're done for now, but stick around. We may need to ask you more questions once we've heard from everyone. Send over the next most senior professional on your team. Thank you."

The Director of Laboratory Operations, Martin Brown, came with some assistants who passed out snacks and drinks to everyone in the parking lot while we waited. He took me aside. "There seems to have been an accident, a very serious accident, with Ewan in the irradiation laboratory. It is unlikely that Ewan will survive, but if he does, he will not work another day in his life. I'm very sorry."

"Thank you. I appreciate it. The member of the team who found Ewan told me that he was unconscious and bleeding heavily under a running radiation machine."

"Yes. Yes. That is our understanding. We will keep you informed about Ewan's condition as we find out new information. Do you feel comfortable communicating with your team about this? If not, Lance can do it."

"I'm sure I can manage. Thank you."

"Great, I also wanted to check with you about something more personal."

"Okay…."

"Ewan has been working for the laboratory for almost a decade. HR tells me that his emergency contact is a cousin that lives in Vermont. That has not likely been updated though since he was hired. Do you know if he is in a relationship with anyone locally?"

"Yes, actually, he has been steady with someone named Rita for a few years."

"Oh, well. Do you, ah, do you have her contact?"

"No, but one of the team members might."

"Good. Good. Can you check on that for me?"

"Sure. Do you want me to call and tell her what happened as well?" I asked, not really knowing why Martin was acting weird.

"No. No. That needs to be done by the Legal department."

"By legal?" I asked.

"Yes, you see Virginia, Ewan was likely fatally injured on the job. It looks like it was an accident and the laboratory might be sued if his working conditions were unsafe in some way. Regardless, the media will be interested in amplifying the story as much as possible, potentially making this into something that it's not. Public relations are very important to us and we want to try to get ahead of the media as much as we can."

"I understand. I'll go check and see if a team member has that contact information for you."

"Before you go, Virginia. Can you confirm that Ewan was trained on the instrument he was found under?"

Then a light bulb went off in my head. "No, he was not."

"He wasn't!" cried Martin, startling another employee nearby. Angling his body away from the crowd, he lowered his voice and through gritted teeth, he whispered, "What do you mean he wasn't trained...? If he was doing life threatening work without training, we could be in for a serious lawsuit."

I responded quietly, "Irradiation was not part of Ewan's duties."

"It wasn't?"

"No, Ewan was responsible for automation of a variety of our tasks. He's never been trained on the irradiation equipment because that was not his job."

"What was he doing there then?!"

"Ewan has been very different since the incident with Shelly. Quieter. More reserved."

Martin lowered his voice, "Did he seem unhappy?" Martin almost looked like he was suppressing a smile.

"Yeah, maybe."

"Oh, we may need to... umm. You find Rita's contact info for me, and I'm going to chat with one of the officers. Oh wait. Before I forget, we need to discuss special access to the building. We want to keep as many people out of the building as possible while the police finish up their investigation, hazards are removed, and cleanup is complete. However, I am aware that your team does experiments in Building 9. Does anyone absolutely need access in the next few days?"

"No."

"Great. Let's meet again soon under better circumstances. Excuse me, I need to go talk with these police officers."

"Certainly."

Two hours later, suicide was decidedly unlikely because of prolonged suffering. The prevailing thought was that Ewan had a tragic accident, everyone's stories checked out, and we were allowed to leave.

Two days later I was called by the Laboratory Director, Elijah Whitham, who told me that Ewan had died from radiation poisoning and that the whole Smoky Mountain National Laboratory family was mourning the loss of our friend and colleague.

"Did they determine a reason for his death?" I asked.

"The forensics indicated that Ewan moved the instruments and knelt below them by his own will. Since he was freely kneeling below the beams, we have to assume…this was purposeful."

I took a deep breath, but before exhaling a sigh of relief, I switched to a sigh of sorrow, frowning, lowering and closing my eyes, and hunching my shoulders.

"I'm so sorry, Virginia."

I remained silent with my head down, trying to conjure tears. The exciting relief of escape made it too hard to force more than a gloomy expression. I was dry.

Even so, Elijah stammered, clearly not wanting to break professionalism, "You… your team… can take the rest of the week off… paid… for bereavement if you wish… longer if you need. Your building will be open though next week…"

When I continued to stay silent, he got up and walked toward the door, which made me get up.

Elijah said as he opened his office door to show me out, "I, uh, hope you feel better."

Later that day a news statement was made by Elijah about the unfortunate lack of resources available to individuals suffering with mental health issues and suicidal thoughts. "The laboratory family grieves the loss of Ewan… We hope that events like these and the new CDC report from the U.S. Secretary's task force on youth suicide will provide enough reasons to create resources for struggling individuals. Thank you. That is all."

Monday, when everyone returned, Skii came to my office and told me something was wrong with our data. I freaked out until we determined that I had slotted the hard drives into the housing in the wrong order. They simply needed to be remapped. Skii asked me why I took the hard drives out in the first place. I said I was worried about them getting destroyed in a fire or something before I found out what the emergency actually was last week. This satisfied her and the last loose end was tied up.

The end of the week came and then the weekend was horrible. I was in the clear but the image of a bloody, roasted Ewan on the floor haunted me. So, I busied myself with work, analyzing data, and writing reports and grant proposals to purge the thoughts from my mind. I intended to persist right into Monday in workaholic mode, but received a derailing trainwreck email from Major Lance that the VIP project was shut down.

Chapter 73: The Horsemen

Much of what the return-to-work week was about was making sure that my team was emotionally and psychologically stable. The death of a teammate can be really hard on some people. I didn't want anyone to mourn Ewan alone.

I was hard at work writing reports and grants leading up to the incident and therefore thought I could take a break during the return-to-work week to spend time doing emotional check-ins with my team members.

My interest in staying at SMNL was growing because of the incredible resources/facilities we developed over the years, including the genotype-phenotype database, human genomic DNA collection, REV gRNA collection, mouse house automation, virus collection, and others. I thought NIH or NIEHS might not be the greener grass I use to fantasize about. I just needed to get awarded a grant. Researchers were pretty much obligated to publish with all of the standard funding mechanisms. Getting a grant proposal funded would also give the Department of Defense reason to promote me to a junior member role, which is similar to the level of an assistant professor in academia. My dreams were shattered though when Reagan's defense funding dried up and my project was canceled.

A few months prior, in 1989, George H.W. Bush took the office of U.S. President, and started shifting a lot of spending around. My grant was not renewed. I wasn't mentally or emotionally prepared when I found a warm contemplative-looking black man in Major Lance's office chair Monday morning.

"Please come in," he beckoned.

His unreadable strabismus eyes boosted my anxiety, and I thought my heart stopped when he introduced himself noticeably without giving his name.

"I'm from SMNL HR."

"Human resources?"

"Yesss," he seemed to hiss. "Did Major Lance send you an email this morning indicating that it was decided that funding for your project would terminate effective immediately?"

"Yes," I admitted.

"Good. I am here to elaborate a little more. Thank you for your service."

My heart sank and I felt lightheaded as he went on.

"Your project is no longer supported under the current administration and therefore your position in the United States government has been terminated. Your lab space will be repurposed, your data will be archived, and your chemicals and biologicals will be safely discarded."

I interrupted, "You can't discard our collections! We've collected over a million individuals' genomes, tens of thousands of viruses, and…!"

"Ma'am, please do not discuss the specifics of your research with me. I am not authorized to receive this information. I am part of the HR department and this is a standardized message for exiting scientists. May I continue?" Asked the HR representative.

'This bureaucratic corporate mouthpiece and the politicians have no idea what they are about to throw away. We need to save the collections!' bellowed my desperation.

"Can I speak with Major Lance?" I asked.

"No, you cannot."

'We need to go talk to him or someone on the team,' urged my responsiveness.

My brow wrinkled and as I looked around and discovered that two security guards were now standing just behind me outside the door. Hopelessness came upon me like a straitjacket.

My thoughts were drowned out as the HR representative continued, "Your work must never be stated explicitly on resumes, during future interviews, or in any context other than with individuals with Q-clearance." He turned the page and scanned it for a moment. "You will receive a generous two-year severance package, a pension commensurate with the length of your service upon retirement, and life-time health benefits upon retirement." He handed me an opened folder and pointed to the documents inside. "To accept these benefits, sign the highlighted portions. You must do this now or forfeit these benefits."

They really made it hard not to comply. I signed the documents.

"We greatly appreciate all that you have accomplished, your devotion to protecting the people of the United States from its enemies, and advancing freedom and democracy. Thank you and we wish you the very best in your transition back to civilian life. Unless you have any questions, you will be escorted to your vehicle and to the gate."

"Now?"

The abruptness felt like colliding at high speed into a brick wall. At the same time, the way he said these things made me feel so small and discardable.

"Yes. All your personal items have been collected and boxed. These gentlemen will now take you and your belongings to your vehicle and then escort you to the gate," he repeated. "Here is my card, if you have any other questions, please give me a call."

'More like, call me if you want to hear the word no,' quipped my sarcasm.

I wasn't going to let that be the end of it. I'd wait outside the gate and flag down coworkers' cars if I had to. First, I decided to try getting in contact with Major Lance through the white pages. He wasn't there but I was able to find coworkers in the white pages who asked him to call me back. Major Lance told me that the decision was made at a much higher level than himself and that doing something to save the collections would put his livelihood at risk. When I tried calling back coworkers, they told me that they were sorry and that they wanted to help, but they didn't want to lose their jobs either.

The month of May I internally felt like Mount St. Helens, Mount Agung, Mount Galunggung, Mount Usu, Nevado del Ruiz, and Mount Arenal, all erupting at once. My rage poured out like volcano blasts. I would be sitting at one moment accumulating magma and the next minute blowing my top. It wasn't just inside the private seclusion of my rental house. I erupted in public a few times; screaming at the top of my lungs walking down the street, in the bank, and at the grocery store. Having accomplished so much, but nothing I could publicize, was enraging. It was just too much emotion to keep inside.

June and July were calmer but hard on my self-esteem. I was falling into new unemployment routines. My days mainly consisted of modifying my resume for company-tailored and position-specific applications, reading the newest developmental biology journal articles, taking long walks around my hilly neighborhood, and trying to learn how to cook. I also had to fill out several forms to start and perpetuate unemployment benefits. After submitting about a hundred applications with no reply, I started getting very anxious and depressed. My thought life often centered around reflections about what led me to this dead-end. I wondered if these thoughts during my walks were at all influenced by the long streets terminating in cul-de-sacs.

I could really use some of Milli's bravery right then, some of her encouragement. It was a tragic thing; waiting to see her once I had substantial success in science but never having a breakthrough. My pride wouldn't let me go back to her with my hat in my hand. I mean, sure, I had my Ph.D. and a handful of papers, but this was all I had to show. Milli was right in every way. Men *had* hidden my greatest achievements. I decided not to go to her, but sent her a letter about a month before my termination when I was anticipating that my success would come soon. The static influences from my childhood were always there, but I wanted more. I wanted to know how she was and see her again. The Hell with my self-serving fantasies of showing I was in control of my life and destiny. I wanted my mother, and I decided that as soon as I sorted where I'd be moving, I would make a stop in Kalorama, D.C.

The lack of responses from employers made me second guess the positions I was applying for. Chinese takeout became automatic after throwing out about a dozen of my culinary creations. Jogs and walks stretched on which helped my physical health and lowered my stress, but my ruminations stretched on too, and this eventually turned into cry exercising. Even though it was public, there wasn't really anyone outside in the middle of the day to see me.

Poor in spirit, recognizing my need for Him, I prayed to God, "I know you are the God of hills and valleys. "Deliver me from my troubles as you delivered your people Israel from Ben-Hadad's army."

On the first of August, a courier came to the house a little after lunch and hand-delivered a letter with no indication of who it was from. He didn't have a clue either. Very curious, I went back inside, opened it immediately, and started reading.

"All laboratory equipment, frozen collections, and computers were moved to a new location for continued research and development of your technology."

I fell on my face, praising God for the good news. Then, realizing I hadn't finished the letter, I returned to the revitalizer like a desert traveler dying of thirst.

The next paragraph read, "We are familiar with your work and wish to offer you an opportunity to lead a private company. Your title will be CEO, but you will be wearing several hats as you hire employees to fill different roles and build the company from the ground up. The board of directors will be meeting in Aspen, CO in two days."

'What?' my suspicion objected. 'This sounds ridiculous.'

'Read on!' demanded my curiosity.

"If you wish to accept the offer, fly to Aspen with this letter and enclosed tickets."

I shook the envelope and six first class tickets fell out. The inbound set was scheduled for tomorrow and the outbound set a week later.

'These are real,' noted my surprise.

'Read on!' exclaimed my curiosity again.

"A driver with a sign will take you from the airport to the meeting lodge. No action is necessary if you are not interested."

'What kind of scam is this?' inquired my suspicion.

'No scam! It's God!' declared my faith.

'Right!' A Billy Graham-like providential preaching came from my amusement, 'It all makes sense now! We needed to suffer Jim to make the move to Clingman, and work on SMNL trade secrets and inventions. He was never going to lead us to an academic laboratory. God was always leading us to a corporate position. Even Milli urged us to avoid academia and do something in industry. This is our real calling! This is who we were meant to become!'

With no further hesitation, I packed my suitcase and practiced answering common interview questions. The letter didn't say anything about an interview, but I wanted to be prepared just in case. Even if they did offer me the position without an interview, they would probably still want to know what ideas I had for my first 30, 60, and 90 days as CEO. Sleeping was still a struggle, but for the first time in months, it was due to positive reasons.

The next morning, I taxied to the Knoxville airport. I had to connect through Atlanta and Denver airports to finally make it to Aspen's small airport. I exited the plane onto the tarmac where a man in a tuxedo with a sign that said my name greeted me with a British accent. He took my bag, and escorted me to a Jaguar XJ-S in the parking garage. I asked him for his name.

"You can call me Felix," he said.

My memory went to Felix the Realist, the young dutchman from the Maryland marshes, who now sat in my mind, and occasionally reminded me of the wisdom to let go of things I can't control and focus on what I could. British Felix so far didn't really display any obvious similarities, but maybe God's purpose for him was to call attention to Felix the Realist's wisdom again.

British Felix put my bag in the trunk, and helped me in the car, opening and closing my door for me. There were some skiing magazines inside the door. He retracted the roof of the convertible. The temperature was a little cooler than I would have liked, but I was trying to go with the flow. Felix didn't say anything during the half hour drive. Normally this would bother me, but I was captivated by the giant mountains of basalt surrounding us. Yellow Aspen trees shown in the sun, like golden rivers running between the evergreen spruce. The mystery, Felix's name, the lack of control, and the surrounding beauty made me think, maybe God was actually trying to communicate that *He* was the one in control and I didn't need to worry.

We turned down a street without a street sign. Then another, and another. A solitary house was tucked away on the mountain side. The dark brown house we arrived at was very modern looking, yet the maids and butlers within reminded me of the Victorian era. Artifacts from the Napoleonic Wars and War of 1812 ornamented the walls.

A butler brought me a letter on a silver platter.

It read, "Consider this house your home. We will arrive tomorrow. The servants are yours to command this weekend. There is a jacuzzi out back. A servant will provide you with a bathing suit if you need one. There are many hiking trails, a golf course, and a ghost town nearby if you enjoy history. Our meeting will begin tomorrow at 7pm."

When I was finished reading the letter, the butler handed me a menu and asked what I would like for dinner. Moose, elk. buffalo, bighorn sheep, black bear, and trout were on the menu with paired wines. I chose the bighorn sheep with a glass of Sangiovese. The meal far surpassed all the Chinese I had eaten lately. Before bed, I pruned in the hot tub.

The following day, I ate Belgian waffles for breakfast, trout for lunch, and sheep again for dinner. In between meals, I went for a hike, visited the ghost town, and practiced answering more interview questions, just in case.

At quarter of 7, I was brought to the basement. It was a large room with wooden paneling on the walls and ceiling. Tall bookshelves stood beside my entry and the doorway on the opposite side of the room. On my left was a crackling fire in a gigantic hearth, and on my right was a glass case with more artifacts. Two long tufted black leather couches faced each other and were parallel with the hearth and glass case. I was instructed to sit. I sat on the couch opposite the fire, and the butler left me alone.

I had a flashback of the mountain cabin Jim and I used to live in. Our wooden paneling looked much cheaper than the rich dark wood paneling of this luxurious cabin. Our green shag carpet looked trashy in contrast to the oriental rug below my feet. Then, I saw Jim's contorted face look up at me. His phantom looked confused, like he was wondering how I had gotten the better of him. I counseled myself to crumple the memory up and throw it in the fire. Burn it away. Renew my mind.

The recessed lighting was suddenly dimmed and the fire shone brighter. Four tall, large men with horse masks and business suits appeared from the opposite entry I came in. The horse masks had bulging eyes and exaggerated fixed expressions of fright. The first mask was white, the second was red, the third was black, and the fourth was pale green. I was paralyzed with dread. They had colored gloves on that matched their masks. A profound sense of impending doom came over me. The men sat on the couch opposite mine completely silent.

After settling in, the black-masked Horseman finally asked, "How was your flight?" The voice that came from the mask sounded altered and very deep.

Sheepishly, I answered, "Fine."

"I guess you're not impressed by first class amenities. Neither am I," the black-masked Horseman said graciously.

"Has your food here been good at least?" the red-masked Horseman asked. It became clear that the masks were changing all of their voices.

"Very good." I said with a strangled voice.

"Glad you liked it. The game actually came from some of this year's hunts," the white-masked Horseman boasted. They seemed to be trying to calm me down.

When I didn't respond, the black-masked Horseman started, "We apologize for scaring you with our masks. Keeping our identities a secret is important to the activities of our organization. You may call us The Horsemen."

"I'm sorry, but couldn't you just wear plain white masks?"

They laughed. "Yes, but that wouldn't be nearly as fun," the white-masked Horseman answered.

"We know you as Virginia Marshall, but would prefer if you started using your nickname Vir and your maiden surname for identity concealment."

My name had been legally changed when I married Jim. Since 1977, there were no public records of a Virginia Goreman, and there had never been records of a Vir Goreman.

"Why the secrecy?" I asked.

"Very well. Let's get to the point. Vir, are you familiar with United States history and the different wars we've been involved in?" asked the red-masked Horseman.

"Not especially. I'm more familiar with more modern conflicts because of my mother's work," I answered honestly.

"Yes, you're the daughter of a successful journalist," the pale green Horseman said, sounding somewhat sarcastic.

"I am. How did you know?" I asked.

"We know many things about you, Vir. That's how we were able to offer you a job without an interview," the red-masked Horseman answered smugly. "Now to answer your first question. Our families rose to power through the founding and advancement of our nation locally and abroad. Our ultimate goal is to make the World a better place for future generations."

"By nation, do you mean the United States?" I asked.

"Well, yes now, but also The New World, The United Colonies, The United States of North America, The Confederacy, The Union, and other prior names," the red-masked Horseman explained.

The white-masked Horseman continued, "Our operations are covert, discreet, behind the scenes. We sway public opinion, ensure the election of specific officials, get legislation passed or rejected, conduct espionage, influence foreign government policies, execute special operations, and more. Our activities impact everything from crime prevention, to welfare, to education, to national defense, to trade policy, and much more. For the sake of national and international security, our identities must remain secret."

It was around that time that I had started hearing the term "deep state" in the news. Deep state was coined as a group of unelected government and military officials who secretly manipulate or direct national policy. While that term became increasingly popular, other names were also used - dark state, the cabal, the fifth column, the illiberal democracy, the parallel state, the power behind the throne, the Propaganda Due, the shadow government, the military-industrial complex, the 4th branch, and meetings in the smoke-filled room. It made perfect sense that they wanted their identities to remain a secret.

"Why hire me though to make a biopharmaceutical company?" I asked. "Why are you interested in cancer therapeutics?"

"Vir, I think you have the wrong idea. We know that the technology you were working on was positioned for cancer therapeutics for the sake of team morale at SMNL. That was not the real intention though, was it?" the white-masked Horseman queried.

Their knowledge of the intention of my project for military applications was proof that they were deep state. "No, it was not," again responding candidly. "So, are you asking me to lead a company that produces biological weapons for national defense?"

"Not quite," responded the black-masked Horseman. "A major issue that we and future generations are facing is the ever-growing human population and their demand on resources. The ecological footprint of humanity is about 1.5 times

411

greater than the biocapacity of Earth. That means we require 1.5 planet Earths to sustain the lifestyles of the inhabitants. Since we do not yet have a way to transport humans to terraform and inhabit other planets, we have a hard decision to make."

The Horsemen paused to let the statement sink in. I couldn't help but think of the arcade game I used to play sometimes, Terraform Tracy. The scientist hero would build domes, initiate cyclical chemical reactions to change planetary atmospheres, grow crops, and save stranded space explorers from space monsters.

"Are you saying you want to kill large populations of civilians?" I asked frankly.

"Yes, but not something that evenly impacts all populations. The power of nations is strongly impacted by their people. If the people are weak, poor, uneducated, violent, etc. they reduce the peace and prosperity of the nation," said the red-masked Horseman.

"The power of a nation is also relative to that of its enemies," said the white-masked Horseman.

"Some nations and subpopulations also consume more resources than others," said the black-masked Horseman.

"Population levels must be decreased to pre-turn-of-the-century numbers, about half of what they are now. Specifically, we want you to reduce the populations of the Chinese, Indians, Russians, Arabs, including North African Arabs, and Hispanics by at least 50%. Within the United States we also would like at least a 50% reduction in Black Americans, Native Americans, genetically handicapped and diseased Americans. Other populations can be reduced by as much as 25% to avoid suspicions," said the pale green-masked Horseman.

"This is relabeled Eugenics! You're racists!" Is what I wanted to yell. Instead, I asked, "Why target these groups?"

"Was that not clear? These are the groups that carry the largest resource burden on the planet. They are enemies to our nation and values, and populations that weaken our nation when they become too abundant," snapped the pale green-masked Horseman.

I didn't respond.

"Can you accomplish these goals?" Asked the white-masked Horseman.

'Can and will are two different matters,' challenged my respect.

After some hesitation the black-masked Horseman said, "Maybe you don't like the targeting of specific populations."

"I don't like the idea of killing *any* people," I responded sincerely.

The black-masked Horseman continued, "Right, but the Earth's resources and capacity to recycle waste are limited. Human activities are causing climate change, altering the weather patterns, increasing the extremes of heat, cold, droughts, and wetness. This translates into fiercer fires and storms which are killing our planet."

"And in so doing, we are killing ourselves," finished the red-masked Horseman.

"I still don't like the idea of killing people," I repeated.

"You knew that's what your technology would be used for when you were working on it at SMNL," replied the white-masked Horseman.

"No, I assumed it would be like nuclear weapons, never used because of mutually assured destruction," I lied, but I really didn't think it would be used before all other options were exhausted.

"Vir, we used nuclear weapons on the Japanese, and unlike nuclear weapons, your technology offers selective killing similar to what we were able to do with smallpox against the Native Americans in the 19th century," said the white-masked Horseman.

I was taken aback, suddenly realizing that my technology could be more devastating than nuclear weapons and used with less apprehension since it wouldn't pose a direct threat to the population using it. I started to feel sick. While the nuclear race had to end in a treaty, a race to make these kinds of weapons would inevitably end in genocides.

"Verily, verily, I say unto you, except a grain of wheat fall into the earth and die, it abideth by itself alone; but if it die, it beareth much fruit," the black-masked Horseman quoted John 12:24. "Death now will be like a seed promising new life. Things are accelerating too fast and we don't have a good solution to our resource issues. There is no chance that this planet will survive humans for another century. We need more time. There is no hope without a reprieve now. Your technology can slow things down, give us another chance to fix what is broken. Humanity needs you. If you don't help us, humans will die from lack of resources. Their deaths will yield nothing, like plants withering in the sun, swept away by erosion, or terminated by an early frost. It will be too late. You hold the key to the door to humanity's future. Will you leave us stuck, piled up on this side, dead anyway, or will you give us a chance?"

Humanity *was* struggling. We didn't have good solutions to our resource problems. That was true. Planet Earth, and by extension humanity, was in trouble. Reducing the population now *would* offer a chance for lifestyle reform and technology advancements that could save humanity's future, perhaps until space travel was possible. Did the ends justify the means, though?

Chapter 74: Damned If You Do

The prospect of becoming the CEO of a new biotech company was extremely enticing. Serious power was within my grasp. I wouldn't just be managing a lab of one or two dozen people. Hundreds, thousands, even tens of thousands of employees would be under my leadership. Financially, I would be set, even very wealthy. The only bosses I would have would be the Horsemen, and it seemed like no authority was above them besides God. Since they were apparently busy running the World, I'd probably be left to my own devices for the most part. Pretty much everything sounded amazing. The only thing preventing me from accepting was that the tech they wanted me to develop would definitely be used to kill people. Not maybe, definitely.

I used to believe that defense was the only valid reason to kill, but could no longer hold to this standard after killing Ewan. I killed him for being a traitor, trying to sabotage national security. I killed him to avoid progress being set back by years and hundreds of millions of dollars. Last but not least, a part of me killed Ewan because he threatened my professional future. So, in multiple ways my psychological restraints for killing were compromised. Still, genocide was too far.

At the same time though, I wasn't naïve about my value to the Horsemen. Yes, my experience and knowledge were unique. REVs were my discovery and I knew more about how they worked and what they could do than anyone else on the planet. However, my team did an excellent job documenting everything related to the technology and the Horsemen had the computers, the databases, the equipment, and the freezer stocks. A handful of talented scientists, maybe even one very clever scientist, skilled in the arts of molecular and cellular biology, developmental biology, virology, and computational biology would figure it out. If I didn't accept the position, the Horsemen would find others to do this work, and they would probably kill me. For now, staying alive was the priority.

"I see what must be done. Yes, I will help give humanity another chance," I answered, playing along.

"Excellent. Thank you, Vir!" said the black-masked Horseman. He stood and extended his gloved hand to me. The others lined up behind him. I stood and shook each of their gloved bear paws. They towered over me.

"You're a good person. You are making a hard but good decision," encouraged the white-masked Horseman shaking my hand with both of his.

"If you pull this off, you will save us all," added the red-masked Horseman.

The pale green-masked Horseman didn't say anything and gave me a limp fish handshake.

"Thank you for accepting this position, Vir. One of our people will be in contact with you soon to discuss the specifics of your compensation and benefits. Now that you understand what we need you to do, please prepare a presentation to explain how you plan to accomplish these goals. Let's plan to meet again next week. Until then, we hope you enjoy the cabin, its amenities, and the local charm," concluded the black-masked Horsemen before following the others to the exit.

"Madam, please follow me," a butler beckoned. As I turned to look in his direction, the lighting in the room brightened again. I turned back toward the Horsemen's exit, and they were gone like a hallucination or bad dream.

The butler took me to the dining room where decadent desserts were laid out and the compensation committee was waiting. They explained that the average C-suite executive was making $1.8 million this year and that the package they were offering included an annual salary of $10 million, more than five times the average. I did the math quickly in my head. That was more than $25,000 a day. Two days of salary was more than I was making in one year at SMNL.

Perks included private residences in strategic locations around the world, private planes, hired drivers, assistants, and a security team. The way the committee worded my performance incentive was that I would receive an additional year's salary for every 10% reduction in global ecological footprint. The committee underscored that there would be no severance package if my employment was terminated for whatever reason. I accepted the offer and signed the legal documents to start my employment the following day.

I kept thinking that I was going to wake up. The historical artifacts and décor of the grand cabin, the servants, and the gourmet food options all assured me that I had spoken with some very powerful people. The whole thing was very taxing and I decided to retire to my room.

On the way, a butler recommended, "Madam, consider visiting the nearby resort town, Vail, and the Colorado Snowsports Museum & Hall of Fame sometime during your stay. You can learn about the skiing spy camp that trained Tibetan freedom fighters in guerrilla warfare to fight against their Chinese oppressors."

"Thank you for the recommendation."

"Certainly, my masters were involved in creating Camp Hale," he added pridefully.

Other stories of the Horsemen's influences were shared throughout the week with what seemed like genuine enthusiasm from the staff. In their eyes the Horsemen were something between men and gods. Perhaps they *were* demigods. Like legendary heroes of mythology and folklore, they had made and were making momentous impacts on humanity.

As I lay in bed, I thought about Yahweh plaguing the Egyptians. If I made the Horsemen the viruses they were asking for, viruses that would kill people in target nations and ethnic populations, would it be like plagues? Would I be the angel of death?

The people of Egypt must have hated Yahweh for murdering their family members, their children. When people read the story today, I think many are bothered by Yahweh murdering the Egyptians. I was bothered until I considered the alternative, perpetual brutal slavery for the Israelites. You feel bad for the Egyptians until you think about them whipping the backs of the Israelites, forcing them to build pyramids, and working them to death. Yahweh was their liberator. Perceptions of Yahweh are thus relative and emotions run high. However, no one finds fault in the angel of death, or worships him. The angel of death was just doing his job. Even still, do I really want to be the angel of death in this narrative? No.

Did the angel of death have a choice as to whether or not he would kill the Egyptians? I assume the angel of death was/is more than just an unfeeling instrument. If Satan and a third of Heaven's angels could choose to disobey Yahweh and be cast down to Earth, why couldn't the angel of death? I would think he could have. So, it seems he chose to murder the Egyptian children. I suppose he would have said it was justice, a defense of the Israelites, not murder.

I wondered if the angel of death had a knowledge of how things would play out or if he just trusted Yahweh. I mean he could have acted without remorse if Yahweh had a place in Heaven for the innocent children. I imagine much is sorted in Heaven. It would only feel like a punishment to the Egyptians still living their finite, mortal lives. If Yahweh killed the adult Egyptians guilty of oppressing the Israelites, then they would have no chance to repent before an eternal judgment. From the eternal perspective, killing the innocent children instead would be a severe mercy. The guilty adults would still have a chance to repent and join their children in Heaven.

That line of thought could only get me so far. Felix's wisdom came to mind. The more important question was whether or not I had a choice to disobey the Horsemen and what would be the consequences? I realized that if the Horsemen had no issue with killing hundreds of millions of people, then they wouldn't have an issue killing one, me. Then again, why would they want to kill me? Just to silence me? The

Horsemen would only need to silence me if my voice could harm their efforts. How could I say or do anything to inhibit them though? The only power I have is what they have bestowed on me. If they knew I was against them, they would just take the power back.

I think a more likely consequence to disobeying the Horsemen would be the death of my loved ones. They started with the carrot – C-suite position, wealth to build a massive company, and a mission to save the planet and humanity. At some point though, if the carrot wasn't working, they would use the stick. If I said I didn't want the carrot, they would have to go with a stick. And what would be the only stick that would force me to do their will? Killing the three people I cared for the most.

The idea of the Horsemen killing those I love made me very fearful. I wanted to protect them. I wanted them to live long happy lives. Even more than that though, I wanted more time with them to be confident that they were spiritually saved. I mean perhaps Dan was, but I couldn't tell if Gina was, and my mother certainly was not. The present health and eternal destiny of these three were more important to me than billions of faceless victims. Still, I wanted to find a way to avoid killing anyone, except maybe the Horsemen who threatened everyone else's lives.

After a few days of anguish and contemplation, my determination took over. I iterated through scenarios like an AI machine learning how to walk for the first time, and found a way to move forward.

Chapter 75: Autonoma Inc.

"Making large amounts of virus and dispersing it in various sovereign nations will require facilities in those nations," I started.

"Why?" asked the white-masked Horseman.

"Well, what would you do? It's not like there's an international postal service that can deliver viral laden packages to every major metropolitan area in every country. Even if there was, viruses are generally unstable on packaging materials, they have limited ability to survive outside of a biological host, especially with changing temperatures and humidity during shipping, and you can forget about effective transmission with postal systems that include irradiation as part of their processes. The viruses will be inactivated before they get to the targets."

"So, you are saying viruses must be made and dispersed quickly?" inquired the black-masked Horseman.

"Yes, which means local facilities in populus areas," I simplified. "But sovereign nations will not allow a company to construct just any facility on their soil. We need a legitimate cover, a legal profitable business."

"Okay, what do you propose would be the legal front?" asked the red-masked Horseman.

"Diagnostic testing for infertility. This is an area that is near and dear to me. I could utilize the rapid sequencing platform my team developed at SMNL to screen blood samples for genetic infertility biomarkers."

"Sounds like a very expensive front," commented the pale green-masked Horseman.

"I anticipate making profit within three years. Here is my business plan." I handed the Horsemen printed packets.

"Why not something simpler like textile, agriculture, or food processing plants? Wouldn't it be faster getting those up and running as fronts?" reasoned the red-masked Horseman.

"Well actually, we already know the diagnostic biomarkers responsible for infertility from the SMNL genotype/phenotype database. I could have our legitimate business up and running very quickly. I don't even need to offer diagnostics for all of the infertility biomarkers. I could have them patented in waves and market new diagnostic panels each fiscal quarter."

They looked at me and each other but didn't speak.

"One major advantage to starting a diagnostic company is avoiding suspicions of auditors. An auditor is less likely to raise an alarm finding viral production technologies in a diagnostic research and development or manufacturing facility than if they found such technologies in a textile factory," I explained.

"Let's say we allow you to start this diagnostic enterprise," posited the pale green-masked Horseman sarcastically. "What will you do after that?"

"In phase two of business development, we would apply our testing expertise to select blastocysts for *in vitro* fertilizations (IVF), and provide IVF services. In phase three, diagnostic testing, we would expand to all other genetic diseases. Phase two and three activities would provide a smokescreen for the creation, testing, and dissemination of the population reduction viruses," I explained.

The Horsemen were again silent.

Then, the pale green-masked Horseman challenged, "You do realize that we are trying to reduce population levels? Why would we agree to fund a business that helps infertile couples have children?"

"Great question." I said, "I can edit specific genes in developing blastocysts preimplantation. I can make the babies infertile. Not only will the mature adults be unable to have children, any fertile human that engages in a monogamous relationship with them will also be unable to have children. That's an average of two to three fewer children on the planet with each IVF."

"How impactful could that be? I mean how many babies will be born by IVF? Seems very niche," challenged the red-masked Horseman.

"Well, right now it's about a hundred thousand people globally, but by 2000, it's anticipated to rise to about a million."

"So, you are saying this initiative will increase the global population by one million people in a decade, but prevent the births of two to three million. A net of negative one to two million people?" the red-masked Horseman clarified.

"Yes," I answered.

"That's good, but you're still burdening the planet with more humans now, and this takes time away from the main project, which should reduce the global population by billions," argued the red-masked Horseman. "Stick with the infertility diagnostics and maybe expand into the genetic disease testing if the time investment is low and you need the additional auditor smokescreen."

I could tell that wasn't a request. "Yes, sir," I agreed.

"Are there any other anticipated barriers with this idea?" asked the white-masked Horseman.

"Fertility and genetic disease testing are desired to some extent in all countries, but the ability to afford these tests and services is limited in many countries. Developing the markets and the infrastructure in less wealthy, less developed countries and regions, could translate into major challenges," I said.

"That's not really an issue. The local and national governments will actually appreciate the employment opportunities and other economic benefits from construction of facilities and utility grids. I'm assuming these facilities will be just outside populated metropolises?" asked the white-masked Horseman.

"Yes," I answered.

"Right. So, governments won't inquire why your company is setting up operations in their country. They will just assume your company, like other companies, are interested in cheap labor," said the white-masked Horseman.

The Horsemen paused. Then, the red-masked Horseman asked, "What will workers in these facilities be doing though? Can the labor from those regions actually be trained to do high-tech activities? How can you hide the viral production activities from your employees?"

"Many of these facilities can be testing facilities. Blood samples can be taken in countries and regions where gynecological tests are more routine, the DNA can be stabilized and shipped to the testing facilities, and yes, we can train the locals to do a couple of laboratory procedures. The laborers can learn how to do things safely without learning what and why the procedures are being performed. For the most advanced procedures in the R&D departments, things like engineering virus, I will need to come up with very creative mendacities. In some cases, I may need to have contracted employees that we pay especially well to keep quiet," I answered.

"Yes, and what do you anticipate the timeline will be for engineering and dispersing the viruses?" asked the pale green-masked Horseman.

"It's hard to say at this point," I admitted.

"What do you mean? Having a plan to accomplish these things was the primary topic of this meeting," spat the pale green-masked Horseman.

"Yes, and we talked about a critical aspect of this, getting in position to release the viruses. We will probably only have one shot to disperse the virus before alarms are raised. People will hunker down to prevent transmission, authorities will close roads and cancel flights to stop spread, and epidemiologists will find the viral release source and shut us down," I argued.

"Why don't you have anything prepared beyond this?" challenged the pale green-masked Horseman. "Didn't you manage a team that engineered viruses that could target human populations?"

"Yes and no. I managed a team at SMNL that engineered a virus that could kill individuals with a specific genetic sequence in their genome. The technology can theoretically be applied to target populations, but it hasn't been done yet."

"Vir, that doesn't exactly inspire a lot of confidence from your board," said the black-masked Horseman.

"Well, it's one thing to target one population. It's another thing to target many different populations, and come up with a strategy that kills at least 50% of those target populations, as well as up to 25% of non-target populations, all-together amounting to about half the human population. It's a tall order. Determining the best genetic sequences to target is not something I can do in a week, a month, or even a year. I need to hire a bioinformatics team to help me with that. We need to make and test the enzymes that cut the DNA of target populations, and we need to conduct tests to make sure those cuts in the DNA activate apoptosis of the cells. We need to make sure enough cells die to kill the human. We also need to screen and modify the actual viral vectors and their receptors to infect target populations. We also need processes and equipment that quickly makes lots of virus. *We also need* to run models to figure out the most effective strategies for dispersing the virus. Then, we need to put everything in place and execute. I want to give you a Gantt chart but I need to hire some teams and do some preliminary work to be able to provide you with meaningful time estimates for specific project goals."

"Give us a moment, Vir. Just wait right there," said the black-masked Horsemen. They all got up and exited the room.

In the low light with the crackling fire, I wondered if my new position would be short-lived, if an assassin would just come in the room and shoot me, if my blood would stain the carpet and wood floors, and what Heaven was really like. After a few minutes, the Horsemen came back into the room and stood towering over me like NBA basketball players.

"Vir, we understand that making milestones for your project without data would be ill-founded. So, we've decided to give you a year to hire the teams you need to make a preliminary project timeline and get your facility constructions organized and contracted. With that, we require a plan to work from and refer back to. The plan can be modified based on new information and new data, but we need a place to start. Okay?" asked the black-masked Horseman, extending his black gloved hand.

I stood up and shook it. "Yes, thank you for understanding."

"Certainly," affirmed the black-masked Horseman. And the others shook my hand and thanked me before leaving.

Later that night, while I was falling asleep, the name for my biotech company came to me like a vision, *Autonoma*. I was thinking about the Automatons of Greek mythology. The god Hephaestus crafted metal animals and beautiful women that could move. He did this for himself and other gods. Though the Automatons were powerful, they never rebelled. Somewhat contrary to this idea is the word Autonomos, which in Greek means "having its own laws," and autonomy means self-governing.

I took a Greek language elective in college to better understand all the Greek-derived scientific nomenclature. The suffix "oma" generally refers to cancer, like carcinoma (from epithelial tissue), sarcoma (from connective tissue), or lymphoma (from the lymphatic system). While most cells have a limited number of times they can divide before reaching replicative senescence, many cancer cells can avoid senescence, apoptosis, and replicate continuously, making them "immortal". I imagined Autonoma Inc. to be a powerful Automaton, and while the company is beholden to the Horsemen, I would learn to control it for other purposes and persist like a cancer.

Chapter 76: Destroyer of Worlds

As one does when faced with a massively stressful situation, I distracted myself, renting workspace, hiring teams, and making plans for the diagnostics front of Autonoma Inc. These were things I much preferred over planning how to kill billions of people. After I completed the checklist items that I wanted to do, I was faced with boxes of tasks that became unavoidable.

The Horseman put me up in an estate in Historic Brookhaven, Atlanta while my house outside the city was constructed. Tormented by my stressful reality, I paced around the living room trying to come up with a way to avoid killing people. At least avoid killing *so many*. The Horsemen wanted me to kill *billions* of people.

I thought, 'You already know you are not going to go through with this. The death toll will be so much greater than the Mongol massacre and the wars of the Crusades. For God's sake, it would be two orders of magnitude higher than the deaths from WW2. No one will speak of Hitler anymore, only of Virginia Goreman. Whose Oppenheimer? They will only remember and speak about Virginia Goreman, destroyer of worlds.'

'We are not that though, and we don't want to become that. We don't want to kill all those people, especially not the children. We learned virology, molecular, and developmental biology to answer the question of broken-hearted parents, "Why can't we become pregnant or stay pregnant?" We wanted to lead a laboratory to find therapies to help the 25% of couples impacted by fertility issues,' argued my success.

"Running is not an option." I reminded my reflection in the mirror. "They will find you. They will kill you and find someone else to do the work. I can't kill them. They're too well guarded."

'They'll also kill us if we take too long,' noted my anxiety.

'We can pretend to make progress,' suggested my relaxation.

'We need to make them happy in some other way,' recommended my amusement.

'The Horsemen want substantially reduced target populations. What if instead of killing people, we sterilized them?' offered my pensiveness.

The thought sickened me.

'How could we entertain something that's practically the opposite of our life's aspirations?' asked my discouragement.

My responsiveness answered, 'We know what inhibits and prevents the complete development of a fetus from our work at SMNL.'

'Stop! We can't do that,' responded my disgust.

My prudency chimed in more calmly, 'No, we can't. We might create ethnic wars. If target populations suddenly see that they can't have children, but others around them can, they will assume the others are to blame. Imagine the hostility if they realized someone took away their ability to reproduce?'

Then, my pensiveness suggested a compromise. "What if we just reduce the fertility of target groups to lower their birth rate? Conception will take longer, more failed attempts, but they will see their friends still having kids. So, they will be less suspicious. They'll think it's caused by air or water pollution, or something else that everyone contributed to; not something diabolical, intentional, targeted. It's still a horrible thing, but at least you wouldn't be outright killing them."

I sent a late-night email to the Horseman requesting a meeting and went to bed.

We met at a seaside 5,000 square foot "cottage" on Mount Desert Island, Maine. The estate was located where millionaires row used to be, before a fire swept through and torched nearly all of them.

Rather than entering through the front door located prominently on top of the bluff, a tender took us through the shallow water to a cave. Inside the cave were steps hewed into the contorted, thin bands of white and gray quartz and feldspar rock. The steps led to an oxidized copper metal door with a camera situated above it. A guard unlocked the door and let us into a cellar. Wine racks lined the walls except where there was another set of stairs, which I found out later led to the first floor. On the opposite side of the cellar there was a nearly bare wall. The guard pushed a section of the rock wall, causing it to retreat and reveal a hidden room. The room was empty except for a table and chairs. I sat down and the Horsemen entered behind me a few moments later.

"Welcome to Mount Desert Island, Vir, the place in the continental U.S. where the sun touches first each day," boasted the black-masked Horseman.

"With the exception of a few weeks around the equinoxes," corrected the red-masked Horseman.

"Thank you," I acknowledged.

"What did you want to discuss with us, Vir?" asked the black-masked Horsemen as he and the others took a seat at the table.

"I have been thinking about the backlash that might occur after the viral release and disproportionate population deaths," I started.

"Yes, and?" said the white-masked Horseman.

"I am concerned that statisticians will run the numbers and show the World that some populations had significantly different death toll impacts. Conspiracy theorists will come up with all kinds of stories to give the emotionally-charged target populations plenty of reasons to fight, but the doubt will hold them back. That is, until the molecular biologists find the genetic markers of engineering in the viruses. The conspiracies will be validated and there will be war. Innocent people will kill each other, and groups will hate each other more than ever."

"We are not opposed to war, Vir. War is sad and can be very harmful to the planet, but it is a viable option for population reduction," replied the white-masked Horseman.

"Okay, but wouldn't it be better for your children and grandchildren if there was less strife in the World?" I asked.

"Yes, of course, but how do you propose to accomplish this?" Returned the white-masked Horseman.

"Instead of a sudden glaring pandemic event, what if I gradually reduced their fertility with a stepwise reprogramming of their genes. They won't know it's happening because the infections will feel like common colds."

"That sounds interesting," perked up the black-masked Horseman.

"I would use modified cold viruses to infect the respiratory tracts, the virus would spread and replicate, and it would also infect the genitalia, spreading into their reproductive organs, and editing their genomes," I explained.

"A cold virus that infects reproductive organs? That sounds fictitious," scoffed the pale green-masked Horsemen.

"Actually, ACE is a transmembrane protein on the surface of a variety of cell types including lungs, testis, and ovaries. It's also a receptor for Coronaviruses that cause common colds."

"Each year, my seasonal colds would edit their genomes, reducing the viability of target populations' gametes. Demographic stats would show this trend. It would be visible but not alarming. Within a few decades, I could cut the birth rate by half or more and people would just think the changes were due to shifts in ideology," I surmised.

"Like shifts toward individualism or postmodernism, for example?" inquired the black-masked Horseman, supportively.

"A 50% birth rate would have a much more profound impact in the long run than a one-time 50% cut in the population. For instance, the U.S. population growth rate is 1.3%. At that rate, the population will double every 54 years. At 0.65% growth rate, it would take 108 years."

"Yes, and if you cut the population in half, it would take 108 years to reach the same population size," challenged the pale green-masked Horseman.

"Yes, but," I started.

The pale green-masked Horseman cut me off in mid response, "Except there would be fewer people in the United States, which means less burden on the planet for the majority of that time."

"Yes, but after 108 years," I started again.

"We will have things sorted before then," interrupted the pale green-masked Horseman.

"It's a good thought, Vir. We've gone down this road before, and tried reducing birth rates with the Eugenics Movement," apologized the black-masked Horseman.

"We had some decent success with sterilizations. Percentage decline in Native American births from forced sterilizations was about 25%, which translates into tens of thousands fewer redskins today. Not bad, but not great. The per person cost is very high, and forced sterilization has become increasingly taboo, even in the South," explained the red-masked Horseman.

"The impact of the Miscegenation Laws and their legacy continues to be significant. Some models have estimated that multiracial undesirables are roughly half of what they could be today in America if it were not for these laws. We are talking on the order of tens of millions, and passing laws is much less expensive than paying for surgical procedures," added the white-masked Horseman.

"Birth control has had the most impact so far and is very economical," noted the black-masked Horseman.

"What did Margaret Sanger write in 'Woman and the New Race'? It was great," asked the pale green-masked Horseman.

"Birth control itself, often denounced as a violation of natural law, is nothing more or less than the facilitation of the process of weeding out the unfit, of preventing the birth of defectives or of those who will become defectives," quoted the red-masked Horseman.

Hardy laughs echoed around the room. I curved my mouth and eyes to hide my disgust.

"Margaret was one of my favorites. God rest her soul," commended the pale green-masked Horseman.

"The global fertility rate has dropped by about 9% to 4.4 children per woman over the last decade because of birth control, and Margaret and others' promotion. Models suggest that this trend will continue so that it will be about 2.6 children per woman by the turn of the century," declared the red-masked Horseman.

"Yes, but this has disproportionately impacted whites. Despite free birth control programs, the most irresponsible cretins continue to replicate like rabbits. So, this has backfired some," qualified the pale green-masked Horseman.

"Among other reasons, we need you to quickly reduce the Negro population, so they are not democratically elected into power," directed the red-masked Horseman.

"Reducing their birth rates by half is a great idea, but it would be better if you worked on that after you have first reduced their total population by at least half," guided the white-masked Horseman.

"Keep up the good progress on your viruses, and you will be more impactful than Margaret, birth control, and perhaps even the whole Eugenics Movement," encouraged the black-masked Horseman. "It was good to see you, but we have some pressing matters to attend to. Feel free to stay and enjoy the island, carriage trails, and seafood for a few days. You've earned it, Vir."

"Thank you for your time and your hospitality," I replied as we shook hands.

As they left the room, I thought, 'What kind of villain could enjoy bicycling carriage trails and eating lobster rolls with a billion souls on their kill list?' The thought depressed me. Still, I decided that these minor distractions would be healthier than others.

Chapter 77: Lock and Key Engineering

Late October, 1991, the Horsemen asked me to meet with them at a mansion in Lake Forest, Illinois. They talked to me briefly the Friday evening I arrived.

"Vir, we are impressed with your progress. You've coordinated the construction and procurement of facilities and started diagnostic operations in twenty-eight high-population countries, two months ahead of schedule." The Horsemen clapped, and the white-masked Horseman continued, "As a small token of our gratitude, we wanted to offer you three million dollars to donate to the charity of your choice."

This was rather surprising as it was not part of my compensation package.

'What were they trying to achieve with this gratuitous gesture?' my suspicion asked warily.

I think they saw the confusion on my face because the black-masked Horseman explained, "Sometimes we play God and like to bless organizations or even individuals anonymously. We find discrete ways of introducing the money through anonymous donation channels, purchases with cash, and we have also started doing it with ecash."

"What's that?" I asked.

"It's a cryptographic electronic currency," answered the black-masked Horseman. "We thought you might enjoy helping someone have an extra good year. Does anyone come to mind?"

"Who would you like to bless the most?" urged the pale green-masked Horseman.

"I don't know. That is a very nice offer. Thank you very much. I'll need to think about it," I stalled.

"We're really quite busy. Who's the first person that pops in your mind?" pressed the pale green-masked Horseman.

"I'm just not sure. No one is coming to mind," I lied.

Then, there was an uncomfortable silence.

"Okay. No problem, Vir. Let us know at your earliest convenience so we can try to make that happen before or near the upcoming holidays. People spend a lot more money around this time of year so it will be less suspicious. Also, the holidays are a great time of year to bless people anyway," concluded the red-masked Horseman.

Later that night, a mixture of anxiety and relief came over me as I realized that they were just trying to gain more leverage over me by gauging who or what was most important to me. I was so glad I didn't give them a name. While the most powerful men in the world certainly have access to my family records, my phone call records, and who knows what else, *they don't have access to my mind.* So, they couldn't know for sure who was important to me unless I told them. My hope was that they would think that no one mattered to me based on the fact that I stopped talking to everyone. I stopped talking to Milli after our fight; Dan, Alice, Nancy, Warren, and Phoebe after Jim started drugging me; and Gina after meeting the Horsemen. I didn't try to send any of my loved ones mail, wire any of them some of the exorbitant amounts of money I was being paid, email them, nor anything else. After I learned what the Horsemen wanted, I knew they wouldn't be safe. The Horsemen's ploy just confirmed my concerns.

The next evening, we had a longer scheduled meeting. I asked them to donate the money to Greenpeace.

"Really?" blurted the white-masked Horseman. "There isn't any other organization or individual you'd like to bless more than Greenpeace?"

"No, I liked that they purchased the rights for the ozone-safe hydrocarbon alternative refrigerant from the German technological institute and made it an open-source patent. Maybe with this money, they will do more of that kind of work," I feigned care.

"We'll do our best, Vir. Donating to Greenpeace is a little tricky because they are very circumspect about where donations come from and don't accept government, corporate, or political contributions. If we can't figure out a way to donate to Greenpeace, is there any other group or person you would like us to bless?" Asked the red-masked Horseman.

"Probably the Sierra Club…Yeah," I lied, trying to think of another progressive environmental organization.

"Vir, I don't think we knew you were so passionate about environmental protection and preservation. That's wonderful!" exclaimed the black-masked Horseman.

"Oh, yes, I do care, a lot!" I replied, trying to sound convincing.

"What other environmental organizations do you favor?" Asked the pale green-masked Horseman, calling my bluff.

I was trying to remember other ones that I had seen commercials for on television or seen in advertisements in magazines. "The Rainforest Fund and World Wildlife Foundation," I replied.

"I think you mean The Rainforest Foundation and World Wildlife Fund," said the red-masked Horseman.

"Yes, you're right." Trying to bring the conversation away from the deviled details, I redirected, "I care a lot about this planet. We…" I gesticulated, "…will all be making a great and worthy sacrifice for Mother Earth in the coming years. Yes, a very worthy sacrifice to protect and sustain her for future generations. Of course, she is very important to me and all of us."

"You will do more for Mother Earth than anyone else has ever done, Vir. Very good choice for your donation," commended the black-masked Horseman. "We will work on getting those funds to Greenpeace, or the Sierra Club."

"Thank you," I said appreciatively.

"Now according to your Gantt chart, some of your next milestones involve making ethno-specific viruses. Can you please take us through some of the details on that?" Asked the pale green-masked Horseman.

"Certainly. The effectiveness of a virus in killing a large number of people will depend on three factors: (1) wide distribution, (2) high-lethality, and (3) limited response time. The challenge with combining these features is that they are contrary and unnatural," I began.

"You see, viruses are generally not considered to be living things. Yet, like living things, they want to perpetuate their existence through replication. A reason why viruses are considered not to be living is because they require a host. If they kill their host, they are less likely to be transferred to a new host for continued replication. *Thus*, our number two factor, high lethality, is contrary to a virus's survival and our number one factor, wide distribution.

The way viruses naturally accomplish wide distribution is by evading the immune system of a host, gradually spreading from host to host, and harboring in reservoirs (other hosts with little or no immunogenicity). It's typically a slow process for viruses to spread far and wide. Some factors quicken spread like international travel but others limit spread, like border control. Therefore, a virus spreading so fast that there is no time for a response, or third factor, would be unnatural. Humans typically have enough time to respond to viral outbreaks and are getting better at travel restrictions, quarantines, vaccine production and distribution."

"Anything else?" inquired the white-masked Horseman.

"Another *modus operandi* I learned from my studies is that viruses will evolve - mutate to become less fatal - to avoid killing their hosts. The benefit to becoming less fatal is that there's a greater chance for the virus to spread and replicate."

"So, how do you intend to overcome these undesirable unnatural and natural virus features? We don't really have ways of significantly changing human response time, I don't think…" The white-masked Horseman's voice trailed not entirely confident in his last statement.

"Perhaps you do or perhaps you don't, but my idea will not rely on you all from delaying human response by creating mass confusion, hysteria, or whatever. What is unnatural in biology can often be engineered or synthesized. My idea is to engineer a control mechanism into viruses that activates their lethality after they've spread around the world and had a chance to replicate throughout their target hosts' cells," I proposed.

"Wow! That sounds like a promising strategy. Please, go on," encouraged the black-masked Horseman. He was almost always very positive about my ideas and efforts.

"I believe there are a number of different ways to accomplish control over viral lethality. Micro and molecular biologists have started to discover and characterize a number of inducible systems. In the presence or absence of stimuli, such as a chemical in their environment. Problem with inducible systems is that they would be difficult to control."

"What are the difficulties?" Asked the black-masked Horseman.

"There are many. Let's say I engineer an inducible system into a virus that activates lethality in the presence of an unnaturally high concentration of a common chemical. Let's say something benign, like oxygen. You can imagine the logistical issues with production of enough oxygen to be significantly different than the 21% in the air, like 40%, or reduction down to say 10%. That sounds like an extreme example, but oxygen is actually one of cheapest natural compounds where low or high concentrations activate a number of inducible systems. NaCl or table salt is another extremely common compound that can activate inducible systems to change gene expression. Can we somehow get everyone in the World to consume extra salty food one day? Maybe your global media influence could get everyone to eat extra salty food one day, but how would you stop Americans from consuming extra salty foods the rest of the year? Do you see what I mean?"

"Yes," responded the red-masked Horseman. He seemed to be the most logical oriented one in the group. "You're saying inducible systems can be used like switch on lethality but a harmonized condition that triggers the inducible system will be extremely challenging if not impossible."

"Right. That is true for natural inducible systems. A more tenable solution, logistically speaking, would be to create a synthetic inducible system that is activated by very low concentrations of a synthetic chemical, something unnatural and found nowhere on the planet. Just a sprinkle, just a pinch, just a spray or a dust, a sniff, a taste, a lick, and the lethal activation begins. While this is certainly possible, there are a few problems with this approach though. Creating a synthetic system is hard, screens to ensure that natural compounds don't activate the system are also challenging, and synthesizing a novel compound for global distribution would be very expensive, even if you only needed a low concentration to activate the inducible system."

"Please, enough with the preamble," said the pale green-masked Horseman. "What's the solution?"

"Okay. Something I started working on at SMNL was virus activated viruses. A strong candidate that I was going to seek funding for was sequential application of engineered herpesvirus strains."

"How does benign herpesvirus kill large populations of people?" challenged the pale green-masked Horseman.

"Let me explain," I asked firmly, but trying not to irritate him further. He was typically the most cantankerous of the Horsemen.

"Herpesvirus HHV-6B is a virus that everyone gets within the first few years of life. People spread it through close contact. Yes, it is relatively benign, and can live dormant in cells for an entire lifetime."

I paused to see if there were any questions.

"Go on," politely urged the white-masked Horseman.

"HHV-6B can also come out of dormancy during times when its host is immunocompromised, start replicating, spread to other cells and other humans, and then go back into its dormant state. If it integrates into a chromosome, it can also pass laterally from parents to children. So, lots of avenues of spreading without killing anyone."

"When does the killing start?" Pressed the pale green-masked Horseman.

"Let me explain," I defended with a careful and respectful tone. "HHV-6A is another commonly acquired Herpesvirus with similar features. At SMNL, we found 90% DNA sequence homology between the HHV-6A and HHV-6B strains. What's interesting is that 6A can reactivate a dormant 6B."

"A virus that activates another virus!" exclaimed the black-masked Horseman.

"Exactly!" I affirmed.

"You still haven't answered the question," reminded a frustrated pale green-masked Horseman.

"Simply put, my idea is to engineer RENDS into 6B, let it infect everyone over the course of months, and then activate 6B with 6A to produce RENDS, causing apoptosis through the host, resulting in organ failures, and death," I quickly concluded.

"That sounds promising, but what are RENDS?" asked the black-masked Horseman.

"Ah, sorry, I thought you knew from the reports or however you learned about the project at SMNL."

This might have come across too casual a response or challenged his or their competency or thoroughness. The black-masked Horseman's tone and response sounded much less warm and more cautious than normal.

"We might have missed some details."

Trying to run out of whatever I stepped in, I explained, "RENDS is an acronym for restriction endonuclease nuclei death shredders. They are just REVs, type five restriction endonucleases, that target highly repetitive sequences in the human genome. So, they cut many times, or shred the genome into an unrepairable number of pieces. This causes cells to go into programmed cell death, or apoptosis. Enough of that and you have organ failure and death."

"Okay, but what prevents the 6A that's already in the environment from activating your engineered 6B with RENDS?" Inquired the logical red-masked Horseman.

"Nothing. That's why we need to install a new molecular lock and key. It will take time but I feel confident that Autonoma employees can do it," I assured them.

The Horseman ultimately accepted my proposal. Before leaving, they suggested that I spend a few days in town to relax, enjoy the leaves changing colors, attend the Fall Festival, go on a ghost tour, and see the newly famous Home Alone House down the street. I was in no hurry to start making biological weapons, so I relished the minor distractions.

The initial problem the Autonoma Inc. team ran into was that too many other things reactivated 6B. Everything from cold virus, to hormonal changes, even temperature changes reactivated 6B. So, we tried engineering 6B to overexpress the dormancy genes to prevent unintended reactivation. Modified versions of 6B are referred to as m6B. We also added several activation genes to 6A. Modified versions of 6A are referred to as m6A.

I really wanted to call Gina and see how she was doing. She was always the person I could go to when I was stressed about something not working. Sometimes our conversations helped me think of good solutions, but talking to Gina always reeled me back in. Hearing about what was going on in her life also reminded me that work wasn't paramount. I couldn't call her though because it would put her, her mother, and potentially even her boyfriend or maybe husband at this point in danger. I couldn't be sure what the Horsemen were or weren't monitoring.

Months later, my Autonoma scientists got reactivation with the m6A to work great with m6B-infected cells in a test tube. The problem was that m6B was now so sedated that it couldn't replicate and spread in an actual human host without the presence of m6A. Once m6A was present, m6B would kill only a small number of infected cells. Models showed that it was too few cells to cause organ failure and kill a human. We needed the m6B to be present in a significant percentage of the cells in at least one vital organ when it was reactivated for the host to die.

My team screened hundreds of thousands of combinations of m6A and m6B variants on cells and tissues, but we still failed to solve the problems by the milestone due date.

The truth is that I was sabotaging our progress.

'These are *valid* problems. The red-masked Horseman will appreciate the logical path we took to trying to solve the engineering issues,' emphasized my security.

'What if they don't care about our excuses? What if meeting milestones is all that matters? I mean the white-masked Horseman is so results oriented,' submitted my inadequacy.

'Yes, but the black-masked Horseman will advocate for us,' my appreciation uttered nervously.

'Will it be enough to counter the pale-green masked Horseman's condemnations?' inquired my discouragement.

'We're going to die!' Cried out my anxiety with fearful certainty.

When the Horsemen requested a progress report, having to tell them that the tech in its current form could not be used for genocidal applications made me very anxious. However, the Horsemen seemed surprisingly fine with my progress, even jolly, when I broke the news to them.

"How do you propose to fix this problem?" asked the white-masked Horseman.

"The strategy and techniques we've been employing may work eventually, but we've transitioned from rational design to high-throughput screens in desperation," I responded.

"You mean you ran out of ideas?" Asked the white-masked Horseman.

"Just with the current methodology. I have a whole new strategy to get around the issues we are having."

"Go on," said the white-masked Horseman.

"My idea is to create human clones with RENDS preloaded in every cell," I started.

"Human clones?" asked the black-masked Horseman. "You mean copies of human beings?"

"Yes. Sort of. I mean a clone's genome starts the same as the donor, but I can use the REVs to add genetic variation, as little as one base or more extensively than siblings and strangers," I answered.

"Okay, but what do you mean you want to create human clones with RENDS preloaded?" asked the red-masked Horseman.

"We have found in our testing that we can control activation of some of our variants of m6B with variants of m6A. The new door lock and key we talked about before. However, the new m6B variants do not spread well through tissue and organs. If I preload our m6B variant that contains the RENDS into zygotes, I could ensure that all cells would contain it. Remember that not having enough infected cells, meant that not enough cells would die, causing organs to die…"

"Yes, yes, and the human host dying," the white-masked Horseman finished my explanation.

"So, you make clones that have m6B with RENDS, and when you expose the clones to m6A, the RENDS kill the clones. Sounds like a zero-sum game," growled the pale green-masked Horseman.

"Currently, yes, but I believe we can further modify m6A to delete m6B's dormancy genes. Thereby, making m6B capable of quickly spreading to others nearby, and killing not only the clone but others in the home including the target leader." I responded.

"Like a Trojan horse," proclaimed the black-masked Horseman.

"Yes, like a Trojan horse," I concurred.

"Just to play devil's advocate. Why would clones be in close proximity to the leaders for them to be infected?" Queried the white-masked Horseman.

"Because the clones will fulfill their primal desires in some way- to live forever, carry on the empire, be the perfect child, etc. They will be by their side, the apple of their eye, their most precious possession."

I had anticipated this question and practiced the response in the mirror.

The Horseman asked me to leave the room to confer. When they asked me back in, they had a few more questions.

"We see value in this tech in targeting people who could mount a response against an outbreak, order quarantines, lead the masses, and mobilize resources for vaccine development. People who have means of physically separating themselves from the general population, and protecting themselves and their loved ones from infection. Leaders with large gated guarded compounds can mount responses from a safe distance," started the red-masked Horseman.

The white-masked Horseman continued, "Once enough of these Trojan horses were in the field, you could send the gifts containing m6A to the leaders on a single date or about the same time. We can provide intel to guarantee receipt. My question is, what percentage of the leaders would actually die and how fast?"

"We will need to do additional testing and modeling, but based on initial models, about 90% would die within two weeks. The warning signs would be too minor and the end would come too quickly to respond." I answered.

"What would be the death toll that results from these elaborate assassinations?" Demanded the pale green-masked Horseman.

"I guess that would depend on combined tactics," I replied.

"What do you mean?" Inquired the white-masked Horseman.

"Killing the leaders would just kill the leaders, but simultaneously starting an epidemic, war, or famine, could increase the deaths by millions without leadership, right?" I asked, actually not knowing what to expect.

"And who would start the epidemic, war, or famine?" The pale green-masked Horseman forced me to say it.

"You."

The Horsemen grumbled.

"See, she's worthless," judged the pale-green masked Horseman. "We just need to shoot down more planes."

I wasn't sure what that last comment meant, but the grumbling stopped and the Horsemen all looked at me. I sat up in confidence, burying my fears.

I declared, "We will have one shot to achieve your population reduction goals. If it is executed poorly, falling short is only one potential failure. It's actually more likely that these viruses could kill everyone, including you."

The Horsemen looked at each other but remained silent.

Then, the white-masked Horseman asked, "Assuming that we did help with that, what would be the death toll estimates for each of those scenarios?"

"I do not have that data."

'How would we even estimate the impact of one or more leaders' deaths on the survival of a population in the midst of major calamities?' argued my pride.

There was more grumbling, and then the white-masked Horseman addressed me, "Vir, we see some value in this program, but there are just too many unknowns for us to get behind this idea."

My proposal was kiboshed. Thankfully, they were in a good mood and didn't give me a one-way ticket to eternity.

The next day, I saw on the news that over two hundred thousand Tutsi and their sympathizers had been killed just a couple of weeks after the plane of the Hutu President of Rwanda, Juvenal Habyarimana, was shot down. I then understood what the pale green-masked Horseman was referring to when he said, "We just need to shoot down more planes," and why they were in such a jubilant mood. I'm pretty sure the success of their assassination-triggered Tutsi genocide was why I wasn't killed that day.

Chapter 78: Trojan Horse

The Horsemen rejected my ideas of sterilizing *in vitro* transplant babies and elaborate resource-intensive methods for simultaneously killing leaders with human clones. Hell, I would have rejected my ideas too if I were in their NBA player-sized shoes.

Unleashing a virus to kill billions was what they wanted but it was too horrible for me to work on it. I wanted, no I needed, them to let me do something else. Limiting births was a palatable option. I killed two people, but killing hundreds of leaders and therefore being responsible for the indirect killing of many more people was already an enormous moral compromise for me. I realized I was happy they rejected those ideas because those ideas wouldn't get me any closer to absolution with God.

I needed to take killing people off the table. It was definitely a sin to kill and it might be too great a debt to pay off. I wasn't sure if God would forgive me for the sins I had already committed. However, I thought maybe I could make it up to Him by creating a technology to aid in birth, and being responsible for the generation of more life compared to death.

'To even have a chance at this, we needed the Horsemen to let us develop a cloning pipeline,' reasoned my contentment.

'How can we, though? How would they benefit?' questioned my skepticism.

'Maybe we could appeal to other interests the Horsemen have besides population reduction?' offered my hope.

'Like what? They seem pretty myopic,' pointed out my discouragement.

'What about making a healthier labor force? Wouldn't that be important to them?' suggested my discernment.

'Hm. We could accomplish that with clones,' assured my optimism.

'What would we say? "You see, Mr. Horsemen. Altering human DNA is much easier when they are just a small mass of a few hundred cells than when they are fully formed with 37-trillion. We can fix the errors and supercharge them at that stage,"' mocked my skepticism.

'Yeah! And "Wouldn't you agree, Mr. Horsemen, that fitter disease-free humans are more productive and will help fix our resource issues faster than normal disease-ridden humans?"' added my confidence.

'That's a shameful ideology,' guilted my respect. 'There are countless examples of how persevering through challenges, genetic or otherwise, has molded famous and highly impactful historical figures. Unique perspectives and revolutionary ideas have often come from people with differing abilities and those whose minds are wired differently.'

'Yes, we know,' my insecurity answered dismissively, 'But, it's what the Horsemen believe, and we have to sell this idea to them, right?'

A few months later, I was teleconferencing again with the Horsemen.

I started my proposal by saying, "The REV tech was being developed at SMNL for targeted killing of enemy populations based on their genetics. However, the scientists working on this technology believed we were developing it for cancer therapeutics. It was easy to convince them because REVs can be used for that purpose."

"Vir, we do not wish to invest in a cancer therapy company. You will need to find another way to motivate your scientists to create and test the REVs," the pale green-masked Horseman said assumptively.

"What I was going to say, is that there is another application for the REV technology; to edit out disease-causing mutations from a human genome at the early stages of fetus formation," I paused so the Horsemen could follow.

"And…" said the pale green-masked Horseman.

"While genome editing is challenging to do with natural reproduction because the early stages of fetus formation take place in a mother's womb, editing is easier with human cloning because the early stages take place in a Petri dish," I explained.

I continued elaborating when the Horsemen didn't respond.

"We can fix the DNA errors with REVs before implanting the blastocyst into the womb. With this technology, we can make future generations of humans healthier!" I declared, concluding my proposal thesis.

The Horsemen started to laugh. I was a little surprised by this.

"Hold your horses, Vir…" the white-masked Horseman paused for colleagues to finish their chuckles. "You already proposed developing human cloning. At least in your first proposal you were going to help us kill target population leaders which would theoretically cause more deaths during disaster, disease, or war. We rejected this proposal though because you couldn't quantify how many would die without their leadership. Did you really think we were going to say yes to investing in healthier human clones? What's the point if these Trojan horses, for lack of a better term, are going to be detonated anyway?"

"I was thinking that if parents were assured that their children would be more or less disease-free, they would switch from natural birth to cloning. Healthier humans would be a more productive workforce."

"A more productive workforce *was* the pursuit of our father's fathers," said the pale green-masked Horseman. "*Not ours!*"

"Also, also," started the white-masked Horseman, speaking in a more controlled calm tone, to deflate the tension. "There would be no way to prevent your presumably sterile clones from just cloning themselves."

I hadn't thought of that and didn't have a good answer.

"We could … claim that you can't clone a clone."

"Ah, but they can," insisted the white-masked Horseman.

"Yes," I conceded.

"There will be other companies competing in the same space in twenty years, when the clones are ready to procreate. Hypothetically, if we let you do this and you were successful, you better believe that others would seek to get a piece of the market. The lie would be discovered very quickly and the competing companies would be happy to help the sterile clones have their own clone babies," argued the white-masked Horseman.

I couldn't say anything. The debate was won.

"Vir, we wouldn't disagree with you that healthier people are better than unhealthy. That is why we would like you to alleviate the burden of the genetically diseased and handicapped populations," added the white-masked Horseman. "Starting a Department of Therapeutics at Autonoma Inc. to reduce disease in our citizens could be a good project down the road, but we need large population reductions now."

"Come on, Horsemen! Improved health would help the Trojan horse marketing," joked the pale green-masked Horseman.

They all laughed again. I was frowning.

"Sorry, Vir. It's just too much of a rabbit trail. Too big of an investment for too little return," concluded the black-masked Horseman.

Human cloning would in fact be an enormous undertaking. I'm actually glad that the meeting ended early because I didn't have a good idea of how much time and resources it would take. Animal cloning successes since the 1950s up to that point were limited to a small number of frogs, mice, and rabbits. Predicting resources and timelines for milestones was very challenging. They would have roasted me if we had reached that point of the proposal.

A better idea came to me a couple of weeks later while I was lying in bed. One that would both capture their interests and mine.

I requested another meeting with the Horsemen, and they teleconferenced with me a couple of days later.

"Are we going to develop weight loss clones this week, Vir?" chided the pale green-masked Horseman. One of the others chuckled.

I ignored this and asked, "What if cloning was the only way to procreate?"

The Horseman paused. I could see the gears turning, even behind the masks.

"Hypothetically speaking, that would mean whoever can produce clones, controls reproduction," the red-masked Horseman responded.

"And control of population levels," emphasized the black-masked Horseman.

"Now that would be worth a huge investment. Three hundred thousand people around the World are born every day. We could stop the birth of roughly 110 million people every year. Since there's a similar death rate, that would mean significant population reductions. But, how could you make cloning the only means of procreation?" asked the red-masked Horseman.

"I could delete a gene or genes for gamete formation (eggs and sperm) in the genomes of clones using the REV technology. In the case of the rest of the population who already have gametes, I could design a virus to deliver the REV to the gametes, inhibit sperm mobility, fusion with the egg, and/or other key processes," I explained.

"World-wide infertility?" the black-masked Horseman asked.

"Yes, no one could have children without access to cloning technology," I affirmed.

"Do you see any loopholes, any methods someone with your skillset could overcome the monopoly?" inquired the white-masked Horseman.

"Yes, just as gene deletions are possible, so are gene insertions," I conceded.

Disappointed grumbling echoed through my speakers.

"Is it useful at all then?" asked the white-masked Horseman.

"Yes, just because a reversal could theoretically be done, doesn't mean it could actually be done. There are *tremendous* barriers to reversing a genetic deletion that causes infertility," I emphasized.

They were all ears.

"First, the cause of infertility must be discovered. Is it something environmental, chemical, hormonal, a pathogen, etc.?" I started.

"Go on," they urged.

"Second, if someone hypothesized it was genetic, they still would not have the databases to test their hypothesis. One must have access to a Human Genome-Phenome database. Some drafts of human genomes are public because of work done at the NIH and private contributions from wealthy philanthropists. However, these drafts include a very small amount of human diversity. Even more scarce is characterizations of how mutations in the genome impact or even correlate with phenotypes. Currently, SMNL and Autonoma Inc. are the only ones that have in-depth understanding and data resources for relating Human genotypes and phenotypes. If you could make it so that only Autonoma Inc. has access to the Human Genome-Phenome database, that would build a billion-dollar barrier," I declared, grinning.

"We can do that," assured the red-masked Horseman. "Go on."

"The third barrier is that someone would need to know what genes are responsible for procreation." Then, I realized, "Actually, no. They would just need to know what was different between the genome of the target cells and the genome of all other cells. I suppose a Southern blot hybridization experiment could be done to find large differences like a deleted gene or genes."

"Hell, Vir…" started the pale green-masked Horseman.

"Wait, I know…" The solution came to me, "Instead of targeting whole genes, I could target a promoter, enhancer, ribosome binding sites or even a small portion of these. Instead of thousands of bases, I could target just a few bases. That would be much harder to detect, something between searching for a needle in a haystack and a coffee grain on a beach."

"Just to be clear, you're saying the Southern blot wouldn't work in that case? What would an investigator need to do to find the cause of infertility?" asked the white-masked Horseman.

"If I created a virus that disrupted a target gene's expression with a small deletion of just a few bases, a Southern blot wouldn't work. At that point, the easier path for an investigator tasked at finding the issue causing sterility would be to determine all of the genes in the Human Genome that are responsible for procreation and characterize each one in terms of how a loss of the encoded protein impacts the appearance and/or function of the gametes. Once they found some similar dysfunctional phenotypes, they would need to develop a technique for replacing the gene or genes they suspected were broken. And I could make things much harder on the investigators by disrupting multiple targets at the same time."

"Why couldn't they all just be replaced?" asked the red-masked Horseman.

"What do you mean?" I replied, unsure of his meaning.

"What if instead of characterizing each gene, they just replaced all the genes with healthy ones, and why not replace all the genes simultaneously?" he clarified.

"Ah, good question. Adding extra copies of healthy genes would cause dosing issues. More specifically, multiple copies of these genes being expressed causes diseases like Klinefelter Syndrome, Triple X, or XYY Syndrome, and X-linked intellectual disability," I explained.

"Not add. Replace," replied the red-masked Horseman sounding a little frustrated.

"Ah, sorry. No, it can't be done. That would require removing and introducing whole chromosomes. The Y-chromosome is the smallest at 58 to 59 million bases. It's possible outside of an organism with a powerful microscope and molecular tweezers, but the technical barrier is very high. It's actually easier to replace the whole nucleus, what we do in human cloning, than to replace a single chromosome. *In vivo*, it's impossible because there's no delivery method for something the size of a chromosome. So even if one could delete the entire Y chromosome, you couldn't replace it with a new one," I assured.

"What if it was reintroduced in pieces?" asked the red-masked Horseman.

"Currently, the viral vectors I'm using have a capacity of thousands of bases, about four orders of magnitude less than the size of a chromosome. Even if someone figured out how to introduce bacterial artificial chromosomes *in vivo*, they would need to introduce around one hundred to replace just the Y-chromosome. Not going to happen. Even if someone did accomplish that, they would still have the problem merging them all together and getting them to wind up and function like a normal chromosome. *It's impossible*," I emphasized.

The Horsemen were silent.

After a few moments, the black-masked Horseman asked, "Are there any more questions for Vir?"

"Yes, what about other companies wanting to develop cloning?" the white-masked Horseman asked. "What are the barriers preventing them from doing the same thing?"

Things were feeling really positive. It seemed like the right moment to give the disclaimer that would protect my butt for a while. "This is new territory. It hasn't been done before in humans. In animals, researchers are observing abnormally large offspring, enlarged or malformed organs, compromised immune systems, developmental issues, and more. Miscarriages and stillbirths are more frequent than normal, and the causes of these are mostly unknown. We have an accelerated schedule for mastering human cloning because of the Mouse House experiments done at SMNL, but there's still a lot to work out in animal models before we transition to humans."

"So, you're saying cloning has been done with animals, but the efficiency of producing a healthy animal clone is low and it's unclear why?" clarified the white-masked Horseman.

"Yes."

"And what's the problem with transitioning to humans now?" inquired the white-masked Horseman.

"There would be a high incidence of malformations. Rates of healthy clones will likely be in the single digit percentile range," I warned.

"That is not a problem," replied the pale green-masked Horseman. "That is an opportunity for scientists! Dissect, interrogate, characterize the malformed failures and the healthy successes. Find the problems without government oversight, outside of legal purview, and accelerate your development progress. Then, burn the remains."

While he conveniently left out words like "human" as in "human remains" and "babies" as in "malformed babies", my mind didn't leave them out, and I almost vomited.

Thankfully, the white-masked Horseman asked an open-ended follow-up question to stop my mind from dwelling on these sickening thoughts, "Any other significant challenges?"

"Human cloning has raised numerous ethical debates under normal circumstances in which most humans can procreate naturally. These debates can sometimes create hostility. History has shown us that this often starts with picketing and escalates to arson and bombings. I imagine that people will shelve the ethical debates if there is no other way to have children without using this technology. Still, you should be ready for activists trying to stop operations. We need redundancies for all technologies, data, freezer stocks, etc., and additional security, just in case," I warned.

"Anything else?" asked the white-masked Horseman.

"Yes, lots more, but we've gone over what I think are probably our biggest challenges to accomplishing your objectives," I guaranteed.

They turned off my speaker while they deliberated. When they returned, I was told that I needed to send them a complete science and business development proposal. If it was approved, the Horsemen would take care of the legal, security, and competitive aspects.

They requested that I include Trojan horses to be part of the proposal as an add-on rather than a main focus.

The desire to kill myself came again, knowing what I must do. That would be the easy way out, but it wouldn't solve anything. They would just have someone else take over the project. There was no way around the hard road ahead. Taking away people's dignity was an inevitability, and so was taking human lives. I would be like Josef Mengele, certainly, but I also hoped to become someone like Irena Sendler someday. There seemed to be no path to become the latter without first becoming the former. I just hoped that God would forgive me.

Chapter 79: Early Access

The Horsemen ended up giving me a very generous fourteen-year deadline, after some negotiations. I would have until June 2010 to develop, test, refine, and optimize human cloning and the infertility viruses. Part of the agreement was that all clones that we produced while we were developing the cloning technology would be Trojan horses carrying a dormant inducible lethal virus, which was different from the infertility viruses. The Horseman assumed that most of the early clones would be sold to wealthy target patrons, and wanted to eliminate those individuals. I agreed, but was already thinking of loopholes for not including dormant inducible lethal viruses in some, even the vast majority, of the clones.

Shortly after the agreement, surprising news hit on July 5, 1996. A sheep named Dolly was successfully cloned using the same tech we planned to use for humans, somatic cell nuclear transfer, or SCNT. Prior to that, mammalian cloning was done simply by splitting embryos. Embryo splitting is kind of like the process of monozygotic twinning, which is the natural process of identical twin formation, except embryo splitting is done *ex vivo*, or outside the organism. It makes twins, so it's technically considered cloning. Not trivial, but it's junior league cloning compared to SCNT.

The SCNT technique involves a single egg cell having its nucleus removed (enucleated) and replaced with another nucleus. The egg nucleus must be replaced because it only has half the chromosomes (the mother's contribution) of a complete human chromosome set. The sperm cell provides the father's contribution in natural reproduction. With SCNT, a replacement nucleus comes from a donor cell, like a skin cell. The donor cell's nucleus must have a complete set of chromosomes. So, if I broke natural reproduction by altering the DNA of sperm or eggs, reproduction would still be possible through SCNT. If we could perfect this technology before any other entity and sterilize the human population, then the Horsemen would have a monopoly over human procreation.

The news of Dolly was a shock to me. I thought academic laboratories were at least a decade away from success with SCNT. The Horsemen made me explain the significance of this innovation. Two years were taken from my projected timetable. March 31, 2008 was my new due date for achieving SCNT in humans.

447

Three years later though, it was discovered that Dolly had twenty percent shorter telomeres than her peers. Telomeres are repetitive DNA at the ends of chromosomes that shorten with each cell division, a genetic marker of aging. A year later, she was discovered to have arthritis, much too early for her age. These problems helped build back the Horsemen's confidence that I knew what I was doing. I wasn't allocated any additional years though for the project.

Around the same time Dolly was discovered to have these ailments, Autonoma Inc. produced about two dozen healthy human clones that were sent to target leaders. Thousands of other clones died or were prematurely terminated because of obvious malformations and diseases. I told myself that they were suffering and that ending their lives was merciful. I still felt terrible about this, which affected my sleep. While my R&D team at Autonoma Inc. worked to discover the causes of these issues, I went on the road to speak with potential patrons and sell clones.

I didn't have to do sales. I could have hired a sales team to do that, but I thought it would be useful for me to understand the market so that I could lead them better. Selling clones with viruses to target leaders was necessary for the success of the Trojan Horse program. This was critical for the continued support from the Horsemen to develop the cloning pipeline. I was therefore keenly interested in learning about what the market wanted and strategies for getting them to buy. The Horsemen were also supportive, providing me with intel about key targets (leads). To appeal to elite target leaders and entice them into purchasing the Trojan horses, they recommended that I use marketing like "human clone early access program".

Indeed, this marketing appealed to a variety of patrons including one Bola Adebayo who welcomed me to his private residence in Lagos. When I met Bola, he was wearing a camouflage military uniform. Rising from his chair to greet me, he looked like an elm tree, very strong, and wide at the top.

"Hello, Dr. Goreman." Bola's voice was rich in timbre.

He extended a bulging muscular arm which I couldn't help notice was connected to Atlas shoulders and barrel-like pectorals. Despite the imposing build, Bola had a kind face with rounded cheeks and chin, a winsome smile, and a clean-shaven face that probably made him look younger than he actually was. He was very handsome.

"Hello, Mr. Adebayo."

"Please call me Bola," he requested with another warm smile.

"Thank you. In that case, please call me Vir," I replied, returning the smile.

"Please sit down," he said politely, with an openhanded gesture.

He waited for me to sit down and followed.

"Were your travels here okay?"

"Yes, thank you for asking."

"And how are your accommodations? Are they acceptable?"

"Yes, they are excellent. The rooms are very nice and the wait staff is exceptional."

"Perfect! So, what is this I hear about your company cloning humans?"

"Just that. We have developed a technology that can make a copy of you or anyone you choose."

"I very much would like a copy of myself, and I'd like to know, would this copy be exactly like me?"

"Genetically yes, but you are both a product of genetics and environment. So, a large part of making another you would require education, molding, etc. Like you might do with a child."

"I see, and would the clone be an adult right away or start as a baby?"

"A baby."

"So, he would need to be raised up."

"Yes."

"Who would be the mother?"

"That would depend on whether you had someone in mind or if you wanted to hire one of our surrogates."

"Oh, I was hoping you might be the mother," he said grinning.

I blushed at the implication.

Wanting to maintain a cordial composure, I laughed this off and joked, "That's quite a proposal for a first date."

"Yes, well, I'm also curious about how the chosen mother impacts the child," he added.

"That's actually a loaded question as we suspect that she is not simply a vessel. Without going into the details, I highly recommend picking someone who will take great care of themselves nutritionally, keep active, and avoid high stress situations."

"I see, and would her genetics contribute to the clone's?"

449

"No, the genomic DNA of the clone will be the same as the donors. Nothing genetic would come from a surrogate mother."

"This sounds very interesting."

Bola paused. He looked unsure about something. Then, he continued.

"Is it possible to clone someone who can't have children?"

It seemed like Bola was probably talking about himself and that he was ashamed.

"Yes, fertility is not a requirement for cloning," I responded without compromising his discretion.

Bola took a deep sigh of relief.

"That's very good to hear, Dr. Goreman, I mean Vir."

"Are there any downsides to cloning? Any problems? I don't know exactly what to ask, but is there anything I should know about that might be negative?"

"Well, this is a very new technology, and it's not perfect. Rather, a large number of clones are deformed, and we're not really sure why."

His brow furrowed. "Oh. So, some of your customers get deformed clones?"

"Unfortunately, there is still a very high risk that clones will be imperfect. We offer testing for preimplantation, *in utero*, postpartum, and during the first year. Patrons have the option for us to terminate humanely during this time and provide one additional attempt, free of charge."

"Mm." Bola thought for a moment.

"We are working to reduce the chances of an issue. I believe it's just a matter of time before the rates are similar to natural birth or even better."

"In that case, I don't see a reason to rush."

Bola stood up. So, I did the same. When he walked around the desk, I also noticed that he had prominent leg muscles too.

He extended his hand again to shake and when I placed my hand in his he held it saying, "Can you please come visit me again when…" He wasn't sure how to phrase it. "…when the chances are better?"

"Certainly."

Still holding my hand gently but firmly he continued, "And please let me know if you would like to visit for any other reason! I would love to have you as my guest anytime!"

His hospitality seemed genuine, and part of me really wanted to meet with him outside of a professional context.

"I will," I agreed with a smile.

"Perfect."

Before releasing my hand, he guided me as if we were dancing toward his office door. Then, he moved that hand gently down to my back as he walked beside me. Rather than calling the wait staff, he guided me to the front of his home himself and bid me farewell.

Later in bed, I found myself thinking about Bola, and decided that I would find other reasons to travel to Nigeria this year.

Chapter 80: Patrons

Bola seemed to struggle with infertility and saw Autonoma Inc.'s cloning technology as a way to overcome this issue. He was an ideal customer, exactly the kind that I imagined and wanted to help. Despite the help of my mind sage, Felix, I still suffered with some regret of having failed to achieve my pre-college dream of developing therapies for infertile people desiring to be parents. Assisting Bola to have a child through cloning would allow me to move forward with less existential regret. In my sales travels, I discovered that these cases were rare, and that the desire for power and control inspired other dehumanizing applications for the clones.

Many of our patrons were willing to take the clones that had diseases at significantly reduced prices. I didn't understand why at first. I thought that perhaps the patrons still felt a connection with the clones because their DNA had been used to make them. After hundreds of clones were sold, I found out that they were training these clones to be suicide bombers. These humans were undocumented, impressionable, and often intellectually challenged. Their disfigurements and handicaps invoked human compassion and brought the enemies' guard down, which enabled them to get closer and do more damage than healthy humans. Once trained, these suicide bombers enabled a level of precision and destruction rivaling that of missiles with sophisticated guidance systems in mechanized militaries (like $1.5M Tomahawk cruise missiles), but for 100X lower cost. In my mind, this disturbing application made solving the issues with cloning critical.

By 2002, my team understood the key issues in the cloning process that I mentioned above. We considered these issues solved in 2004 after two years of observing no statistical difference in the health or developmental milestones of clone and control cohorts. That's because most infant deaths occur within the first year (global rate of about 5.1% at the time) and several developmental milestones can be measured by two years. We could not know if our clones would continue to develop and age normally, but we felt confident enough to start producing dozens of clones per month.

Other companies were also having success with cloning in 2004. Dolly wasn't doing so well at that point, suffering with severe arthritis, but many other mature animal clones were doing fine. About four hundred farm animals had been cloned, a mixture of mainly cattle, sheep, pigs, and goats. 77% were determined to have no health problems, which was similar to natural populations. The main purpose of the successful cloning organizations was making immune-compatible animals for organ donation. Even though these companies were working with animals, they were still my competition since they were identifying and solving the challenges with cloning.

The barriers for transition from animal to human cloning weren't Himalayan but were at least Alpine.

Once Autonoma started producing healthy clones, we no longer had discount clones available for sale. Many of the groups who were using suicide bombers transitioned to ultra cheap armed drones. With a higher production success rate, we were able to bring the prices down to about twice of what it would cost to give birth to naturally conceived humans in a U.S. hospital.

At this price point, we attracted warlords interested in superior child soldiers and political leaders interested in gold-medal Olympic athletes. Both were interested in undocumented elite spies. I gave the patrons exceptionally strong and fast clones, some that could feel no pain, some that were fearless, some that were strategically brilliant and agile, and all absolutely loyal to authority. One also requested that we make some "Navy SEALS" that were generally athletic as well as averse to sea sickness. They could hold their breath like Houdini, and swim in the sea for days at a time. I didn't love what the patrons were planning for the lives of these clones, but I consoled myself saying that better days were ahead. These were just the stepping stones to the goal of human cloning at the scale of natural births.

Autonoma Inc. had frozen cell samples from millions of people, but this wasn't the main reason we could provide customized clones to patrons. It was because I had the genotype-phenotype association data from SMNL and my REV genetic engineering tech. We didn't just offer clones. We offered disease-limited functionally-enhanced human clones. We can't actually produce disease-free humans. Disease-free is impossible because of how the environment factors into disease. For example, skin with less melanin is less protected from UV radiation. So, about 2.6% of white people will have melanoma in their lifetime compared to just 0.1% of black people. So, by "disease-free" we really meant "disease-limited". We inform patrons of the inherent risks by choosing phenotypes, like skin color, and help them select lower-risk mutations.

We actually had a product called Me2s, which were genetically cleaned and upgraded versions of the patrons. That was the marketing before the #MeToo Movement. After the #Me Too Movement, the sales team would ask if the patrons were interested in a Me2.0. The sales team would have them imagine living forever through the transfer of genetics and accumulated wisdom. One salesperson told me his pitch before I fired him, "Your Me2.0 wouldn't be just your child, he would be your successor. You would know he wasn't a fool, some idiot offspring diluted by the genetics of their mother. No, your son would be a guaranteed improved copy of yourself. With your intellectual capacity, he would just need some mentoring and molding to become your successor and perpetuate your empire." While that salesperson had closed some sales, he conceded that many of the prospective buyers laughed at his pitch and would say things like, "I just imagined Mini Me from *Austin Powers: The Spy Who Shagged Me*." The ones that were interested in Me2.0 also wanted loyal friends and advisors cloned too for their successors.

Managing so many departments of Autonoma became unsustainable. I decided to start building some layers of leadership so I could delegate my responsibilities. One of my hires was a VP of Clone Engineering and Design. Besides the issues with having too much work, I really didn't want to be so involved with human genetic manipulations anymore. Patrons were shallow, exacting, and all kinds of other evil. It was reflected in their cloning requests.

The most common patrons were rich powerful heterosexual men interested in undocumented female sex slaves. My former VP of Clone Engineering and Design contracted scouts to sample the most beautiful women (mostly professional models) from all over the world. Autonoma Inc. scientists sequenced their DNA and searched for enrichment of specific genetic signatures in these populations relative to our entire database. The bioinformatic scientists were double blinded so they had no idea what they were doing. The categories they were evaluating such as being a model, having voluptuous firm breasts, round bottoms, proportions, long legs, thin midsection, etc. were labeled as PhenotypeM1, PhenotypeM2, etc. They also searched for genetic signatures that were commonly absent in the models relative to the database. Donor eggs were screened for these "anti-model" signatures. Model cells and donor cells edited to include model signatures were used for source DNA to generate a variety of clones to satisfy the sexual desires of the patrons.

While female clones were generally only valued as personal slaves, commodities, and gifts, occasionally a client would request a clone of their deceased daughter or wife. And a couple of clients requested femme fatales with irresistible beauty, loyalty, ninja agility, precision, speed, stealth, and ruthlessness.

Selling clones to warlords and politicians for mostly unsavory purposes put Autonoma at risk for federal lawsuits. So, I made a shell company to separate the liability.

Chapter 81: Competitive Advantage

Sales travel was really starting to wear on me, but I kept making my rounds to target countries so that I could see Bola without altering the Horsemen's suspicions. Our fondness for each other grew over the years and eventually became romantic. Spending time with him became my respite. There weren't many other things that made me happy or could relax me like a weekend with Bola.

With our growing tenderness, I felt increasingly guilty about my many decisions. For a while, I pretended like we were still working on lowering the rate of deformed clones. I would ask, "Is 50% okay?" and then immediately advise him to, "Say, no. We can and will bring the rate down."

"You're the expert, Vir," he'd say. "Since you're here, how about we have some fun?"

Then, I'd respond, "What did you have in mind?"

And every time, he had some wonderfully charming experience ready for us.

Eventually, I did tell him that we fixed the issues with deformations, and he decided to buy a clone. I made sure that his clone did not have the dormant lethal virus embedded inside. One of his sisters agreed to carry the child to term. Bola invited me to the birth. I came and stayed for a couple of days. His feelings of joy and appreciation lead to a very romantic day at the ocean complete with playing in the waves, sex on the beach, and a proclamation of love.

"You're the most brave, brilliant, and beautiful woman I know."

"Come on. Beautiful?"

"Yours isn't just an external beauty, though your freckles drive me crazy. They make me want to explore and follow them like a trail of crumbs to your sweets."

"Stop," I implored, while relishing the compliments.

"Your inner beauty is gushing with creativity, kindness, compassion…"

"How?"

"How!" He bellowed. "Look at what you've done. You've given new life to a barren man."

I suspected the remark was meant to be a double entendre.

"I love you, Vir."

I didn't really see it coming and was a little afraid to reciprocate given my romantic history. The best I could say to him at that time was, "I care about you deeply, Bola. You make me incredibly happy."

I was thankful when he didn't make an issue about me not saying *the* words.

After one of the best weeks of my life, I had one of the worst weekend business meetings with a ruler in the Middle East.

Hassam, an oil prince, agreed to meet with me in a boardroom with chaperones sitting beside us. He wore a ghutra (white head covering) and thawb (white robe) secured with an agal (black chord).

I was required to wear a black headscarf and an abaya (loose fitting black cloak).

Hassam's interpreter sat beside him and translated Hassam's Arabic and my well-rehearsed pitch. Hassam seemed very intrigued.

He asked through the interpreter, "Who can I speak with to answer my technical questions?"

I answered, "You're talking to the best technical support specialist. I'm the inventor of the technology."

"I see," he replied through his translator. Then, he whispered in his translator's ear. From below the table they raised automatic firearms and the jarring blast of shots resounded.

"Stop!" I yelled, but an instant later, my guards were dead.

"What the Hell are you doing?" I demanded.

"Blind fold her, tie her hands behind her back, search her, and bring her to the lab," commanded Hassam.

I got into a fighting stance but was quickly overcome by the guard. It happened so quickly that I wasn't sure how I ended up on my face.

They put me in a high-riding vehicle like an SUV or truck and started to drive, keeping my blindfold on.

Anxious about being abducted, I asked where we were going.

"The lab. Weren't you listening?" mocked Hassam.

The guards laughed.

"Why are you doing this?" I demanded.

Something hit me in the side of the head. My vision blurred and a sharp and throbbing pain followed. "That is not a respectful tone!" someone barked.

"Yes, Vir. I do not answer to you, but you answer to me now," stipulated Hassam.

We drove for about a half hour while they spoke fervently in their language that I didn't understand. The blindfolded drive brought unwelcome memories of the drive to the mountain house Jim and I used to live in, the one that became a torturous prison to me for a year.

When we stopped, I tried to run, but they pulled and pushed me through a door, down a hall, and into an elevator. I counted that we went three levels down. Perhaps, I could use the information to escape, I thought.

Once we were out of the elevator, my blindfold was removed. I was surrounded by Hassan and the two guards that abducted me. My daring wanted me to try and fight them, but before I made a move, Hassan started to speak.

"See, you're in a lab."

Looking around, I saw benches, shelves, centrifuges, burners, glassware, etc.

"Yes," I agreed. "Why though?"

One of the guards was about to hit me again so I turned and closed my eyes reflexively. The impact never came though. Opening my eyes, I saw Hassam with a hand on his guard's shoulder.

"This is a scientist. They have been trained to ask questions. We should not beat that out of her, since I want her to be our scientist," declared Hassam.

"I am the CEO of Autonoma Inc. I am no one's scientist!" I exclaimed.

"Correction, you were CEO of Autonoma Inc. How many clones did you sell?"

"That is proprietary."

Hassam nodded his head at the man behind me.

A sharp pain exploded from my right kidney, radiating to my abdomen and growing. A terrible memory of being immobilized in the hospital with excruciating pain and fear rushed to mind. I buckled feeling a strong urge to vomit, but only dry heaves came.

"I am being nice by allowing you to ask questions because you are a scientist. You must answer all of mine because I am your new boss, understand?"

It wasn't really a question. I wanted to tell him to go to Hell, but knew it wouldn't be prudent for my survival and escape.

"Yes," I acquiesced.

"Good. How many clones?"

"Hundreds probably."

"That's how many orders or how many clones were actually delivered?" he clarified.

"Delivered."

"Excellent." He sounded pleasantly surprised.

"Okay, I answered your question." Now, no longer nauseous, I was kneeling submissively in the seiza posture, and requested carefully, "Please, can you tell me why you abducted me?"

"Sure, why not?" He stated, "Your cloning services are for sale."

"Yes," I agreed.

"So, the wealthier your customers are, the more clones they can buy, right?"

"Yes."

"And they can buy better clones with more money?"

"Yes."

"Is there anyone who you won't sell to?"

"Generally speaking, no."

"Exactly."

"Exactly, what?"

"That's why I needed your services exclusively. I couldn't have any of my competitors buying more and better clones from you. Now, I have the advantage! You will make me hundreds, even thousands of clones," Hassam insisted.

"And how am I supposed to do that?" I inquired, remembering to put my push-back in the form of a question.

"You will have the supplies and resources you need to make your clones. We can get whatever you need."

"Sure. Can you provide the following - billions of dollars, exclusive technologies, and dozens of brilliant scientists? The best you can hope for is to wait three decades because that's how long it took me to establish my current facilities."

Hassan took out his pistol and held it inches from my face. His guards each backed up a couple of steps.

"If I can't have your services, no one can."

"Wait!" I bellowed narrowly avoiding execution. "May I please have some time to think about how I might be able to expedite the R&D?"

"You have two days to come up with an affordable solution."

A bullet rang out and startled me. Tinnitus followed and the sound of their shoes walking away was muffled. They got into the elevator and left me there alone.

After taking a few minutes to recover, I stood up and looked for exits. There were no windows. Side doors were closets, and the elevator was badge access only.

Feeling frustrated, I considered filling the room with gas from the burner and blowing it up, but ultimately decided against it. When no one came down that evening, I laid a stool on the ground and used the backrest as a pillow.

I was shaken awake a few hours later. A man in a black mask and night vision goggles shocked me.

"Dr. Goreman, you are being extracted," a hushed deep voice explained concisely.

Looking around, I realized that there were five in tactical attire around me. Attempting to get up, back and neck pain, muscle soreness, and joint stiffness assailed me. Before I could object, one of the operatives flung me over their shoulder, and within minutes, they had me on the roof leaving in a helicopter.

A couple of months later, I was abducted a second time in an adjacent country. This time, when the extraction team came to get me, I had them hold the client down on the ground, face up to see me. I punched and kicked him. Then, I shot him in the neck aiming for his chest. I felt guilty about killing him later, but in the moment, I was angry and it felt good to get some power back after having my life threatened once again.

The Horsemen had given me power by making me CEO of Autonoma Inc. The caveat was that I was only allowed to lead the company in directions that accomplished their goals. While it's not unusual for the Board of Directors to set the overall strategy of a company and for the CEO to execute accordingly, it is unusual that the CEO would be killed rather than simply fired for lack of progress. After two attempts by clients to enslave me and force me to perform or die, I became acutely sensitive to my power and who was trying to take it from me.

Chapter 82: Too Far

I was in India the following month, had finished my business meeting, and was walking on the tarmac to get onto my private jet, when a few men approached me and my guards. We moved into a defensive formation to prepare for a fight. One of the men announced in a reassuring tone, "I am Vijay, one of the sons of Lahiri Ghatak. My job is to firm up my father's business deals. He is intrigued by your offer but wants to know more."

"Well, I am in a hurry to get to a meeting in Abu Dhabi," I responded.

Before I could say, "Let's set up another meeting," he cut me off with, "That's fine, we can talk terms on the plane."

I stopped for a moment, thinking this was presumptive, but then kept walking and agreed, "Yes, that's probably better than coming back. You may come along, but we don't have enough room for your men."

We boarded and buckled up.

Vijay bragged, "I've previously procured large labor forces, armies, and weapons for my father's interests, but what you have to offer is quite novel!"

"Thank you. We are unique," I admitted, carefully accepting the compliment.

The service came through and provided drinks as we were preparing to take off.

Vijay was gazing at me as the plane rose into the clouds. This made me uncomfortable. So I asked, "Why are you looking at me that way?"

Vijay answered, "I know you. The voice and the way you walk with such long strides. While my sister was at Nettie Maria Stevens University, I came to the end of a Bible study, and then went out dancing with the group. I remember walking behind you and the reverend, trying to keep up so I could listen to your conversation."

'That's kind of creepy,' noted my judgment.

'Who is this guy?' wondered my suspicion.

"You were in love with the reverend. My sister was in love with the reverend too. She was impressed by his ability to create a diverse congregation. My sister had

461

long conversations alone with him, which I didn't like. She told me that she imagined being his wife and was very sad when he chose you instead."

A memory suddenly came to mind. The person who must have been Vijay's sister was a congregant named Aarna. She danced with Jim at the disco one night, and I remembered feeling jealous.

"What is your sister doing now?" I asked.

"After you and the reverend were married, it was easier for her to finish her studies at Harvard. She has since married a friend of the family and started her own. She seems happy but sometimes talks with me about her alternative reality with the reverend," said Vijay.

I was glad for Aarna, that she avoided Jim's abuse.

"It's truly amazing what you have become. From a reverend's wife to an international merchant of genetic superhumans. What did you study while you were at university?" Vijay asked.

An explosion of memories rushed in my mind starting with the night that I killed Jim, then selling the house, moving to Tennessee, making a project team at SMNL, developing the REVs, and my first meeting with the Horsemen. I answered with a slight delay, "International trade."

"That makes sense. Except you didn't." Vijay pressed, "My sister said it was something related to biology and how humans develop. Did that background knowledge help you get the job?"

I was a little perturbed by his catching me in a lie. "Right," I responded, wondering where this was going.

"Except that's not quite right because why would a poor hyper religious reverend's wife be hired for this position? Not exactly a great fit for negotiation with rich and powerful men and extensive travel. Did you make a business connection at Nettie Maria Stevens University?" Vijay pressed.

"No," I answered with growing disdain on my face.

"Or a connection in a position you had after college? After the reverend's accident, as it were." Vijay probed.

"Stop," I barked, greatly irritated by this interrogation. He had obviously done some background checking of my past, and was working on filling in the gaps.

But he kept going, "Or was it some secret knowledge you gained at the national laboratory?"

"I'm warning you," I growled, baring teeth. My blood was starting to boil.

"Did you develop some of the technology?" Vijay continued.

My emotions were flooding, but there was nowhere to go. Not that I was one to retreat but I could tell that my anger was ready to take over. I just needed time to decompress.

When I didn't answer Vijay right away, he gawked in amazement and declared, "You did help create the technology! A *poor, religion-and-husband-distracted woman* helped create this incredible technology! Unbelievable!"

"I didn't just help! It's my invention! I lead the project team!"

"I can't believe that. How could someone dumb enough to join a cult and marry the leader, create something like this?"

Before I had a chance to respond, he added, "Well, if you're capable of that, I probably underestimated you in other ways too. The reverend's death wasn't an accident, was it?"

My eyes and mouth widened in shock, betraying my confidence and revealing my secret.

"Wow! You're a murderer too! You aren't the typical reverend's wife, are you?"

'He knows too much about us!' exclaimed my anxiety.

"Now, *Virginia Dare Goreman...*" Vijay slowly articulated my name to point out the fact that he knew my identity. "I know who you are, what you've done, and who you care about." He winked, cupped his hands around his mouth to prevent my guards from lipreading, and whispered, "Ocracoke."

He paused for emphasis.

'How does he know about the Ocracoke crew?' yelled my anxiety.

"Now, you're going to give me the best deal you can on clones or you might have some unwanted information exposure," Vijay threatened.

'There's nothing else to do. He's too much of a risk,' decided my feeling of being overwhelmed.

"Throw him out of the plane!" I commanded. Three of the guards grabbed him, unbuckled his seat belt.

"What? No!" He struggled as they ripped him out of the seat and quickly dragged him to the emergency door.

The air lock and door were opened. Wind rushed around. "Please don't do this!" He cried out.

"Maybe you'll be reincarnated and clever enough to keep your mouth shut in your next life. Oh, wait, you're too smart for religion. Too bad."

I waved him goodbye as two guards held his arms and the third kicked him square in the chest, sending Vijay flying out of the airlock door into the open sky.

Coming back down to Earth from the emotional flood, I realized the potential folly of my deed. I still felt strongly that Vijay had to die because he clearly knew too much about me and my loved ones, and he was threatening to control me with the knowledge. It was an unacceptable risk. The problem was that three of Vijay's men saw him get on the plane with me. When we arrived in Abu Dhabi, someone would be expecting him. Either there would be someone waiting for him to walk off the plane, or someone back home would be expecting a phone call. This meant I only had two hours to figure out what to do. The Ghatak family would come after me if they discovered what I did to Vijay.

I thought about calling the Horsemen. They could probably clean this up. Then my autonomy asked, 'Why can't we fix this ourselves?'

My opportunistic side asked, 'What more could we get out of taking care of this ourselves?"

My defense answered, 'We could instill a little fear in the patrons, not just for our own safety but for our future sales team.'

My prudence echoed my opportunistic side with a different emphasis, 'What benefit would there be of us cleaning things up compared to the Horsemen doing it for us?'

My guilt said, 'Many people will need to die to contain this.' I imagined at least family would need to be killed, but possibly some friends wanting to avenge Vijay too. This was very upsetting.

My defense reminded me, 'Vijay was cornering you and he was going to try to control you. He was a threat to your loved ones. It's his fault. He put you in this position. Your actions were in self-defense, and now you need to defend yourself from revenge.'

My opportunistic side suggested, 'What if we use this as a way of distributing more clones, a sales tactic? We could offer 10, 20, or 30% more clones for free to a customer or customers that eliminate our enemies.'

Nothing in me could think of a better plan.

My urgency asked, 'So, how can we set this up quickly?'

My strategist answered, 'There's too little time to negotiate with someone new. We need a current patron. Someone significantly more powerful and unsympathetic to the Ghatak family. Also, we need someone who is looking for a deal.'

My relationale suggested, 'Bola!'

My prudence chimed in, 'Bola might be too overt and cause an international incident.'

'Sato family might work,' offered my relationale.

'No, we would need to meet with and talk to all six family representatives,' returned my strategist.

'What about Toofan Ghilji?' asked my relationale.

'No, he won't talk to a female over the phone. Same with Ali Ali,' answered my strategist.

'Apirak Anuman, Melchor Catapang, Joyo Bakrie, or Wei Neo might do it.' My relationale went through my mental rolodex.

'Yes, they might,' agreed the strategist.

'I can't think of any long-term concerns,' supported my prudency.

After a few phone calls, one of my patrons agreed to my proposal, negotiating for 25% more free clones. The Ghatak family was eliminated, but some of their allies took issue with their murders. The patron I hired to do my dirty work was killed, but not before one hundred clones were sent to his compound for training. When leadership broke down, the clones escaped to the streets. This was fine with me. While bloody hostilities were tragic, I learned that creating and cultivating strife could be an effective strategy for dispersing more clones. In other words, while some ruthless businessmen were losing their lives, many more innocent clones gained freedom. The balance of life was positive.

Taking this logic a step further, I thought, 'Maybe I could make the World a better place by having some especially loathsome patrons eliminated in exchange for clone promotions.'

'It's an opportunity to create and distribute more clones, *more life*,' emphasized my guilt.

'And it's an opportunity to make the Horsemen happy for once,' added my strategist.

I tried it a couple of times and the Horsemen were indeed very happy to learn that patrons were willing to fight and kill leaders from target ethnic groups in exchange for clones. Those eliminated were enemies of the United States which helped set my mind at ease.

Trade was another method I used to create and disperse clones. Customers were willing to give me land, houses, vehicles, visas, passports, and other things in exchange for clones. Many of these things I kept for myself, imagining that they might become useful for escape and retirement someday. However, the primary purpose of this bartering strategy was to get dispersion numbers up to maintain Horsemen support for development of the cloning pipeline.

With implementing these strategies, sales volumes were picking up, and the trajectories were good enough for me to step away from the sales side of things, hire a team for that, and go back to being a CEO.

During my last sales trip, I had a bittersweet reunion with an old friend.

"Virginia!" Dan exclaimed, waving, trying to get my attention.

Chapter 83: Better Left a Memory

I turned my face toward him and realized that there was no way I couldn't pretend like I wasn't Virginia and he wasn't Dan, one of my best college mates.

"Hi, Dan! Crazy running into you here." Suddenly aware of my escorts stopping beside me, I said, "I'll catch up with you. Go on." They took the hint and kept moving.

"It's great seeing you! Do you have a little time to catch up before your flight?" Dan asked.

"Yes," I replied, still a little stunned that I was seeing Dan after so many years.

"How about we grab a coffee?"

"Sure," I replied, accepting his invitation even though I already had my two cups earlier.

We walked over to Bunna and Dabo.

"How are things with you?" Dan started as we waited in line.

I hadn't been asked that in a very long time. "Okay," I said, not really thinking of any particular part of my life being okay.

"Can I get you something?" asked the barista.

"Black coffee, please," I ordered.

"Hazelnut latte, please," Dan requested. "Put it on one check."

"Thank you, Dan."

"I owe you for all those Ninja Stix," His words activated the reeling of a million great early college memories. I turned and walked toward the end of the counter where others were waiting for their orders to be made. I took a napkin from a dispenser and wiped my eyes, hoping that Dan wouldn't see.

Dan always paid careful attention to me though, and was checking in even now, "Are you okay, Virginia?"

"Yes, thank you." I wasn't okay. Wiping dead youthful hope and expectations from my eyes, I changed the subject, "How are things with you, Dan?"

"I'm doing very well," Dan started. "Getting back from presenting a talk at the annual American Society for Developmental Biology Conference. Looking forward to getting back home."

I was kind of surprised. "What was your talk on?"

"Dendritic cell heterogeneity in human and zebrafish organs. Differential expression analysis of dendrites sorted from organ samples allowed us to predict the presence of functionally unique dendrite subpopulations. With that information we constructed reporter cell lines for *in vivo* tracking of dendrites during development. We got some stunning fluorescent images of zebrafish organ sections enriched with specific dendrite subpopulations. The most exciting finding was highly conserved gene expression between the dendrites isolated from zebrafish organs and those isolated from human organs. I submitted a few grant proposals last week requesting funding to construct neurodegenerative zebrafish disease models," he declared passionately.

"That's incredible work, Dan," I congratulated. I was genuinely impressed. The Human Genome was only just made public by Francis Collins and team six years earlier in 2001, so using transcriptomics now in 2007 was extremely cutting edge.

Dan smiled. "Thank you. I don't think I would have been doing this level of scientific research if it wasn't for you pushing and leading me, Gina, and Bobby to write that literature review as undergraduates. It introduced us to scientific collaboration and gave us early understandings of the frontiers of developmental biology, the areas where we could really make an impact, and methods that could help us achieve those objectives; everything we needed to start writing solid grant proposals and conducting rigorous experiments."

"Okay, okay." I tried to brush off his compliments.

Dan locked eyes with me and spoke very sincerely, "Virginia, I'm serious. Thank you for putting me on a trajectory for success."

I smiled, happy for Dan, but a little jealous. He was living the life I had envisioned for myself years ago, and was doing very well.

"And look at you! Leading a big international company. I mean someone has to lead the giant pharmaceutical and biotechnology companies. You just don't expect to know those people."

He didn't really know me. Not the person I had become.

"Black coffee and hazelnut latte for Dan!" announced the barista.

Changing the subject back to him I said, "Thank you again for the coffee. You said you were anxious to get home?"

"Yes, to my lovely wife and teenage kids." He pulled out his phone and showed me some pictures of his family posing on a mountain side. He had two girls and one boy. The middle child, a girl, looked more like her mother.

"Beautiful family, Dan, and everyone looks happy. Do they all like hiking?" I inquired, imagining some teens not appreciating hiking too much.

"Yes, thankfully we got them hiking early. Everyone in the family enjoys it. These pictures were from last weekend. This weekend we have some church events related to international adoption. We volunteered to host some informational session speakers and taxi them around," Dan elaborated, smiling.

"That's very nice of you, Dan," I encouraged, sincerely.

"When did you get married?"

"A while back. Actually, you asked me about Jacquee. You saw us flirting once outside the lab. I told you she was my girlfriend."

The memory flashed in my mind, and having seen the recent picture, I recalled the young woman's face so many years ago. The same cheery smile. Apparently, she still wasn't sick of his doting, and I'm sure he enjoyed her appreciation.

"Wow! Who knew I was witnessing the beginnings of a match made in Heaven?" I said excitedly.

My memory of what followed shortly after seeing them caught up with me though; Jim abusing and enslaving me. These things sucked the enthusiasm right out of me, leaving nothing but depression.

Dan, picking up on the swing in my mood, consoled me unaware of the Hell I had been in and my bloody escape. "Um, Virginia, so sorry about what happened to Jim. The terrible scene came on the news. I tried to call but the phone line was always busy. I didn't want to just show up without invitation or at least your awareness. And you were reasonably depressed. So, I sent a card. Not sure if you ever got it?"

"I'm sorry. I didn't. I appreciate the thought though," I lied. Jim always got the mail, and after I killed him, I didn't bother retrieving it until a few days before I did the short sale. Mail was overpacked inside the box and spilling out all over the ground, some pieces blown clear across the road. Most of it was junk anyway but I did find Dan's card.

The letter was annoyingly Dan. Felt like he was hugging me through the card. I hated it because it made me wonder for weeks if I chose the wrong guy. Ultimately, I invoked the ghost of my wise realist, Felix, whose memory told me to stop worrying about the past and what I can't control.

Then, Dan asked a really annoying question to me. "Did you remarry?" As if that's all there was to life. Sure, it would have been nice, but it was never centric to my values and there were too many barriers after Jim.

"No, I never remarried," I replied, not wanting to discuss it further.

There was a long pause. I think he expected me to say more and wasn't really sure how to respond when I didn't explain my preference or reason for not remarrying.

He made a non-specific noise, and considerately changed the subject. "Did you find another church?"

"No...," I trailed off. I didn't really know how to be part of a congregation anymore after I poisoned Jim. Even though it had to be done, I couldn't confess my sins. Everything had to remain hidden after that.

"I can see how that would have been hard and how things probably got overwhelmingly busy when you started Autonoma. I want you to know that I still pray for you, and if you ever want to come to church with my family, if you are feeling lonely on Christmas or Easter, you are more than welcome to join us."

It felt like the conversation was ending. "Thank you for the offer. I'll keep it in mind, Dan. I have to run and catch my flight."

Getting the hint, Dan replied, "I'm really glad we ran into each other, and I hope we can talk more sometime. Here is my card with my contact information." Then, Dan gave me a small hug. Seeing me smile, he enveloped me into an even bigger one, the Dan-kind I remembered from years ago. "Great seeing you, Virginia!" he said as I started to walk away.

"Great seeing you, Dan." I replied.

"Oh, I nearly forgot. Uh..." He jogged over to me, but then looked unsure if he wanted to say what he planned to say.

"What?"

Dan scratched his head. "I don't know. Maybe we should talk about this another time. Not a great thing to end our conversation on. How about you just give me a call?"

"What is it, Dan?" I insisted.

He took a deep breath. "Gina was really upset when you stopped calling her."

My heart sank.

"She got married..." He did some quick math "...about seven years ago. It really hurt her that you weren't there."

My insides crumbled with those words. It was too much to bear. I needed to escape.

"I'm sorry Dan, I really have to run and catch my flight," I eked out just barely holding back my tears.

Trying to stifle the sadness, I turned to anger.

'What *the* Hell! The Horsemen kept us from our loved ones, and now our best friend believes that we abandoned her!' yelled my hurt.

'We need to contact them!' bellowed my responsiveness.

'No! Not contacting Gina is what is protecting her. We can't contact anyone we care about. We have to make the Horsemen believe that no one matters to us. Then, they won't try and use any of them for leverage,' reasoned my security.

'That's not good enough. We have suffered! Our friends have suffered! We cannot live this way! We cannot allow this anymore!' insisted my hostility.

'The Horsemen have to die!' demanded my pain.

'That's not something we can just will,' responded my strategist. 'We need time to think on this.'

I scanned around and found my guards pretending to be occupied in a T-shirt shop. They found me as soon as I started walking toward my gate. They didn't say or ask me anything, which was how I liked the relationship. Still, I was anxious about them (my new world) coming so close to Dan (my old world). I wondered if they might tell the Horsemen about this encounter and if they took any pictures of Dan. I couldn't think of any way to find out. If I asked, they might report something they wouldn't have otherwise mentioned to the Horsemen. I couldn't tell them not to mention the encounter because then they would definitely tell the Horsemen.

I had a brief memory of throwing Vijay out of my plane. That threat to Dan and his family was at least neutralized, but was there no way I could end the threat of the Horsemen? My mind went in a million directions. In a myriad of parallel universes, I imagined that if Dan and I were married, I never went to work at SMNL, never developed the REVs, never was summoned by the Horsemen, and never founded Autonoma Inc.

Why did I always blow Dan off? Just because he wasn't charming or exciting or exceptional? And I then remembered what it was, his lack of exceptionality. Even though he seems impressive now, he just wasn't at the time. Then, I wondered what if I had been forward thinking and had seen him for his potential instead of what he was? Still, I decided that I probably wouldn't have been happy being his wife. I might have ended up his stay-at-home wife, hating that he was the professor and not me. Then again, maybe we would have been teaching at the same school. To quell another storm of sadness, I protected myself by saying that it didn't matter because that's not the reality in this fiery universe.

I got in the back of the Land Rover Range Rover HSE and was chauffeured back to my house in Atlanta.

Chapter 84: The Surrogacy Program

In 1984, well before Autonoma Inc. was established, the first gestational surrogacy was performed. The child of the intended parents was named Ishmael after the first recorded surrogate child, the son of Abraham and Hagar. Unlike *traditional* surrogacy, which made it possible for infertile women to have children, *gestational* surrogacy made it possible for fertile women to become biological mothers without experiencing pregnancy. Autonoma Inc. made it possible for all women (fertile and infertile) to become biological mothers without experiencing pregnancy through a combination of cloning and gestational surrogacy.

I initiated the surrogacy program as soon as we started the cloning program back in 1996. The number of customers who could or would carry their own clones to term was a small fraction of the total. Again, most customers were warlords and politicians. Beyond filling the need for mothers to carry developing clones to term, I had a vision to do more with the program. After experiencing an abusive relationship with Jim and hearing about other women's stories of abuse with their male partner, I wanted to help women have more independence from men when having children. I'll use the umbrella term, "reproductive freedom". For women who didn't want to carry babies, we could offer surrogacy as an option. For women who wanted to earn extra money by carrying fetuses to term, they could be surrogates. I was able to keep this program off of the Horsemen's radar simply by not bringing it up in meetings. If they ever asked me about it, I would justify the expansion of the program as a requirement for ensuring a large enough pool of surrogates for the cloning program.

The surrogacy program was very popular with Autonoma Inc. employees. They liked the dual income and many signed up to be surrogates multiple times. Several employees also stopped working in the positions they were hired for, after they became mothers, and instead did surrogacy work for Autonoma Inc. while raising their children.

Autonoma Inc. initially favored recruiting employees for the surrogacy program because they already had completed background checks, the program managers could more easily coordinate with them, and they were already set up for a direct deposit. However, we had to look externally for more candidates with the increase in requests for services. It wasn't long before we needed to employ thousands and even tens of thousands of surrogate mothers to meet the demand, and contracting so many was challenging. Questionnaires and background checks often revealed drug abuse, poor health habits, unstable living conditions, victims of chronic domestic abuse, and other factors that could cause harm or death to a fetus. Unfortunately, many women were disqualified from being part of the surrogacy program.

Increasing payment helped expand the pool of candidate surrogate mothers, but we could only go so high before the cost became unaffordable for many patrons paying for the services. To mitigate this issue, we ended up creating different tiers of guaranteed and prioritized services. Premium packages meant patrons had less or no time waiting for surrogacy services.

Autonoma Inc.'s diagnostic tests enabled us to avoid implanting surrogates with high-risk gene mutations. Our algorithms could tell us the probability that a fetus would make it to term and the probabilities of the genetic issues they would have in their lifetimes if they survived. All of our genetic-phenotypic data came from naturally born human populations. Therefore, the models could not make accurate predictions for clones. Clones had diseases that were rare in naturally born human populations. Our lack of knowledge of these rare diseases made it challenging for us to avoid miscarriages, stillbirths, births of deformed children, and birthing complications caused by oversized and/or oddly shaped clone fetuses. There were increased cases of Cesarean sections, prolonged or obstructed labor, shoulder dystocia, vaginal tears, perineal lacerations, episiotomies, and postpartum hemorrhages. A few women even died in the two years we were figuring out why our clones were not developing like naturally born humans.

A few things protected Autonoma Inc. from getting in major legal trouble for having surrogate mothers carry clones without their knowledge. I had a great team of attorneys that produced an ironclad waver protecting the company from litigation in all cases of harm or death of surrogate mothers or intended children. We also had a policy for our surrogate mothers not to see sonograms or the newly born children "to avoid psychologically damaging bonding and separation". So, the surrogates would never see the deformed babies. There was even a tape of a recorded crying baby that was played when the intended fetus did not cry for whatever reason, and doctors and nurses would clap and cheer to assure the surrogate mothers of their success. Doctors and nurses working for Autonoma were also required to sign ironclad non-disclosure agreements to work for the company and remain silent about everything they witnessed.

One of the major outcomes of the surrogacy program was seeing an enormous need for artificial wombs. It was very upsetting to me when I came to grips with the truth - we were using deceptive and unethical practices on women to progress the cloning program. Neither that, nor expanding women's reproductive freedoms, were robust reasons for dehumanization. The women in the surrogacy program were unwitting experimental subjects.

Besides disliking what we were doing to the women, there were a number of other reasons why we needed artificial wombs. I needed to protect the company from lawsuits, lower our costs, alleviate the bottleneck of surrogate mother recruitment, and realize the unparalleled control that an artificial womb could offer throughout the fetal development process. Of course, we couldn't immediately transition away from utilizing surrogate mothers for producing clones. Surrogacy was the only option before the artificial wombs were developed.

To take steps toward Autonoma Inc. producing artificial wombs, I baptized a dedicated joint-department or section of multidisciplinary scientists. I did this just a few months after we started observing the birth complications with clones. I called it the Joint Artificial Womb Section, or JAWS, thinking about the phrase "snatched from the jaws of death". This brought to mind the babies and women whose lives we would save with the technology. A major investment toward this end was creating a series of prototype fetal bioreactors. They were bulky tanks that could be sterilized in place and had numerous inlets, outlets, and probes. They weren't very impressive. They seemed like something between a fish tank and beer brewing equipment. However, the bioreactors would help us understand what growth factors were needed to bring a fetus to term and ultimately decouple the surrogacy and cloning programs.

Parallel to these efforts, I commissioned a Department for Clone Development, or DCD, to figure out why our clones were not developing like naturally born humans. I hoped that JAWS would develop the artificial womb quickly so that the surrogate mothers would be protected from the additional risk associated with birthing clones. The artificial womb would have also removed the variability in their tests associated with the surrogate mother. For better or worse, the DCD proved to be quicker than JAWS, solving the issues with the malformities. Though the additional perils with birthing a clone were eliminated, we still needed the artificial wombs. The key reason being that we would never be able to recruit enough surrogates as we scaled the cloning pipeline toward natural birth levels.

While the vast majority of customers used our surrogacy program, some customers did want to carry their own clones or had someone they wanted to be the surrogate mother.

Sarai Vader was a very memorable surrogate. On September 5, 2009, she became the first virgin to give birth in a non-miraculous way. Her baby girl was given the name, Emmanuella Diedonne, which means God with us and God-given, which I think was meant to be mockery.

Amma Vader was the biological mother. She somehow acquired my phone number and called me in early 2009 and asked if Autonoma could clone her, and if Sarai (her companion) could be the surrogate mother. I said of course, pending answers on questionnaires, background checks, medical checks, and diagnostic testing. Then, she asked if I could ensure that no men were involved in any part of the process. I thought this was odd, but said that we could accommodate that request - that her doctors, nurses, and lab technicians could all be female. It wasn't that hard. Autonoma Inc. employees were mostly women anyway.

Then, Amma asked if Sarai's hymen could be kept intact during the implantation procedure. This question surprised me, but I didn't feel super comfortable having a discussion about why this requirement was important. So, I told her that I would need to confer with one of my medical doctors to be sure.

Later that day, I called her back to confirm that a catheter would be used to insert the blastocyst, and we could avoid damaging her hymen.

Finally, she asked if we could provide official documentation with our letterhead signed by me stating that she "was the sole biological parent, Sarai was the gestational surrogate mother, and that no man participated in the baby's conception, development, medical monitoring, or delivery." In early 2009, we were very accommodating because of the financial crisis and because we didn't have many patrons at the time. I agreed to all of her unique requests.

Amma and Sarai came to one of our facilities after they were approved for their respective roles. Samples were taken from Amma. Sarai returned for preparation of the uterine lining, implantation, checkups, and delivery. Autonoma Inc. employees followed through with all I had agreed to, and Amma and Sarai were delighted with the birth of their daughter.

Amma sent me a link to a video posted on social media roughly a month after the baby's birth. In it she declared that men were obsolete. She said that Sarai was a virgin and held up multiple documents from official medical examinations of Sarai's hymen before and during her pregnancy. She said Sarai was a virgin, and yet bore her daughter, Emmanualla Diedonne. Amma said that while there is no medical proof of the virgin birth of Jesus, she had abundant medical documentation from multiple sources proving that their daughter was indeed *born of a virgin*. Amma said that no man contributed in any way to her daughter's birth. Sperm was not an ingredient of her daughter. Amma showed and read the Autonoma Inc. documentation that I had signed. She said Autonoma Inc.'s medical professionals took her skin and egg cells and made an embryo that Sarai was impregnated with. Amma said that the baby's development in Sarai's womb was monitored by female medical professionals and that female medical professionals delivered their baby on September 5, 2009. It was actually a blastocyst that Sarai was impregnated with, but she was correct about everything else. I was floored by this video and the message that men were no longer needed for continuation of our species.

I wondered if viewers would believe what Amma was saying in the video. The claim that men were obsolete was hard to believe, but even just the success of human cloning might be unbelievable to many. Several prior public videos with claims of human cloning were found to be unsubstantiated or fabricated over the last decade. The Horsemen were probably behind many of them to make it difficult for average citizens to know the difference between fact and fiction. That way they could control the narrative. If you remember, our plan was to use a virus to sterilize everyone and control procreation through monopolized human cloning. Their messaging wouldn't be that though. Their messaging would be "A plague has come upon us that threatens the continuation of our species, but over the years we've been perfecting a new way to carry on..." Human salvation would come through cloning and they would be saviors.

Later that night, I was considering the potential impact of Amma's act on Christendom. Without a simple English word for the concept, I turned to my Greek college elective training. I created the word "thaumadynato", which translates to "making the miraculous achievable or possible".

My question was- what would Amma's thaumadynato act lead people to do? Would more people turn away from the Church and the Trinity, and more turn to science as their god? Would virgin births become a fad, a mockery, or a new way to emulate Mary and Jesus? Would reading the Christmas story continue to be so extraordinary without the uniqueness of the virgin birth? Would confessing the third article of the Apostles Creed (i.e. *qui conceptus est de Spiritu Sancto, natus ex Maria Virgine*) be less of a confession of faith?

During my drowsy contemplations, I decided that "thaumadynato" was a great slogan for Autonoma Inc. With this last fleeting thought, my mind finally let me fall asleep.

The next morning, I opened a browser on my phone to watch the video again. The video had been taken down. I searched around the internet to see if it was moved or posted anywhere else, and came up empty handed. I should have known that such content would not be allowed to exist. The message wasn't just about improving women's reproductive freedoms. They had challenged man's relevance in the continuation of the human species. I never heard from Amma, Sarai, or Emmanualla Diedonne again. They were a threat and probably eliminated. With Amma specifically mentioning "Autonoma Inc.'s technology" I wondered if the company, members of the company, or I would now be a target for elimination too.

Chapter 85: The Chopping Block

While many scientists were ready to make use of cloning for a variety of applications, much of the public in leading countries were strongly opposed to it. Science fiction books since the 1960s and more recent blockbuster movies like Jurassic Park, Multiplicity, Gattaca, and The Sixth Day generally had themes warning against cloning. These seemed to have a major impact on U.S. and most democratic nations' laws and funding for at least the first decade or two that cloning was actually possible.

When many of the leading science nations decided not to throw their hat in the ring, others did, and started with animals. Amur Tigers were saved from extinction in 2003 when clones of the species were perfected after trialing a variety of alternative egg donors (pig, cow, and domestic cat) and surrogate mothers (tigers and lions). While one lion developed a hernia and did not survive, the cloning strategy was considered a major success. Dae-Seong Choi, the South Korean scientist leading these efforts went on to amass his fortune cloning the loyalist dogs, the meatiest cows, the speediest horses, the most gigantic camels, and more.

Others followed Dae-Seong's lead, harvesting cells from medically dead family pets and applying SCNT to clone them. Autonoma Inc.'s competitor intelligence team estimated about 1600 dogs were cloned between 2005 and 2009. The experience with cloned pets helped patrons understand that cloning didn't mean perfect personality copies or even physical copies of their beloved companions. Competitors started using sales messaging similar to ours, like Fido2.0. The positioning was very different from our Me2.0. Fido2.0 solidified the understanding that clones would not be the same as the original pet. This was actually helpful to the Autonoma Inc. sales team. While more and more patrons were inquiring about cloning deceased human family members, they understood that a genetic clone did not mean a physical or emotional copy of their loved ones. Many competitors tried to meet the demand, but none were successful.

In early 2008, the U.S. Food and Drug Administration approved the sale of cloned animals and their offspring for food. This seemed like a major sign that concerns were shifting away from cloning in the U.S. However, the administration quickly reverted and banned the sale because of public safety concerns related to the introduction of unnatural genetic elements and viruses, as well as allergy inducing proteins and prions. Restrictions have only been lifted in recent years for use of cloning in food production.

How deeply the Horsemen were involved in the media and other influences to stop other companies from developing cloning technologies was unclear, but Autonoma Inc. had no competition for human cloning until 2009. Autonoma Inc.'s monopoly was foiled along with the potential to control procreation when the Obama administration issued an executive order to ease restrictions on federal funding for embryonic stem cell research that were in place during the entire Bush administration from 2001 – 2009. This relaxation resulted in a surge of grant applications, approvals, innovations, and competition.

By 2010, other entities with public affiliations were privately making human clones with SCNT at a scale similar to Autonoma Inc. Less than 47% of clones on the black market were produced by Autonoma Inc. This made the Horsemen very unhappy. With many other companies now capable of making human clones, the Horsemen would not be able to restrict procreation by sterilizing everyone and limiting access to cloning services. The other plan to kill inaccessible leaders by triggering the dormant viruses inside of their Trojan horse clones was also a failed project. Besides having other companies to purchase their clones from, the clones we sold to these leaders were often considered trifles and given away rather than cared for and groomed to take over empires.

The Horsemen called a meeting. It seemed likely that I would be losing their support of the human cloning program.

"The cloning program is a good investment for the future of Autonoma," I argued.

"What makes a good investment is the return you get for the investment. The ROI is too low," contended the white-masked Horseman.

"Human cloning is an extremely complicated technology. Profitability takes time."

The pale green Horseman cut me off, "We don't care about profit. We care about the death toll, and your clones aren't killing anyone."

"You are right. The Trojan horse clones have not been used to eliminate any leaders of target ethnic groups. The plan was always to trigger the Trojan horses to ensure death of leadership at the same time as a broader attack on the target ethnic groups. Plus, some patrons are killing others in exchange for clones."

I thought this objection handling started very well, then I put my foot in my mouth.

"Most clones are sterile, and therefore inhibit population growth by reducing the opportunities of non-sterile humans to procreate. Limiting reproduction is better for a myriad of reasons compared to killing."

"We will decide what is better," the green-masked Horseman barked, reminding me who was in charge. "How hard would it be to end the dormancy of the lethal viruses, kill all the clones, and everyone in their proximity?"

"Well, the vast majority of clones are not Trojan horses. So, that would be impossible."

"We were under the impression that all of the clones were Trojan horse clones. Isn't that what we approved?" chimed in the black-masked Horseman.

Realizing my error, I tried to reason my way back to safety.

"Tracking all clones would have been an impossible logistical nightmare. We only track the Trojan horse clones, so that we can trigger their dormant viruses when the time comes."

The black-masked Horseman raised his voice, sounding annoyed.

"No! You don't need to track any clones if they are all Trojan horse clones. You can just trigger them all and kill everyone in the vicinity."

"That would pose a serious risk," I warned. "The dormant virus in the Trojan horse clones is not ethno-specific. They just can't spread very far because the progression of infection is so aggressive that they kill the host and others in proximity before there is a chance to spread. That strategy works with leaders that shut themselves up in ivory towers during times of turmoil. However, that would not be the case with our other clones which are often released in crowded populous cities. Since international travel is so prevalent in populous cities, the virus would have a chance to spread much farther by way of airports to destinations far from the target ethnic groups, killing unintended populations."

"That is fine," the pale green Horseman said flatly.

"You don't understand. It's very difficult to predict." I stammered, "There's no way of ensuring that triggering numerous Trojan horse clones would achieve your ethnic population reduction goals."

"Well, it sounds like you might overshoot the targets we gave you, but that wouldn't be so bad, right? You'd get a bigger bonus," minimized the white-masked Horseman.

My heart was beating wildly. I did not want to release this highly lethal virus into any general population.

'Think, think. What is important to the Horsemen?' urged my desperation.

Then it came to me, and I blurted, "That strategy could backfire because the busiest airports in the World are U.S. airports. Even if Trojan horse clones were triggered in international cities, populous U.S. cities would be disproportionately impacted."

The red-masked Horseman replied, "Sounds like you need to get working on ethno-specific viruses then."

With that, my heart fell. A total backfire, and I had no choice but to agree.

"Yes," I replied, and asked sheepishly, "Do the Horsemen agree that producing sterile clones to limit reproduction is still a valuable endeavor?"

"For now," answered the red-masked Horseman.

While limiting reproduction did contribute to the Horsemen's goals, the impact we had in this area was small. Autonoma Inc. was currently only able to produce and distribute hundreds of sterile clones per week at best because of limitations with our technology. I was always trying to increase the number of lives we were creating, even if there weren't patrons to buy them in a given month. Extra clones were released. I wanted them to be free and hoped that they would survive and thrive, but sadly, many died in the streets.

Autonoma Inc.'s scientists had no idea that the children we were creating were sterile, that many of them were released into the streets to fend for themselves, or that some of them contained deadly dormant viruses. It wasn't their fault. Autonoma Inc.'s scientists thought they were just helping people that were unable to have genetically-related children, people who wanted to adopt healthy babies, people who had trouble adopting from specific countries, wealthy families who would love and care for them, and other positive or neutral reasons.

The distribution increased some when costs for clones came down because of the increased competition. Still, dealings remained private because of the lack of public acceptance. This continued to limit demand. There were also limitations with releasing clones into the streets. It had to be done in a careful and controlled manner to avoid suspicion from local authorities.

Since Autonoma Inc. no longer had the monopoly on human cloning, there was no longer a good case to make a virus to sterilize everyone. In my mind, sterilizing everyone was a much better scenario than making genocidal viruses. Certainly, it was better on my conscience. That ship had sailed, though. If we sterilized everyone, a myriad of companies would step up to provide SCNT services. As it was, people were not sterile and human cloning was generally perceived as immoral. The market for human cloning was therefore limited, which meant that there was little opportunity to replace fertile naturally born children with infertile clones. The project and all potential variations contributing to population control was a failure. The Horsemen became very short with me when I brought up cloning. That didn't stop me from speaking with them about it though.

Cloning had become more to me than just a way to tilt the scales of my contributions of life and death when God accounted for my sins. Over the years, Autonoma Inc. had become a profitable success, especially with regards to diagnostics. Leading my company to success made me happy. It was the only thing in my life that made me happy. Well, that and Bola, my romantic intrigue. I wanted Autonoma Inc. to continue to be successful and grow. I believed that cloning would be very popular one day and I wanted Autonoma Inc. to lead the market. So, I kept abreast of competitive activities, threats, and opportunities, and something significant came on the radar in 2010. Researchers in Japan successfully reprogrammed *fully mature, fully differentiated adult skin cells* back to a pluripotent state. That is, they were *like embryonic stem cells.* Not only that, these researchers figured out how to then differentiate those pluripotent cells into gametes, sperm and eggs. So, they figured out how to turn skin cells into sperm and egg cells! Then, they showed that they could combine these sperm and eggs to form zygotes. This technology was truly revolutionary, offering many advantages over SCNT for human cloning. These included not having to harvest female eggs, not having to hollow them, not having to inject a new nucleus into them, and the list goes on.

When I presented the new cloning technology to the Horsemen in a subsequent meeting, they inquired how this would reduce target ethnic populations to 50% of their current levels? I didn't have a good answer for them. The meeting abruptly ended with the comment, "We do not have time for discussions unrelated to ethno-viruses. Have your proposal ready by June. Your current funding is terminated."

Even though the Horsemen no longer wanted to support Autonoma Inc.'s cloning services and products, I still cared about this part of the business because it contributed to the success of the company. Autonoma Inc. didn't rely on the Horsemen for funding, it just made innovation faster. We had strong revenue from diagnostics and other departments.

Support from the Horsemen was more important for another reason. The meetings we would have and being on the same page about our goals and milestones gave the Horsemen reasons to keep me above ground. They still hadn't outright threatened me, but again, they didn't really have to. Their values were very clear. My life was only as valuable as how many lives I could extinguish. As much as I wanted to work on updating our cloning pipeline, I only had time then to prepare a new proposal for ethno-viruses. The original due date for my infertility virus project, June 2010, was just a month and a half away. I didn't want to create ethno-viruses or even make proposals related to ethno-virus development. Still, I was motivated by fear of my own death and the desire to continue leading Autonoma Inc.

I realized that to get Autonoma researchers to work on such a project, I needed a viral system that could be used as a therapeutic tool. Any virus that was easily spread would be a red flag for a scientist, and I couldn't think of any viral vectors that checked all the boxes of low immunogenicity, scalability, and deliverability. So, I also considered non-viral delivery methods for the REVs.

The main solution I considered was nanoparticles with lipid and/or protein outer shells. These could be used in therapeutic applications. It was unclear whether or not I could weaponize them though because they were difficult to secretly disperse. I thought about sending it through junk mail, 58% of which is opened. Even if this percentage was 5.8%, that would be more than enough to initiate the spread. However, biosecurity might be tough to get through in most developed countries. Dispersal might be limited in less developed countries.

Then, I thought of using wildfires and smoke pollution to deliver the nanoparticles. Smoke disperses well and goes into the lungs of people every year without very many people thinking much of it besides some researchers at the U.S. Environmental Protection Agency. I looked into this but couldn't figure out how to stabilize the nanoparticles or their REV payloads in the heat and dryness of the smoke. I also thought of rain clouds and delivery through rain, but people are generally not outside when it's raining. Rain also isn't breathed in. There are viruses that infect skin, but REVs would not be very effective in killing individuals by skin infection.

I was running out of time, started to panic, and decided to escape.

'If they can't find us, they can't kill or threaten us, and if they can't threaten us, there's no point in killing our loved ones,' reasoned my strategist.

Chapter 86: Escape

I remember looking over the porch of Bola's coastal mansion in Cape Town, South Africa. The warm sun was perfectly balanced with a cool breeze coming off of the crystal blue ocean. A picturesque scene only tarnished by gunmen scattered about the private beach.

Bola embraced me from behind. "You're safe," he assured me. For a fleeting moment, I actually felt safe in his arms. Far out on the horizon a black helicopter was headed right for us. We could see attached rockets and other weaponry as it came closer.

Gunmen pointed their weapons toward the helicopter ready to fire in range.

Earlier that week, Bola listened to my vague description of an impossible situation with no good outcomes. Autonoma Inc.'s board of directors, made of the richest, most powerful men in the world, were forcing me to lead the company to do things I found morally and ethically wrong. They would kill me and my loved ones if I refused. I told him that I wanted to escape, and that I could escape, but they would come after me to either recover or kill me. He said that he could protect me. I told him that protecting me would be a huge financial risk and place him in mortal danger.

I was overcome with affection for Bola when he replied, "You're worth it. I'll risk it all for you." I rendezvoused with him in Nigeria and he brought me to Cape Town. There, he owned a mile-wide fortress. The three-sided wall that lined the perimeter and jettied into the ocean seemed formidable when we entered. Now, these ramparts seemed entirely inadequate for what was coming.

We saw the ominous helicopter loaded with missiles and guns headed straight for us. Bola said, "Don't worry, it will be stopped."

Suddenly rockets tore out of the ocean water, exploding the back of the craft, and dropping the front a couple of hundred yards from the shore. Two boat teams finished off the survivors with the exception of one. He wasn't someone I recognized from my guard.

He was dragged from the beach into the kitchen and tied to a chair. Blood streamed from a gash on his head mingling with brown hair. Little could be read from his stony face. His demeanor and build suggested ex-military. Various questions were asked. The most important question to me was why he was there. Was his mission to retrieve or kill me? He didn't say anything in spite of a severe beating. He was dragged back out to shallow water, shot, and then thrown on the burn pile with the other bodies. The bones were later buried after the dogs had their fill.

Weeks passed and no one else came. I started thinking that I might actually be free. I wondered how that could be. The lack of urgency to retrieve me at least suggested that I wasn't needed or wanted anymore. Perhaps the Horsemen found someone else to run Autonoma Inc. Someone smarter. They didn't want to waste any more resources on my failings. Even with unlimited resources and a huge head start, competitors were gaining ground and leapfrogging us with brilliant solutions.

If they did find someone else to run Autonoma Inc., would that really mean I was off the hook though? Could they really just let me live with everything that I knew about them and their plans? This seemed unlikely to me. So why not fire a rocket at the house if I'm just a liability at this point? Maybe that would be too flashy. The Horsemen would probably prefer to avoid Cape Town publicity. They could just wait for me to leave the compound. Silence me with a sniper shot.

Bola asked me a couple of days later at dinner if the Horsemen's compulsion had anything to do with the clones. Up to that point he hadn't asked me any follow-up questions. It was kind of him to trust me without knowing the full picture, but he deserved a better explanation.

I sat there wondering what I could tell him. It didn't seem possible that Bola could still love me if he knew what I was involved in. I also worried that he would try to go after the Horsemen if he knew they were trying to mass murder non-white ethnicities. I was sure he would fail. Defending us was one thing. Executing a successful offensive strike was another.

Just as I was about to concoct a story, Bola interjected, "Bullshit. That was way too long of a pause. You're not going to tell me the truth."

This response caught me by surprise, and I was worried that I might have offended him. I was relieved when he swiveled me around to face him and sympathetically observed, "Whatever this is has you really scared. I hope you know that you can stay here as long as you need." Bola's unconditional acceptance made me feel secure and powerful again.

It felt like the rug was pulled out from under me when he added, "I'm going to need to go take care of business back in Nigeria." I considered trying to convince him to stay, but knew I didn't have a leg to stand on since I was unwilling to tell him the full truth. He left the next day and was gone for two weeks.

Bola's absence gave me time to reflect, and I realized the importance of being honest with him. This was a formative time in our relationship, and without a strong foundation of trust, our home was doomed to crumble. I was ready to tell him everything about the clones and ethno-viruses. To soften the blow, I thought that it might be best if I first properly thanked him for saving me.

I roused his romantic appetites with soft kisses. I let him nibble, bite, and devour all of me. I told him that I hungered for him and asked him to fill me to the brim. We consumed each other in courses, and between each passionate dish, we played, joked, and laughed. When we were both full and happy, I fell asleep snuggled in his arms. Virginia, the bird, was no longer locked in a cage. I was held safely in the branches of my tree.

When I woke the next morning, ready to tell Bola the whole truth, he was dead beside me. My screams brought no one to help. Running out from the room, I found bodies in the hallways, kitchen, and scattered around the property. Everyone in the compound but me was dead.

The eerie quiet was suddenly broken by a buzzing that filled the air around me. I saw something that looked like a large black hornet hovering in front of me. "Open the gate," a voice demanded. It took me a moment to realize it was coming from the hornet. I turned to run, but another was there. "We are here to collect you, dead or alive. It's up to you."

Chapter 87: Haplogroups

A helicopter transported me to Sandton, Johannesburg, and I was taken to a boardroom on the top floor of one of the buildings.

My eyes smoldered seeing the Horsemen there at the table. I sprang forward, grabbed a microphone and with vindictive passion I hurled it like a tomahawk toward them.

Immediately I was tackled from behind, which prevented me from seeing how true my aim was to the mark, but I heard the Horsemen stir.

"For God-sake. Sit her in a chair and restrain her," demanded the white-masked Horseman.

"How did you kill everyone in the compound?" I spat.

"What, no small talk?" mocked the pale green-masked Horseman.

"Go to Hell!"

"Hornet drones with botulinum toxin A," declared the white-masked Horseman, ignoring my curse.

The red-masked Horseman elaborated, "For 95% of humans on the planet, the lethal dose of botulinum toxin A is two hundred nanograms. Obese individuals need more. One hundred times this amount, 20 micrograms of toxin, plus various stabilizers are loaded into each hornet drone. Normally, a human can survive for days after an injection with the lethal dose of botulinum toxin A. However, the hornet drones inject ten times the lethal dose. So, expiration only takes as long as it takes for blood to circulate, less than a minute. The concentration is just too high for the immune system and kidneys to fight."

I gritted my teeth. "Well, you sure know your toxicology."

"We have AI assistants in our masks that help us," explained the red-masked Horsemen. "Says here that botulinum toxin A is a neurotoxin that cleaves SNAp REceptors or "SNARE" proteins. These proteins enable the release of acetylcholine, the principal neurotransmitter at the neuromuscular junction. Blocking the release of the neurotransmitter, which causes muscle paralysis. So, various muscles are paralyzed rapidly, lungs stop working, and the person suffocates."

"My AI is telling me that you, being a virologist, might appreciate that the toxin genes are actually contained in a phage, or bacterial virus, that's integrated in the bacteria's genome. Does that interest you?" finished the pale green-masked Horsemen cheekily.

"What I would appreciate is if you would go kill yourselves."

"Is this belligerence because we killed your Bola?" The pale green-masked Horseman inquired.

I didn't respond.

"Did you know he was cheating on you?" Asked the black-masked Horseman.

"No, he wasn't," I contended. While we hadn't stipulated monogamy, there was an unspoken agreement, and mutual love and respect.

"No? Are you sure?" challenged the pale green-masked Horseman.

Before I had another chance to respond, the screens at the front of the room immediately turned on.

"Here is some video footage of them at the beach," annotated the black-masked Horseman.

"Here they are eating together at his home in Nigeria," he continued as he changed the video clip.

"And here they are having sex in his bed," he concluded.

My blood boiled as I watched the clips. "Taking care of business is what he called it when he left the Cape Town compound."

"Yes, he deceived you. Are you still mad at us for eliminating him?"

I didn't respond. I had no words, only fiery anger for the Horsemen, Bola, my situation... I was sick of it all.

"You don't need to thank us. If you want to live though, and we think you do, you are going to need to hurry up and make us *ethno-specific viruses*," insisted the black-masked Horseman, slowly emphasizing the last words.

I didn't respond. I wanted to strangle them. I wanted to be strong enough, fast enough, powerful enough to actually strangle them to death. I wanted them to run in fear but be unable to get away, and feel so much terror and pain as they died in my hands.

"*Virginia, do you want to live?*" inquired the black-masked Horseman.

I didn't respond. I regretted not preparing for this moment better. I just assumed they would never dare to meet with me in-person again lest I expose them to some of their own medicine, a Horsemen-specific virus.

"Virginia!"

"Yes!" I yelled back.

I was so angry, but I knew there was nothing I could do to them. They held all the cards. Biding my time was all I could do.

"Good. Then, we will expect your new proposal and timeline next week. Do not mistake our cordiality and long-suffering for slow-wittedness. We are running out of patience and you are running out of chances. Do you understand?"

"Yes."

With that, I was taken out of the boardroom and thrown into a hotel room. A note instructed me that this was where I would remain until I met with the Horsemen to present my new proposal and timeline. '

'Fiery Horsemen!' exclaimed my rage.

'Fiery men!' exclaimed my hostility, implicating Bola.

'We can't forget the patrons, Major Lance, my male professors, Jim... It's all the Y-chromosome-carrying prick-bearing lot,' generalized my hurt.

'They're always deceiving us, trying to control us, use us,' complained my hate.

'We've fought back though. Haven't we?' asked my power.

'Indeed!' agreed my pride.

'It's not enough! We need more justice!' demanded my vengeance.

Looking at the note demanding a new proposal, the idea came to me.

'I can make Y-chromosome haplogroup-specific viruses.'

'No, it's too general,' challenged my thankfulness. 'We're going to kill the Dans of the World.'

'We've been through this. There is no way to release lethal viruses and not kill some innocent people,' reminded my pensiveness.

'With Y-chromosome haplogroup-specific viruses we can at least avoid killing the more helpful, caring, nurturing, loving sex.'

'Yes. Yes!' agreed my strategist. 'Men are territorial animals, so the Y-chromosomes haplogroups are highly concentrated in geographic regions and within ethnicities. Y-chromosome haplogroup-specific viruses *are* ethno-specific viruses!'

'Maybe we could make some that would kill the Horsemen as well, just in case we get another chance to be in the same room with them again,' suggested my opportunist.

A week later, when I presented my proposal to the Horsemen over a teleconference, I didn't explicitly tell them that I was targeting the Y-chromosome. I just indicated that I was targeting regional and ethnic genetic signatures. What they wanted to hear was that the targets represented hundreds of millions of people, which they did. The Horsemen approved my ten-year plan.

Scientists at Autonoma Inc. thought they were developing a therapy for Klinefelter's Syndrome, also known as XXY Syndrome. I told them the viruses would be used to shred the Y-chromosome *in utero* before there was time for the fetus to develop testis. While the technology could work for that application, it would be developed for its ability to eliminate up to 50% of a target population. A second target could be developed later to kill females I surmised, but I wasn't in any hurry to work on that.

Chapter 88: Sweetvirus

Even though I had a target population (men), I still faced four major challenges to killing them.

1.   How do I prevent the human immune system from stopping the virus from replicating and spreading *in vivo?*

2.   How do I make enough virus to spread across the World?

3.   How do I spread the virus across the World?

4.   How do I prevent degeneration of REVs so that they will remain specific to a target population and not shred everyone's DNA?

The way I stated these challenges to my researchers at Autonoma Inc. was:

1.   How do we avoid patient immunogenicity (immune system response)?

2.   How do we make scaled production cost effective?

3.   How can we make delivery easy?

4.   How do we eliminate off-target cutting?

The challenges were giant, but over the years my Autonoma Inc. teams tested different ideas and came up with a truly brilliant idea for a virus that overcame three out of four of the issues.

My researchers engineered a plant virus that could infect human cells. The team called their great achievement the Sweetvirus because they performed many tests on fruits initially. Subsequent tests showed that the Sweetvirus also infected vegetables, weeds, and insects, but the original name stuck. There was no selective evolutionary advantage for humans to develop immunity against plant viruses, so there was no immunogenic response to the Sweetvirus. That solved the first challenge. The second challenge was solved by the fact that it could be propagated in low-cost plant cells.

The solution for the third challenge came as a surprise when one of my researchers ran into my office and declared, "Eureka!"

I waved off the guards who were converging on her.

"Hi Lily! You have some great news to share?"

"Yes, Dr. Goreman. Sorry for barging in."

I liked Lily's spunkiness, so I forgave her with a smile.

"Please." I directed her to sit in the chair in front of my desk.

"Thank you. I didn't want this news to get delayed."

I was sure what she meant was that she didn't want anyone else getting credit for her finding. 'Clever and diplomatic', complimented my discernment.

"That sounds promising!" I encouraged.

"I'm not sure if you know, but I'm leading the Sweetvirus life cycle characterization project."

"Yes, I did, and how is that going?"

"Well, I was isolating Sweetvirus from different samples of plants we infected and…" she paused for dramatic effect, "…found that Sweetvirus was in the pollen!" she exclaimed, beaming.

Not following, I asked, "Sorry, why is that so exciting?"

"Your third challenge was making delivery of a virus for gene therapy easy. We can use pollen inhalation as a delivery method!"

My eyes widened, initially thinking this could be a great idea. Then, some objections came to mind.

"Pollen can cause immunogenicity."

"Of course you're right, Dr. Goreman, but different people have different allergies. Many kinds of pollen have low immunogenicity."

"Yes, and when people move to new regions, it can take time for their immune system to develop a response to certain pollen…" I was thinking about people from different target countries being exposed to pollen from foreign plants.

"We might also be able to find ways to modify plants so that they produce pollen with reduced immunogenicity," Lily offered.

"Yes," I agreed, still thinking through the implications.

"I guess what I'm trying to say is that we don't need to introduce the Sweetvirus intravenously, orally, or topically. Our therapies can be introduced by inhalation, and we don't even need to aerosolize the Sweetvirus."

"This is a very good idea, Lily. Before we get ahead of ourselves, we're going to need to test whether the virus is stable in pollen and if it can spread from the pollen through host lung tissue. Keep up the good work and tell me if you have any other discoveries like this."

The key to keeping my scientists innocent from wrongdoing was keeping their efforts siloed. The lie that they were developing gene therapies was easy to maintain as long as they didn't have a view of the whole picture. I assigned other researchers besides Lily to work on testing pollen delivery.

Months later it was confirmed that pollen inhalation was a viable method for Sweetvirus delivery. So, I started buying rooftop space on skyscrapers in cities all over the World and had greenhouses installed. Knowing pollen could travel hundreds of kilometers from a tree, I mathematically modeled the spread from skyscrapers to determine what I needed for rapid delivery to hundreds of millions of people in days. After a few years, Autonoma Inc. owned rooftop greenhouses on skyscrapers in 366 cities. With that, the first three challenges were solved.

I was vainglorious going into the progress report presentation with the Horsemen, but left deflated when I couldn't answer their simple question, "When will you release the virus?" I didn't know the answer because we still had a major technical issue left to solve, off-targets.

Thankfully the Horsemen agreed that there was too much of a risk with not perfecting the specificity of REVs.

'How do we prevent REVs from cutting in places that they shouldn't?' I asked myself and the Autonoma Inc. researchers.

Some of my researchers didn't think it would be possible. "All enzymes are imperfect, Dr. Goreman!"

Nevertheless, I reallocated thirty scientists to tackle the issue. The team mined nature for higher-fidelity orthologs of REV enzymes. That is, they searched in the soil and animal stool samples taken from Brazil, Ecuador, South Africa, and Madagascar, the most biodiverse locations on the Earth. They found millions of enzymes similar to the one we were working with. This brute force screening helped us identify enzymes that were orders of magnitude more specific than the original REV when testing our model mouse genome and human genome. Even with this improvement, the enzymes still didn't have high enough fidelity and continued producing more off-target cuts in longitudinal experiments. That is, when REVs were given enough time, they produced off-target cuts.

Years flew by and the pressure kept mounting. Meetings with the Horsemen were nerve racking. I'd say things like," It took Edison 2774 attempts to make a working light bulb," and they'd reply, "Yes, but it only took him 14 months." The off-targets haunted my dreams. Snoring turned to clenching my teeth, and clenching turned to grinding. I sleepwalked, yelled out often, and woke up gasping in hot and cold sweats after having nightmares of wiping out the human race.

Chapter 89: Hidden in Plain Sight

The fidelity issues of the REVs seemed insurmountable, but not everything was going badly. I teleconferenced with the Horsemen to discuss a major cloning pipeline upgrade, recognizing an opportunity to make my balance of life giving to life taking more positive. Tensions had built up with each new progress report meeting though that I was wary of how the Horsemen would be for this meeting. Right at the beginning, I was hit with some antagonism.

"Why are we still talking about this? The sterilization virus project is over!" barked the white-masked Horseman.

Staying calm, I replied, "Yes, the cloning pipeline upgrade will speed the development of the ethno-specific viruses."

"How?" demanded the white-masked Horseman.

I offered some semi-genuine reasons.

"Clones have orders of magnitude fewer variations than regular human test subjects. The genome differences can be compared to identical twins."

"Skip to the end," ordered the pale green-masked Horseman.

"Without variation, it's easier to conduct experiments with ethno-viruses, test changes, engineer features, fix issues, and iteratively improve designs."

I paused to see if the Horsemen needed any clarification or had any other rude comments.

"Why?" inquired the red-masked Horseman with less vinegar.

"Simply put, if I test different viruses on different people, I won't know if the person got sick, recovered, or died because of the person or the virus. If I have the same test subject, at least subjects with the same genome, then I can remove that variable and compare the effectiveness of different viruses."

The pale green-masked Horseman grumbled, "The viruses just need to be highly lethal."

Ignoring him, I explained, "Another massive benefit to creating clones for viral testing is avoiding the logistical challenges of abducting test subjects. Capturing and

495

disappearing thousands of documented citizens or at least humans with family networks, work or government assistance connections, and/or other community associations is very difficult."

The Horsemen didn't argue. They gave me money for the upgrade I requested.

I didn't really want to use clones as test subjects, but I knew that I would need to test the viruses on people. A benefit to this proposal was that I could upgrade my Autonoma Inc.'s cloning pipeline and create far more clones than the ones I used in experiments.

As it was, Autonoma Inc. pipeline using SCNT was very manual, and much lower throughput than what I desired. Dexterous hands could hollow out about 100 egg cells and inject nuclei into these each working day. Manual extractions were very hard on the egg cells though and many of these newly formed diploid cells never grew. Automating the process to improve the success rate would have been an incredible engineering accomplishment with robots directing molecular tweezers. When the idea to automate first came up, the huge investment didn't make sense since we were struggling to fulfill surrogate mother services.

Now we had artificial wombs (AWs) though, which removed the surrogate bottleneck. I was also seeing more publications demonstrating that reprogramming skin cells back to sperm and egg cells was possible. There were numerous advantages to this new technology. In terms of automation though, liquid handling of egg and sperm was far simpler than trying to automate our current manual process. With Horsemen support and funding there was really nothing stopping Autonoma Inc. from upgrading.

The new cloning pipeline was completed in about a year. The long and short of it is that we turned skin cells into gametes, combined them to make zygotes, and used artificial wombs to carry the baby to term. Amazingly, everything was fully automated!

Anoushka, one of the team members, showed me around when it was completed.

"The pipeline begins with robots taking skin biopsies. The extracellular matrix is digested with enzymes to release dermal fibroblasts."

I watched the tissue being microcentrifuge tubes.

"Microfluidics then takes the fibroblasts and nutrients into long veins of microchip plates where they attach and proliferate. After a couple of iterations of enzyme release, passaging, attachment, and expansion, the fibroblasts achieved a high titer for reprogramming with Yamanaka factors (Oct4, Sox2, Klf4, and c-Myc)."

Yamanaka factors were familiar to me. I knew they were biomolecules that reprogrammed the mature cells back to stem cells. Rather than just calling them stem cells, the researchers who made the discovery called these reprogrammed cells induced pluripotent stem cells (iPSCs).

"The iPSCs are flow sorted and expanded. Artificial intelligence checks for pluripotency markers before transferring them for differentiation into gametes."

She pointed to the extremely high-resolution cameras that were able to take pictures of single cells.

"We then convert the iPSCs into egg cells. Robots monitored by AI apply chemical factors and conditions found in the ovarian follicles."

From my studies, I was familiar that the primordial follicle stage normally occurs over years between early development in the womb until puberty in women. Our team discovered the factors for accelerating this stage to just a couple of months. That was a huge breakthrough for developmental biology. An additional month and various stimuli were then required for other maturations that normally occur during follicular growth, Graafian follicle development, meiosis I, and ovulation.

"To differentiate iPSCs into sperm cells, these robots apply chemical factors and conditions found in the seminiferous tubules and epididymis of the testes."

Thankfully we didn't need to speed up spermatogenesis because it only takes weeks.

One of my Autonoma Inc. team members called it "G sperm". She said it was a double entendre: "G" for girl, since the sperm could be made from a woman's skin, and "G" for Gertrude Ederle. Gertrude was a female athlete who, in 1926, became the first woman to swim the English Channel. She finished with an incredibly fast time of fourteen and a half hours, beating five men that had swam the channel before her by two hours. Gertrude's time remained unbeaten for almost a quarter century.

At one point, the swimming enthusiast Autonoma Inc. team member suggested that if we ever needed an improved version of the "G Sperm", we could call it the "F sperm" for female and Florence Chadwick. Florence was the woman that broke Gertrude's record in 1950 by more than a half hour.

We did end up improving "G sperm" by editing out known genetic disease markers and adding various fitness improvement markers. Also, to the team member's delight, we did internally call them "F sperm". I didn't care. Time was ticking and I was slave driving. So, it was helpful when I could balance my spurring with low-effort low-cost positivity.

Annoyingly, my public relations and marketing teams were much more particular about the names that were being circulated. Human resources had us do a training on keeping the phrases and meanings of "G sperm" and "F sperm" terminology internal to avoid potential controversies. Cloning alone was a controversial topic. We did not want the public to connect the dots and realize that we found a second way to make humans without the involvement of men. The first method being SCNT.

After G/F sperm were mature, the next part of the Autonoma process involved transfer into artificial capillaries with hostile chemicals and conditions found in the vagina, cervix, uterus and fallopian tubes to test their quality. Only thousands of the most resilient sperm per sample made it through. These were all dispensed for fertilization into a single microwell of a 384-well chip, each containing a single egg cell. After 24 hours, the zygotes were checked for two pronuclei by AI. Media with growth factors were refreshed daily for six days as blastocysts formed. Five to ten cells were sampled from the trophectoderm of the blastocysts. Nucleic acids were amplified by polymerase chain reaction, and libraries were prepared and sequenced. Artificial intelligence searched for biomarkers in sequencing data calculating probabilities of disease, fitness, and other potential attributes. We tried several preimplantation genetic optimizations. Selected blastocysts were implanted into our AWs. A feedback loop of machine learning algorithms improved and expanded biomarker analysis and blastocyst selection with our criteria.

AWs were multi-layer thick but flexible plastic bags with a uterus and an endometrium-like inner lining. Tubes for zygote introduction; exchange of waste and growth factors - nutrients, gasses, and hormones; and wires for heat and sensors were attached.

AWs were an extremely sophisticated technology when we first introduced them. A fetus in an AW was provided with whatever it needed based on signals received from sensors. For example, they were provided small molecule hormones like thyroxine for fetal thyroid, brain development, and overall growth; cortisol for lung maturation; melatonin for regulating sleep-wake rhythms; and cytokines for fetal immune development.

Whole facilities had to be organized around the AWs. In an AW building, AWs were three floors below ground (L3). They were suspended by the ceiling. Robot arms on tracks controlled the movement of AWs, and they were frequently "walked around" and "rested" to simulate natural maternal movements. This operation looked somewhat like garment bags going around in circles at a dry cleaners or suspended seats on a rollercoaster ride.

The floor above this one (L2) was where growth factors were sterilized, stored, and dispensed. L1 was where automated fetal developmental testing was performed. Floor 1 was the lobby and security. Floor 2 was where skin samples were converted into iPSCs. Floor 3 was where blastocysts were produced and tested before implantation. Floor 4 was office space where all operations were monitored. Floor 5 was the nursery.

I had great pride knowing that Autonoma Inc. in 2012 was the leader in human cloning with the most advanced pipeline in the World and the most facilities.

As time ticked by, I saw our competitors start to gain ground on us. Researchers in China publicly announced successful cloning of a rhesus monkey. Most people were unaware, didn't care, or didn't understand that there was an increasing enterprise of livestock cloning for food. The only news that penetrated into the mainstream was the successful cloning of a wooly mammoth by a Vietnamese scientist, Dr. Chi Pho. He was found guilty of fabricating data in stem cell and cloning research years earlier. Still, a U.S. company interested in tourism paid him 15 million to transform a wooly mammoth carcass from Alaska into nun cho ga, or "big baby animals". A few years later, the Mammoth Alaskan Zoo (MAZe) was opened. This would become a key factor in the acceptance of human reproductive cloning less than a decade later.

Chapter 90: End of Safety

Many people have issues with cloning. I can appreciate the ethical debates that have been raised over the decades. Many concerns became reality in the 2010s. Naturally born humans frequently put clones in a different value category lacking the same rights and consideration. A huge flaw of my Trojan horse project was that I assumed our clones would be cherished, and treated like children. Instead, the rich were abusing, killing, and giving away the clones as trifle gifts. Clones were often used as sex slaves and replaced when they bored the clients or became too old for their tastes. Many considered it the end of human dignity when human clones started being used for spare parts. Some scientists wanted to create human-animal chimeras through cloning techniques. The U.S. National Institutes of Health (NIH) imposed a temporary moratorium on funding for such research in 2015. The vast majority of these scientific interests had to do with making humanized animal models to characterize diseases and develop therapies without using humans. However, some unsavory characters had aspirations similar to the fictitious Dr. Moreau. While there were several private markets for the hybrids, the Cirque du Rudaux made hybrids public. The circus was named after the French astronomer and artist, famous for paintings of what humans might look like if they evolved for alternative environments. The "exhibits" are indeed mostly human, but treated more or less like animals.

While many took issue with cloning because of the abominable works, others quickly warmed up or converted their position on the technology when they found out they couldn't have kids naturally.

My mind was in a totally different place than the responsive public, though. I was considering a future where genocidal ethno-viruses were released and only remnants of survivors remained. I put myself in a survivor's shoes and thought, 'I feel responsible for helping repopulate my ethnic group.' I imagine I would also be concerned that if I didn't maintain my culture and history, no one else would. Furthermore, if I didn't have someone (aka children) to pass the baton to, the history and culture would be lost with me.

Another scenario I imagined was the post-apocalyptic World where two people are tasked with repopulating the planet (e.g. Snowpiercer), or the tropical remote island where a couple are marooned with little hope of rescue (e.g. Blue Lagoon). In these scenarios, the human remnants are trying to survive hungry polar bears and the cold from nuclear winters or venomous stonefish and human-sacrificing indigenous people threatening their lives. They are surviving, not thriving. What if there was a tool though that could help a family of two become thousands (or even more) rather than maybe ten. That's what cloning can do now. Especially with our AWs and skin cell-derived eggs. One facility with a footprint the size of Starbucks can produce four thousand eight hundred babies per year, six times the population of the Vatican City. A surviving member of an ethnicity devastated by a genocidal event could utilize inherited wealth, insurance, charity, etc. to finance the reestablishment of a viable population.

Conservation scientists actually think that two people is nowhere near enough people for the continuation of a population. The movie was good but I actually knew the Snowpiercers were screwed. That's because there's something called the minimum viable population size, which is enough individuals in a species to calculate the probability of survival. With fewer individuals, survival is unpredictable and limited genetic diversity is likely to cause major problems down the line (incest => disease). Models suggest that the minimum viable population for humans is about four thousand two hundred individuals. With Autonoma Inc.'s facilities and our gamete genetic modification technologies, a single individual could theoretically be the source of a minimum viable population.

These were the things that helped me sleep at night. While I was haunted with guilt for the people I had killed, some of my other emotions were giving me grace.

'How much could someone really fault us? Are we really that different from an employed blacksmith, hammering out swords for the slaughter of a rival tribe in medieval times?' inquired my appreciation.

'Isn't this somewhat of a Nuremberg defense?' challenged my remorsefulness.

'We weren't just following orders though. We were actually secretly defying our leadership like Oskar Schindler did with the Nazis,' argued my bravery.

'Yeah, we were hammering out the plowshares by making the cloning tech that will enable numerous births and repopulation events,' added my optimism.

'I'm just glad there are other Righteous Among the Nations,' remarked my skepticism.

In 2018, Autonoma Inc. was far from having a monopoly on cloning. Many other companies would be able to assist with repopulation if the Horsemen had their way and we actually released the ethno-specific viruses. Looking farther into the future, I hoped my plowshares might one day be responsible for creating a more equitable representation of ethnicities in nations and powers. That is, underrepresented groups could be cloned to even out populations for improved democracy. I found solace in these dreams.

As time ticked by, I began to wonder if there would be any genocide at all by my hand. Autonoma Inc. was having tremendous issues with making proverbial "swords". I won't bore you with the details of all the things we tried, but in early 2019 we finally figured out a workable solution to the fidelity issue with REVs. My scientists tethered mutated REVs called nickases together. Normally REVs made double-strand cuts, but these nickases only made single-strand cuts called nicks. The tethered nickases were like two headed snakes, each head biting a different nearby section of DNA. Another domain of the enzyme would help displace the strands after each side was nicked. The requirement for cutting two proximal sequences instead of one substantially reduced the off target cutting rate. Furthermore, off-target nicks were less consequential because they could be more easily repaired by host repair mechanisms than double-stranded breaks. The impact of viral mutation on changes in Y-chromosome haplogroup targets was now an acceptable rate of hundreds of years.

After successfully testing the new tethered nickases REVs in tubes with nucleic acids, it took another year to combine the REVs with Sweetvirus and successfully test on tissue samples and clones. After eight ethno-viruses were produced, I had the Horsemen contract a team for me to test them with non-clone human targets. Autonoma Inc. team members were unaware of the human testing. While I was conducting tests, they were busy producing other viruses still thinking they were developing cures for Klinefelter's syndrome. Autonoma Inc. employees were also distracted and heavily preoccupied with figuring out the new normal during the first year of the COVID-19 Pandemic.

Chapter 91: Prototype

Eight prototype ethno-viruses targeting different Y-chromosome haplogroups were ready for field testing by the beginning of 2021.

Test subjects were chosen from our customer database. We had the genome sequences and therefore the Y-chromosome haplogroups of many of our male Autonoma Inc. customers because they had requested cloning of themselves. I also knew many of the customers from my sales travels. The men I selected for test subjects were absolute scum. I assured myself that the deaths of these men would almost certainly make the World a better place.

My first target was Kasib Kaseeb. When I was in field sales, I pitched our cloning technology and he had agreed to purchase a clone of himself. Kasib was interested in the idea of grooming an heir for managing his business empire after he retired. He provided Autonoma Inc. with biological samples so we could sequence his genome and make his clone. However, Kasib ended up changing his mind because he didn't really want the responsibility of raising a child. He asked instead if he could purchase eight female clones and specifically requested "sexy features". Those clones were sold and born fifteen years ago. A salesperson who recently followed up with Kasib to see if he was interested in additional clones reported that the teen girls were scantily clad in his apartment.

While he was far from the only client of ours who was a pedophile and owned deviant enterprises, few clients' perversions were as all-consuming. Kasib was the lead developer and CEO of the Swingverse, the erotic virtual reality platform with sex robots called swingpeople. It was started in 2016, and increased in popularity in the first year of the Covid Pandemic.

My spy informed me that Kasib rarely left his luxury apartment in downtown Riyadh, Saudi Arabia. He had food brought in, laundry and trash taken out, and maids in for cleaning. Kasib exercised once a day, ate twice a day, had sex with the eight girls in the morning and evening, and spent the balance of each day developing the Swingverse.

I didn't just pick Kasib because I despised him and his lifestyle. Numerous clients were just as deviant and depraved, many worse in different ways. He was a great target because of his physical and genetic isolation. He had a very rare Y-chromosome haplogroup for Arabs, haplogroup I, which is occasionally found in

Egyptians like himself, but almost never found in other Arabs. Saudi Arabian laborers that came near him wouldn't be impacted, hypothetically.

Our experimental goals in infecting Kasib included a real-world test to see if the virus targeting Y-chromosome haplogroup I was lethal, and if it could kill people that were not haplogroup I.

To initiate the experiment, we sent a flowering Tiger Lotus plant to Kasib with a note from a fictitious fan of Swingverse. Kasib's Swingverse profile included his ethnicity and that he owned a three-hundred-gallon freshwater aquarium. The Tiger Lotus is Egypt's national flower and is also an attractive addition to freshwater aquariums. It probably seemed like a very thoughtful gift to Kasib. Except that this Tiger Lotus produced pollen with Y-chromosome haplogroup I-specific Sweetvirus.

We monitored the progression of Kasib's illness by listening to conversations and sounds in the apartment. Our team used telescopic electro-optical sensors able to capture minute vibrations through windows and walls, and filter background noises.

Kasib had difficulty breathing on the fifth day. The eight girls tried to help maintain most of his routine. They served him tea to help with his dry cough. Kasib stayed in bed most of the sixth day, presumably because of the exhaustion he felt from all the cellular damage that the virus was causing inside of him. The coughs became worse and Kasib didn't sleep. Kasib tried to call a doctor's office, but we hacked his phone and answered the call instead. My team assured Kasib that a doctor would be over later that day. He was told that under no circumstances should he leave his apartment or have anyone else come in case his illness was contagious. Kasib's breathing became too labored to talk after a few hours. Then, he began gasping and wheezing until he finally expired.

The girls initially were hysterical. One told the others to quiet down. She instilled concern in the group that they might be blamed for Kasib's death. After some deliberation, they decided as a group to pack up and leave the apartment without reporting anything to the local authorities.

My cleanup team removed the body, plant, and letter, and sterilized the room. The experiment appeared to be a success. The virus was deadly, specific, and didn't spread through non-target individuals. However, one other hotel resident was found dead thirteen days later.

A neighbor reported a pungent smell in the hallway to the hotel staff. The staff who investigated discovered the decaying corpse of an elderly man and reported it to the local authorities. The authorities contacted the surviving adult children and requested permission for an autopsy. The next of kin, one Abdullah Hussain Khan, refused the request. The authorities sought a court order because of the mysterious circumstances of his death after his neighbor Kasib was found missing the same week. However, the judge denied the request due to religious discretion afforded by Sharia Law.

Because the body was too decayed, symbolic sacraments were performed rather than the traditional Ghusi and Kafan, the pre-funeral ritual washing and shrouding. With these arrangements Abdullah and other Y-chromosome haplogroup I individuals never came in contact with the virus-containing cadavers.

After his body was taken from the apartment by the authorities, my contract team obtained entry with skillful locksmithing, took swabs, and sterilized the environment. Sweetvirus was detected and he was determined to be Y-chromosome haplotype I. It seemed that he was killed by the Sweetvirus.

What was unclear was how the Sweetvirus made it to the elderly man in the first place. Our best guess was that pollen traveled on the clothing or cart of a laborer who visited both Kasib and the elderly man. It could have been food delivery, laundry, trash or other service personnel.

Review of this experiment made us realize that there were substantial risks associated with our methods. The Sweetvirus was very nearly discovered by an external organization. This could have led to an international incident, appropriation, Autonoma Inc. being linked to the murder, etc. We would have lost control if the virus had spread any further. Therefore, it was decided that all subsequent tests would be performed in a controlled environment.

While there were some changes that we wanted to make with the testing procedures, overall the experiment was a success. What did that mean though? I could kill everyone with a Y-chromosome haplogroup I. Obviously, we would need to test the other haplogroup-specific ethno-viruses, but it's likely they would selectively kill too. After that, we would make and test the remaining haplogroup-specific viruses. Then, as much as I didn't want to, I would need to make and test another set of viruses to target females in each target ethnic population. Viral production would be scaled-up, the ethno-viruses dispersed, and many people would die.

While the idea of killing men was bothersome, the idea of killing women was especially upsetting. I imagined a salt-of-the-earth woman succumbing to the virus the way that disgusting Kasib did, coughing until she was out of breath. My imagination zoomed into dying cells in this woman's lungs. I saw a magnification of the REV enzymes repeatedly cutting the DNA all over, and the cell's repair enzymes trying to reconnect the strands, but eventually being forced to give up because the cuts were too many. My imagination tried to include the target DNA sequences in the abstraction, but I realized that there were no sites that were female-specific. This was irritating, but then I realized something very unsettling. If I couldn't come up with a target that would kill members of the other half of the population, then any strategy that included the Y-chromosome haplogroup-specific viruses would mean substantially disproportionate killing of the sexes.

'Would that be the worst thing though? We would prefer to kill men over women anyway, right?' asked my vengeance.

'Their kind has done so much evil to us,' added my pain.

"Yes," I said out loud.

'And we could fulfill or almost fulfill the Horsemen's population reduction goals since men make up about 50% of each ethnic population, right?' calculated my strategist.

"Yes," I agreed.

'And it would be great if we didn't have to make and test a whole different set of ethno-specific viruses after the Y-chromosome haplogroup-specific viruses, wouldn't it?' supported my contentment.

"Yes!" I emphatically agreed. That would be nice.

'But would the Horsemen be okay with us killing all men and no women?' challenged my inadequacy.

'Why would they?' countered my contentment.

Then, memories from a lecture in my college feminism class, news coverage from the International Criminal Tribunal of Rwanda, and other news stories came flooding into my mind. I responded emphatically with horror, "The Horsemen would likely be happy with me killing all the men and no women!"

I realized that killing most or nearly all of the men in target ethnic groups would start the same pattern that's occurred throughout the ages. Men start wars, one side is victorious, the victors pillage the loser's property, and women are raped. The rapes are often not just motivated by some animalistic urge. No, it's also meant to be a tool of psychological warfare, to humiliate the enemy. It's also often used for the purpose of forced pregnancy, to breed slaves and commit… genocide! "What have you done?" I screamed at my reflection.

A guard came to check on me. I was crying, heaving, and yelled at him to go away. My mind reeled with images from the news and abstractions of women being raped: Tutsi women during the Rwandan Genocide in 1994, Croat women during the Bosnian War between 1992 and 1995, Albanian women in Kosovo in 1998 and 1999, East Timorese women during the Indonesian occupation from 1975 to 1999, Tamils during the Sri Lankan Civil War between 1983 and 2009, indigenous Guatemalan women during the long civil war from 1960 to 1996, Chechen women in the 1990s, South Sudanese women since 2013, Darfur women since 2003, the Kachin and Karen women in Myanmar, the Nubians in Sudan at various periods, Kurdish women in various conflicts at various times...

If I killed the men of specific ethno-groups, their enemies would rape the women. Warriors from America and allied nations would rape the women. We like to pretend that the United States and its allies are above reproach, but we are not. There are documented instances of American servicemen raping Japanese women during World War 2, Korean Women during the Korean War, Vietnamese women during the Vietnam War, even some cases more recently in Iraq and Afghanistan, where the United States has been engaged in the War on Terror. Even if neither the United States nor its allies overtly raped the women of nations devastated by Y-chromosome haplogroup-targeting viruses, many of the women would likely still end up having children with men from the United States and allied nations because of the limited options they would have for male partnership in their own nations.

Once women had children with men from other nations, they would begin losing their identity. Generation after generation the influence of the fathers' nations would dilute the genetics and culture of the mothers' nation. I wouldn't just be responsible for reducing populations. If I released these viruses, I would be responsible for destroying cultures, at least massively diluting them.

Chapter 92: A Silver Lining

I couldn't release the Y-chromosome haplogroup viruses and allow this female, genetic, and cultural oppression and slavery to happen. I needed viruses that were not male-specific. Something that would impact demographic subpopulations more evenly. Thankfully, necessity is the mother of invention, and a new strategy came to mind: targeting *mitochondrial DNA (mtDNA)* haplogroups.

All people in the World have mtDNA. It's DNA that's inside of our mitochondria. The mtDNA comes from their mother. More specifically, the mitochondria are in the cytoplasm of egg cells when sperm and egg fuse together. So, everyone has mtDNA.

As with the Y-chromosome haplogroups, there are mutations that distinguish mtDNA haplogroups. One concern that I had was that dispersion of the mtDNA haplogroups might be too homogenous across the nations. Unlike Y-chromosome haplogroups, the mtDNA haplogroups are dispersed across the planet. That's because throughout history women have been taken as wives, lovers, concubines, slaves, etc. and taken to the locations where the men lived. The men don't move. The women are moved. Still, my bioinformaticians confirmed for me that higher percentages of certain mtDNA haplogroups could be found in specific regions and within specific ethnicities. So, looking at that quality alone, mtDNA seemed like a good candidate for ethno-virus target biomarkers.

Targeting mtDNA haplogroups would have a critical challenge to overcome though. mtDNA has far fewer differences in their sequences than Y-chromosome DNA sequences. Therefore, most of the gains we achieved with tethered-nickase REVs would not help when targeting mtDNA. Yes, I'll admit that targeting the Y-chromosome haplogroups was a very illogical plan. Normally, setbacks like this were fine with me, even orchestrated by me, but this was a major oversight, and now I was running out of time.

A silver lining was that I wouldn't be starting from scratch. We learned a lot from troubleshooting off-target issues with the REVs used in Y-chromosome haplogroup-specific viruses. I knew right away that we could not use gRNA to target mutations in mtDNA. There just were not enough differences in mtDNA. The lack of fidelity of REVs using gRNA would cause an abundance of off-target cuts. We needed something that we could count on to cut target sites and only target sites, and we needed a solution that would retain its fidelity for hundreds of years or more.

Thankfully, Autonoma R&D had already started developing something called homing endonucleases about a year earlier to combat the off-target issues we were having with REVs. Homing endonucleases were presented to me as a way of removing gRNAs from the equation. That sounded good because that was one less part to troubleshoot and one less thing that could cause problems. I agreed to shunt some resources toward that, but was reluctant to stop all progress on REVs at that time.

Homing endonucleases didn't have the same off-target issue as REVs because they are entirely protein. With REVs, you have the protein component that does the cutting and the nucleic acid component (gRNA) to tell it where to cut. A single change in the gRNA changes the target. Mutations in the homing endonuclease gene rarely impact the specificity of the enzyme. It's actually more likely for a mutation in the catalytic site to stop the function of the enzyme altogether than for enough mutations to accumulate elsewhere in the gene to change the target of a homing endonuclease. Computational models suggested it would take eons for enough mutations to accumulate in homing endonuclease sets used in ethno-viruses (we used five or six) to impact non-target populations.

We chose five or six homing endonucleases per virus to give us a better chance at making lethal viruses. My computational biology team told us three cuts in the 16.6 kb long mtDNA should be enough to trigger apoptosis. That would be a similar or greater density of cuts compared to what was used for the 60 Mb long Y-chromosome and would cut several locations in and around genes that are critical for generating cellular energy. We also made a Pan Y homing endonuclease as a control since we knew that we could generate apoptosis by cutting the DYZ1 site, the repetitive sequence only found in the Y-chromosome.

The major disadvantage of using homing endonucleases for cutting DNA targets is that they take months to make, a process of many engineering and testing iterations. Making new gRNAs for REVs only took a day. We didn't see a path forward though with REVs. Only homing endonucleases could help us obtain the necessary precision and fidelity for ethno-viruses.

The Horsemen approved my proposal to replace the REVs with homing endonucleases, but offered me no additional time for development. My whole point of meeting with the Horsemen was to obtain more time. I desperately needed more time to determine if the mtDNA haplogroup-specific viruses were going to kill non-target populations. While it was unlikely, there was a chance that these viruses were not specific at all, and I could kill everyone. So, I looked for other justifications to request more time.

About two months later, my corporate espionage report indicated that a human cloning competitor was quickly progressing toward commercialization. They were in stealth mode, so their name and mission were unpublicized. However, my spies discovered that they were called Androgene Inc. In the Greek, "andro" refers to men and "gene" means born of or produced by. So, it made sense to me when I read in the report that they were producing embryos from sperm. What surprised me was how they were doing it.

Sperm (X and Y-chromosome containing) are first separated by flow cytometry. Then, two (XX or XY combinations) are injected into a single enucleated (nucleus removed) egg cell. Since each sperm contains 23 chromosomes, the full set of 46 is achieved with two sperm, and the embryo is constructed. There is no need to artificially activate the embryo to begin developing as with SCNT because sperm naturally activates egg cells.

The reason why this process is advantageous compared to SCNT cloning is because it avoids mitochondrial interference, telomere shortening, and somatic epigenetic memory, all of which accompany somatic donor cells. The challenges Androgene were still working through included problems with imprinted genes, X-chromosome inactivation, and dosage compensation. The report indicated that Androgene's experiments in mice were very promising.

Autonoma Inc.'s new process of reprogramming skin cells to gametes (eggs and sperm) followed by fertilization had huge advantages over Androgene's process. We no longer had to harvest female eggs. Egg cells would be a limiting resource for Androgene's pipeline and a major process cost for them. Egg removal from women's ovaries is a very invasive, painful, and challenging procedure. Autonoma just made their egg cells.

I wasn't actually concerned about Androgene being a serious competitor and taking the market from us. However, I was very stressed with the deadlines for the ethno-viruses coming. My fear was just looking for minor distractions, and I thought scheduling a meeting with the Horsemen to propose funding to squash this potential competition would scratch that itch. I wasn't looking for anything huge. Just a little bit of funding.

I called a meeting with the Horsemen and after sharing Androgene's competitive activity and my proposal for how Autonoma Inc. could maintain the market to ensure distribution of ethno-viruses in Trojan horse clones, the Horsemen took a brief recess to talk between themselves. They returned laughing before going completely silent.

Then, the black-masked Horseman who had always seemed to be supportive of my proposals pushed back, "Vir, we have had little to no interest in your cloning technologies over the years, especially in the last decade."

The pale green-masked Horseman added, "We definitely don't want to develop some technology for gay men to make children."

They clearly hadn't been listening very closely. I wondered if the Horsemen knew that Autonoma Inc.'s current cloning technologies enabled gay men to have children.

The black-masked Horseman continued, "We put up with it because you were passionate about it and you gave logical reasons for us to allow you to continue development. The chance to control procreation is no longer possible. Human cloning is not exclusive to Autonoma Inc., and you've given up progress on the sterilization viruses."

The pale green-masked Horseman continued, "The Horsemen will no longer support new cloning proposals. Additionally, this is a warning that our interest in your ethno-viruses is waning."

The red-masked Horseman went on, "We have a variety of alternative tech in our pipeline for culling the masses. We have ultra powerful lasers that can slice through walls of buildings and rooms full of people. We are manufacturing and testing hundreds of chemical agents more toxic than VX. We are developing hordes of autonomous killer robots as large as fighter jets and as small as bacteria. Your ethno-viruses will have little value to us once we have nanobots that can quantify skin pigment concentrations."

'Nanobots?' I thought. At the time I was completely unfamiliar with the technology, but after the meeting I read that these were indeed robots the size of bacteria. The peer reviewed literature was limited, but this was also the case for viral engineering thirty years ago.

The white-masked Horseman added, "Your window to satisfy us is narrowing quickly, Vir. We will achieve our goals with or without you. We might spare your life and let you have a nice retirement *if* you complete your mission objectives." This was the first time they overtly threatened my life.

The truth is that there are likely thousands or tens of thousands of ways to make deadly ethno-viruses and I could have led Autonoma Inc. to make them years ago, at least a decade earlier. Autonoma Inc. had the resources to develop many different technologies in parallel. I chose to try different strategies sequentially to bide my time.

I sabotaged our progress by choosing to pursue my third or fourth best options before working on the better options. Shortcuts were never permitted. No experiments were quick and dirty. Rather, all experiments had enough samples to be statistically powered. The company was process heavy with decision-making channels and committees to supposedly reduce risks. Very little decision-making power was actually given to my managers. I took on as much as I could handle to slow progress. Despite the overengineered stagnant environment, turnover was low because pay, benefits, and other aspects of company culture were great.

The Horsemen offered me retirement if I was successful in reducing target populations, but I knew there was no way they would let me go after I completed this objective. The liability was too high, and I would be worthless to them once the viruses were released.

"You will not live if you fail, and neither will your loved ones," the white-masked Horseman threatened.

"We will begin executing your friends and family beginning with Gina if you do not start releasing virus," promised the red-masked Horseman.

'No!' cried my anxiety.

I was starting to believe that the Horsemen would never discover my vulnerability, but they had. There was no question in my mind that they were serious. Before they finished the meeting, I tried giving some reasons why my team needed more time, but they just responded, "If you are unable to deliver in one year, we will kill you and everyone you care about. That is all." And the video conference was abruptly terminated.

I feared that I wouldn't be able to protect my loved ones, that I would fail to get the virus out in time, and they would be killed. Grinding my teeth late into the night and early the next day, I pondered how I could shorten the testing and production timeline. Autonoma Inc. R&D had presented their plans for testing last Friday showing me a two-year Gantt chart for testing their thirty-three mtDNA haplogroup-targeting prototype ethno-viruses on human *tissue*, not even humans. There was no time for any of this though. I only had time for an abbreviated human testing schedule before I would need to start producing virus in large quantities for dispersion.

Chapter 93: Human Testing

mtDNA is the DNA passed down to all humans exclusively from their mothers. mtDNA is not present in sperm. It's inherited through the mitochondrial organelle of an egg cell and is now present in all of your other cells with few exceptions like red blood cells. Over the course of two hundred thousand years, there have been over five thousand four hundred mutations relative to the Mitochondrial Eve, making as many haplogroups and sub-haplogroups (which I won't distinguish here). Some of these mutations are rare, found in small populations, just hundreds or thousands of people. Other mutations are carried by billions of people.

R&D developed thirty-three mtDNA haplogroup-targeting prototype ethno-viruses because my bioinformaticians found thirty-three sets of mtDNA haplogroup mutations that distinguished a goldilocks range of people, something in the high tens or low hundreds of millions of people per set of mtDNA mutations. Logistically, engineering tens of viruses was manageable for construction and testing. The major bottleneck was the six-month process of producing each set of homing endonucleases for the viruses. With no way to speed up the process of producing one homing endonuclease, we decided to simultaneously produce one hundred and ninety-two at the same time. This was enough homing endonucleases for cutting five to six sites in each target haplogroup mtDNA.

The thirty-three ethno-viruses were designed to target 91.77% of the global population and about half of the haplogroups. You might be wondering how 91.77% of the world could make up only half of the haplogroups. This is because throughout human history, women moved or were moved to the location of men. This dispersed the mtDNA haplotypes far and wide, as opposed to the Y-chromosome haplotypes of territorial men, who remained more segregated by continent and region (patrilocality).

My teams at Autonoma Inc. were told that these viruses were being developed for mtDNA replacement or repair; therapies for age-related and genetic mitochondrial diseases. They were not involved in any human testing or viral dispersion. The Horsemen contracted personnel for these activities.

Choice, something that widens as you wait and tapers in your haste. That was a riddle I came up with late one night thinking about what I would do to accelerate testing of the ethno-viruses. Perhaps I could have done some good in the World by eliminating more perverts like Kasib. Instead, I would do evil and sacrifice the innocent, specifically one thousand three hundred and twenty homeless people from populated cities. I buried my guilt, made my choice, and set to work.

A one hundred and fifty thousand square foot facility outside of Atlanta was rapidly but discreetly reconditioned for captivity in two months. Homeless people were drugged, abducted, and their mtDNA haplogroups were sequenced. If they were the type we were looking for, they were flown to the facility outside of Atlanta.

Thirty-eight people plus or minus three from every target mtDNA haplogroup were collected. A minimum sample size of thirty-five individuals would be enough for 70% of our confidence intervals to be correct, that the virus would kill 90% of an estimated subset of one hundred million people out of eight billion total, and with a 10% margin of error. Greater confidence ballooned the sample size, and we just didn't have the facilities to accommodate thousands more people or the time to coordinate such experiments.

The design included two experiments. First, we grouped everyone by their haplogroup and exposed them to all of the alternative viruses simultaneously (in other words, the ones that didn't target their haplogroup). If any of these alternative viruses had off-target activity, we would have been able to determine which one caused it by sequencing. The genetic sequence of the virus or viruses that successfully infected the non-target group would be abundant in the tissue of the decaying bodies. In the second experiment, we would expose each group to their mtDNA haplogroup-specific virus. We separated the control group who were being exposed to Sweetvirus Pan Y since it theoretically would shred all Y-chromosomes and kill any exposed male.

Once the experiment was over, the bodies would be incinerated on site in ovens. A field was plowed for the ash remains to be spread. Soil would be layered over. The planted leguminous alfalfa fixes its own nitrogen but benefits from the calcium phosphate minerals.

What actually happened was that the control group exposed with Sweetvirus Pan Y all died but only one person who wasn't part of the control group died. The homeless man's death wasn't from a virus according to sample analysis, but some precondition. I wondered if someone made a mistake and somehow didn't expose the mtDNA haplogroup-specific viruses to the subjects. So, we repeated the experiments. No deaths occurred the second time.

I had no idea why the experiments failed. So, I was very stressed out that evening.

My house outside of Atlanta was a three-level industrial-style building on ten acres. Dozens of monitored cameras are scattered all over the property. I was exercising vigorously, trying to exhaust myself, so I could fall asleep.

Suddenly, a SWAT team came through the woods in camouflage with assault rifles. One of my guards pulled me off of my chest press machine and ushered me out on the adjacent enclosed helipad before SWAT blasted through the backdoor. My helicopter warmed up, the rooftop retracted, and we were out of there in a few minutes. My house had major security features preventing any intruders from getting to me easily. I had AI entry (cameras that can detect approved and unapproved residents and guests), blast resistant doors, bullet proof glass barriers on the stairs and between rooms, and localized release of smokescreen and tear gas.

I was flown to Mexico City and brought to a hotel. The Horsemen scheduled a morning meeting. We didn't know how officials had come to find out about the abductions. The Horsemen told me to sit tight at least for a couple of days while they investigated.

To my surprise, the raid had nothing to do with the abductions of the human subjects for my ethno-virus testing. A warrant was out for my arrest for child trafficking, transportation of victims, contributing to the delinquency of minors, nonsupport, abandonment, and child endangerment. INTERPOLE was working with law enforcement agencies around the World under international conventions treaties. Basically, they were seeking to capture and try me for releasing thousands of children into the streets without guardians. In reality, Autonoma had released tens of thousands. They probably were just aware of a single dispersal.

Crimestoppers offered a fifty-thousand-dollar reward for any information on my whereabouts that would lead to my arrest. They described me simply as 5ft 8in tall with a medium build, long curly red hair, and blue eyes. A few pictures from last year's corporate events were circulated.

I was a fugitive on the run.

Chapter 94: Escape Goat

I was sitting in the back middle seat of a black Escalade between two guards unsure of where they were taking me.

'They're going to kill us!' declared my anxiety.

'No, we're the Horsemen's scapegoat, at least, for now,' assured my security.

'Yes, they're going to hide us so we don't get captured,' agreed my value.

'Won't be long though. They'll need to sacrifice the queen to win the chess match,' warned my discernment.

'The chess match?' inquired my surprise.

'Once we release the virus, international organizations will isolate the viruses and discover the signs of engineering. People are going to be looking for the engineer, and the Horsemen are going to pin everything on us,' explained my discernment.

'Yes, they'll probably just have some Autonoma Inc. R&D teammates tell the World that we deceived them. They say we hid the true purpose of what they were making, which is true,' suggested my strategist.

'Yes, but we can just tell everyone that we were being forced by the Horsemen,' growled my frustration.

'We won't say anything because at that point we won't be breathing. Carefully placed evidence and records will be found after our body is discovered. They'll probably make it look like a suicide to end the line of questioning,' surmised the strategist.

'Like what we did? How would that be for karma?' quipped my amusement.

Ignoring, my strategist finished, 'Of course the evidence will prove we were the mastermind behind the genocides.'

'Yes, and the cabal will just remain in the shadows, off the chess board; players not pieces,' concluded my discernment.

The Escalade stopped at a gate. We were let in and down a curved driveway with tall hedges. Suddenly, the bushes ended and before us was an expansive landscape with gardens and a large private residence in the back center of the property. We parked out front and the guards took me to the door. A man with an unnervingly wide-eyed gaze directed toward me welcomed us in. His balding head was tilted slightly forward further accentuating his piercing blue eyes.

"Hallo! Welcome! Welcome!" he exclaimed with a light German accent.

"Thank you," I replied, trying to be polite.

"You must be Vir. You may call me Picasso."

'His name makes this situation even more unnerving,' commented my wariness.

"Please go through." He directed me into, what looked like, an at-home surgical unit.

I was very apprehensive, unsure what was happening.

"Do not be scared. You are here to be metamorphosed, like a beautiful butterfly! Let me say zough, za caterpillar is lovely, very lovely indeed," he flattered.

This made me feel a little better, even if it was insincere. Then, I noticed that Picasso seemed to constantly have inexpressive moderately pouty lips which only gave hints of emotion, even when he was being very positive. I wondered if he might have given himself botox. Perhaps not though. His mouth seemed to compliment his intense stare. There was no point in discussion though. Picasso had been directed by the Horsemen.

"What do you want me to do?"

"Remove ze clothes and lay on ze operating table."

"They will need to leave," I insisted, referring to the guards.

"Yes, take your positions outside za door, please," ordered Picasso.

I stripped and lay on the cold operating table as he instructed.

"Now, it's time for night night. Count down from ten if you please!"

When I woke, I felt very sore.

"I have suctioned de fat from your stomach, inflated de lips and cheeks, and lifted de nose and buttocks."

"Once you've had time to recover, my assistant, Hannah, will dye your hair brown, cut and straighten it."

Picasso had a servant take me to a bedroom where I stayed for a couple of days. At which point he encouraged me to, "Get out of bed, walk around ze gardens."

I wasn't in a good mood, feeling like a sheared sheep, ready for slaughter.

However, Picasso insisted. "You must not ruin ze work. You need blood flow to help with ze tissue recovery!"

So, I did as he said. After the swelling subsided and my hair was done, to my amazement, I looked ten years younger.

Hannah also gave me a new wardrobe.

"Sorry, we would like to do ze fashion show, but we are instructed to make you blend in."

I was sure the changes were all meant to fool the AI recognition software used in public surveillance.

There were televisions in my room and other places in the house, and during my recovery I watched news of Mario Volpe, the former CEO of InvivoSeq, taking my position as the new CEO of Autonoma Inc.

Picasso would find me stewing and say, "Vir, try not to stress. It's not good for ze recovery."

I requested a meeting with the Horsemen and they accepted.

"Are you ready to get back to work, Vir?" asked the white-masked Horseman.

"Yes."

"Good," replied the white-masked Horseman.

"Glad to hear you're recovering well," said the black-masked Horseman, again playing the good cop. "What's your reason for requesting the meeting?"

"Why did you let Mario take my place?" I queried sharply.

"Are you not pleased?" replied the green-masked Horseman, pretending to be surprised. "It was either that or dissolve the company. We didn't think you wanted that."

"Don't worry, Vir. You will still have control, at least of a large portion of the operations. Mario will just be your go between," explained the black-masked Horseman.

I was racking my mind, trying to think of some other way.

As if reading it, the red-masked Horseman added, "Your invisibility is critical to avoid being recognized, arrested, and prosecuted."

I imagined being dragged to the town square for the guillotine. With regards to a method for leading Autonoma Inc. more directly, I couldn't think of any good ideas.

After a few moments of silence, the black-masked Horseman inquired, "Did you have anything else you wanted to discuss?"

"No," I answered, a little annoyed by his fake politeness.

"Okay. Since you're ready to resume work on the ethno-viruses, we will have you brought to your new facilities. Thank you," concluded the white-masked Horseman. "Oh, and just to be sure. Vir, this event doesn't change your due date. We are going to start killing your friends and family if you don't start releasing viruses. Is that clear?"

"Yes."

With no time to waste, I called Mario. He was a little bit tricky to work with because he had been a CEO previously and used to managing his own company. So, he operated more independently than I would have liked. Me being his ventriloquist would have been the ideal situation. The Horsemen had their hands up his rear, but I didn't have that same level of control. My oversight of Autonoma Inc. and power quickly dwindled.

Perhaps even more frustrating, my company was served a class action lawsuit for human trafficking, identity theft, and other crimes committed. Settlement negotiations were agreed upon quickly. Autonoma Inc. was preparing for an extended bankruptcy where they would continue to operate and generate profit to be paid to the victims' families for the next 15 years. After which, my company would be dissolved. The Horsemen didn't care. To them, Automona Inc. was simply a front to produce and distribute ethno-viruses. To me though, it was my baby, nourished from one employee to thousands of employees. I had raised it to be a global leader of diagnostics, surrogacy, and *ex vivo* services with annual profits in the billions.

A public relations team also damned me in the media with various interviews and advertisements. In one commercial, they likened me to a cruel master beating and caging my pet employees. With the company's reorganization the pet employees were safe and free to frolic in huge backyards and be loved by their benevolent adoptee, Mario. The legal team probably advised using symbolism and fanciful imagery rather than characterizing the wrong doings. Describing the crimes would be admissible evidence in a court of law and could make the company even more vulnerable to lawsuits by legal avenues of vicarious and corporate liability.

That's when part of Autonoma Inc. was spun off and given the name Good Parents Better Children Inc, often shortened to just Good Parents. The corporate mission of this new company is: *Helping parents pass on the best parts of themselves and keeping their children safe from genetic diseases.* They were well positioned for this new direction with Autonoma Inc.'s technologies. I was disassociated from all of their activities and required to stay focused on ethno-virus engineering. Knowing little more about Good Parents than what was online made me increasingly bitter.

Months passed and what ended up irritating me the most was how much interest there was from the market in spite of all the crimes that had come to light.

My jealousy exclaimed, 'No one cares!'

My surprise exclaimed, 'Good Parents had record quarterly profit increases of 52% and 94%! It's ridiculous! Hardly anyone wanted clones before all this blew up in the media.'

'No, it makes sense. People know what happened. It's just that the public relations team did their job well. All the blame has been placed on us, and there is so much new coverage that more people are learning about the option to clone than ever before,' grumbled my irritation.

'Yeah, it was taboo, but people are openly talking with their friends and family about the news and one discussion leads to another, and then clones maybe don't sound so odd anymore,' contributed my awareness.

'Right. Clones are cheap now,' noted my appreciation.

'Because of all the work we did!' sneered my fury.

'Yes,' my appreciation continued calmly, '...and parents want their kids to be strong, healthy, and disease resilient. It's no wonder why Mario and Good Parents are doing so well.'

'Whatever! It's enraging to watch fiery Mario have all this success on our shoulders!' spat my jealousy.

'Why can't we just be happy our technology is a success and helping people?' asked my appreciation.

My emotions went quiet.

'Ugh!' huffed my depression.

'What?' inquired my anxiety.

'It's just that… we're not the prominent CEO queen piece anymore. We're not even sure if we're on the Horsemen's chess board anymore,' my depression said despairingly.

'Maybe a scientist pawn,' suggested my inadequacy, not really helping.

My frustration stewed. 'Fiery Mario!'

My jealousy stirred that pot, too. 'He's the one who actually gets to help people. He's the one running the company. He's helping families and kids.'

'We would have done better, helped even more people,' contested my pride.

'We say that, but how do we know that's true?' challenged my insecurity.

'Of course we would! We know our company and this market better than anyone, definitely more than Mario! The success he is having is entirely coming from the fortuitous circumstances,' argued my pride.

'Meanwhile, we're a disgrace. Our reputation is worse than that corporate charlatan who was on the news all last year,' complained my frustration.

'Who?' asked my confusion.

'Liz House,' answered my frustration.

'Well, she didn't kill anyone,' noted my appreciation.

'Only because she didn't have a chance to,' debated my pride. 'If those so-called urine strip tests started giving false negatives and people didn't get their cancer treated in time…'

'Would never have happened because the strips would have never made it through clinical trials,' countered my strategist.

'That's probably true,' admitted my pride.

'It is true,' concluded my trust.

'Fine, whatever! I think we can agree that we should have been more successful. Far more successful!'

'Yeah!' cheered a few emotions.

'Would we have been?' my inadequacy queried this time. 'Aren't we here because of the Horsemen?'

'Yes, we are here because of the Horsemen! Is this success?' demanded my pride.

'Well, no…it's not,' conceded my inadequacy.

'Ugh! This just isn't fair!' complained my success.

'Yeah, how can the Horsemen's horse be the Devil and a fugitive?' questioned my justice. 'It's the fiery Horsemen who have been spurring us on the whole time!'

'Is this not the same toxic pattern that we have been repeating?' posed my pensiveness.

'What?' asked my pride, surprised.

'We've been allowing all the significant men in our lives to use us for their purposes,' submitted my pensiveness.

'We see that,' admitted my embarrassment.

My pensiveness elaborated, 'We knew Jim was using us to get money for his church, that Major Lance and His management were using us to make precision weapons to fight communists, and we knew that the Horsemen wanted us to commit acts of genocide, and still do. Did and do we want to do these things? No.'

'No, our ambition was to help people with infertility issues,' recalled my hope. 'We worked hard to position ourselves for a great job in academia. Yet we compromised over and over again.'

'Why?' demanded my pensiveness. When no emotions answered, pensiveness urged, 'Come on! We know why.'

'It's because subconsciously we've been looking for something,' started my discernment.

'Yes! What though?'

'A worthy authority, someone stronger and more competent than us. Someone we could respect who also respects and validates us. We were looking for courage, honesty, and integrity. Most of all we were seeking power. We didn't care about their surface objectives - amassing congregants and business or eliminating opposition. We knew deep down that they had power and were seeking greater power,' propounded my discernment.

'Right,' affirmed my pensiveness. 'So, we supported their efforts really because we wanted to experience the proxy or derivative power. Subconsciously we drank it up; we couldn't get enough. Well, we couldn't have our cake and eat it too. Their work left no time for anything else, and it cost us our dreams.'

'And we followed for too long,' confessed my shame.

'We *cannot* allow our subconscious to rule us *because* continuing to submit to these authorities *will be the end of us*,' asserted my pensiveness.

'Yes. After we're worn out, the Horsemen will put us out of our misery,' quavered my anxiety.

'And get another steed to ride the rest of the journey to their goal of applying genocidal weapons to the masses,' added my insecurity.

'Well, we're not going to be controlled anymore!' declared my pride.

'The pawn does not move the chess player!' challenged my helplessness. 'Nor the queen.'

'No, they don't. We must transcend. This cannot just be about outwitting the Horsemen. *We* must decide what's best for this World,' resolved my power.

'But what is best?' queried my confusion.

'And how are we qualified to decide?' disputed my insignificance.

'The position we find ourselves in is what qualifies us,' answered my confidence. 'We can either choose to be played by the Horsemen or play the Horsemen. Do what they want us to do with the weapon to enhance their power, or elevate and diminish who we want with it.'

'Do we not already know in our heart of hearts who should wield the power in a new world order?' asked my pensiveness.

My hurt recited, '*For from within, out of the heart of men, evil thoughts proceed, fornications, thefts, murders, adulteries, covetings, wickednesses, deceit, lasciviousness, an evil eye, railing, pride, foolishness: all these evil things proceed from within.*'

'*And Jehovah saw that the wickedness of man was great in the earth, and that every imagination of the thoughts of his heart was only evil continually,*' added my hate.

'*The heart of the sons of men is full of evil, and madness is in their heart while they live, and after that they go to the dead,*' contributed my hostility.

I knew these verses were written about humans rather than just men, but what I saw throughout my life was that men specifically did more harm to other men, women, children, the environment, etc. than women. I had far more data points of selfish, aggressive, and violent behaviors from men than women. My own father planned to abandon my beautiful and brilliant mother because she wasn't helping him achieve his family goals fast enough. Gina's dad abandoned her and her mother, saddling her mother with his enormous gambling debt. Men had hindered, derailed, and blocked my success in having children, completing my Ph.D., publishing, obtaining funding, getting promoted, and leading people to create beneficial technologies. They fooled me, manipulated me, tortured me, corrupted me, and soured me. They weren't just my problem though. Men were a problem to basically everyone and everything within their reach, often even themselves.

Professor de Pizan posited that women were better for everyone and everything around them and supported her assertions with statistics. While her data was shockingly telling, living gave me the proof. I was raised by my single mother; financially supported through college by my grandmother; emotionally supported by my best friend for many years, and longer if it wasn't for Horsemen; Kacy Burch and Jill Burmeister helped me publish my first manuscript in a peer-reviewed journal; Colleen Blake allowed me to finish my Ph.D.; Olga Nikolaev expanded my technical expertise at SMNL; and my primarily female staff at Autonoma helped me build a multibillion-dollar international company.

Could I find exceptions to my generalization? Yes, but they would be just that, exceptions.

'What would be best for the World?' inquired my pensiveness.

"More women relative to men,' I concluded.

Chapter 95: Reciprocity

Creating a world ruled by women and free of the Horsemen was worth many lives. I was sure that not everyone would feel the same way, but not everyone knew the alternative. If I didn't act, there would be a comparable scale of death, just less men and more women, and the World would be further steeped into the Horsemen's tyranny.

We already knew the fruit of the man-led world and how it perpetuated and bore numerous crises. The women-led World would have more solutions for resource disparities, international peace, the environment, and so much more.

The first generations of women would have it the hardest. Adapting would be challenging to most wanting a male significant other. Furthermore, some vocations that were previously dominated by men would require female laborers to step up. However, it's not as if the severe depletion of men would be permanent. Other scientists would figure out a way to confer immunity to my viruses and repopulate a desirable quantity and quality of men through cloning.

In the new world, I'm sure that women will want tighter control of reproduction. The main reason being to avoid returning to the environmental crises we find ourselves in now. I think men's fertility will be controlled more since men can impregnate thousands of women in the same amount of time it takes for one woman to give birth. Leadership will also probably want to limit the male population simply for the sake of maintaining power. Last but not least, I believe as men are repopulated, sterilization will become more common to prevent unwanted pregnancies and cloning will be utilized far more frequently to realize the health, wellness, and fitness benefits they provide compared to natural births.

One control that I could also imagine is that some countries will decide to quickly repopulate their male populations through cloning. I predict that these countries will begin experiencing renewed turmoil and see how much better things are in the countries that decide to limit and control male populations. Then, they will take corrective measures. The failed second chances will solidify policies for the suppressing men. While many may not understand in the short-term why I chose to deplete the men, I think the evidence of failed second chances will substantiate my actions. Not that I have to prove anything to anyone.

I was very comfortable with my plan and I knew that I was no longer a pawn of the Horsemen or my subconsciousness. Convincing the Horsemen that my ethno-viruses were tested and ready for scale-up was step one to setting the wheels in motion.

Chapter 96: The End of Man

The Horsemen contracted the men helping me with the testing. They were not scientists, but they also weren't idiots. The thirteen hundred plus test subjects would need to die. They wouldn't necessarily need to die from ethno-viruses, but it would need to look that way. I did not take the decision to kill these people lightly. It was a necessary sacrifice though for the betterment of the World.

Sweetvirus Pan Y was added to 33 vials. The contract workers thought I had provided them with 33 different viruses to conduct the tests. All the test subjects died, the bodies were vaporized, and the ashes were used as fertilizer. I pretended to be excited and relieved. The lie I told the Horsemen to explain why the first set of testing didn't work was that all of the viruses had a frameshift mutation in their genomes that prevented replication in the host. The researchers had copied the error over and over as they developed the other mtDNA-specific viral strains. This was an easy fix involving amplifying the viral packaging plasmids with new primers that incorporated the correction. The contractors bought it and their reports to the Horsemen aligned with mine.

The Sweetvirus Pan Y was released the day that I received the news that my mother died. It was this past Palm Sunday. A fire of hatred toward men was raging unchecked inside me for months. I simply saw them as cancer at that point, and only had the smallest apprehension about initiating the metaphorical surgery. The news that I could no longer reunite with my mother triggered me.

The date also added to the intensity of my emotions. Years earlier, Jim had explained to our Bible study group that Palm Sunday was special because it was a day when the oppressed cried out Hosanna ("please, save") and they were rescued. I had cried for Hosanna on this day for many years, sometimes with great conviction and belief that He might come, but He never did. I wanted Him to defeat the Horsemen and protect me, my family, and friends, but He never did. The threat of their deaths always loomed heavy on my mind. Releasing the virus was taking the opportunity to eliminate the threat myself. At this point, it was less about saving Gina or other individuals. I was now driven by the idea of making a safer and better world for everyone with the priority of making it safer and better for women.

The Horseman allowed me to go to my mother's funeral with supervision after I told them the virus was released. They were happy because they thought the virus was targeting several of their target ethnic groups.

Chapter 97: Regret

I loved and admired my mother, even though we hadn't been on speaking terms for decades. She heroically overcame major challenges, was highly accomplished, and enjoyed her life. My impressions of her were mostly confirmed by the funeral eulogies and reception stories. Milli was a highly-regarded journalist with well-known articles covering key events like the Watergate Scandal. She helped expand the impact of photojournalism, and helped pave the way for the success of other female journalists.

New details emerged about the earlier years of Milli's life. As a child, I didn't realize how much it cost to live in Kalorama, for my mom to drive a Jaguar E-Type, to have a nanny, for her to own a variety of Hasselblad and Leica cameras… We didn't have a cluttered home, but we had very nice things. Her excessive spending habits left little savings for a rainy day. Until the funeral, I never knew about the metaphorical deluge because we stopped talking after I went to college.

"Hi, Virginia. Good to see you all grown up. Your mother said you work for SMNL. How is the secret government work? Can I take a statement?" joked Cathy, my mother's old newspaper friend. Margaret, another journalist, joined us and reminisced about Friday night dancing. The Lindy hop and Calypso were favorites with hunky guys in Jazz and Rock'n'roll clubs. Others talked about impactful off-diary stories and exposés. My mother had several opportunities to cut some rug with dignitaries and even host politicians in our home. "That neighborhood was so much fun. It's a shame she lost her brownstone with everything that happened," they said.

The members of her church blessed me and tried to encourage me with their belief that I would get to see my mother again in Heaven. While the sentiment was appreciated, I couldn't help thinking, 'If they only knew about my work and my mother's long-time irreverence for religion, they might not make such promises.'

The way they talked about Milli was remarkable though. She seemed to have become an entirely different person than the one I remembered. They noted her exceptional service in the church ministry and celebrated her fearless evangelism of the Gospel.

"Your mom was excellent at planning and hosting charity events to raise money for school supplies for children of low-income families!" one elderly woman with a hearing aid yelled.

"And don't forget about the holiday meals and medicine drives," reminded her frail sarcopenic friend.

"What?!"

"Holiday meals and medicine drives!" the other elderly woman said louder in her friend's hearing aid.

"Oh, yes! Milli always made sure to care for people's physical needs before attending to their spiritual ones!"

The hard of hearing woman pressed the button a few times on her aid.

"Your mom used her connections with politicians and celebrities outside of the congregation. I think she even got some donations from deep-pocketed heathens outside the Church!" The frail woman chuckled. I thought she was going to crumble like a house of cards. She saw that I wasn't in much of a cheery mood, regained her composure and thankfully her stability, then added, "Seriously though, her ministries and evangelism were as much a blessing for the donors as the recipients."

One long-bearded man with a walker slowly made his way over to me. When he came close, I noticed the blood vessels and spots in his eyes. It was almost certainly retinopathy. When he shook my hand, I saw dermopathy. After realizing he was diabetic and that he had braved painful neuropathy to share his condolences, I grabbed a nearby chair and asked him to please sit.

"Thank you."

I held his hand as he slowly sat down.

"Your mom was a part of our small group for the past fifteen years."

"Really?"

"Yes. You could always count on her for an encouraging word."

I was very surprised to hear that my mother who had faithfully critiqued politicians, businessmen, and me, would have regular words of encouragement for the members of her Bible study, and for fifteen years? I realized that would have meant she got involved with this Bible study around the recession.

"Was my mom struggling with financial challenges during the recession?" I sheepishly asked.

"Well, she did lose big in the stock market. We took care of her though."

"Who?"

"Our Bible study group."

The man didn't shame me. Nevertheless, I felt guilty for not knowing about this and helping my mom. I never saw Milli as someone who would ever need help from anyone.

"Milli was also diagnosed with emphysema and chronic bronchitis around the same time."

Thinking of her simultaneously facing health and financial issues without the support of family made me feel worse. I got angry with myself. 'Why didn't I just call?! I should have tried to reconnect and mend things years ago!' My face must have given away my brewing emotions.

"Don't worry, Virginia. We battled alongside her in the physical and spiritual realms, and she came out of it a new creation, a healthy whole person."

I started to tear up. God had taken care of my mom through His Church, in my absence. He didn't stop there though. He repurposed her for good works, blessing her congregation and many others. A warmth came over me, feeling more assured that she really was with the Heavenly Father now.

Suddenly, another stranger approached me.

"Hi Virginia. Wow! You've grown up to be such a stunning woman. You kind of remind me of Nancy Pelosi a little with your smart red coat and brown hair. Why didn't you keep your beautiful natural red hair though?"

"Sorry, I don't believe we've met," I replied.

"No, you are right, and I'm very sorry it's taken as long as it has. I'm your dad's sister, Marie, and I have something important that I would like to talk to you about."

Chapter 98: Identity

My newly discovered Aunt Marie and I went to a late-night diner and sipped some bitter coffee while we talked.

"Your mom has not been completely honest about the quality of man your father was."

"How do you mean?" I inquired.

"He wasn't a perfect man by any means, but he was a good man," she said with admiration.

I wanted to believe her, but I was skeptical because my mother had painted him to be a man with a wandering eye, eager to spread his seed far and wide.

"Your dad wanted children very much, but to my knowledge, he was never unfaithful to your mom."

It was very tempting to believe this good news, but I didn't understand why my mother would talk the way she did about my father if that were the case.

As if reading my mind, Aunt Marie took a deep breath and uttered, "I'm sorry, but your mom didn't want to have kids. She said and did all kinds of things to avoid having kids, so she could focus on her career."

'Well, too fiery bad,' I thought, feeling irritated and hurt. 'Good thing for her that I was pretty self-sufficient.'

"Your dad found her putting spermicide on a diaphragm, and figured out that she was avoiding him and making excuses on the most fertile days of her cycle."

The waitress came by to check if we wanted anything to eat. It took me a moment to register this. 'Didn't I say I just wanted coffee? Can't she see that we are talking!' "No!" I barked, and the startled waitress took flight.

"Sorry, we're good," my aunt apologized with a remorseful wave.

My mind raced. My mom always told me they had fertility issues, and that I was a miracle child. That was the driving force for wanting to dedicate my life to researching why some parents could have children and others couldn't.

"Your dad felt so betrayed. Rather than try to repair the broken trust, your mom only defended her actions, and said she needed to do more before becoming a mother. She'd say *mother* like it was a derogatory word. When pressed, she wouldn't give specific achievements that would satisfy her or timelines to meet her goals. She just said, it's too hard to say. You never know what kinds of opportunities might come.

Your father had a lot of conversations with me, trying to process what your mom was telling him and what that meant for their future. It became clear that having children was not a priority for your mom. This was something expected of her by society, and she really wanted to be married to your dad, so she played along and talked about how many kids she wanted while they were dating.

Something that demonstrates the character of your father is that he sympathized with your mom despite this deception. He actually offered to work part-time and even be a stay-at-home dad so they could have children and she could pursue her career in journalism. That kind of reversal of traditional roles would have been extremely stigmatizing for your dad in the 1950s.

Milli said she just was not ready and didn't know when she would be ready to complicate her life in that way. The more she talked, the more it became clear that it was less a question of *when* and more a question of *if* she wanted children.

Your dad told me that he loved your mom deeply, but that he didn't think it was fair that he would have to give up children for her.

Divorce papers were drawn up a week later. Your father told me that he was going to leave the document on the kitchen table for your mom to find in the morning after he'd left for work.

Your dad's coworkers told me that he was melancholy throughout the day, but didn't say why. He was making small mistakes, seemingly distracted by something, and then..."

I teared up and croaked, "No." I asked, "When did that happen?"

"May 2, 1955," Aunt Marie answered.

I did the math and blurted, "That's about seven and a half months before I was born."

"Yes. At your dad's funeral, my parents and my husband and I asked your mom if we could help support her in any way while she was figuring out what to do. She politely declined. We still dropped off a card that said if she ever wanted or needed anything to please let us know. It was unclear if she knew then that she was pregnant.

About seven months later, around Christmas, I stopped by to check in on her and she was obviously pregnant. I asked if it was your dad's, and she said "no". I was confused, questioning in my mind how that could be. Was she unfaithful to my brother? Was there actually enough time for her to have had relations with another person and been this far along? I think your mom realized this was a bad lie and blurted out, "Yes." I reignited with excitement when I knew the baby was his. I immediately started offering ways we could help her. I suggested taking her to appointments, bringing her groceries, cooking for her, taking her to the hospital when the time came, and helping to watch you.

Your mom explicitly told me not to tell my family and that she did not want our help. She exclaimed that your dad wanted to divorce her and that they would have been divorced if he had not died. I started to say, "But, if he had known," and your mom cut me off, and said, "No, he would have finalized the divorce before finding out. He wanted to leave me, and now you need to leave. I do not want you or your family involved in my life or her life." "It's a girl?" I asked. She frowned at this. I said, "But, she is one of us, too." "No, she is not! I would have had custody after the divorce, and unless you want a legal battle, I am requiring that you stay away from us."

At the time, we were not in a position financially to fight for any custody rights. It seemed likely that we wouldn't win any custodial time if we did fight. A lawsuit would probably just drain our resources, as well as your mother's, which would have meant less resources for your upbringing. Giving her space and time to think seemed like the best option. Certainly, this seemed like a good plan while you were still in the womb. We thought it might even make sense to wait until you were old enough to understand who we were. I also didn't see any purpose in telling my parents. It would just hurt them to know your mom was keeping their grandchild from them. Then, the two of you moved a few years later and I didn't know where.

I lost track of you for two decades, until I saw your husband's gruesome accident on the evening news. I wanted to comfort you, so I took time off work and purchased a bus ticket to New York. You were gone by the time I arrived though, and no one could tell me where you went.

I decided to try the Salvation Army's Family Tracing Services. This was before the internet. They couldn't find you, but they were able to find your mom's address. I met her at your beautiful home in Kalorama and told her that I was sorry for the loss of her son-in-law. Your mom let me in the house. We sat at your dining room table and we talked for a while. She wasn't aware that you had gotten married. Your mom shared with me that you two had a falling out right before you went to college."

Some memories of the fight about me going to college to study human development and fertility came rushing back along with Milli's words, "No, I had you. Don't do it for me. I won't care. It's a hellish waste of time! You don't have my support and won't have my help!"

I was crushed. It didn't make sense at the time why Milli said these hurtful things to me. Now I understand that my mother and father didn't actually have fertility issues. Her lie sent me in a direction she didn't want me to go, and she was too proud or maybe even too afraid to tell me the truth.

My mother couldn't financially stop me. I had my grandmother's trust money for college, including room and board. Sticking to my guns, I followed through with seeking this educational plan, and Milli never tried to call or send mail while I was in school.

Aunt Marie continued, "Your mom told me that she was wrong for not contacting you. She believed that you were wasting your time and college money, and that you were going to end up regretting your decision. Your mom was very sad when she told me that she wished she could do it all over again and join you in the struggle anyway, rather than leave you to struggle on your own."

That struck a chord. A tear streamed down my face.

"Your mom said that you sent her a letter once. You simply wrote that you were a scientist at the largest science and energy center in the United States of America. She framed it and showed it to me. It was evident that your mom was very proud of what you had accomplished. If your father were here, I know he would have felt the same way."

I began to ball. It was too much to think about their love for me, how right my mother was, the truth of the terrible things I was involved in, and how they wouldn't really be proud if they knew what I had become. I left the restaurant sobbing uncontrollably and ran to my car. Aunt Marie got in the passenger side a couple of minutes later and waited until I caught my breath. She could tell that I didn't want a hug.

"I know this is painful, but I think it's important for you to know. Do you agree?" she asked.

"Yes," I croaked.

"May I continue?"

"Yes," I answered, less throaty.

Aunt Marie proceeded, "Your mother and father had their honeymoon in the Outerbanks of North Carolina. They went to Roanoke Island and read about the first English colony. Your namesake, Virginia Dare, was the first English child born in the New World on August 18, 1587. Your father told me that God came to him in a dream that night. God told him that he would have a girl and to name her Virginia Dare because she would be the first to accomplish many great things."

"Your mom obviously didn't have to go along with this when your dad died, but she did. You have to give her credit."

"And please don't think too badly of your mom for not allowing us to know each other while you were growing up. She was heavily influenced by your stricken grandmother."

"I'm sorry to tell you, if you don't already know, but your grandfather on your mom's side was a womanizer. His infidelity was widely known and an embarrassment to your grandmother. He got away with it though for a long time because he was rich. She divorced him at a time when the law made it very hard for a woman to divorce a man. However, she was strategic. Your grandmother made a name, a brand, and a business for herself in accounting. She was in charge of training and managing a team of all female accountants that did everything from bookkeeping to payroll to tax preparation for your grandfather's many businesses. Your grandmother was able to take most of the accountants with her, and started a successful company after the divorce."

"Your grandfather sought revenge on your grandmother, and sued for custody of the children. It's not like it is now. Your grandfather won custody of all their children that had been born. However, your grandmother denied that your mother was his and didn't include your grandfather's name on the birth certificate. He didn't want to have another legal battle, so your grandmother retained custody and never interacted with your grandfather again. Your mom was named Millicent because it means strong in work and in purpose. Your grandmother made sure to cultivate these qualities in her."

"Your grandmother was doing a lot of good, employing women and paying them the same wages as their male peers, proselytizing the positive feminist ideologies. However, she was bitter and frequently warned women of the serpentine nature of men, referencing her ex-husband's bad behaviors."

"Your mother knew all the stories. I'm sure she was fearful that she too would be victimized like your grandmother when your father had the divorce papers prepared. She could not allow that. So, she put her guard up, lied, and maneuvered to protect herself. The truth is that your father thought the divorce papers would be a wakeup call, that your mom would realize how unreasonable she was being and that they could find a compromise that worked well for both of them. He felt very bad about this tactic, but..."

"But what?" I asked.

"You have to understand Virginia. I couldn't have known what would have happened. I was just trying to help," she stammered.

"What?" I urged.

"I told your dad that he should have the papers drawn up," she finally admitted.

"You did what?!" I was enraged.

"I'm sorry, Virginia."

"Get out," I demanded.

"But, Virginia?" she pleaded.

"Get out!" I yelled.

"I just wanted…" the door shut in her face. I might have run over her foot. I don't know and I didn't care.

I drove off, speeding faster and faster down Route 97. I was increasingly enraged by the implications. This aunt had meddled in my parents' business and advised my father to get an attorney to draw up divorce documents to change my mother's position on having children. Instead, my mother was put on the defensive. She vilified my father. My father was probably regretting his decision when he absentmindedly electrocuted himself to death at his dangerous job. My father might have been able to salvage his marriage if he returned and explained himself. Without the explanation, all my mother knew was he had given her divorce papers. My family was fractured. I lost a father and extended family; their love to help guide me as a child and a teen. All because of this terrible counsel of best intentions.

If the divorce papers were never introduced, my mother would have been showing in a matter of weeks, my father would have been overjoyed, and we would have been one happy family. "Goddamn her!" I screamed. Then, I saw police lights appear about a quarter mile behind me.

I started to slow down, hoping they didn't see me. One of the Horsemen's guards who was monitoring me from a distance called my phone and asked if I had been drinking. I hadn't. He asked because if I was suspected of DUI or DWI, they would take me to the police station.

Maryland State Police Officer Smith pulled me over. I didn't care. I would have just paid a lawyer to fix it. But the police officer saw I had been crying and asked me why. When I told him that I was coming back from my mother's funeral, he let me off with a warning.

Deciding I was in no condition to drive, I got a room at a nearby hotel. Drinking was not of interest. I wanted to destroy something. I swung a floor lamp into the TV and then slammed the TV down onto the coffee table. I threw the iron, ironing board and hangers across the room, causing some of the art to fall off the wall. I flipped the desk chair and tore the shelves out of the refrigerator freezer. A concerned hotel patron knocked on the door asking if I was alright.

"Do you smell something burning?"

"No, Miss."

"Then, go to Hell!"

They left, murmuring.

That night, I was lying in bed thinking about the influence of parents on their children. Both my name and my mother's name were intentional. Our parents hoped that we would do impactful things with our lives. However, they didn't assume that the names alone were going to drive our success. They worked to mold us in our formative years into successful people. My mom developed into a triumphant journalist, and she tried to steer me in a good direction. Why do some children listen to wisdom and others don't?

My father claimed that God named me and had great purposes for me. How could God be thwarted though? And, if my father was so tuned into God, why would he take counsel from Aunt Marie? There are certainly many mysteries about my father. I don't know much about him. One thing I was able to learn though from Aunt Marie was that he loved my mother and he loved me. And if he had lived, I would have liked to have him in my life.

I wept for hours, realizing the consequences of my meddling. Billions of daughters and wives were going to lose their fathers and husbands in the coming weeks, not to accidents, but to murder.

Men are not the only evil ones. Women can be quarrelsome and fretful, fools and drunks, slanderers, tempters and adulterers, witches, idolaters, jezebels, and more. As for me, what man could match the evil I have done? And if my evils were worse than the sum of millions of men, how could the result of those evils be what's best for the World? There was nothing that could be done about the release of the Sweetvirus, but there was still time to save some men.

Chapter 99: The Year of the Lady

Hiding in my old study nook at Rosalind Elsie Franklin Public Library, Ocracoke, I confessed my sins to the World. I knew that it was only a matter of time before someone came with swift justice. Thinking I could hear my assassins coming, with great fear and trembling, I finished up my weblog.

My final plea was to the Women of the World, that they would forgive me for killing their husbands, fathers, grandfathers, brothers, uncles, sons, and friends, and for depriving many women from ever having the experience of those relationships.

Even though I knew there was no use to the appeal, I suggested that rather than coming after me, women should try and preserve as many men as possible. Time was of the essence. I even challenged women to find a way to undo what I had done.

However, knowing the inevitability of men approaching extinction, I felt obliged to encourage women to prepare for and think carefully about male repopulation. Birthing men immune to the Sweetvirus was one thing, but somehow restarting the former family dynamics was the greater challenge.

Careful of the way I phrased it, I essentially asked what I believed to be rhetorical questions:

1.   Would young men feel a new kind of fear when they discovered that their sex was once eliminated?

2.   Would they fall into existential despair when they realized that their sex was unnecessary for the continuation of the species?

Emotional stability in men would require encouragement from women, putting the men at ease and reassuring them that their lives really do matter.

I fully expected that I would be gunned down before I was able to share everything I wanted to in the weblog, but my assassins still had not arrived even after I finished typing my concluding remarks. The ever-present awareness of imminent death brought me pleading in all humility to God. I glorified Him, appealed to His love and mercy, and recited Psalm 34. Even still, I felt hopeless.

Chapter 100: Epilogue

Gunfire thundered through the library stacks. I shook with fear, unable to decide how to face whatever was coming. Hormones flooded in and my instinct was to run, but my old study nook offered no escape route. My heart rate skyrocketed as I imagined black uniforms coming around the corner at any moment, guns pointed right at my chest, earsplitting bursts ringing out from their weapons, and bullets ripping through my body and throwing me backward. My muscles tensed at this terror, but no one came for what seemed like an eternity. I dropped to the ground, deciding to lie flat on my stomach with my hands on my head.

My strategy suggested, 'They might demand this kind of compliance, and if whoever comes around the corner doesn't immediately kill us, they might take us in if we offer ourselves in complete surrender.'

The shooting ceased, but now I could hear radios, boots, and swishing of pants. The shuffling grew louder and louder. I was sure they were surrounding me.

There had been times during my travels when I feared for my life, but now I was sure death was coming. What wasn't clear was the afterlife. Justice might send me to immense unending pain, deservedly for all the suffering my technologies had and would inflict. How can Heaven, if it's not just space out there, ever accept me? My only hope was the unlikely scenario that the Gospel of Jesus Christ was true, and faith in Him was all I needed.

The last Easter service hymn came to mind. "What can wash away my sins? Nothing but the blood of Jesus. What can…" I stammered fearfully, singing and weeping simultaneously.

The boots surrounding me stopped moving. I trembled, lying face down, unable even to muster enough courage to look up. I continued, '…make me whole again? Nothing but the blood…"

"Cover for extraction," someone commanded in a high female voice.

Hearing those words, I froze, listening intently.

"Confirmed," responded two other female voices.

"Dr. Goreman," declared a woman, putting her hand on my shoulder.

I remained petrified.

"Dr. Goreman, you're safe, we're getting you out of here," she assured me.

Memories of extractions executed by the Horsemen came to mind.

"Oh no, I'm not going back to work for them!" I exclaimed, wriggling up. "I might be on my way to Hell, but the Horsemen will have to live in this Hell if they can even find a way."

I felt my knees give out from a non-damaging but forceful thrust, and I was quickly brought back down on my face. "We don't work for the Horsemen," the Commander Woman assured me. "We are the Women About Systematic Progress, WASPs."

I turned my head to look up and saw six women with armor and assault rifles. They formed a fortress around me with their guns facing toward the direction they had come from. Some peeked over their shoulders to look at me.

"It is great to meet you in person, Dr. Goreman," started the commander. "You need to keep your head down though. There are still hostiles in the building."

The commander prompted, "Extraction ready?"

Three responses returned, "Ready."

After a short pause, the commander issued the order, "Execute."

"Let's move, Dr. Goreman."

The team formed a line. I was the second to last and was guided by a hand on my shoulder.

I couldn't believe it. This group was trying to protect me.

"Why are you doing this?" I asked nervously.

"The men will be gone soon. They are dropping like flies. Women will dominate the population and rule, regardless of what governments implement. We want you to lead at the highest level," the commander answered.

'Lead? At the highest...? I can't.'

Boots stomped in front of me. The WASPs weaved from cover spot to cover spot. I could feel the acid in my body from the anxiety alkalizing. The adrenaline from the fear was wearing off. I felt warmth from the vasodilation. My muscles were relaxing, and a devious smile crept across my face as the many emotional voices of my inner legion came to a decision. I heard my lips pronounce the contrary.

"I can."

About the Author

Let's connect!

X: @JMWhithamAuthor

Instagram: jasonwhithamauthor

LinkedIn: Jason Whitham

ResearchGate: Jason Whitham

Email: jmwhitha2@gmail.com

Jason M. Whitham, Ph.D. is a new sci-fi author with a rich history of applied science. Made Not Begotten (#1 How Women Took Over The World) is his debut novel. If you would like to find out what happens next, share an encouraging comment on social media. You may directly contact him at any of the social media platforms above.

Made in the USA
Columbia, SC
22 November 2024

46713933R00298